# UNMENTIONABLES

## DAVID GREENE

Unmentionables Series

### BOOK ONE

*For my dog "Asia" who gave me "Venus"*

# PREFACE

My purpose in writing *Unmentionables*, which was first published in March, 2010, was to tell a story that had never before been told about people whose lives had been ignored by historians. I wanted to fill in a piece of history that had been omitted—an account of enslaved men whose love for each other was considered by society to be unmentionable.

I spent twenty years researching this book. I traveled to Madison County, Tennessee, and visited the sites where this story is set. I read published first-hand narratives of enslaved people and books about the lives of enslaved people published by historians. The experiences and situations described in this story are primarily based on precedents I found in these recorded histories. I was unable to find, however, any recorded precedent that described the feelings and experiences of enslaved gay men, which is why I wanted to tell this story.

I've endeavored to ensure that the language used in the novel accurately reproduces American speech as it existed in the mid-nineteenth century, including words, idioms, and expressions. I want to caution readers that some of the dialogue includes hate speech, including the n-word, a word that was commonly used by white people of the time, and also used, without the same malice and for their own purposes, by enslaved people themselves. It is a painful word. And many of the experiences depicted in the novel are painful to read.

This story depicts some of the horrors enslaved people experienced—near total regulation of personal freedom, children sold away from their families, restrictions in movement by roaming slave patrollers, grueling manual labor, and domination of the black body through rape, whipping and confinement.

Nonetheless, this is a story of resistance and resilience. Despite everything, many enslaved people through their own courage, fortitude and actions were able to experience ordinary happiness, humor, love and joy, which I consider an extraordinary spiritual achievement.

David Greene
   July, 2020
   for the Tenth Anniversary Edition of *Unmentionables*

## SAMMY SPEAKS

"Stop your fussing, Ella," Wally said.

"Just swat a fly, mama."

"Must be the sugar. They smell that sugar you spilled on your dress. Now you'll have no end of flies."

The sugar was for a bowl of raspberries that Wally picked from a bramble. The raspberries were in a new bowl she bought in town with her Sunday money. Slaves were not obliged to work on the Sabbath, but if they did, it was the custom to remunerate them with modest pay. Over the years, Wally had devoted most of her Sunday money to the purchase of wooden bowls, which she prized especially because they did not break if someone should drop one.

Ella settled back with the bowl, and pondered whether to eat one berry at a time and make them last or just …. She stopped, and turned toward the sound of a horse's hooves behind her. Mr. Holland maneuvered the buggy into the yard from Christmasville Road, towing a clapboard utility wagon. He whistled to Willis to come unhitch Maple. Ella and Wally went to see what Mr. Holland had in the wagon. There in the back, wrapped in a gray blanket, was a small dark boy, a stranger.

Wally was the first to speak, "Well I'll be ...."

Willis ran up alongside Maple and took the rein from Mr. Holland's hand. He looked at the boy in the back. "And who's that you brought along here?" he asked.

The boy clutched the blanket around his shoulders. He turned and shot a glance at Wally, Ella and Willis, who stood around the wagon to inspect him. He turned his eyes away and stared straight ahead at a spot where no one stood. For a moment no one spoke. Leaves rustled from a light breeze in the courtyard.

"This is Samuel," said Mr. Holland at last. "Boy of five years old. Regrettably, the boy's mother passed away in June. So his people sent him up to Memphis with traders. And when I got into town, I ...."

He stopped. Aroused by the sound of the buggy, Mrs. Holland had come out of the big house with Sarah and Dorothy. They walked quickly toward the wagon. From the other direction, Jimmy strode out of the slave cabin and joined the group. In the twilight, Mrs. Holland squinted at the boy bundled in a blanket.

"George, what in the world ...?" Her hand waved.

"I was just saying," said Mr. Holland, "that this boy is named Samuel. His mother passed away in June and ...." He paused, trying to anticipate his wife's reaction as he considered his words.

George Holland's wife wore a pale blue dress with lace trim, which she often wore in the evenings, but which was nevertheless insufficient for the cool night air. She put one hand around her bare shoulder, and the other firmly on the wagon's sideboard. She scanned the wagon's contents. "George, did you purchase this ...?"

"Yes, Henrietta, the boy was put in the charge of two gentlemen who happened to bring him into the dry goods store where I was transacting business. They said he was a most obedient and right-acting lad at an especially low price … I …." He turned to the boy. "Look at him, my dear." He swung an upturned hand toward the boy as if he were presenting the Prince of Wales. "I thought he'd be fine with Wally and Jake." He looked around the group. "We need to think of the future," he said.

Mrs. Holland stared at the blanketed boy in the back of the wagon, who continued to look straight ahead, as if he couldn't hear what anyone was saying. His wide eyes were two chestnuts set sunny side up in a dark-colored face. No one dared speak. The entire assembly waited to see if Mrs. Holland would be angry or not. The boy turned for a moment, bravely flashed his bug-eyes at her, and quickly turned back.

"Oh Lord help us," said Mrs. Holland. "I hope he won't be much bother. I hope he's quiet." She shivered, rapped her knuckles on the side of the wagon and turned to walk back toward the house.

Mr. Holland clambered out of the wagon to follow her. "Yes, yes," he said. "He's been as quiet as a mouse for two days. You'll see, my dear, a good investment at a bargain price. The child cost but a trifle, Henrietta."

The master and mistress disappeared into the house. Dorothy and the assembled slaves pressed in on the wagon, while the boy sat inside, not moving.

For a moment, no one was sure what to do. Willis led Maple away toward the barn. Wally reached into the unhitched wagon and put her hand on the boy's shoulder, "How d'ye do, young Sammy," she attempted a formal tone. "Welcome to our house." The boy didn't move. "Looks like you're going to live here now." She rubbed his head. "We're going to be your people."

Wally shook her head as the weight of this realization sank in. She clasped her hands together as if she were about to pray. The boy sucked in a breath and craned his head back to look up at the sky. His chestnut eyes rolled around, searching for stars, some of which twinkled faintly in the evening twilight.

Wally unclasped her hands and climbed into the wagon. She was a slim, strong woman. She was short, but when she stood up straight in the wagon next to Sammy and looked up at the October sky she seemed tall. Wally surveyed the group around her. "OK now," she said.

She knelt and took hold of the boy by both his arms. "They call me Wally," she said. She looked at Dorothy, who was craning to see over the side of the wagon, bouncing on her tiptoes. "And down here is Miss Dorothy, Massa Holland's daughter. And there on Miss Dorothy's right is Sarah, the cook. Her husband, Willis, is the man who took the horse to the barn. Sarah and Willis live with the Hollands up in the house and they are the house servants."

The boy cocked his head but did not speak.

"And over here on Miss Dorothy's left is my Ella." Wally pointed at Ella, who still held the bowl of raspberries in her hand. "And this here," she pointed at a tall, crow-black boy with a bright orange rag tied around his head, "is my son, Jimmy. I reckon Ella and Jimmy are going to be your new sister and brother."

Jimmy stuck out his hand and held it in front of the boy's face. "Hey, brother," he said.

Sammy closed his eyes, then opened them and looked around the group. He saw that Jimmy was holding his hand out and that he was supposed to shake it. He looked at the orange head rag on Jimmy's head, and then into Jimmy's eyes.

"It's OK, brother," Jimmy said. "We gonna look after you. You gonna be all right now."

But Sammy closed his eyes again, pulled his arms out of Wally's grip, took the blanket from around his shoulders, raised it over his head, and pulled it down until he disappeared beneath it.

"Poor child," said Wally. "What a sorrowful time he's had!" She put her hand over her mouth for a moment, then let it drop. "Oh I guess …." She looked around the yard trying to think what to do next. "I guess we better take him in the cabin."

Jimmy climbed into the wagon, scooped the boy up, holding him with one arm, and gently tugged the blanket off his head with his free hand. "I'm gonna take you in the house now, Mr. Sammy," he said. "You don't have to worry about nothing or say nothing." Jimmy hopped to the ground with the boy in his arms and led the way toward a cabin across the yard from the Hollands' house. The whole group, including Willis, who had returned from the barn, filed in a procession to the slave cabin where Wally, Ella and Jimmy lived with old Jake.

Inside, Jake snored in his wooden bed. It was unusual for a slave to have a wooden bed, but Jake had belonged to George Holland's father, Walter, who in his lifetime was a furniture maker in North Carolina. Walter, when he died, bequeathed Jake not only the bed, but also a wooden table and three good chairs, which sat in the center of Jake and Wally's cabin. Walter also bequeathed Jake himself to his son, George Holland, which, though not unexpected, had ended Jake's unspoken hope that he might someday be set free.

Jake, as was his custom, had gone to bed early. But when the procession streamed into the room, he sat up and rubbed his eyes.

5

"Jake, what do you think? We got us a new member of the family," Wally said. "Massa Holland done bought this child up in Memphis on account of his mama passed away and his people sent him up to the traders in Memphis."

Jimmy held the bundled boy aloft and sat him down slowly on the side of Jake's bed as evidence of Wally's truthfulness.

Wally sat on the bed, too, and once again took the boy's hands. "Sammy, this is Jake. When Jake was a boy, just like you, the traders got him in Africa. Them traders brought him over to North Carolina. Jake was the first ever slave of Massa Holland's father. Back in Africa his name was Juba, so we call him Juba Jake."

Juba Jake glanced at the child's face. He bowed his head remembering his first encounter with the new world. He reached out to put his hand on the boy's shoulder and closed his eyes. For a moment his eyelids trembled. Then he opened his eyes and looked at the boy tenderly. "Ain't nothing I can say to make it better—but you gonna be better by and by." Jake coughed to clear his throat. "You got to know you lucky to come here now. Massa Holland's a good one, 'bout as good as can be, I suppose." As he spoke, Jake realized Dorothy was standing in the group, along with the others. But he continued, "And we all had our lot thrown in here together and you got to know we gonna look after you. You gonna get by, child." Jake looked up at Wally. "Is Massa Holland fixing to have him live here?"

"Yes, that's what he said. He said, 'He'll be fine with Wally and Jake.'"

\* \* \*

THE NEXT MORNING Jimmy and Ella gave Sammy a tour of the farm. Sammy held Jimmy's hand.

"We live in the first cabin," said Jimmy. "In the next cabin is Daniel, Jefferson, Little Andrew and Solomon."

"One, two, three, four," said Ella. "Four men."

"They're all field hands," said Jimmy, "like me."

"Me too," said Ella.

"Nah, you don't work in no field, Ella." Jimmy turned to Sammy. "Ella is the water girl. That means she brings the water out to us when we're working in the field."

"Yup, I bring the water," Ella said, "but nobody works today 'cause it's Sunday."

"Right," said Jimmy. "And here in the last cabin we got Luke, Big Andrew, Paymore and John Henry."

"John Henry has two names," said Ella, "but he's just one man. Little Andrew and Big Andrew are two men. Big Andrew ain't really so big. But Little Andrew is short, so since he's littler than Big Andrew, we call him Little Andrew."

Sammy stared at the unadorned clapboard cabins, which seemed small to house so many men. He looked back at Jimmy and Ella, but said nothing.

"I don't think he's ever going to talk," said Ella.

"He don't need to. You talk enough for both of you."

"I ain't either."

Jimmy continued. "Over in the big house is where Sarah and Willis live. They live behind the kitchen. Then upstairs is Massa Holland and Mrs. Holland."

"And Dorothy," Ella said.

They had come to the barn, a large painted wood building with a chicken coop attached to one of the exterior walls. Inside the barn were two horses, seven mules and a milk cow. On the right side of the barn were ten stalls, one for each animal. The first two stalls held the horses; then came a slightly larger stall for the cow, with room for a stool and assorted pails. Then came the smaller stalls of the mules. Bales of hay sat stacked like giant loaves of bread along the opposite wall with pitchforks stuck in two of the loaves.

They stepped inside. The smell of animals and hay was pungent. Jimmy led them to the horses' stalls. "Little brother, this is the horse that drove you in last night." said Jimmy. "Her name is Maple. And the dark horse, his name is Walnut."

Sammy nodded, but still did not speak.

Ella tugged them on to the next stall. "This is the cow," said Ella, "Her name's Basheba."

"Bathsheba," Jimmy corrected, "Bathsheba is the milk cow." Then he pointed at the mules' stalls. "Massa Holland named the mules like a music scale. They're names are 'do,' 're,' 'mi,' 'fa,' 'sol,' 'la,' and 'ti ' I can't say for sure which one is which, but Paymore knows each one by name. He says we got a pack of musical mules."

A chicken waddled in through the open barn door. Ella pointed at it and giggled. "Jimmy, don't forget rooster."

Jimmy smiled. "Oh yeah, we got one rooster and we call him George Junior."

"Cause even before it's daytime," said Ella, "George Junior, he wakes everyone up and Massa Holland's name is George and so you can't say nothing about it, cause Massa Holland don't know about it."

"He won't say nothing," said Jimmy.

Sammy tugged out of Jimmy's hand and went to stare at Bathsheba more closely.

"I don't think he ever saw a cow before," said Ella.

"Could be there weren't no cows where he lived," Jimmy said. "Someday maybe he'll tell us where he comes from." He took the boy's hand again. "But don't worry, little brother; you don't have to talk about it today."

There were three short barks out in the yard. In through the open barn door ran a medium sized yellow dog with floppy ears just shorter than a rabbit's. The dog's tail wagged furiously as it rushed up to Ella.

"Venus!" Ella exclaimed.

Sammy clung to Jimmy's hand, but Jimmy beckoned the dog over to them.

"Come on, Venus. Come over here; meet our new brother." The dog approached Sammy with its mouth open in a silly grin. Sammy tentatively put one hand out. The dog sniffed it, and Sammy pulled away. "She won't hurt you," said Jimmy. "She's a real nice dog."

Sammy let go of Jimmy and leaned toward the dog. His eyes widened. With both hands, he brushed the dog's back. The dog turned to lick one of Sammy's hands. Sammy's eyes lit up. He looked up at Jimmy. Jimmy nodded.

"Venus," Sammy said.

Instantly Ella ran out through the barn door and down the line of cabins to the first one in the row. She burst into the room where Wally was scrubbing the table.

"He talked!" Ella shouted. "Sammy said Venus!"

---

# 2

# "A CHILD DON'T KNOW"

Christmasville Road was the main thoroughfare from the Hollands' farm to the town of Jackson, Tennessee. It was a dirt road—a mix of clay and sand with a yellowish tinge. There were farms and plantations all along the road. A strip of woods, mostly narrow, sometimes wide, separated the road from the private properties. Occasionally, an entry gate or service lane interrupted the wall of trees, which lined the length of the road from the county line to the town. There were scaly bark hickories, sweet and black gums, that turned bright orange in October. There were mulberry trees that scattered purple splotches of fruit on the ground all around.

Slaves made good use of these woods after dark. If a slave was out without a pass, a slave had to sneak. And the best way to sneak was in the woods. At night, paddy rollers and dogs patrolled the road. Most often, they peered into the woods with whale oil lamps, and cursed the darkness that hid dark faces.

The woods were a sanctuary in another way. The slaves held

prayer meetings and church gatherings in the woods on Sundays. Their meeting place was in a grove along the banks of Dyer Creek. The creek formed the left side of a V of which Christmasville Rd. made the right side. The spot where the creek and road met was the halfway point from the Hollands' farm to the town of Jackson. Since woods lined both the creek and the road, their juncture was where the woods were thickest. It was there that the road crossed a wooden bridge over the creek.

It was 1857. Ella and Dorothy stopped at the bridge, as they always did. Dorothy was on her way to school. Ella was on an errand to buy potatoes for the Hollands' dinner. Dorothy was 16 and Ella was 15, both wavering between youth and adulthood.

Dorothy was supposed to ride one of the mules so she wouldn't tire on her way to school. Ella was supposed to walk alongside the mule and carry Dorothy's books. But Dorothy refused to ride. She said she'd rather walk. When they left the farm, Ella carried Dorothy's books for show, but once they got on the road, Dorothy took half the books herself. Dorothy's discomfort with slavery had been evident since she was little.

Ella was her best friend. Dorothy could not square that with being Ella's mistress. Dorothy half-heartedly acted the part when her family was present. But even that effort waned. By the time she reached 16, Dorothy felt old enough to disagree with her parents. Nonetheless, she bided her time. She understood that the thoughts she had were radical. She watched and waited—looking for signs—for anything that might help her understand why slavery existed. She felt she must be older before she passed judgment.

Ella, for her part, saw Dorothy as an exception, as not really part of the Hollands in particular or of the white race in general. Ella had accepted the fact that she was a slave. Because she liked Dorothy, she was more willing to play the slave with Dorothy than she was with any of the other Hollands. But Dorothy's questioning of the status quo sometimes made her feel worse. When Dorothy wondered aloud why Ella couldn't go to school with her, it was the first time Ella thought what it might be like to go to school. Dorothy's reordering of assumptions made it harder for Ella to come to terms with her situation.

"Don't you want to learn things? Don't you want to learn how to read?" Dorothy asked.

Ella took her time answering. "This child has no time for reading. Besides, I don't need to read to do what I have to do. I learnt cooking from Wally and Sarah. I learnt cotton picking from Paymore."

Dorothy smiled. "From Paymore?"

"Yup," said Ella. "Why, you thought I was born knowing how to do it? You think it's easy?"

"I don't know."

"It's not really that hard—not for me anyway." Ella thought back to her first day picking cotton. "After your daddy bought Sammy, he decided Sammy would carry the water instead of me. He said it was time for me to learn to pick cotton. So they gave me a bag and took me out to the field. They wanted Jimmy to teach me what to do, but I said no. I said I have enough trouble with him telling me what to do all the time. I said let Paymore teach me, 'cause he's always polite to me."

"Was he a good teacher?"

"He knows how to pick cotton. When he showed me what to do, I said, 'Is that all there is to it?' and he said, 'Miss Ella, that's all there is to it, and soon enough you gonna wish there's more to it than there is.'"

Dorothy laughed. "I guess it must be boring."

"Yes'm, if you're just doing it, it's boring. But you got to play a game. You got to be quick with your fingers. You got to watch out not to break the buds that ain't bloomed. Your hands got to fly around like a butterfly. You got to drag that sack up and down the rows. That sack gets heavier and heavier just when you get more and more tired. When I'm picking cotton, I say to myself, 'Somewhere somebody must be using a whole lot of cotton.' With all the cotton I personally picked, you could make clothes for half the people in the world."

"The world is bigger than you think."

"Course I don't pick as much as some do."

"Who picks the most?" asked Dorothy.

Ella was reluctant to admit it. "Jimmy picks the most."

"Oh, I cannot believe that!"

"He likes to work, but don't tell him I told you, cause he'll say it ain't true. When he works, it's like he's dancing. He gets going. Then you see him catch himself. He slows down. But it's his mind that slows him down, not his body. If he wanted to, he could pick circles of cotton round the rest of us."

"Why does he slow down?"

"He don't like bein' a slave."

"Oh."

"'Course he gets upset about everything. He gets upset with me 'cause I ask too many questions. He gets mad at Wally 'cause she don't let him do what he want. The only one he never gets mad at is Sammy. They stick up for each other. When Sammy first carried the water, he always took the bucket to Jimmy first. Jimmy would stop his picking and say, 'Oh, little brother, I been waiting on you. I been dreaming of that water for the longest time. Oh, I'm a thirsty cotton picker, and here you come with all that good water to give me.' He'd make a big show of it. Sammy would giggle and dip the gourd in the bucket real slow. And Jimmy would fall on his knees and spread his arms wide and let Sammy pour the water in his mouth, while Jimmy threw back his neck and slurped and ooohed and ahhhed. Well it was quite a show for the rest of us, cause we all standing around thirsty waiting for them to get through playing. And you know Sammy would sometimes start to pour a little too fast and spill water on Jimmy's face and nose, and they'd both fall out laughing. Your daddy was never too happy about this."

"He probably wished someone would pour water all over his face too," Dorothy said.

"One day it went too far. Sammy got carried away. While Jimmy was on his knees, Sammy poured the whole bucket down onto Jimmy's face. Jimmy fell back on the ground, soaking wet. Then Sammy fell down next to him and they both laughed and laughed. But when your daddy saw, he came up and stood right on top of them. Your daddy was real mad. He was hot and thirsty, and all the water was spilt. With one hand, he reached down and grabbed Sammy by the back of his shirt. He picked that boy up and held him in the air. He started to shake him. I thought for sure he's gonna go get the whip. But just then, Wally ran up and grabbed him out your daddy's hand, and scolded the boy real loud. She said, 'Child, you got to behave. You got to behave. We not out here playing games child. You wasted all that water and now Massa Holland and the rest of us is thirsty. We working hard out here and won't be too long 'fore you know what I'm talking about. Now you run like the devil and bring back some fresh water for your Massa before we all come get you with the whip."

"Your mama's smart."

"Mmm, she turned to your daddy and said, "Look here,

the boy don't know what he's doing. A child don't know. I'll see to it that he brings the water from now on straight to you."

Ella and Dorothy had tarried on the bridge too long. Dorothy grabbed Ella's hand. "Come on," she said, "we're going to be late. You make me forget the time with your stories."

After they'd walked a quarter mile past the bridge, they heard the rumble of horse hooves behind them. Dorothy had been holding Ella's hand. Now she yanked her toward the side of the road. "Watch out!"

A carriage rushed toward them at tremendous speed. As they turned, they saw a plume of dust rise like a windstorm behind the carriage. There was a break in the dust plume as the carriage clattered onto the bridge over Dyer Creek. At the end of the bridge, the clatter stopped, and the rumble and dust cloud resumed. In an instant, the horses and wheels whooshed upon them. A uniformed black coachman peered at them and cracked the whip on the horses. Dorothy and Ella lurched from the road to a shallow ditch, where they turned to look back at the coach. They glimpsed a white man in a tall black hat. His hands rested on a black walking stick, propped between his knees. He cupped a pair of white gloves, which sat folded on the polished silver crown of the stick. The man looked at them from the carriage glass—but his eyes glazed over. He did not see them.

The dust storm trailing the carriage erupted all around them. Their dresses flew up. Each girl instinctively put one hand out to hold her dress down, and another to her mouth to keep from choking. When the dust died down, they climbed back onto the road, and swatted their clothes.

"Who was that?" asked Ella.

"Augustus Askew," Dorothy said.

"So that's what he looks like," said Ella.

"Seems like he doesn't care who he runs over," said Dorothy.

"I don't think he saw us."

"Oh he's a selfish, cruel old man. May his carriage tip and fall and end his misery," Dorothy said.

## 3

## THE LIGHT WITHIN

*I*n May of 1860, a traveling painter arrived in Jackson. Erastus Hicks painted "anything that wants an artist's hand," including portraits, signs, keepsakes, lithographs, and Biblical illustrations. Word of the artist's arrival spread. Within a week, Mr. Hicks received a commission. Mr. Augustus Askew engaged Mr. Hicks to paint two paintings: first, a portrait of his wife, Lucille, and, second, a painting to illustrate one of Mr. Askew's favorite Biblical scenes, in which Mary of Bethany, sister of Martha, washes the Lord's feet.

Mr. Hicks began his work at the Askew plantation, which bore the name Hickory Grove in honor of the row of stately hickories that lined both sides of the lane from the gate on Christmasville Road to the plantation house.

As he calculated his financial expenses, Mr. Askew briefly explored with Mr. Hicks whether the artist might combine the two projects by inserting the portrait of his wife into the Biblical allegory in the role of Mary. However, Erastus convinced Augustus that he would do better with a likeness of his wife piously reading the Bible, than to subject her to the uncertain implications of foot washing, even though the foot would be that of the Lord himself.

Mr. Askew gave the task of assisting Mr. Hicks to his twenty-year-old slave Cato. Everyone at Hickory Grove, except for his wife, Lucille, knew that Cato was the offspring of Augustus' rape of the slave Josline in 1840, three years after he met and married Lucille Watford.

Lucille might see as well as anyone that Cato's lineage was not pure. His skin was more the color of butternut than walnut. His hair and features disclosed mixing of blood. What Augustus hoped was not obvious to Lucille was how much Cato resembled the way he himself had looked when he was a boy of a similar age. There were no portraits to reveal the appearance of the young Augustus. Since Lucille had not laid eyes on her spouse until he was past 40 years old, she had no basis upon which to make a comparison between her husband and this fair-skinned young slave, who was always kept close at hand.

Relying on the invisibility of the familiar, Augustus calculated that keeping Cato ever present would lessen the possibility of Lucille's happening upon him at chance intervals in which the uniqueness of his appearance might arouse her curiosity. She watched the boy grow for twenty years; yet so accustomed was she to his presence that she did not notice the particulars of his eyes, or of his nose or lips. She did notice that Cato was deferential to her in an odd, sometimes anxious way. However, this eccentricity gave her nothing she could ever put her finger on.

Mr. Erastus Hicks, on the other hand, a close observer of all things visual, did notice the particulars of Cato's features. When Mr. Askew informed him that Cato would be his assistant, Erastus sought to gain the boy's friendship. He saw eagerness and curiosity in Cato's wide eyes. He also noticed that the boy abruptly changed from exuberant youth to humble servant whenever Lucille entered the room.

Cato, for his part, soon learned to trust Erastus. When they were alone together, he did not hide his enthusiasm. Not only was Erastus an artist, but he told stories of his travels across the country. He was different from all other white men. When he spoke, it was with an accent that Cato took to be a Northern dialect. His speech was full of mysterious words. He spoke to Cato as if speaking to a kindred spirit. This above all else set him apart.

As the portrait of Lucille progressed, Cato marveled at the ability of the painter to bring the blank canvas to life with an accurate likeness. Cato saw that Mr. Hicks gave his customers just what they wanted. In her portrait, Mrs. Askew sat beside a small table upon which rested an open copy of the Bible. Her hand lay outstretched on one page of scripture, as if pointing to a particular passage, while her face entreated the viewer with a stern smile that conveyed her piety. Mr. Askew was pleased with the portrait. More important, so was Mrs. Askew.

The day after that project was finished, Erastus moved his painting operation from the parlor, in which Lucille had sat, to a shrubby corner of the garden, where a bank of closely planted dogwood bushes provided shelter. As assistant, Cato had begun to learn the practical aspects of making a painting. While Mr. Hicks set up his easel, Cato fetched charcoal sticks, paints, cloths and sundry brushes. He also carted out two chairs and a bucket of water.

When they were ready, Erastus explained the project to the boy. "Son, I will now commence to paint a Biblical illustration, depicting the washing of the foot of Jesus by Mary, or more explicitly, the drying of the Lord's foot with her hair, since I reckon that particularity of the story is one that your Master Askew is most apt to find inspiring."

"Yes, sir, Master Hicks," said Cato, with the wide-eyed look of a puppy watching a bone.

Erastus smiled at the boy. "Now, Cato, my lad, here we are quite alone, don't you see. And as we will be working together hereabouts in the garden, quite out from under the eyes and ears of your master and mistress, I propose that we dispense with formalities and commence with the familiarities. Why don't you call me Erastus, and I, for my part, will call you Cato?"

"Yes, sir, Master Erastus," replied Cato.

"No, truly, you needn't say 'sir' or 'master', Cato. It makes me feel—what shall I say?—too immodest, and truth-be-told, I'm a Quaker, you see, and we Quakers believe in modest ways."

Cato nodded. He wasn't sure what a Quaker was, but he could see that they were strange. "All right, Erastus," he said.

"Fine, now, do you know your Bible? Have you heard this story of Mary washing the feet of Jesus?"

"I don't recall as I have," said Cato. "I don't recall that Reverend Zeke has mentioned it."

"Reverend Zeke?"

"He's our preacher, the slaves' preacher. We go to him on Sundays down by Dyer creek. He tells many fine stories, but I don't recall him telling a story about washing the Lord's feet."

"Well, Cato, this story is connected to the story of Lazarus."

"Lazarus? I know that story. Reverend Zeke told us that Jesus raised him from the dead."

"Yes, well then no doubt you know that Jesus raised Lazarus from the dead because his sisters, Mary and Martha were quite distraught. When Mary wept, Jesus wept too; so he was right fond of Mary, you see. Sometime after Jesus brought Lazarus back to life, the whole group, Lazarus, Martha, Mary,

Jesus and the disciples, they all sat down for a pleasant supper. Mary brought in a pound of costly ointment, anointed Jesus' feet, and then wiped his feet with her hair. Well, old Judas, he didn't like that. He said, 'Why was not this ointment sold and given to the poor?' And Jesus said, 'Let her alone: against the day of my burying hath she kept this. For the poor always ye have with ye; but me ye have not always.'" Erastus quoted the gospel with a devout intonation.

Cato's eyes searched Erastus for an explanation of the moral. "So I reckon Jesus was thinking about his death," Cato ventured.

"Yes, and I think in truth he was moved by Mary's love and gratitude," said Erastus.

Cato hesitated, then asked, "Do you suppose she was good-looking?"

"Yes, Cato, I do suppose she must have been good-looking. Anyway, that's how I expect to paint her, don't you think?"

"Yes," Cato agreed, "but how will you draw her? Will you make her like someone you know?"

"Oh I expect I will use my imagination for Mary. That would be best, in this case. But I'll want to work with a model for Jesus ... especially so I can draw his feet. Feet are considerable hard to paint, you see."

"A model?" said Cato, who was not sure of the word's meaning.

"Yes. A model, you know, is someone who stands in for somebody else."

"Will you ask Master Askew?"

Erastus laughed. "No, no, I don't suppose old Askew will have the time or patience to sit as a model, much as he might hanker to see himself painted in as the Lord. No, I need a body with a pair of good feet to model." As he spoke, Erastus looked down at Cato's bare feet, then back up at him with a wink.

"Me?" Cato was astonished. He looked down at his feet in dismay. "Oh but my feet are all dirty."

"Well, lad, I'd allow that Jesus' feet were dirty too, and that's why Mary thought to wash them for him."

"But what if Master Askew finds out?" Cato asked. "I don't believe he'd think it fitting for me to be a model for Jesus."

"No, Cato, I expect you're right about that." Erastus agreed. "So that's why we've come out here in the garden, where all these fine dogwood shrubs and bushes block the view from the house. Nobody can see us here. And if someone should happen upon us while I'm sketching you, I will surely pretend to cuss you out as if I'd just caught you sitting down on the job. No one will be the wiser."

Cato was not convinced. "But won't they recognize me in the painting?"

"Well that depends." Erastus scratched his chin. "I calculate that if I use your face and body, I'll disguise it just enough so no one will know it's you … except you and me, of course." He winked again. "I can alter your complexion, and fix you up with a fine beard."

"Gracious!" said Cato with a broad smile. "I'll be the model for Jesus!" His eyes shone as he paced beside the chair. "A beard! I don't know what I should look like with a beard. … Do you want me to sit here on the chair?" He looked at the chair, and then at the bucket beside it. "Should I wash my feet first? Is that what this bucket of water is for?" He sat down on the chair. He sat on his hands to keep them still. Then his eyebrows arched, "Oh Erastus, what about the ointment?" His hands flew up. "We haven't any ointment!"

"Now, now lad, let's be methodical here," said the artist. "The first thing I need is some libations for the artistic muse. Tell me, Cato, do you happen to know where Mr. Askew keeps his anti-fogmatics? I need something to embolden my palette. A dram of bourbon and sugar for a julep should do the trick."

"Do you mean liquor?" asked Cato.

"Yes, my boy, I do indeed. I mean to have a smile of a drink before we commence, and if you can fetch that for me from the house, I'm inclined to suggest that you might join me in a swallow to our health."

"Ah, to our health ... yes, but the bourbon is locked in a cabinet," Cato said. "I'd have to ask Mrs. Askew to open it." He hesitated. "I do believe it might go better, if you wouldn't think it too inconvenient, if you were to ask Mrs. Askew for it yourself. Otherwise I fear Mrs. Askew would question such a request from me, and wonder if I'd taken leave of my senses."

The artist considered this. "Well, yes, I suppose it would be better if I inquired after the bourbon myself," he concluded.

While Erastus went to the house to negotiate the liquor, Cato busied himself arranging the easel, paper and charcoal sticks. He contemplated whether he ought to wash his feet. He was uncertain whether the artist wanted him to model with clean feet or dirty feet, so he decided to wait. He was beside himself with excitement. Never in his life had he imagined that such a moment might fall to him, to have his portrait painted in a likeness of Christ, by a white man who offered him bourbon and asked to be called by his first name.

As Cato was contemplating these things, Erastus returned from his mission with a beaker of bourbon, a small pouch of sugar, and a glass. Then with yet another wink, Erastus, reached inside his waistcoat and pulled out a second glass, which he had secreted from the pantry.

"Now, we'll have a proper toast to launch this project," he said. He placed the glasses on the ground, poured a half inch of sugar in each, and then topped the sugar with the bourbon. He handed Cato one of the glasses. "Are you partial to juleps?" he asked.

"I've never tasted one before," said Cato.

"Have you had liquor ever at all, my lad?"

"No, Erastus, not as I can recall."

"Well, I do believe you should recall it had you done so," said Erastus. "So here is a start; and here's to your health, my friend." He handed Cato a glass and clinked it with his own. "May all the dreams of your heart someday come true."

Cato had never received a toast before. He tasted the sweetened bourbon, which felt warm in his throat. "And, well, to you also, Erastus." He clinked his glass on the artist's. "May the dreams of your heart also come true."

"Ah, my friend, thank you," said Erastus. His eyes narrowed. "You know, I think I can say that the dreams of my heart have indeed come true. Look, don't you see, here we are on a fine summer day in a splendid garden, about to commence upon the undertaking of an inspiring artistic depiction, and you are as fine a model as I could ever hope to paint." He put his hand freely on the boy's wrist, and held it there.

Cato felt the blood rush to his head. Perhaps it was from the bourbon. He was not sure why, but he felt as if he wanted to grasp the artist bodily and clasp him to himself. However, he simply looked at the ground and said, "Yes, Erastus, it is a fine day to model for Jesus."

"Well, let's get to it then, shall we?" Erastus swallowed the last of his drink, then turned to the easel, which sat a dozen feet from the chair and water bucket. "Now let's see, have a seat there, and I'll sketch out the basics of the scene. I'll commence with a study, a charcoal sketch, proportional to but smaller than the final painting."

"Do you want me to wash my feet first?" asked Cato, recalling his earlier dilemma.

"Ah …." Erastus considered this. "I have a surprise," he said.

Cato sat on the chair, and rolled up his pant leg in preparation for modeling. The artist observed this, then came up in front of the boy, knelt and slid the water bucket round in front of him. He reached into a pocket of his waistcoat and pulled out a small vial and a cloth. He popped the stopper off the vial and passed it under Cato's nose. "And when Mary washed his feet," Erastus said, "the house was filled with the fragrance of the ointment."

Cato inhaled the rich flowery aroma, which recalled a perfume he'd smelled on Mrs. Askew at Christmas time. He felt his eyes roll back in his head.

Erastus poured the contents of the vial into the bucket of water, which had sat warming in the sun for half an hour. He placed his hands in the bucket and swirled the water, gently stirring it. Then, with his wet bare hands, he cupped Cato's foot and began to rub it. Startled, Cato raised his head, which had sunk back, and stared down at the man at his feet as if he were dreaming. He felt the warmth of the water and the smooth, massaging strokes of Erastus's hand. He heard himself murmur, "Ah, that feels …." He let the sentence trail off.

Erastus washed and kneaded Cato's foot, while he gazed at the boy's face. He appraised the head of soft sepia curls, the warm, hazel eyes, the nut-brown whiskerless skin, the mulatto medley of features: Caucasian nose and cheeks, Negro lips and eyes. "Yes, Cato, you're as handsome a lad as I can recall, and I shall paint the Lord as an older version of you, so no one but you and I will know it."

Cato was not sure what was happening. The warmth of the water, and the sensual touch on his foot, shot up his leg in a way quite similar to the way the bourbon had glided warm and sweetly tingling into his throat. He felt a strange, comfortable feeling. Instinctively, he placed his hand on his leg and squeezed it. He saw the artist's eyes watch his hand, and then felt the man's grip tighten, rubbing up and down his foot. There were goose bumps on Cato's neck.

Cato wanted to say something, but he was speechless. He had never before felt sensual pleasure at the hands of any person. His whole life now seemed as if it had been a yearning for a kind touch such as this; and here was this gentle man, washing his foot, anointing it now with a sweet perfume. He wanted to thank him, to say something to convey the gratitude that flowed in his heart for the Quaker's friendship.

Erastus peered at Cato with an earnest look. He pulled himself slightly forward using Cato's foot, and seemed, for a moment, as if he was going to lay his chin down on the chair right between Cato's legs. His gaze froze there in midair, as if to appraise a rare jewel. Cato could not decipher the transfixed look in his eyes. The painter seemed almost frightened. He stayed that way awkwardly long, staring at Cato's lap, his head suspended, not moving down or up, but poised above Cato's legs.

Then Erastus sucked in his breath, turned his head, and closed his eyes. He said, "Someday my lad, you shall have the dreams of your heart come true, for you are one of God's finest creations." He pulled back, lifted his head and smiled. "All I can do is tell you this: You will find this dream, someday. For God has given me the gift of vision, the gift of imagination, and I can see the happiness of that time, when you shall know the yearnings of your heart, and the truest joy of life shall come to you."

Cato did not know what Erastus meant, nor could he see what place or yearnings the man imagined, but he felt the kind intentions of his friend's wishes. He placed his hand gently on the artist's head, and, as he did so, Erastus voice squeaked, "Oh … God help me."

Erastus shook his head, as if brushing off a fly, and stood. He shrugged his shoulders. "Yes, God help me lad, we've got much work to do and I'm inclined to say we could fritter away the hours with no accomplishment if I don't set about my work."

Erastus returned to the easel and took up a pencil. "All right, now let's see you extend your foot there. Find a comfortable position, and I shall commence to draw."

Cato lay back in the chair and propped his leg on the bucket with his bare foot extended. He folded his hands behind his head and looked up at the sky. His body tingled. He thought of a time past, when he'd sat by himself on a stool in a room adjacent to the parlor. The Askews were entertaining. One of the guests played the piano. The pianist had announced that the music was a nocturne written by a man whose name was "show pan." Cato had thought at the time that those moments he sat listening to a nocturne, had been the best moments of his life. Now he considered that this moment in the garden might supplant that in his memory.

"Erastus, do you know famous piano music?" he asked.

"I do."

"Do you know music written by a man called 'show pan?'"

The artist smiled. "Why yes, Frederic Chopin, composer of etudes, nocturnes and waltzes. I have heard his work. But where in the name of gracious did you hear of him, my young friend?"

"A man came to visit the Askews last year. He played the piano in the parlor. I was in the next room. I thought it must be how it is in heaven, to hear music like that."

"Yes, well, you have a sensitive soul, my lad. I hope that someday you will rest in heaven, and hear all the great music of the world. I do believe that humankind has done its best when it comes to music, Cato; better than at any other art."

Cato had never thought about humankind in this way. "Where does music come from?" he asked.

"I should think it comes from God," Erastus answered. "In fact, anyone who might doubt the Almighty's existence, should only have to hear the music of Chopin or Mozart to know for a fact that it must come from the Holy Spirit."

"Where did you learn to paint, Erastus?"

"I studied it as a boy," the artist replied, "with a man my father knew. His name was Thomas Fields. He painted portraits in my home city: Philadelphia, Pennsylvania."

Cato had heard of Pennsylvania. Master William told him about it, as he had told him of so many things. William talked about the North as if it were quite another world. "What is Pennsylvania like?" he asked.

"It's full of woods, my lad. The name Pennsylvania means 'Penn's woods' after Mr. William Penn, a great man, a man of peace. He was a Quaker, you see, like me. He was the first governor of the colony."

"How come you are a Quaker?"

"My people in Pennsylvania are all Quakers, and so I was brought up in the Quaker faith."

"Are Quakers the same as Shakers, Erastus?"

"Now lad, how ever did you hear of Shakers?"

"From William, he's Master Augustus' son. I was his servant until he went to college. William said there were Shakers in Kentucky. He said they shaked when they were in church."

"Well the Shakers split off from the Quakers, Cato. I guess you could say we quake and they shake."

Cato laughed. "How come you quake?"

"Well that's what Quakers do when they are moved by the

Holy Spirit, you see. It means you feel the power of God upon you, and it causes you to tremble."

Cato tried to imagine the feel of the hand of the Holy Spirit upon him. "I think I would like to be a Quaker," he said.

"Well, my lad, we don't just quake. We call ourselves the Society of Friends. We believe in brotherly love, mainly. Quakers founded the city of Philadelphia, which means the city of brotherly love."

A city of brotherly love seemed fantastic. Cato could not imagine what it would look like. "Do the Quakers have slaves too?" he asked.

"No, lad, no." Erastus looked toward Cato with tender eyes. "That is not our way. We believe in love and friendship … among all God's creatures."

"I expect it is right that creatures should be friends with each other," Cato said.

Erastus smiled. "We Quakers, we Friends, speak of the light within, which means the light of God that shines in everyone. When I paint, I try to capture that light in my painting."

"Is that's why Missus Askew's portrait glows so?"

"Well, it is a question of how you use the paint, you see, Cato. Each man can put himself in the service of the Lord, no matter what job he does. You only have to look for the light within each person you meet."

"I can't say as I ever saw the light within Missus Askew, Erastus. She's generally strict where I'm concerned, though she's always been kind to William."

"Well Cato, you have to consider if you may be sometimes unfriendly toward her. I've noticed that your manner is different when she's about."

"I … well …." Cato was not sure if he should confide in

the painter. "I'm afraid that she might find out about me," he said.

"Find out what?"

"About where I come from."

"Weren't you born here?"

"Yes ... well ... that's just it. ... I was born here, and my mother was, well, she was a servant to Master Askew and he .... well ... I reckon, from what everyone says, that he was my father."

"Ah ...."

"And you know Erastus, I think everyone in the whole county knows about it, excepting for Missus Askew; and I do believe if she knew it, she would not glow so."

"Perhaps not ...," the painter conceded. "But what does Askew think of you. Does he treat you well?"

"Yes, mostly he does. But ... well ... he never does look me in the eye. I think he always looks to my left or my right. Only once did I see him look at me. It was in the mirror, once ... in the dining room. That's the only time I recall him looking right at me, and I think he was staring then for certain."

"Well, now, I expect he can see himself in you, wouldn't you think? But it must be considerable hard for him to see it."

"Yes, considerable."

"And what of your mother?"

"My mother passed away ten years ago."

"I see."

"I was ten then. They wouldn't let me see her when she died. She was sick with fever. I guess it was catching."

"Ah, my gracious."

"So, now I'm mostly on my own."

"Yes. Well, Cato, that is the truth, we are all on our own, you see, in a manner of speaking. There's nothing wrong with that. But you have the light within."

"Do I?"

"Ah, lad, it glows powerful strong in thee. I can tell you that. But look now, you must look for it in others, that's the thing. Look for it in the people you meet. That's how you can see it best."

"I'll try, Erastus."

"The more you're able to see the light in others, the more brightly it will glow in you. Watch and see."

"How do you make the paint glow, Erastus?"

"It's a trick of the eye my boy. When you control the whole world within the painting you can choose the relative glow of anything within it."

"I wish I could paint."

"Ah, well …." Erastus looked at the boy with tenderness. "I wish it was a world in which you could do all that you are capable of doing. For I think you could learn to do anything you put your mind to. But you must make the most of what God gives you. If you were born to serve, always remember that you can serve with grace."

4

## A POT TO CATCH THE SOUNDS

The reverend Ezekiel Daniel's life changed upon the death of his owner, James Greer. Greer whipped Ezekiel regularly in his early life. But near the end of his life, when the specter of his demise was before him, Greer grew repentant for his sins. It came to him in a dream to strike a bargain with his slave. He told Zeke he would set him free, if in return Zeke would take a vow to spread the word of the Lord among his people.

At that time, Zeke had not come unto the Lord. But when Master Greer put forth this proposition, Zeke accepted salvation on that day. They struck a bargain, and each was as good as his word. Greer brought in a tutor to teach Zeke to read, so he could study the Bible. Zeke came each Sunday to the back row of Greer's Methodist church to hear the teachings of its minister. When the old master saw that Zeke had learned to read the Bible well enough to quote chapter and verse, he signed the papers that set Zeke free upon his death.

The night the old man passed away, Zeke knelt next to his master's body and kissed his forehead. Zeke had both his freedom and a sizable sum of money, which Greer left him for good measure. Zeke might have done any number of things, but the very next day he set upon his mission. He spread word among the slaves in the northern districts of Jackson to come to the woods along Dyer Creek near Christmasville Road on Sunday morning, there to hear the word of the Lord.

The Forked Deer was a narrow river, brown from Tennessee mud, which did not run straight for any meaningful distance. Even so, it was navigable for the flat-bottomed boats that carried cotton west to Memphis then down the Mississippi. Several tributaries along its course fed the Forked Deer, and these creeks crisscrossed the farms and plantations of Madison County. Dyer Creek was one of the largest of these, wide-enough to require a bridge on Christmasville Road, and deep enough in late spring or early summer to accommodate a full baptism.

The slaves gathered in a clearing along the banks of Dyer Creek, surrounded by woods thick enough to assure conceal-ment. A big clay pot sat tipped on its side near the stump from which Reverend Zeke held forth. The slaves believed the pot could catch the sounds, the amens and exhortations of the faithful. The pot would prevent wayward words from reaching white ears. This was an important precaution, because the forum at Dyer Creek provided an occasion for frank talk, permissible in only a few places in the life of a slave.

When he wasn't preaching, Zeke was a quiet fellow. He lived in a shack on the edge of the old Greer farm. He was a big, heavyset man, much given to perspiration and blowing his nose. Apart from food, his principal temptation came from clothes. In this, he held himself to moderation, lest he become too worldly. His natural inclination was to dress nattily, and to keep himself oiled and sharp. But in deference to modesty, he focused his love of ornamentation upon a single collection of accessories: his handkerchiefs.

Drawing from time to time upon his financial endowment, Zeke collected handkerchiefs from the humblest plain white cotton to the most fanciful embroidered silk. These he bought from merchants and traveling salesmen. Others he received as gifts from members of his congregation of followers.

Zeke put his ever-present handkerchief to good use when he preached. It came and went from his vest pocket as he spoke. Sometimes, in an impassioned moment, it rose up to wipe the sweat from his brow. Sometimes it hung in his hand by the side of the tree stump that served as his pulpit. Sometimes it waved in the air making a point. It could be the flag that parted the waters of the Red Sea. It could be the trumpet that sounded in Jericho. It could be the prodigal son working his way back from the excesses of sin to the simple redemption of home. It could be the crown of thorns on Jesus' head, or the whip that scourged his body. It could be the cross itself, carried up Golgotha, heavier than any sack of cotton ever dragged to the gin, or it could be the great stone which rolled away from Jesus' tomb on Easter morning.

Soon enough, Zeke found a good crowd gathering on Sunday mornings to hear him preach. As it happened, the slaves' yearning for the Lord and their yearnings for each other found a common purpose at the Creek, as there was no better place to begin a courtship or learn the news of the land than while pursuing salvation. Slaves from a dozen farms and plantations mingled together, and the opportunities for the slaves to enjoy social intercourse were greater at the Creek than at any other place in Madison County.

Wally accustomed her children to attending Zeke's services on Sunday mornings. At age 18, Ella went willingly, not only because she wanted to hear the gossip, but also because she enjoyed Reverend Zeke's sermons. Reverend Zeke and his handkerchief kept folks shouting, fanning, and leaning forward. The sermons roused her. Emotions yanked at her heart. But then a sober voice in her head would see that the flag, or the stone, or the scourge was just a handkerchief, that it was made from cotton cloth, that back home when he was by himself, Reverend Zeke must surely have blown his nose in it.

Jimmy, who was 23, had no patience for hearing about yet another Master who set forth commandments and required obedience. He was indifferent to gossip, and though he was of age, he was indifferent as well to the opportunities for romantic advancement. He endured the weekly ordeal only because Wally gave him no choice. But one Sunday, events conspired to bring Jimmy's simmering resentment to a head.

Sara, a slave from the Askew's Hickory Grove plantation, had been caught stealing food from a locked storehouse. In reprisal for this, and by way of setting an example to others, Augustus Askew had arranged to have one of Sara's children, her son Charles, sold to traders who would take him to a distant county. Mr. Askew told Sara he would use the proceeds from this transaction to replenish the stolen storehouse supplies.

"You have taken from me. Now I will take from you," he told her. "The child will be gone by the end of the week."

Within a quarter of an hour, the whole gathering at Dyer Creek had heard the story. Sara herself came to the side of the stump, where Zeke stood with his head bowed. She knelt in front of him, and said simply "Help me."

Reverend Zeke stood over her. He was a big man, big as a mountain. When he looked up at the sky, his eyes flashed. They flashed as though lightning struck the mountain from a cloud. There was a storm of emotion brewing. Reverend Zeke moved to take control of the storm. He raised his hands to quiet the congregation.

"I know you got a hurt", he roared. His voice boomed with the power of the mountain behind it.

"I've been there," he whispered. His whispering voice cracked.

"I've been there," he said yet again, even more softly. It was hard for him to say it, hard for him to let the pain of it back up, to let it out of his soul, to show it so clearly to his people.

Sweat beaded on Zeke's face. His eyes closed. His face wrenched into a question, and his eyes opened. "Anybody else been there?"

He looked around the clearing in a sweeping arc. All around the bank of the creek, hands shot up and waved. The slaves leaned forward with their arms stretched out, leaning so far across the backs of those in front of them and waving so hard that the whole congregation seemed on the verge of toppling over.

Zeke smiled. "You've been there?" he asked. "You know what it is to hurt?"

Sara, on her knees, could not speak. Several days of tears had choked away her voice. Her face was raw and soggy. She looked around the clearing at the faces that mirrored her pain, at the arms stretched out and waving at her.

"I know you ask, 'How'd we get this way, Lord?'" Zeke was imploring. He spoke upward to the sky.

"I know you ask, Lord, why? – Why, Jesus?" Zeke got lost in his question. He didn't know the answer. He hadn't prepared an answer before he spoke.

He asked again, "Why?" He wanted God to hear him clearly.

His voice grew louder, "Why would you let this happen?"

His voice grew angry. "I mean to say, why should it be this way?"

Zeke forgot about the people around him. He straightened himself up and raised his arm up toward God. He yelled now, angry and shaking his fist. "Why should this woman ...?" His hand pointed down at Sara. He took a step forward and then a step back, as if he were preparing for a fight.

"Why should Sara ...?" His voice cracked when he said "Sara," and his eyes fell closed again.

"Why should Sara – a good mother ..." He began shaking his arm as he pointed down at Sara. "... a woman who loved her little children." There were shouts now in the congregation. Zeke was saying too much, saying it too clearly, more than anyone could bear.

"No, I'm gonna say it now." Zeke shook his head. "... a woman who loved her children, a woman whose only thought, whose only thought was to get some food for their hunger."

Zeke opened his eyes again and cast them out over the congregation. "What mother wouldn't?" He looked at a slender woman who leaned against a tree while she slapped her head with the back of her hand. "What mother wouldn't?" he asked again.

Zeke stepped forward to the edge of the tree stump. He pulled out his handkerchief to dangle it in front of him like a hungry child. "Little boy says, 'I'm hungry.'"

A woman in the back shouted, "That's right!"

Zeke smiled, swung the handkerchief back behind him, and said, "Well, let me get you some food then."

Several voices answered, "That's right!"

"Gonna go over to that store house," Zeke said, and waved the handkerchief to his side. "Gonna go over to that house where they got all that food locked up!"

"Go on."

"Got to go and get my little boy something to eat."

"Amen."

"Don't care about Askew!"

"No!"

"Askew don't need that food."

"No!"

"The plain truth of it is, Askew's got too much food."

Zeke began laughing now. "That's why he's got to keep it locked up!"

Everywhere heads nodded.

"But the Bible says ..." Zeke paused, and dropped the handkerchief to his side. "... The Bible says, 'Thou shalt not steal.'"

The congregation fell silent. Zeke had come to a trap. He didn't know where he was going. He closed his eyes again, seeking to implore his heart.

"God says, 'Thou shalt not steal.'" Zeke repeated it slowly. He looked hard at the commandment, looked for a way around it. But it seemed locked tight. Silence rippled across the creek.

Zeke turned around. He turned to face the water for a moment. Then he raised his hand above his head and turned back to his flock. "Now some might say that Askew stole – that Mr. Augustus Askew stole that child from his mama when he determined to sell that boy away from her."

Several slaves looked at the pot. Others turned and peered into the woods behind them. No one was there. There was no sound except the echo of Zeke's defamation.

Zeke shook his head. "But Askew, he says, 'No, I didn't steal. These children, they're my property. Sara, she's my property.'"

Ella moved to the edge of the rock she was sitting on. Jimmy was glaring. Sara looked up now at Zeke with vacant eyes. Zeke stared at her for a moment, and then wiped his face with the handkerchief.

"But I say … I say, if Sara took some of Askew's food, well that's not stealing. No, that's not stealing."

He raised his voice now to drive home his message. "Those children put that food in their mouths. That food went down in their stomachs. If Askew owns the children, then he still owns the food even when it's down inside them. So Askew didn't lose none of his food. He still owned it. Ain't nothing got stole!"

This line of reasoning stunned the congregation. Zeke had found a way past the commandment. "You see, brothers and sisters, that's just one piece of Askew's property eating another piece of his property!" Zeke boomed.

"But old Askew," Zeke cocked his head, "he don't see it that way. Askew say he's gonna make an example."

Zeke screwed up his face and looked back over his shoulder. He said, "An example?"

He looked down at Sara. "Now brothers and sisters, we have here before us an example."

Zeke stepped in front of the stump. He reached down to take Sara's hand. He raised her to her feet.

"We have an example of the sadness of losing a child." Sara stood meekly, tears glistening on her face.

Zeke raised his eyes and looked at the sky. "But what can this teach us?" He looked back down at his congregation. He said, "I say to you and I say to the Lord, 'What does this teach us?'"

Zeke let go of Sara's hand and stepped back behind the stump. "Jesus said …" He paused and looked around slowly at the slaves, "Jesus said, 'If a man strikes you – you ought not to strike him back.' Jesus said, 'You've got to turn the other cheek.'" Zeke turned his face to the side as he said this.

Then, with his head sideways, he turned his eyes back toward the listeners. "Well, alright ..." He turned his face forward again.

"Alright, I turned my cheek." He turned his head to the other side, "and then I turned the other cheek," he turned his head once more, "and then I turned back to the first cheek again!"

"I'm 'bout run out of cheeks." He raised his handkerchief in front of his face. "But I say ..." he shook the handkerchief. "I say you got to keep on to the last." Zeke was trembling now, summoning the power of his faith from within himself.

"Listen to me!" The light began to shine in his eyes again. "Listen to what I say." Zeke was summoning back the storm.

"After Jesus had been whipped ..." Zeke paused. "... whipped and scourged! ...." Zeke looked at the sky, at a soft white cloud. "Do you know what that's like?" Zeke put a twisted smile on his face. "Do you know what whipping feels like?"

The congregation was silent. Everyone knew how often Zeke had been whipped in his youth.

"After Jesus was whipped, they nailed him ..." Zeke's voice faltered. "... they nailed him..." Zeke swallowed his voice completely now. "... to a cross." Zeke's eyes glazed with the vision before him. The sun was beating on his face. Beads of sweat dropped from his chin, but he did not feel them.

"And when Jesus was nailed on that cross, he had something to say." Zeke opened his eyes. His eyes were full of his pain and anger. They held the storm that was raging in his heart, in the hearts of all those present. And for a moment, it looked as if he couldn't go on, as if he'd reached the limit of what he could say. He was teetering on the edge of the small rock upon which he stood behind the stump. His muscles strained against his weight.

A passing cloud caused the sun to darken, stretching a shadow quickly and quietly across the clearing. Several slaves looked up —surprised by the sudden chill. Then the cloud passed and the sun leapt back into the clearing. The expanding brightness soothed the hurt in Zeke's eyes. His weight settled back on the rock. His upstretched arm slowly glided down to his side.

"When he was nailed to the cross, Jesus said, 'Forgive them.' He said, 'Forgive them, for they know not what they do.'" Zeke's voice was gentle now. A glint of tear showed in the corner of his eye.

"I say, 'Alright! Askew has given us his example. Now let us give Askew ours!'" Zeke shouted the last word so abruptly, that several heads jerked forward.

"We have a higher example, an example that puts Askew to shame. We can be better than Askew. We can do what that man has never done! We got to say, 'Forgive them. Forgive him brothers and sisters. Forgive this man! For as God is my witness, this man does not know what he do. He doesn't know it!'"

Zeke paused and shook his head. "This is a man who has seen fit to put his own son into slavery." All eyes darted around the clearing for Cato, looking for the slave that everyone knew was the offspring of Askew's rape of his house servant Josline. But Cato was not there this day.

"This is a man who has whipped and punished and taken and given nothing but suffering to those who work to care for his home, his land, his property, even his wife and his children."

This is a man who does not know, cannot know, will never know, until that day when he finally stands before God almighty, what he do."

Zeke wiped his face with the handkerchief. "They know

not what they do. And Jesus said, 'Forgive them, Father. They know not what they do.'"

Zeke finished his sermon with his face bowed. He took Sara's hand again. Her face was empty. Zeke said, "Let us now join our hands brothers and sisters, in prayer for our sister Sara, and for the well-being of her precious son Charles."

With that, Ella reached to take Jimmy's hand, but Jimmy pulled his hand away. His chest was heaving. He seemed to be struggling to breathe. He was so incensed, so outraged by the forgiveness that Reverend Zeke proposed that he could barely speak. He stood and crackled these words to Wally, "I will never come here again." And with that, he pushed past the people near him and walked back into the woods.

# 5

# BEL CANTO

*A*s the summer of 1860 ripened, so too did Erastus Hicks' painting of the washing of Christ's feet by Mary of Bethany. Having completed an assortment of charcoal studies, the painter began preparations for the painting itself. One morning, he became a carpenter, fashioning stretchers with wood and glue. In the afternoon, he coaxed the canvas onto its frame, then brushed its surface with sizing of rabbit skin glue. The next morning he primed the skin with a coat of lead white paint. A week later, he painted the entire area with a ground using burnt umber, a dark, neutral pigment, which would allow the flesh of the figures to incarnate with three-dimensional force.

At first, the characters emerged from the background without context. The figure of Christ sat in a space that would eventually hold a stool. In front of Christ, the specter of Mary, on her knees, dried his foot with her hair. The body of Jesus leaned back on the invisible stool in a yielding, dreamy posture, his left leg raised toward Mary. The face of Jesus—a delicate, sable-brushed sheen of color--was wrapped in hog bristle strokes of chestnut hair and beard. Erastus, seeking a heretical realism, intended to paint Christ as an ethnic Jew, with Semitic blood in his veins. So the hair, a flurry of passionate paint strokes, was coarser than that of the pious fine-haired Protestant Christs Erastus had seen in a New York museum.

While Erastus had painted most of the face of Jesus, he had not yet painted his eyes. A plain umber wash still showed in the spot where he would render those eyes. As he prepared, the painter looked toward Cato, who sat on a tree stump, in the same yielding posture as Jesus, his left foot similarly raised. With great concentration, the painter stared at Cato. He wanted to capture the eyes in quick, deft strokes of his brush.

Cato sat patiently watching the painter. He asked, "Why do you paint, Erastus?"

Without interrupting his staring, Erastus spoke. "I don't know if I can explain it well, my boy. It has to do with yearning ... yearning to get hold of what I see. Sometimes I'm overcome, Cato, truly ...." He looked away from Cato now, and swept his eyes around the Askew garden. "When I look at this world and see it, I wonder if what I see ... is this what others see too?" He looked back at Cato. "Because I think if others saw it as I did, they too would be compelled to take up paints and brushes—to try to rope the magnificence of this world onto a canvas ... just to try to get hold of it .... I'd say it's like putting a saddle on a horse. Of course, when I paint for folks like Askew and when I paint for myself, it's like the difference between riding a Shetland and riding a Mustang. One's a pleasant enough journey, but the other ... my boy, I hold on for dear life."

Cato's eyes were wide as he pictured the painter on a charging horse. "I wish I could see things through your eyes," he said. "I think I only have my eyes half open most days. I get to thinking … and my thoughts take over, and I walk around, and I do my work, but inside I'm thinking so very hard … I don't know what I do see."

The painter smiled. "Your thoughts light up your eyes, my boy. You carry that depth in your eyes. And I want to get that look in Jesus' eyes. There's a whole inner world that looks out from those eyes." He turned to look at the canvas with a critical gaze. "I don't know if it can be painted, God help me. Things like that, they're more than just light and shadow. I'm not sure that I can paint it. It's like a twinkle or a moon ray. Such fleetingness can't be fixed in pigment through repeated effort. I can't work it and re-work it. I must get it in a few certain strokes."

Cato sat listening to his mentor. "Erastus I don't know what I shall do when you leave. I wonder if I will ever again meet someone like you. I fear my whole life will come and go with no one to talk to about the things that you talk about."

The painter blinked his eyes in a befuddled way, and thought for a while. Then he said, with sudden optimism, "Truly, my lad, the best thing for you would be to take up reading."

"Reading?!" Cato shook his head. "Oh, no."

Erastus picked up a small brush. He balanced it in his hand as if he were sizing up the trueness of an arrow. "You'd meet many a fine mind in the great books," he said. "And it would comfort you right well, I know it."

"It's not possible," Cato insisted. "If I were caught, I'd be punished. You don't know Master Askew. He's terrible strict— and no one dares cross him."

"Yes, I know it's dangerous," the painter said. "But … well my boy …" He arched an eyebrow. "Surely you do things now in secret."

"But how would I learn to read?"

"You'd learn from me, of course. I can start you off ...,
teach you the alphabet. Once you get the idea of it, you can
learn the rest on your own."

"But I don't have any books."

Erastus frowned, as he saw that there was to be a host of
objections. "Doesn't your Master Askew have a library? Aren't
there scores of books on his shelves? I should think you could
find a way to take a volume out, now and then, without
leaving an empty space." The painter mimed taking a book
from the shelf with his hands and replacing it with the brush.
"That's the key ... you must always leave a place holder." He
returned to staring at the painting. "I can give you a proper
book for that purpose: a nice plain volume, one that won't call
attention to itself."

"No. No. He'd find me out."

Erastus shrugged this away. "Do you think he inspects the
library day by day?" He took a rag and dabbed it at the canvas.
"I've seen enough of the man to know his mind. I'd wager he's
read but a few of those books." He looked back at Cato again.
"His library's for show, my boy. Askew is not a man who
hungers for the written word."

"But Missus Askew ...," Cato said. "She reads the books.
I've seen her. And she watches me close." He looked around
suddenly, as if Lucille might be watching him even now. "I
don't know where I would hide a book, either."

"Oh my gracious, hiding is easy," the painter asserted,
looking exasperated. "You can make a hiding spot outdoors.
Somewhere seldom visited. You can fashion a fine hiding spot
with an arrangement of rocks." He kicked a nearby rock to
make his point.

"And how would I carry a book from the library to the
rocks and back? And where would I read them?" Cato shook
his head. "If anyone should come upon me reading! Don't

you know? It's strictly forbidden. No slave is allowed to read."

The painter's exasperation melted. He looked at Cato now with the patience of a kind parent. "Knowledge gives a man power, my boy. That's why they've made that rule." His eyes widened. "I know it will be dangerous for you. I know there will be risks. But any risk is worth it if it saves your life." Erastus gestured for emphasis with his brush. "And I fear that your life may be in greater danger if you are without this companionship, without this counsel, without the life-giving knowledge that is stored on the printed page. Your mind will not rest. I see how you are. Your soul will be forever yearning. You must have this friendship of reading." Erastus set down the brush, came up to Cato and knelt in front of him. "You must let me give you this gift." He put his hand on Cato's foot. "Someday, my boy, you will understand my reasons. I know it must seem fearful strange to you to take this step. But I have a special book, one book in particular that I want you to read."

"Is it the Bible?"

"The book I have in mind for you is a book of poems … a poetry book."

"Poetry?" Cato cocked his head. "What is that? Is it something religious?"

The painter smiled at the slave's innocence. "Poetry is like a painting made of words, my boy. It is a fine and subtle thing. And, yes, these poems are religious in their way. They are imbued with spiritual passion. These words carry the inner light of which I spoke. You'll see it plain and true in this book." He reached inside his vest and removed a worn volume. "I have but this one copy. I can find another. I want you to have this." He handed the book to Cato, whose hand hesitated when he took it, as if it were a precious jewel.

Cato looked at the markings on the spine: gold letters on

dark green leather. He knew enough to know that there were three words at the top and two words at the bottom. That was all he understood. "What is this book called?" Cato asked.

"If I tell you the title, you will have begun your reading lesson. Are you ready to begin this journey?"

Cato opened the book. He turned over a few pages. He stared at the printed marks. How strange that these funny marks could speak, could tell stories, could become ... through mysterious magic ... his friend.

"I've never heard Master Askew, or Missus Askew or William or anyone ever speak of poetry," Cato said. "But in my heart I know I would feel the rest of my life ... what was the word you used? ... yearning, if I had no one to talk to, no one to teach me. So if reading and poetry and books can be my friend when you are gone, then yes, teach me to read."

"Bravo! And courage, my lad." Erastus reached out, closed the book in Cato's hand, and pointed to the first word on the cover. "This first word is 'Leaves,' " he said. "The next word is 'of' and the last word is 'Grass.'"

Cato repeated it. "Leaves of Grass?"

"That's right. 'Leaves of Grass', written by the poet Walt Whitman. When you first learn to read, you'll find it easier to speak the words out loud. So you must practice in a place where you can't be heard. This is a book meant to be spoken out loud, my boy. The poet is an admirer of bel canto, which means 'beautiful singing' so you must practice reading with a beautiful voice."

"Bel canto," Cato repeated.

"You have to say it like an Italian," Erastus said, "Bel canto." And he gestured with his hand, raising it, and at the same time closing it, as if he was grasping, then shaking a piece of paper. "Say it like you're about to sing."

Cato laughed. "Bel canto," he intoned. And he imitated the hand gesture. "But what does it mean, 'leaves of grass?'"

"Well you see that's how poetry is, my boy. You might think of the pages of a book as leaves. That's what printers call them: 'leaves'. So perhaps the poet wishes you to think of the humble beauty of something as common as a leaf of grass when you hold this book of poems. As you'll see, these poems find beauty in many common things. After reading them you might well see the world differently."

Cato turned the pages of the book again, looking hard at the printed markings and letters. "Will you read something to me, Erastus, to let me hear how it sounds?"

He handed the book to the painter who looked at the open page and smiled. "These verses," he said, "are on page 92 … I'll read a few lines to you."

> It is no little matter, this round and delicious
>     globe, moving so exactly in its orbit forever
>     and ever, without one jolt or the untruth of
>     a single second;

Cato giggled. "…this delicious globe …," he repeated. Erastus continued reading.

> I do not think it was made in six days, nor in
>     ten thousand years, nor ten decillions of
>     years,
> Nor planned and built one thing after another,
>     as an architect plans and builds a house.
> I do not think seventy years is the time of a
>     man or woman,
> Nor that seventy millions of years is the time of
>     a man or woman,

Nor that years will ever stop the existence of me
  or any one else.
Is it wonderful that I should be immortal? as
  every one is immortal,
I know it is wonderful . . . . but my eyesight is
  equally wonderful . . . . and how I was
  conceived in my mother's womb is equally
  wonderful,
And how I was not palpable once but am now .
  . . . and was born on the last day of May
  1819 . . . . and passed from a babe in the
  creeping trance of three summers and three
  winters to articulate and walk . . . . are all
  equally wonderful.

Erastus closed the book. "There now what do you think? It seems the poet has a lesson to teach us about wonder."

"Could there really be ten decillions of years?" Cato asked. "I didn't know there was such a number."

"Well, my boy, this may be what we call 'poetic license' … that is, the poet invents a figure of speech to evoke an image or a feeling—even if he makes things up a bit. It's no different really than using you to model for Jesus. Jesus may not have looked just like you … but how you look … for me … evokes the right image for Jesus. That's 'poetic license'"

"Poetic license …," Cato repeated, and shook his head. "I don't know if I'm going to understand poetry. But I do like how it sounds. It sounds 'delicious.'" Cato smiled broadly.

Erastus was looking hard at Cato. "There now. That look in your eyes when you said 'delicious.' That's what I want to capture." He dashed back to the easel, picked up the brush, twirled it once in his hand, held his other hand behind his back, dabbed the brush on his palette, took one last look at

Cato, then, while holding his breath, executed a series of quick strokes. When he was done, he let his breath out in a sigh, panting heavily, as if he'd just finished a sprint. "Ah, now" he said with great self-satisfaction. "I think I've done it!" With that, the painter took up a rag and wiped his hands. "Now, my boy, it's time for us to eat."

# 6

## TEA AND CAKE

*D*orothy's nineteenth birthday party promised to be a
special affair. Mrs. Holland invited several of
Dorothy's friends. She invited a few of her own friends as well.
She instructed Cora to make a teacake. But ongoing tensions
between Dorothy and her mother had worn them both out. As
far as Mrs. Holland was concerned, Dorothy would wear the
new dress she'd bought for her, a dress that any girl in her right
mind would be thrilled to wear to a party. As far as Dorothy
was concerned, it was her birthday, and thus she ought to have
her way. The pale green embroidered silk dress and its accompaniment of petticoats were, in Dorothy's mind, silly and
uncomfortable. The wide neckline and short sleeves made her
look, she thought, coquettish. But Mrs. Holland would hear
none of that.

So on the morning of the party, Ella stood in Dorothy's
bedroom helpfully holding, pulling, strapping and otherwise
maneuvering Dorothy into the corset and corded petticoat,
while Dorothy made faces and held her arms and legs in stub-
bornly uncooperative ways. The sight of Dorothy's cinched

figure with the hoopy petticoat amused Ella, but out of loyalty, she suppressed a smile.

"You're laughing at me!"

"No, ma'am."

"Don't 'no ma'am' me," Dorothy replied. "I swan, I look like a walking church bell in this contraption." She swung her hips as if to ring the bell.

"Don't get puckered at me," Ella said. "It ain't my fault you got to wear this outfit."

"Oh prittle prattle," Dorothy said. "Sometimes I think I'd have been better off to be a servant like you. You never have to wear anything except one simple get up, and really it just seems so much more sensible."

"Never thought of it as sensible," Ella said. She circled Dorothy with a whiskbroom, brushing down the sides of the crinoline.

"Well, really, it is. You don't have to wear stupid clothes, or have cussed lickfinger parties, or sit around sipping tea with a bunch of old ladies."

"Ooh eee, listen to you talk. Which old ladies are you speaking about?" Ella asked, taking a few extra swats at Dorothy's backside.

"Stop it. Mother's invited the ladies from the Methodist church who always sit around waving their fans like their hands were tied to a steam engine."

"Uh huh." Ella continued brushing, working her way around the lower regions of the fabric near the floor.

"Then they'll be gossiping about this and that, and raising their eyebrows and humph-ing and frowning, and twisting around this way and that in their big silly hoop skirts. It's enough to make me dizzy. Oh and on top of that Mother has asked that Askew boy William to come."

"William Askew? I thought he was gone away to school."

"He's back for the summer."

"How come you don't like him? Here, put this on." Ella held the gathered bodice so that Dorothy could slip it on.

Dorothy slid her arms in deftly, then tightened the waist to see how snugly it fit over the corset. "William doesn't know which way his clock is wound. Besides, he's only coming because his mama and papa want him to find a local girl to court, and I'm the handiest one around."

"You think he likes you?"

"Who knows? He's so awkward when we talk, I can't tell if he's tongue-tied or bored or just plain daft."

"He's not bad looking." Ella brought out the embroidered skirt and belt. While Dorothy held one end in place, Ella again circled around her with the other end.

Dorothy said, "Hmmm, he's not half as good looking as his brother."

"William Askew has a brother?" Ella stopped gathering up Dorothy's skirt and thought for a minute. "Wait now, you don't mean …?"

"Yes," Dorothy said, "you know just who I mean … that half-white half-brother of his, now he's handsome."

"You talking about Cato?" Ella clucked her tongue. "You must have gone off your rocker, Miss D." She wrapped the belt around Dorothy's waist. "Now you know you better not let your mama hear you talk like that. Ain't nobody even supposed to know those two are brothers."

"Well, don't you like him?"

"Who, Cato?" Ella blinked. "What would I want with some fool like that?"

"That's exactly how I feel about William," Dorothy said.

"Well, far as I know," Ella observed, "nobody's invited Cato to come visit with me."

Dorothy stuck out her tongue. "You see, that's just what I mean. It seems to me you get to manage all your own private affairs, while I have to jump to Mother's tunes, and all Mother's tunes have to do with getting me engaged."

"I don't know as I get to manage all my affairs. Most of the time I have to help you manage yours."

Dorothy nodded. This wasn't the first time she'd argued the advantages of being a slave only to be brought back to the one fundamental disadvantage. "Yes, I know. I know it's unfair, worse even than my own picayune problems. At least when I grow up I'll be able to do what I want." She looked at Ella with sudden intensity. "You know, if I ever have the power myself, you'll be freed too. We'll be freed together someday."

Ella had a hard time thinking of both of them being freed in the same way, but Dorothy's renewed pledge to grant her freedom moved her anew. "So you say, Miss D, and I truly would be thankful for that gift. I just don't see how your mama and papa will ever let you get that chance—especially if they get wind of what you're fixin' to do."

"Goodness' sakes, Ella, you know I wouldn't tell Mother and Father my plan if my life depended on it." Dorothy closed her eyes. "The way I figure it, I have to play my cards just so until I'm about 21 or thereabouts ...."

"Playing your cards just so," said Ella, "means you're gonna have to jump the broom with somebody like William Askew. They won't let you be lest you be married."

"Oh no," Dorothy said. "No siree. That's not my idea of freedom. I'm going to have to find a way to get along on my own, with just you and me and no one else."

"I don't know how you're going to do that," Ella shook her head. "You got to get married. Once you do, then your husband will take over the whole thing, me included."

"I'd rather be an old maid."

"You know your mama won't let you be an old maid. She's mighty set in her mind about things like that." Ella busied herself arranging the long, embroidered end of Dorothy's belt to lie just so on one side of the skirt. "You need to find somebody you can trust," she said. "Maybe William feels the same way you do about things."

"William?" Dorothy rolled her eyes. "I don't think so. He comes from a rich family. The Askews must own a hundred slaves. I don't think he's going to give up any of that."

"I mean, maybe he's like you …" Ella wasn't sure how to put it. "… Maybe he won't want to marry anybody."

"If he doesn't want to get married, I don't see how that would help anything."

"His mama and papa will want him to get married. They'll make him."

"They won't make him. Boys can do whatever they want and nobody cares. Now I wonder what happened to that bottle of perfume."

Ella fetched the crystal atomizer bottle filled with amber liquid from the bureau. She held it at arm's length pointing at Dorothy, her eyes turned away, as if she didn't want to contaminate herself with its contents. "Where should I squirt it?"

"Right on my foot. I think my foot smells a little peculiar."

Ella squirted copious amounts of perfume in the direction of Dorothy's feet. "My mama calls this 'stank good,' " Ella said. "Phew! This is one way you can keep William Askew away."

"Ha. You're funny."

"And Jimmy calls it 'puke good'", Ella added.

"Your brother doesn't like girl stuff much." Dorothy lifted her leg up toward her face, tilting the bottom of the hoop as close as she could to her face and sniffed while wafting the smell toward her with her hands. "I think Jimmy might be right." She mimed nausea. "I smell like an overripe peach mixed with hog stink."

Ella turned and pointed at Dorothy's feet. "It's those stanky stockings," she said. "You wore those same stockings yesterday." She carried the perfume back to the bureau, and returned with clean stockings from a middle drawer.

Since she couldn't bend over very far, Dorothy stuck out her feet one at a time, and Ella removed the offending stockings. Making a face, Ella held them away from her body.

Dorothy giggled. "You look like you're about to faint from holding those things."

Ella had her mouth scrunched up. "I'm not breathing." She inhaled with a short gasp. "Till I get them out in the hall." She marched across the room to the hall with her arms stretched out, while Dorothy held the clean stockings in front of her, looking helplessly at her feet, beneath the petticoat hoop below.

"I just don't know who invented these outfits," Dorothy said. "It had to have been a man. Anyone who's actually ever tried to do anything in one of these getups would know how impossible it is. I can't even put on these stockings."

Ella returned, rubbing her hands on her own skirt, as if to clean them. "Give them stockings here," she said. Taking the stockings, she stooped and slid them brusquely onto each of Dorothy's feet. "Keep your leg out," she instructed. She dashed over to the closet and returned with shoes.

"I don't like those shoes," Dorothy said. "They're too shiny."

"Can't nobody see what shoes you're wearing underneath all this dress." Ella worked the shoes onto each foot and commenced to tie up the laces.

"You're right." Dorothy said. "I should wear roller skates

down there; that way I could just float around the room like a ghost and spook all the old ladies."

"You'd skate right on out the house, right out onto the porch, and then right on down the front stairs."

"No, I'd fly off the stairs," Dorothy said. "And this hoop dress would catch the wind like a sail and carry me off away from this blasted place."

"And leave me here alone?" Ella asked. "I'd run and haul you back in, afore you blew that far away."

The exchange made them both grow silent. It revealed the heart of their dilemma, a desire to get to somewhere else, but not to be separated in the process.

"Did you ever feel," Dorothy asked, "like you were born in the wrong place at the wrong time? Sometimes I feel like there must be some world that you and I belong to, but it just isn't here. It's not anywhere near Madison County or even in Tennessee."

"You mean up North?"

"Maybe. I don't know. The North seems strange to me too. I think the place I'm imaging doesn't even exist yet. It's like a world of the future where all this no account silliness is gone, and people don't waste their time on foolishness."

"And just what would you do in this place you have in your head?"

"I think it would be a world run by women, or maybe a world run by the slaves—anybody but these foolish men hereabouts. I'd spend my time growing roses or reading or traveling the world."

"A world run by the slaves," Ella repeated it. "Now that would be skeery. You think the slaves would be doing things right?"

"All the slaves I know are thoughtful, and courteous, and

kind." Dorothy went to the mirror and began to study her hair. "Why shouldn't they run the world?"

"I don't know about that," Ella considered the idea. "Some slaves can be just as mean as the white men that own them. I heard tell about the overseer they got at the Dobson place. Say he's worse than old man Dobson ... won't let nobody catch they breath."

Dorothy pulled on a spit curl, wanting it to have less spring. "Well then, let's just say the world is run by kind people, whoever they may be. Why not?"

Once again, Ella found herself thinking about things she would never have thought about on her own. Dorothy gave her this gift, to make her think strange thoughts, to imagine the impossible. "You think there are kind people all over the world?" she asked. "I mean mixed in with everybody else."

"Yes," Dorothy said. "Mixed in with everyone else!" Her eyes lit up. "I bet if all the kind people in the world could just get together and form their own country ..."

"Then all the other countries would probably send in their armies, and put all the kind ones in slavery." Even as she spoke, Ella was surprised by her own cynicism.

"No," Dorothy said. "I don't think they would. Not if the kind people kept to themselves. Not if they didn't bother anyone."

"Well the people back in Africa," Ella said, "I bet they kept to themselves. I bet they didn't bother no one, and I know it didn't do them no good."

Dorothy looked crestfallen. This was a familiar impasse between them: Dorothy's idealism bounded by Ella's cynicism. And when it came to it, she could not deny Ella her cynicism, because the truth of Ella's point was unassailable. "I suppose that's why I'm thinking that this world is some place in the future," she concluded. "I don't know how else it can come to be."

"Well I hope I can be there too," Ella said. "I mean when this world you're talking about gets here."

"Yes, I hope we can be there together," Dorothy said. "And then you can wear the hoop skirt, and I can wear something sensible."

"I'm not wearing no corset 'n' hoop skirt," Ella said. "I'm gonna wear just what I got on."

The party attendees had gathered in the parlor of the Hollands' house. Three Methodist church ladies, Mrs. Baker, Mrs. Sneed, and Mrs. Greer, sat fanning themselves in a cluster along one wall. Four of Dorothy's girlfriends—Martha Greer, Clara Baker, Edna Sneed, and Lena Madison—sat along the other wall, where they giggled and tapped their feet with nervous energy. William Askew, looking trapped, paced back and forth in the center of the room, admiring the chandelier from various angles. He was twenty years old, fit and handsome, and stood to inherit a sizeable property. For all these reasons, he was the most eligible bachelor around. Though his visit marked the occasion of Dorothy's birthday, any of her friends would have been happy to have his attention. But William was socially clumsy, and none of them could tell if he was simply shy, or if he had no real interest in any of the girls present.

George Holland made a brief appearance in the parlor only to realize that, with the exception of William, the room was filled with women. He quickly excused himself with the explanation that the mule Fa was feeling poorly and that he must, with Willis's help, attend to the mule forthwith. This did not sit well with Henrietta, who believed her husband to be chronically oblivious to the social activities that might lead to a satisfactory betrothal of his daughter. In truth, George understood what was wanted better than he let on, but he did not have the stomach for tea and teacake with Mrs. Sneed and Mrs. Greer, and so he adopted an air of heedless naiveté when it came to such matters.

Just as her father was leaving, Dorothy made her entrance, gliding down the stairs, her legs and feet hidden beneath the mammoth pale green skirt, while Ella clomped down behind, with somewhat masculine exaggeration, in her sensible but mundane outfit. Mrs. Holland beamed her approval of Dorothy's appearance, then gave Cora, who stood in the doorway, an impatient look. "Bring in the tea, Cora," she said, and then, "Ella, mind the stairs with your shoes. You'll scuff up the wood walking that way."

"Yes, ma'am." Ella softened her stride, and slipped quietly to the side of the table by the window, eyeing the cake.

Cora had placed the teacake on the table. Beside it beckoned wrapped gifts, and the Hollands' nicest teacups, waiting to be filled with tea.

Turning her attention back to Dorothy, Mrs. Holland said, "You remember William Askew."

William, hearing his name, stepped forward as if on command, and held out his hand. "How nice to see you, Miss Holland," he said, with impeccable manners.

Dorothy was the most beautiful of the girls in the parlor, but to William, she was as formidable socially as he felt socially ineffectual. She had a reputation for being uncommonly bright. She was an avid reader, and well informed on many diverse subjects. But she was never quite as feminine in manner as in her figure, which made for a complex reaction in William. He found her agreeable to look at, but unnerving to talk to.

Dorothy took his hand. "You must tell me about life at school," she said. "I suppose things are quite exciting there, and must seem rather dull back here."

William instantly lapsed into an awkward state, unsure of how to respond to Dorothy, who seemed, as always, to be posing a trick question. "Well not so dull," he began. "… that I'd want to stay away. I mean, I'd never say it was dull to come to such a fine party." He didn't know if he'd answered successfully.

Before Dorothy could reply, Mrs. Holland burst in. "William has told me, Dorothy, that his father has acquired additional property up near Oakton."

"My, my," said Dorothy. "Soon your property will be so large, you'll need to pack a lunch and drive a carriage to get from one end to the other."

"Yes," William tried to laugh. "I suppose we will."

"Dorothy," Mrs. Holland said. "Why don't you show William the garden? Ella, help Cora serve the tea to our guests."

The room, full of people who'd been sitting quietly watching the formalities, suddenly sprang into a fever of activity. The two youngest of Mrs. Holland's friends, Mrs. Baker and Mrs. Sneed, immediately lined up at the cake table. The third, Mrs. Greer, who was a good deal older, struggled to get up, looking to be in need of a cane, but also too proud to carry one. Dorothy's four friends dashed in a group over behind the two church women, then stood watching as William and Dorothy, under Mrs. Holland's commanding gaze, exited the house toward their ordained tryst in the garden. Ella, fearing that Mrs. Greer, who was struggling mightily to rise from her chair, might tip over onto the floor in the process, went to help her get up.

Out in the garden, Dorothy began the conversation with an apology. "You'll have to forgive my mother," she said. "When she gets an idea in her head, her approach is always direct."

"I don't mind," William said. "My parents are the same."

They came to a bench near Mrs. Holland's hydrangea bed, and Dorothy said, "Shall we sit here." They sat for a moment, neither of them knowing what to say.

"I suppose your parents expect you'll settle down at Hickory Grove or somewhere thereabouts after you're done with school," Dorothy began.

"Yes, I'm sure that they do," William said.

"If I had the chance," Dorothy ventured, "I believe I'd move out of this area—I'd move to somewhere more …." She searched for a word. "… civilized."

William studied her face. Once again, he could not tell if this was a trick question. "I'm sure there are more interesting places to live," he said. "But I like the familiarity of home. It's strange to be somewhere where people don't know you."

Dorothy had heard that William was attending a school in Louisville. "Is that how it is in Louisville?" she asked.

"The Kentucky folks all know each other," he said. "Up there they grow tobacco, race horses, and make whiskey. They think anyone from Tennessee is backward."

"Have you been North?"

"You mean to Illinois?"

"I mean North, anywhere."

"No, have you?" Again, William couldn't tell where Dorothy was going.

"I haven't, but I think I'd like to see what it's like up there," Dorothy said.

"I heard that it's not that different," William said. "… except that they're kind of poor because they don't have any cotton farms and they don't have any slaves."

"I heard that they have cities, where people build steam engines."

William nodded. "The railroad is coming through here,

you know. I believe the tracks are going to split in two right down below your land."

"That's funny," she said. "I mean it's funny to hear you talk about my land. I never thought of it that way."

"Well, doesn't it belong to you?"

"I suppose it does. It belongs to my family."

"Ofttimes," William ventured. "… girls receive a portion of land in their dowry."

"Do tell," Dorothy said. "Do they let girls keep their servants, too?"

"Ofttimes," William said.

"Ella is, in fact, my best friend," she said, "… even though she's a servant."

This took William aback. Nevertheless, he said, "I know what you mean." Then he added, without thinking, "My servant Cato knows all my secrets."

"Secrets?" If Dorothy had a fan, she would have waved it. But lacking one, she merely fanned herself with her hand.

William blushed, wishing he could withdraw the word 'secrets'. "I mean," he began. He was not certain what he meant. "I mean only that Cato knows about almost everything I do, since he's always around."

"Why Mr. Askew, whatever do you do …," Dorothy persisted, "… that you must keep secret?"

"Well I reckon that's a secret." William was flushed, but he held his ground.

A gentle breeze billowed Dorothy's skirt, and rustled the nearby bowers of garden shrubs. Both William and Dorothy sat in silence, as each seemed reluctant to push their relationship in any particular direction. Each was willing to let it unfold as it might. Dorothy remembered Ella's idea that perhaps William may not want the bonds of a marriage. At the time, Dorothy couldn't see how that would help her own marriage dilemma. Now, as she thought more about it, she wondered if William might enjoy the advantages of a marriage, if he were married to someone independent, who would not much intrude on his life.

"I believe every woman should have her own private life," she began. "Some things are quite personal—and every woman should be free to follow her heart in personal matters. If I were married, I'd want to make my own decisions about matters of personal importance. Of course, my husband would also be someone who enjoyed his privacy."

William, still wary of Dorothy's conversational maneuvers, said, "Ah yes, a private life sounds well and good. But what binds two people together if each has a separate life?"

"There are many benefits to marriage," Dorothy said. "These benefits come just from being married: social standing, property, the opportunity to have children. Two people do not need to live separately in order to have privacy in their lives. If two people enjoy each other's company, wouldn't they enjoy sharing some activities even while other matters remained personal?"

"All this sounds quite practical," William said. "But it says nothing of love, romance, or …" He hesitated. "… desires."

"As for me," Dorothy replied, "I don't view romance or desire as necessary for two such people. Such desires as someone may have should be private concerns."

"You're not like any of the other girls around here," William said. "I'm never sure when you're serious, and when you're teasing."

"Oh I'd never tease about a subject like this," she said. "I might tease someone about his shoes, however."

William instinctively looked at his feet. "Shoes?"

"Yes, when a man has shoes that seem peculiarly large, it makes me wonder what that largeness says about the man."

"Well I suppose," William said, "it means the man has big feet."

"Ah, big feet. Well, I might have a mermaid's tail instead of feet, and no one would be the wiser with a dress like this." She laughed. "But you see..." She stuck her feet out from under the skirt. "... My feet are quite petite." Dorothy continued pulling her skirt back, to let more of her leg show. She watched William to see how he responded.

"Oh ...," William was blushing. "Your feet are lovely, even so."

"I wonder how much of my limb I ought to show you," she said.

"I shouldn't want to see any more than was proper," William said. "But I would find it agreeable to see a proper portion."

"I wouldn't want you to see more than was proper, either," Dorothy said. "But I'm not sure where I ought to stop. Shall it be here –?" Dorothy slid her skirt just below her calves. "Or here?" Dorothy slid the hem up close to her knee. "Does this portion seem proper?"

"That portion seems powerful proper," William whispered, his face still flush, his eyes wide. Then he said, "But I think I hear your mother calling."

It was true. Mrs. Holland was calling Dorothy's name, and calling out about the cake and tea and gifts. But Dorothy continued to hold her skirt at the cusp of her knee, and she winked. "Someday, Mr. Askew, perhaps we shall discuss more of these personal matters."

"Yes," his voice cracked. "I shall look forward to it."

Back in the parlor, Mrs. Greer sat at the table working at her slice of birthday cake with a fork. However, she had misjudged the effects of the frosting and smeared a quantity of it around her lips, where it stood in unseemly disarray about the edges of her mouth. Ella, uncertain as to how she might intervene to rectify this embarrassment in such a way as to spare Mrs. Greer's feelings, chose to come along with a large napkin and said, as if it were part of the service, "Would you care to have a napkin, ma'am?" As she spoke, she tried to indicate with her eyes that something was amiss in the direction of Mrs. Greer's mouth.

Mrs. Greer, for her part, still intent upon dispatching the teacake with gusto, took Ella's attention as an unwanted interruption. She said, "Must you stand about here making bug eyes? Aren't there other guests to attend to?"

"Oh ma'am, it's only that I forgot to serve these napkins, and Mrs. Holland said the napkins ought to be served, on account of there'd be such frosting on the cake as to make the napkins most useful to the guests." With this, she mimed wiping her own mouth with a napkin, being careful not to actually touch her mouth in the process.

"Oh very well, set the napkin on the table then."

Ella did as she requested, then shrugged, shaking her head as she walked away.

Mrs. Greer seeing this disapproving gesture, harrumphed and—having been sufficiently interrupted—returned to the cake-eating task before her.

In the meantime, Mrs. Baker and Mrs. Sneed, sitting at the opposite end of the table, had finished their cake, and commenced to drink their tea. Each held a cup in one hand and a fan in the other. Their fans were held up near their mouths in order to affect a barrier to their voices, as they discussed something discreet. Ella, curious if they were discussing the frosting smeared about Mrs. Greer's mouth, edged closer, straining to hear exactly what the Methodist church ladies were saying, while she busily mopped the table with a napkin.

She heard Mrs. Baker say, "… soiled the sofa in my parlor, and not with cake crumbs, I can tell you …"

Just then, Mrs. Holland came in from the porch, with Dorothy and William in tow. All three of them stopped at the table and turned to look at Mrs. Greer, who had just finished her cake. She held her plate in one hand, and was attempting, again without success, to raise herself. It appeared that she wanted to obtain a second slice, as there were still a few good slices to be had from the remaining cake.

Mrs. Holland, not one to mince words, said, "Lilah, you need to wipe your mouth." Then she added, in a sweeter tone, "Would you care for another slice of cake?"

Mrs. Greer grasped the napkin and waved it in a nodding gesture to indicate her assent to the additional slice of cake, then coughed and pressed the napkin to her face as if to block her coughing spell, while she sniffled and wiped her face generously. These maneuvers had the unfortunate effect of smearing the frosting even further around the contours of her face—so that the creamy frosting and the caked coating of her face powder were commingled inextricably, resulting in an appearance that could only be described as uncouth.

Mrs. Holland, having busied herself cutting another slice of the cake, turned back to see Mrs. Greer's debauched appearance. She set the plate of cake down abruptly on the table. "Ella," she called, "Come help bring Mrs. Greer to my dressing room. Now, Lilah," she said, "we must attend to your face, and then we'll come back, and you may have more cake."

Mrs. Baker and Mrs. Sneed, whose fans had begun to flutter during these events, now scooted their chairs back, as if they might also get up. But Mrs. Holland said quickly, "Ladies, do not trouble yourselves. Cora will be in to serve more tea and cake to those who wish it."

As Ella and Mrs. Greer hobbled by her, Dorothy rolled her

eyes at Ella to attest to the foolishness engendered by her mother's social ambitions. Then she turned to William and said, in a lowered voice, "So you see, when I spoke of seeking a more civilized life, I meant a life without silly social occasions."

William nodded. But he was not sure what Dorothy's vision of a civilized life entailed.

# 7

# THE SCHOOL OF COTTON AND PICKIN'

On Sunday morning Wally, Ella and Sammy put on their Sunday clothes and traveled on Christmasville Road toward the woods at Dyer Creek to receive their weekly guidance from Reverend Zeke. Jimmy, as was now his custom, went with his family only as far as the split rail fence at the edge of the Holland farm. There he bid the family farewell, and perched on the fence to watch the passers-by. Venus, as was her custom, kept Jimmy company. She pawed at the ground in front of him, then sat at the foot of the fence. Together they observed the steady stream of slaves coming down the road from the Askew plantation, the Hobson plantation, and the smaller farms near Oakfield.

Most of the travelers were going to the creek to hear Zeke. Jimmy had not returned to the Sunday gatherings since the day Reverend Zeke proposed forgiveness for the selling of Sara's son by Augustus Askew. Even now, as he thought of that occasion, he spat.

Sunday morning was Jimmy's favorite time of the week. All the other Holland slaves went to the creek. The Hollands themselves went to their own church in Jackson. Jimmy was alone and, for a few hours, he could do as he pleased. He sat on the fence, tossing stones at a sapling across the road. He counted his hits until he reached twenty-five, then stopped. The March day was unusually warm. All the snow from February had melted. The air was moist and full of promise. Planting time was at hand.

Jimmy didn't like planting. He could not help but think, as he'd done many times before, about how he might someday escape from slavery, how he might leave Tennessee, make his way across the Ohio River, and travel on to Illinois and freedom. He'd heard by word of mouth that the Ohio River was wide. He puzzled about how he could cross it. He didn't know how to swim. He thought there must be a rowboat he could steal, or perhaps a canoe. He imagined it vividly … paddling across the river in the dark of night, reaching the other shore, stowing the boat, then climbing onto Illinois soil, Northern soil.

He looked down at Venus. He considered what it would be like if he took the dog along. She might help protect him from the paddy rollers and bounty hunters. "What d'you think, old girl? You think you could swim the Ohio River?" he asked her.

Venus looked at him with the same puzzled look she always wore when she saw something was wanted of her but wasn't sure what it was.

Jimmy, for his part, looked at Venus with envy. He longed for his world of troubles to be as simple as that of the dog, who knew nothing of work, who was always fed, who would never puzzle over the complications of running away. He said, "Naw, I guess you'd best stay home so you can look after Sammy and Ella. I expect I'll have to cross that river by myself." Jimmy threw a stone hard at the sapling, but it missed.

A voice assailed him. "Is it safe to pass, or you aim to hit someone?"

Jimmy was startled. A young man, who seemed to have come out of nowhere, stood in the road directly in front of him. The stranger wore a gold vest and a black waistcoat. His skin was white. Jimmy jumped from the fence to the road. He wondered if he'd almost hit the white man with his stone. The man had a questioning look on his face.

"Sorry, sir!" Jimmy said meekly. "I didn't see you." Adrenaline flushed his body. He saw in a flash how easily his action might be ascribed to malevolence, and how quickly he could be punished for it.

But the stranger said, "I see that," and then he added, as if to make an excuse for Jimmy, "It appears that your mind is off somewhere else."

Jimmy stared warily at the stranger, trying to size him up. The man didn't seem hostile. But Jimmy didn't know him, and he was mistrustful of any white man. "I was aiming at that tree," he said.

The stranger looked at the trees. "Which one?" he asked, as if to verify the plausibility of the excuse.

Jimmy pointed. "There, the sapling ...."

"It's not too big," observed the stranger. "Can you hit it?" he asked.

"Yes sir, I'd say I hit that sapling twenty-five times already, or thereabouts." He said this in a boasting way, but underneath was a veiled warning about his prowess in throwing stones.

"How many times did you miss?"

Jimmy shrugged. He wasn't sure what to make of this question. "Don't know," he said. "I don't count the misses."

"That's a fine philosophy," said the stranger. "A positive attitude." He walked over to Jimmy and extended his hand. "I'm Cato," he said.

Jimmy shook the fellow's hand tentatively, and looked at him closely. "Cato?" he asked, "from Hickory Grove plantation?"

Cato looked surprised. "Yes," he said. "You know who I am?"

Jimmy nodded.

"Goodness' sakes," Cato was flustered. "Seems like everyone in Tennessee knows who I am."

Jimmy felt the tension melt from his body. He staggered back a bit, as if he might almost fall back against the fence. Now his voice changed. No longer the quivering transgressor, he said, as a reproach, "You just about look white." There was undisguised disdain in his voice. "I bet you could pass for white."

Cato eyed the dark man who appeared to be his own age. He wore a head wrap, brightly colored. It was strange to see a man wearing such a thing. "What's that you got on your head?" Cato asked.

Jimmy rolled his eyes up, as if to look at the top of his head. "Oh that," he said. "That's my head wrap, or rag, or whatever you want to call it."

"How come you wear that?" Cato asked. "Seems to me, usually only females wear something like that."

"Females?" Jimmy sneered. "That's a funny way to put it. What do I care who's supposed to wear what? I wear it 'cause I like it." He took the question as a challenge. Now he looked at Cato's vest, which sparkled with gold threads. "Look here, what about your vest?"

"This?" Cato adjusted a button on the vest. "This is my Sunday vest. I got it as a gift. Master William spilled gravy on it one day, and then he gave it to me—but I got the stain out! I wear it on Sunday, going to church."

"Is that so?" Jimmy cocked his head. It didn't surprise him

that this white-looking slave was the church-going type. "You headed down that way now?" he asked.

Cato nodded.

"You're gonna be the last one there. All the other folks passed by here some time ago."

"What about you? You're not going?" Cato asked.

"I don't go for that Bible stuff. I got my own church." Jimmy leaned up against the fence, with his elbows propped on the top rail, and his knee raised so his foot was on the bottom rail.

Cato too, now, leaned onto the fence with one arm, as he faced Jimmy. "What church?" he asked.

"Me and Venus here …," he pointed at the dog, "… are the church members. I preach and she listens. She never says, 'Praise the Lord,' and that's how I like it."

Cato laughed. "So … she just barks?"

"That's right." Jimmy was annoyed by Cato's questions, but he made light of it. "When I say something worth barking about, she barks and licks my hand."

Cato looked at the dog, which looked back at him with her tongue hanging out. "Your dog …. What'd you call her? … Venus? … She looks kind of old," Cato observed.

"Well, she's an old girl," Jimmy allowed.

"So what is it you preach that's worth barking about?" Cato wondered.

Jimmy inspected Cato more closely. He could see, now, some of the ways in which the man was indeed not white. His hair was soft, but it hung in tight curls from his head like ringlets. His lips were full like his own. His brown eyes were wide and piercing like Sammy's. Cato looked at him with the same kind of puppy dog look that Jimmy remembered Sammy had when he arrived in the wagon nine years ago. He was becharmed by that look. He said, "Oh I expect I could preach a lot of things that would have you barking."

Cato seemed surprised by this. "You don't say?"

"Oh yes. I'm known hereabout as a wicked soul …," Jimmy said. "That's what my family thinks. I don't go to hear Reverend Zeke. I don't think much of the Lord. Besides that, I don't think much of white folks."

Cato frowned. "I'm not white," he repeated.

"So I hear, brother," said Jimmy. "So I hear."

Cato lowered his head, and shuffled his feet. Then he looked up at Jimmy with a friendly look. "You don't look all that wicked to me," he said.

Jimmy wasn't sure what to make of this. Jimmy didn't have any friends. He generally avoided pleasantries with the other slaves. But there was earnestness in Cato's eyes, and something else he couldn't put his finger on. The half-white slave intrigued him. He said, "Oh I'm only nice to you on account of Venus likes you." Jimmy reached down and stroked the dog's back. "Otherwise, you'd see how wicked I am."

"How d'you know she likes me?" Cato asked.

"Cause if she didn't, she'd of attacked you by now, and tore you up," Jimmy explained matter-of-factly.

"Man you got to be kidding," Cato snickered. "That dog is too old to tear up anything. I bet her teeth are about to fall out."

"Look here; don't talk that way about Venus," Jimmy only partly feigned his indignation. "I might not think you're as righteous as you appear to be."

For several minutes, Cato had been standing with his hands in the pockets of his waistcoat. He took them out now and slipped his thumbs in his pockets. "Well some folks think I look like Jesus."

"Like Jesus? Shoot. Why you want to look like Jesus?"

"Because I modeled for Jesus," Cato boasted. "It was for a painting. This summer a painter came to Hickory Grove. He got hired to paint a story from the Bible about how Mary washed the feet of Jesus. His name is Erastus and he asked me to model for Jesus."

"Erastus?" Jimmy said the name like he was speaking Greek.

"Erastus Hicks." Cato continued. "I reckon he is a great painter. He's a Quaker. He comes from the city of Philadelphia."

"A white man?" Jimmy's eyes narrowed.

"Yes …," Cato said, as if it was obvious. "But he's not like any other white man I ever met. He gave me some bourbon to drink, and he toasted me, and called me by name, and he …." Cato stopped suddenly, embarrassed to tell the rest.

Jimmy couldn't imagine where this was going. "He what?'

"He washed my feet, and anointed them with oil."

Jimmy let the picture of this form in his head. The notion of a white man bending down and washing a slave's feet— putting oil on them even—was too incredible. He had to stop himself from laughing. "Oh man, you must have fallen asleep someplace and had a crazy dream."

"No, I'm serious. It all happened, just like I'm telling you."

Jimmy was puzzled. This story did not fit in with his worldview. "How come he did all that?"

"Well …." Cato fumbled for a reason. "… Because he's a Quaker, and the Quakers believe in brotherly love."

"Brotherly love?" Jimmy repeated the phrase, with curiosity. He added, "Sounds like this white man was out of his mind."

"No, Erastus said it's all in the Bible."

"Oh, the Bible …," Jimmy made a sour face. That reference

obliterated whatever interest he had in the concept of brotherly love.

"I forgot," Cato said. "You don't think much of the Bible."

"I told you. I'm wicked."

"All around?"

"Right." Jimmy returned. "All around". There was something probing about Cato's question. No one before had ever wondered about the degree of Jimmy's moral waywardness. He wasn't sure what Cato meant by "all around"—but he was certain his answer must be consistent with his unholy self-image.

"So what do you do on Sunday morning, besides throwing stones at trees?" Cato asked.

"Not much …." Jimmy looked about him. "I just take it easy, sit on the fence, scratch the dog, throw stones … no work." He said all this as if it described the obvious course of action.

Cato looked down Christmasville Road. The air was quiet; no one was in sight. "You want to go for a walk?" he asked.

"What, with you?" Jimmy's wariness surged again.

"Yes, with me," Cato replied. "Why not?"

"No, man, I told you, I don't like that Reverend Zeke stuff."

"I'm not talking about going to Reverend Zeke," Cato clarified. "I just mean going for a walk."

"I thought you were going to church." He couldn't figure out what Cato had in mind. He'd never just 'gone for a walk' with anybody.

"I go there every Sunday," Cato said. "I don't think the Lord will mind if I miss one time. Besides …" he lowered his head "… folks there look at me like I was … different."

The word 'different' resonated with Jimmy. He looked at Cato, as if seeing him in a new light. He recalled how he himself had mistaken him for white. "You mean 'cause Askew's your daddy?"

Cato nodded.

"Shoot, that don't bother me," Jimmy said, and spat. "You didn't have nothing to do with it, did you?"

"No."

"I didn't have nothing to do with it either," Jimmy winked. He felt a glimmer of fondness for his fellow misfit.

"No, I guess not …."

"Not by a jugful," Jimmy said, warming to a friendlier tone. "So all those righteous church folks can just absquatulate."

"Ab … what?"

"Absquatulate, it means skedaddle, disappear." Jimmy couldn't remember where he'd heard the word, but he knew it was right.

"Where'd you pick that up?"

"That's how educated folks talk," said Jimmy, turning it into a boast.

Cato raised his eyebrows. "So you're a educated cotton picker?"

"Me?" Jimmy nodded playfully. "Oh yes, I went to school …"

"What school?"

"The school of cotton and pickin'." Jimmy grinned.

"Oh well!" Cato returned. "I went to the school of waitin' and servin'." He paused for effect. "That's just down the road from your school."

They both laughed such that Venus stood up with her tail wagging.

"What about the dog?" Cato asked. "Do you take her along when you walk? Or is she too old to make it?"

"Man, I don't generally go on a walk," Jimmy said. Then he

looked at Venus. "What you say, old girl? You want to take a walk?"

Venus, not knowing the word 'walk' but sensing the excitement of adventure in the air, wagged her tail furiously.

"I think she does," Jimmy said.

They set off down the road toward town.

"It will be better to walk in the woods," Jimmy declared suddenly. "I know a path we can take. That way we won't run into any crackers."

Cato eyed the looming wall of trees. He had never entered the woods this far up the road from Dyer Creek. "All right," he said. "You lead the way."

Jimmy scrambled off the road and down across a shallow ditch, then up toward the forest. Cato followed. As Jimmy strode in front, Cato took stock of him. Jimmy was obviously a field hand. He was an inch or two taller than Cato, and more broadly muscular, especially in his arms and legs. He wore a brown cotton vest with no shirt. He cinched his trousers around his waist with a piece of rope, which bunched the fabric before it stretched across his thighs, then fell loose at his knees as it hung down to his calves. He walked effortlessly in his bare feet, inured to the stones and twigs of the ground by a leathery skin. Then there was the mysterious wrap on his head, the only odd note in Jimmy's appearance. Its bright yellow glowed against the deep brown-black of his forehead. Cato saw that Jimmy wore it unabashedly—and that he was undaunted by the notion that it was peculiar. Cato had never before seen anyone but a woman wear a head rag. The brazenness of it awed him.

Venus was sufficiently advanced in years that she ought to have had trouble keeping up with them. But the outing excited her to such a degree that she was impervious to her age. She easily pushed ahead of them. She held her tail straight up.

From time to time, she trotted a few steps toward Jimmy, then turned and dashed forward, looking back over her shoulder, as if to egg him on. The dog's pleasure in the walking, and her attachment to Jimmy, set a picture in Cato's mind of how fine it would be to have a friend, someone to explore the world with, an ally against those who whispered about his skin color. Cato hoped Jimmy was truly indifferent to his parentage. Why else would he have said that the church folk ought to absquatulate? But then he recalled his hostile remarks about whites and his belligerence about the Bible and Reverend Zeke. Jimmy's outspoken opinions reassured him, but they also made him hesitant to hope for friendship.

Just as they began to get some momentum going, Venus barked, and turned back toward the edge of the woods, her tail coming to an alert stop.

"The dog sees something," Cato said.

Jimmy turned toward Venus. "What's up, old girl?" He cupped his hand to his ear. "Something's coming on the road," he said.

As they listened, the sound of a carriage drew upon them. The two slaves and the dog edged toward the road to see who it was.

"Oh gracious," Cato cried, "It's my Master! That's his carriage."

The carriage whooshed past them, clopping down the road at high speed. Jimmy strained to look into the carriage. He saw the thin white man in his lace cuffs, sitting in a stiff upright posture, impervious to the three onlookers in the woods.

"Shoot," Jimmy said. "Where's he going in such a hurry?"

"Master Askew always takes the carriage into town and back. I don't know what he does when he gets there," Cato said.

"How come he's not in church?" Jimmy wondered.

"He never goes to church," Cato explained. Then he added, "I guess he's the same as you."

"Same as me?" Jimmy spat. "Yeah, just like me."

"Course, he always says grace at supper time, before anyone at the table can eat. But he never does go to church. Only Lucille goes."

"Lucille?" Jimmy didn't know the name.

"That's his wife. They married before I was born." Cato fidgeted with his hands. "Master was married to her when he … when my mother …." Cato was flustered. "Anyway, Missus Askew doesn't know about me."

Jimmy wasn't sure how to interpret this. "You work in the house?"

"Yes."

"And this wife of his sees you all the time?"

"She sees me, but she doesn't know he's my father."

Jimmy rolled his eyes. "Well shoot. You reckon she'll find out?"

"I hope not." The look in Cato's eyes made it clear that he didn't like to talk about it.

"Dang! Well … ." Jimmy searched for something to say. "That Askew, he looked a whole lot peakeder than you … ," he ventured. "And he's all stuck up … you know. I don't think you look like him much. He's kind of plug-ugly." Jimmy couldn't tell if any of this was reassuring. "Besides, he's a lot older'n you are."

"Considerable." Cato said, uncertain how to interpret Jimmy's observations.

"So I reckon his wife, she'll never know. I mean you're kind of … well … good-looking … just seeing him, I wouldn't guess that old cracker was your daddy."

The balm of Jimmy's compliment crept up on Cato. "Good-looking!" No one but Erastus had ever called him that.

He often wondered how people thought he looked. He was certain that people stared at him, but he was never sure what it was that made them stare. He assumed it was because of his "secret." He saw that Jimmy wanted to put distance between him and his father, whom Jimmy disliked the way he must dislike all white men.

"Let's absquatulate," Cato said, suddenly eager.

Venus was already headed back into the woods. She turned and looked around at the men behind her, who were unbearably slow, who did not pant, who showed no visible excitement, who had the strength to leap with their legs, but for some reason did not, who held their tongues improbably in their mouths, who were all at odds with her sense of right behavior. However, she knew, from long years of experience, to wait patiently for them—after all, they were just humans. And then too, she knew that they, like her, were set upon adventure.

8

_____

# THE PRICE OF A PAINTING

*T*he painter, Erastus Hicks, remained in the county for most of the year. He had spent four months working on his Biblical painting, longer than he actually needed to do the job, but long enough to afford him an entire idyllic summer with Cato, who was not only his assistant, but also, in secret, his model and his student.

Each day that summer, weather permitting, he and Cato retreated to the furthermost part of the Askew garden, where behind a veil of dogwoods and thorny rosebushes, Erastus spent his days alternately painting and conducting lessons in reading, using the book of poems that he kept hidden beneath a rock. Gradually, the boy mastered an ever-increasing number of words, until he had, as Erastus declared, got the hang of it.

During this time, Cato also began to walk down the road to the Holland farm every other Sunday morning. He alternated his activity from week to week. One week he'd go to Dyer Creek to hear Reverend Zeke, and the next week he'd spend sitting on the split rail fence or walking in the woods with Jimmy.

As the summer wore on, Cato's friendship with Jimmy and his friendship with the painter amplified each other. For as much as Cato eagerly wanted Jimmy to be a confidant, with whom he could share the marvelous secrets of his adventures with the painter, he also found in the painter a mentor, who encouraged his burgeoning friendship with Jimmy.

Jimmy, for his part, regarded Cato's stories of the painter as fantastic. Because he accused Cato of making it all up, one Sunday Cato brought, hidden in a sack, the much-discussed book itself. He read aloud a poem from "Leaves of Grass." Even so, Jimmy's skepticism was not allayed. He examined the book and its strange markings closely, suspecting a trick. The content of the poem, with its charged images and exuberant words, seemed to him like a foreign language. Jimmy could not imagine a white man who behaved as kindlily and as generously as the painter in Cato's telling of it did. But he was too fascinated by the improbability of it all to dissuade Cato's visits or to discourage him from sharing his secrets. Cato's enthusiasm and optimism amused him, and, in its way, was a counterweight to the cynicism and tepidity of his own life.

The delicate balance of this situation ended when the painting was finished. Hicks achieved considerable success in the county with his painting. Augustus Askew was so pleased with his two paintings that at summer's close he held a ball of unprecedented size to unveil them for his fellow planters. Not surprisingly, after that, Hicks was sought for other commissions. While there were some raised eyebrows regarding the liminal erotic nature of the foot washing of Jesus by Mary of Bethany, and especially regarding Hicks's provocative depiction of a dark-haired—and one might even say tanned—Savior, the virtuosity of the painter's technique and his plainspoken religious piety outweighed these uncertainties. A consensus arose in the local community that to commission the Quaker painter for a portrait was to achieve a distinctive social standing.

Henrietta Holland saw in this an opportunity to bolster the connection between the Hollands and the Askews, and at the same time to raise the status of her daughter in the eyes of the community. She beseeched her husband to commission Hicks to paint a portrait of Dorothy. But Hicks, upon seeing how well the wind was blowing with his local reputation, had raised his fee. George Holland told Henrietta that they simply could not afford it.

Henrietta was not to be dissuaded. She reminded her husband of various occasions when he had indulged himself in purchases that were of no interest to her. In particular, she seized upon the memory of her husband's purchase, without her consent, of a useless young boy in Memphis, an acquisition toward which she had never warmed, since she regarded young Sammy as an ineffectual slave, constantly playing games, laughing, and distracting the others. In fact, she observed, they could easily sell Sammy, and invest what capital gains he might engender in a number of more engaging domestic improvements, including not only the painting commission, but also the acquisition of a new sofa for the parlor, since, in her opinion, the parlor as it stood was not sufficiently furnished to accommodate the social events she envisioned.

George was not keen on this plan, but he saw that his wife was so set upon it that she would not let it go. The prospect of constant reminders of his impulsive purchase—and the fact that he did agree that the boy was not essential to the running of the household—led him, at last, to acquiesce. And so it was settled: Sammy would be sold, and the money would be used to buy not only a sofa worthy of social entertaining, but also a painting, which would itself become the occasion of an important social event. While George agreed to the scheme, he was adamant that nothing should be said about the plan in advance of the sale itself, since he sensed, quite rightly, that his daughter and his slaves would not take well to this redeployment of the Hollands' assets. And since he did not expect to pay the artist —or for that matter, purchase the sofa—until after the portrait was completed, George chose simply to let the matter of the sale of Sammy remain a secret during the five weeks that Erastus Hicks spent in September and October of 1860 rendering the reluctant Dorothy Holland in paint.

For Henrietta, nothing would do but that Dorothy should wear the same extravagant dress she had worn for her birthday party in the summer. This meant that every day she sat for her portrait, Ella had to bind her, tie her and shoehorn her into the corset and hoop, in a repetition of the elaborate ritual of donning the dreaded outfit. The dreariness of this routine, however, was offset by the painting sessions themselves. Dorothy found Erastus Hicks to be just the breath of fresh air for which she longed.

As with Mr. Askew, Mr. Hicks had requested of Mr. Holland that one of his slaves be assigned to help him. George at first thought to assign Sammy to the task—but then, thinking of the financial scheme he had in mind, he thought better of it, and, at Dorothy's request, he gave the job to Ella.

For Ella, the experience of meeting Erastus Hicks was unnerving and thrilling. He had an unprecedented way of regarding her. When she and Dorothy were both present, Erastus would say something like, "Now, ladies, shall we commence with our work." For Ella, to be characterized in the plural—with Dorothy—as a lady--made her drop her jaw. And when Erastus wasn't looking, she often gave Dorothy a puzzled, conspiratorial look, or simply rolled her eyes.

The portrait itself commenced, as was Mr. Hicks's custom, with a series of charcoal sketches. After observing the workings of the light in various locations, Mr. Hicks settled upon the Hollands' front porch as offering the best combination of steady light and modulating shadow. The work began on a warm morning in mid-September. The porch was filled with a delicate bouquet from the sweet autumn clematis vine that grew up one of the columns and out onto the railing. Dorothy, in her special green dress, leaned against the back of a chair on the porch, as she watched Mr. Hicks set up his drawing easel in the walk at the foot of the stairs. Ella stood at the back of the porch where the parlor window looked out. She picked up a wet rag with an eye to washing the windowpanes.

"Ladies," he began, "our first task is to create a scene. I like to create a portrait that tells a miniature story—that is, I like to put my subjects into a narrative context, so that they're not just sitting in the painting and staring out at the viewer like a bump on a log. Rather, I prefer to have my subjects present themselves as characters—you might say—as players imbued with a visual personality augmented by the telling artifacts of their existence."

"Well, Mr. Hicks," Dorothy replied, looking about her on the porch. "I'm not sure what telling artifacts of my existence there might be upon this porch, nor even that I ought, if I had such artifacts, to be telling them to the world in this painting."

"Please," the artist said, "won't you—won't both of you—call me Erastus, and won't you be so kind as to allow me to call you Dorothy and Ella?"

"Yes, of course," Dorothy said, "as you prefer."

They both looked at Ella—who held her window washing rag in midair as she stared at the painter with her head tilted. She realized that he had also addressed her in this request. "Yes, sir, Master Hicks, I mean, Master Erast... how d'you say that name?"

"Erastus."

"Yes, sir, Master Erastus."

"And truly," he said, "I'd prefer it if you simply called me 'Erastus,' for my skill is not so great that I can be called a master."

"Yes, sir." Ella looked at Dorothy, as if to ask her somehow to explain this odd bird to her.

"Ah, the formality of the South," the painter said. "Very well. Now Dorothy you seem to presume that an artifact must necessarily reveal, when in fact, some artifacts might have the effect of imbuing a subject with mystery."

"Well I should hate to think that this silly outfit, which my mother has insisted that I wear, might be regarded as an artifact of my existence. The only use I might personally have for this hoop skirt would be if it were to launch me like a hot air balloon and transport me to a less frivolous society." She took several steps toward the stairs, as if to suggest that she might leap off, if required.

"Ah my dear," said the painter, "you are a rare jewel to have come to such an assessment of the world around you. But I must say, the image of you floating into the air in your hoop skirt excites my visual imagination."

Dorothy smiled. "Truly, I believe my mother would faint dead away if you painted my portrait thus. She has it in her mind that this portrait will render me attractive to the young man whom she wishes me to marry."

"Well," Erastus said dryly, "perhaps this young man might find the image of your skirt billowing up quite attractive indeed."

Dorothy smiled. "Yes, William Askew may very well find such an image to his liking."

The painter, who had been holding a stick of charcoal in his hand, set it down. "Ah, so it is William Askew, is it?"

"Do you know him?"

"I've never met him," Erastus said. "But I've worked with his servant Cato, who speaks well of him—even in confidence."

Dorothy raised her eyebrow. "In confidence?"

"Yes." The painter shrugged. "It is always my goal to earn people's confidence. For I am aware that my itinerancy provides an opportunity to confide in me, knowing I shall hold information only in transit, as it were."

"I'm not convinced," Dorothy said. "You may well be like a bee that carries confidences like pollen—from flower to flower."

"Another charming visual image, my dear" said the painter. "But I shall not press you for any—as you call it—pollen. Perhaps we can achieve the desired effect with just a hint of billowing in your dress. If, for example, you were to stand astride the porch steps, with each foot upon a different step, so that, seen from profile, the hem of the dress would seem to be raised."

"Very well," Dorothy said as she adopted the suggested pose, standing astride the stairs, fluffing the bottom of her dress a bit to billow it. "You mean, like this."

"Yes, that's lovely," Erastus said. "And what about Ella? She is your companion, is she not?"

"Indeed," said Dorothy. "She is my closest friend."

"Then why don't we include Ella in the portrait?"

They both looked at Ella, who was wiping the panes of the window in order to make herself useful. Ella, realizing that her name had again been spoken, turned round from the window to look down at the painter, who stood at the bottom of the stairs. "You want me to stand in your picture?" she asked.

"Why not?" Erastus said. "You might stand behind the porch rail, looking on at us."

"I don't know," Ella said.

"Don't you want to be immortalized in paint?" Dorothy asked.

"Imm ... what?"

"Made famous." Dorothy clarified, swatting a fly off her arm.

"No ma'am," Ella said. "I think if you're going to put me in the picture, you better have me busy with something, or Miz Holland—every time she sees it—she'll think I'm famous for standing around doing nothing."

"I suppose you could dust the porch rails," Erastus offered.

Ella looked down skeptically at the railing around the porch. She said, "Mister Erast, pardon me for saying so, but I never knew nobody who dusted no porch rails."

"I have it!" Dorothy said. "You can help me put on my shoe. That will really get my leg up in the air." She lifted her leg by way of demonstration.

Ella scratched her head. "Pardon me, Miss Dorothy, but I don't see why I'd be helping you slip on your shoe while you're standing up here sideways on the front steps of the porch. That just won't make sense!"

"Indeed," Erastus agreed. "I think I'd best avoid further foot handling paintings for now, or it will seem as if I'm in a visual rut."

All three of them pondered the dilemma of how to include Ella in the painting in an active role.

"I don't suppose you play the banjo?" Erastus ventured.

"Ha!" Ella laughed at the image. "I don't, but Juba Jake does," she said. "Why don't we ask him to come in the picture?"

"And Ella can dance," Dorothy said. "You should see how she dances!"

"How'm I gonna dance in that painting?" Ella asked. "He'd

have to paint me pretty darn quick to get that down in his picture."

Erastus smiled. "I've thought of just the thing. Surely, Ella, you must ofttimes assist Dorothy with her hair. You might well come out on the porch of a summer morning, and brush Dorothy's hair, as she stands upon the stairs contemplating the garden."

"I don't know that we've ever done such a thing," Dorothy said. "But I suppose it would not seem too odd—maybe a little odd."

"It would allow me to show you with your hair down—a rather enticing idea for young Askew, and with hair as lovely as yours—I can make the sheen and texture of it—as Ella strokes it out—quite charming in the morning light."

"I think you'd better see what mother thinks," Dorothy said.

"The best way to propose the idea," Erastus said, "is for me to sketch it. Then I can show your mother the sketches, and see what she says before anything is committed to paint."

"I'll fetch your hair brush," Ella said, and with that, she dashed into the house.

Once she was gone, Erastus said, rather matter-of-factly, as he fiddled with the drawing pad on his easel, "I believe Ella is a good companion for you."

"I appreciate your tact, Erastus," Dorothy said, "in choosing such a cordial word as companion. Of course, she is a slave. Do you think it odd that she and I are friends?"

"Not at all."

"It does not seem odd to me either," Dorothy said. "But I feel as if people hereabouts view such friendship as limited in a way that I don't. I can imagine that Ella and I would be friends even if she weren't bound to me." Dorothy looked the painter in the eye. "I would prefer it, in fact, if she were free."

"Ah, well there indeed is pollen that I would not carry about," said Erastus. "But your wish reflects a wise and loving heart. I think you are quite right to feel so."

"I'm glad you agree. Sometimes I've wondered if I would ever in my life encounter anyone who did agree with that." Dorothy sighed. "The problem, Erastus, is that both Ella and I are bound by circumstances that may interfere with her freedom. Custom demands that I marry, and once I do, my husband will—I fear—own us both."

"Ah, young Askew." Erastus scratched his head. "Have you broached this topic with him?"

"I've spoken to him about my desire for independence. But really he's too—infatuated—to understand what I'm saying."

"How do you feel about him?"

"His main appeal, I must confess, is that he seems—pliable —and I need someone to marry who will accommodate my independence."

"Ah my dear, it would seem a pity to give your heart to someone that you do not love."

"But whom shall I love? If there were such a man, I have not seen even a wisp of him. Indeed, you are the first man I've met to whom I feel I can speak frankly."

"You honor me."

"Are you married, Erastus?"

"No, it has not fallen to me to marry."

"You are fortunate—to be a man and an artist. You can be odd without being suspect."

Erastus smiled. "I would not say that I am not suspect! But surely, you must also have the fortitude to resist custom. Why do you feel you must marry?"

"In short, it is what my mother lives for."

"Ah."

"I have no brother or sister. The future of the family depends upon me."

Ella had returned to the inside front door with a hairbrush, where she stopped to wait discreetly. She imagined that Dorothy might want to speak privately to the painter. She thought about going back upstairs, but then she saw the painter waving to her.

"Come, Ella," he said. "We must begin our work."

Ella positioned herself behind Dorothy. She looked at Dorothy's head tentatively, and said, "Took half an hour to get this hair done up like this. You sure you want to take it all down?"

"If you don't mind," Erastus said. "The hair will be the focal point of the portrait. The morning light falling on Dorothy's hair; the garlands of clematis on the porch column framing you. It's perfect!"

Ella removed the hairpins and undid the tidy rolls in which Dorothy's hair was firmly held above her neck. As Ella did so the hair fell upon Dorothy's shoulders, and Dorothy shook her head gently, as Ella slipped her hand beneath it to smooth it out.

"Shall I brush it?" Ella asked.

"By all means," said Erastus.

Ella lifted a handful of Dorothy's hair and, with her other hand, brought the brush down upon it. Dorothy tilted her head back slightly from the pressure, as a weightless smile formed on her lips. The rising morning light, which had completed a long, slow crescendo, fell brightly but softly upon Dorothy's hair, her face, and her neck, which glowed in pale, delicate contrast against the halo of Ella's dark round head and nappy black hair. For a moment, Erastus held his breath. For he had often seen a conjunction of light and shadow and color materialize before him this way. It formed an evocative image that, despite its brilliant shimmer, was one that would not last. His eyes gulped as a dog eats, with greed and relish. He strained to memorize what he saw. For he knew, in an instant, a passing cloud, or a shift in position, or even a change in his own power of seeing, could alter the poignancy of this vision: a shared affection between mistress and slave, between friend and friend, between Dorothy and Ella.

And without thinking, his hand was drawing on the page. "Just so," he said. "Hold that pose, please." The glowing colors of the scene: the green silk of Dorothy's dress, Ella's calico, the cream-painted, vine-entwined columns, the auburn strands of Dorothy's hair, all these danced in his mind, while his hand sketched lines in black and gray. The very things that had called him his whole life—light, forms, shadows, colors, texture, sheen—filled him, as they could, with adrenaline. He lost awareness of his breathing, of his movements, of the physical mechanics of his work. He was wholly his eyes, given over entirely to seeing, to distilled vision—as sound, touch, taste, smell all receded, and his iris narrowed to crisp the focus through which his soul saw the world. He felt then only the inadequacy of his skill, the poverty of the medium in which he labored, his incarnate weight—each of which seemed an obstacle to overcome as he reached for the truth of the two young women before him.

In stolen sideways glances, Dorothy watched the feverish work of the artist as his gaze moved from her to the paper and back. "Why Erastus," she said, "I do believe you are sweating. Should we fetch you a drink of water?"

"No, no," he said. "Just hold still as long as you can."

Ella held her right hand and arm akimbo in a frozen tableau of brushing. She imagined herself already as a painting, and she knew that figures in paintings did not change position. Even so, she felt her arm begin to tremble, and the expression on her face, which had started out as a fond smile, began to waver such that she could not be sure what kind of look she would end up famous for. She imagined herself appearing as a big set of white teeth floating in the dark behind Dorothy's shimmering hair.

Dorothy, whose head tilted backwards, already felt the strain in her neck muscles. She found herself staring at the ceiling of the porch—which, she realized, she had never really noticed before. The paint in the ceiling boards bore a web of crackling that made it appear as if a finely etched net or strainer had stenciled a pattern upon the paint.

And so an essential truth of art-making impressed itself upon each of them. Being immortalized was tedious. It was contrary to all the impulses of the present moment: to fall upon a chair, to scratch an itchy elbow, to fetch a drink of water, to answer the call of nature. But the call of all these natural things beckoned them away from the very rendering that might endear them to the world. For Dorothy could imagine William Askew as he looked upon her portrait. And Ella could imagine Wally and Cora slipping into the parlor to admire it. As for Erastus, he did not imagine the human witnesses to his work. His testimony was made entirely for himself, and for God—the only sets of eyes able to judge.

It was during this collective in-breath of holding still and rapidly sketching that the front door swung open and Sammy burst onto the porch with such momentum that he was barely able to stop himself before crashing into the frozen tableau.

"Sakes alive," Dorothy said.

"Lordy," said Ella.

"Gracious," said Erastus.

Sammy had reflexively swung his arms out and was now embracing Dorothy and Ella with a big smile. He was so star-tled to find them standing on the porch that he could not understand what was happening. His eyes darted from Dorothy to Ella to the painter, and his smile grew sheepish as it dawned on him that he had interrupted something. But he could think only to say, "Excuse me, Miz Dorothy, Cora—she said I should tell you all lunch is ready."

"Mr. Hicks," Dorothy said. "This is Sammy, one of the more exuberant members of our household."

Erastus, whose irritation vanished in the wake of the boy's playful spirit, was disarmed. Even now, after a moment of chagrin, the boy grinned broadly—as if the whole scene was the greatest amusement. And Erastus found himself wondering from what source a young slave found reason for such cheery good humor.

"How do you do, Sammy?" the painter said.

The boy looked at him with some surprise. "I do well, sir," he said. "And do you do too?"

"Yes, I expect I do," said Erastus.

So it was that Erastus first encountered the young slave who would be sold to pay for his painting. But in that first encounter, Erastus sensed only the boy's improbably happy spirit.

9

## A WALK IN THE WOODS

*V*enus had to slow herself down despite her age. The humans plodded beside her in their typical lumbering fashion. She still did not know what sound the new one was. Of course, she knew "Jimmy" was the sound of Jimmy, just as she knew her own sound was "Venus." But the humans never tried to teach their sounds to her—they only did that with each other. She had to listen to the whole chatter of their speech in order to catch the part that signified the sound by which they called each other.

Their sounds would be easier to sort out if they always called to each other, just as they always called to her. There was hardly an interval when someone didn't call her sound —"Venus"—then wait expectantly for her to come. If they would only do something as obvious as that, call each other's sound, then wait for each other to come, she would not have to concentrate so hard to figure out the new one's sound.

Of course, even without knowing the new one's sound, she could tell a lot about him. He did not smell like Jimmy. He smelled more like the ones who kept the food. Like them, he had a lighter color than the ones who did the work. The new one's color was somewhere between the ones who worked and the ones who lived in the house and kept the food.

It had not escaped her that the new one walked faster and was more eager and energetic than Jimmy. She liked that about him. If she could get him by himself for a while, she might teach him a reasonable way of behaving—with lovely running and playing. He was not as ponderous as her dear Jimmy.

Of course, she loved Jimmy above all others—for he was the one who repeatedly talked to her, who worried what she was feeling, who paid attention to her hunger, and who always looked at her with love in his eyes. But Jimmy was hopelessly human in his habits, taking every opportunity to sit down, to rest, to do, essentially, nothing—as if sitting, resting and doing nothing were what life was all about.

Jimmy walked as if he had lead weights attached to his feet. Getting him to move was like pulling against a chain. When he did walk, he sauntered along. If that weren't bad enough, when something worth stopping for appeared, he kept right on going. He'd pass by the most powerfully fragrant smells— enough, really, to knock over anyone with half a nose—and, though she, of course, was swept into an ecstatic rush by the swirling smells and odors, Jimmy trudged on, heedless, altogether oblivious.

She had long since concluded that his nose was broken—or at least that he could hardly smell at all. Then again, all humans were at a disadvantage. Walking as they did with their noses so high up off the ground, one could hardly expect them to catch most of the essence of the world. For what was the earth if not a sniffable, whiffable, smorgasbord? The world was a bouquet of fumes and traces, redolent, spicy, sometimes sweet or savory, sometimes foul or fetid. There were stinks of rot— and there were lovely perfumes. There were damp smells like creek water, or wet grass, or spring mud. There were dry smells like hay in the hot sun, or the grainy, dusty smell of weeds, browned and desiccated from days without water. There were exciting, erotic smells of urine, sweat and body aromas: those powerful, heady wafts that brought the atoms of one body into the nose of another. How could humans not read these sexual signatures, the intimate imprint, the very particular smell of each being, traveling like a cloud of emissions, the fumes of physicality, dragged in a trail of musk behind all creatures? Ah, it made Venus sniff just to think of it. But poor Jimmy, he might lay his head down on her back with affection; then stroke her fur—all the while sighing outward instead of sniffing inward, so misguided were his instincts, so hopeless his human-ness. If only he saw how easily he could bring her being into his, with a simple inhalation.

And this, of course, is what she did with him. She inhaled him with pleasure whenever she could: his shiny, dark skin— beaded with sweat, full of molecules, and bits of odoriferous identifiers that belonged to no one else. She took him into her brain in one in-breath—or, if she really sniffed—she might reassemble his whole molecular structure inside her, to fill her heart with unfiltered love.

Oh yes, she could smell them all quite clearly. And each one had a precious smell, unique and particular. She thought of the smell of the one whose sound was "Sammy," to whom she had passed the gift of joy when he was a boy. How simple it was, when you found fertile ground, to open their senses and awaken them to a rightful feeling for the world. If you got one of them young, while they still leapt and bounded, the way any normal creature would who had air in its nostrils and food in its stomach, then you might get them to understand, to realize the joy of being a physical body in this thoroughly physical realm.

Sammy had seen the light. It had been easy, because he was scared and lonely. He would not open himself to see into the eyes of another, until she looked at him with a straightforward, tongue-hanging, tail-wagging smile. That opened him. She alone had not looked at him with pity, but with a clear declaration of the loveliness of being.

Ah, patience, patience—such is a dog's fate. To sit patiently with the density of humans and their somber preoccupations, knowing how easily they might run and laugh or roll on the ground if only they understood. But there they are, lumbering along, deep in thought; their eyes glazed over, no longer seeing the very world before them. They are trapped in their ruminations and deliberations—lost to their own senses by their sensibility. It was frustrating enough, really, to make her bark, to startle them back to the here and now.

Jimmy was behind the new one. They'd been silent a long time. But now they made sounds with each other. She knew something was forming between these two. Since the day they met, their sounds had become more animated and loose. They laughed more often now, and looked at each other knowingly. The new one stopped and waited for Jimmy to catch up. He pointed at a tree, up high in its branches, which made Jimmy tilt his head back. She looked up, too, but she saw only the colored leaves rustling in the wind. She ran back to Jimmy's side to be sure she had not missed any telling effluvium from where the new one pointed. But there was no new information there—only Jimmy's heightened smell, which told her he was feeling happy and excited. That was good. The new one had done that. He had awakened excitement in Jimmy, just when she had been ready to give up hope for him. And the new one was happy and excited too. His movements were graceful; he walked like he almost might skip. He smiled and made sounds and looked at the sky. All good signs. The colored leaves in the tree, it seemed, made him happy.

They progressed as a group through the woods toward the creek. Although the day was warm and sunny, the trees had already begun their annual change. Even now, dry leaves lay crunched and withered on the ground. Soon the days would dim and the air would chill, and the time would come when, without warning, the mysterious snow would arrive and sit upon the ground like a mammoth frozen treat. The trees prepared themselves for snow time in their methodical way. One rarely caught them unprepared for anything, really. The trees were more stuck up and full of themselves than the humans, but it was pleasant to be within the protective embrace of their shelter, the hallmark of which was that you could count on them never to do anything unexpected. Oh, they might drop a branch occasionally, but only under the most predictable circumstances.

What a sour stench! Something was rotting just beyond the path, and beneath a fallen branch, where one might well expect to find decaying matter. It was tempting to go investigate, but Venus felt she must concentrate on keeping her people moving along. The new one was making odd sounds. She'd heard such sounds before. When Wally, Ella and Cora washed clothes at the creek, they sometimes joined their voices together in this odd way, louder, harmonious, and abstractly vocal, like the way birds do. The new one was sounding notes up and down merrily, and his eyes were twinkling. Jimmy wore a tight, serious face, but his legs betrayed him. Jimmy was ever so subtly bouncing along to the sounds coming from the new one.

Just then, behind the merry notes, Venus heard something new. Someone was approaching. She stiffened her tail, and dashed in the direction of the oncoming distant sound. Then she looked back at the humans to see if they understood her message. They didn't. The new one still trilled away. She dashed six steps toward the sound again—how clear did she have to make it?—then barked once, while looking in the sound's direction. It worked. Jimmy made her sound, "Venus," and he looked in the direction she indicated. The new one fell silent; the smile left his face.

Jimmy made sounds to the new one. They moved closer together—to form a phalanx against whatever approached. Venus positioned herself alongside them. All three of them peered into the kaleidoscope of trees to see what was coming. Jimmy saw something first, because his body went stiff. His smell changed to fear. He pulled at the arm of the new one, until they moved off the path toward a thicket twenty yards away. Their movements were anxious but deliberate. They wanted to move without making sounds, but they had to pick their way across the underbrush with their big, clumsy feet, while Venus padded soundlessly beside them.

She wrestled with what to do. Her primary instinct was to bark and charge headlong at the threatening thing that was coming. And doubtless, in her youth that is exactly what she would have done. But time had taken its toll on her bravado. And, in her way, she had learned from Jimmy that not every impending threat required attack. Jimmy held a finger to his mouth—a gesture she'd seen often enough to know what he meant by it. So she focused her mind and muffled the growl in her throat.

They came to the thicket, where she saw that they would hide themselves. She scanned the ground for a hole, or depression, anything into which she might burrow. Jimmy and the new one pulled themselves close in behind the widest tree in the thicket, and strained their necks to see what was approaching.

Venus scrunched low until her feet disappeared beneath her. With her head raised up just a little, she spied three humans coming down the path. They were like the ones who keep the food, not like the ones who do the work. They walked heavily on their feet. They did not make sounds to each other. They peered about—as if they knew someone was hiding close at hand. None of them smelled familiar. How easily she might leap out at them, and scare them away with fierce growls and threatening fangs. But Jimmy kept looking at her with his finger raised to his mouth. So she waited, and let only a low, muffled growl escape from her throat.

She sniffed at the intruders. Though they were far away, and though their smell was complex, she perceived the odors of fear and hostility distilled together. They wore big boots. Their hats were furry like an animal's skin. They carried iron rods wedged between their arms and bodies. The three men stopped, then veered toward the woods, still a good distance ahead of the thicket, but moving into the woods, on the same side of the path as the thicket, but toward a different point.

Venus heard another sound. Something else moved. She turned her head to the right and caught a trace of smell. She heard a rustle, and then the sound of scamper. She looked at Jimmy. He stood motionless behind the new one. Jimmy stared at her, as if he meant to control her with his look. The new one stared with wide eyes at the iron rods held by three men in the hats. She looked at them too just as one of the men lifted up his iron rod so that one end of it was at his face, just below his chin. The man peered down the length of the rod—staring hard in the direction from which the smell trace and scamper sound had come.

Venus caught the smell trace again. As she turned her snout, she saw the owner of the smell. It came from an animal she knew. She'd seen these animals before. They looked like big

dogs, on long legs, with pale brown fur—and white spots—
and turned up noses. She'd seen them in the woods from time
to time. She knew that they were cowards. She had only to
dash in the direction of one of them, and the frightened thing
would dart away. She'd seen them eating leaves off the bushes.
And it was no wonder they were cowards, for they didn't seem
to have any teeth at all. At least, she'd never seen one of them
bare its teeth.

Just then, she heard a loud explosion—a tremendous bang
that startled her and frightened her all at once, and she trembled. She looked in the direction from which the awful noise
had come and saw the man with his raised iron rod. A wisp of
grey smoke curled up from the end of his rod as he lowered it.
He and the other men were looking in the direction where the
long-legged animal was. Jimmy and the new one were looking
too. Venus looked and saw that the pale brown, long-legged,
coward animal was down—lying on the ground. The men with
the fur hats began to rush toward it. And they made sounds to
each other.

Suddenly, Jimmy moved closer to her with exaggerated
steps—and he pulled on the arm of the new one. The men
with the fur hats, as they approached the animal on the
ground, were also approaching the other side of the thicket.
Jimmy signaled Venus with his hands. He wanted her to follow
him. Jimmy and the new one began moving away from the
men and the animal on the ground—back toward the path.
Venus followed them closely. And as they moved, she noticed
their long, awkward steps grow smaller and faster—until they
were walking quickly, and then faster, and then finally when
they got to the path, they ran. Jimmy and the new one looked
around, back toward the men with the fur hats. But Venus
didn't look back. She just bounded along beside them, and
thought, "At last, we're moving like we have legs!"

So the three of them, Venus, Jimmy and the new one, ran along at full speed on the path in the woods—back the way they'd come—away from the creek, and back toward the house. She knew some wrong thing had happened, something that had scared Jimmy and the new one—and then there was that awful bang! But, she didn't care, because now at last they were having some fun. She wanted very much to bark, and nip at their heels—to remind them how much fun it was to play like this. And there was a torrent of smells rushing past her now— smells left over from when they'd come this way an hour before —which were mixed in with smells from others who'd criss-crossed the path—who had themselves, no doubt, inspected the smell collection. She noted the smell of the little gray animals with bushy tails, the ones who always clambered up the trees. And there was the smell of those long, round, brown, crawling little creatures that came up out of the dirt in the rain.

Just here was the familiar smell of another dog, one she knew only from smells, but had never seen. It was a mystery dog. She hoped to meet it someday. All these smells whipped through her thoughts as they ran, and she was panting now in a most breathtaking way.

Suddenly, Jimmy stopped, and then the new one stopped too. Jimmy bent down and was breathing hard—looking back, but now no longer fearful. The new one also bent down with his hands just above his knees, catching his breath. Venus over-shot them, doubled back, and circled around Jimmy in a cooling down prance. When she stopped, she panted hard, with her tongue stuck out—a look that conveyed the afterglow of exertion. Jimmy held his hand out to her. She approached, and sniffed his hand. He said her name, "Venus," and reached into his pocket and pulled out a piece of bacon. She knew all along that he was carrying it. She could smell it in his pocket from the beginning, but this was how they played it. When he was ready, he pulled it out and gave it to her, and, naturally, her tail went straight up. Then, as his hand neared her snout and the smoky meat smell enthralled her nose, he flicked it out toward her, and she chomped it down in one gulping bite. Eating bacon was so good that it was worth all the trials that came from being a dog. Ah, Jimmy, he was absolute loyalty, a dog's best friend. Her wagging tail bespoke her appreciation for his efforts to procure, carry, and dispense this special treat. It wagged furiously of its own accord—no thinking involved, just pure, instantaneous reflex. Wagging conveyed and was in itself an aspect of her joy.

The new one made sounds at Jimmy. Venus imagined that the new one wanted to know where his bacon treat was. The new one was undoubtedly hungry, too! But Jimmy petted her now, and he looked in her eyes—as he often did—with fondness, but also dismay at the gulf between them. He petted her as if he wished to reach across the barrier and join his heart with hers. For her part, she turned and licked his hand to mirror that impulse back to him. And the new one, too, added his hand to the petting, crouching down to kneel beside her. She looked at the new one with sparkling eyes. There was much hope for him. He was full of the right kind of spirit. She could feel the hands of both of them stroking, overlapping, and caressing her back. It was almost too much. For the heart can sometimes overflow and suck a dog down into the well of affection so quickly that it's frightening. Venus pulled back. She moved a few yards away, toward a faint sweet smell emanating from a cluster of delicate yellow flowers. She fixed the smell in her memory, where she collected moments of joy.

## 10

## "WE'RE THE SAME COLOR"

When Jimmy and Cato returned to the Holland farm from their walk in the woods, they happened upon the patient ensemble, which after two weeks' work, was still engaged in the production of Dorothy's portrait. Erastus held a position five yards in front of the Hollands' house, where he meticulously worked his brush upon the canvas. Dorothy and Ella stood steadfast on the porch, remaining obedient, as best they could, to the demands of their tableau. Each of them, however, glanced discreetly sideways upon hearing the sound of approaching visitors.

"Erastus," Cato called. "Hello!"

The painter turned, but had to squint into the sunlight behind him. "Hello?" Then as the two men drew near enough to block the sun, he saw them clearly. "Ah, Cato!" he said. "And this must be your friend Jimmy."

"Yes!" Cato's breath quickened. Jimmy and Erastus had not yet met. Cato held a faint hope that despite their differences, each of them would in some way be pleased to meet the other.

"Erastus, this is Jimmy. Jimmy this is Erastus Hicks, the painter I told you about."

Jimmy nodded his head and said, "Hello," but he did not offer his hand to the white man. Instead, he looked up to the porch. Civility required that he, too, ought to make an introduction. "Miss Dorothy," he said, "this is Cato, from the Hickory Grove plantation," then turning to Cato, "Cato, this is Miss Dorothy Holland, and my sister Ella."

"Pleased to meet you, Miss Holland ... Miss Ella," Cato said, nodding at each of the women.

"I'm pleased to meet you, Cato," said Dorothy. "I'm well acquainted with another member of your household at Hickory Grove."

"Yes," Cato said, "Master William speaks of you often."

"I hope he speaks of me fondly," Dorothy said.

"Oh yes indeed, Miss, most fondly."

"I haven't seen Mr. Askew since my birthday party last spring," Dorothy said. "Is he at home, or has he returned to Kentucky?"

"No, Miss, he is at home now. He's all done with school. He graduated in June. I expect he's hoping you'll have another party so he can call on you again."

"Well you may tell him for me that he is welcome to call on me any time, party or no. I should be happy to receive him."

"Yes, Miss."

Ella, who, unlike Dorothy, continued to hold her position for the portrait, looked quizzically at Erastus. "Can I put my arm down now?"

"By all means," said Erastus.

Ella eyed her brother and Cato. "Y'all been running in the woods with that dog," she asked.

"We were in the woods," Jimmy acknowledged. "But we had to skedaddle. There were hunters."

"I thought I heard a gunshot," Erastus said.

"They shot a deer," Cato said.

Heedless of the artistic arrangement, Venus climbed up onto the porch in order to sniff Dorothy and Ella.

"That dog's got stickers sticking every which way on her back end," observed Ella. "You'd better not let her get in the house, and spread those stickers all over Missus' furniture."

"Don't worry, I'll pick them off," Jimmy said. "Come on, Venus," he called the dog, who dashed down the porch steps more quickly than she'd climbed them. "Let's get you fixed up."

"I'll help," Cato offered.

Jimmy and Cato turned to leave, but the painter took Cato's arm. "How are the leaves of grass these days?" Erastus asked, with a barely perceptible wink.

"Very well, thank you," Cato said. "I've covered a lot of ground since we last spoke."

"So have I," said the painter, nodding at his canvas.

Cato looked at the painting and felt a tinge of jealousy. He looked at the women on the porch. "Miss Holland, Miss Ella," he said, "you both look fetching in this painting."

Ella harrumphed, but Dorothy said, "Why thank you, Cato. You are indeed a gentleman. Please remember me to Mr. Askew. Perhaps you can tell him of my fetchingness, perhaps that might fetch him over for a visit."

"I will remind him of your fetchingness," Cato said. "And knowing how he feels, I'm certain he'll want to call on you."

Jimmy led Venus back toward the barn, with Cato trailing behind. Inside the barn, Jimmy retrieved a horse brush from Walnut's stall, then situated Venus between a pair of straw bales upon which he and Cato might sit and clean her up.

"You want to brush, or pick stickers?" Jimmy asked.

"I'll pick the stickers," Cato said. "Venus likes it when you brush her."

Jimmy began to brush the dog in long, gentle strokes. "You're something else," he said.

"What do you mean?" Cato surveyed the stickers in the dog's fur with fastidious attention.

"Not too often you hear a slave tell a white woman she looks fetching."

"I told her she looked fetching in the painting, that's all. It was just to say something nice about the painting …, about Erastus, really. And I didn't only say it about her; I said it about your sister, too."

"Do you think she's pretty? Miss Holland, I mean."

"Oh she's pretty enough." Cato plucked gingerly at the stickers adorning Venus's backside, in response to which the dog looked around at Cato dubiously, but she kept still.

"You ever wonder what it would be like to get with someone like her," Jimmy said.

"Get with her? Not much chance of me getting with someone like that," Cato said.

"Naw, I guess it's your white brother she likes."

"Yeah," Cato said. "My brother. Can't say as I ever think of him as my brother." Cato pulled hard on a sticker that was stuck deep in the fur, and Venus whimpered. "But he does like her, no doubt of that." Cato held the sticker in his hand, unsure where to drop it. "All William talks about is how beautiful Miss Holland is—how hard it is to say anything to her on account of she's so smart."

"Smart mouthed," Jimmy said. "Most times, you don't need to do any talking when she's around, since she talks enough for two or three people."

"William's mother, Lucille Askew …, she talks a lot too," Cato said, deciding finally to drop the stickers in a pail which sat nearby. "But she's not the same as Miss Holland. Miss Holland looks at me like I'm actually a person."

Jimmy tried to grab onto Venus's tail, which was twitching about, so that he could steady it and brush it. "Lucille Askew," he said. "Damn, now that sounds like someone I don't want to meet." He tried to imagine the woman who was married to Augustus Askew. "What's she like?"

"She acts like she's bored most of the time. She struts around the house looking for someone to give orders to. And even if you do something perfectly fine, she'll find a problem with it, just so she can make herself seem needed. Like she wouldn't have any purpose if she didn't go around finding fault with how people do their work."

"They're all uppity like that," Jimmy shrugged. "Like no one but white folks can ever do anything right …, like they're the only ones can do anything right." He kicked the dirt in exasperation.

"And the truth is," Cato said, "they don't hardly know how to do anything at all. You take Missus Lucille …, she can't cook or sew. She wouldn't know how to clean something if she had to. The only thing she knows how to do is give out orders."

"Anyone over there that you do like?"

Cato shrugged. "I don't know. No one pays any attention to me except William. I guess he's the only one I like."

"You like him?" The idea of liking a white man was inconceivable to Jimmy.

"Yes, of course …, why not? … He's the only person at home who's a friend to me."

"No women you like over there?" Jimmy spoke into the ground, somewhat embarrassed by this question.

"Like I said, they all treat me as if … I don't know … like someone who's neither this or that. I'm lighter than all the

111

others. I talk different. Everyone knows my story. And they all move around me like I'm some kind of strange something."

"You are some kind of strange something," Jimmy said. "Nothing wrong with that." He scratched his head.

"The world is strange," Cato said. "I think you and me were just born in the wrong place and time." Cato watched Jimmy brushing Venus. "You should have been born a dog,"

"A dog! Now, why'd I want to be a dog?"

"'Cause I bet you'd like to have a master that picked out your stickers, and brushed you, and gave you bacon, and stroked your ears and all."

"I don't want nobody stroking my ears."

Cato laughed, jumped up, and playfully stroked one of Jimmy's ears.

"Cut that out," Jimmy said, swatting away Cato's hand.

"Come on, you like it," Cato said.

"Says you." Jimmy stood to move his head out of Cato's reach, but he said, "Am I gonna get some bacon too?"

"No, I'm gonna pick out your stickers." Cato reached down and pulled at some stray stickers caught in the bottom of Jimmy's trousers.

"Man you are something else—some kind of strange something." Jimmy sat down again on the straw bale, and stared at his friend.

"Jimmy, do you think I have the light within?"

"The light where?"

"The light within. That's what Erastus told me. He said I had the light within, and that I can look for it in other people, and that other people can see it in me."

"I don't know, maybe that's how come you're so pale." Jimmy made a face.

"No I'm serious," Cato said.

"What light are you talking about?"

"It has to do with the spirit inside people. It means that some people have a light in their spirit … and they're different, and you can tell they are because they don't act the same as other people, because they're gentle, like the Quakers."

Jimmy nodded. "Yeah you're gentle all right …, too gentle, if you ask me."

"Too gentle! Why's that?"

"Because you got to be strong if you want people to respect you." After a pause he added, "Of course, I respect you, but other folks …."

Cato looked away …. He stared out the window in the barn. "Erastus thinks that gentleness is more powerful than physical strength," he said quietly.

"I don't see how," Jimmy said. "You can't wrestle someone all gentle like and expect to win."

"No, you don't understand, it's about … I don't know how to explain it … about how when a gentle person comes up against an ungentle person the gentle person is the one who can … ." Cato wasn't sure how to end the sentence.

"Can what?"

"Can stand his ground," he said finally. "– If he believes in his own power."

Jimmy shook his head. "I wish I knew what you're talking about. I don't understand it." Jimmy looked at Cato with plain bewilderment. The mystery of Cato was that he was half-white. He had the blood of old Augustus Askew in him, but as cruel as his father was, Cato was the opposite. Even so, Jimmy wondered if these strange ideas about light and gentleness that Cato shared with the painter were thoughts that sprang from his white blood— because they didn't feel like anything he recognized in his own thoughts.

"I see the light within you," Cato said.

"In me?" Jimmy laughed and looked down at himself—as if to check whether something was in fact visible on his chest.

"It's in you," Cato said. "In your spirit."

"I don't think so," Jimmy said. "Only thing inside me is the hope to someday get free of this place, and all these paddy rollers, and all these ugly ass crackers and their guns and their fur hats."

"That's what I mean," Cato said. "I saw how you were back there when we saw those hunters. You hate those violent people?"

"Huh?"

"And when you're petting Venus, that's when I see it in you. You have dark, angry feelings ... but they're all mixed up with light feelings too."

"Only one around here who has light and dark mixed up in him is you, judging from your appearance." Jimmy meant to be funny, but Cato didn't smile.

"I told you, I am not white," he said.

"So you say."

"You act like you're angry," Cato said. "But I think somewhere inside you, you're just ..."

"Just what?"

"... I don't know, just waiting for something, or someone, to change you."

"So you think you're gonna change me?"

"I don't mean me."

"I can't figure you out," Jimmy said. "Half the time I talk to you I don't even know what we're talking about."

Cato stood, stepped over Venus, and sat down on the straw bale next to Jimmy. "It's something I feel," Cato said. "I can feel things about people. You're different from other people. I've always felt it."

"Different how?"

"Look in my eyes," Cato said.

Jimmy turned to look at Cato, but it was awkward. Cato stared at him with intensity. Reflexively, he blinked. "What are you looking at?" Jimmy asked.

"I'm looking inside you."

"You know it is scary when you look at someone like that," Jimmy said. "You should see how big your eyes are. Your eyes look like some big black-eyed peas in a pail of butter."

"Well yours look like glowing coals just before the flames leap out."

"What flames?"

"Yes and your nose is kind of peculiar."

"What? Oh man!" Jimmy stood up, and covered his nose with his hand. "You're crazy," he said.

Venus, who had lain down during their conversation, lifted her head to see what was happening.

"Yup, and your nostrils flare up and down when you get embarrassed," Cato went on. "And it's really kind of nice because your nose is like an animal that lives on your face and it does things you don't know about."

Jimmy shook his head. "OK. I just don't know what to say. Do you talk like this with other people?"

"No."

"Then how come you talk like this with me?"

"Because, like I said, you're different."

"I don't know how different I am," Jimmy said. "Look," he held out his hand with the horse brush to illustrate a point. "If I had a knife and if I was mad enough, and if I thought nobody would know about it, I'd take that knife and stab your Master Askew with it if I could. I know what he's done to people. And I'd stab that old bastard with a knife just like that if I could get away with it. I'm not this gentle person you seem to think, do you understand? I don't go in for turning the other cheek. And I don't know what I might do someday if they ever try to lay a hand on me or on someone I care about."

Jimmy began to pace, holding the horse brush now like a pointer he might use to underscore his remarks. "I never told you this," he said. "I walked over to see you last week. When I got close to Hickory Grove, I saw slaves working the fields out there. They were in a gang, and there was an overseer with them. When I looked close, I saw a little boy down on the ground. He was down on all fours, and that damn cussed white bastard was whipping him. And right then, right then, I just about lost myself. I thought I ought to run in there and beat the shit out of that son-of-a-bitch. I was shaking, Cato, I was shaking so hard … and I almost couldn't stand up on the road any more. He was just a little boy. And that cuss-assed cracker was whipping him as hard as he could. Why?" he shouted … and now his hand, exaggerated by the brush, began to shake. "Why shouldn't I fight back?" Jimmy's voice trembled. "Why should anyone think there is light in a world like this—in a world where that is what they do to us?"

Cato stood up. "Don't," he said. "Don't ever do anything like that. They might kill you. Don't you know? You can't do anything about it. There isn't even any point in trying to do something like that. You'd just end up getting yourself hurt. I …," his voice broke off.

Jimmy glared. "What?"

"I wouldn't want to see you get hurt, that's all," Cato said.

"They'd have to catch me first," Jimmy said.

Cato sighed heavily. "Look, I don't think it does any good to beat people up or to run away. The only way we can get by in this world is to be loving with each other, and be good to each other."

"Oh cuss that," Jimmy spat.

"You get mad because you feel it so deeply," Cato said.

"You get mad when someone is wronged—because your heart is good, and it hurts you when you see someone doing an evil thing like that."

"You sound like Reverend Zeke," Jimmy said. "Next thing you'll be talking about forgiveness. But you better not, you better not ... not if you want to be my friend."

Cato was stunned, and hung his head. "I won't say anything more," he said.

Jimmy knew his anger had spilled over, that it had poisoned his feelings. But the image of the little boy lying on the ground, crying helplessly, danced in his mind—and in his righteous wrath, he felt that Cato and Reverend Zeke and all those who stood by and abided such things were guilty for it. He paced, saying nothing, and just stared at the floor of the barn.

After a while, he came and stood over Cato, who had crouched down beside Venus and stroked her, as if to take refuge from the anger. "You look like a scared rabbit down there," he said.

"Yeah, that's me, Cato the gentle rabbit." He sighed. "I wish I was more like what you want in a friend."

Jimmy knelt down, picked up a clump of straw, and then dropped it. "Oh man. Who says you're not what I want in a friend?"

Cato looked up at Jimmy. The lines on his forehead uncreased.

"You're just some kind of strange something," Jimmy said. "I was wrong to say what I said. I guess I'd be your friend no matter what." He rocked back on his feet. "I don't know. Maybe it's like you say. Maybe there is light and dark mixed inside me."

Cato smiled. "You're dark on the outside ... that's for sure." He grabbed Jimmy's hand, and held it in front of his eyes, like an object for inspection. He turned the palm up to examine it. "Your palm is the same color as me," he said finally. "Look." He placed Jimmy's hand, palm out, next to his cheek. "We're the same color."

Jimmy smirked. "Yeah, I guess so, except I'm better looking."

"What?" Cato laughed. "William says I'm the best damn looking darkie he ever met."

"Oh, man … he just says that because he thinks you look like him."

"I do look like him."

"Shoot man, you don't look nothing like him. If you looked like him, I wouldn't even come within ten feet of you."

"And who told you you're good looking?" Cato asked.

"Didn't nobody tell me. I just looked in the mirror."

"Where'd you run into a mirror?"

"Oh you know, I go in the big house once in a while. I'm not just always a field nigger, you know. Sometimes, I help Willis serve dinner, when they have guests for supper."

"I see," Cato smirked. "And I suppose you get all dressed up in some fine outfit when you do that."

"I do," Jimmy said. "I got a special suit Cora made for me. What? You laugh?"

"I do laugh."

"Why?"

"Because the picture of you in a suit is funny."

"What's so funny about it?"

Cato tried to stop laughing. "I'm sorry," he said. "I'm sure you look fetching in a suit. You'll have to model it for me sometime."

"Hell no," Jimmy said. "With you laughing like that! I'd sooner walk around naked."

Cato giggled.

"Look here, I'll have you know, when I put on my suit, and serve dinner, all the ladies turn their heads."

"What ladies?"

"Missus Holland, Miss Holland, Cora … don't think I can't tell."

"Tell what?"

"That they're looking at me and thinking, Mmmm, Mmmm, that is one fine-looking buck in that suit."

"Oh do they?" Cato said.

"Well," Jimmy said, "I know you're vain too. You've got that gold vest. You've got that wavy hair. And you walk like you got some kind of strut you can't help in your legs."

"Strut? Hah, you should talk. Did I ever show you how you walk?" Cato said. "Watch this." Cato aped Jimmy's walk, walking as if he was four inches taller and twenty pounds heavier, with his hands swinging, and his hips rocking, exaggerating the pelvic movement.

"Man, you got to be kidding," Jimmy laughed. "Did I ever show you how you walk? Look here, you walk like this …" Jimmy made himself thinner and lighter, and walked on his feet like they were delicate spindles. He lifted his nose up too.

Venus stood, and began to pace during these demonstrations. Suddenly she barked.

"See that," Jimmy said. "The dog thinks I've gone and turned into a octoroon or something, and she can't tell who I am no more."

"She thinks you've turned into a horse, and that you're about to prance out of here."

Venus barked again. Jimmy laughed, and reached down to pet her. "It's OK girl, I ain't turned into no horse. I'm just your plain old Jimmy." He picked up the brush, and held it in front of her nose. "Truth is, nobody's quite so fine looking as you, girl."

"That's right," Cato said, and knelt down to pet her as well.

Venus looked at each of them in succession. She knew something was going on with them. She knew that Jimmy was happy. She'd never seen him as happy before. And she knew it had to do with the new one, that together they were having fun.

She barked at the new one.

"That's Cato," Jimmy said. "Cato!"

She barked again.

"Cato," Jimmy repeated. "Cato is my friend."

---

## "AND THE BEE JUMPS IN"

ato duly delivered Dorothy's message to William, who that same evening sent Cato back to the Hollands' farm with the message that William would call on Dorothy on the following Saturday afternoon. William was beside himself from the moment Cato said that Dorothy wanted to see him. For months, he'd lived with the conclusion that he had made a poor impression on Dorothy at her birthday party, and that any chances he might have had with her were lost. There was no argument behind this conclusion beyond his knowing that he had been tongue-tied in her presence, and his belief that she had toyed with him idly, like a bored cat with a too meager mouse. But now she was offering another chance, and he was determined that he would acquit himself well this time. The last time had been a social occasion, at which he was the only male in attendance. Some men might have relished such circumstances, but for William it was awkward. He had no interest in any of the other girls, and he had not known how to convey that fact. Now he would see her alone, and he would feel himself to be on firmer footing.

When he arrived, however, Dorothy seemed intent upon renewing his awkwardness. "William Askew!" she exclaimed. "I do believe you've grown an inch since last I saw you." Dorothy's attention shifted to the face of her suitor. "And is that a beard you're growing?"

"No, I … it's just that I haven't shaved. I may grow whiskers."

"Well then," Dorothy asked, "did Cato tell you that I wished you would call on me?"

"Yes, he did. … I was surprised."

"Why William …, why ever were you? I've always enjoyed seeing you."

"I was not certain that was true."

"I suppose you're just awfully shy. I don't know what else it could be. Come now; let's go out in the garden and talk, just as we did at my party."

Dorothy was in simple attire, the sort of clothes in which she felt comfortable. Her plain cloth skirt fell straight from her hips, with no hoops or structure to extend it. William, however, had dressed for the occasion, wearing a pair of new boots, and a vest made of silk.

"Cato tells me that Mr. Hicks is painting your portrait," he began

"He is indeed."

"I would like to see it, when it's finished."

"Mr. Hicks is painting the portrait in a way that he hopes you'll find agreeable. He said he'd rather please you with the painting than my mother, though it is Mother who has been hounding us to get it finished."

William was surprised by this. "Why would Mr. Hicks consider my feelings above your mother's?"

"He said that he would rather take a young man's point of

view in his work than the point of view of a mother. Altogether he has the most unusual ideas about everything."

"He's a Quaker."

"Yes, so I've heard. But come now, let's sit here on the bench, and pick up where we left off."

As they sat on the bench, Dorothy realized that her ordinary skirt did not lend itself to flirtatious manipulations in the same way that her green party dress had done.

"Oh dear," Dorothy said. "I fear I shan't be able to tease you this time."

"Why do you tease me?"

"Because, you're so earnest and bug eyed."

William turned his head away. "I'm sorry. I didn't realize I was staring. I'm just not used to being this close to you."

"Goodness, you talk as if I were the queen of England."

"I know," William said, "that I'm ... awkward. You told Cato that you'd like me to call, but I don't know, really, what your feelings are toward me."

"I enjoy talking to you, even teasing you a bit. I think you are agreeable looking. But I wish, really, that we might talk more frankly about things."

"You are most agreeable looking to me," William said. "I guess you know that."

"Yes, I can tell."

William reached out, without warning, and put his hand on Dorothy's leg. "Don't you ever want to just feel touched by someone?" he asked.

The unexpected warmth of his hand on her leg gave Dorothy pause. She thought she ought to scold him, and shoo his hand away ... but she let herself feel it lying there for a moment, just to see what it was like. It did feel nice to be touched. "Ah William," she placed her hand on his. "It is good to be touched. But you must learn the art of seduction. You can't just jump into touching someone like you're taking a plunge at the swimming hole." She gently lifted his hand off her leg. "Let us explore each other with our thoughts first. Touch as bold as this must be reserved for a greater intimacy than we have at this time."

"But you do think, someday, we will arrive at a time for that kind of touch."

"Perhaps."

"Then I can wait." He folded his hands in his lap, and looked around the yard—as if to discover a topic of conversation. "What would you like to talk about?" he asked.

"About how someday I might leave this backwater to find my place in the world."

"But why? You have everything you need here, surely."

"I'm not entirely aware of what it is I'm missing," Dorothy said. "But I'm certain that I am missing something. I hope there is a place where people think more as I do. Mr. Hicks, for example, speaks of intriguing places."

"Are you sweet on him?"

"Honestly, Mr. Askew, you surprise me. He's far too old for me. I find him refreshing, but I wouldn't say I'm 'sweet' on him."

"He's kind of odd, isn't he?"

"I count that among his virtues," Dorothy said.

"So if I were odd, you would find that appealing too."

"Yes."

"I'll try to be odder."

"Oddness isn't something to be tried on like a new pair of boots. And you miss the point. It is the way that Mr. Hicks is odd that is appealing. It has to do with how he looks at the world, with how he regards people."

"He's been quite friendly with Cato," William observed.

"Well there you are," Dorothy said. "The very fact that Mr. Hicks would pursue a friendship with your servant sets him apart. He doesn't heed social class or custom. He has a direct appreciation for the world as it is, rather than as it pretends to be."

William nodded his head, but he said, "I'm not sure what you mean."

"I mean that when I look at the society hereabouts, to me it feels unreal. It feels like an elaborate stage production, written by a windy old plantation owner. Everyone is playing his part. Everyone is wearing the proper clothes, going through the proper rituals. ... But it has nothing to do with reality. It's just a play. It's a play in which I feel miscast."

"I've never thought of it that way."

"I should think not. You're cast perfectly. You're the son of a wealthy planter. You have power, independence, education. As far as I can see, you have a plum part in this play."

"But your part's not bad. You too have means and education. And you have something I don't."

"What's that?"

"You're beautiful."

"Ah," Dorothy blushed. "If I am, it is more evidence of how miscast I am—for I do not value being attractive. I'd rather be independent. I'd rather have control of my own destiny."

"I think I would do anything to be attractive to you. That aspect of my casting was overlooked."

"I've told you, you're not disagreeable looking. You place more store on that quality than I do. What matters to me is what you say and do, and how you think. If you had thoughts that I wanted, I'd want to be filled by you."

William imagined filling Dorothy with thoughts, but how he would fill her he did not know, since she seemed immense. Even so, the sexual overtones of her remark aroused him.

"All right, I will try to think some very fine thoughts," he said.

Dorothy smiled.

"I will think about something important. I'm going to think about …." He looked around, as if to find an answer. "This!" he said, as he picked a long, pendulous bloom from the hydrangea bush behind them. He held it in front of him, sniffing it. "It has real smell, real delicacy. But in fact, it is only here for a moment. Then it will be gone. So many things that are beautiful fade quickly. Except you, you always grow more beautiful with time."

"Honestly, Mr. Askew, you keep returning to flattery."

"I can't help that. It's really how I feel."

"Let me smell the flower," she said.

He handed her the blossom, and she inhaled its fragrance.

"It's so sweet!"

"Sweet, but doomed to fade," William said.

"Why be gloomy? Why not just enjoy the sweet, delicate flower, in all its ripeness?"

Feeling a burst of courage, he said, "It is my desire to enjoy the flower in its ripeness. That's why I put my hand on your leg."

"Ah."

"And why I wish the flower would be glad of my pleasure in it."

Dorothy looked at the flower and grew serious. "You're right," she said. "It would seem unfitting for a flower not to be glad for its beauty. Beauty is its principal quality. Flowers have a purpose which beauty satisfies—to attract the bee."

"And the bee jumps in," William reminded her. "Just as if he were taking a plunge at the swimming hole."

"Yes, I suppose he does." Dorothy said. "However, we are more than flowers and bees. We may share some of their instincts. But what is the point of being human if we are not more thoughtful, more deliberate in our actions."

"If we deny our instincts, if we act only after deliberation, we may miss the pollen."

"Ah, the pollen." Dorothy raised an eyebrow. "Does it matter so much?"

"It must," William said. "Otherwise the desire would not be so strong."

"What I desire," Dorothy said, "has less to do with pollen than with the garden. I want to be planted in a place where the climate is more to my liking."

"If I could be with you, I'd plant myself anywhere that was to your liking."

"Would you?"

"Truly."

"I wish I could believe you, but it is in my nature to be skeptical of an amorous bee's intentions."

They sat in silence for a while, listening to the birds and the sound of crickets. Dorothy saw that William wanted to talk about important matters. She was pleased by that. But she was skeptical of his ardor, and especially of his certainty. She'd never been certain of her attraction toward anyone. It seemed improbable to her that such certain attraction could be genuine. She believed herself capable of detecting insincerity. She'd had plenty of practice honing her skill in a roundabout fashion in the company of her mother's friends. Those women were so routinely insincere that with them the trick was detecting the rare moments of sincerity that occasionally slipped through. She knew sincerity when it appeared. By that measure, William seemed sincere, yet the feeling he espoused remained suspicious to her.

William, for his part, wondered if speaking more boldly might be the way to draw her closer. She was formidable, but he liked her lack of superficiality. In this respect, she was so unlike his mother. He realized he must tell her this. He must tell her that it was not just her beauty that he admired. He tried to think of how to say it.

"Miss Holland," he began, "you're not like my mother."

"I've never met her. I presume Lucille feels our family is not of sufficient means to warrant social connection."

"No, it's not that. She has hardly any social contact with anyone, really."

"Does she know you're calling on me?"

"No. I don't tell her much about what I do."

"That sounds appealing. If only my mother didn't manage my every breath."

"What I mean is that my mother only cares about things ..., things like clothes and furniture and having the house look just so. She lives on the surface of things. She doesn't question the way things are."

"That part does sound like my mother."

"And this is what I'm trying to say ... that it is how you do question the way things are ... that I ...." He felt himself going red. His tongue tied just when he wanted to say something important.

Dorothy saw his blush. She saw that he was struggling to say something he couldn't articulate. She asked, "Are you saying you like that about me?"

"No. 'Like' isn't an adequate word."

"Ah."

He sat in silence, looking helpless. He stared up at the sky, wondering if there was a way to will the amorphous feelings racing in his head to coalesce. He watched a cloud gliding along. He thought about how it slowly, imperceptibly changed its shape. Suddenly he thought of what to say. "It affects me. It changes me. It makes me wish I were someone else. It makes me feel like a cloud."

"Like a cloud?" Dorothy smiled.

"And I don't know if I will evaporate or turn into a thundercloud, but I know that I want to be changed by you."

Without thinking, Dorothy kissed him. It was quick and impulsive, but sincere. William was so startled by the kiss that he did not know how to respond, and so he sat still, and said, "You kissed me."

After a time, Dorothy spoke. "Well, Mr. William Askew, I would like to see you turn into a thundercloud. I think that would be most attractive."

"Really?"

"I'm not sure I want to be struck by lightning. But rain … rain that cools and breaks the humidity; that would be most refreshing."

"Do you know what makes it rain?" he asked.

"I'm not sure."

"It's the water from all around us, from the rivers and lakes. I learned about it at college. The water evaporates and rises to the clouds, and eventually the clouds have so much water that they break open and it rains."

"Ah, the clouds break open."

"Really they are just fragile vessels … delicate pouches of water floating in the sky."

"Is that how they described clouds in your college classes?"

"No. I'm being poetical."

"Yes. You are."

"What makes them break?"

"I suppose it's just that they can only hold so much."

"Like people," Dorothy said. "People break too. They can only hold so much."

They sat again in silence, looking up at the sky. Though it was October, the weather in Tennessee remained benign. Only the faintest hint of cold rustled the tops of the trees. At ground level, the earth was warm, and still alive. There was no rain in sight.

## "VENUS WOULD LIKE IT"

"You kissed him?" Ella was shocked. She made clucking sounds to show it.

"Well he said something charming, and I just suddenly did it. I didn't even hardly think about it."

Ella was helping Dorothy get ready for their final day of portrait posing. Though Dorothy regretted that their visits with Erastus Hicks would come to an end, she was giddy over the prospect of never having to wear the green silk dress again. Ella was just to the point of lacing her up.

"I thought you said you didn't like him all that much," Ella said. "I thought you said you didn't want to ever marry nobody, and you were gonna start by not marrying William Askew."

"Who said anything about marrying him? I only kissed him on the cheek. He didn't kiss me back, really. He just sat there tongue-tied. Though he did put his hand on my leg earlier, and I had to remove it."

"Where'd he put it?"

"Here," Dorothy said, and pressed Ella's hand onto her dress at the thigh.

"Oh my. What else happened?" Ella resumed lacing.

"That's all. But he said I made him feel like a cloud, and he wanted to be changed by me into a thundercloud."

"Sounds like crazy talk to me."

"Ouch, don't tie it so tight." Dorothy made a face, but straightened her spine to be helpful.

"I got to tie it so it holds together. This dress is just about on its last legs." Ella fiddled with the knot, and then patted Dorothy on the shoulder. "You're ready. I just got to get the hair brush, and we can go down."

"My legs are on their last legs," Dorothy said.

"You and me both," Ella agreed. "My hair-brushing arm is definitely on its last legs. I wonder how many hours I've held that brush in the air above your head." Ella picked up the brush from the top of the bureau. "Do you think he'll show you the painting today?"

"I'm not sure if I want to see it," Dorothy said.

"Don't worry—you look fine and dandy—just like an angel," Ella said.

"What?"

"I took a look at it the other day when I carried that pitcher of water out to him."

"What do you mean I look like an angel?" Dorothy wasn't sure this was the way she'd want to look.

"Well, you kind of glow I reckon."

"How about you? How do you look?"

Ella shook her head. "I didn't look at that part. I squinted my eyes sideways so I could only see you in there."

When they arrived on the porch, they found Erastus sitting on the ground at the foot of the stairs with his head in his hands. The canvas and all the painting tools stood ready and waiting.

"Is something wrong?" Dorothy asked.

"I'll be leaving town after I finish your portrait," Erastus said. "I'm going to miss many fine souls in these parts."

"Must you leave so soon?"

"I received a letter," Erastus said. "My father is ill. I must return to Philadelphia."

"I'm sorry," Dorothy's face showed sincere emotion. She hadn't considered that Erastus would have a father. "Is he terribly sick?"

"He is. And he's quite old now. So I don't know if he'll survive until I get there."

Ella spoke. "I'm sorry for your troubles, Mr. Erast. Would you like me to fix you a sandwich, or a glass of lemonade? I know Cora has some lemons saved up."

"No, thank you, Ella, not just now. I propose that we all toast our achievement with lemonade once we're through here today. Dorothy, I hope to show the portrait to your mother and father this evening."

"Have they paid you your wages yet?" Dorothy asked.

"No, not yet."

"Well I hope that won't delay you," Dorothy said. "I expect father will have to go to the bank tomorrow. Does he know you're nearly done with the painting? He's planning a trip to Memphis, and I heard him say he was planning to leave tomorrow."

"I just mentioned it to your mother this morning," Erastus said. "She said she would inform Mr. Holland straightaway."

The October air had grown decidedly cooler. Ella took her pose for the last time, holding the hairbrush just above Dorothy's carefully brushed hair. She tried, as always, to adjust the expression on her mouth until it felt proper. Dorothy, in a much easier pose, stood with her hands resting on the porch rails, looking off into the distance. Today her eyes wore a distant, searching look, as she peered out toward Christmasville Road, and tried to imagine the city of Philadelphia. She wondered if William Askew would ever want to travel there.

When the last stroke of paint was laid down on the canvas, Erastus stepped back and nodded. "OK, ladies, you can relax now. We're all done. Would you like to see the painting?"

"Shall we see it now, just like that?" Dorothy said.

"Why not?" Erastus said. "The late afternoon light shows it a bit redder than it really is. But I think you'll see it to better advantage here than in the house."

With a mix of excitement and uncertainty, Dorothy and Ella climbed down the stairs of the porch. Dorothy came first. She stood and stared at the painting with her eyes wide. Ella, too, came around and stared, this time without squinting.

"Gracious, how'd you make me look like that?" Ella said.

"Like what?" Erastus asked.

"I look kind of all right," Ella said. "I think I look skinny or something."

"Perhaps a bit," Erastus said. "I didn't change you very much though."

"Mr. Erast, you got me with a nice expression. I can't believe that's how my mouth came out after all these weeks."

"What do you think, Dorothy?" Erastus asked.

"I think it is extraordinary," Dorothy said. "I'm sure my mother will like it. I'm sure my father will like it. William Askew will undoubtedly kiss me when he sees it. He may even kiss you, Erastus. I think, perhaps, you've changed me, too. You have been flattering to both of us."

"Well, I merely painted you as I see you," Erastus said.

"And my eye habitually makes small adjustments to render the world in a beautiful way."

"It must be fine to see the world through your eyes, Mr. Erast" Ella said.

"Thank you," Erastus said. "That's a fine compliment."

"Can I show Wally and Sammy?" Ella asked. "Maybe they could see it out here before you carry it in the house." Ella's excitement was palpable.

"That's a good idea," Erastus said.

Ella instantly called out, "Sammy! Sammy! Go on and fetch your mamma and come out here and see this picture Mr. Erast has painted. Sammy, where are you at, little brother? You come out here now and take a look at this."

Even before the front door of the house burst open, they could hear Sammy's feet running inside. Trying to get Sammy excited about something was like trying to get rain to be wet. He rushed out onto the porch, seeming already to know what was happening. "Is the picture all done?" he asked.

"It's all done, now go and fetch mama and then come back here and take a look at it out here in the light before they bring it in the house."

"Can't I look at it first?" Sammy's legs were poised to sprint in either direction.

"All right. All right," Ella said. "You take a quick look," Ella beckoned with her arm. "But hurry up before Mrs. Holland comes out here and finds us all standing around."

Sammy dashed down the porch steps and turned as quickly as he could to look at the canvas. With his head tilted, he looked back and forth from the painting to the porch. Then he pointed at the painting as he assessed its merits. "It looks just like the porch. Ella, it looks just like you. And it looks just like you Miss Dorothy, but it isn't you and it isn't the porch, it's all just a picture. It's the most nice picture I ever saw. Can I go get

135

Venus? I bet Venus will think it's really you in there. I don't know if she ever saw a painting before."

"You go on and get mama. You can't show a picture to a dog, don't you know that?"

Sammy shrugged. "OK. But I bet Venus would like it." With that, he ran off toward the cabins.

The front door opened again, and this time Mrs. Holland herself came out. She stood on the porch, at the top of the stairs, surveying the situation.

"The portrait is completed," Erastus said. "Would you like to see it now, or shall I bring it in the house?"

"I'll wait until you bring it in," she said. "But Mr. Hicks, I'm afraid we won't be able to pay you until Mr. Holland returns from his trip to Memphis. He must dispose of some property intended to raise the funds for your fee."

"Ah," said Erastus. "When do you think Mr. Holland will return from Memphis? He hasn't left yet, has he?"

"No," Henrietta said. "Mr. Holland is in his study now. He plans to leave for Memphis tomorrow."

"What property?" Dorothy asked, "Why would father need to go to Memphis to dispose of property?"

"I'll speak to you about that later," Henrietta said.

A quizzical look crossed Dorothy's face. "Excuse me," she said to the painter. "I'd like to go and speak to my mother about this." She turned to her mother. "Let's go in the house."

"Very well," Henrietta said. "Ella you stay out here and help Mr. Hicks put away his things."

The two women went into the house, and Ella set about helping the painter clean his brushes. After a few minutes, she said, "Mr. Erast, can I shake your hand?"

"Of course," Erastus said. "Why do you want to?"

"Because I never shook the hand of a famous painter before, and I don't reckon I'll get too many chances for it."

Erastus stepped forward and held out his hand. "It's my pleasure," Erastus said. "Though my fame is not so widespread as you may imagine, I am glad to count you among my admirers."

Just as they were shaking hands, a scream erupted from the house. Ella recognized Dorothy's voice.

"Oh good Lord," Ella said, and she dropped both Erastus's hand and the paintbrush that she was holding in her other hand. She ran up the stairs. Just as she got to the top, Dorothy stumbled out the front door. She fell straight into Ella's arms. "What's happened?" Ella asked.

Dorothy tucked her head on Ella's shoulder, whimpering.

"Are you all right? Is your mama all right? What's happened?" Ella repeated.

Dorothy raised her head. "I don't think I can tell you. It's too horrible. I can't even say it."

"Say what?"

Erastus stepped halfway up the porch. "Is anyone hurt?" he asked.

"Oh why did I have to be born in a place like this," Dorothy said. "I should have known they'd plan something like this. I don't know if I can tell you what they plan to do."

A fearful look came onto Ella's face. She took Dorothy by the shoulders and shook her, as if to shake Dorothy's hysteria out of her. "Tell us," she said.

Dorothy inhaled deeply, closed her eyes and said it all in a single stroke. "My father is going to Memphis to sell Sammy to raise money for your fee, Mr. Hicks."

"What?" Ella's hands began to shake. "Sammy? You don't mean our Sammy? No, they wouldn't do that. You mean something else, don't you?"

Dorothy shook her head.

"Oh God help us," Ella threw her hands up in the air. "And

the boy's just gone to get his mama." Suddenly Ella could no longer speak. She saw that Sammy and Wally were coming toward them. They approached with rapid steps. Sammy carried a glass pitcher, which he struggled to hold steady while keeping up with Wally, who maneuvered a tray of glasses. Ella felt her mouth go shut, and at that moment, she wondered if she would ever open it again.

Erastus Hicks sat down on the steps of the porch. He leaned his head back against the stair rails. His breath came heavily, as if the oxygen in the air had suddenly diminished. He clasped his hands together, then squeezed them as hard as he could. He looked up at the sky, speckled with clouds lit orange by the late afternoon sun.

Wally arrived at the side of the house wearing a big smile. Her gaze was fixed upon the rear of the canvas, which sat still upon its wooden easel erected at the base of the stairs. "I knew that picture would be done today," she said. "So I made y'all some lemonade! Oooh, and let me tell you, this sure is some good …." Wally turned to look at the painter, who sat on the stairs, and then at Ella and Dorothy above him. She saw the glint of wet on Dorothy's cheek and the fearful expression on her daughter's face. She did not finish her sentence.

"What's wrong?" she asked. "Did something happen to the picture?"

Balancing the pitcher of lemonade, Sammy ran around to look at the painting again. But this time he peeked up at the canvas with his head bowed in a manner that seemed to suitable to the mood around him.

Erastus looked at the boy with his pitcher of lemonade. He looked at the mother with her tray of glasses. He felt his head nod as a thought entered his mind. He had felt this way before. He had once before felt the course of his life change in an instant. It had happened one day as he sat in the Quaker meeting house, and found himself compelled by an urge to speak. He had stood and declared to the Society of Friends that he would travel the country and paint, that he would endeavor to bring God's light to his fellow men one painting at a time, that he would use whatever opportunities he had to speak to those who would listen, and for those who were not ready to hear, he would simply offer his art. He had not planned to speak that day in the church house, nor had he planned to change his life so dramatically by leaving Philadelphia. But the realization of what he was born to do fell upon him with such certainty, he never doubted the rightness of his decision.

Now it was the same. This new thought had come to him out of nowhere, in circumstances he had never imagined. But as soon as the thought entered his mind, he knew it was inevitable. Perhaps it was God's plan all along. For there had been many times in his life when he would not have been able to do what he now knew he must do. He stood. He grasped the handrail on the porch steps. He spoke first to Wally, "There's been a disagreement about the painting with Mrs. Holland," he said. Then turning to Dorothy, he said "Dorothy, don't say anything just yet. I'm going to speak to your mother." Erastus climbed the porch steps. At the top, he turned to look at the fidgeting young boy who stood behind his painting.

Sammy saw him look and called out, "Would you like some lemonade Mr. painter?"

Wally dashed over to Sammy's side. "Hush up," she said. "The man's got business with the mistress."

But Erastus found his voice. "Not just now, Sammy. Keep some for me until I return."

As he passed her on the porch, Erastus looked at Ella, who stood with her back against the porch post. Her hands lay folded on the top of her head, as if to hold her head in place. But Ella did not see him. Her eyes darted back and forth like the great gold colored pendulum on the grandfather clock back home in his father's study. Tick tock, the eyes that did not see marked some kind of time, not for music, nor for measuring the hours. But as surely as the wagging tail of a dog, they revealed the inner state of her mind, as it tried to see what it could not look at.

# 13

## "I MIGHT SET THINGS ARIGHT"

When Erastus entered the Hollands' house, it seemed particularly dark. Mrs. Holland had drawn tight the heavy damask drapery in the sitting room and in the dining room. The contrast in brightness from the outside to the inside magnified a gloomy effect. No candles were lit. The only light entered from the front door. Erastus felt as if he'd entered a sealed crypt. He walked slowly to allow his eyes to adjust to the light, and to avoid tripping on an unseen object. Henrietta Holland stood in the rear of the main vestibule, from which she watched his hesitant progress into the house. Erastus asked Henrietta if he might speak to Mr. Holland regarding the settlement of his fee. Although she sensed some purpose in the painter's request beyond that which he stated, she obliged his wish. After a brief exchange with Mr. Holland, she showed the painter to her husband's study, then deferentially closed the door behind him, and remained outside.

After instructing Wally and Sammy to return to the kitchen, Dorothy came into the house to find her mother eavesdropping outside the door of the study. Dorothy inferred that the painter and her father were inside. She approached her mother in order to dally with her in the vicinity of the closed study door. The two women strained to hear, but they could not make out what the men were saying. Dorothy was certain she heard her own name mentioned. She saw her mother scowl at that, and realized, from this demonstration, how frustrated her mother must be to have the matter discussed without her.

Dorothy presumed that the whole wretched scheme to sell Sammy must be her mother's idea. When her father bought Sammy on impulse, Henrietta had let it be known she thought it a foolish waste of money. No doubt, she had waited years for an opportunity to redeem that expense. But now decisions were once again being made without her. Though Dorothy had no sympathy for her mother's plans for Sammy, she was sympathetic to her frustration at being excluded from the men's discussion. In this Dorothy saw her future self, consigned to wait behind a future closed door, while men spoke and made decisions. Dorothy whispered, "I hope Mr. Hicks has some kind of plan. He was distressed about his father's health. I don't know what his state of mind might be."

Henrietta said, "I told your father he should have settled this business of selling the boy weeks ago. But, whenever something has to be done that he doesn't wish to do, he procrastinates. He hasn't the fortitude a man ought to have in these matters."

"He has fortitude, mother, he just doesn't have the nerve to be heartless."

"Heartless! You would think his family's welfare would matter more to him than the fate of a useless, lazy servant."

"Sammy is neither lazy nor useless. He may be slow-witted. But he's dedicated and spirited. Besides, I hardly think a painting of me can be regarded as our family's welfare."

"The painting may yet play a role in securing your future. And I can tell you, the sale of the boy would pay for more than just the painting. The furniture we have from my parents was old when they gave it to me. Now it's almost beyond repair."

"You'd sell Sammy just to get a new sofa? Really, mother. You are short-sighted. When he's older Sammy should produce far more income in the field than father would get for him in Memphis."

"I have no hope that this boy will ever amount to much in the field. I can only wish that some buyer in Memphis will be as foolishly optimistic as your father was about the wastrel's prospects."

Dorothy was about to reply when the study door opened. Erastus emerged holding a piece of paper. He said, "Miss Holland, might I speak to you about the arrangement I've made with your father? Perhaps we may converse in the sitting room?"

Not knowing why the painter addressed his remarks to her, Dorothy looked at her mother, who seemed equally baffled. But before Henrietta could speak, Mr. Holland asked his wife to come into his study, which she did. Dorothy followed the painter to the sitting room where they sat.

"Do you mind if we open the drapery? The room is too dark. I am a man who depends upon light."

"Allow me," Dorothy said, and she set about tying back several of the draperies, which emptied the room of its pall.

Erastus spoke in a subdued voice. "I have combined the money your parents owed me for the painting with an additional sum from my own pocket upon which your father and I agreed, so that I might purchase the boy Sammy as my own servant."

Dorothy started to speak, but then held her hand to her

mouth, as she saw that Erastus had more to say. She sat down in a chair across from him.

"I cannot take the boy with me at present. Hence, I have asked your father, and now I must ask you, if I may leave the boy in your care."

"In my care?"

"Yes. I would be grateful if you would look after him on my behalf and use his services as you see fit. In return, I ask that you spend what time you can to teach the boy skills that would befit a painter's assistant. You may find some help with that task from Ella. Should you be willing you might also seek assistance from the boy Cato at Hickory Grove, who spent many weeks with me during my work at the Askews, and who learned all the skills I would require of an assistant. Perhaps your friend William Askew would lend you some of Cato's time for that purpose."

"How long do you intend to leave Sammy in my care? When will you return for him?"

"I cannot say at present." Erastus smiled mischievously. "I may not return until the boy is grown. I shall be interested to know, when he is grown, what his own ambitions for his future will be."

Dorothy sat back in her chair. She had expected the painter to do something, but nothing as extreme as this. Her breath quickened. This was something new in her world. She inquired, "May I ask why you wish to leave him in my care, rather than in the care of my parents?"

"As I explained to your father, I wish to have the boy trained for a specific purpose. My purpose will not be abetted by sending him to work in the field. Your father fears that your mother will find it an imposition to supervise the boy in household tasks. Yet we both thought it fitting that the boy should perform work to earn his keep, since you are to clothe and feed him until I return. If he is put in your service, he is more apt to learn the skills I require. I suggested that you might take up the responsibility of managing the boy's work and undertake his training. Your father agreed. All that is left is for you to agree."

Dorothy stood and said, with a slight bow, "I would be honored to do so," and then she sat down.

"Thank you. I know that I may rely upon your good judgment in all the boy's requirements. You must see that he provides good service to this household."

"Mr. Hicks, I must say it seems improbable to me that you, a Quaker, and a traveling painter whose home is in the North, would find it sensible to part with a great sum of money in order to purchase a slave."

The painter looked at Dorothy a long moment, while he pondered how freely he could speak to her. He could only rely on small clues and his own intuition to imagine that he might speak freely to Dorothy at all. But having already transformed so much on impulse, he decided that he may as well trust his instincts with Dorothy still further. He said, "I find it sensible to let life unfold as it will. There are few opportunities for a man like me to do something meaningful in response to the institution of slavery, which, I confess to you, is an institution I find morally unsound. If I cannot by myself give freedom to a whole race of people, I can at least give refuge to one of its members, and in doing so I expect, if I have understood the situation properly, I may give comfort to an entire family."

"An entire family?" Dorothy grasped for his point. "Do you speak of Sammy's family, about Wally, Ella and Jimmy? They will indeed be comforted by what you've done."

"I'm talking about your family, slaves and masters alike. I have only been with your household these several fortnights, but what I have seen is a family, and I do not comprehend how anyone in that family might choose to see it divided."

"I appreciate your candor, Mr. Hicks," Dorothy said in an earnest voice. "I can't tell you how much I appreciate it. But tell me, how did you come to this resolve so quickly? I saw you. It was but four or five minutes after learning of my parents' scheme that you came to a decision about what to do about it."

"Those four or five minutes, I suppose, were the product of a lifetime of intentions."

"But what are these intentions?"

"If I may use an analogy, I strive to paint for myself the life that I want. But in painting, discovery sometimes supersedes intention. If I've learned anything in life, it's that so much of what is beautiful happens in an instant. It does no good to ponder. The hand of God guides all things. You can allow great things more easily than you can pursue them. All that is required is to keep your eyes open, and to recognize the Divine breath when a breeze strikes you in the face. When I paint, I sometimes disappear. I am more skilled as a painter than as a man. But I have striven toward this end, to give the Divine hand more liberty to paint the canvas of my life."

"Your spiritual ideas reach beyond those considered at our Methodist church!" Dorothy widened her eyes to signify the widening of her point of view.

"My spiritual beliefs derive less from my being a Quaker than from my being a painter. I commend you to this path, Dorothy. Find a creative endeavor for your life. You'll profit from any such practice. In fact, I would be obliged if you would encourage my young servant in this regard. I will leave some brushes and paints for him. It would be good for you both. Tell him I want him to learn to paint something that … what's that dog's name?"

"Venus."

"… something that Venus will appreciate. I tell you truly it was that very act, when the boy revealed his desire to show my painting to the dog, which caused me to feel myself kin to him. I believe his declaration made my response to the subsequent events easier for me."

Although the painter had advised against pondering, Dorothy felt that each new statement the painter made was unexpected. For each question answered, a new one arose in her mind. She inquired, in an unpresuming tone, "Do you mind if I ask how it is that after many weeks of work you are able to go without wages, and to summon up additional sums of money on impulse?"

"Ah, well, my work is something I do, but it is not something I need to do. I have been blessed with an income and an inheritance from my father. I suppose if he is now at the end of his life, as his letter suggests, I shall come into an even greater sum when he passes."

Dorothy attempted to restate what she'd heard, to see if she understood. "So this itinerant life you have, traveling about, making paintings, living with strangers, this is what you prefer to do?"

"It is my greatest pleasure. Do you not recall the first day I began to sketch you and Ella on the porch? As I said before, so much that is beautiful in life happens in an instant. But one must contrive to be in the right place at the right time and have one's eyes open."

Dorothy wondered how the occasional instant of beauty might warrant such an eccentric existence. "What about a wife, a family, a comfortable home? Do you not wish for these things?"

"There are certainly times when I wish to be in the company of old friends. And I have some old friends that I see from time to time in Philadelphia. But in general I prefer the adventure of the new to the comfort of the old."

"I wish I were your age," Dorothy said impulsively. "And if I were, I would want a husband just like you."

"Ah well." The painter smiled. "Have you no faith in young Askew?"

"Neither he, nor any man that I have known, is comparable to you," Dorothy said with all sincerity. "The comparison, in fact, seems beyond logic. You are like a force from another realm."

"There's nothing unworldly about me. I doubt I was much different from young Askew when I was his age. There are countless seeds in all of us, my dear. One has only to choose which seeds are nurtured."

"I shall miss you very much, Mr. Hicks."

"I would be grateful if you would write to me from time to time," Erastus requested. "I will give you an address in Philadelphia to which letters may be sent. If you're willing, I would like to hear news of my boy and, indeed, about all of your family."

"And will you write to me, to tell me of your adventures?"

"By all means."

"Then we both shall write."

With that, Erastus said farewell to Dorothy. The two embraced with a degree of feeling that might seem unseemly to an outside observer. But for each of them the conventions of society were ill-suited to accommodate their situation. Despite their differences in age and gender, Dorothy envisioned in Erastus the clearest flowering of the seeds she wished to nurture in herself. And Erastus found in Dorothy the fulfillment of the mission that drew him out from Philadelphia and into the world. They hugged each other meaningfully, and even after that, they still shook hands, as if to relinquish each other more slowly.

The painter departed from the house, but stopped at the

front porch. Now that his intents with regards to Sammy were settled, Erastus considered a further intent, one that had loomed in his thoughts from the moment he knew he must leave. He contemplated how he might arrange the rendezvous he desired. Seeing Ella, who stood dead still on the porch, just as he had last seen her, resting against the column, but now with her head turned to the side in a sullen gaze, he stopped at her side, both to reassure her and to engage her in a plan.

"My dear Ella, do not be sad. I have made arrangements with the Hollands for your brother to remain here with you. They have sold him to me as payment for my painting, but I shall leave him here in Dorothy's care until such time as he is older. When he is grown he will have the opportunity to venture with me in the world, or, if he prefers, he may choose to stay here at home indefinitely."

Ella's eyes, a little dilated, fixed themselves on those of the painter. She saw that the world, which but a short time before had been torn in an instant, would now be stitched back just as quickly. But it was changed. It would never be the same. And she felt, in this new instant, as if she might topple over into a dark ditch … as if peril had been unleashed and was nipping now at her feet to undo her balance. She felt her eyes roll back. She began to swoon, but Erastus clutched her from behind to steady her feet. The abrupt movement made her start. "Gracious," she said. "I felt almost faint."

Ella leaned back and fixed her gaze upon the roof of the porch. She clasped a hand onto the painter's shoulder, while her head remained tilted back. She held him thus for several moments as she replayed his words in her mind. She asked, "What does it mean, Mr. Erast, 'indefinitely'?"

"It means Sammy can stay here as long as he likes."

Ella turned her head now to look the painter in the eye again. A tear showed on the ridge of her cheek. "When I shook your hand, it was because you paint so fine. But now, what you mean to do for my family ...." She stopped unable to say more. Instead, she slid her hand down from the painter's shoulder in order to grasp his hand. She placed her other hand upon it, and rocked their hands gently to and fro as if their handclasp formed a cradle in which a child might be lulled to sleep.

"It is God's grace," Erastus said, "that I might set things aright."

After a passage of some minutes, Ella resolved to focus her mind on a task. "Lemonade," she said. "You were fixing to have some lemonade. I can get it for you. Wally and Sammy, they took it back to the kitchen."

"No thank you," Erastus said. "I have another favor to ask of you."

Ella could not get used to this white man who asked favors instead of giving directions. Life had not taught her how to respond to such things. She said, "Can I fetch you something else?"

"I'd like you to speak to your brother. I'd like you to ask him to convey a message to Cato, his friend from Hickory Grove."

Ella nodded, though her eyes conveyed doubt.

Erastus spoke slowly, to underscore the importance of his message. "Ask your brother to ask Cato if he will meet me tomorrow ... Sunday ... at the Hickory Grove gate at Christmasville road just before sundown. Tell him I'm leaving on Monday morning and I wish to say farewell to him."

Ella was consumed with concentration and did not speak.

Erastus asked, "Can you repeat what I just said?"

"You said to tell Jimmy to tell Cato to meet you tomorrow at Christmasville Road."

"At the Hickory Grove gate," Erastus added. "Just before sundown."

"At the Hickory Grove gate before sundown," Ella repeated. "And you're going to go away on Monday, so you want to say goodbye."

"Yes, that's right. Will you ask Jimmy to request that of Cato?"

In the newly stitched-back world, this seemed strange to Ella. She could not think why the painter would want to say good-bye to a slave from the Askew plantation, but she knew it was not her place to question such things. She nodded and said, "Yes, sir, Mr. Erast. I'll tell Jimmy straightaway."

14

## "WHY WOULD A WHITE MAN DO
## THAT?"

*B*ack inside the house, when Henrietta Holland entered the study, she took a seat in the solitary austere chair that faced her husband's oversized desk.

"Now what have you to say, George?" she asked.

"Really, my dear, I think the circumstances are most fortuitous. Mr. Hicks has chosen to purchase the boy. In fact, he has agreed to pay fifty dollars more than the price you and I discussed. And, happily, he has determined to leave the boy here in Dorothy's care, for her personal supervision, for an indefinite period while he returns to Philadelphia. All he asks is that we see that the boy is trained in the skills of a painter's assistant, so that when he is older, he may assist Mr. Hicks in his work. But in the meantime, we shall make use of the boy's services, just as we have all along—and collect the money from his sale. It's a windfall, really."

"And you agreed to this?"

"Of course, why not?"

"How are we going to explain this to anyone? Training a nigger boy to paint! Hicks must be crazy as a Betsy bug. If we agree to this madness, people will think we're daft as well. The whole point of selling the boy is to get rid of him. But you and Hicks with your mad scheme! We'll bear all the costs of feeding the boy and clothing him. And what about the aggravation of supervising him? It will fall upon me, I can tell you, just like all the others. He'll slowly sap our resources. In the end, we'll have nothing to show for it. Really, George, I thought our agreement was clear. I detest having the boy here. It is more than just the money at stake."

"Henrietta. I do not understand why you dislike the boy so."

"He's half-witted. He's lazy. He moves like a glacier when he's working. He darts around like a banshee when he's not. Worst of all, he has only three or four moods—each of them relentlessly cheerful. He sashays about emitting the same insipid happy sounds all day long, even when it's perfectly clear that there is serious work to do. It is dissonant. It grinds my teeth. Truly, George, I don't know what he has to be so cheerful about. He's homely, smelly, and stupid even for a nigger. He was worthless when you bought him, and he has not improved. Indeed he has grown worse, as his poor habits have become vexingly fixed."

"Surely, my dear, there are worse faults to bear than those of a boy who is always cheerful."

"George, you're not here each day. You don't have to put up with it. It wears upon me. I endure a daily ordeal. I have no choice but to explain everything to him again and again. Despite this, he smirks and smiles as if it were all delightful. I've told him to stop it, but he doesn't. I tell you, he means to provoke me. He acts as if he doesn't understand what I'm saying—yet I make myself perfectly clear!"

"Yes, yes, I know. He's playful. He's not too bright. It's not as if I don't know that. When he brings the water bucket to the field, it's all a game to him. But look now … surely … this is something we can bear. Mr. Hicks has asked to have the boy put in Dorothy's care. He's out there speaking to her about it now. She will have all the responsibility. You need not supervise the child in any way. Dorothy will keep him from under foot. She'll find a way to make good use of him. You won't have to worry about him at all. In the meantime, we have the painting, the money, the extra money, my dear, remember that. I could never do so well in Memphis. You must keep sight of your goals. There will be enough to buy new furniture. You must reconcile yourself to see the advantage in this, Henrietta. I have already signed the bill of sale."

"You've signed it? Oh, God help us. Is that what the man was carrying when he left? Heaven save me. Really, George, would it be too much for you to discuss such an important matter with me before acting on impulse."

"I had to act! Mr. Hicks has reason to leave urgently. His father is ill. Time is of the essence. And frankly, I could not see anything to object to in his proposal, so I agreed to it, and that is that. I'm a patient man, Henrietta. But you step outside your bounds. It is not a woman's place to make these decisions."

"So, is it a woman's place to live with the consequences? How many years will I have to put up with this boy? You are a fool to think that Dorothy will somehow keep the boy in line. She's oblivious to his faults. She'll do nothing to improve him. I tell you, it will all fall on me. Not even a new sofa is worth the bother. It will fall badly on the boy, too. You'll see. I shall punish him. It will not go well for him. You'll have that to sleep on, George." With that, Henrietta Holland stood and left her husband's study. She saw the painter, just at that moment, leaving by the front door, which prompted her to mutter to herself a curse on the man whose meddling had interfered with all her plans. Then she saw that Dorothy was seated in the sitting room, where, Henrietta observed, the drapery had been opened.

"Dorothy I've told you not to open the drapery. When the sun shines in here, it fades everything. The sun and heat bearing down on everything ages the fabrics twice as fast as they would normally age. Drapery is to be opened only on social occasions, or in winter when the light is low. You have no sense of the value of things."

"You're just upset, mother. I understand why."

Henrietta busied herself, untying the drapery and letting them fall closed. "Do you? And I suppose you think you're going to play along with this foolishness?"

"Father appears to have decided it already."

"Well I don't like it. Am I to have no say in the affairs of my own life? Must I live with things I detest?" Henrietta sat on the old family sofa in the darkened room, her voice cracked as though she might be on the verge of tears. "I think it is only right that I should make any decisions that concern the house-keeping. Your father's business is to produce the crops. My business is to run the household. It is intolerable!"

"I agree with you," Dorothy said in a sympathetic tone. "It isn't fair for father to make all the decisions on his own." But from this, she extrapolated to the essence of what vexed her about marriage. She said, "And you wonder why I don't wish to marry? Shall I end up consigned to a husband's whims? Is that what you want for me?"

For a moment Henrietta, who still seemed lost in an appreciation of her husband's injustice, did not appear to follow the unfolding of her daughter's logic. But then as she digested what Dorothy had asked, her tone turned from self-pity to irritation. "Dorothy, please, do not twist this for your own purposes. I haven't the energy to argue with you right now. Can't you try to see things from my point of view?"

155

"I do, mother. I do see things from your point of view. That's the irony of it."

"I fail to see any irony. If you understood things from my point of view, you'd understand that what is wanted is a reasonable husband, a husband who trusts his wife to manage the affairs of the house. You talk as if the only solution is to become a spinster. You miss the point entirely. The fault is with your father, not with having a husband."

Dorothy looked as if she were ready to admit that there might be some truth to this; but after thinking about it, she said, "The fault is with the whole system, we're all just slaves, I think ... a hierarchy ... yes, a pyramid of masters and slaves, and at the top there are a few wealthy men who run everything."

Henrietta's face set into a grimace. "Really, Dorothy, you talk in wild exaggerations. I don't know how I can converse with you, if you're going to talk nonsense."

Dorothy said nothing for some time. She knew that the decision that her mother would make in the current matter, if she had the prerogative, was itself odious. But she was sympathetic to the dilemma of being a woman who could not control essential aspects of her destiny. She decided to take a conciliatory tone. "If what you say is true, that the problem is not having a husband but having a reasonable husband, then I think you would agree that it is important to find the right man to marry. What do you think about William Askew? If I married him, do you think he would allow me to be independent? Would he let me manage my own affairs? Or would he be more like father?"

"What kind of a question is that? Dorothy, marrying a man like your father would be quite sensible. It would make both your father and me happy. As to this one aspect of your father, and whether or not William Askew would behave the same way, I cannot say."

"Do you think I should ask him?"

"Ask him? Ask whom?"

"I mean, should I, for example, describe to Mr. Askew the situation that has occurred here, regarding the sale of a slave, and ask him whether he thinks a decision like that should be made solely by the man; or by the man and wife together; or made, as you suggest, solely by the wife, since it is a domestic matter."

"Dorothy, you have no experience with courtship. How do you suppose you're going to find a man to marry you if you put a question like that to him? You need to expend your energy on attracting a man, not submitting him to an examination."

"Then how is a woman supposed to know what kind of man she will marry?"

"Well, I admit, it isn't easy," said Henrietta, warming to this direction in the conversation. "But that's where you must be clever. You can find out the kind of thing you want to ask about, but you have to get it out of him in a roundabout way."

Dorothy was curious about this bit of strategy. "How?" she asked.

"Well you might tell a story, like you said, about some situation, and in the story you might say that the wife felt she ought to make the decision. But you don't ask him a question about the story, or even ask for his opinion, you just say, 'Isn't that interesting?' That's all you say. You just tell the story, and then see how he reacts, and listen to what he says. You can tell his opinion just by taking note of what he says without ever asking him directly."

"Is that how you operate with father?"

"You seem very dense about these matters, Dorothy. Once

you are married to a man then it is an entirely different situation."

"So this coyness you are advocating, that is merely an aspect of courtship?"

"Well, yes … though, of course, even after marriage it is always good to let a man believe that he is making decisions, even when he shares them with you."

"It strikes me, mother, that there is much contrivance in being a woman. I don't know how you keep straight about what to say and what not to say."

"Well it's really quite simple. Before marriage, you must always be agreeable. After marriage, you must be assertive, but deferential."

Dorothy considered this advice for a few moments, then, with a shrug, decided it was best to change the subject. "So what are we going to do about Sammy?" she asked.

"As you say, your father has made his decision, dubious as it may be, and we must adhere to it. Your father thinks you are going to keep the boy out from under my foot—I wish I could believe that were true."

"Why shouldn't it be true? If that's what you wish, I'll tell him to give you wide berth."

"The boy won't be able to grasp what is meant by wide berth. He will come chirping around me, just as he always does."

"I'll have a talk with him, mother. I'll make it clear that he isn't to speak to you."

"He isn't to emit any sounds to me at all!"

"I'm going to speak to Ella about helping me with him. Mr. Hicks would like me to teach him to work with paint-brushes. I think it shall be quite pleasant, really. I may take up painting myself."

"The whole idea is ridiculous."

"Perhaps I will propose the idea of my taking up painting to William Askew and then, as you suggest, I will see what he has to say about it. I know he was very keen to see my portrait. Now that it is completed, I don't see why I shouldn't ask him over to view it, and talk about it."

Henrietta remembered that this was the main reason they had commissioned the painting in the first place. "Yes, you should have him come to see the painting—by all means. I suppose I'll have to go and have a look at it myself, seeing how much it has cost in one way or another."

Just at this juncture, Ella entered the house, having finished her conversation with Mr. Hicks on the porch. She had the painter's message for Jimmy to give to Cato fresh in her mind, and so she hoped to find Jimmy right away and deliver it. But it occurred to her that she'd do better by not divulging the content of her message to the Hollands, who would only press her for an understanding of the message that she could not give them. "It seems to be particular hot today," she said, "Shall I carry some water out to the field?"

"It doesn't feel very hot to me," said Henrietta.

"Well, ma'am, I was working out in the sun for a spell, and I felt like I might perspire. The sun itself is more hot than the air is right now. You don't feel it so much in the house, though."

"Very well, very well" said Henrietta with irritation. "Go on and leave us be." Then she added, "I suppose I'd rather see you carry water out there than that little devil."

"Yes, ma'am," Ella said, "I'll fetch it right away." With that, she left before any more discussion might occur.

Ella wasn't sure why Mrs. Holland had referred to Sammy as a little devil. She supposed it had something to do with the fact that he now belonged to Mr. Hicks. This truth, in fact, had not really sunk in with her. All she could think was how quickly it all had happened. One minute they were getting ready to drink lemonade, and the next minute, her brother was sold to someone else. Even though Sammy's domestic status was unchanged, it felt as if something consequential had taken place, and that things would henceforth be different. She understood with new clarity that something similar or worse could happen to her, or to any of them, without warning. She also realized that she would have to figure out a way to tell Jimmy what had happened. She knew he would be enraged.

Since Mr. Holland was still in his study—not in the field, when Jimmy got angry, at least Mr. Holland wouldn't see it. But she worried how a new source of anger would affect her older brother. He already festered with so much resentment that a new grievance was likely to drive him to unpredictable behavior. If only she could express the news to him as an entirely good thing, and overlook the fact that there was a brief moment when their brother might have been lost to them forever.

As she drew the water into the bucket at the well, Ella's thoughts turned to Reverend Zeke, and to his teachings about God's love. When Dorothy told her that Sammy was to be sold, it felt as if God was nowhere to be found. In that moment, the world was not governed by any goodness. And though she had been moved by Reverend Zeke's exhortation to turn the other cheek, it had been an abstract idea. It had to do with people she didn't really know, like Sara at Hickory Grove. Now she saw that when cruelty came close to home, it was another matter. She did not think she would be able to forgive the Hollands for selling Sammy away—even if, as the Reverend said, they knew not what they did.

But less than an hour after that cruel prospect had been presented, something divine had intervened. If ever there was a man through whom God worked, Ella felt sure that the painter was such a man. She did not understand him. He was unlike other men. Even though he was white, she felt an accommodation in his presence. His kind eyes and mellifluous voice conveyed a sympathetic regard. When they talked, she heard herself anew. She heard how her own words seemed cynical and fussy, by contrast to his—and yet, he never looked at her with judgment. He seemed to grasp all the good intentions of her soul, as if he could see inside her. He twinkled, and chuckled, and seemed amused no matter what she said.

In some ways, the painter was like Reverend Zeke, but his manners and methods were different. Whereas Reverend Zeke seemed a normal sort of man, transformed by circumstance into a preacher, Mr. Hicks seemed like a man who had never been normal, and who must have always had an odd effect on people.

She had observed—or rather felt, through instinct, from his manner—that her brother Jimmy held a grudge against the painter, a grudge she couldn't explain. Yet it seemed to be part of another brewing bitterness in her brother's stew of vexations. At the time, she attributed this to the painter's odd effect—but upon reflection, she guessed there was more to the story than she had yet discovered. This additional uncertainty nagged her as she wondered how she could describe what had occurred in a form that her brother might find acceptable.

The sun was low in the sky when she arrived at the field, but it was not yet time for Jimmy to quit his post behind the plow. She set the water bucket in the dirt, not bothering to offer him any, choosing instead to walk behind him, following him by a few steps as he trailed the mule and plow.

She told him this: "The painting was finished today."

Jimmy said nothing.

"We was fixing to celebrate when Mrs. Holland come out and told Mr. Erast that there was some problem with getting him his money. So Dorothy went inside with Mrs. H to find out what was the problem; and then she came out and said Mr. and Mrs. H had figured that the only way they could pay for the painting was to sell something; and they figured that what they would do would be to sell ...." Ella stopped; she couldn't bring herself to say it.

Jimmy kept walking, but he turned around now to look at his sister, confused by her abrupt silence. Sweat, from his efforts with the plow, dripped from his forehead. "What's wrong?" he asked.

"Nothing's wrong. Everything turned out fine. But it started out that they was going to sell Sammy to pay for the painting, but then Mr. Erast ...."

Jimmy interrupted her "What? What you mean, 'sell Sammy?' What kind of ...?" Then he stopped, yanked hard on the rope to stop the mule in its tracks, and the plow ground to a halt. Jimmy dropped the rein, turned, grabbed Ella by the shoulders and shook her. "What are you saying?" Then, like a heavy weight, he fell onto his knees, and thrust his hand in the air behind his head, as if he was trying to reach and squeeze onto some invisible support that resided there. "They wanted to sell Sammy?" His words were formed as a question, but expressed as a crescendoing exclamation. "To pay for a God damn painting?!"

In Jimmy's words and gesture, Ella saw the mirror of her own reaction to this news, yet she could not bear to see it relived in her brother's temper. She threw herself down onto him, as if to throw a bucket of water on a fire. She encased him in her arms and said, quickly "He's not leaving. He's staying with us. The painter bought him. Mr. Erast is leaving him with us to raise him."

Jimmy pulled back away from her, and stared at her with wide, disturbed eyes. Then slowly Ella saw the torn world restitching itself as it had for her—but in Jimmy's case the needlework seemed reckless—on the verge of tearing an even greater rent in the fabric of normal life. The sheer power of his anger made her take quick breaths, and set her heart thumping. But matching her breathing, he, with her, grew breathless, until his breathing began to attenuate into a slow, sighing, series of inhalations.

"Something is not right with that man," he said at last. "Why would a white man do that?"

Ella was relieved to see that Jimmy had understood what she had said. "I think he did it," Ella said sincerely, "out of the goodness of his heart. I don't know what else it could be."

"But it's queer for a white man to do something like that. He doesn't even know Sammy, does he?"

"I don't think so. But he said that when Sammy is grown, he can either stay here or go off on adventures with Mr. Erast."

"I don't believe it. There's something odd about him. I don't trust him."

"He asked me to give you a message to give to your friend Cato."

"Cato? What's he want with him?"

"He asked you to tell Cato to meet Mr. Erast down by the Hickory Grove gate at sundown tomorrow."

"That's just what I mean," Jimmy said. "What business could he have with Cato?"

"He said he just wants to say good-bye to him on account of he's leaving on Monday."

"Where's he going?"

"I don't know. He just said he was going away."

Jimmy shook his head. He knew that there was a strange friendship between Cato and the painter, and he didn't like it. It made him suspicious of them both. There was no reason for it. Then there was this business of teaching Cato to read.

Jimmy was sure it would lead to no good. He could only imagine that with time, Cato would become more stuck up. Sooner or later, he'd have no more interest in an ignorant field hand like Jimmy. That was what most galled him, the way the painter felt free to come into people's lives and turn them upside down. Now he was doing it to Sammy.

"Has anyone told Sammy what's happened?" Jimmy asked.

"I don't think so. Unless Dorothy told Wally, but I doubt it. Dorothy's just sitting up there in the parlor looking like two day old bread."

"Well, don't say anything to him until I'm there and Wally's there and Juba Jake's there and we're all together. I want Sammy to have his whole family with him when we tell him."

"In that case," Ella said, "we'd better be sure Venus is there too."

# APPETITE FOR DEVOTION

*J*immy walked to the point of exhaustion. Walking was the only way he could calm his emotions. First, he'd walked to Hickory Grove to deliver the painter's rendezvous message to Cato. This had led to an argument. Jimmy grew angry. He accused Cato of having white ambitions, of being a pawn in the painter's meddling peculiarity. Cato grew sullen, which was not what Jimmy wanted. Jimmy didn't know exactly what he did want. He was vexed that there was little he could rightfully complain about in the situation, beyond that which had been intended, but averted. Yet he was quite certain that grievances had been committed, and that more were bound to come.

On Sunday morning, when Cato did not stop to see him, but went instead to Dyer's Creek to join the apologists with Reverend Zeke, Jimmy could no longer sit still. He set off into the woods with Venus, where he purposefully walked an unfamiliar route. He hoped that if he immersed himself in strange scenery, it might somehow illuminate him about what to do. Ella, Wally and Jake had agreed that they would gather the family together on Sunday afternoon to tell Sammy about his new owner. But Jimmy insisted that he should be the one to explain what happened. He walked and thought and practiced what he might say. Yet he could not summon the right words, nor could he get past the essential point of the story without ranting. He wanted to find a way to emphasize the Hollands' villainy and the painter's wiliness, to warn the boy against naiveté, but without—and this was the hard part—saying anything that would corrupt his brother's inherently cheerful disposition.

Although Jimmy believed that Sammy's innocent optimism was a poor strategy for managing the realities of the world, he felt protective of Sammy's naiveté. He struggled with how to open his brother's eyes without souring the boy's view. Jimmy saw no justification for anything other than a cynical view of the world, but he felt that innocence, especially in one so young, ought to be protected, just as one might protect a treasured garden from the encroachment of nature's inevitable weeds.

Jimmy himself did not recall ever being innocent. From his earliest memories, he knew life was unfair and that he, in particular, had been dealt a bad hand. He saw it as a strength of his character that, unlike some others around him, he had never imagined that this inferior position was in any way his fate. He was righteous. He had no reason for shame. He saw that the world conspired to justify its oppression, that white people had no compunctions, that nothing would induce them to forgo their greedy exploitation of innocents, that everything unfortunate in the world was entirely their fault. Even when someone like the painter came along, someone who confounded the clarity of this view, he supposed that this confounding was the result of some hidden motive, some dissembling of the natural evil of the white race, which he guessed must be an even more wicked expression of that same corruption.

That the painter should be working his wiles on his friend, who, like Sammy, was essentially gullible, made his blood rise. In the neutral emotions of the woods, he regretted the spat with Cato. He only wished that Cato would not be so reckless in his embrace of the painter's influence. And he worried, yet again, that Cato's racial chemistry was itself a predisposition to such influences. He felt it his duty to counter that influence. But the painter was a formidable rival.

He resolved to make amends. He would go to Cato after the family's talk. He would find a way to mend the breach. It would be easy, he knew, since Cato, like Sammy, could be relied upon for good will. As he thought of this, his mood lightened. Venus, sensing the change, turned to him with a playful look.

"What are you looking at girl?" Jimmy smiled at his dog. "You think everything is just a game? Maybe for you it is, but you're a lucky dog. You got Jimmy to bring you bacon and take care of you. Ain't nobody gonna watch out for me but me."

The dog made a look as if she begged to differ. She was, after all, ever alert to protecting her master.

"Oh I know you're looking out for me, too. Sure. But you don't know what it's like to be a person. I got to put up with all kinds of evil. I don't think you'd like it."

Venus responded with a short bark and a wag of her tail. The day was comely, and there was no point standing about in a perversely human way. She dashed around in a circle, as she had done many times before, to remind Jimmy of the purpose of legs.

"All right, All right," Jimmy said. "Let's go this way." He set off in a direction that he believed would take them past Dyer's Creek.

But Venus was not to be dissuaded from her playfulness. As they walked, she tapped Jimmy's leg with her snout to make this clear.

Jimmy stopped, abruptly squatted, then rocked back and forth on his haunches in a way that was clearly playful. He swiped at her with his hands. Despite her age, she reared back on her hind legs and raised her forelegs to paw back at him. Her tail thumped on the ground like a drum. Her tongue was sloppily extended. When Jimmy made such gestures, which throughout her life had been the signal of his willingness to play, Venus reverted instantly to a puppy-like physicality, which age had transformed only by small degrees. She was now obliged to mime the playful gestures. This more stylized play of her old age bespoke the history of their relationship. They had learned shortcuts in the dance of their play, which came from many years of playing together. Jimmy would move his body unpredictably, in an effort to fool her about which way he would lurch, as if he were trying to block her path. Venus, with an animal's nimbleness, could match his every feint and even, some-times, anticipate his movements so accurately that he could not block her. She invariably darted past him again and again, tremendously enjoying both her agility and the aban-donment that these dancing movements signified for each of them.

As they played, the escalation of Venus's emotions led her to more and more physical contact, nuzzling, light nipping, and heavy breathing. Sometimes it led her to bark. The game led Jimmy to ever livelier dodging and stroking movements. This was how they communicated their feeling for each other. It was the physical expression of a strongly held affection. It built to a climax—a point of exhaustion, when they both fell back to rest. Jimmy embraced her fur with his arms, hugging her, and vocalizing softly. She, for her part, licked him mightily.

That afternoon in the cabin, when the family had gathered round the table, Wally announced that Jimmy had something to say. He began by talking about the day eleven years before when Sammy arrived in the back of a wagon. He recalled how for three days Sammy had said nothing until the moment he met Venus, whereupon his first utterance had been to speak Venus' name. He spoke of how since then, Sammy had been his favorite little brother; how he had brought daily cheer into Jimmy's life, and indeed into everyone's life; how Jimmy would never let anything happen to him. Then he turned to the subject of the painter; how the crafty white man had spent these last many weeks working on Dorothy's painting; how the Hollands had indulged themselves in this extravagant endeavor; how Mrs. Holland had schemed to raise the money for this extravagance by selling a valuable young slave; and how the painter had stepped in to purchase the boy at the last minute. During the telling of this, Jimmy watched Sammy to see his reaction, but the boy sat with rapt attention, never giving any indication that he understood that he was the worthy young slave to whom Jimmy referred. For a while, Jimmy worried that Sammy had missed the point. But as Jimmy explained that the painter left the boy in Dorothy's care; that Sammy was to be trained to someday be the painter's assistant, and that in the meantime he would remain at home with the family who loved him, it was clear that Sammy was smiling, that he had recognized no misfortune in these predicaments, and that he was on the whole fidgeting to say something, though he waited until Jimmy had finished.

When Jimmy at last paused and looked at Sammy earnestly, Sammy exclaimed, "Can I paint a picture of Venus?"

Venus, hearing her name, stood up and looked around the

cabin at the faces of the group expectantly.

Wally said, "When the time comes, I reckon you can paint any picture you want, if Miss Dorothy will let you."

"I just don't know if Venus can hold still like Ella," Sammy observed. "Ella, can you teach Venus how you stand still like that?"

Ella was startled by the direction of Sammy's response. "I don't know," she began. "I don't think Venus can stand still so good. I don't believe she likes to hold still much." Ella looked at Jimmy, as if to get help from him. She said, "Maybe your brother will sit with her and hold her, that way she might keep still."

Jimmy was baffled. Sammy's reaction did not exhibit the sort of feeling that Jimmy thought appropriate. He wondered if he ought to have said something more forceful to convey the gravity of the situation. But since Ella had handed the dilemma of the conversation back to him, he rallied to the spirit of Sammy's request, "Oh yes, little brother. You know I believe I can get old Venus to hold still for a spell." Then he added, "But I just don't know what Miss Dorothy will say about that."

Wally chimed in, "Sammy, your brother's right. You gonna have to mind Miss Dorothy now and do as she says. Right now we don't rightly know how much painting Miss Dorothy's gonna want you to do."

Sammy was not deterred. "If I learn to paint good, I think Miss Dorothy will like it. Then I can paint everybody's picture and Missus Holland won't have to pay nothing for it."

The force of Sammy's logic was such that no one in the room could disagree with him.

"And I think Venus would like to see herself in a picture," Sammy went on. "And I think that's what God would want me to do," he said with innocent authority.

Juba Jake, who had been listening to all this in silence, now lifted his eyes and looked at Sammy with affection and wonder. "Yes, boy," he said. "The Lord works in mysterious ways. The Lord brought you into our house and you showed us all …," he paused, groping to find the words. "You showed us all how to smile. You come to us like an Angel of the Lord. We thought we'd all have to cheer you up, but you done cheered everybody up. You got the Holy Spirit, that's all there is to it."

"Yes, Lord," Wally said, with her eyes raised and her hands clasped. "Lord, we're grateful for Sammy, and that You see fit to let him stay with us."

Jimmy, at this point, saw that the entire conversation was going in a direction he abhorred. He was mortified, once again, to realize that he'd been cast into a house full of people whose strategy for coping with reality was to close their eyes to the truth of things. He wondered if he was the only slave in Madison County who saw things for what they were. It was bad enough to be born to such an intolerable state, but it piled insult upon injury to be saddled with a group that seemed intent on persuading themselves that everything was lovely.

"Don't y'all start talking about the Lord. Save that talk for Reverend Zeke. You know you can't just make everything right by pretending it is. Am I the only one who sees what's going on?" Jimmy hadn't meant to get upset, but as he spoke, he found the anger rising in his throat. "They sell Sara's boy, who never did nothing wrong! And y'all talk about turning the other cheek. You think that's right?" Jimmy's voice grew louder. "Up at Hickory Grove the overseer whips little boys no bigger than Sammy here. You think that's right?" Jimmy looked at Juba, who had bowed his head, and turned it slightly away from the sound of Jimmy's voice. "Jake, they took you out of your home. They carried you a thousand miles from where you were born. They put you here on this cotton farm just like a dog. They made you a slave. You weren't born like that. You weren't born a slave. You think that's right?" Jimmy saw that his words were angry and provocative, but he could not stop himself. "Mama, you worked your whole damn life for these cuss ass Hollands, and what you got for it? A couple of wooden bowls, that's what you got. Y'all think you can just 'praise the Lord' and everything gonna work out fine! That's just bullshit. That's just what they want you to do."

Wally stood up to calm her son's feelings. "Everybody's got to find their own way," she said. "We see how things are. You feel it so hard, baby. You feel it hard for everyone else. You got such love, I know you do!"

Jimmy wondered, for the first time, if he somehow could seek restitution for everyone else—if that was part of his destiny. He felt alone, and the forces arrayed against him seemed formidable. He wondered if the power and clarity of his understanding of things might be sufficient to adjudicate the evil. He would bring something new into the world, something born of his tremendous insight, which he was certain surpassed that of everyone around him. He was, in his way, filled with a holy spirit—insurgent, mutinous, the quiet hand of retribution. Perhaps he too was an angel of God.

Sammy worked his thoughts mightily to think of something to say to Jimmy, and in the end he said, "Jimmy, don't worry. Venus loves you. She loves you more than anyone else. I don't think Missus Holland can ever sell Venus."

"Yes, little brother," Jimmy said. "I know it."

Jimmy could not remain in the room. He went outside, where he sat on a rock. His mind raced. His feet tapped. After half an hour, Venus wandered out. She sat on the ground next to him. He let his right hand fall into the reach of Venus' tongue. She, with certain understanding of her master's needs, licked his hand until, with time and patience, Jimmy's anger was consumed by the dog's appetite for devotion.

## 16

THE WORLD OUTSIDE THE WINDOW

*A*n hour before sunset, Erastus positioned himself near the Hickory Grove gate on Christmasville Road. He sat on one of two substantial rocks, which had been installed on either side of the gate to mark the entrance to the Askews' plantation. He watched yellow leaves fall from the maple trees across the road. They added to the crisp autumn aroma that permeated the air. He marveled that fate had conspired to send him back to the North just as winter was approaching. He had hoped to spend that season in the more temperate Tennessee climate.

At the same time, he thought about how much he had accomplished during his visit. He had launched Cato toward a new destiny. He taught the boy to read and filled his head with initiative. Even if Cato didn't fully understand his motives, Erastus knew the boy had started down a path that would take him to a vantage point from which he could someday look back and understand them.

He couldn't call it love in a conventional sense. It was too subtle to be equated with romance. But it was as close as

Erastus could get to what he considered true love. It was mentoring, yes, but also vicarious. He wished that he could arrange for the boy to have even more. If only he could fill the boy's world with pianists playing Show-pan. He wished he might set him loose in a great library of adventures. How splendid it would be to take the boy on a tour of the old world, and to share with him the handiwork of artists whose dazzling skill left Erastus feeling like a poor echo.

But, like so many possibilities Erastus imagined, he knew this was not to be. He must settle for the boy's creation of private adventures, to suppose that the boy would have quiet moments engrossed in books, to fancy that he would embark on happy private expeditions. Erastus was content to envision that life would continue to sustain the boy's curiosity and idealism. He prayed that whatever adversity befell him, it would be no more than enough to deepen Cato's appreciation for good fortune. He did not know if and when he would see Cato again. But he did wonder if this were the last time he would see the boy in the fullness of his physical beauty.

"Ah," Erastus thought, "This is the fate that befalls the most perfect of fruits. Such fruits are not eaten. They are reserved for seed. They are kept as the source from which future produce will germinate." And so he resolved to imprint his mind with the beauty of Cato's form. He would, in his mind, artistically copulate with that imprint, and produce progeny in pigment to share with the world the season of ripeness he had beheld. Through his art he would betroth himself to the boy he loved.

As he mused on this, he saw Cato walking toward him down Hickory Grove's main road. In Cato's gait, he saw the exuberance that he knew the boy felt. Erastus wished he might somehow protect this exuberance. But he could not shield Cato against the impending loss. And Erastus felt himself shaking, shaking like a nervous child. For he felt the coming moments to be so portentous, so demanding of all his skill to impart the last seeds, that he suddenly felt inadequate to the task he had set for himself.

When Cato approached, the boy saw that the painter did not look at him, but sat upon the rock looking down at the space about his feet.

"Why don't you look at me?"

"I've suddenly lost all my competence. I am so intent upon an outcome that I cannot find the path to it."

Cato had no idea what this meant, so he said, "Jimmy told me that you're leaving tomorrow. You will come back to visit sometime soon, won't you?"

Now Erastus disengaged his gaze from staring at the ground, and looked at his friend with kindness. "Ah, yes," he said. "I will come back to visit. You can rely upon it. But I don't know when. Often it is best not to know exactly when something will occur. That way you can imagine it to be sooner or later as suits each day."

"You're talking strangely. Is it because you're sad to be leaving?"

"I am."

"I'm going to miss you," Cato said with all sincerity.

Erastus returned to looking at the ground. He shifted around on the stone uneasily. In a quiet voice he asked, "Have you ever seen a fly caught in the house, buzzing against the window, trying to get out?"

Cato nodded.

"That's how I feel," the painter said. "I feel as if an invisible barrier blocks me from the world I want to fly to. The more I buzz and strike against it, the more baffled I am by this thing that seems not to be there."

"But I thought you were leaving for Philadelphia."

"Philadelphia is not the world outside this window I refer

175

to. The world outside the window I speak of is the space in which you live."

"Erastus, you're not making any sense."

The painter sat still on his rock. He had lost his way in his own emotion, speaking more than he'd intended. Now he said, "I know. What I'm saying is not meant to make sense to you, just to me."

Cato was puzzled by his mentor's metaphor and did not wish to let it rest. "Well, why don't you just open this window that blocks you?"

"Ah, you make it sound so easy."

"It is. I open windows all the time."

"Do you?"

"Oh yes, it's one of my duties! I judge when the house needs to be cooler or warmer, and then I go about the house and open or close the windows as the weather requires. I have a very good sense for temperature. So the Askews rely on me to do this without even having to tell me when to do it."

"Ah well, my boy, truly I don't know why I don't open this window of mine. I suppose that a painter relies on having a window through which to view things. It is good to frame one's view in some way, even if the window is also a barrier."

"Well surely Erastus, if anything was stopping you from flying off to the world you speak of, you, of all people, would find a way to overcome it. I don't believe there is anything you can't do."

"Ah, my boy, it is flattering to see myself reflected thus in your eyes."

"But it's true. You know everything. How could anything stand in your way?"

Erastus was amused by the boy's vision of his omnipotence. But then for a moment, he wondered if, with Cato's encouragement, he might do more than he'd planned. He wondered if he might, at the very least, raise the window that stood between them a few modest inches, and reach out his head into the cool paradise beyond. Ah, how the fresh air would renew him! But then he saw himself in this vision, in sharp contrast to the boy. He had let too much time elapse. He had grown old. Time, he realized, had sealed the window shut. The decay of a thousand moments of inaction had left him firmly seated with his face behind the glass. There was no single moment when he had lost his chance. Throughout his life, he had hesitated on the cusp of this aperture, and now it could be no different from how it had always been. He must content himself with the vantage point he had chosen. But, he told himself, he could still have an effect. "Have you ever heard the story of Johnny Appleseed?" he asked.

Cato shook his head. "Who is that?"

"He was a man named John Chapman. He spent his life traveling about the Northwest Territory. He searched the land for likely places, and then he planted the seeds of apple trees in those spots. He only stayed in one place long enough to clear the land, to give the saplings a good head start, and then he moved on—and did it all again. He did this over and over because he had a vision. He imagined the wilderness, someday, all abloom with apple trees. He imagined orchard after orchard of trees, with fragrant flowers that would provide a bounty of fruit for future citizens. In his lifetime, he planted thousands of seeds. He was a good Christian man."

"Why do you tell me this story?"

"The answer to your question is one that I want you to discover on your own. After I'm gone, I want you to consider this story I've told you, and see if you can conclude what I meant by it."

"All right." Cato was silent a moment. "I'm glad you came

to say good-bye to me. I will always consider you my greatest friend."

"Will you walk with me down the road to the Hollands' farm? Let us say good-bye there."

As they walked down Christmasville Road, Erastus spoke to the boy such wisdoms as he could summon. "Don't be distressed by the troubles of this world," he said. "Keep your attention on what is eternal: kindness, trust, loyalty, forgiveness … and patience. Patience is what you need right now, my boy, and, after all, with practice, you can learn it. The sun will rise for you. But the sun rises at a slow pace. Since you are young, I will tell you a secret. As you get older, everything moves more quickly, until at last it moves so very fast that you come to wonder how to slow it down again. So try to set aside your natural youthful impatience, and let yourself savor your ripening."

"What does 'savor' mean, Erastus?"

"It means to enjoy something patiently, to take your time with things, and relish every part. So when the day is fine, like this one, you must not let it escape you because of some trouble. See how glorious the trees appear." And indeed the black gum trees were flaming orange, while the maples were yellow.

"But your going away is trouble!" Cato said. "I don't see how I can enjoy the day when I'm sad that you are leaving."

"Yes, I know it is hard," Erastus said. "But this is precisely what I want you to practice. Practice turning your attention away from those things that trouble you, and put it on anything good: the beautiful color of the leaves, the fine fragrance of autumn in the air. Most important, put your attention on the lasting nature of friendship. You and I are friends. This is something we will always have. Nothing can undo it. That is an example of something that is real and eternal. My going away is just a change in our proximity, but it has no bearing on our friendship."

Cato walked with his head hung, refusing to yield his sadness to this hopeful perspective. "As time goes by, we'll forget," he said. "You'll forget me. I'll forget the things you taught me."

"I won't forget you," Erastus said. "And you won't forget what I've taught you, though how you understand it may change. You must not confuse forgetting with changing. Remember the story of Johnny Appleseed, Cato. Seeds are just mere bits of woody flesh, yet the seeds change. They change tremendously from small grains to full-grown trees. Despite this transformation, the tree does not forget its origins. Indeed its memory is so complete that it can reproduce a bounty of seeds, just like the one from which it came. Through this ever-repeating cycle, the living tree does not forget. It grows. It learns from experience, improving with each generation. A great man, Mr. Charles Darwin, has written a book about this. God, you see, works like a great sculptor. He chips and edits and carves away. He discards the imperfections. But this He does slowly over vast eons of time. He works with great patience. Patience, you see my boy, is God's great power, which is why you must learn it too. It is necessary in this physical world, where the interval between our visions and our executions is tedious. But you must always remember that our evolution, Cato, is most certainly our growth, our steady, patient progress toward God's ideal. You will grow and carry with you all that we have shared. I have witnessed this, my boy. I have seen the seed become the seedling, which in turn becomes the sapling, which someday stands tall and firm with sheltering presence. Someday I will return, and take refuge in the shelter of what you have become."

Even as Erastus spoke, they came upon a great tree. It stood on the left of the road with a colossal rooted trunk, from which spread long thick branches in all directions. The crooks and gnarls of the tree's great arms rose like massive muscles within the shedding veil of its tawny leaves, which lay, also, like a discarded skirt upon the ground around it. The tree was set apart some twenty yards in all directions from its nearest neighbor. Its solitary position spoke of both its independence and dominance within the grove. But for the creatures who came upon it, it was a welcoming sight that promised shade in summer, or protection against any storm.

Now the painter and his young friend paused freely to admire it. Erastus had seen the tree before and noticed it with appreciation. But this was the first time he'd seen it partly divested of its leaves, which revealed more of its might. Here was a physical manifestation, an archetype, to illustrate the very vision he held. He felt himself inhale the spectacle of it with his eyes, which, as was their habit in the face of beauty, grew moist, as if to temper the glaze through which beauty entered his soul. At such times, he experienced an involuntary reflex to record, to hold on to what he saw, to cast an inner net of artistic technique upon it, whereby he might learn to etch it back into life. For more than anything else, Erastus wished to show the world its own beauty.

"From now on, whenever I see this tree, I'll remember you," Cato said. "This is halfway between Hickory Grove and the Hollands' farm. So whenever I come down this way to visit Jimmy, I can rest here, and try to remember what you taught me."

Erastus nodded. "Yes, this will be something for me to remember as well," he said.

They walked on in silence now. Erastus felt he had said to his friend all that he could say. Now it was left to simply be aware of the boy's presence, to feel the proximate movements of the physical creature striding beside him. He tried to sense the warmth emanating from the boy's body. He drew as close as he dared beside him. He glanced, yet again, at the sheen of curls on his head, at the smooth glow of his skin. Then, when this visual stimulation grew too much, he turned away his physical eyes, and summoned a vision with his inner eyes. It was through these inner eyes that, from now on, he would interact with his beloved. Memories, though formless, had no less forming power to recreate his emotions.

When, in time, they reached the gate to the Hollands' farm, Erastus's breath quickened. He could not bear to draw it out. The painter turned, grasped Cato's bare biceps, held him face to face, looked as deeply and kindly as he could into the boy's eyes, then kissed him once, hard and fast, on his lips.

"Farewell," was all the Quaker said, and he turned, before Cato could bring himself to speak. Erastus walked down the course of the Hollands' driveway, with determined steps. Cato saw, in the force of this gesture, that the painter meant that he should not follow.

# 17

# THE PERFUMED HANDKERCHIEF

o honor the promise she made to her parents, Dorothy began her stewardship of Sammy by giving him instructions for avoiding her mother. She told Sammy that her mother, Henrietta, was considerably unhappy, and that for a sad woman like that to lay hapless eyes on a happy young man was intolerably distressing. She explained that contrary to what he might think, any effort Sammy might make to brighten Mrs. Holland's day would have the opposite effect. If he were to smile at her, she would be obliged to frown. If he were to be polite to her, she would be forced to be rude. If he were to show concern or express kindness to her in any way, she would of necessity become quite nervous. Mrs. Holland was so upside down, Dorothy explained, that the best thing for Sammy to do was to avoid her altogether. In fact, Dorothy proposed that henceforth, for each day in which Sammy could truthfully say that he had not allowed himself to be seen by the eyes of Mrs. Holland, Dorothy would provide Sammy with a penny, which he might save or spend as freely as he wished.

Sammy was perplexed by this proposition. But being as

earnest as he was cheerful, he promised Dorothy that he would do his best. He was not certain, he admitted, how it might be possible for him to keep himself out of Mrs. Holland's view, since his duties involved various activities that were normally conducted within the very rooms of the house where Mrs. Holland was most likely to be found.

To address this problem, Dorothy conceived a plan that would entail the assistance of the other household slaves. Cora and Willis were in charge of the house. Cora did all the cooking and most of the cleaning of dishes, pots and pans. Willis served the food, and looked after the barn and the animals. Willis also tended the garden from which the family's food was supplied. Wally assisted Willis in the garden, but she was principally in charge of the laundry and of the management of clothes and fabrics in general. Under Wally's guidance, Ella performed much sewing and darning, and was, of course, attendant upon Dorothy to assist her with any personal needs.

Most of Sammy's duties involved assisting the other slaves. If Willis needed a bundle of straw with which to mulch a plot of strawberries in the garden, Sammy would be sent to gather it from the barn. If Cora needed water for cooking or cleaning, Sammy would be dispatched to the pump in the yard to draw it. If Wally filled a basket with freshly laundered sheets, Sammy would be requisitioned to transport this cargo up to the linen closet, which meant a trip into the house. If Ella required assorted botanicals with which to concoct a batch of shoe polish, Sammy would be sent out of the house to the woods to procure the necessary ingredients. All these activities arose in a fashion that it was impractical to plan in advance. To this was added the complication that Mrs. Holland's own transversal throughout the household domain was itself impossible to predict. Thus, the objective of keeping the machinery of the household running smoothly—a goal which in some small part depended on the reliable lubrication that Sammy's fetching, gathering and transporting provided—was at odds with the goal of having Sammy perform these tasks without encountering Mrs. Holland.

Dorothy assembled the slaves to strategize. Her idea was simple. Each of the adults would keep an eye out for Mrs. Holland's whereabouts. If any of the adults saw that a particular task might cause Sammy to cross her path, he or she would defer the task until a later time. Sammy himself submitted an additional creative proposal that would enlist the services of Venus. Sammy's idea was that he might have Venus travel about with him to and fro. Before Sammy entered any room, Venus would be dispatched into the room alone to see if Mrs. Holland was there. If the coast was clear, Venus would beckon Sammy to enter the room with enthusiastic tail wagging, and perhaps a short bark. If, however, the pigeon were in the roost, Venus would exit the room and inform Sammy of the dilemma with a brief growl.

There was general skepticism of the practicability of this scheme, owing to the difficulty of tutoring Venus in the intricacies of her mission without actually using Mrs. Holland herself as part of the instructive process. Ella, however, hit upon the idea of taking advantage of the perfume that Mrs. Holland wore with such regularity that it was in everyone's mind part of her characteristic smell. Ella suggested that they might take a handkerchief liberally sprinkled with the perfume and place it in this room or that as a starting point for educating Venus with respect to the requirements of the proposed campaign.

Dorothy thought there might be something to this idea. She proposed that she could obtain a workable sample of the perfume in question from her mother's supply, which she would then sequester in a bottle kept in the bottom drawer of her bureau. It was soon realized, however, that the only person capable of teaching Venus the complex tasks required was Jimmy. So Jimmy, after initial protestations, was pressed into service for the training.

Since Jimmy could only supervise this project at night, when his daily work in the fields was finished, he decided that he would use the slave cabins to stand in for the rooms of the big house. Jimmy had taught Venus some useful behaviors in the course of her life, such as "come," "sit," and "stay." However, he'd taught her only two tricks. One trick was to "speak." Jimmy would say 'speak' and Venus would emit a short quick bark just louder than a yip. The second trick was to shake. Jimmy would say "shake," and Venus would first sit, then extend her paw upwards with the expectation that the speaker would then yank it.

Jimmy opted to begin Venus' education by demonstrations of what she was to do. He reasoned that she had at times revealed a facility for imitation, and that if he pretended to be a dog doing the things that were wanted, she might grasp the rules of the game. The first order of business was to demonstrate what was wanted with respect to the fragrant handkerchief. Jimmy would go into a cabin, examine it for the presence of the special perfume smell, then come back out and provide a signal to Sammy about whether the smell had been detected or not.

At first, Jimmy performed this routine on his hands and knees, the better to give the appearance of being like a dog. However, he soon realized that this aspect of his technique was confusing to Venus, who was quite struck by the sight of Jimmy crawling about in an unnatural way on his hands and knees, which was a behavior she found most engaging. However, since she herself had no comparable means for crawling about unnaturally, the imitative premise of the exercise was compromised. Moreover, Jimmy's crawling itself was so stimulating to her emotions that all other subtleties of the exercise were lost on her.

So Jimmy began again, this time simply walking into his cabin, from which all occupants had been duly evicted, and in which there was placed a handkerchief upon which the scent of Mrs. Holland's favorite perfume had been splashed. Jimmy went into the cabin containing the handkerchief, then came back out with a menacing air, came up to Sammy and growled. Then the trio moved to the adjacent cabin, which lacked a handkerchief, whereupon Jimmy again entered, but thereafter came out with a very pleased look, and said the word, "speak", as if to himself, after which he emitted a strange little sound intended to be understood as a discreet yip. This sequence was repeated half a dozen times, with Jimmy demonstrating the desired behavior and Sammy, each time, handing Jimmy a small token of bacon as a reward.

Then the class advanced to the next stage, in which Venus herself was coached to join Jimmy in the ritual of investigating for the handkerchief. On the first attempt, Venus accompanied Jimmy into the cabin where the handkerchief was kept, and was shown with great precision exactly what had to be done. Jimmy sniffed all about the cabin, pulling Venus along with him as he went, until at last he came upon the handkerchief, whereupon he growled as he sniffed it. He then dangled it in front of Venus' nose and growled again. Venus took note of all this with great interest and growing excitement; however, she did not, as yet, undertake an active role in imitating any of the goings on.

Next Jimmy and Venus left the cabin and came out to Sammy. Jimmy growled and Sammy handed him a small piece of bacon. Then they both looked expectantly at Venus, who returned their expectant looks with an expectant look of her own, since she surmised that a piece of bacon was in the offing. However, upon this point they reached an impasse, since Venus did not growl and thus had not yet caught onto the rules of the game. No bacon was proffered to her. Once again, Jimmy took her into the cabin and repeated the sniffing about; the discovery of the handkerchief; the growl; the dangling of the perfumed cloth in front of her nose; and finally the emergence from the cabin to Sammy's dispensation of bacon, which came straight upon Jimmy's sounding of a growl.

Now again, Sammy and Jimmy looked to Venus to show some indication of grasping the concept. But again, while Venus was most attentive to the pocket of Sammy's breeches in which he was hiding the bits of bacon, she did not growl, but looked from Jimmy to Sammy and back again with a mixture of excitement and confusion.

Seeing that this approach was not successful, Jimmy embarked upon a new tactic. He told Venus to go into the cabin, which she did. Then, after a suitable pause, he called her back out and out she came. Again she came up to Sammy filled with great expectations, since she had with aplomb carried off the going and coming that Jimmy had requested. But since she did not growl, no treat was dispensed to her. On this point Venus took umbrage. In fact, her sense of injustice was sufficiently aroused, that when Jimmy once again took her collar to lead her back into the cabin, she turned her head, looked back at Sammy and growled, by way of conveying that from her point of view the exercise was proceeding in a way that was entirely unfair.

Instantly upon hearing the growl, however, Sammy removed a bit of bacon from his pocket and dispensed it into her mouth, while both Jimmy and Sammy lavished great praise on her.

At this point, Venus was compelled to ponder greatly. By

now, she understood that some tremendous thing was being asked of her. The earnestness of the praise delivered by the humans told her that the game they had in mind was one of much import to them. She wished in all sincerity to accommodate them. It had not escaped her attention that the bacon and praise had come quickly upon the heels of her growling. Therefore, it struck her that it was well worth taking a chance on repeating this sequence. With this in mind she, somewhat tentatively, growled again. More bacon was doled out, and thus she grasped that this was indeed the key to the game. But, alas, she soon found out it was not to be quite as simple as that.

Every night after supper, the game was resumed. Venus learned with certainty that a little growl was just the thing to procure the bacon, and by degrees she came to understand that the growling was to ensue in proximity to the aroma of the perfumed handkerchief. But many more nights were then required to advance her to the point of understanding that she was not supposed to growl immediately upon smelling the perfume, but only after exiting the cabin and reuniting with Sammy. In the fullness of time, the night came when Venus performed the entire sequence exactly as wanted. She was dispatched into the cabin. She pretended to sniff around, although she knew perfectly well where the silly handkerchief was placed; she came upon it; she suppressed any inclination to growl; then she departed, went straight up to Sammy, and, finally, with a much-practiced technique emitted a perfectly formed, if somewhat affected, growl. At this instant, Venus was given such a helping of bacon, and so much praise and affection, that she was nearly overwhelmed by her own achievement.

In a likewise fashion, which required considerable patience from all concerned, and the effort of advancing subtle aspects of the wanted behavior by degrees, Venus was also taught to go into the adjacent cabin, where no handkerchief resided, and to return to Sammy, wag her tail and emit a pleasant yip.

Now what remained was to put this business to the test in a real life encounter with Mrs. Holland. In this, there was much uncertainty. Jimmy himself could not participate in it. It would be incumbent upon Sammy to carry out the most authentic part of the exercise on his own. Yet it was Sammy who was most unable to recover from any failure in the process, since if Mrs. Holland were to lay eyes upon him during these exercises, it would not go well for him. Moreover, it had not as yet been ascertained to what degree Venus might be able discreetly to roam about the house without herself becoming the object of Mrs. Holland's displeasure. Finally, there was considerable anxiety over the possibility that Venus might, under the pressure of such an important performance, forget the intricacies of her routine, and growl directly at Mrs. Holland upon smelling the perfume.

With all these uncertainties, the conspirators concluded that it would be best to begin by perfecting the "coast is clear" aspect of the enterprise, which was an objective that could be pursued, by design, in Mrs. Holland's absence. Thus, when Mrs. Holland was known with certainty to have left the house, Sammy and Venus were called in to practice. This part of the plan went quite well.

Then one day, Dorothy, who was principally in charge of the campaign, noted that her mother was gone from the house. Dorothy walked to Jake and Wally's cabin to suggest that Sammy and Venus might undertake yet another round of practice. Sammy and Venus entered the house by the side door, which placed them in the kitchen. Sammy took Venus to the threshold of the dining room door, where he indicated that she should go into that room and inspect it. She did. She came back, wagged her tail, yipped, and received her treat. Now

Sammy entered the dining room, which was duly noted to be unoccupied by Mrs. Holland. Then he took Venus to the threshold of the adjacent room, which was the parlor, and again indicated that Venus should go into that room and inspect it.

Venus entered the parlor, whereupon she came directly in contact with the figure of Mrs. Holland, who, unbeknownst to Sammy, had returned via the front door. Venus found Mrs. Holland sitting on the sofa in the company of Mrs. Greer, with whom she was having a visit. Venus was naturally cautious in the presence of Mrs. Holland, since that lady had throughout Venus' life made it clear that dogs were a particularly inferior element in the domestic hierarchy. Nevertheless, Venus pursued her objective as cautiously as possible, with her tail notably pushed down, since she was well aware that her activities might be regarded by Mrs. Holland as punishable. Mrs. Holland, however, was so engaged in her conversation with Mrs. Greer, that she did not pay any heed to the dog, as it moved around the room sniffing discreetly. Then, however, Venus was compelled to approach Mrs. Holland, since she had noted from the very first moment she entered the room, that Mrs. Holland bore the perfume smell that was indelibly associated with the growling variation of the game.

She came up to the sofa where Mrs. Holland sat. To remain true to the formalities of her mission, Venus drew in a substantial draft of the perfume smell. At this point, Mrs. Greer noticed and remarked upon the presence of the dog. Although Venus could not know what was said, Mrs. Greer's statement characterized the parlor as having been invaded by a beast. Mrs. Holland turned and glanced at Venus with a look of severe annoyance. Seeing this, Venus rapidly withdrew from the room, whereupon she, quite instinctively, growled at Sammy.

Sammy believed Mrs. Holland to be out of the house. He did not understand why Venus would growl. He feared that Venus had made an inexcusable error, which was bound to undermine all of their endeavors. He took her by the collar and, despite her resistance, pulled her back toward the parlor, so that he might show her the error of her ways. But before he had ventured more than a few feet into that room, he himself caught wind of the smell of the fateful perfume. With quick reflexes and great agility, he threw his body down to a crouching position next to Venus. Together they crawled back out of the parlor and into the dining room. All this was accomplished without Mrs. Holland having noticed anything, but Mrs. Greer, owing to her position on the sofa, observed these proceedings with great curiosity. She was just upon the point of commenting to her hostess about the odd behavior she had just witnessed, when, by luck, Dorothy, who had noticed Mrs. Greer's buggy in the driveway, and had herself ascertained that her mother might well have returned, burst into the parlor with an intentional degree of commotion. Having passed Sammy and Venus crouching in the dining room, Dorothy concluded that the situation called for a diversion.

"Ah, Mrs. Greer," she said loudly. "How nice it is to see you. You're looking very well." Recalling the lady's previous interest in cake, Dorothy asked, "Wouldn't you like a small piece of cake?" Dorothy was not at all sure that there was any cake in the house, but she was desperate. "And a nice cup of tea?" she added.

"Cake?" Mrs. Greer exclaimed. "Oh yes, most certainly. Cake and tea would be quite nice."

Henrietta was startled by this unusual behavior from Dorothy, and looked at her daughter with a degree of suspicion. Nevertheless, being keenly sensitive to her obligations as a hostess, she also consented to the prospect of cake and tea, though she had no knowledge of the existence in the house of any cake that might be brought forth.

Dorothy went to the kitchen and asked Cora if there was any cake in the house. Cora said that there was none. Dorothy instructed Cora, nonetheless, to prepare tea for serving to Mrs. Holland and Mrs. Greer. In the meantime, Dorothy had remembered that when she'd gone to fetch Sammy that Wally had been in the process of cooking a pan of cornbread, which was intended for the slaves' evening meal. Now she dashed across the yard to Wally's cabin, and, as briefly as possible, explained the situation to her. How quickly, Dorothy wondered, might Wally and Cora working in tandem, concoct a batch of exceptional icing? Might that icing then be deployed on the cornbread with sufficient generosity that the cornbread might be taken for cake? It would certainly be taken as a cake of dubious quality, but Dorothy hoped that the tastiness of an abundant amount of very good icing would appease Mrs. Greer, whom she knew to be particularly fond of that delectable ingredient.

And so it was that when Jimmy came home from the field that night, there was no cornbread for him to eat with his meal. However, Jimmy was told a most satisfying story. Venus had acquitted herself admirably in the detection of Mrs. Holland in the parlor. Sammy had not believed Venus, but had been rescued from discovery by the swift intervention of Dorothy. A distraction had been created with the rapid preparation of an impromptu cake. Mrs. Greer had, in fact, eaten the cake with gusto. Although Mrs. Holland only consumed a few bites, Mrs. Greer had requested a second piece. The thought of Mrs. Greer eating the slaves' cornbread was a source of great amusement to all concerned. For had Mrs. Greer known, in fact, the true pedigree of the food she so enjoyed, she would have choked on the very thought of it.

In subsequent months, Sammy and Venus were quite successful in their approach to detecting and avoiding Mrs. Holland. Mrs. Holland, for her part, was truly surprised by how well her daughter carried out the promise of keeping Sammy out of her sight. She almost never saw the boy in the house, and only observed him at some distance when she was out on the grounds. Mrs. Holland did, however, gradually notice that the dog could be seen lurking about the house much more than usual. She thought she detected in the dog's manner an element of guilt that, she was certain, must be the result of some malfeasance. However, whenever Mrs. Holland looked about the house in order to uncover whatever mischief the dog might have made, she could find no evidence of any misbehavior, and this, over time, became a mystery to which she became inured.

In time, Sammy accumulated one dollar's worth of pennies from Dorothy, which meant that he'd evaded Mrs. Holland entirely for one hundred days. Sammy diligently saved this money, for it was his intention to use the money, when a sufficient amount was put aside, to furnish himself with the supplies necessary to commence his career as an artist.

# 18

## "PLEASE DRAW THE DRAPE"

*I*n the spring of 1861, William Askew's courtship of Dorothy Holland reached a new threshold. By this time, William had passed several of Dorothy's examinations with excellent marks. The previous fall, when put to the test suggested by Dorothy's mother regarding the question of who ought to make decisions about domestic slaves, William had unequivocally declared that Dorothy should make any and all decisions concerning matters affecting her household domain. When queried about the locations in which he might be willing to live, he had assured Dorothy that he would live anywhere where she was present. When studied for any signs of infidelity, he had exhibited only a constant gush of devotion.

There were two areas, however, where Dorothy felt William fell short. First, she concluded that his intellect was not all that she had hoped for. Although he occasionally surprised her with insightful observations, she determined that she could not probe the great questions of life with him in a way that would satisfy her thirst to do so. Second, she perceived him to be emotionally flat. And though there was much that was reassuring about the steadiness of his temperament, he did not evince strong passions, either happy or sad, beyond his one-pointed dedication to Dorothy, which Dorothy supposed was mainly a consequence of his sexual desires. She wondered what might be left of him emotionally once that sexual inclination had been satisfied.

The question of William's emotional repertoire took on new significance when, in March, his mother Lucille became gravely ill. Lucille began to cough one day, and then, with each subsequent day, her coughing grew worse. The doctors spoke of consumption, or of pneumonia—there was no clear agreement on this, and Dorothy could not discern how much of the disagreement was equivocation designed to foster the hope of uncertainty in the family, which daily grew more alarmed.

During this time, William kept close proximity to his mother at Hickory Grove, which gave Dorothy greater opportunity than had previously been afforded her to visit him in his own surroundings. A notable drawback of these visits was that she had more than one occasion to meet William's father. Augustus Askew was, in Dorothy's mind, a significant deficit in William's catalogue of assets and liabilities. She disliked the man. He mistreated his slaves. He lacked charm. He wasn't even cordial. He seemed particularly unpleasant toward Dorothy, since, she supposed, he did not deem her to have a social standing worthy of his son.

With time, Augustus' fear and concern about his wife further spurred his most disagreeable tendencies. He began to mete out punishments of outlandish severity to slaves whose infractions were innocuous. He altered between outbursts of anger, and episodes of withdrawal behind the locked doors of his study, from which he would emerge only at night to look in on the sleeping form of his wife. Although the latter behavior worried William more than the former, each retreat to the study brought a spell of relief to members of the household staff, who became wary as cats whenever the master emerged from seclusion.

Like his father, William also withdrew. He stopped calling on Dorothy at her home. He became less and less articulate whenever she visited him. If he spoke, it was generally to express a gathering hopelessness, both about his mother's prognosis and about his father's morose mental state. If he had been emotionally flat before, now he was positively thin. Single syllable words furnished the bulk of his conversation. His face, never greatly animated to begin with, became transformed by degrees into a persistent glum expression. If she tried to get a rise out of him, he only tamped his feelings down further.

On two occasions, Dorothy was presented to Mrs. Askew. On the first, William's mother was too distraught by her illness to convey more than a courteous response to Dorothy's wishes for her improved health. But on the second, during a reprieve from coughing, Mrs. Askew attempted to have a serious talk with Dorothy. She asked William to leave them alone for a quarter hour, so that they might have a woman-to-woman discussion. After William had gone, Mrs. Askew invited Dorothy to sit on the edge of the bed. She solemnly asked Dorothy to take her hand.

"There is something I want to ask you about." She spoke in a soft, halting voice so as not to trigger her coughs. "It's of rather a delicate nature, and I cannot think of anyone suitable to ask about it. Neither my son nor my husband is in a position to be frank with me. I know from William that you are kind and bright, and I hope that you will do me the favor of answering a question that I have no right to ask you."

"If it is something I can answer, I assure you that I will," Dorothy said, politely matching the soft tone of Mrs. Askews' voice.

"Are you acquainted with William's manservant?"

"Cato? Yes, I know him," Dorothy replied.

"What do you know about him?"

From the look in the sick woman's eyes, Dorothy understood what it was that Mrs. Askew wished to know. This was not what Dorothy had expected. She had not thought in advance about the topic of Cato. She hesitated as she considered what she ought to say. "I know that William likes Cato a great deal," she began. "And that he treats him just as he would a member of the family," she added, moving closer to the point.

"I'm told," said Mrs. Askew, "that Cato's mother died many years ago, from an illness similar to my own."

Hearing no question in this, Dorothy simply nodded.

"However," Mrs. Askew continued, "no one has ever mentioned to me anything about the boy's father." With this statement, Lucille stopped and stared at Dorothy expectantly.

Dorothy looked into Mrs. Askew's eyes. She could not read the woman's intentions. It seemed unlikely, given the lady's grave illness, that Mrs. Askew meant to squander her remaining strength on an act of retribution against her husband. But Dorothy was less certain of what Mrs. Askew might contemplate with regard to Cato. Taking revenge on a slave was ridiculously simple. Mrs. Askew would only have to give instructions, and a great deal of harm might be done.

"Why is it," Dorothy asked, "that you want to know about Cato's father? Would you find fault in the boy for the consequences of acts that preceded his birth?"

"Are there acts that preceded his birth which deserve fault?"

"Certainly no fault on Cato's part," Dorothy said.

"Then it's true," Lucille sighed.

"I cannot say," Dorothy said quickly. "I only know of rumors and hearsay."

"Do you believe those rumors?"

"I would say," Dorothy said carefully, "that they seem plausible."

"Plausible?"

"You must forgive me." Dorothy decided she would have to speak plainly. "I am not sure of your inclinations, and I would not wish to make assertions that might result in some harm befalling a boy whom I believe to be innocent, regardless of what may or may not have preceded his birth."

Mrs. Askew disengaged her hand from Dorothy's. "Do I seem vindictive?" she asked. "I am past all that," she said flatly. "I only wish to have a clearer view of my husband, and of the circumstances of my life."

"As to the circumstances of your life," Dorothy said more gently, "there is no dishonor in your innocence any more than there is in Cato's. I suppose your husband saw no benefit in being candid about a subject that would not be a happy one. He strikes me as a man of practical inclinations."

Lucille laughed as best she could. "Practical, indeed!" This produced a small cough. "Will you have him for your father-in-law?" she asked abruptly.

"I would not let my assessment of your husband override my assessment of your son," Dorothy said. "And my assessment of your son is quite favorable."

"Please tell me as directly as you can. Is my husband the boy's father?"

"I have no way of knowing for certain," said Dorothy, "but my impression is that there is a notable family resemblance with your husband."

"Would you ask Cato to come in here, then?" she asked. "I would like to have another look at how my husband's character is reflected in this boy. But make no mention of our discussion to anyone," she added.

"What will you say to him?" Dorothy asked.

"If you will do me the favor to bring him here," said Mrs. Askew, "you shall hear for yourself."

Once again, Dorothy hesitated, as she considered what might happen. She realized she was being asked to play a role in a drama that was a consequence of Mrs. Askew's circumstances—and that she could hardly begrudge a dying woman the satisfaction of discovering the truth. But the situation made her anxious, since she did not know just how dramatic such a drama might become. Nevertheless, she said, "All right. I will get Cato."

When she left Mrs. Askew's bedroom, Dorothy found William waiting twenty feet beyond the bedroom door, a distance calculated to be as close as he dared come without seeming to eavesdrop on their conversation. "Where can I find Cato?" she asked him.

"Cato?"

"Yes, your mother would like to see him."

This information seemed like the kind of thing that ought to raise a response of some sort from William, but he merely raised his eyebrows and said, "He's polishing silver down in the dining room."

In the dining room, Cato was worried when Dorothy informed him of Mrs. Askew's request to see him. Like the rest of the household staff, he was on edge because of Augustus' erratic displays of temper. A look of dread crossed his face, as he speculated about what mistake he might have made that would warrant an audience with the mistress. He surveyed the silver he was polishing to see if the answer to this question might lie in some aspect of his present task.

Since Mrs. Askew had asked Dorothy to make no mention of their discussion, Dorothy did not feel she could explain to Cato the real purpose of their visit. But she felt it would not violate her discretion to say, "Mrs. Askew is speaking to those she considers a close part of the family. She's quite ill. She may be dying. She asked me to fetch you."

When, in due time, Dorothy brought Cato into her bedroom, Lucille lay with one hand on her forehead, staring at the ceiling. As she turned her eyes toward her visitors, she showed no sign of agitation, but a strong curiosity, which over-rode the weakness of her condition.

"Dorothy, please draw the drape, and let some light into the room."

Dorothy did what she was asked to do. The room, which was distinctly a woman's bedroom, was decorated with soft colors and lacy fabrics. The pink silk drapery was backed with heavy fabric, by which it effectively obscured the light. As Dorothy pulled one of the draperies to the side, the sun streamed in, and the somber mood of the room was trans-formed. The light fell heavily on Cato, who squinted momen-tarily as his eyes adjusted. Mrs. Askew, also squinting, covered her eyes with her arm, which she used as a visor from under which she might peer out at her son's servant.

"Come closer," Lucille said to him.

Cato stepped nearer the bed, and faced Mrs. Askew in an awkward state of attention, with his hands clasped behind his back. He was not certain if he should look her in the eye, so he stared at a spot a foot or two above her head.

For a while no one spoke. Lucille studied the boy, who, she had determined from previous inquiries, was twenty-one years old. His skin was light brown, and of such a smooth texture that it glowed with a sheen like velvet. His muscles, though firm and well-shaped, were more modest than those of most of the slave men, since his household tasks were of a lighter nature. This gave him a delicate appearance that struck Mrs. Askew as like the prettiness of a beautiful girl. Yet there was no question that he was handsome. The boy bore features that resembled but improved upon her husband's, which made her wonder briefly if Augustus had looked as fetching when he was twenty-one.

Dorothy moved from the window and stood next to Cato. Unlike Cato, she looked Lucille directly in her eyes.

"I've called you two here," Lucille began, "because I don't expect I will last much longer. You two are the closest persons to my son. I want to ask each of you to look after him. He is not as strong as his father. He is more sensitive than you may think. You must help him cope with my ...." She stopped and sighed, feeling suddenly the weight of her situation and the difficulty of her task. "... with my passing. I'm beyond the point of polite conversation," she continued, "and I will speak frankly. Dorothy, my husband is not fond of you—but he is not fond of most people, so you mustn't take his attitude personally. What matters to me is that my son is fond of you— I trust his judgment." She paused again. "It's odd how clari-fying death can be," she said. "I've spent most of my life distracted by things that mean very little to me right now. If I could transfer this insight to you I would, but I know that I cannot. I'm sure I would never have come to it had I remained healthy." She paused again, not because she seemed to be finished, but because her energy failed her.

During this speech Cato's awkward discomfort was displaced by an unexpected feeling of tenderness. He shifted his gaze from the wall to look her in the eyes. He had never seen Mrs. Askew in the light in which he now saw her. He felt regret that she was dying. He realized that he had spent years fearing and distrusting her. In this respect, he shared her insight. He too had been distracted by feelings that he had never questioned. He felt, suddenly, that he must say something while he still could. "I'm sorry, Missus," he said, "that I have not been more kind to you."

Lucille was moved by this. She covered her eyes with her arm, and said, "I might well say the same to you."

Cato continued, "I told Mr. Hicks ... the painter, that you seem to glow in the portrait he painted of you. He told me it was because he can see the light within people. Right now, I can see you as he did. You have a glow. I will think of it when I look upon your portrait."

Lucille shifted her arm to peer at Cato again. For a moment, she said nothing. She fought to stifle a cough. Then, she said, with regret, "I wish I might have lived up to that portrait." After a further silence, she lifted her hand toward Cato, and he stepped forward to take it. She said, "Look after William, will you?" Lucille spoke softly. Her voice had little power. "He was raised an only child," she whispered. "But you must treat him like a brother."

With this, Cato understood that she knew. Feeling the import of her acknowledgement, his eyes grew moist. "I shall," he said. "I shall serve him as I would my own brother."

Then Mrs. Askew dropped Cato's hand, and spoke, with much effort to form her words, addressing both Dorothy and Cato. "Please do not judge my husband too harshly. Part of what is good in William comes from him. But you have to take the first step with Augustus. He will not take it." With this, she turned her head to the side in a gesture that signaled that she needed to rest, whereupon Dorothy and Cato left the room.

Outside the bedroom, William again stood waiting. This time the look in his eyes conveyed that he wanted to know what had been said.

"Your mother called us in," Dorothy said, "to ask us to look after you. She does not think she will last much longer."

William's face twisted into an awful expression. He seemed

to want to cry, but he could not. "I must go for the doctor," he said.

William went for the doctor, but several hours later, with the doctor in attendance, and both William and Augustus at her side, Lucille Askew breathed her last. She was only forty-four years old.

Now it was Dorothy and Cato who stood outside the bedroom waiting. First, the doctor came out, and told them what had happened. When the doctor had departed, William came out by himself, bearing grief on his face, but with eyes shocked and waterless, unable to focus directly on either Dorothy or Cato. Dorothy, who, in response to the misery of the moment had begun to cry, merely looked at William with a sense of helplessness. But Cato, seized with a desire to act upon the dispensation given him, went up to his brother and clasped him in his arms.

William was startled by this. He resisted the embrace with a stiff posture. Undeterred, Cato pulled him closer, and laid his head across his brother's shoulder. Presently, unable to find any other response, gradually set loose from his shell of numbness by the force of Cato's affection, William by degrees began to tremble. Then in an abrupt, acquiescing eruption, he clutched hard onto Cato's body, likewise laid his head across his brother's shoulder, and began at last to weep. He sobbed with convulsing jerks, each cry rising in a crescendo, until at last his tears flowed so freely, that Cato felt the warm wetness of them dribble onto the cloth of his shirt.

It was upon this scene that Augustus Askew emerged from his wife's bedroom. When he viewed the poignant spectacle of his sons' anguished embrace, he was merely filled with acrimony. He was embittered by the injustice of his wife's death. The one person whom he had invested with kindness had left him with no good reason. He would no longer have anyone to comfort him. Nothing in his vast holdings could provide him with solace. He saw only the endless emptiness that lay before him. With a sense of finality, he realized that he was beyond the age and aptitude ever to replace what he had lost. Without speaking, he pushed past William, Cato and Dorothy, descended the stairs, went into his study, locked the door, and collapsed onto the sofa across from his desk. He did not emerge from that room for the next three weeks.

# 19

# IN SEARCH OF THE CLOUDS

*A*fter his mother's death, William spent as much time as he could with Dorothy. He had become emotional. Emotion poured out of him freely. He sometimes sat with Dorothy and cried for no apparent reason. Whenever he did, she was tender. She took his hand. She stroked his forehead. To his surprise, the less stoically he behaved, the more affectionate she became. In the past, he had not imagined he could show his feelings to her or to anyone. But his mother's death uncapped a new spontaneity in his conduct—and now he was struck by the marvelous freedom he felt when he gave his grief free rein. The loss of his mother only heightened his desire for Dorothy. She became the focus of this emancipation of his feelings. Grief rolled easily into passion. Unstopping one emotion intensified the other.

Dorothy, for her part, was encouraged by his transformation. Whereas William had once seemed imperturbable, grief forced him out of his self-control into a more genuine, less studied behavior. Dorothy believed this new version of her suitor was more authentic. He was not at all like his father.

Where his father had become closed by grief, William had been opened. Even his posture seemed different, as if he'd let himself loose from muscles that had held him rigid. When he spoke, his voice was more melodious. He did not edit his thoughts. He spoke freely of silly or serious things.

As soon as William proposed it, Dorothy acquiesced to an un-chaperoned visit. She was privately thrilled by it. She felt confident, grown-up, no longer a child. She was determined to be no simple replication of her mother. While her mother was scheming and calculating, Dorothy repudiated all pettiness. She was honest, incautious, uncritical, and spontaneous. She allowed William's new flow of feeling to wash over her. She felt the malleability of her own passions. She let herself fall in love. It was without rhyme or reason. She thought, for the first time, that she might let her mind relax its vigilant seriousness. She allowed herself to imagine acts that had once seemed unthinkable. Erotic daydreams lit a flame within her. She began, like William, to yearn.

On the first warm evening in April, 1861, he came to visit her after supper. William knew that George and Henrietta Holland had gone to visit Henrietta's sister in Memphis. So he arrived at a later hour than he would otherwise dare. Dorothy was alone in the house with the servants. William calculated that on this night there would be no impediment to the advancement of his courtship.

He arrived on the front porch with a bouquet of yellow tulips. He was specially dressed for the occasion. He wore a ruffled shirt, a white silk vest, a black frock coat, black pantaloons, and a new pair of Hessian boots. He'd brushed his hair forward to form a cowlick, and shined it with perfumed Macassar oil. His face was offset by fashionably bushy whiskers, which contrasted with the ruddiness of his lips.

At first, they sat and talked politely in the parlor, letting the twilight advance until just that point when, by rights, an oil lamp should have been lit. But rather than striking a light inside, William proposed that they step out to the garden. The wafts of air that came through the window felt warm and inviting. Winter had loosened its claim on the night air. The allure of a balmy April evening beckoned them to the garden, even though the damp air hinted at rain.

They went to sit, once again, on the bench where they had often sat and talked before. Without warning, William pulled a silver flask from his pocket. He tilted it back slowly to nurse a few drops of bourbon onto his tongue. He did this as much for dramatic effect as to taste the liquor. Dorothy watched him as he held the flask out to her. She knew instinctively that this was a crucial moment for her, that she would accept the ritual of adulthood signified by the alcohol. She knew too that it marked a change in her relationship with William, that it portended intimacies never discussed, but which she had imagined while staring at the ceiling in bed at night. Even so, she wondered if she could lose her head from a simple drink. She took the flask and sipped. She felt the warming liquor slide down her throat. At first, the odd sensation of it distracted her. Then she noticed the first gush of intoxication unwind something in her body, like a tight spring that clicked a notch looser. The loosening surprised her. It was more pleasant than she had imagined. A layer peeled away, a layer of stiffness, which she now realized could not really belong to her, because the looser truth of her beneath that layer felt more alive, and so it must be, she concluded, more real.

Dorothy's eyes turned toward the ancient swing that was tied to a massive limb in the oak tree. Though she had swung on that swing routinely as a child, it now appeared as a symbol of something in her that she'd lost. How odd that in this ritual in which she sought to pass into adulthood she should find herself wanting to be childish. Like William, she was dressed for the occasion. She had lightly rouged the fine white skin of her cheeks. She had adorned her neck with simple, virtuous pearls. She wore yet another satin dress that her mother had bought her. But this evening she enjoyed it. Its strapless elegance posed a contrast to the prospect of the swing. She stood and ambled toward the swing, conscious of the disjunction between her attire and her sudden desire to swing.

Dorothy giggled. She sat on the swing, stuck out her legs for a moment, and then let them drop. William crept up next to her, walking like a cat. He did not want to make any move that might break the unfolding spell. Smoothly he pulled the flask from his pocket without making a sound. This time he took a substantial drink. When he handed it to her, she held the rope of the swing with one hand, leaned back, and lifted her legs until the swing floated freely. She tilted the flask toward her mouth in what she imagined was a graceful gesture. But she lost her balance as she sipped. She lurched forward just as she swallowed a gulp of bourbon, and this set her laughing.

William only smiled, and said, "Do you want a push?"

Dorothy looked up at him, aware of lifting her eyelashes upward, as she clutched the flask to her belly and said, "Why, yes, William, I should like a push."

William stepped behind the swing. He held his hands above her bare shoulders, hesitating at the prospect of touching them. He lowered them slowly onto her skin. The live contact with her flesh amazed him. Certainly, they had shaken hands and brushed each other in passing before. William had even once put his hand on the fabric of her clothed leg. But now his touch was skin on skin. The heat he felt in his palms, and the warmth she felt in her shoulders focused both of them on that point of pressure. Dorothy said, "Mmmm" just as William unconsciously let his fingers spread lightly over her skin.

William lingered; his fingers explored her shoulders until Dorothy said, "Come now, Mr. Askew, you're supposed to give me a push."

William pushed his hands, but, surprising himself, he let them slide all around on her shoulders.

"I can't seem to get my hands to work right," he said. He genuinely believed he was trying to push, but his hands performed on their own. They slid up to the side of her neck. He lowered his head, and buried his nose in her hair.

"William." Dorothy turned her head to the side, to look around at him. And as she did so, he found her ear beneath his tongue. He licked it. "Mr. Askew," she said, "I'm going to fall off this swing if you do that."

William took hold of the ropes of the swing to steady it. Dorothy threw her head back until her head rested against his waist. She stared up into his face. Without deliberation, he lowered his head and touched his lips to hers. She let her legs sink to the ground.

William pulled his head back. His muscles sprang to life. "Are you ready?" he asked.

"What?"

William pushed on the ropes and set the swing in motion. Dorothy raised her legs. He stepped back, and pushed her till she began to swing in a gentle arc.

Dorothy smiled, feeling her inner spring click looser. "Higher," she said.

William pushed her harder. She began to pump with her legs. The ancient swing picked up speed.

Dorothy let her head fall back. Her hair hung down like a counter-pendulum in the breeze. "Higher," she said again.

He pushed her hard, and again, and again, until she was swinging in the widest possible arc.

"Higher," she said again.

William laughed outright. "You can't go any higher." And it was true, the ropes of the swing pulled mightily on the great branch of the oak, which creaked under Dorothy's weight. She whizzed up and down with such speed from her own pumping that William had to step to the side and push lightly, lest the branch itself give way.

Dorothy squealed like a child, in crescendos that matched the rhythm of her arc.

"Sing to me," William said. "Sing to me while you're swinging."

Dorothy breaths came hard and fast. "Boy … woo … you're crazy … you …."

William pushed harder, the ropes and the oak branch groaned.

"Oh William …. Hold on! I …."

"Are you tingling," he shouted.

"Yes … I … oh, stop! Please. I need to stop." In the distance, she heard the low, deep sound of thunder.

William grabbed onto Dorothy's back, and with great effort brought the swing to a halt. Her body was quivering. He held her tight, with his legs pushed up against her back, aware of the pressure of her shoulders pushing into his thighs.

"Come with me," he said, and he pulled her off the swing.

"Where?"

He pointed toward the barn.

She knew what he meant, and she was shocked to realize that she was ready to go with him. It had seemed so improbable only a month before, but now she understood that it was right. "How odd," she said aloud, by which she meant the sudden welling up of desire. Something in the air, the bourbon, the warmth of his touch, the sensation of his tongue on her ear, the giddy pleasure of swinging, the urgent, affectionate look in his eyes, rent open a flood of desire within her—and made her want to do the thing she had only imagined.

There was a flash of light in the sky. "Imagine!" she said, by which she meant the unexpectedness of her wanting William Askew in that moment as much as he clearly wanted her. Echoing the flash came another low rumble of thunder.

"It's going to rain," he said. He took her hand and pulled her toward the barn. She bounced along just slightly behind him as the first drops of rain fell on her shoulder. The barn was fifty yards away. The rain began to plunk, with a gathering percussiveness. But they did not notice—so inward was their focus, as their thoughts raced on to the prospect of the barn. More and more drops plopped, drumming a rapid escalation. But neither of them spoke. They felt the communion of an unspoken accord pass between them. Through their hands, which were joined, they felt a pact. The rain itself was part of that pact. It joined them with heaven, earth, and all the things that might feel as alive as they felt in the rain. The rain itself was water that had risen from the creeks and rivers and the distant oceans. It had departed silently from the soil, dried up off houses, roads, and treetops. It had abandoned the sweaty skins of animals and humans. It had risen to the heavens, molecules of water beckoned to a cosmic reunion, to an ancient ritual of coming together and entangling into clouds, and gliding and flying in unison across the sky, across valleys and fields, over the plantations and farms, until the swelling molecules, the liquefied ambassadors from all reaches of the region, so full of attraction and the impulse to fuse, that the water cried out in thunder, and flashed bolts of power, then fell, purified, unburdened, in a mad rush back to earth, to new creeks, new rivers, new rooftops, new trees, new animals, new human skins. The rain poured now, and through this water, through this rain, came a feeling of familiarity. The intimacy that seized them felt timeless. They shared a sense of all that was still impending, but which swept over them like nostalgia. For they knew that they were about to make love, that they would, in fact, be lovers, that their souls on this night, in this rain, would become enmeshed.

When they got inside the barn, their clothes were drenched. He pulled her tightly against him. There was no reason to speak. His hands explored and found the secret things that held her dress. The dress came off, but he did not look at her. He grabbed a horse blanket, which he folded like a towel. He closed his eyes and dried her body with it, feeling her, but not wanting yet to look.

When he was done, she took the blanket and wiped his hair. She undid his shirt, opened his belt, rubbed the water from his chest with the blanket, then felt his skin with her hands as if it were a mysterious rock face. When they were naked and dried, they stepped together at ease, as though they had done so many times before. Each was shocked by how familiar and relaxed their shared nakedness felt. Then the silence in the barn gave way to gasps of heavy breath, to small sounds emanating from the backs of their throats, to the sound of breath sucking in through their noses, rising in pitch, becoming frantic, as they fell upon the straw pile, their mouths locked together.

William, who normally was as refined a southern gentleman as he could be, now heard himself snarl. He was unconscious of the source of his sounds, which were predatory, resonating in timbres he hadn't realized his voice possessed. Dorothy, too, began to exhale unfamiliar short, hot cries which felt like William's name, but which had no relation to those syllables, naming him instead in the mysterious language of her desire. Thought drained from their minds. Their helpless muscles swept them onto each other in a force they could not stop.

William looked at her now, at the pale, naked softness that had been sheathed for so long in skirts and petticoats and so many veils of propriety. His eyes widened with the spectacle, as if he beheld the treasures of the unseen tomb in the great pyramid, as if he alone now viewed the very thing that all mankind must dream of knowing. And for a moment, he stopped, gulping at the enormous portent of this precipice. She was naked except for the strand of pearls. His gaze went from the contours of her breasts to the firm brown fleshiness of her nipples, then down to her pubic hair and on to that coveted space which now emerged before his eyes as she spread her legs just a bit.

He called out "Ah!" He held his body above her, looking down, scanning again the precious surfaces, cataloguing like an explorer, wanting to savor all the visual revelations. He wished for a moment to stay the plunge, but the aching momentum of his desire pulled him like an arrow shot from a bow, and he could not hold it back. He took hold of her knees, spread her legs further apart, and was borne along with the arc of his craving to its home.

Tears formed at the corner of Dorothy's eyes when he entered her. She saw herself nod her head. William fought against the instinct of his body to thrust violently. He used all his strength to temper his muscular lust into slow, gliding arcs in and out of her, thrusts that nonetheless bore the power of his penetration, which probed the reaches inside to answer her "Yes" with his.

And she, seized by the realization of his being flagrantly inside her, felt the blood and chemistry come up suddenly to a boil, to an intensity that surprised her so much that she moaned. He moaned with her, until his voice cracked and then she took him over.

Control passed unspoken. In a single moment, they were transformed. He on his side became yielding, his body loosed and passive, his attention focused like a gleaming lens upon the raw sensation of his flesh inside her. She pumped herself upon him as he lay back and felt himself falling, as if he was falling from the sky. She rocked upon him in frenzy. Her voice made noises he had never heard before. He wanted to let go, but he didn't want it to end. For a few moments, he held back the entire cascade. He fought with all his strength to hold it back, but he could not. "Dorothy!" he cried. She felt liquids, hers, his, theirs, flowing, spraying, gushing, as she cried out, "William!" And throughout the reaches of time and space, that human event which defies description, the knowing of which is so essential to life, toward which so much human endeavor secretly winds, which is marveled at by the nodding heads of souls who have been, and imagined by those who are yet to be —the moment of orgasm revealed its essential truth.

Their bodies shone with sweat. Again, they were wet. Again, the water began its journey. Again, the water, imperceptibly, departed their panting skin, returned to the warm dry air in the barn, seeped out the open window to renew the cycle, once again in search of the clouds.

# 20

## THE NIGHTSHIRT

On March 4th, 1861, when Lucille Askew first struggled with a cough, President Abraham Lincoln was inaugurated in Washington. By the time Mrs. Askew died in late March, the country was in turmoil. Seven states seceded. Tennessee was torn. Those in the east wished to stay in the Union. Those in the rest of the state cried out for secession. The crisis, in the beginning, did not press close upon the Askew family. All their attention was turned at first upon Lucille, then upon their own grief. For Dorothy, the dramatic national events unfolded in the background of romance, where they added notes of hope and dread to her escalating emotions. The institution of slavery had at last erupted into a wedge that split North and South into enemy camps. Dorothy, and her father, George Holland, were not, by local sentiment, in the favored camp. Virtually all of the white, land-owning population of Madison County endorsed secession. George and Dorothy were lone dissenters. Dorothy was outspoken. George was circumspect. He read Lincoln's inaugural address in the morning paper. He took the President at his word. Lincoln promised he would not interfere with the South or any of its institutions. George believed a peaceful solution would be the most practical … and the most desirable.

Dorothy was unabashedly Republican and an abolitionist. The crisis emboldened her point of view. William Askew, by contrast, was open to all political points of view. When asked, he agreed with his fellow citizens. It made sense to secede. He believed the grievances posed by slavery should be addressed by benign slaveholders, by Southern gentlemen who would act as morally as he would. Yet he was not opposed to staying in the Union. He bore no ill will toward the North. At school in Louisville, his chums were two lively fellows from Ohio. They left him with the impression that Northerners could be quite decent. He was not zealous for war. Yet he recognized its inevitability as a consequence of secession.

For William, the troubles of the world seemed remote in the afterglow of the barn, which left him feeling so agreeable that he would agree with everyone if he could. But a few days later, Fort Sumter was fired upon. Then, two of his friends enlisted in the army. His father informed him that by virtue of his station and his education, he ought to be commissioned as an officer. Officers, his father pointed out, were permitted to travel in the company of a personal servant. With Cato in attendance, William would make a fine officer in the Tennessee Sixth Regiment, which was assembling nearby in Jackson. He would be, his father assured him, a genteel figure. He would be self-evidently superior to any Yankee abolitionist. The prospect of war roused his father. Augustus Askew was ardent to defend the South against the threat to slavery. The imperative of saving sacred Southern traditions yanked him from his withdrawn depression.

By degrees, William came to accept his father's belief that he should join the Provisional Army of Tennessee as an officer.

A feeling of invulnerability begat by his youthfulness was now coupled with a fearlessness engendered by his personal joy. The trouble would not last, he thought. It was, he was sure, not much more than a family squabble. Dorothy would object, of course, to his going off to fight for a month or so. She would miss him. He would miss her. But her passion for him, he was certain, would override her objections. When he pictured himself in an officer's uniform, he saw gallantry. Surely, he would look dashing in Dorothy's eyes. Nevertheless, as a precaution, and merely as a way to avoid a petty argument, he decided it might be best if he pursued an officer's commission without telling her. It would be a surprise.

With his father's help, William's credentials were put forth. Very soon, a uniformed man brought him the papers of notification. He would be commissioned as a second Lieutenant. He would be assigned as an officer in the Tennessee Sixth Regiment at Camp Beauregard in Jackson. He took a swallow of Tennessee bourbon, then signed and returned the form of oath —a loyalty oath that pledged his fidelity to the Confederate States. The die was cast.

At Christmas the previous year, Henrietta Holland had presented Dorothy with a copy of "The Ladies Self Instructor," a publication that provided patterns for dressmaking and millinery. Though Dorothy had been taught sewing, she had shown no particular affinity for that art. The dressmaking patterns in the book exceeded her ambitions. But on the day after her adventure in the barn, she found several yards of a nice flannel fabric in a closet, which had been meant for a project her mother had abandoned. Dorothy had an impulse to make a nightshirt for William—a practical gift —yet one which she now thought might be pleasurable to make. There was no pattern for this endeavor in "The Ladies Self Instructor," and so she turned to Ella for guidance. Ella had assisted Wally in the creation of many practical garments.

"It couldn't be easier," Ella assured her. "You cut two pieces of flannel like so. You make a cut out for the collar. You sew the pieces together, add some sleeves, and hem the edges. Anyone can do it."

"How can I be sure it will fit?" Dorothy was optimistic, but she doubted it could be as easy as all that.

"Don't worry. I have an eye for fit," said Ella. "He's about Jimmy's height, but his shoulders aren't as wide. His arms are about yea long." She held up her hands to illustrate. "Besides, you can't go wrong with a nightshirt Miss D. It's got to fit kind of loose so's you can slip it on and off easy." Ella winked. "I 'spect you'll want to slip it off for the most part."

Dorothy blushed. They sat in the parlor. Ella, in a chair by the window, mended socks, and gestured with needle and thread to augment her comments. Dorothy drank tea. She sat comfortably on a divan with her legs stretched out, enjoying her parents' continued absence. She felt tremendously transformed by what had happened in the barn: older, happier, in a state of reverie.

"Oh, you got to tell me one more time," said Ella, "about last night. I saw him comin' down the road in those boots, you know, with them flowers, and lookin' all fine. I said to myself, 'Oh, Miss Dorothy is gonna have trouble tonight.' Next thing I see you out there swinging in that dress."

"You were spying?"

"No ma'am. I was minding my own business over by the cabin. But when I heard you squealing like a piglet I stepped round the corner to make sure nothing was wrong. Then I saw you flying on that old swing—with your legs up in the air. Next thing I hear thunder and lightning and I see you and him hightail it toward the barn."

"We had to get in out of the rain."

"Seems like you could've gone back to the house if staying dry was all you wanted. Nothing in that barn but them mules. Ooooh what those mules must have thought. Do, re, mi!" Ella chuckled.

"I thought you wanted me to tell the story."

"Well I just hadn't thought before 'bout how those mules must have felt. I don't s'pose those mules get much company."

"Oh, bother the mules. They didn't pay any mind."

"I don't s'pose it was the mules you were looking at."

"No." Dorothy giggled. "I did not look at the mules."

"Ah," Ella held her needle in a provocative position. "I wonder if I'm ever gonna see a sight like you saw."

"Why shouldn't you?"

"'Cause I don't want the Lord to strike me blind."

"Oh, posh. You can jump a broom as well as anyone. Someday you'll be seeing a sight."

"I wouldn't know what to make of it. I mean, is it …, does it …?" Ella seemed unable to complete her question.

"Does it what?" Dorothy asked.

"Does it look like how you thought?"

Dorothy held out her fist, and extended her forefinger. She touched her extended finger with her other hand and said, "Ping," then stuck it straight up.

Both women convulsed in laughter.

Suddenly Venus appeared in the room, sniffing out the scene. Venus sauntered up to Dorothy, then sat on her haunches, looking at Dorothy with some uncertainty.

"What are you looking at?" Dorothy asked, speaking to the dog.

"Maybe she thinks you turned into your mother," Ella said. "Now that you done what you done, you might seem different to her. Maybe she's wondering whether to warn Sammy against you now."

"Oh, honestly!" Dorothy waved her hand to shoo Venus away. Venus cocked her head, then turned and trotted out of the room. After a brief moment behind the dining room door, she scampered back in and once again went up to Dorothy and sat. "Well?" Dorothy spoke to the dog with a voice she would use with a child.

At this, Sammy burst into the room and hurled himself, giggling, into a ball onto the sofa. Venus followed him straight to the sofa with her tail up, and looked around the room panting.

"Child what's got into you," Ella said.

"I was only playing," said Sammy. "I knew it was just you."

"You ought not be standing around eavesdropping, you know." Ella admonished him.

Sammy sat up on the sofa. "You don't want me to drop what?"

Ella attempted a stern look. "It means you ought not be listening in on folks when they in here having a private conversation."

"I didn't listen in on folks," Sammy protested. "I just told Venus to go in and see if ... you know."

"Mr. and Mrs. Holland went to Memphis," Ella explained. "They won't be back till Tuesday. So you don't got to send that dog in and out no more until Tuesday."

"What day is today?" Sammy asked.

"Today's Friday." Ella said.

Sammy looked at Dorothy. "Will I still earn a penny?"

Dorothy smiled. "I suppose so. Since you're keeping in practice. But why aren't you helping Willis today?"

"I am helping Willis. He asked me to come ask you if it's all right if he picks some asparagus for us folks to eat for supper. He said he has a whole lot of asparagus coming in all at once, so you might not mind it."

"Tell him I don't mind it," Dorothy said.

"And Cora said I should ask you if it's all right if she takes out some extra butter for us too. Cora said that Bathsheba came out with a whole lot of milk all last week and so she's got to use up all that buttermilk."

"What a coincidence." Dorothy observed.

"Buttered asparagus!" Ella smacked her lips.

"Tell Cora that since my parents aren't home, she can use up any food she would have made for them."

"Yes ma'am." Sammy shrugged. "Oh gosh, I reckon I'll have to be at the churn all morning." He cleared his throat. "Cora told me I have to sing to make the butter come faster. Is that true Miss Dorothy?"

"Cora's right," Ella said. "Butter won't come unless you sing 'Waiting for a butter cake, come, butter, come'—and you best do a little dance too."

"Come on, Venus," Sammy said. "We got to go churn butter."

Venus went up to Dorothy one last time, then turned and dashed after Sammy as he left.

"I don't know if I want to see Sammy grow up." Dorothy sipped her tea, and looked out the window at the boy and the dog. "I'm not sure how long his happy ways will persist."

"I used to have happy ways," Ella said. "Now look at me."

"I don't know," Dorothy replied. "Ella, it seems to me you have always been inclined to a certain cynicism .... At least, you've always seemed rather disenchanted about most things."

"If I seem disenchanted," Ella said, "it's on account of I used to be enchanted." Ella put down her knitting and peered out the window, looking with Dorothy at the lively young boy outside. "When I was a little girl, I was just like Sammy. I'd run into a room, and I'd see all the adults sitting around in chairs, and I'd think … oh, that's all these grownups ever want to do. All they like to do is to sit in chairs. When I grow up, I'm not going to be like that. No, sirree. I'm going to always be the same as I am now, and I'm never going to want to just sit in a chair and do nothing more than that. What's wrong with them? I used to think—they just sit there! And now look what's happened. Here I am, all grown up, and I'm sitting in a chair … and don't talk to me about getting out of the chair unless I have to."

"I do recall," said Dorothy, with a wistful smile, "that you and I would get so excited by simple things—like seeing the first snow."

"Oh Lord," Ella sighed. "I remember waking up one winter morning. It had been the quietest, darkest night. Nary a sound had crossed my ears. Then Wally opened the door to see what the day looked like. I could see from under my bedcover that the entire outdoors had been covered—every inch—with that heavy wet snow. The outdoors had gone all white—everywhere and everything. I couldn't believe it. Nothing looked the same. It was as if the whole world had been turned upside down, and it just suddenly went white. I thought it was such a big change. How could so much happen in just one night? How could the world be so differ-ent, so completely upside down, from one day to the next? And how could it happen so quietly? That was the part I could hardly believe—that such a huge change happened—and there was no sound of it. I might lie in bed and hear a thunderstorm make a commotion, roaring and booming all night long. Then I'd get up the next morning and look outside. It would look as if nothing at all had happened. But the snow! It came, and it completely changed everything. And it never made a sound!"

"Sometimes a thunderstorm can change things too," Dorothy said. "Last night …."

"Your world got turned upside down!"

"Yes."

"So will you get married now?"

"I suppose so."

"He didn't ask you yet?" Ella stopped her darning, as if she could not continue such a task until this question was answered.

"No," Dorothy shrugged. "It's odd, I haven't even thought about it. I just assume that he'll ask me. He's very shy."

"Except when the mules are watching."

"Yes," Dorothy rolled her eyes. "When the mules are watching, he's most bold."

"So Dorothy … honey … do you think he's going to be the one you hoped for? … Someone who'll let you be who you want to be?"

"Yes … I do. I believe William wants more than anything that I should be happy. I believe he'll want me to have the life I want."

"You reckon I'll come along with you once you're married?" There was a slight tremor in Ella's hand as she asked this.

"Oh I'm sure of it. My parents wouldn't begrudge me that. I will insist!"

"Where d'you suppose we'll live?"

"We could live in Louisville," Dorothy said. "It's not so far away … it's almost in the North, but it's like being in the South."

"Hmmm. I can't see how your mother would like it if you went to Louisville. And then I'd be far away from all my people. I wouldn't know anybody but you."

"I wouldn't know anybody but you either," Dorothy replied. "But don't you see? That's the fun of it. It's like starting a new life. It's like being a child again … and seeing snow for the first time."

"Well," Ella admitted, "the more North we go, the more snow we'll see."

"And I suppose William will want to bring Cato," Dorothy continued. "Can you picture the four of us, starting a new life in Kentucky? We could breed horses!"

Ella shook her head. "If Cato came with us, it'd make my brother sad. He and Cato are good friends. Come to think of it, I suppose I'd miss ol' grouchy Jimmy, too. But don't tell him I said so."

"Maybe I can bring both of you," Dorothy proffered. "My parents have never discussed any of this with me. I don't know what kind of dowry I should have."

"Don't forget Sammy," Ella reminded her. "Mr. Erast already put him in your care. You got to take him along, don't you?"

"Yes, of course!"

"And if you gonna bring me and Jimmy and Sammy, you better figure to bring that dog along too. Those boys won't go without her."

"Yes … I suppose that, at least, will be a relief to my mother."

"Yes, ma'am, it's going to be quite a honeymoon. You won't need no mules!"

"Really, Ella! He hasn't even asked me to marry him yet."

"He'd better ask you," Ella said. "After what happened last night. Supposing you was to have a baby?"

"A baby?" A look of terror crossed Dorothy's face. "I suppose that could happen. But surely not from just one time."

"From what Wally told me," Ella said, jabbing her needle into a sock. "One time is all it takes. Somehow I have a feeling there's gonna be more than one time before all is said and done."

Over the next five days, Dorothy could think of nothing else. She wondered about a baby. She wondered about getting married. She wanted to discuss all these things with William, but five days passed, and still he did not call. She thought about going to Hickory Grove to call on him. But then it became a matter of curiosity on her part—to see how long he would wait to see her again. She began to wonder if something about their night in the barn had put him off. She was certain it had not. She was convinced she knew his heart. But why would he stay away?

Then her parents returned. The news from the world was awful. Everyone talked of war. Dorothy grew increasingly anxious. Finally, after more than a week had passed without a word from William, she sent Jimmy to Hickory Grove with a note requesting that William come to see her as soon as possible. He sent back a reply saying that he would call on her the following Wednesday afternoon at one o'clock. His behavior was not what Dorothy expected. She could not understand why he'd stayed away during the few days her parents were still in Memphis—and by Wednesday afternoon it would be almost two weeks since she'd seen him. None of it made sense.

She was in an agitated state of mind while she awaited him Wednesday afternoon. Her anger at his absence simmered, but her ill feeling was mixed with alarm. Something must have gone terribly wrong. Again, Ella sat with her in the parlor, once again mending socks by the window. Dorothy sat by the window too this time, holding the now completed nightshirt in her lap. Knowing Dorothy's agitation, Ella said nothing. They sat in silence, listening to the ticking of the grandfather clock ..., which sat in the vestibule like a tapping foot, awaiting William's one o'clock arrival.

At five minutes to one, both women heard the sound of a horse cantering down the Hollands' drive. Dorothy thought it odd that William would ride a horse instead of taking a buggy. She looked out the window. In a matter of seconds, she was able to discern him, sitting on the back of a commanding horse. He wore a uniform, gray with gold trim, and a snug gray wide brim hat. "Look at that," she said, about to laugh at the oddity of his appearance. Then the meaning of it hit her. She dropped the nightshirt on the table. She reached out and grabbed Ella's arm. Ella, too, saw what it meant. "Oh Lord," she said. "Oh, Dorothy!"

Dorothy stood. Instantly there were tears on her face. Ella stood, too, and grabbed her in a hug. "Don't now," she said. "Wait and see. It might not mean anything."

But the meaning was all too apparent. Dorothy knew it all in an instant. In an instant, her dreams slipped away. They were replaced by a horrible reality. Now anger and dread mixed in her like kerosene and fire. She did not know which was more outrageous, that he should choose to go off to war—or that he should do so for the Confederacy. And that he should do any such thing without even discussing it! She looked around the room, wondering if she could run away. She did not know what she could say to him. He who ten days before had entered her like a missing piece of her soul. She blinked her eyes. It was unbelievable. Even with blinking, it was unde-niable. She couldn't think. There was nothing to prepare her for this. Nothing in her entire life had ever caught her so completely off guard. She was lost in uncharted waters. She hardly knew if she could speak at all.

Ella opened the door, and William stood in the doorway. Like a fool, he had a smile on his face. How could he not know? But then he saw. Dorothy did not turn around to approach him. She stood in the parlor by the side window—her back turned against him. He could hear her crying.

"Dorothy," he began. "Are you crying?" He came up behind her. He tried to put his arms around her, but she shrugged him away.

"Don't!" she shouted. "Get away from me!"

"Oh Dorothy," he said. "I just wanted to surprise you. I didn't want to hurt you. I thought you would like to see me in uniform."

She turned, but her face was hard and icy. She peered at him through a wet film that blurred her eyes. "You know that's not true." Her glare seared through the film of tears. "I have nothing to say to you." Her voice was bitter. She spoke with a tone of finality.

"But, Dorothy!" William now realized the full brunt of his miscalculation. And as he digested the bile of her animosity, it poisoned his throat. His heart beat wildly. He felt his arms and legs tremble. Inside, he fought the urge to fall on his knees. Everything about the moment was happening in an opposite way from what he'd imagined. His uniform cinched him like a stiff binding. It demanded that he swallow his emotions. But he could not. His voice cracked. He tried to say something, but only a cracking, whimpering sound came out—as if he were saying her name again.

"Leave," Dorothy said. "Just leave. I have nothing to say to you. Nothing ever again!"

And now a solitary tear leaked from William's left eye, despite all his efforts to fight it back. "Oh God," he cried. "Oh God! I've made a terrible mistake!"

"Yes," Dorothy replied. "You have!"

# 21

# "BECAUSE HE'S MY BROTHER"

"Jesus said, 'You will know the truth, and the truth will make you free.'" Reverend Zeke exhorted. The reverend stood in his accustomed spot in the clearing near Dyer Creek. His handkerchief was held up as the truth. One could see that it was true. But just then, he let it float like a leaf to illustrate what it meant to be free.

There were more slaves than usual at the service. Everyone knew that the war had begun. And there was talk that the war would seal their fate. They might indeed be made free. But at what peril? The seams of the familiar world had begun to come apart. Everyone was uneasy. The white men carried guns at all times. There were rumors that the slaves might be kept home —not even allowed to gather—and the prospect of that had encouraged everyone to gather while they could.

Reverend Zeke had his Bible open. "This passage is from the Gospel of Matthew," he said, and he commenced to read. "Ye have heard that it hath been said, Thou shalt love thy neighbor, and hate thine enemy. But I say unto you, Love your enemies, bless them that curse you, do good to them that hate you, and pray for them which despitefully use you, and perse-cute you." Reverend Zeke closed his book. "Who today is our enemy?" he asked. "Is it the Yankees?"

Many hands went up and many voices shouted, "No."

"Is it the Confederacy?" he asked.

This time there was silence. No one was quite certain what answer Reverend Zeke might favor.

"Is it," he asked again, "the Confederate Army?" He looked around the clearing—noting the heads, which neither shook yes or no. "There are those," he continued, "who have despite-fully used us and persecuted us."

Many heads nodded at this.

"You know who I'm talking about."

Several amens were shouted.

"And those selfsame men have sent their sons into the army to fight. They will fight to keep us as slaves. They will show no love for their enemies."

The reverend paused to ensure that everyone was following his line of reasoning.

"What are we to do?" he asked, and at this, he raised up his handkerchief in such a way as to embody the very question he was asking. "Are we to join this fight?" The handkerchief leaned to the left. "Are we to oppose it?" The handkerchief went now to the right. "Are we to stand by while these Johnny Rebs and these Yankees tear at each others' throats?" The handkerchief went into convulsions with itself. "No," he asserted, and the handkerchief deflated. "There is one thing we can do. We can pray!" He took the handkerchief now and folded it between his folded hands.

"Dear Father, we pray to You to help us find our way. We want to do what is right, Lord—even when right and wrong get all mixed up." Zeke raised his folded hands to his brow. "Help us to know Thy will. Help us to follow Thy word and open our hearts to love. Let us love those who persecute us. Let us also love the enemies of those who persecute us. Let us neither by word nor deed be a party to the hatred we see around us. We are Thy servants, Lord—but servants to no other!"

More amens were heard in response to this last remark.

Zeke continued. "Let us therefore, each of us, hold our hearts in peace, as we pray that the highest good may come— even such good as may come from this terrible war. Let us have faith during these dark nights—faith that the dawn will bring a new day for all who have served Thee—so that we may rise up in that dawn as free and obedient servants of Thy Son. Until then, let us not turn to the ways of hatred. Let us not raise up our arms against any. Let us rather give comfort to each other, to strengthen each other in our patience—for we must wait yet a little longer, for that new day to come."

There was another round of amens. And then, as it appeared that Reverend Zeke had concluded his sermon, there was a general murmuring—as the faithful took up discussions among themselves as to what, in fact, Reverend Zeke had instructed them to do.

Cato sat next to Ella. And as he had a particular reason to want guidance, he turned to Ella for advice.

"William informed me I'm to go with him," he told her, "when he leaves next week for Camp Beauregard as an officer."

"Go with him?" Ella was confused.

"The officers are allowed to bring their personal servants," Cato explained. "He said it would be just for a few months … until the war is over. But I don't think I should go."

Ella said nothing as she considered what to say. Then she said, "Maybe you should ask Reverend Zeke for advice."

"Will you come with me if I ask him?"

Without answering, Ella stood and took his hand. She led

him to the stump where Zeke was conversing with Sara. When Sara had left, Cato explained his situation to the reverend.

"You say he's going next week?" asked Zeke.

"Yes."

"Have you told him you don't want to go?"

"No. I don't know what to do. I've never contradicted his wishes."

"Tell him your feelings. Tell him you will look after his interests here at home until he returns."

"I think he might be afraid to go without me," said Cato.

From this remark, Zeke deduced a quality about Cato he had not previously understood. "Are you willing to go for his sake?" Zeke asked this with gentleness in his eyes. He had seen the light-skinned slave sitting in the clearing on odd Sundays. Zeke never understood why Cato came some weeks, but not others.

"I don't want him to be lonely," Cato said. "I don't want him to be hurt. But I am more afraid for myself. I don't know where they'd take me … if they told me to shoot Yankees; I wouldn't be able to do it."

"Do you think they'd make you fight?" asked Ella.

"I don't know what to expect," Cato said. "I don't want to fight. I don't want to hurt anybody."

"Tell your master how you feel," said Zeke. "You must speak to him of your conscience, of your Christian faith."

"Miss Dorothy might feel better, if you went with him," said Ella. "But I don't think you should go. You got no place fighting. That's the white man's fight!"

"Ella," Zeke turned to her, "Are you talking about your Miss Dorothy?"

"Yes, sir, Reverend … you see, Miss Dorothy and Master William, they … well …." Ella paused, finding herself unsure of how much she should say. "Can I borrow your handkerchief for a minute?"

Reverend Zeke handed her the handkerchief. Ella took it and deftly tied it into a knot.

"They got kind of like this."

"You mean they're married?" asked Zeke.

"Well, not exactly married, but they got kind of tied up anyway."

Cato's eyes went wide. "When did that happen?" he asked. "William never said anything to me. I know they were courting, but you mean they …?"

Ella nodded.

"Well," said Reverend Zeke. "And now he's joined the army!"

"Yes, and Miss Dorothy is none too happy about it," said Ella. "Fact is, when she found out he was fixing to go to war, she told him to leave and never come back. She hasn't spoken to him since … and she won't even speak his name now … but she ain't fooling me. She won't think of anything but him once he's gone."

"I just don't understand why he wants to go and fight," said Cato. "Especially if Miss Dorothy doesn't want him to go. He told me he's got nothing against the Yankees."

"I wouldn't be surprised," said Reverend Zeke, "if his father has something to do with it." Zeke was all too familiar with the philosophy of Augustus Askew.

Upon hearing this, Cato made a strange muffled sound in his throat and looked down at the ground. After a moment, he raised his head. "I think I have to go with him," he said.

"But why?" asked Reverend Zeke.

There was a new intensity in Cato's eyes. "Because he's my brother."

## 2 2

## "SO IT'S A GAME YOU PLAY?"

illiam Askew knew he had little time left at home. He wished he could sit at his father's side and ask for advice. He wanted to speak frankly, to declare his love for Dorothy, to proclaim his intention to marry her. But how could he say it, now that she had spurned him? If he told his father why she had rebuffed him, if he admitted that she was both a Republican and an abolitionist who opposed his going to war, he feared his father would have no sympathy, and might even congratulate him on being well rid of such a lover.

But William's love for Dorothy was so critical to understanding his state of mind that he felt he must declare it. He didn't want his father to be deprived of this insight. Not to know how deeply he was smitten was not to know him at all. He hoped his father could perhaps sympathize with his agitation at Dorothy's repudiation of his love. Surely his father had himself fallen in love with his mother. Surely his father could comprehend that the reasoning of love is sometimes not reasonable. And shouldn't a father see fit to respect a son who has, however unwittingly, placed honor and duty above the longings of his own heart?

William asked himself a great many questions, and gave himself a great many answers, but he longed for a friend to confide in. Such a friend was Daniel Watson. There had been little occasion for them to see each other in recent years, but when William discovered that Daniel was himself in the grip of love—and, moreover, that he was enlisted in the Tennessee Sixth Regiment, they rekindled their friendship. Daniel, too, would be mustered in at Camp Beauregard in three days' time. Since Daniel's parents had perished in a fire, he lived by himself in a small house in Jackson, where he worked at the lumberyard. When the day of their departure had been set, Daniel called upon William at Hickory Grove to plan their journey. He brought a flask of whiskey and a young dog. Since the dog wanted walking and the whiskey wanted drinking, they set out upon a stroll down Christmasville Road to discuss their predicaments.

Daniel was smitten with Dorothy's friend Lena Hopper. Their relationship had not progressed to the degree of intimacy reached by William and Dorothy in the Hollands' barn. But the prospect of such a progression was very much on Daniel's mind. He wondered how, given the forces of propriety, William had achieved such an advancement with Dorothy. William told his friend everything that occurred. He spoke of a warm April evening, of the bouquet of yellow tulips, of his white silk vest, and of the flask of whiskey, which was not unlike the flask the two men now shared. He spoke of Dorothy's satiny dress, of her bare shoulders, of the thunder, and of the swing, which had swung them in a trajectory that led them to the barn just as the rain commenced. He told Daniel of the removal of petticoats. He professed that he had beheld the treasures of the pyramid. He spoke with wistful reverence, and the very act of recounting those moments filled him with yearning.

William's story emboldened Daniel. It was still spring. There was still one more warm evening before their journey to Camp Beauregard. Daniel wondered if there was some counterpart to the swing in Lena's domain, some amusement that could be used to advance his courtship. But before Daniel was able to follow this line of thought too far, William cautioned him as to the risks and consequences of such love. He told Daniel that Dorothy disowned him as soon as she saw him in uniform. Everything William achieved through dint of perseverance ended in a rebuke that stung like a slap. He wondered if Lena too might resent the military obligation Daniel had undertaken. But Daniel already knew this would not be the case. Unlike William, Daniel had told Lena about his intention to enlist before he actually did so.

"I should have done that," William said. "But I had the idea that I would surprise her."

The two men commiserated about their coming fate. Since they would be in the same regiment, they wondered if and how often they would see each other. They speculated about how long the war would last, how long they might be kept away from home. Daniel mentioned that in addition to Lena he had another matter to settle before his coming departure. As he lived alone, he had no one to look after his dog. He did not yet feel sufficiently intimate with Lena to ask her to take the dog. He had no relatives living nearby.

"I don't want to just let him loose in the countryside," said Daniel. "He's not used to fending for himself."

William looked at the dog, who was no longer a puppy, but who still dashed and darted about with puppy-like enthusiasm. "What's his name?"

"Scout."

"I don't suppose you can take him with you in the army," said William.

"No," affirmed Daniel, and he handed William the flask for a drink.

After taking a drink, an idea arose in William's mind. "I suppose," he said, returning the flask to his friend, "that I could ask my father to look after the dog. He's been lonely since my mother died. Since I'll be gone, it might do him good to have a dog to keep him company."

"Your father must be a busy man. Would he have time to take care of Scout?"

"I would hope so," said William. "But if you agree to it, and my father accepts, I'll speak to Henry, who manages the household. If Henry keeps an eye on the dog, you may be certain that the dog will be well cared for."

And so it was agreed, that William would propose to his father that he look after Scout during Daniel's absence—and that Daniel would pursue a farewell rendezvous with Lena, properly prepared with a floral bouquet and a toddy of whiskey. Upon reaching these decisions, they decided that William should bring Scout home right away—so that there might be time to make other arrangements, should Augustus refuse the request.

Thus, William came to the door of his father's study with the about-to-be-homeless dog at his side. As it happened, his father, just then, was pacing about his study, ruminating about how to endear himself to his son. Augustus Askew was most satisfied with his son's decision to join the war, which, from his point of view, was fitting and proper. But as the moment of William's departure approached, the father found himself, as he paced to and fro, contemplating the dangers inherent in war. There began to stir inside him a mixture of fondness and concern for his son. He was well aware that he had been sour and withdrawn since his wife's death—and that his company had been disagreeable. He did not reproach himself for that. Yet now, as the time of separation grew near, he hoped that he would part with his son on an agreeable note, that they might share a few happy moments together.

The timing of William's request, therefore, was fortuitous. Under other circumstances, Augustus Askew might not have considered such a request. But when William entered the study and entreated his father to look after the dog, as a favor to his orphaned comrade in the regiment, and as a favor to himself, the father could hardly refuse. Augustus had never had any thoughts one way or the other about dogs, but he did not see why he could not manage such a thing if he could oblige his son in doing so.

His father's surprisingly cheerful acquiescence to this request encouraged William to try for a further objective. He broached the topic of Dorothy. First, he made certain that his father understood whom he was talking about.

"That Holland girl?" his father asked.

"Yes, father, Dorothy. She was with me at home, of course, when mother died. She's been a great comfort to me since then. I had thought even … well if it weren't for the war, I would have thought it likely that she and I would soon marry."

"I see," said Augustus, who was not at all sure what he thought of the girl in question.

"But she is most distraught about my leaving," William added. "She doesn't think much of the war, you see. Some women are like that I suppose."

His father raised his eyebrows … but in the spirit of endearment, he did not comment on this blasphemy against 'the cause.'

"And truthfully, now that I'm leaving, I think I shall be

rather distraught myself, for I shall miss her … just as I shall miss you."

His father nodded. "Well it shouldn't take our boys too long to rout the Yankees," he said, by way of puffing up his confidence. "You'll have plenty of opportunity to think of marriage when you come home. In the meanwhile, if you like, I can call on George Holland from time to time, to keep abreast of your young lady's situation."

"Yes!" William was surprised by how closely his father's instincts matched his own. "I would like that. But listen, father, she's angry with me now. I did not confide in her about my plans before I sought my commission."

"Women don't like surprises," said Augustus. "Unless they are pleasant ones." Without wishing to, Augustus recalled his wife's dismay when, in their last conversation, she revealed that she was surprised to learn of her husband's filial connection to her son's servant. This train of thought led him to ask, "Has Cato prepared your kit for the journey to Camp Beauregard?"

"Yes, everything is prepared."

"So then, you leave tomorrow?"

"Yes, we'll leave at sunrise."

"I'm proud of you, William."

"Thank you, sir."

"And don't be …," Augustus bit his lip as emotion suddenly welled. "Don't be frightened, son. I know that you'll be …." Despite his efforts, Augustus felt his voice crack as he spoke. "I know you'll be fine." He stepped forward, awkwardly … aware abruptly of the void created by his wife's absence, and of the difficulty of conveying the parental feelings without her help.

Since childhood, William had not been physically touched by his father except through a handshake. Now as his father stepped forward in a way that might be regarded a prelude to an embrace, William felt his face flush. He did not wish to cry in front of his father, but his resolve ruptured as his father's arms fell upon him. He gulped as he tried to speak. "Don't worry," he managed to say. "I'll keep safe."

"Yes, yes, my boy," said the father—and he looked across his son's shoulders through his old damp eyes at the eyes of his new charge, who sat curled and quiet in the corner, watching the scene from a considerate distance. Like a mirror, the dog's eyes looked sad. Augustus did not know what sadness might trouble the dog's heart. But he took the dog's look as one of sympathy. And in that moment he resolved that he would fulfill his commitment to take care of the animal without resentment.

Elsewhere another emotional scene unfolded. Cato had come to the Hollands' farm to say good-bye to Jimmy. Jimmy's reaction to the news that Cato was to leave home and join William in the army was similar to Dorothy's reaction to seeing William in uniform. Jimmy was livid. The idea of any self-respecting slave aiding and abetting the Confederacy was abhorrent—unforgivable. He shouted and railed and stewed over the treachery of it from the moment Cato delivered the news. Gradually, he calmed down sufficiently to give some credence to Cato's claim that there was no choice in the matter —that he had been ordered to go.

"But you could just run away," Jimmy said. "It would be better to do that than to go off to this war."

"I have to go with him," said Cato. "I have to look after him. He's my brother."

"What kind of brother is that?" asked Jimmy. "What kind of man takes his brother as a slave? What kind of man takes his brother into a war? You don't owe him anything!"

"I may not owe him anything," said Cato. "But I'm

worried about him. Though he would never say so, I think he's afraid to go alone."

"What?" This was too much. "He should have thought of that before he joined the damn army. And what about you? Who's going to worry about you?"

"I'm worried about myself," said Cato. "Sometimes I'm afraid."

"Oh, Cato!" Jimmy felt his anger bubble again, but it quickly turned to concern. He managed to keep the concern out of his voice. "What is it you have to do for him? Hold his hat? Drag around his sword? Are you supposed to fight beside him, too?"

"I don't think so," Cato replied. "It doesn't matter, because I won't fight—no matter what happens, I won't fight anybody."

"Damn!" Jimmy saw there was nothing he could do to stop this. "You better stay far away from the fighting. If something should happen to you, I'll come out there and kill that brother of yours myself!"

"Don't worry. I'll keep away from the fighting. I just hope they don't shoot cannons at us."

Jimmy could not bear to speculate on that possibility. "How long are you supposed to stay with him?"

"William thinks the war will take several months."

"But what if it doesn't?" said Jimmy. "Nobody knows how long it will last. If you don't come back here by the end of summer, I'm going to come after you and bring you home myself. You understand?"

Cato thought about this. Indeed, it was true. The war could last a long time, and he did not like the idea of being gone more than a few months. Perhaps a few months would be enough to do his duty by William. "All right," he said. "I'll tell William I don't want to stay with him past October. That should give him time to get used to his situation."

"When are you supposed to leave?"

"Tomorrow. We're going to Camp Beauregard to join the Sixth Regiment."

Jimmy shook his head. "Why don't you run away? I could run away with you. We ought to be fighting with the Yankees!"

"I don't want to fight anyone," said Cato.

"How will I know if you're safe?" Jimmy asked.

"William will write to Dorothy," said Cato. "I'm sure of that. But I don't know if she will read his letters. She's mad at him now."

"She's mad at him?"

"Yes, because he didn't tell her he was going to fight—and she doesn't want him to go."

Jimmy nodded. "She's right to be mad at him. I'll talk to her."

"That's it!" Cato's eyes lit up. "You can tell Dorothy she has to read William's letters. And I can tell William he has to write something about me, because you'll be back home asking Dorothy about me. If he wants her to read his letters, he'll have to write about me. It's a good plan!"

"It's awful," said Jimmy.

"And you must do the same," Cato continued. "You have to ask Dorothy to write about you and Ella in her letters to William. That way I'll know how you are doing too."

"OK" Jimmy acquiesced. "I'll talk to Dorothy."

"I'd best get started," Cato said.

With this, Cato signaled that he was going to leave. Jimmy raced his mind to think of something to say to keep Cato from leaving. But he couldn't think of anything more to add. "It won't be the same around here," he sighed. "Venus will miss you."

"Yeah, well ...." Cato lowered his eyes. He did not think he could look at Jimmy directly. "You take care of her. Tell her I'll be back when the leaves turn colors. We'll go for a walk. She likes the fall, doesn't she?"

"Yeah, she likes it," Jimmy said.

Cato put out his hand to shake good-bye. Jimmy took it, and felt, briefly, that his hand trembled. He wondered if he'd see his friend again. Cato looked up before turning. There was a long, heartfelt look between them, but neither man allowed his worry to be seen—and then Cato turned and walked away.

At sunrise the next morning, Daniel arrived at Hickory Grove to join William and Cato for the journey to Camp Beauregard. Although his weary eyes looked as if he hadn't slept a wink, Daniel's uniform was smart and unwrinkled. He wore a smile on his face, which suggested that his aspirations with Lena had swung in a happy direction. Knowing Daniel's limited skills in matters of laundry, William surmised that Lena had also ironed his uniform.

William, Cato and Daniel were to be transported by Henry to nearby Camp Beauregard in Augustus's brougham. Augustus accompanied the carriage to the gate at Christmasville Road, where he stood with Scout by his side. Scout had been agitated from the moment Daniel arrived. Now the dog paced back and forth between Augustus and the ominous wheels of the brougham. Daniel peered through the window at his dog. It was impossible to explain to his friend what was happening. He thought for a moment that he should climb out and pet Scout one last time, and perhaps whisper something. But in truth—everyone was anxious to accomplish the farewell without delay.

William sat stiffly in his seat, showing no emotion. His uniform, like Daniel's, was freshly laundered. Beside him sat Cato, who wore his finest Sunday outfit. As they drove out the gate, Daniel leaned out the window, removed his hat, swirled it in the air, and yelled a hearty whoop to convey his enthusiasm for their mission.

The brougham set off at a smart gallop down Christmasville Road, whereupon Scout instantly ran after it. Augustus, who had no knowledge of what to do at such a moment, stood watching at the gate. The dog ran after his master for the better part of a mile. But Daniel had retreated into the carriage and did not look back. Daniel did not feel it was bearable to look back at Scout. In time, Scout saw that he could not keep up with the horses. He saw that there was to be no turning back on Daniel's part. At last, the dog slowed down and stopped his pursuit.

He trotted in a circle around the middle of Christmasville Road. He looked at the carriage disappearing in the distance one way ... then back at the man standing at the gate the other way. Then he came again to a stop and fell back on his haunches, waiting for something to show him what to do.

In time, Augustus decided that he should walk down the road and fetch the dog. As he walked, it occurred to him that he could not remember the last time he had walked on Christmasville Road. He was accustomed to riding in his brougham. But the morning was fine and the air smelled sweet. He had his walking stick with him, and he used it now to good advantage as he made his way down the road.

When he approached, he saw that the dog continued to sit on his haunches, panting, looking up and down the road, but without venturing either to run away or come back to him. When Augustus arrived at the dog's side, it occurred to him that he had never before spoken to a dog, and as he considered what to say, it suddenly struck him as foolish to say anything at all. So he said nothing, and attempted instead to indicate by his movements that the dog should follow him.

Scout watched Augustus with great curiosity. But he did not move from his secure spot on the road.

Once again, Augustus made movements and gestures with his walking stick that, to his way of thinking, conveyed a clear meaning that the dog should follow him.

But the dog remained still, feeling his spot on the road to be the only certainty left to him.

Growing impatient, Augustus at last said out loud, "Well I can't carry you. If you're going to come with me, you're going to have to walk."

Scout cocked his head and looked at Augustus as though he were the most baffling figure imaginable.

"Very well then," said Augustus, and he turned and began to walk back toward the entrance to his property. He walked about twenty paces, then paused and looked back. The dog sat still upon the same location. The dog seemed disinclined to move, and stared back at Augustus with questioning eyes.

Augustus shrugged and turned again to continue walking away, determined now to be blithe in his manner, for he was certainly indifferent as to whether the foolish little beast should follow him or not.

But once more after twenty paces, Augustus stopped and turned to look back. The dog still sat on its haunches. But now Augustus pondered if the dog wasn't just as near to him as the last time he'd looked.

Augustus shook his head. Perhaps his eyes played tricks on him. He turned and recommenced his journey. He marched emphatically back toward the Hickory Grove gate. But as he walked, he wondered about his eyesight. He did not know if his judgment of distance could be relied upon. So he could not be sure whether the dog had come closer. Of course, it was of little consequence to him, since he did not really care one way or the other. The dog could sit upon the road for the rest of eternity if that was what the creature wished to do.

Soon his mind was occupied, as he trudged along, with the irregularities of the road and the maneuvering of his stick. Yet again after twenty or so paces, Augustus paused and looked back. The dog remained seated, unmoving on the road, but it had clearly advanced as many paces as Augustus had walked in the interval. Augustus smiled. He knew his depth perception could not be that amiss.

"Ah, so it's a game you play, is it?" said the planter.

Now Augustus resumed walking, but he strode with decided jauntiness in his gait. He walked all the way back to the Hickory Grove gate, determined not to look around until he arrived at that threshold. He was confident of his strategy. He could play a game as well as anyone.

When he arrived at the gate, he turned with a flourish. But the dog was gone. Augustus steadied himself on his feet. He raised his hand to shield the sun from his eyes, so that he might peer down the road with maximum acuity. There was nothing to be seen!—just an empty road inhabited only by occasional swirls of dust. With his hand still shielding his brow, he cranked himself around to scan the road in the other direction. Again nothing. His heart sank. He had been so sure of himself. And now the dog was nowhere to be seen.

Just then, he felt something nip at the back of his leg. He turned round with a start, and there was Scout, looking up at him with an expression that Augustus could only regard as a smile.

"Oh you got me! Yes you got me that time!" he said. And he laughed. And as he laughed, he realized it was the first time he had done so during the entire time that Abraham Lincoln had been president.

23

---

## SAMMY PAINTS

*A*s the summer months of 1861 dragged along, there was little reason for cheer on the Holland farm. Dorothy was out of sorts. Jimmy was sullen. Ella was anxious. Wally was more preoccupied than ever with her wooden bowls. Mrs. Holland was especially cross with her furniture, and Mr. Holland was quiet and withdrawn. The slaves continued their ordinary chores—but everyone had a growing sense that the order of the world was creeping off balance. Only Sammy was cheerful. He continued his routine patrols with Venus, who by now had reached her sixteenth year.

Venus was quite old in dog years, and lately had begun to show signs of enfeeblement. Her back legs were stiff. She groaned audibly whenever she rose up or sat down. But by no means did her troubles cause her to forsake her dedication to Sammy's patrols. Nor did she abandon her mission to remind Jimmy each day of the virtues of play. Since she was sensitive to the state of mind of her family, new challenges betook her. The increasing aura of gloom in her friends obliged her to work harder to cheer them, just at a time when her own grasp on zest was itself in peril. Venus knew nothing of dismay. Discouragement could not get any hold upon her. But in her quest for righteous joy, she had to rely more and more on Sammy, who seemed to be the only human who kept his sights on the goodness of life.

Sammy undertook to advance his painting career by painting the barn. Mr. Holland was more than happy to find that someone among his charges was eager to perform this tedious task. And how well Sammy did it! He proved resourceful in finding clever means of elevating himself to various heights from which he might dispense the paint on ever higher portions of the barn's façade. Then too, increment by increment, Sammy had Walnut pull the buggy wagon around the entire barn. The wagon was outfitted with a chair, a stool, a table, and an old chest of drawers. These objects, including the drawers themselves, in various architectural combinations, furnished Sammy with increasing altitudes from which to carry out his task. As the buggy wagon was drawn into each new position, Sammy wedged logs about the wheels to secure the entire contraption, and then continued his work. Although Venus could not contribute anything directly to the effort, she dutifully followed the platform apparatus as it progressed around the barn, seating herself in propitious positions from which to observe the proceedings, and show her loyal support to her comrade.

It was in view of Venus's dedication to the painting operation that Sammy hit upon the idea of portraying his noble companion for posterity on the back wall of the barn, a vantage point that would reveal his masterpiece only to informed enthusiasts. Toward this end, he made use of several brushes and paints, which Erastus Hicks had left for Sammy's artistic education. Sammy had no actual instruction to guide him, but he was sufficiently filled with creative fire that he was not troubled by mere inexperience. He situated his portrait fairly high up on the wall, just below a shuttered window, which was occasionally used to pitch out hay.

Alas, Sammy's initial rendering of his noble companion was not of the highest caliber. Fortunately, he was well stocked with whitewash, and was thus able to clean the slate and start again. Many aspects of the painting exercise challenged and perplexed him. He stood on the buggy, on a table, on top of two drawers. He frequently stared down at Venus with probing calculation as to her proportions and shape, but he found it difficult to recreate these proportions on the wall of the barn. Her head was too big. Her body was too small. Whitewash after whitewash, he struggled with the ratios. Then there was the further problem of dimensionality. He was not sure how it was that he should make her head look solid or make her tail seem to arch away. Thus, there was a great deal of trial and error, and many rounds of whitewash, before he began to acquire the rudiments of those illusions and deceptions that accomplished painters so effortlessly deploy.

Throughout this process, Venus was most cooperative. Whether it was because she understood the importance of holding still, or because her joints were too stiff to budge, she held steady her faithful countenance, which was interrupted only by the slightest nodding of her head and by the occasional hanging down of her tongue.

It was Sammy's desire that his debut painting should be kept a surprise from everyone around him. He feared that his intentions might be greeted with skepticism and that his failures would be taken as a sign that he should desist. Consequently, no one observed the evolution of his handiwork, from his most primitive initial attempts to his ever more effective renditions. And just as with other transformations that sometimes happen unobserved, like the budding and blossoming of a flower, the startling effect of his efforts was all the more striking.

On a Saturday evening in June, when Jimmy and Ella were done with their day's work, and while the summer sun still amply illuminated his efforts, Sammy marched his brother and sister around to the back of the barn to behold the fruits of his labor.

"What's this?" Ella said. "Is that a horse you painted?"

Sammy's face was immediately crestfallen. But Jimmy deduced his brother's intentions. "No, you fool," said Jimmy to his sister. "That's Venus!"

"Venus!" Ella squinted a bit, and then nodded slowly. "Well I'll be switched." She looked at Sammy, who was now beaming. "Well boy, you did a nice job. That's near about as good a painting as Mr. Erast could do."

This was just the kind of encouragement the young artist needed to hear.

"Yes," said Jimmy. "That's very good. You even got how she hangs her tongue." And in demonstration of this, Jimmy hung his tongue out of his mouth in a goofy gesture designed to make Sammy laugh.

"Ha. Ha. Ha." Sammy did laugh. "Do you like it?"

"It's the best painting ever, little brother," said Jimmy. "I'm proud of you. You did this all by yourself?"

Sammy nodded.

"How come you didn't tell us before?"

"I had to practice," he said candidly. "It took me a lot of times to get it right."

"You mean to say," inquired Ella, "that all these weeks you've been up here behind this barn all day long painting that old dog?" Ella was doubtful as to the consequences of this activity. "Supposing Mrs. Holland was to catch you up here."

"I didn't do it all day long," Sammy protested. "Just some

of the time. Venus would've warned me if anybody came back here."

"I don't think Mrs. Holland has been back of the barn her entire life," observed Jimmy.

"Well you sure got a knack for painting," said Ella. "I bet Mr. Erast would be proud of you."

"Will he come back to visit us?" asked Sammy.

"I don't rightly know," said Ella. "Especially now with the war on; I don't think folks travel about much these days."

As they stood admiring Sammy's work, Venus herself came wobbling around the corner of the barn and sat down next to Jimmy. Jimmy smiled to see the old dog approach. He knelt down beside her, which comforted Venus. She sensed that her meditations with Sammy had broken the gloominess swirling all around the place—and she looked up at the faces of her loved ones, Sammy, Jimmy and Ella—glad of the moment.

"We ought to show this painting to Dorothy," Ella said.

"Yes," Jimmy agreed. "And then she can write about it to William, and he can let Cato know about it too."

Having reached a consensus, Ella was elected to go and fetch Dorothy, which she did straightaway. When Dorothy arrived and saw the painting, she was visibly pleased.

"Oh but that's wonderful, Sammy! Mr. Hicks will be delighted. I must write to him."

Jimmy, seeing his opportunity, spoke up. "Maybe you can write about it to William Askew too. That way he can let Cato know all about it."

Dorothy was aware of Jimmy's friendship with Cato, and was sympathetic to their wish to have some form of communication with each other, which had been privately expressed to her by Ella. But in the four weeks since William had departed, her anger had not diminished. She disdained to hear his name mentioned. It occurred to her, however, that she might send a letter in an envelope addressed to William, but which would in fact contain a letter written exclusively to Cato. Such a gesture would certainly be appreciated by Cato and Jimmy, and would at the same time be pleasingly spiteful.

The next day Dorothy composed two letters, one addressed to Erastus Hicks and the other to Cato. Insofar as regular mail service between the South and the North had been suspended, Dorothy was obliged to post her letter to Mr. Hicks by forwarding it to a private carrier, the American Letter Express Company, which accepted northbound letters at Nashville.

The letter to Mr. Hicks was as follows:

My dear Mr. Hicks,

I am pleased to inform you that your apprentice Samuel has, on his own volition, and with considerable care and practice, completed a painting of our beloved Venus. This portrait was executed on the rear exterior wall of our barn, which Samuel had been commissioned by my father to improve with a new coat of paint. Although the likeness is undeniably raw and naïve, it is nevertheless much better than any of us might have expected.

Needless to say, this delightful accomplishment comes as a pleasant diversion from the general state of doom hereabouts. For reasons that I cannot begin to fathom, William Askew saw fit to become commissioned as a Lieutenant in the Provisional Army of Tennessee, and was four weeks ago mustered into service. I regret to tell you that Mr. Askew has also seen fit to take his servant Cato with him. Southern officers, it seems, feel it necessary to have their slaves traipse around with them while they fight.

I know that you became friends with Cato during your visit here, and I hope that I may be able to write you of his safe return, once this maddening war has been abandoned. I will confess to you that William Askew's decision to fight disappointed me a great deal. I have no sympathy for 'the cause,' and on this point, I seem to be alone in all of Madison County. I had become most particularly fond of William, but his decision to join the fight and take Cato with him was presented to me as a fait accompli. His actions came as a complete repudiation of my beliefs, my principles, and thus of my person. I have, therefore, had no communication with him since he appeared at my door in his uniform.

I know that you join me in my abhorrence of this conflict. I wish indeed that I had someone like you nearby to whom I could speak my heart. I hold you in the highest regard, not only as an artist, but also as a man of principles and great wisdom.

I trust that you are well, and that I may have the favour of seeing you again under better circumstances than the world now provides us. Would you be kind enough to let me have a note in reply? Pray loan me the wisdom of your words in this troubling time.

Believe me to be

My dear Mr. Hicks

Your assured friend,

Dorothy Holland

Holland Farm, Jackson, Tennessee,

Sunday morning, 7th July, 1861

The letter to Cato read thus:

Dear Cato Askew (care of Lt. William Askew, Sixth Regiment),

I am writing to you on behalf of your friends Jimmy, Sammy and Ella here at home. I should hasten to add that I have been particularly requested to report that Sammy has completed a portrait of Venus, which he painted on the wall of our barn these past several weeks. We are all quite proud of this accomplishment. Though she is getting on in years, Sammy has managed to imbue Venus with a most lively look. With respect to the barn, it is the nicest thing to happen there that any of us can remember.

Jimmy has asked me to inform you that he has recently acquired a new outfit for serving dinner in our household on special occasions. He says that you will recall with certain envy that he is notably handsome when so dressed, and to this, I can duly attest. Ella reminds me that you may soon face colder evenings as autumn approaches. Toward that end, she has knit you a pair of warm socks, which I am sending under separate cover.

We are all very proud of your dedication to serving Lieutenant Askew. We trust that he will not lead you into harm's way, and that he will return you as soon as possible to the shelter and safety of home. Perhaps you can prevail upon Lt. Askew to send a note as to your current condition, as such would be most appreciated by those you have left behind.

With best wishes for your health and safety

Most faithful Cato

Your loyal friends,

Dorothy Holland,

on behalf of Jimmy, Ella, Sammy and Venus

Holland Farm, Jackson, Tennessee,

Sunday morning, 7th July, 1861

When William Askew received this second note, he was duly spited. Dorothy's remark about nothing nearly so nice happening in the barn since she didn't know when was not lost upon her lover. And yet, he saw—or rather, he chose to see—something hopeful between the lines. For one thing, she had to some degree broken her silence by writing. She had encouraged him to write in return. And though all her references to him in the letter were cold in tone, they were at least an acknowledgment of his situation. He chose to believe that her wish for the avoidance of harm's way was meant to apply to both himself and Cato.

William read the letter out loud to Cato, who blushed when informed that Ella had knit him a new pair of stockings. Cato asked if he might hold on to the letter as a keepsake.

"But you can't read it," William said.

"Be that as it may," said Cato. "I can remember what it says, so I'd like to keep it."

Cato could, in fact, read the letter—and so he did, a hundred times, while hiding in the outhouse or behind a tree. Like William, he was keen to read between the lines. The lines about Jimmy's new uniform—and how he looked therein—were particularly scrutinized. And in Cato's imagination, the painting of Venus on the side of the barn rose hundreds of feet in the air, and looked every bit as big as the picture of Jefferson Davis that adorned the exterior of the Provisional Army Head-quarters at Union City.

Dorothy's letter to Erastus Hicks also had an effect. Erastus was shocked to learn that Cato and William were traveling with the Army. Erastus had considered joining his fellow Quakers who had volunteered their services as doctors and nurses to treat the wounded. He felt he could serve as a nurse's assistant. He had no medical training, but he had studied anatomy. He wanted to learn onto which field of battle William Askew and Cato would be deployed. He had planned to provide ministration to members of either army who needed care. But he was especially desirous of providing aid and comfort to friends who might need it. In order to learn William and Cato's exact whereabouts, Erastus first needed to know the regiment to which William had been assigned, because Dorothy had not mentioned this detail. Toward that end, and also to respond to Dorothy's clear request for advice, Erastus wrote a reply to Dorothy and posted it straightaway.

William Askew also did not waste any time in writing a reply to Dorothy's letter. His letter read:

Dear Miss Holland,

Although I wish to oblige your request that this letter be limited to information about Cato, I have also taken the liberty, if you will allow it, to enclose an additional letter from me personally, which is on a separate sheet of paper. If you do not wish to read it, you may avoid it by reading only this sheet.

Cato is most grateful to you for your letter. He has taken the letter and carries it with him at all times. He appears to have memorized the letter in its entirety from my single reading of it. As amazing as this seems, I can attest that he can recite any line from the letter at will.

He has asked me to inform you that he is in good health, and that he is most pleased to learn of young Sammy's artistic advancement. He is touched by Ella's thoughtful gift. As with the letter, he is never parted from his socks, and I must confess that I do wish that he washed them more often!

He has also expressly requested that you inform Jimmy that he too is in possession of a new uniform, and that without taking anything away from Jimmy, he feels that his appearance therein is most striking.

As you will no doubt have read, our regiment moved on May 23rd to Union City with 851 strong.

Cato sends his best wishes to you and your family, and hopes that you will enjoy health and safety until we are all returned together.

With gratitude

Dear Miss Holland

Your humble servant,

William Askew

6th Regiment Encampment, Union City, Tennessee, Saturday evening, 13th July, 1861

Dorothy received the set of letters from William before any reply from Erastus Hicks had arrived. Consequently, she had not yet received the benefit of Mr. Hicks's advice when she was faced with the predicament presented by William's two letters. Her first impulse was to tear up William's second letter without reading it. She was annoyed by the very fact that he had contrived to slither past her ill feelings with this device. But a vestige of sentiment compelled her to stash the second letter in the bottom drawer of her bureau, thinking that she would leave it there unread as a testament to her convictions.

In the meantime, she fetched Ella, Sammy and Jimmy and read the letter regarding Cato out loud to them. She skipped the first paragraph and began with the second. After she had read the letter to them several times, and saw that they were well satisfied with it, Dorothy took Ella aside so that she could read the letter's first paragraph to her. She wanted to tell Ella about the second letter so that she might have someone to whom she could express her outrage at William's conniving ways. Dorothy likened the second letter to a Trojan horse. Dorothy explained to Ella exactly what that ancient episode entailed.

Ella, however, was not entirely allied with Dorothy's point of view on this matter. She agreed that it was rather a sneaky thing to do—but then she observed that William must have resorted to this horse trick out of some desperation. She also pointed out that if William had been really as conniving as the ancient Greeks, he would not have warned her of the second letter's contents, or invited her to ignore it if she wished. It was Ella's opinion that so doing was thoughtful of him.

But Dorothy was unmoved. "He only wrote that because he's being cleverly devious. He thinks he can pretend to be thoughtful and that it will fool me."

"Hmmm," said Ella.

"Do you think he's not pretending? You think he's actually being thoughtful?"

"I don't know," admitted Ella. "All I know is, from what you say, those Greek gentlemen didn't give those Trojan gentlemen any warning. They just jumped out of the horse and killed everybody, didn't they?"

"Well, warning or no warning," said Dorothy, "I have no intention of being killed."

And so she left the letter in her bureau drawer, and went to bed that night fretting and wondering about its contents, but not yielding to read it.

# 24

# THE TROJAN HORSE

*A*ugustus Askew did not, at first, realize how much attention a dog like Scout would require. Augustus imagined that he would give the dog a bit of food, pet him every now and again, give him leave to run outside for a while, and that would be that.

But Scout was not one to spend his time in solitude. There was very little satisfaction in solitude, and so Scout was determined to make himself a constant companion to Augustus, who, it was evident, was otherwise completely without companionship.

Augustus had spent his life giving orders, therefore it came easily to him to command Scout to come, or sit, or fetch, or lie down—with august authority in his voice. On this score, Augustus did not disappoint the dog. And on these terms things went well enough between them, as long as the activities were limited to coming, sitting, fetching, and lying down, each of which had been taught to the dog by his recently departed master, Daniel.

However, after a round or two of such elementary activities, Augustus eyed the easy chair in his parlor, then hobbled over to it, and collapsed therein with a great sense of accomplishment. Not so Scout. When Augustus sat in the chair, Scout trotted up beside him and proceeded to nuzzle Augustus's leg with his snout.

"That's enough little dog," said Augustus. "Now it's time to sit and relax."

Scout would hear none of it. He dashed around the chair one or two times, then again, with gentle insistence, nuzzled the man's leg. When nuzzling the man's leg had no effect, he nuzzled the man's foot. When nuzzling the man's foot had no effect, he insinuated himself in between the man's legs, effectively wedging them apart in the process, and jutted his face onto the man's lap. From this vantage point, he stared up into his friend's eyes with an imploring countenance.

"Well, well," said Augustus. "By George, what's the matter with you? Do you have to go out? I don't see why you should. You haven't had a drop to drink these past few hours."

But Scout did not feel that this observation put the matter to rest. He continued to nuzzle and implore—with gradually increasing emphasis.

At last, Augustus was forced to capitulate. "Very well then," he said. And he rose from his chair, got his walking stick, and proceeded to exit the house with the dog dancing at his heels.

Scout was very well pleased with the progression of these events. He strutted around, dashed and feinted, looked up, looked down, and whirled around. He ran out to the edge of the road, then sprinted back, all in the time it took Augustus to walk a few steps. There was no indication that Scout had any intentions regarding urination or other such activities. Indeed, it was evident that his sole purpose in coming outside was to run about. As Augustus gradually surmised this state of affairs, he began to grow impatient with the dog. He did not like to be duped into foolish activities. He turned to go in the house and, with particular emphasis, he loudly commanded Scout to "come."

At this very moment, however, a squirrel came into Scout's purview, and the squirrel had the effrontery to engage itself with the disassembling of a hickory nut, rather than scampering away, as would have been the proper behavior when approached by a larger creature, according to Scout's way of thinking. This outrage was sufficient to compel Scout to chase the squirrel, which he did, and a mighty chase it was. Scout's attention was fully directed on the trespassing squirrel. The territorial adrenalin flowed in his blood. Indeed his pique at the squirrel's impudence so consumed him, that his ears were temporarily out of service. Thus, he did not hear Augustus call "come" and so he did not desist from his chase.

When Augustus saw this disobedience, he was angry. He was not used to being disobeyed—certainly not by one who could only be considered the lowliest of the low. He set out after Scout, waving his stick and shouting epithets at the dog as he approached him. When at last Augustus came upon the dog, who was stranded at the bottom of a tree, up which the hapless squirrel had escaped, he gave the poor creature a mighty whack with his stick. Scout yelped, and instantly cowered. His tail shot down between his legs. His head lowered. Scout deduced that he was guilty of a venal transgression—but he could not, in the flush of so immediate a verdict, calculate what he had done wrong.

Years of mastering disobedient slaves had led Augustus to believe that where one whack was good, two were even better. And so he whacked the dog again. Now, the dog cried out with an even louder yelp, and not just with the physical pain. Scout was mortified to find himself so guilty as to require such measures from his commander. He hung his tail as low as he possibly could. He crept penitently along the ground—looking over his shoulder at the angry eyes of the old man, to whom he endeavored to convey an expression of deepest remorse. But the fire of punishment burned hot in Augustus Askew. He was not one to be scorned by a dog. He whacked the dog again—and this time the dog began to tremble, for he started to fear for his life.

Augustus raised his stick high in the air, taking aim for another whack. Now Scout ran with all his might to escape the impending blow. He dashed away a good twenty feet and stopped. Augustus, having expended all the energy of his displeasure, hobbled back now to the house. When he opened the door, he turned to look at the dog. Once again he spoke in a firm voice, "Come!" The dog scurried up and into the house, running quickly past the legs and stick of the man who stood at the door.

Augustus returned to his easy chair and sat, once more. Now he was upset. What ought to have been a simple enough thing had turned into a great exertion. It had raised his pulse in a poisonous way. He sat and stewed. Scout, keeping a goodly distance away, also sat in abject stillness. And so the two of them sat for the better part of an hour.

Little by little, Augustus's anger wore away. The arms of the chair held him comfortably. Slowly his head leaned sideways, until it came to rest upon the wing of the back. Scout observed these gradual diminutions of Augustus's anger. And after a credible time had passed, Scout ventured noiselessly to relocate himself a small number of feet closer to the chair of Augustus. Then again, after another interval of ten minutes, Scout moved still closer. This process Scout repeated, until he was finally situated at Augustus's feet. By this time, the old man was asleep.

At one moment in his nap, however, the master opened his right eye and spied the dog at his feet. The dog looked up also, as if he were as surprised as Augustus to find himself in such close proximity. Augustus muttered something—a quiet curse on the dog, and then went back to sleep.

It would have been well if Scout had been able to learn the errors of his ways and adjust his actions accordingly. But the earnest creature had not the capacity to do this—and so even as he tried harder and harder to please Augustus, he found himself ever more frequently at the sharp end of the master's stick. Thus in the weeks and months that followed, there was little joy in Scout's life—and Augustus, for his part, came to feel that the trouble of keeping a dog was a constant irritation. Had he not impulsively promised his son to commit himself to caring for the dog, he would have had the creature sent away for good. But as he did not feel he could do this, he continued to dispense punishments to impel the dog's behavior toward a state of absolute obedience.

Throughout his life, Augustus Askew had demanded obedience from those who were beneath him. He had no illusion that in so doing he would in some way acquire love or affection from those who had to obey him. Respect, yes—a certain grudging gratitude for the livelihood he provided, perhaps. But he was used to being alone, aloof, and largely unloved—such was the price of domination. So it was confusing, even disconcerting to Augustus that despite repeated punishments and severe corrections, Scout continued to seek reconciliation. The end point of each reconciliation was an unabashed display of affection from Scout, who, upon regaining proximity, or finding a less hostile mood from Augustus, would lick the old man's hand, or nuzzle his foot, or lie at his feet with a demeanor of loving devotion.

In time, Augustus came to realize that the dog loved him no matter what he did. This realization was unsettling. He had never before considered the possibility of unconditional love, except perhaps as it behooves a mother to love a child. His own mother had loved him well enough. But she was an alcoholic. His mother had been a great disappointment to his father. Augustus had found little comfort in his mother's affection, for he, like his father, judged her harshly. Augustus's wife, Lucille, had loved him—but she too, in the end, was unable to forgive his youthful transgression. Her last words to him had been words of scorn and regret.

Augustus believed that love was nothing more than a bargain, an exchange of good will designed to be a practical aid to coping with the challenges of life. So he regarded these displays of love from Scout as a matter of practicality. He assumed that the creature had made his bargain, just as Augustus had, to make the most of their situation. They had their lots thrown together, and, by George, they would have to make the most of it. So it was that Augustus viewed Scout's love with skepticism. Yet he found the dog's companionship comforting. And in time, he concluded that he may as well treat the dog pleasantly, since he found it quite cordial to have the dog lying at his side, or licking his hand. It occurred to him that he might overlook the dog's behavioral lapses, and treat him as he would someone he cared about—someone, for example, like his absent son. In time, Augustus came to behave in a more kindly manner to Scout. Scout, for his part, was gratified by this transformation. For in his heart he had resolved to give Augustus all that he had to offer.

* * *

ANOTHER CHANGE of heart took place on the Hollands' farm. It happened when Dorothy received her reply from Erastus Hicks, which read thus:

My Dear Miss Holland,

I was dismayed to learn that your friend William Askew and his servant Cato have joined the army. We receive news here in Philadelphia of battles occurring on several fronts. I trust you will be kind enough to write to me with more information about the particular regiment to which your friends have been attached. I will want to keep alert to their progress in our local papers.

I understand how disappointed you must have been by this unfortunate development. If the boys in Tennessee are anything like the ones here in Philadelphia, they all rush off to join the fight with very little forethought. It is, I fear, in the nature of men to be swept up by the general passions that surround them without much thought to the consequences of their actions. The feelings on both sides are quite strong. Men have got their hackles up. Then too, men are wont to put their courage on display—and no doubt, Mr. Askew imagined that he would in no small degree display his courage to you in particular. Clearly, he did not probe the matter sufficiently, or he would have realized—as would anyone who knows you—that you would oppose all elements of this terrible conflict.

Nevertheless, since you ask for my advice, I must not withhold it from you. My advice is that you forgive Mr. Askew. My advice is that you open your heart, that you not judge him too harshly for his decision. I doubt very much that he meant to offend you by his actions. It is not helpful to dwell upon what may or may not have been his motives. It has been my experience that the only way to effect a positive change on those we love is to show them love—most especially when they disappoint or oppose us.

If it is your desire to counter this war, I advise you to write to your friend. Tell him of your feelings. Use the power of your friendship to sway him with your insights. You will not stop him from committing violent acts by turning away from him now. If you love him—and he loves you—you can make a difference.

I know this is not easy advice. But I have seen enough of your heart to hope that you will grasp the truth of what I say. You cannot oppose this war with anger or harsh judgments. You can only do so by increasing your love in proportion to the hate that rises in the world around you. That means you must show love even to those who offend you. All that any human being desires in this life is love.

I also beseech you to undertake this campaign of persuasion for the sake of his servant and brother Cato. You are right to presume that Cato's health and safety are of great concern to me. With your permission, should you inform me of their location, I will also write to them, so that I too may encourage them to reconsider their actions.

Despite all these troubles, I am truly delighted to learn that Samuel has painted a portrait of Venus—especially on such an ambitious scale as the barn wall. You cannot know how deeply this piece of information satisfies me. It is a tonic to my soul.

I shall remain

My dear Miss Holland

Your devoted friend,

Erastus Hicks

West Street, Philadelphia, Pennsylvania,

Sunday evening, 14th July, 1861

When Dorothy read Erastus Hicks's letter, she found she could not disagree with anything the painter wrote. She knew that William had acted impulsively. She knew that he had been swept up by the local fervor, by the prevailing bravado expressed by his friends. She recognized too that one thing she could do in response to her horror at the war would be to convince her lover that he should not participate in it. Having read the painter's advice put forth so plainly, she wondered how she hadn't thought of this herself—for it struck her as thoroughly self-evident, once she had the idea of it in her head.

Being thus moved by Erastus's advice, she decided that she would read William's letter after all. She went to her bedroom, with her heart racing, and pulled out the sheets of paper from the bottom drawer of her bureau.

This is what she read:

My Dearest Dorothy,

I know that what I have done is abhorrent to you. When I did it, I did not well consider how you would feel about the war itself. I only thought about how you would feel about me being an officer. As I have reflected on this, I've realized that I was really thinking about myself and my father. For my father's sake, I wanted to do something that would make him proud of me. I also knew that I would myself be proud to wear an officer's uniform. I have heard it said that pride goeth before destruction. So it was for me. When I realized how deeply I had disappointed you, I fell to the lowest feeling I have ever had in my life.

If there were some way I could undo this—some way to restore your good will—I would do it. I have not been able to hope to do so, for I see that you are tremendously angry with me. Yet, I can hope that if you are even now reading this letter, then perhaps there is some opening in your heart to forgive me. You must realize how much I love you. My only consolation in this desolate predicament is to recall the greatest night of my life, which is one that I know you are well aware of. Even if I shall never be able to restore myself to your favour, I will always cherish those moments when we were able to hold each other in such deep affection.

My regiment will soon be moved to Camp Blythe across the river in New Madrid, Missouri. We will make our winter encampment somewhere near there. We are still training, and as yet we have no word as to when we shall join the fighting. I cannot know what my fate will be. Having no other course of action known to me, I must follow my comrades to battle when the time comes. But I have decided that I will send Cato back home before we move to Camp Blythe. Cato told me that he loves me as a brother. It is only now, as I face the specter of mortality, that I have come to realize the truth of what he has already understood. Our blood unites us more than our race divides us.

My father told me that he may pay a visit to your father. My father promised this because he intended to inquire about your well-being on my behalf. My father is a difficult man, but he is not without merits. I hope that if he should call on your household, you will not regard him unkindlily on account of your grievance with me.

I will confess to you that I am sometimes beset with fear about going into battle. I know I have no right to ask for your comfort—but the one thing that would give me courage when the time comes would be to have a note from you, any kind word that I can carry with me into the coming conflict.

I shall always remain

My beloved Dorothy

Your most devoted admirer,

Lt. William Askew

6th Regiment Encampment, Union City, Tennessee, Saturday evening, 13th July, 1861

Like the Greek gentlemen before him, William penetrated the heart of the citadel. His words were well chosen. Dorothy's heart was conquered.

## "I CANNOT BETRAY MY OATH"

hen word came that the Sixth Regiment would move to winter quarters near New Madrid, Missouri, William asked Captain Henderson for permission to escort his servant Cato back to his father's plantation in Tennessee. He told the captain he had received word from home that his father had developed an urgent need for Cato's services in conjunction with important matters at the plantation. This was not true, but William found it expedient to lie. He could hardly tell Captain Henderson that the Negro Cato was his brother, and that he wished his slave to go home because he had come to the realization, since arriving at the camp, that he did not wish any harm to befall his brother when the time came to join the fighting.

As Cato's presence was entirely optional, the captain granted permission for William to make the journey home, upon the condition that he return in an interval no greater than two days' time. To facilitate this, Captain Henderson provided the travelers with a buckskin nag upon which William and Cato could ride. As Cato had little practice in horse riding, he had to straddle the back end of the horse and grasp tightly onto William, who sat in the saddle and held the reins. It took seven hours to travel from Union City to Hickory Grove. They arrived after sunset. William decided not to take Cato directly home, but rather to take him to the Holland farm. William knew that Cato would certainly want to see Jimmy and Ella, just as he himself quite certainly wished to see Dorothy.

So it was that on a Saturday evening in late July 1861, Lieutenant Askew, in his still unblemished gray uniform, and Cato, who tried to look dignified as he clutched onto William and held onto his duffle, rode up the lane to the Hollands' farm on a pale old horse. No person saw them ride in. But the ever-alert Venus hobbled out from her place of repose in a corner of the yard, whereupon she sounded two friendly barks, both as a greeting to the visitors and as a signal to the house-hold that someone had arrived.

The first to come out was Ella. Upon seeing the two long absent travelers, Ella let out a shout, while at the same time she put her hand up to her mouth to muffle it. Although she had heard a recitation of the contents of William's second letter, and knew that Dorothy had officially forgiven him, she felt it safer to commence the reunion by summoning Jimmy to come and greet Cato. This would give her time to prepare Dorothy.

Jimmy, when he heard Cato's name, ran out from the cabin at full speed. He had just been eating; he had a cloth napkin tied around his neck and a large chunk of cracklin' bread in his hand. Jimmy hugged his friend awkwardly, then broke off a piece of bread to offer him a taste. As he accepted, Cato gestured with his eyes, and Jimmy, seeing the direction indi-cated by Cato's eyebrows, broke off another piece of the bread and asked, in a less enthusiastic manner, if Lieutenant Askew would care for a bite as well.

"No, thank you," William said. "My only desire at this time is to see Miss Holland. Is she, by chance, at home this evening?"

"I'll go and see," said Ella, who knew quite well that Dorothy was inside the house eating dinner with her parents.

Ella rushed to the Hollands' dining room, where with a meaningful look in her eyes, she said, "Miss Dorothy, there's a gentleman here to see you. He's just outside."

"What gentleman?" Henrietta Holland wished to know, presuming to speak on her daughter's behalf.

"It's Mr. William ... I mean ... Lieutenant Askew," said Ella, "and he's brought Mr. Cato back with him, and they're both outside waiting to see Miss Dorothy."

"What!" Dorothy could not believe it. "Outside now?"

"Yes'm."

"Well for heaven's sakes," said Henrietta, "invite Lieutenant Askew into the parlor. We should all like to see him."

To Ella's surprise, Dorothy did not hesitate or deliberate. With no attempt to disguise her feelings, she ran out of the house, leapt directly into William's arms, and in so doing, poked herself on the handle of his sword, which sat sheathed at the side of his gray coat. William, with no less alacrity, kissed her unabashedly on the mouth—while Cato and Ella stared, and Jimmy chomped on the remainder of his cracklin' bread.

In an attempt to recover her dignity after this display, Dorothy said, "Pray come into the parlor Lieutenant Askew, so that my parents may greet you."

"Can't we be alone?" William pleaded. "I have to ride back to the regiment tomorrow. I don't know when I'll see you after tonight."

"Come into the house," Dorothy suggested. "After a few minutes, I may announce that we will go for a walk. Then we can spend some time alone."

Hearing this, Ella turned to Cato. "Why don't you come with us?" she said. "Wally's just fixed supper, but she can fix up some extra food in no time."

So the slaves went off to the quarters, and William and Dorothy climbed the front stairs to the house and entered the parlor. Inside the house, there was much formality. First, there were greetings. Then Mr. Holland inquired about William's health. Then Mr. Holland inquired about William's opinion as to the prospects for the war. After all this was duly discussed, Mrs. Holland let it be known that insofar as she had no fore-knowledge of William's visit, and as they had just finished their evening meal, she had no ready provisions to offer the Lieu-tenant a supper, but if he could but wait half an hour Cora might be able to assemble a suitable repast. William thanked Mrs. Holland, but told her that there was no need to trouble the servants. Far greater than mere appetite, so he declared, was his desire to visit with Miss Holland.

Dorothy took this as her cue. She proposed that they adjourn for a walk to the garden, which they did. With beating hearts, they returned to their bench. But all that they wished to say overwhelmed them, and so they found themselves at first unable to speak.

At last, William tried. "Dorothy. Dorothy." He could hardly get his lips to give utterance to the disarray of his heart. "I'm sorry …."

But before he could finish that word, Dorothy put her hand up to his lips. She said, "It is I who should apologize. I did not even give you the chance to explain."

"My explanation would not have changed your opinion."

"No, not about the war," she agreed. "My opinion about this war will not change. But was that a reason to be fickle in my opinion of you? When I saw what you had done, it fright-ened me. I was frightened for you. I was frightened for me.

What came out of me was anger. It was only later, with time, that I saw my anger might be no more than an expression of fears."

"What I did, I did without thinking of you as I should have. But Dorothy, since then, I have had so much time to consider what I'm about. At the very least, I had to bring Cato back."

"Can you resign?"

William looked gravely at the ground and shook his head. "Last week they shot a fellow from our company for desertion. He was absent from the camp without permission. But he was absent only because he was drunk. He was not disloyal. It did not matter. They gave him no quarter. They shot him."

"This news does nothing for my fears!"

"I'm sorry," said William. "I have thought a great deal about it. But I cannot think of an honorable way to undo what I've done."

"But if you ran away ... if they couldn't find you?"

"I would give up my freedom. I would forever live at peril. I would live all my life in hiding."

"We could go to the North."

"Oh Dorothy," William cried out. "I cannot betray my oath. I cannot become a Yankee. What good is my word? What good would my life be if I did?"

"Then you must find a way to see this through without doing harm to anyone, or letting any harm befall you."

"How can I avoid harm? We are going into harm's way."

"I have written to Mr. Hicks. I will write to him again for advice about what to do."

"What advice can he give?"

"I don't know. But I know of no one else who might think of something wise to suggest."

"Very well, but for now ... Dorothy ... let us pretend for a few hours that none of this has happened. Let us be as we were. I want so much to kiss you."

"We'll say no more about it tonight," Dorothy promised. "I will ask Mr. Hicks to write letters directly to both of us."

Dorothy put her hand on William's leg. He put his hand on hers. From that point on there was no more talking between them.

## 26

# OUT OF HISTORY'S EARSHOT

*J*immy walked on Christmasville Road toward Hickory Grove. He was not aware of anything around him. It was dark. He was out at an hour when he should not have been on the road. But his feet were taking him to see Cato.

When at last he arrived at the back of the Askew home, he had to throw pebbles against the window of the room where Cato slept. The night was still. The pebbles seemed to crash against the window more loudly than they should have. Jimmy held his breath, because he did not want anyone else to see him, and yet his breaths came short and quick. After several volleys of pebbles, Cato came to the window and looked out.

Jimmy looked wild-eyed. He called up, trying to whisper yet shout as best he could. "I've got to talk to you. Something's happened."

In two minutes, Cato came down from his room. He tiptoed out the side door of the house. He found Jimmy standing with his head hung down. "Come on," Cato said.

"Let's go back behind the smokehouse. There's a woodpile back there. I can chop some wood. You can sit and talk to me."

"I ain't supposed to be out here after dark." Jimmy's voice was barely audible. "But I had to come and see you."

"If anyone comes," Cato reasoned, "you can hide, and I can say that I couldn't sleep, that I decided to get up and chop some wood."

They stumbled in the dark toward the smokehouse. A thick crescent moon lit up the sky, but trees along the path blocked the moonlight. They made their way to the woodpile at the back. There the unobstructed moon rays cast a glow on the logs, and the murmur of crickets surrounded them.

After looking about to be sure no one was nearby, Cato crept up to an oddly shaped rock in the corner of the woodpile. He lifted it and retrieved something hidden beneath it. "This is the key to the tool shed," he said. "In the old days, Henry kept the key in his pocket all the time. Then he'd give it to me whenever he'd want me to chop some wood. But one day the key fell out of a hole in his pocket. We spent the whole day looking for it. Ever since then he's kept the key hidden under this rock, 'cause that way he knows he won't ever lose it."

Cato walked to the tool shed, at the back of the smoke-house, opened the padlock, stepped in, and quickly came back out with a large wood ax. Even in the moonlight, Cato could read the emotion in Jimmy's eyes. "What's wrong?" he asked.

Jimmy plunked down on a log, propped his hands below his ears, and hung his head. Cato stood holding the ax, as if he might actually chop some wood.

"It's Venus," Jimmy said to the ground, "she's gone."

"She ran off?"

"No, she ...." Jimmy closed his eyes. "She's dead." He sat still, saying nothing. He kicked his foot at the dirt in front of him. He squirmed around on the log, then lifted his head, opened his eyes, and looked off to the side. A glint of moisture showed at the edge of his eyes in the moonlight. "She was feeling bad all day," he began. "And I tried to help her out. She had to shit real bad—but she couldn't get her legs to work right. So I held her, you know. I held her up so's she could shit. But she looked miserable. She couldn't get nothing to come out. So then, I just sat with her. I sat with her for, I don't know, hours ... till I fell asleep. Then when I woke up, she was lying there next to me. I touched her and she felt cold. And she was ... dead."

Cato held the ax handle in front of him, as if he were pointing at something on the ground. "She had a long life," he said.

"Yeah."

"She was a fine dog."

"Yeah. She was."

Cato looked at Jimmy's face. He saw the muscles of Jimmy's forehead crease, as he tried to control his expression. The sound of the crickets pulsed, rising and falling. The smell of the spruce trees behind them perfumed the air.

"I just wish I could have done something for her," Jimmy said. "She looked so miserable. And I didn't know what to do."

"Wasn't nothing you could do," Cato said.

"I tried to hold her up, so she could shit. But she looked at me, Cato, and she knew it was no good. I think she didn't want to try any more. I think she just wanted to be done with it, because you know when you can't shit, when you can't even do that, what point is there anymore?"

Cato nodded, holding the ax now like it was a baby in his arms. He didn't know what to say. So he said, "Venus loved you. I'm sure that when she knew she had to go, she wanted you to be with her."

"I fell asleep," Jimmy said. "I sat for hours, Cato—and then I don't know why I did, but I fell asleep."

"She knew you were with her. That's how I'd want to go too. Knowing you were right there beside me."

An owl hooted in the distance. A cloud drifted across the moonlit sky, and swept its shadow swiftly across the woodpile. Jimmy's face screwed up like a squeezed mop. "Damn," he said. "Damn, damn, damn. The only damn thing in the world I love so much and ...." He stopped speaking. He looked up at the sky, as if he were looking for a sign from heaven to answer him. He sucked his breath in hard, then heaved it all out in an uncontrolled moaning sigh. "Venus," he said. His voice cracked. Tears, suddenly, streamed down his face.

Cato couldn't bear it. He threw down the wood ax, leapt over to Jimmy and threw his arms around him. "Oh Jimmy ... I'm sorry ... I know you loved her."

"She was the only one in the world I always knew I could count on—the only one who I knew loved me," he said.

"That's not true," Cato said. "You know I love you, don't you?"

"Yeah."

"I do," Cato implored. "I love you, just like Venus."

"You've been good, Cato. You've been a good friend."

"I'm more than a friend," Cato said. "I mean it. I love you."

"Yeah?" Jimmy, overwrought, wild-eyed, looked back into Cato's eyes, trying to make sense of his words. But Cato brushed Jimmy's hair with his hand. He squeezed the back of Jimmy's neck.

"I love you," Cato said again. "Just like Venus."

Jimmy looked at him with bewilderment. He felt as if a fountain of emotion must be streaming out of him. He wanted to let everything go, to succumb, to let himself cry in a way that he had not done for many years. "Just hold me," he whispered.

Cato sat down on the log next to Jimmy. He put his arm around Jimmy's back and hugged him. He leaned his head onto Jimmy's shoulder. Jimmy sat still, breathing roughly. Tears fell without restraint from his eyes. They felt like wet waves of anguish, washing down his cheeks. And in that anguish, he felt the comfort of Cato's embrace. He stared at his lap, and at Cato's lap—not really seeing anything—just visually aware of their proximity; of the solace that it gave him to see that he was not alone. And as he stared, he put his hand onto Cato's leg and squeezed it. His mind filled with images of Venus, of that awful, helpless expression when she knew it was all over. He realized in that instant that he had never before let anyone see him cry. And here he was, sitting on a log next to Cato, crying freely, and it was all right. It was a surprise to him that it could be this way, that his friend could be so comforting, that Cato could give him the freedom to cry and not feel any embarrassment. He watched the unfolding of it, as Cato, also, placed a hand on his leg, and gently squeezed it.

Jimmy had not expected to feel this way. Venus was only a dog, after all. He had loved her as a dog. He knew that she was old. He knew she would someday die. But something in the way it had transpired had raised such an awful feeling inside him. There was something beautiful and tragic in the looks of helplessness and regret that passed between them. There was something profoundly intimate that arose from their inability to speak or communicate except by looking into each other's eyes. He had looked into the old dog's eyes and realized that this creature was the one thing he loved without complication or doubt. And he had seen from how the dog looked at him, that she too loved him with a certainty that seemed ancient, as if they had always known each other and had always felt a deep and abiding bond.

The tears in Jimmy's eyes glazed his vision. His vision was blurred and unfocused, but still he felt something catch his eye, so he tilted his head to adjust his sightline. He looked at Cato's lap, at the folds of brown cloth in Cato's trousers, where they bunched up between his legs. Emotion had carried Jimmy into an altered space. He no longer had any control of his mind— nor did he care to. Everything that might normally demand that he think clearly had been subverted. He was in a place where there no longer was any order or logic, only feelings that were so intense that they seemed more than he could bear. He tried to put his mind onto something else. He was staring at the folds in Cato's trousers, and he pushed his mind to think about Cato.

It was strange to think of Cato's body beneath those clothes. And as he stared, with a distracted sense of curiosity, he wondered how pale Cato was down there. Once, on a hot summer day, Cato took off his shirt, and it surprised Jimmy, then, to see the delicate hairs on Cato's chest, and the contrast of the dark brown of Cato's nipples against his skin. His own body seemed like just one big run of slick darkness, but Cato was a study in contrasts. Cato's lips, his nipples, his eyebrows, his hair, all were a dark brown pigment set against the paleness of his butter brown skin. It was odd to wonder, but here he was staring and wondering what exact colors Cato might have between his legs, and what the color of his hair might be down there.

And as he stared he could feel Cato's hands squeeze his leg, and he thought he saw something stir in Cato's lap—a quiver or twitch of the cloth in Cato's pants, as if something had pulsed in the folds. His mind raced, for he had never in his life let himself be roiled so completely and uncontrollably by the thoughts that began to bubble up within him. He felt as if a vast store of steam had built up inside him, and it hissed now and pushed against him on his insides. All his attention focused itself on the feeling of Cato's hand as it squeezed his leg. And he realized that his hand too squeezed back on Cato's leg. He smelled the scent of Cato's hair, moist with a smell of some sweet herb, which pressed against his neck. Cato's damp, delicate hair, which felt so unlike his own, nuzzled against his skin, like soft fur.

And he saw, from the corner of his eyes, his own lap, with his trousers folded and bunched between his legs. And he felt, to his amazement, the first glimmerings of something—the first small pulse of swelling up in his groin, and he was shocked by the unexpected twitch of it. He heard his breaths grow short —and all at once, he was aware how silent Cato was—and that Cato too was breathing hard and short, and that neither of them spoke or looked at each other. He knew that they were staring at each other sideways, as if they didn't want to look. He knew that they were staring at each other's laps.

And he realized now that something was happening there, in Cato's lap, that the small creases and folds in the cloth had moved, ever so subtly, the fabric had lifted, he was sure of it. And again, there was a slight but unmistakable twitch—and the very sight of it, which registered in his right eye, made him feel a resonant swelling in himself. And he saw that there had been a lift in the folds of fabric in his own crotch. He held his breath—for the reality of what was happening filled him with fear and desire. He could not guess what Cato was thinking. It was too strange, and the grief he felt, his sense that the world had been turned upside down, catapulted him into an unfamiliar openness, one that he had never imagined. He recalled Cato's declaration of love, and all the while, he watched the undeniable physical phenomenon of the rising bulge of cloth between Cato's legs. And with a sudden rush of impulse, Jimmy put his hand down on the side of the log and leaned back. He leaned his long body back, and spread his legs until his right leg pressed against Cato's leg. And as he leaned back, he let himself go fully erect, so that Cato could see unequivocally the ballooning tent of fabric stretch up like a pole from his crotch.

Cato gasped and, without speaking, put his hand onto Jimmy's crotch and squeezed it. And the feeling of Cato's hand squeezing there made Jimmy moan, "Oh, Jesus!"

With his free hand, Cato grabbed at Jimmy's head, and pulled his ear toward him. He leaned his mouth up to Jimmy's ear—as he squeezed and stroked on the fabric covering the stiff flesh between Jimmy's legs. "Pretend I'm a woman," Cato whispered. "I want you to love me like that."

And as he spoke, Cato's fingers fumbled onto Jimmy's pants, trying to pull on the cord of rope that held them together. Jimmy, with his mouth open, and his head tilted back, lifted himself up on the log with one hand, then grabbed at the rope on his waist with the other. He quickly untied his pants as he arched his body up off the log. In one swift stroke, he pulled his pants down to his knees, and the length of his penis sprang up—as if he had never before been so full of desire. He stared into the heavens where he tried to see himself looking back down on the scene that was now unfolding. He felt he could see for the first time what had always been hidden. He refocused onto the twinkling stars, which swirled on an axis, in synch with the swaying of his head. He closed his eyes and a vision came into his mind of the chestnut hairs and brown nipples on Cato's chest. He opened his eyes and turned to look at his friend. "Take off your shirt," he said.

Instantly Cato stood, and frantically pulled off his shirt. He turned to face Jimmy. He, paused only for a moment, then undid his pants. He let them fall to the ground around his feet, and his own erection sprang free in the cool evening air. He stood and quivered, aware that he was naked in front of Jimmy's eyes. Jimmy saw now the darkish field of Cato's pubic hair. And he saw too that the color of Cato's penis matched the color of his nipples. And he saw that all the darkish colored things on Cato's body, his hair, his lips, his nipples, his penis, were stiff and tumescent and stretched taut. Jimmy looked with amazement at the erect points of Cato's nipples. He raised his hand toward them in a beckoning gesture.

Cato crouched down, and, without hesitation, put his mouth between Jimmy's legs. "Oh, Jesus," Jimmy said again.

Jimmy felt the blood pour from all parts of his body into that point of contact with Cato's mouth. His hand reached out, groping, until it found the smooth round curves of Cato's chest. His fingers brushed against the stiffened nipple, which he squeezed hard. Then as if an alarm had gone off, Cato yanked his head up from Jimmy's lap, pulled on Jimmy's body, pulled him down off the log and onto the ground alongside him, until they lay pressed together on the wood chips and the grass. "I want you," Cato said. "I want you to do something." And he took Jimmy's hand and guided it down, around, and behind him. "Do me here," he said.

Jimmy felt around to the plump mounds of Cato's backside. He pictured the muscled ass cheeks in his mind. He could imagine the dark center, the beckoning hole with the chestnut hairs nestled around it, against which his finger brushed. In a single move, Jimmy rolled Cato onto his back. He lifted Cato's legs up, and spread them apart like the wings of a bird. He reached down to the exposed passageway and felt with his fingers for the opening. He globbed a wad of spittle onto his hand, and smeared it on his dick.

"Do it," Cato said, rolling his eyes. "Go ahead."

Jimmy pushed his erection in past the initial resistance, until something abruptly loosened and he slid, with a sudden, exhilarating thrust, three more inches inside. And as he did so Cato's moans, which began low and deep, grew higher and louder. Then all at once, Jimmy pushed in as far as he could, and stopped. He looked down into the eyes of his friend. The tears had dried on his own cheeks, but he saw that tears had formed at the corners of Cato's eyes.

"I love you," Cato said.

"Yes," Jimmy said. "I know it." He began to thrust again, in measured, forceful strokes.

"Do it. Do it. Do it." Cato said, with rising urgency. "I want you. Oh God, I want you to fuck …." There, he said it. "Fuck me, like I was your woman."

"I am," Jimmy said. "I am fucking you, brother." He looked at Cato's wide eyes, brown centers burning in their egg white sockets. "I'm loving you sweet friend." He looked at the half smile of Cato's mouth, at the way his nostrils flared. "I'm loving you because I will always do for you. I will do for you now and forever." He looked at the soft, silky curls of Cato's hair, amazed, as he had always been, at the rich soft texture. "I'm fucking you because you are so all to pieces handsome, Cato. You are beautiful."

"Ever since I first saw you," Cato said. "Since that first day on the road, when you were throwing rocks at a tree, I wanted you—but I couldn't say it. I couldn't say it to you or to anyone. But you are the only one I've ever wanted." He gasped for breath, his eyes darting wildly. "I have been dreaming of you. I know it isn't right. But I can't help it. I have been dreaming of you—of being with you like this. When I look in your eyes, I see all that I want—all that I want."

Sweat poured off their bodies as the glistening coal black of Jimmy's skin and the glazed creamy brown of Cato's skin wove into an intricate knot of contrasting legs and arms and torsos. Jimmy's nostrils pulsed open, and as he snorted for air, he lowered his head toward Cato's, where in a sudden, unstoppable impulse, he kissed Cato full on the lips. And as he did so, he felt Cato's tongue press against his mouth. He opened his mouth, and instantly Cato's tongue pushed inside. It was too much. The warm salty taste of the half-white man's tongue filled his mouth. "Oh Jesus," Jimmy said. "I'm gonna shoot it."

And even as Jimmy spoke, the view of these events had already begun to recede from history's memory, until it was less and less possible to behold the two slave men roll over a full turn as they climaxed, spurting into and onto each other, each convulsing as the waves of orgasm gushed out of their bodies, while incoherent sounds leapt from their throats. They could hardly understand what they were feeling—for neither of them had ever had sex before, nor had they imagined how it might be. They felt as if they were lost in space, clutching each other as tightly as they could, as if they were a single object orbiting the heavens. And in that moment they fell into a gaping hole, out of history's earshot, into the reaches of time and space where all the things that are thought never to have occurred are buried, until that day when the unimagined truth finds its way out of the not being, rends the veil of denial, and says, "I too. I, too, was love."

285

# 27

## LOYAL TO EACH OTHER

*A*t the Holland farm, there was collective sadness at the death of Venus. Ella and Dorothy sat together with long faces. They spoke of how sorry they were that the family's loyal companion was gone. Sammy, who throughout his life had striven to bring cheer into every situation—no matter how trying—could not hold up his head when he learned that his faithful guide was gone. Instead, the reach and extent of his lifelong happiness now became, like the recoil of a rifle, the reach and extent of his sadness. As he had done when he first arrived at the Hollands' farm, he became mute. He performed his duties in silence, with merely mechanical animation. When he had time to himself, he retreated to a spot behind the barn, where he sat with his back to the picture he had painted. This was his gesture of mourning. He placed himself in proximity to that which he had lost, but he could not bear to look at it.

Since no one else had the strength to do so, Wally buried Venus in the spot behind the barn, where the painting on the wall had become the chief monument to the feeling the yellow dog had evoked in all who knew her. Even Mrs. Holland remarked that she missed the old mongrel, recalling how the dog had been ever attentive to her presence.

On the night after Venus's burial, the slaves joined together in the yard to build a fire. In due time, all the members of the Holland household, slave and master alike, gathered round the fire.

"We have lost a special friend," Dorothy said. "Right to the end she showed us how to live fully in this world."

Jimmy, like Sammy, was unable to speak. The two brothers sat side by side and stared into the fire. Without taking his eyes off the fire, Sammy put out his hand to take hold of that of his older brother. Even in this gesture, he did not forsake his mechanical muteness.

After a long hush, Willis, without the aid of whiskey or the strums of the banjo, began to hum a spiritual melody. Willis hummed the tune slowly, tenderly, with reverence. When he had finished, he sat back and folded his arms.

Ella stood to say a word of eulogy. "I think that I knew Venus all of my life," she said. "I can't even remember what it was like before she was here. She was ever someone among us who always liked everybody. She liked folks, and folks could see that she liked them. She made us all feel good."

Juba Jake stood up next. "It don't seem fair," he said, "that a dog should live so short a time. I've lived long enough for five dog lifetimes, and I have seen great changes in the world. This life is full of trials and tribulation, but that dog had a happy spirit that sometimes lightened my burdens. I pray that she is now in a better place, and that she has gone to the angels up in heaven."

George Holland felt moved to say something, to console the members of his household. "I recall when Venus was a puppy," he said. "I brought her home from the Dobsons' house, where she was one of a litter of five. As it turned out, she was the only one of that litter who lived a long and devoted life. When Venus was a pup, she was frisky. She was not trained to be in the house. So I asked Wally to keep her, and to let the children play with her. In time, the dog moved freely among us all. As others have said, she had a happy spirit, and she brought pleasant moments to our whole household. I know that if she were among us now, her tail would wag and her eyes would be bright."

"Yes," said Dorothy. "She would not want us to grieve her loss, but to wag our own tails, so to speak—for life is a precious gift, is it not? And we must honor that gift by our own good deeds."

There was a round of amens at this.

Then Mrs. Holland, feeling moved by an impulse that was not at all familiar to her, stepped up to speak. "I never realized," she said, "how much that dog meant to everyone. I don't know what the world is coming to now, with the war upon us. But it's good for us to be like the dog, loyal to each other." With this, Mrs. Holland walked over to Sammy and extended her hand down to him. The entire assembly was stunned by this. Seeing the object of all his campaigns of invisibility looming above him, Sammy rose to his feet. He took Mrs. Holland's hand, but still he did not speak. She pulled the boy ever so slightly toward her, then, looking around in embarrassment, she quietly walked away.

And so it was that in her death Venus drew the Holland household closer together, at a time when the world around them was splitting apart. The inhabitants of the region, who grew ever more watchful for the coming conflict, felt a great deal of apprehension. That gathering menace made other grievances seem petty. And so for a time, each person in the household fell upon a new sense of belonging with each other.

Lieutenant William Askew went back to New Madrid with

a changed heart. The knowledge that Dorothy still loved him had bucked him up. But he did not know how he would honor his promise to do no harm. Nor did he feel that he could speak in confidence to anyone in his company about his dilemma. He waited for the letter to come from Erastus Hicks. He hoped that in it he would find some illuminating pronouncement that could set everything aright.

He spoke sometimes to Daniel Watson, who was a private among his company. He told Daniel how things were back home, that he and Dorothy had been reunited, that Dorothy had given him a message from Lena, declaring that she faithfully awaited Daniel's return, that Scout was doing fine, and that his father had grown fond of the dog. When they had moments off duty, the two friends sat and wistfully spoke of home. They did not talk about the future, except insofar as it might one day bring them back to those they loved.

Cato, now that he was home, spent as much time reading as he could. Inasmuch as he and Jimmy had discovered their mutual desire, he now lived in a state of rapture. He combed the Askew library for romantic titles. He scanned poems and novels, looking for words that reflected back to him the passion that filled him. He kept books under his mattress. He read late into the night by candlelight. Since the death of Mrs. Askew, he no longer even bothered to replace the books he removed from the library with stand ins, so confident was he that Augustus did not ever look at the library's contents.

At every possible opportunity, Cato and Jimmy stole away to the woods to continue their erotic adventures. What had at first been surprising and strange became, with time, more familiar. And with that familiarity, a new feeling arose between them. They were bound not only by their affection for each other, but also by its taboo. Like William, they had no one to whom they could turn, no one with whom they might talk, no one with whom they could speak of their great new thoughts, no one to whom they dared explain how thoroughly life had changed. This isolation became itself an aspect of their shared experience.

In this secrecy, there was a measure of joy. They soon discovered that neither of them felt guilt or regret, though they both knew that others would be shocked by their actions. For Jimmy, the unorthodox character of his sexual desire bound him more fully to the rebellious spirit that he had cultivated all of his life. The world, he felt, was in so many respects wrongly constructed that he did not care what those who had constructed such a world might think about his behavior. Then, too, a primal mystery had been revealed. He had at last discovered an aspect of his being that stood apart from all those circumstances of his life that were patently unjust. For the first time he could imagine that life might be a worthwhile experience. Against all his expectations, he was in love. He was amazed and awed to find that this love was returned.

Cato, too, was astonished to find that his secret dream had solidified into form. Each morning he shook himself. He had to remind himself that it was true, that it had happened, that God had given him the thing he most wanted. In the beginning, he feared that it might be a fluke brought on by grief and bereavement, or that at any moment a moral force would arise and wrench them away from each other. But with each covert encounter, the two men fell into each other's arms with steady affection. They were confounded by the unprecedented nature of their feelings. They could find no language in which to talk about their relationship, except to express their affection in an erotic vocabulary. Kissing became the parlance with which they articulated their secret yoke. When they were hidden away alone, they kissed and kissed until the need to breathe forced them to pause, and they fell back gulping.

"You amaze me," Jimmy said. "I never knew how you felt. Or maybe I always knew, but how could I?"

Cato laid his head onto Jimmy's chest. He stared into Jimmy's eyes. "How could anyone know," he said. "I didn't know something like this was possible for you and me."

Jimmy looked into his lover's eyes. He recalled the first time he had seen Cato. His first impression had been that Cato was white. It amused him now to remember it. Jimmy could not deny that Cato's difference was an ingredient of his attraction. All the things about Cato that were unlike the ways and manners of the other slaves intrigued him. He was mesmerized by that seductive gilding in Cato's body that had come from his father's blood, like a fragrant flower grown from a poisonous seed. And yet, despite Cato's Caucasian taint, Jimmy felt a deep connection to him. He believed that a shared spirit bound this other man's soul to his, that there was between them an odd sameness that had poured itself into their different containers.

Cato, for his part, was attracted to Jimmy's darkness. His love for Jimmy was his reproach against his father's never tendered love, while at the same time a conduit to the mother he had never known, but whose blood legally defined him. Cato had been made to feel defiled by his white blood. Was it surprising that he yearned for Jimmy? Jimmy replaced both his lost mother and his father. When Jimmy was inside him, he thought every ache he had ever known was healed.

During this time, Sammy continued to be mute, speaking only when no other means of signaling or conveying could be employed to accomplish the necessities of life. If a member of the family tried to comfort him, he nodded his head, but he did not abandon his far off look. Recalling how Sammy had been when he arrived years before, Wally counseled her family to have patience, to give the boy time, believing he would again someday find that core of happiness that had manifested itself so resolutely in the intervening years.

Even though the world had begun to slip into the shadow of war, Dorothy continued her social life as best she could. She attended a party at Edna Dobson's house, which was notable primarily for its lack of males. Nearly all the eligible men of Madison County had joined the army. So when the women gathered to celebrate Edna's birthday, they were dismayed to discover that Lena's brother Walter Hopper appeared to be the only unmarried young man left in town. Walter was a lively fellow, friendly with all the women, but not friendly in an intentionally alluring way to any of them. He was most interested in topics that the women regarded as subjects of interest mainly to themselves: discussions of fashion, etiquette, and the arrangement of social occasions. Walter could be relied upon for an astute judgment as to whether the bodice should be a fitted or "V" bodice or a fan-front or "Y" bodice, or perhaps a gathered or "O" bodice, in relationship to whether the hair was worn confined to the nape of the neck, or with all-over ringlets. Much depended, in Walter's opinion, on how much of the ear was showing. Walter did not condone the gathered bodice on any account unless the wearer had attained at least 40 years of age. He had strong opinions, and his special guidance was sought by many of the women at Edna Dobson's party.

Dorothy, however, was only reminded of how little interest she had in the banalities of fashion. Although she attended the party wearing the requisite full length skirt, she made the mistake of wearing the shiny shoes that Ella was so fond of, but which had lately not fit so well. Consequently, the two-mile walk to and from Edna Dobson's house left her feet in a sorry state. When she returned home, Dorothy complained of this to Ella, whom she held responsible for liking the shiny shoes. Ella offered to rub her feet—to which Dorothy readily agreed.

The two women sat in Dorothy's bedroom. Dorothy was in a chair with her leg extended onto a footstool, while Ella sat on another footstool and rubbed Dorothy's foot. Dorothy described the party and remarked upon the fact that nearly all the young men in the community were now absent.

Then Dorothy corrected herself. "Well, all the white men, anyway. They've all gone except Walter Hopper. At least your women have all your men about you."

Ella harrumphed at this.

"Well, really, Ella—you never talk about any man that you like. Aren't you ever going to fall in love?"

Ella harrumphed at this also.

"You act like such a thing is out of the question," Dorothy said.

Ella believed that such a thing probably was out of the question, but as she sat rubbing Dorothy's foot, she felt that she hardly could speak frankly about this topic. "I don't need nobody else to take care of," she said. "I got my hands full with you."

"Oh really, Ella, you're so grouchy about this subject. Don't you ever yearn for that kind of intimacy?" Dorothy leaned back in the chair. The foot rubbing put her in a state of great relaxation.

"I'm serious," Ella said. "I don't need anyone besides Wally, Jimmy, Sammy and you. And you know me better than anyone else."

"Do I?"

"You know you do. Who else have I spent my life talking to and listening to?"

"It's not just because you have to, is it?"

This question, in its awkward candor, surprised Ella. "No,"

she said. "I suppose I have to carry on with the rest of your family. But it's different with you."

"Oh Ella," said Dorothy, feeling a burst of fondness for her friend. "I don't know why I should deserve your affection."

"The way I see it," said Ella. "I see myself from a different angle when I'm with you. What you say, how you act, what you do—it's like what I would do if I were a white lady."

"I don't doubt that I would want to be like you if I were a Negro lady," Dorothy said.

Ella began, almost as a reflex, to harrumph at this—but she stopped herself. She looked up into Dorothy's eyes—and for a few moments the two women stared openly—with a look of affection, but also trying to decipher the unspoken.

"If you were rich and white and spoiled and married to a planter, perhaps you'd be like Mrs. Greer," Dorothy teased.

"If I was ever anything like Mrs. Greer," said Ella, "I'd hope you'd shoot me right quick."

"You are my best friend, you know."

Ella nodded.

"I wish we hadn't ended up in this position with each other," Dorothy said. "I hate the way things are in this world."

"Things are bad for most slaves," Ella said. "At least for me, I'm stuck with someone I like." Ella stopped rubbing Dorothy's left foot, and turned her attention to the right foot. She attacked that foot with a salvo of deep kneading. Dorothy instantly closed her eyes. The sensation, the sensual pleasure, made conversation seem like too much of a distraction. "I know you like Lieutenant Askew that way," Ella continued. "But I'm not like that. I think what I most like in this world is buttered corn."

Dorothy chuckled.

"And I like knowing I can make a fool of myself in front of my kin folk. When we had that party the other night, I wondered if it might not be the best moment of my life. When I got done dancing, I lay on the ground and looked up at the stars. I watched you dancing." Then after a long pause, Ella added. "I see how beautiful you are." She paused again. "I mean … whereas, I'm just …."

Dorothy opened her eyes and leaned forward. "Oh but Ella …" She reached out to Ella's arm, pulled her up close, and wiped her hand on Ella's brow. "Now look here, you sit in the chair. You sit here and let me rub your feet."

"No."

"Yes, I'm serious," Dorothy said, and she stood up. "Come now. You sit here."

"You're crazy," Ella said, and she eyed the chair warily. But then she sat down, feeling as awkward as she could.

"Now look," Dorothy said, as she sat on the stool. "You see how simple this is. Now stick out your leg." Ella did as directed, while Dorothy removed her left shoe. "Now don't you be supposing that you're not beautiful." Dorothy took hold of Ella's foot and began to work at it. Dorothy had never done anything like foot rubbing before, but she was determined to do it now. "You may be the most beautiful person I know," Dorothy continued. "You have the most beautiful skin. And there is no other face in the world that cheers me up as much as yours, even though you're grouchy half the time!"

Ella leaned her head back and tried to smile, but she had to work to hide the effect of what Dorothy was doing. She really felt like crying.

"Now you see how lovely that feels. And from now on, we shall always take turns at this. For there's nothing quite so lovely in all the world as this, now is there?"

Ella closed her eyes, but still aware that tears might form. She covered her eyes with her hands especially to avoid this. "No, nothing," she said.

"Now I remember many years ago when we were little girls," Dorothy continued. "We were sitting in the dirt and playing with sticks, and I made some very stupid remark about your hair. Do you remember that?"

Ella shook her head no.

"Well, I did, but you see it was because I was so struck by how different your hair was from mine. And I could see that what I said hurt your feelings. And right then I told myself that I would have to learn to think before I spoke. You know it's funny how clearly I remember that day. I made you feel bad, and I made myself feel bad because you felt bad, and that is how it has always been—because we are just like sisters or ...." Dorothy was not sure what words to use. "Or special friends who grew up together, and we've been through everything with each other. Why, bless me, we're immortalized together in Mr. Hicks's portrait, are we not? And there you are brushing my hair. And there I am looking enraptured. Why should it not be so that we love each other as humans do?"

Ella nodded. "Yes," she managed to say. "Now that you mention it, I recollect that day you're talking about. You asked me how come I had nigger hair."

"Yes," Dorothy sighed.

"The next time Wally was brushing my hair, I asked her what you'd meant, and why you'd said it. Wally didn't know what to say. She just brushed me harder with her brush and told me not to pay any mind to those kinds of things."

"I don't know what Wally could have said."

"Yes, but when you said that about my hair, it was the first time I got a bad feeling about myself from you. And that just made me feel extra bad, 'cause I care what you think."

"I hope I have not given you many such bad feelings over the years," Dorothy said. "If I have, I humbly beg your forgiveness. So much fuss is made about white ladies' hair. Ringlets and bangs and braids and this and that. It's just a lot of bother as far as I'm concerned."

"Where you're rubbing there feels good," Ella said. She had managed to regain control of her face, which she hoped had an expression of deep contentment.

"Now, now, you just lie back and let your mind go empty," said Dorothy. "I should think there's nothing so wonderful as letting your mind go all empty while a friend rubs your foot."

But Ella's mind did not go empty. She thought about Dorothy and about the ways in which she both resented and appreciated her mistress.

And so they fell into silence, while Dorothy rubbed first the left and then the right foot. Dorothy felt awkward in doing this, but she pushed herself to do it. She did not know why she should feel any awkwardness about such a thing, and so she told herself repeatedly that it was silly to give it a second thought. And yet she did give it a second thought. She thought about how little there was to guide her in her life. She could not think of a single woman who stood as a model of the woman that she wanted to be. Nor could she think of a man either—except perhaps for Erastus Hicks.

Erastus Hicks, for his part, was also having second thoughts about to how to respond to Dorothy's most recent letter. In it she had described William and Cato's return home, her reconciliation with William, and the fact that they had been unable to think of a way to avoid William's return to the Sixth Regiment. Dorothy had followed Erastus's advice. She had forgiven William and then given her attention to convincing him to turn away from violent acts. Now she wanted more advice. But Erastus knew that it was not possible for a lieutenant to desert his commission, nor would William be able to avoid being called into battle in the coming days.

After deliberation, Erastus decided to write a single letter to both William and Dorothy. He wrote the letter and transcribed it so that there were two identical copies. By the end of August, 1861, all mail service between the North and the South had been suspended, including that which had temporarily been allowed by private mail carriers. Erastus had to resort to sending his letters to a friend of his, a man named Walter McNish, a fellow Quaker who lived in Bowling Green, Kentucky. He asked Walter to take the risk of smuggling the letters across the border to Clarksville, Tennessee, so that he could post them, one to William and the other to Dorothy, within the Confederate mail system. Erastus explained to Walter that the letters "might have a positive effect against the violence of war." In consideration of that possibility, Mr. McNish, who was as committed to pacifism as Mr. Hicks, did as he was requested. The content of Erastus's letter was such that it would have grave consequences were it to be read by the wrong party.

## APPLE SEED

William opened the letter from Walter McNish, which was postmarked Clarksville, Tennessee, and found that within it was a brief note and another, slightly smaller envelope from Erastus Hicks. The note explained that the second envelope contained a private letter from Erastus Hicks and that William should take care to read that letter when he was alone. Mr. McNish explained that he had been asked by Mr. Hicks to transport the letter into Confederate territory, and that he had sent a similar letter to Miss Dorothy Holland of Jackson, Tennessee.

The letter from Erastus Hicks was addressed to both William and Dorothy.

Dear Lieutenant Askew and Miss Holland,

I was glad to hear that you have reconciled your differences. Is it not the nature of life to present us with disagreements? Yet love is required to reconcile these differences. In this, you have demonstrated a worthy feeling for each other, and I commend you for it.

Miss Holland has expressed to me her opposition to the war that now divides my countrymen from yours. She knows that I too am opposed to this conflict. She has asked me to write words of advice regarding how Lieutenant Askew might honor his military commitments, and yet not be altogether complicit in the violence of these hostilities. First, I must point out that we are all complicit in violence of one kind or another, and so the best each of us can do in this matter is to find a boundary of violence that suits each conscience. There is a current of violence, a density of the human spirit, which prevails in times like these, and tends to push the boundary of violent behavior to its limit.

I take my guidance in this matter from the commandment in scripture: 'Thou shalt not kill.' I regard this commandment as a rule given to us with no mention of exceptions. I am aware that many do not agree with so literal a reading of the commandment, and perhaps Lieutenant Askew is among them. Nor can I say with absolute certainty that if faced with my own imminent demise, I would not use lethal force to defend myself. I should like to think that I would not, but it is a theoretical ideal. I can say that it requires courage to aspire to such an ideal. And any man who is guided by this ideal cannot be thought of as cowardly.

I am also well aware that it is impossible for such an ideal to be openly espoused or even hinted at by an officer of the army. And yet who can know the thoughts that lie within any human bosom. Who is to say whether an officer of the army might, in a moment of truth, refrain from discharging a lethal weapon? Or perhaps, that weapon might be purposefully aimed in such a way that it would not have harmful consequences. While such actions might seem at cross purposes with the goals of battle, they would not be, I believe, at cross purposes with the will of the Divine.

I must also reflect that by merely avoiding the commission of harmful acts, an officer like Lieutenant Askew would not himself be kept out of harm's way. For this reason, I am not certain that my advice will coincide with Miss Holland's hopes. Alas, I fear that I can see no other honorable course. To act in the way that I have mentioned will require courage, of this, I am certain. And yet a man can find such courage when it is to honor his beloved that he acts.

A man might do something that goes against his own nature as a matter of gallantry and respect for the woman he loves—but he must also examine his heart to be sure that he does not violate his own moral source. Above all else, I believe that each man must find his own truth, for none of us can claim exclusive knowledge of what is right and what is wrong. I do not know, in short, if what is true and right for me would be true and right for any other man.

I do know that it is right for every person to examine matters so grave as these. Far too many men navigate with an unexamined moral compass, following their brothers in action without regard to who among them is actually leading the way. Whole populations fall into a collective swoon in which only the basest human instincts steer the nation.

While an officer of the army cannot openly condone the behavior I have suggested, such a man can lead others by charitable example toward kindly action. Such a man can comfort his fellows, pray for their safety, offer solace to those in distress, and counter the impulses of hatred that take root among men in awful circumstances. There may appear opportunities for honorable acts of leadership, which only the moment-to-moment circumstances will reveal.

Even if such advice as I can offer is inadequate or impossible to follow—I hope that you will believe how greatly I wish for the safety and well-being of both of you. I hope that our world will some day soon again afford each of you the pursuit of happiness that our forefathers declared to be an inalienable right. I am touched that you would give audience to thoughts such as mine, which seem so un-ratified by the collective judgment of our day.

Regardless of how you judge my advice, I hope you will know the affection I bear each of you. Please remember me with fondness to Cato and to your parents. God grant that we may all see brighter days ahead.

I shall remain

Your devoted friend,

Erastus Hicks

West Street, Philadelphia, Pennsylvania,

Sunday evening, 8th September, 1861

So that was that. William had hoped for more sage advice than the mere strategy that he simply not fire his weapon or aim it so as to avoid hitting someone. Mr. Hicks had implied that he might go against his own nature in this matter, out of a desire to honor Dorothy's wishes. It was certainly not in his nature to march into battle to face the enemy with the equivalent of an unloaded weapon. In fact, it seemed more like madness when he considered it. He had an impulse to tear the letter up. The idea was preposterous.

But it did signify with him that he ought to examine himself; that he ought to be thoughtful about where the boundary of his own morality was drawn. He did not desire to kill anyone, but he could hardly imagine allowing himself to be killed for the sake of that desire. To do so would be suicide. Who could do such a thing?

And yet he was haunted by the memory of the look he found in Dorothy's eye that day he presented himself to her in uniform. He did not want her ever again to look upon him with such ... disgust. He believed her to be a superior spirit. He stood in awe of both her beauty and her wisdom. Even though her point of view on this matter went against the grain, he could not help but credit it.

But what was his obligation to her? She would have no way of knowing the specifics of his actions in battle. Might he not spare her any details that would elicit her disgust? In a practical sense, he realized, all that mattered was his own conscience. All he absolutely needed to tell Dorothy was that he had heeded Mr. Hicks's advice. He would seek his own moral compass. He would not undertake grave actions without consideration. He would not simply follow the herd. He would find the boundary of violence that matched his own ethical standard and then hold to it.

But where did that boundary lie? He imagined aiming his rifle at another man's heart. He imagined pulling the trigger. He imagined watching as the enemy soldier fell dead to the ground. He recoiled from the image. Of course, it was distasteful. No one would do it were it not necessary. But men deemed it necessary. Many men deemed it necessary, most men, even. It was courageous, was it not? And he was after all an officer. It was his duty to be courageous by example. What kind of example would it be to aim away from the enemy? Example! Ha, if any man should even notice the thing, such a man would merely conclude that William was a terrible marksman.

And what other soldier was laden with a desire to please a woman such as Dorothy? She herself admitted that she was at odds with all of Madison County. Of course, he admired her idealism, her grand ideas. But they were not practical. Why, she herself could hardly carry them out if she were in his shoes. No one could. And then there was Erastus Hicks. The man was a Quaker. Such people were expected to be odd. Who else would suggest that "thou shalt not kill" applied even in war. The history of Christianity was itself the history of war. The world would run amok if all men thought such things. Evil men would rise up if righteous men had no force to defend themselves.

And so William argued with himself—an argument that none of his fellow soldiers were troubled to make. He did not fail to notice how absurd it was for him to wrestle with an issue to which no one around him would give a second thought. It was only because of Dorothy. He could see her eyes shining with her great convictions. And those shining eyes were so potent in the chemistry of his love for her. He yearned to fulfill her, and be fulfilled by her. How could they be as one, if on this matter they were so opposed?

He wished more than ever that he had never put himself into his current situation. There was nothing for it now but to try to muddle through and hope for the best. He kept Mr. Hicks's letter. He kept it well hidden away. From time to time, he found opportunities to reread it, but further readings did not help him come to any new certainty about what he ought to do.

Mr. Hicks, for his part, found himself in receipt of a letter, written in a youthful hand. It was a letter from Cato. The letter had been mailed on August 22, just four days before the suspension of mail service. It had been delivered by Cato to Reverend Zeke, who in turn had forwarded the letter via the American Letter Express Company for mailing from Nashville. On the back flap of the letter was written in ink, "Opened by Confederate States Vigilance Committee at Nashville, Tenn."

The vigilance committee had apparently held the letter for three weeks, before choosing to allow it to proceed on to Philadelphia. Erastus saw no evidence that any of the contents of the letter had been censored.

Dear Mr. Hicks,

This is the first letter I have written. I have been practicing writing, but as you can see, my writing is bad. Nevertheless, I had a great desire to write to you to tell you some of what has befallen me. So I have practiced my writing, and will continue to practice.

First, I went away with William to the army for several months, but then he changed his mind about keeping me there, and brought me home. Since I've been home, I've been very happy. Surprise! I have fallen in love. All I can tell you about it is that it has been more than I thought possible. And, thanks to you, I have been reading whenever I can. Oh, I wish I could talk to you about the things I've read. I've read more poems. I like the poems that rhyme. So I wrote a poem for you. Here it is:

*Apple seed.*

*I am an apple seed*
*Whose delicious deeds*
*Were first foreseen*
*By a gallant gent.*

*He decreed I'd read*
*My bound grassy leaves*
*Though I never knew what they meant!*

*Now I seek*

*To read and see*
*What wise men see*
*And be more confident.*

*I seek the light within*
*Though it is dark without*
*My path is like no others.*

*I travel a road*
*Which no one beholds*
*Except my friend and lover.*

*If I could be*
*Anyone but me*
*I would be like a Quaker painter.*

*I'd travel the land*
*With seeds in my hand*
*For what on earth is plainer.*

*Than to wash the feet*
*Of every man I meet*
*I reckon nothing could be quainter.*

So there it is. I hope to make you laugh. And yet I do recall
those days when you painted my portrait and washed my
feet. I don't know what my life would have been if I had not
met you.

Your devoted friend,
Cato Askew
Thursday, August 22, 1861

Erastus did not know what to make of this. He presumed

the Confederate States Vigilance Committee had no idea what to make of it either. They had obviously not realized that Cato Askew was a slave. No doubt they had held the letter for three weeks so that they might ponder the poem long enough to ascertain if it were a coded message. In truth, there was innuendo in the poem. The boy was coy about his lover. What could he mean by "all I can tell you about it is that it has been more than I thought possible." Erastus was not sure that it was more than he himself thought possible. He had to surmise from the poem, "I travel a road, which no one beholds, except my friend and lover" that Cato was speaking of a road that Erastus himself had imagined. But Erastus was beside himself with curiosity to know who it was that traveled this road with Cato. When he thought of possible candidates in Madison County Tennessee, there was no one he could credit as a likely traveler on such a road. He was keenly sensitive to such possibilities in men, and he had sensed no such possibility in any man but Cato. And even with Cato, Erastus was not completely certain. He realized there might be any number of reasons why Cato chose to be discreet about his lover. And yet …. There was only one reason why he would travel a road that no one beholds, unless … he might be referring to his reading! It was true that he had to keep his reading secret, and he may well have shared this secret with his lover.

Erastus read the letter over and over, thinking himself even more vigilant than the vigilance committee, searching between the lines to infer and speculate. After several days, he realized he had become consumed with a desire to elicit the facts from Cato. Yet he did not think it likely that Cato would commit such facts as Erastus imagined to pen and paper. With the confounded war going on, it was impossible to visit Cato in Tennessee or even to write him. If he could only see the boy in person, he was sure that he would learn all.

But the thought, just the possibility of Cato being on a certain road, put Erastus into a feverish state. He tried to imagine the fellow traveler. And then, in his reverie, he imagined Cato traveling on that road. There was no sight upon that road that Erastus did not imagine! In fact, he imagined those sights so vividly and with such fervor, that he was barely able to sleep at night. It could hardly have been more stimulating to him, had he himself been the fellow traveler.

After several days of daydreaming, Erastus decided to write Cato a letter that might convey to the boy an inkling of how well Erastus understood his situation. But then he was struck with another dilemma. Although he imagined he could impose on poor Walter McNish once again to smuggle his correspondence across the border to Clarksville, he could not have Walter post a letter directly to Cato. If such a letter were to arrive at Hickory Grove, it would be evidence to Augustus Askew that someone believed that Cato could read.

And so Erastus wondered if he could dare to use Dorothy as an intermediary. He thought and thought about it, but he could not imagine any circumstances in which Dorothy would betray Cato, or reveal his secret to any other person. Yet, it was presumptuous for him to take any risk in this matter, no matter how small he might believe it to be. Cato himself would be faced with Erastus's presumption.

And that presented yet another dilemma. He might send Dorothy a sealed envelope and ask her to hand it directly to Cato to read. But what if Dorothy were to open this letter out of curiosity? What if she were to read between the lines and surmise, infer and conjecture? How then would he compromise Cato and himself! All in all, the whole thing would be so much easier to manage if he could see Cato in person. But then he would have to wait for the war to be over. And that now seemed like it would be a long time coming.

Erastus decided that he would start by writing a letter, by way of experiment, to see if he could find the right tone, one that would withstand any possible scrutiny from Dorothy without yielding its coded meaning.

Here is what he wrote:

Dear Cato,

My boy you make me proud. You have learned so much, and indeed your writing is not as poor as you suggest. What a lovely poem! And I daresay you have learned much in my absence about poetic license, for you have left me with a decillion questions!

You did make me laugh. You also speak of a feeling that I much understand. I too have traveled down a road that is not well traveled. You are right to seek the light within, for it is only that light which can guide you on your path. As to foot washing, well, I believe Mary of Bethany was no less endeared to our Lord for her efforts in that regard. In such acts, there is much reverence, and, as befits the situation, much adoration.

I do not believe that there are any facts about you that would surprise me—even those which may have been more than you thought possible. It might surprise you, however, to realize that there is more than you've thought possible even now, with respect to what others in this world might share with you.

I wait for the day when this terrible war is finished, for I would greatly enjoy renewing my visit to Madison County. I am sure that if we were to speak in person, there would be much more that we could say than can be managed in letters.

In the meantime, I wish you every happiness in all the things that delight you. I realize that you cannot reply to my letter now that all mail service between our lands has been suspended. I trust that you will continue to be cautious in your habits. Do not forget the strategy we discussed with respect to removing books from the library. Though the war has set the world upon its head, there are still things to be careful about.

I pray that you will continue to love your fellow man, as we are taught to do—and that you will be prudent in all your actions.

I remain your most loyal friend,

Erastus Hicks

West Street, Philadelphia, Pennsylvania,

Monday evening, 16th September, 1861

Having written this letter, Erastus then returned to it day after day. He could not yet bring himself to send it, that is, to send it by way of Dorothy. Once again, by way of experiment, he wrote a letter to Dorothy to see if such a thing could be carried off.

Here is what he wrote:

Dear Miss Holland,

I am writing you once again via my friend Mr. McNish of Bowling Green, Kentucky, with a request that you act as an intermediary. In asking you this, I must betray a confidence. I presume to betray this confidence only because I am hopeful that you will take no offence at the confidence to which I allude. However, I must warn you that the matter that must be divulged is one that could have grave consequences. It is a matter of behavior that is considered illegal in your state, though I hardly think it so in the eyes of God.

Nevertheless, I must ask that you examine your

conscience about this before you take any action. Within this letter, I have enclosed two envelopes, one inside another. If you open the first envelope, you will find the name of the person who is to receive the second envelope. The second envelope is addressed to a person of your acquaintance who resides in Madison County. This person is a slave, and so you can see that the matter of this person receiving a letter could be one that would arouse suspicion and retribution. I must ask, therefore, if you have any qualms or hesitations about the notion of a slave receiving a written letter, intended to be read only by the person to whom it is addressed—that you not open the first envelope. I will trust to your discretion.

If I have presumed upon you to take an action that is not consistent with what you believe to be right, I humbly beg your forgiveness, and ask that you to simply destroy the enclosed envelopes without reading them.

I remain your trusted friend,

Erastus Hicks

West Street, Philadelphia, Pennsylvania,

Wednesday evening, 18th September, 1861

Having written this letter, Erastus found, when he read it, that he was too anxious to send them. And so, for several days, he kept both letters in his desk drawer.

## HOW TO PICK COTTON

$\mathcal{E}$ rastus finally did launch his letters on their journey by way of Walter McNish and thence to Dorothy and Cato. He mailed them on the autumnal equinox, Saturday, September 21st. Dorothy did not receive the correspondence at the Holland farm until a week later, on Saturday the 28th, which also happened to be the day upon which Augustus Askew had planned a visit. Mr. Askew had formally arranged his visit with George Holland. But it was well understood that the purpose of his visit was to see Dorothy on behalf of his son. William had advised Dorothy that such a visit would take place, and so the date for it had been set.

Mr. Askew would call for supper. But Dorothy received the letters in the afternoon mail. When Dorothy read Mr. Hicks's request that she be an intermediary, she did not hesitate about what to do. The idea that a slave might receive a letter to read did not offend her in the slightest. Indeed, she herself had once proposed the notion of reading to Ella, who had merely replied, "This child has no time for reading."

Nor is it to be supposed that the revelation of the name of

Cato on the second envelope was in any way a surprise to Dorothy. She had presumed as much the moment she read the phrase "a person of your acquaintance who resides in Madison County."

There was much about Erastus Hicks that intrigued Dorothy. The prospect of facilitating a correspondence between Mr. Hicks and her lover's mulatto half-brother did nothing to diminish this intrigue. She took the envelope out and carefully examined the penmanship used to write the name "Cato" on its face. It was innocuous enough, written in a simple and straightforward hand.

She was well aware that Mr. Hicks had instructed that the contents were "to be read only by the person to whom it is addressed." This was certainly a reasonable request, and yet there was something suspicious in Dorothy's mind about Mr. Hicks having felt it necessary to make such a request, since it presumed that there was some possibility that she might have otherwise opened the correspondence. She believed Mr. Hicks knew her character well enough to realize that she absolutely would not do such a thing. And yet, his writing it suggested that the letter was of an especially confidential nature. Perhaps it was just a matter of precaution with respect to the violation of law represented by Cato being taught to read. Dorothy did not doubt that Mr. Hicks had played a role in that development. Yet the precaution intrigued her enough to cause her to hold the envelope up to the light just long enough to see if in fact there was anything she could read of its contents. There was not.

When Mr. Askew informed his household of his plans to visit the Holland farm, Cato asked Henry if he might be permitted to drive the master's brougham in Henry's stead. Cato explained that he had a close friend at the Hollands' farm, and that he would enjoy making the trip. Since Henry had no particular desire to go on such an outing himself, he agreed to this request. What Cato did not mention was that what he really wanted was an opportunity to wear the coachman's jacket, which was reserved for those sundry occasions when he was assigned to drive the brougham. Cato wished to present himself in that outfit to his colleagues at the Holland farm. It was a blue wool jacket with a short stand collar and cuffs, brass buttons, lined in red, and was meant to be worn with a red waistcoat. Since Cato did not have a red waistcoat, he wore his gold one instead. He also asked if he might borrow Henry's top hat. Henry asked him why? Cato said it was because it was necessary to make a good impression upon the Hollands for William's sake. Henry observed that the top hat had better come back in excellent condition or it would be Cato upon whom an impression would be made.

So it was that at 6 o'clock Augustus Askew arrived in his brougham at the Holland farm, driven by Cato in his coachman's jacket, brass buttons and top hat. Dorothy saw them arrive from her bedroom window. She had not considered the possibility that Cato would accompany Augustus. But now she pondered how she might conveniently deliver the letter to Cato in some discreet moment. In a sudden impulsive gesture, she picked up the letter, went down the stairs and ran out the door. She stood on the porch with the letter clasped in her hand, which she held behind her back. Then, slowly, she walked up to greet the arriving visitors.

"How very nice it is to see you, Mr. Askew," she said. "We are honored by your visit." And then she bowed, though not low enough to reveal what she held in her hand behind her.

Mr. Askew bowed in return. "It is I who am honored by your gracious hospitality."

"And I see you have been brought here by William's servant Cato. I declare, Mr. Cato, you are most dapper in that jacket!"

Cato blushed, but he also bowed. "I am honored by your compliment, Miss Holland."

Then, as the three of them turned to walk toward the house, Dorothy insinuated herself between Augustus and Cato.

"May I take your arm, Mr. Askew?" she asked Augustus.

"Oh yes, certainly, Miss Holland," he replied.

Augustus held out his arm. As Dorothy slipped her hand around it with her left hand, she simultaneously slipped the letter, which was in her right hand, into the pocket of Cato's coachman's jacket. She did this deftly. Alas, it was managed too deftly! She soon realized that Cato did not register any awareness of what she had just done.

When they arrived at the stairs, Cato stopped. It was evident that he would now take his leave to visit his friends.

"Sir, I will be in the quarters until you are ready to depart," he said to Augustus.

"Very well," said Augustus.

"Ah," said Dorothy. At this moment, she endeavored to give Cato a meaningful look. She tried to indicate the left pocket of his jacket with her eyebrows.

Cato noticed her strange eyebrow movements, but only gave her a quizzical look in return.

"Ah," she said again. "I do hope you will look after that lovely jacket." She realized this was an odd thing to say, but she did not know what else to do.

"Indeed I will, Miss," said Cato. Then he tipped his top hat politely and departed.

"Oh dear," Dorothy said, "Mr. Askew, I fear it is colder out this evening than I realized." And with this, she feigned to shiver slightly.

Augustus squeezed her arm. "Yes, indeed. I must get you into the house, my dear," said Augustus.

Augustus, on this night, had mixed feelings about Dorothy.

He did not at all like the fact that she "didn't think much of the war" as William had put it. Yet he certainly saw why his son was enchanted with her. She was beautiful in her strapless green dress. And she had a way of putting him at ease. In her shiver, he had sensed a mild flirtation, which he thought might have been meant to charm him.

At dinner, the conversation was generally kept to small talk. Then at one point, Mr. Holland inquired about William.

"Have you heard any news from your son about the progress of the war, Mr. Askew?"

"My son's regiment has not yet been engaged," said Augustus. "They are training at New Madrid, Missouri. I believe they are waiting for the enemy to show his hand here in Tennessee."

"Well the whole affair has gone on longer than I thought it would," said Mr. Holland, implying that to some degree he wished the whole affair were over and done with.

"Well sir," Mr. Askew said, "the Yankees are stubborn. They won't let us live in peace. And they have many resources, Mr. Holland. It is no time for us to be impatient. We must see this thing through."

"Oh, yes, of course," said Mr. Holland. "I only meant that the fighting has gotten to be so fierce. And it is drawing closer to us, Mr. Askew. I'm not sure what we shall do if we find the Yankees at our doorstep."

"Well, Mr. Holland, that is the very eventuality against which my son's regiment is training. They will not allow such a thing, I can assure you."

It had not previously occurred to Dorothy that William might actually defend her home against an attack from the Union army. For the first time, she felt a glimmer of pride about his role. "Do you think the Sixth Regiment will end up engaged near Jackson, Mr. Askew?" she asked.

"There's no way to know until the enemy shows his hand. We must certainly hope it won't come to that," he said.

"It's impossible to buy anything anymore," Henrietta interjected. "The Yankees have cut off so many goods from reaching us here. I ordered a dress three months ago, and it still has not arrived!"

Her husband gave her a disapproving look. "We have bigger problems to worry about, Mrs. Holland, than a shortage of dresses."

"Yes, of course," Henrietta agreed, somewhat offended. "I simply meant that a growing number of goods are becoming scarce. I fear what shall happen if we can't get sugar or flour."

"It's the Yankees who should fear that, Mrs. Holland," said Augustus. "Those are products of the South. We shall certainly not go without food or cotton."

"How do you find the mood with your slaves," asked Mr. Holland.

Augustus scratched his head. "The slaves? Why, nothing is different about them. Everyone is carrying on as always. Why do you ask? Have you had problems here?"

"No, no," said Mr. Holland. "But we are like family on this small farm. You have a much larger operation, Mr. Askew."

"Ah, yes," said Augustus, with a note of pride. "But I assure you it is only a matter of having a larger family. None of my people has cause for complaint. They're all fed well enough. In truth, I spend half my time making arrangements on their behalf." Then he added, "Sometimes I wonder if it isn't I who's serving them." And he chuckled at his own joke.

"Oh yes," said Henrietta. "One must spend a great deal of time looking after them."

Dorothy wanted to say something about how unsettling the situation must be for the slaves, how complicated their feelings must be about the outcome of the conflict. But she simply said, "No doubt the slaves are as anxious as we are about the war."

"Well they're lucky really," said Henrietta. "They have so little to worry about. There's something to be said for the simple life."

Something, indeed! As the dinner proceeded inside the big house, the attention in the quarters was all on Cato. Many of the slaves turned out to admire his coachman's outfit. Jimmy was not the least among the admirers. After sufficient time was spent in admiration, and after each slave in turn had tried on the top hat, Jimmy prevailed upon Cato to join him on a walk to the fields so that he could show off the high quality of their cotton crop.

"Now why would Cato want to go look at some ugly old cotton plants?" asked Ella. "Jimmy, don't nobody want to trudge out there to admire your farming work tonight. Just leave the man alone."

"No, I should like to go," Cato affirmed. "I don't know too much about the farming end of things, Ella. I'd like to see how it's done."

Ella shrugged. "Suit yourself."

And so the two men were allowed to go off. They did go out to the fields among the cotton plants. And for several minutes, Jimmy did discuss, with great formality, the ins and outs of cotton farming. But when, in the course of their discussion, they had wandered far enough into the field as to be effectively out of sight from all concerned, Jimmy threw his arms around Cato and kissed him with sufficient intensity that the top hat was knocked to the ground.

"Careful now," Cato said, stooping to pick up the hat and dust it off. "Henry will have my hide. This is his hat. But I wore it just for you."

"You look better than any gentleman," said Jimmy.

"Do you want to try on the coat?" Cato asked.

Jimmy nodded, and Cato took off the coat and held it for Jimmy to put on. Jimmy slipped his arms into the coat, and then stepped off to reprise his imitation Cato walk, walking somewhat on his toes.

"Oh go on!" Cato said.

"Would you care to step into the coach Master Askew?" Jimmy said and he bowed low. He put out his hands. "You can step on my hands Master Askew and I will raise you into the coach."

Cato did as requested, putting his foot onto Jimmy's hands. Jimmy boosted his leg up until Cato nearly lost his balance.

"Be careful Master Askew," Jimmy said. "Perhaps I shall have to carry you in my arms into the coach." And with this, he slid his arms up behind Cato. In a single move, Jimmy swept him up off his feet, holding him in his arms. Once again, the top hat fell to the ground.

"Goodness," said Cato. "My but you are a muscular young fellow."

"I've been working in the field, Master Askew, and I just can't help being strong."

"I fear for you to handle me so," said Cato.

"I just can't help it, Master Askew. You look so fine! When I look at you I just get all mixed up in my head, and all I can think about is how I want to …."

Cato laughed. "To what?"

"To put my big …."

"Put your big what?"

"My big arms around you and squeeze you!" Jimmy squeezed Cato hard.

"Gracious, you are a bold coachman," Cato said.

"And then I just can't help but wish to kiss you, Master Askew."

"Kiss me?"

Jimmy looked now into Cato's eyes as he cradled him in his arms. "Yes," he said. "I want to eat you up." And he lowered his face till it was very close to Cato's face. "I love you," he whispered.

They kissed. And in that moment, standing amidst the cotton plants, where he had stood so many hours of his life, Jimmy in the blue wool coachman's outfit with brass buttons, felt that all the toils of his life had been worthwhile.

He set Cato back on his feet. Cato picked up the top hat, and Jimmy put his hands in his pocket and rocked on his feet.

"What's this?" Jimmy said, as he pulled out the envelope in the pocket.

He handed it to Cato, who looked at it. "What's what?" He turned the envelope around and saw his name on it. "It's got my name on it," he said, in obvious surprise.

"It looks like a letter," said Jimmy. "Who's it from?"

"I don't know. Where'd you get it?"

"It was in your coat pocket," said Jimmy.

"What?"

"I just pulled it out of your pocket and gave it to you?"

"But how did it get there?"

"How would I know?" Jimmy said. "Who's writing you a letter? I thought nobody knew you could read."

"Nobody does," said Cato.

"What does it say?"

Cato opened the letter and quickly looked at the signature line. "It's from Mr. Hicks," he said.

"What!" Now there was anger in Jimmy's voice. "Damn! What does that old Quaker cracker want with you now?"

"He's written a reply to my letter."

Jimmy wasn't sure if he'd heard correctly. "You wrote him a letter?" There was incredulity in his voice.

"Yes, I wrote him," Cato said. "I just wanted to thank him for teaching me to read, and to tell him that I'd fallen in love."

Jimmy couldn't believe it. "You told him that!" Jimmy's voice was filled with accusation.

"I didn't say who with!" cried Cato, in a defensive tone.

Jimmy shook his head and started pacing, while Cato read the letter. Finally, Jimmy asked, "What is it? What does he say?"

"He wishes me every happiness. He says there's nothing about me that would surprise him."

"What is that supposed to mean?"

"I'm not sure," Cato said. "But I think, I think he understands."

"Understands what?"

Cato looked up from the letter. "I mean, I think he understands about you and me."

Jimmy cocked his head. "How come you think that?"

"Well it's just what he says." Cato read aloud from the letter. "He says, 'It might surprise you, however, to realize that there is more than you've thought possible even now, with respect to what others in this world might share with you.' Cato looked up at Jimmy. "You see, I think he knows."

"You think he knows about you and me?" Jimmy was just beginning to fathom what Cato meant.

"Yes."

Jimmy made a disgusted look. "What business is it of his?"

"It's just that he's the same way."

"What way?'

"Like how you and I are."

Now Jimmy's forehead scrunched up into a question. "Why do you think that?"

"Well," Cato said, "he more or less kissed me when we said goodbye."

Jimmy clenched his fist. "What!" Jimmy's stuck out his arm, and bent his elbow, until the clenched fist was held straight up. "And you let him?"

"It just happened real quick. It wasn't anything but a fond kiss. He was saying goodbye."

"Oh man, how come you never told me about this?"

"What could I say? That Mr. Hicks kissed me? It wasn't like what you're thinking."

Jimmy felt rage mix with jealousy into a bitter blend. This white man had interfered in too many matters. Jimmy had never understood why the painter was so interested in Cato. But now, his eyes were opened; he could see it all. The man was in love with Cato. The man was his rival! Despite his anger, Jimmy's voice, when he used it, cracked. He looked Cato in the eye. "Do you love him?" he asked.

"No," Cato said flatly. "I like him," he said. "… as a friend." He looked at Jimmy with tenderness. "That's all. There is no one else but you that I love." Then, after a pause, Cato made an exasperated look. "I don't know how you could even ask me such a question. You know I love you, Jimmy. Look here." Cato returned to reading the letter. "Mr. Hicks even says at the end 'I pray that you will continue to love your fellow man as we are taught to do.' You see, he's given us his blessing."

"I don't want his blessing."

"How come you hate him so much?" Cato asked.

"Why shouldn't I?" Jimmy said. "He's just like all the other white men. He thinks he can do what he wants with us. He even kisses you when he feels like it."

Cato shook his head. "Look, it's just because we were saying goodbye and that he knew we might never meet again. How come you're so jealous?"

Jimmy looked hurt. "Because those cussed white men take whatever they want."

"He can't take me," Cato said. "And besides, he would never do such a thing. He's a good and decent man. I wish you wouldn't say such things about him. If you'd only get to know him better, you'd understand."

"I don't want to get to know him."

"Well we'll probably never see him again anyway," said Cato.

All of this talk of Erastus Hicks had spoiled the loveliness of the moment that had thrilled Jimmy just five minutes before. "So how did that letter get in your pocket?"

"I don't know," Cato said. "I'm certain it wasn't there when I put the coat on."

"Well your daddy sure didn't put it there," Jimmy said.

"I don't know who could have done so, unless it was Miss Holland."

"But she doesn't know you can read. How come she would have the letter anyway?"

Cato's raised his eyebrows as the logic of the situation revealed itself to him. "That's got to be the answer! He must have sent the letter to Miss Holland because he knew he couldn't send it direct to me. He must have known that she would not betray me. So then she knows!" The realization of this made Cato shiver.

"She knows what?"

"It means Miss Holland knows that I can read. Erastus must have told her."

"Shoot! You see, you can't trust him."

"But he's the one who taught me to read," Cato said. "And he knew Miss Holland wouldn't mind."

"Damn, that Hicks spends a lot of time messing with other people's business. What do you suppose he intends to do with my brother?"

"With Sammy?"

"Yeah, with Sammy, now that he owns him. Do you s'pose he'll try to kiss him too?"

Cato sighed. "Look, I know you're upset about that." He took another long breath. "But it's just not what you think, Jimmy, really! Can't we forget about Mr. Hicks for a while? I'd much rather go back to where we were before you found that damn letter." Cato looked at Jimmy with imploring eyes.

Jimmy, who had been pacing nervously, stopped. He could not resist Cato's puppy dog look. "All right. All right. It's just that I didn't think anyone could come between us."

"No one has. No one ever will," Cato said, with a note of finality. Wanting to change the subject, he looked around him at the field of cotton. "So how do you pick this stuff?"

Despite his anger, a smile crept onto Jimmy's face. Cato had put the top hat back on. He was staring at a cotton plant in his gold vest and top hat like he was observing an odd specimen of bird. "You mean you never picked cotton?"

"No."

"Damn, you are a house nigger, aren't you?"

"Well I can't help it if I never did it."

"Look here, I'll show you how you do it. Take this." Jimmy took off the coachman's jacket and handed it to Cato. Then in an instant, he whirled around and rapidly picked half a dozen clumps of cotton from nearby plants. "You got to pick it careful, or you'll hurt your fingers." He pointed at a prime specimen of the cotton. "See when the boll is all the way open like that and it's fluffy, you can pick it easy." He took Cato's hand and put it on the fluffy ball of fleece. "You just pull it like this —and it all comes out easy." Just as he said, the wad came out fully intact in Cato's hand. "But then when you got a boll like this, where the bud's not all the way open, that's when you got to have skill." He guided Cato's hand to the partly open boll, and Cato, awkwardly, pulled on the strands, but only pieces of the cotton came out. "You see, that's what happens. You got to do it like this." And Jimmy deftly extracted the entire clump of cotton from a nearby partly open boll. "It takes practice," he said.

"You've got nimble hands," Cato observed.

"I got nimble everything," Jimmy boasted.

"I bet you could pluck a hair off my chest and I'd never even know it."

"You hardly got any hair on your chest," Jimmy said. "I know. I already looked."

"I do too have hair," Cato said.

"Ha! Where?"

Cato opened his shirt slightly, and tried to look down at his chest, but the top hat made it difficult. "Well why don't you just see if you can find it."

"Find it? Find it?" Jimmy laughed. "You mean you got just one hair on there somewhere."

"Go ahead."

Jimmy stuck his hand inside Cato's shirt and felt around on his chest. He stopped for a moment when he came to his friend's nipple.

"Be careful," Cato said. "If you start doing that, you're going to start trouble."

Jimmy kept feeling around, while Cato giggled. "I give up," Jimmy said at last. "I can't find your chest hair."

Cato took off his hat, and looked down at his chest, in the cleft between his breasts. "I know it was here somewhere."

Jimmy laughed. "Ha. Ha." And he displayed a thin strand of hair, wedged between his fingers.

"You did pluck it! And just like I said, I didn't even feel it!"

"Nimble," Jimmy said.

# 30

# "OH SUCH TREACHERY!"

*A*fter reading and re-reading Erastus's letter, Cato took heed of the painter's reminder to be careful when he borrowed books from the Askew library. After Mrs. Askew died, Cato had grown more careless in his habits. Now he determined to change his ways. He returned all the books he had previously removed from the library. He settled upon just one book, a novel by Jane Austen. He carefully disguised the fact that one of the three volumes of "Pride and Prejudice" was missing from the library shelf by using the substitute book that Erastus had given him.

There was a spot in the woods a mile down the road from the Hickory Grove gate where Cato constructed a reading sanctuary. Within a small clearing, partly hidden by surrounding tall shrubs, Cato scooped out a hole in the ground. He made the hole somewhat smaller than a nearby rock, which he then used to cover the hole. Under the protection of darkness, he brought the novel to this spot at night, and hid it in the hole beneath the rock, so that he would be able to read it during the day.

Whenever he could, Cato found an excuse to steal away to his sanctuary. On those occasions, he walked down Christmasville Road until he came to a certain tree, behind which he had forged a makeshift path to his spot in the woods. When he was confident that no one could see him, he ducked behind this tree, then made his way to the clearing. He moved the rock to retrieve Volume Two, and then removed his shirt, which he placed on the rock to serve as a pillow. He lay on the ground reading with his head on his folded shirt, which was elevated by the rock. In this manner, over the course of several weeks, he progressed with great enthusiasm to Volume Two, Chapter 8 of "Pride and Prejudice."

It was in such a manner that early one Tuesday afternoon Cato was reading Chapter 8, about a gathering at Rosings where Miss Bennet and Mr. Darcy were able to meet. Cato had come to the point where Miss Bennet was about to sit down at the pianoforte to play for Mr. Darcy, whereupon Cato lapsed into a reverie about his own recollection of Chopin being played on the piano in the Askew parlor. He laughed to himself and laid the book down on his bare chest. He placed his hands back behind his head, and stared at the sky as he summoned up the memory. He tried to recall the melody itself. There was one particular phrase of the piece that he could still remember vividly. He closed his eyes, and recreated this refrain in his imagination several times over.

Suddenly Cato heard sounds of movements nearby. He opened his eyes. No more than six yards away a white man and a white woman stood in the clearing. The man wore a Chesterfield, a loose topcoat with a velvet collar and several pockets. The woman wore a cloak. She held a bonnet in her hand. Her hair was disheveled. She quickly put the bonnet onto her head and tied it. The man and woman stared at Cato with a look of disdain on their faces. Cato tried to hide the book by letting it quietly slide down off his chest and then to his side, but it was too late. The man approached him, and stood looking down upon him with an expression that turned to contempt.

"What's this?" the man said. "What are you doing here, boy?"

Cato quickly sat up. "Nothing, sir."

"What have you got there?" The man reached down and picked up the book. He read the title on the cover. "'Pride and Prejudice,' is it?" He looked around to see if anyone else was in sight. "You were reading this?"

Now Cato stood all the way up. He endeavored to put on his shirt as quickly as possible. "No sir, no, I can't read. I just borrowed it. I was going to use the book to press some leaves. I was just going to pick some leaves and press them in the book, but I lay down to rest for a moment."

'Press leaves in the book? Ha, will you lie to me? Do you know who I am?"

"No, sir."

"I am Judge Samuels of the county court. I tell you I saw you reading this book!"

"Oh no sir, I was just looking at it out of curiosity. It puzzles me how anyone can make sense of such a thing. I was just looking at it."

"Do you have a pass, boy?"

"No, sir. I don't have pass just now. I live close by at Hickory Grove, so I should think I wouldn't need a pass."

"You should think, eh? Who is your master?"

"Mr. Augustus Askew. My master is the owner of Hickory Grove nearby."

"And does Mr. Augustus Askew know that you are out here lying about in the woods reading novels all day?"

"No sir. I mean I certainly don't know how to read, sir. I was just looking at the book out of curiosity."

"Was it curiosity that made you turn the pages? Was it curiosity that made you chuckle?"

"Sir, if I chuckled, it was only because these markings inside the book look so odd to me. But I cannot read them."

"Do you take me for a fool? I saw you. I saw your eyes moving down the page. You turned the page and kept reading, and then you laughed at something. Something amused you, I daresay. I should think it quite amusing myself to lie about in the woods reading all day while my master thinks that I am hard at work."

Cato did not know what to say. He thought it would be best if he said nothing further.

The woman, who had stood back in silence since putting on her bonnet, now approached Judge Samuels. "Perhaps we ought to keep going," she said.

"What?" said Judge Samuels. "And leave this boy to sit up here and read to his heart's content. I can tell you what Mr. Augustus Askew would do. I can tell you he wouldn't leave one of his niggers to sit in the woods and read all day. I know the gentleman. He shall hear about this, I tell you."

"But what will you say to him?" the woman wondered. "How will you account for our being here together?"

This question gave the judge pause. Coming upon a slave reading had outraged him. But now his outrage gave way to reflection. "Yes, yes," he said. "I suppose that it might raise unnecessary questions."

Upon hearing this, Cato surmised that the woman with Judge Samuels might not be his wife.

"And you can hardly leave me here in the woods, Jeremiah," the woman continued. "If you took him to his master right now, I would have to go with you, and then …."

Judge Samuels nodded. He turned to Cato. "Now look here, boy. You go straight home and tell your master that I'm going to call on him at three o'clock this afternoon. Then we shall see what Mr. Askew's opinion is of niggers reading in the woods. I'm going to go with you as far as the road out there, and then I'm going to watch you. So don't get any idea in your head about running away. I have a pistol here." Judge Samuels swept back the opening of his topcoat to reveal the firearm holstered there. "You go straight home and deliver that message."

Cato nodded. He picked up the book to take it back with him.

"Give me that," Judge Samuels demanded.

Cato handed him the book.

"I believe I shall hold onto this piece of evidence," he said. "Now get going."

Cato made his way out of the woods back to Christmasville Road, while Judge Samuels walked behind him. When they got to the road, the judge stayed behind the tree.

"Go on now," he said. "I'll be watching you." Once again, the judge pulled back the flap of his topcoat to remind Cato of his weapon.

Cato stepped down the small embankment onto the road, and walked as quickly as he could back toward the Hickory Grove gate. His mind raced as he tried to think of what to do. He held some hope that the judge might forgo the whole matter, if in fact the woman was not his wife, and if the judge feared that somehow the facts of the situation might come out. Cato himself, after all, might mention that the judge was in the woods with a woman. But then Cato also realized that it would be his word against that of a white man. And it would not be good to make more of an enemy of the judge than he had already.

He decided his best hope was to tell Augustus that he'd seen Judge Samuels at Christmasville Road, and that he had been asked to deliver a message that the judge might call this afternoon. He hoped that if Judge Samuels did not show up, the entire affair might be forgotten. The only problem was, the judge had kept the book.

Cato was shaking when he got back to the house. First, he went to his room, where he sat on his bed. He thought for several moments about if and how he might get to Jimmy to ask for his advice. He did not dare to go back onto the road. But there was no other passable route for him to get to Jimmy, who was working in one of the Hollands' fields three miles down the road. He decided his only course of action was to stay at home and deliver the message.

After checking the library, to reassure himself that nothing there appeared out of place, Cato went to look for Augustus in his study. As casually as he could, he told Augustus that he'd encountered the judge at Christmasville Road, and that the judge had asked him to convey a message that he might call in the afternoon.

"Judge Samuels, eh?" Augustus repeated the name, looking up from his desk.

"Yes, master."

"That's odd." Augustus closed the ledger in front of him. "Did he express the purpose of his call?"

Cato did not know how to answer this. He knew that if he gave any indication of the reason for the judge's visit, he would forgo all hope that the matter might be forgotten. He said, "I cannot say. I think the judge suggested the visit on impulse, so I'm not sure if he will remember it later."

"Not remember? Ha! It would not be like Judge Samuels to forget an appointment. Well, we shall see what he has to say. Where did you say you saw him?"

"On Christmasville Road, sir."

"What were you doing out there?"

Cato thought back to his defense regarding the book. "I was on my way to gather some herbs. I was going to make an herbal potion. I've had a small fever today, master."

"A fever? Well boy, doesn't Henry have a potion you can use?"

"I did not wish to trouble Henry about it."

"Very well," said Augustus, returning to his ledger. "When Judge Samuels arrives, have him wait in the parlor."

Cato went back to his room. He did, in fact, feel as if he had a fever. He began to ruminate on possible excuses. He could say that he had gone to the woods to find herbs, and he had brought along the book so that he could press the herbs in it to protect them. Such an appropriation of a book might still be deemed an offense, but it would be a far less serious one than reading. If he were to be found guilty of reading, there would be questions about how he had learned to read. Cato could not betray Erastus. He would rather take any punishment than forsake Erastus's confidence. He could not anticipate how Augustus would react to Judge Samuels' accusation. Cato was certain, however, that if Augustus were to believe Judge Samuels' assessment of what occurred, he would be punished.

Cato spent the next hour in prayer. He entreated God to intervene, to keep Judge Samuels away. And for a brief period, he began to hope that somehow he would be spared any further trouble. But his prayer was not answered. At three o'clock the judge arrived. Henry showed him to the parlor. Five minutes later Augustus went to the parlor to greet the judge. The judge told Augustus what he had discovered. The judge omitted any mention in his telling of the story of having had a companion in the woods.

"You're certain the boy was reading?" Augustus asked.

"As certain as I am a judge," said Mr. Samuels.

"Well I'll be damned!" said Augustus, his voice rising in anger. "I declare these past few months, Judge, some books went missing from my library. Then two weeks ago, the books reappeared. I couldn't imagine who was responsible. By Jupiter, I thought I was losing my mind. Oh such treachery! It was that damned Cato all along. How could a nigger learn to read like that?"

"It's an outrage," said the judge. "It makes you wonder if the Yankees have infiltrated the area. Perhaps they are training them to rebel against us."

"He shall be punished," said Augustus. "You may be sure of that. And I will find out how this came about. I will find out who dared to teach him."

Augustus sent for his overseer, Mr. Flint. He ordered Mr. Flint to fetch Cato and to chain him to the whipping post in the corner of the barn, then to inform him once he had done so. After Judge Samuels had departed, when Mr. Flint had informed him that the boy was chained, and once Augustus had steeled himself with a glass of brandy, he went out to the barn and confronted his slave. Cato was chained with iron manacles that held his hands fast to the post reserved for this purpose. The chains were fastened in such a way that Cato was forced to bend down slightly toward the post, which gave good access to his back, from which Mr. Flint had removed his shirt.

Augustus took the whip down from its hook on the wall. He told Cato there was no use pretending. He told him he had witnessed the books that had come and gone from his library.

"Who taught you to read?" he demanded to know.

Owing to his position facing the barn wall, Cato could not turn to see Augustus. He spoke therefore toward the wall. "No one taught me to read," he said. "I only looked at those books out of curiosity."

Augustus hoisted the whip in his hand and drew his arm

back as high in the air as he could. He lashed the whip forward, striking a bloody line on the smooth surface of Cato's back. "I will not stop," he shouted, "until you tell me who taught you to read."

Cato yelped when the whip hit his skin. But he said again, "No one taught me, master, I swear."

Augustus worked himself quickly up to a punitive frenzy. He struck the boy three more times. Then again, he said, "Who taught you to read?"

Once more Cato repeated, but now in a much smaller voice, "No one, master."

And so it went for more than half an hour. Cato did not speak at all during the last twenty lashes. He cried out sharply each time the lash hit him, then he sobbed haltingly as he sucked in hard breaths between each blow. Each time, before he struck, Augustus repeated his question. But eventually he did not even wait to hear if Cato would answer. The boy's refusal to reveal who taught him to read incensed Augustus. He would not tolerate such brazen disobedience. As it always was with Augustus, the more he lashed the whip, the more enraged he became. It was as if the meting out of punishment was itself an outrage that worked him into a lather.

But Augustus's strength was not what it had once been. When he had delivered forty lashes, he began to tire. After the fortieth lash he told Cato, "I'm going to leave you here tonight to dwell upon your sins. In the morning, you will tell me who taught you to read, or you shall have another forty lashes, you can be sure of that! We will continue in this way until you tell me the truth. So there is no point remaining silent. Do you wish to tell me now, and thus come in to spend the night in the house—or will you be silent, and stay out here all night?"

Cato bobbed his head. He was in so much pain that even if he had wished to do so, he could hardly speak. He simply mumbled the words, "No one ...." Then he let his head fall, and he fell down upon his knees.

"Very well, then," said Augustus. He returned the whip to its hook. He left the barn, and latched the barn door. He went back to his study, where he poured himself a very large glass of brandy. A few minutes later, Scout crept into the room. Augustus waved his arm and yelled a curse at the dog. Scout, who was now quite adept at reading his master's moods, decided to find a seat in the corner of the room, well away from Augustus's wrath.

It did not take long for the news of what had happened to travel about the area. After chaining Cato to the whipping post, Mr. Flint informed Henry of all that he had learned from Augustus regarding what had occurred in the woods. At the first opportunity, Henry mentioned the details of the story as he understood them to Hattie. Half an hour later, Hattie passed the information on to Nettie. Nettie, who did the washing, took the news at 4:30 along with a bundle of laundry down to Dyer Creek, where she encountered Wally and Ella washing clothes. Nettie told Wally and Ella that Cato had been caught reading by Judge Samuels. Nettie further informed them that Cato had been severely whipped by Mr. Askew and even now was chained up in the barn. This is what Nettie had learned from Hattie, who had obtained all of these details from Henry.

Wally and Ella took the information with them back to the Holland farm. But they were not in agreement about what to do with it.

"We can't tell Jimmy anything," said Ella. "He'll just get angry and there won't be nothing for him to do about it."

"We have to tell him," said Wally. "He's going to find out sooner or later."

"It's better if he finds out later," said Ella. "He's only going to get all worked up, and it won't help anything."

So Wally and Ella decided to say nothing. But this strategy was of no avail. Earlier, after Mr. Flint had told Henry the news, he also told the story to his chief assistant Hiram. Hiram was a slave who served as Mr. Flint's helper in overseeing the field hands. Hiram, in due course, told the story to Isaac, one of the Askew field hands. Later, when Isaac was working at the south end of Mr. Askew's southernmost field, he leaned across the fence and told the story to Paymore, who was working the northern end of the Hollands' field. It was Paymore then, who was not in any way aware of Jimmy's relationship with Cato, who eventually told the story to Jimmy—just as the sun was setting.

Immediately upon hearing the news, Jimmy left the field. He ran back to the quarters. Wally and Ella saw him arrive. They quickly deduced that he must have heard what had happened. Jimmy was in a frantic state. He did not speak. He ran into the back door of the big house. He went straight to the kitchen. There, without explaining anything to Cora, who watched him come in, he took a long knife from a drawer in the kitchen cabinet.

Ella saw him come back out of the house with the knife in his hand.

When Jimmy saw that Ella had seen him, he turned and began to run down the lane toward Christmasville Road. Ella shouted and ran after him, but Jimmy did not stop. Ella could not catch him. When she got to the road, she saw she could not hope to catch up with him. She ran back to the house and told Wally what had happened.

"We've got to stop him," Ella said. "He's got a big knife from the kitchen. I'm afraid he's going to get himself killed."

"You can take the horse," Wally said. "You can catch him if you take the horse!"

Ella had little practice riding a horse. She had ridden on a mule once as a girl, back when Dorothy made her try it when she was supposed to be carrying Dorothy's books on the way to school. Now she ran to the barn where she immediately set about attempting to put a saddle on Walnut. But she had no idea how to do that. She wasn't sure which way the saddle went. She didn't know how to fasten it. After several minutes of frantic maneuvering with the saddle, she threw the saddle onto the ground. She climbed onto the railing at the side of Walnut's stall. From that position, she hoisted herself onto Walnut's back. Walnut was not keen on this idea, and let Ella know it. But Ella pleaded with the animal. "We've got to go catch Jimmy," she said.

In the meantime, Wally had arrived in the barn. She saw Ella was now sitting bareback on top of Walnut in the stall, barely keeping her balance. "What are you doing?" said Wally. "You got to have a saddle."

"I don't know how to put it on," said Ella. "Just open the stall gate and let me out of here."

"You're going to fall off the damn horse and break your neck," said Wally.

"No I won't!" Ella insisted. "I won't fall. Come on, we've got to hurry. I've got hold of his neck." And indeed, Ella had leaned forward on the horse, grasping onto the horse's neck bodily in an awkward position.

"You can't ride a horse like that," said Wally.

"Yes, I can," said Ella. "Now open the gate."

But Wally wouldn't budge. "I'm not going to watch two children die today," she said. "You get off that horse. I'm going to fetch Willis and have him ride out after Jimmy." With that, Wally left the barn.

But Ella was not to be deterred. She leaned way down to the side of the horse, reached out and pulled at the latch, which held shut the gate to the stall. She lifted the latch with her fingertips and the gate swung open. Ella repositioned herself squarely on Walnut's back and whispered in his ear, "Come on boy." she said. "We got to catch Jimmy."

Walnut sauntered out of the stall. Walnut tried to look back at Ella, but Ella was pressing forward upon his neck and holding on so fastidiously that he could not manage to look back. Walnut neighed. He made a shaking movement to try to shake Ella off his back. But Ella clung tight.

Walnut walked several steps further, until he had walked out past the barn door, which Wally had left open. Out in the yard, Walnut tried once again gently to shake Ella off, but Ella would not let go. Slowly, Ella tried to sit up. She tried to grasp the horse with her legs as tightly as she did with her hands, so that she could stay on top of him. Once again, she commanded the horse, "Giddy up! Let's go!"

But Walnut was wary of going anywhere. He cantered in a circle around the yard. Eventually, he stopped and walked over to a spot in the yard where there was a clump of Juniper bushes. He stepped into the bushes as far as he could go, then shook himself again, this time more violently. Now Ella was unable to keep her balance. She fell off the horse, toppling sideways into the Juniper bushes, where she landed with her head several branches lower than her feet.

It was thus that Wally and Willis found her. She was not conscious. And so they carried her into the cabin and laid her on the bed. For the time being, any effort to chase after Jimmy was abandoned.

# 31

## "SAVE ME!"

Scout did not move from his out-of-the-way spot in the corner of Augustus's study. This was because Augustus, as he sat sipping brandy in his wingback chair, was still fuming. Augustus thought at great length about who could possibly have dared to teach his slave to read. The only person he could credit with such a task, the only person he could think of who would have had the time and opportunity to undertake a surreptitious training was his son, William. But he could not imagine why his son would ever do such a thing. He knew his son well enough, he thought, to be certain of his innocence. Yet no one else in the household, save his deceased wife, Lucille, even knew how to read. And she, he was sure, would have never conceived of such a pernicious undertaking.

Augustus sipped his brandy and brooded. When at last the sun had set, when the light had grown dim in his study, he rose to light a candle. While he was up, he poured himself another brandy. He came back to his chair, sat down and resumed his ruminations. After an hour of repeatedly coming to a dead end, of repeatedly reaching no plausible conclusion, save that unthinkable conclusion involving his son, he rose and poured yet another glass of brandy. Once more, he returned to ponder in his chair. At last, after he had drunk a good deal of brandy, and after he had worked his mind at great lengths to no avail, he rested his head languidly against the back of his chair and nodded off to sleep.

But when he lit the candle, Augustus had been so preoccupied by his fulminations about who taught Cato to read that he did not notice the rather loose seating that the candle had in its silver holder. The holder was old. It was a silver candlestick holder, which had been given to Augustus and Lucille by his wife's parents. It had served its purpose faithfully for many years. Countless times, it had been cleaned of melted wax, meticulously scraped out by Henry or Cato with the sharp blade of a knife. And as years of scraping the perimeter of the holder's cup accumulated, so too did the circumference of that aperture grow ever so subtly larger. There was no single moment when its size changed in any visible way. It was a slow process whereby from day to day the candle fit imperceptibly less snuggly in the holder's grip.

Augustus snored softly in his sleep while the candle, which sat on a table next to his chair, gradually listed to the side. It had been leaning at a slight angle when it was lit. But as the candle dripped and the melted wax elongated like a lengthening paraffin icicle on the downward-leaning side of the stick, the candle gradually leaned more and more to the side. Finally, it reached a degree of tilt that was so pronounced that the holder could no longer clutch it. Without a sound, it toppled over, fell across the edge of the table, and onto the floor. Then it rolled a few short inches until it came to rest against the drapery, which lay artfully gathered upon the floor by the window.

The flame traveled with zealous speed up the fabric of the

drapery. It made a soft sizzling sound—which may have seemed to Augustus in his dreamy state like the soothing crackle of a cozy fire. Augustus did not awake. Instead, it was Scout who first recognized that something was wrong. After a glance at the enlarging flames, Scout quickly arose, came up to Augustus and wedged his snout in between Augustus's legs. In his sleep, Augustus instinctively pushed the dog's head away. In the haziness of his dream, he mouthed the words, "Not now," which came out of his mouth like a garbled snore. But when Scout saw that he was being pushed away, he barked. Scout barked loudly and urgently until at last Augustus opened his right eye like a slit.

It took untold seconds for the meaning of the sizzling sounds and sparks of light, which little by little dissolved Augustus's dream, to come into focus. But when the reality of the fire did in fact become clear to him, Augustus's heart leapt in his chest, and he in turn leapt to his feet. Despite the urgency, this leap might have been achieved with some nimbleness had Augustus been a younger man, or had he not been intoxicated. But he was old, clumsy, half-asleep and drunk. And so he stumbled on Scout's body, and fell down twisting and hard onto the old oak floor. He knocked his head against the bottommost brick of the fireplace. There he lay for several moments, until once again he roused himself back into consciousness. Now he found that his leg had so twisted itself that he could not, despite many desperate attempts, get back up. And so he was immobilized upon the floor, a helpless man ensnared as if by quicksand. All he could do was look about his study and watch as the fire flaunted an accelerating appetite.

Earlier, just as Augustus had been dozing off, Jimmy had arrived on the grounds of Hickory Grove. Jimmy knew from Paymore that Cato was chained in the barn. When he got to the barn, he found that the side door was locked from the outside with a key. The two large main doors were held shut from the inside by a beam of wood lodged in a pair of braces, affixed one on each door. Jimmy violently kicked one of the big wide doors, but it budged only a little. Then he stepped back and rammed his shoulder into the crack between the doors as hard as he could. In doing so, he forced the doors slightly apart, though he did not dislodge the beam. Straining against them, he was able to force the doors an inch apart, enough so that he could see the beam of wood. He inserted the knife into this opening, eased back slightly on the doors so that the pressure on the braces was lessened, and gingerly wriggled the beam upwards with the dull edge of the knife. After several attempts, he maneuvered the right side of the beam up to the edge of its brace until it slid off and fell to the ground. The left side of the beam remained lodged in its brace. But now when Jimmy rammed his body hard into the door on the right, the top part of it pushed open just enough for him to slip in through the gap.

Chained in the darkness, Cato was in a semi-delirious state. He had been abruptly yanked from his "Pride and Prejudice" reverie by a stranger in the woods. He had been threatened with a gun. He had deluded himself that nothing untoward would happen to him. But then he had been unceremoniously plucked from his room by Mr. Flint, dragged like an animal to the barn, and locked into rough handcuffs. His father whipped him mercilessly, taunted him with the key to the manacles, then threatened more whippings. The image of Augustus angrily slipping the key back into his pocket and stomping away repeated itself again and again in Cato's mind.

The events of the day had unfolded so rapidly and unexpectedly that the events almost did not feel real. Yet Cato was reminded of the reality of what had happened by the waves of pain that pulsed across his back. He had not gotten up off his knees since Augustus had left him alone in the barn. By now, his knees were numb. He felt as if they were locked in a stuck position. When he heard the commotion from Jimmy breaking through the door, he tried to get up. But he was so weakened by his ordeal he could barely move. With effort, he pulled the chains on his wrists against the post to give him leverage. Slowly, achingly, he forced his knees to unbend and stood himself back on his feet. And when he had done so he turned his head in Jimmy's direction. "I'm over here!" he shouted.

There was little light in the barn. Jimmy methodically searched the interior of the place, feeling about with his hands and pressing his eyes close to object after object, until he found a lantern and a box of safety matches. He lit the lantern, and then came up behind Cato. He set the lantern and his knife on the floor. There was not enough room for him to wedge in between the post and the wall so that Cato could see him. Instead, Jimmy gently slipped his hands under Cato's arms, pushed them around Cato's chest, and latched them together so that he could support Cato's weight.

"I've got you," Jimmy said.

Immediately Cato let his body swoon into Jimmy's arms. As he did so, Jimmy saw the wounds on Cato's back. "Oh God!" Jimmy cried. "Look what they've done."

"I got whipped," Cato said.

"It looks bad," said Jimmy.

"It hurts bad," Cato confirmed.

Jimmy buried his nose into Cato's hair. "I'm gonna get you out of here," he whispered.

Cato turned his head slightly. He saw the knife lying on the ground. "How?" he asked, nodding down toward the knife. "With that?"

Jimmy slid one of his hands down Cato's arm. He gently

moved Cato's arm so that he could get a better look at the iron manacle. He inspected the keyhole in the manacle's lock.

"I'm gonna get the key," Jimmy said. "The knife is to make sure that whoever has that key will give it to me." Then, after a pause, he said, "Who's got the key?"

Now Cato tried to twist his face back toward Jimmy. "No," he whispered. "Don't do anything. You'll get in trouble. It's bad enough that I'm in trouble."

"Who has it?" Jimmy said again.

"My father has the key," said Cato. "But you can't get it from him."

"I'm gonna kill him," Jimmy said. "And then we're gonna get ourselves out of here for good."

"No!" Cato's voice was so loud it was startling. "No," he said again more softly, turning back to face the wall. "I don't want you to kill him."

"I have to," Jimmy said.

"You don't understand. It was just because he got so angry," Cato said. "Tomorrow he'll calm down. He's never whipped me like this before."

"He's got the key, doesn't he?"

Cato did not respond.

"Where is he?"

Again, Cato did not respond.

"Is he back in the house?"

Now Cato pleaded. "Just stay here with me. Please stay and talk to me."

"I'll talk to you after I get you out of these damn chains." Jimmy stepped away. He reached down to pick up the knife.

"Wait," Cato cried. "Please … don't go!"

Jimmy looked down at the crisscrossed lines on Cato's back. "Damn him," Jimmy said. "I swear I'm going to kill him!"

"No, you can't. You must not! They'll kill you, Jimmy. I couldn't stand it if they kill you."

Jimmy reached out and grabbed Cato by the chin. He turned Cato's head around far enough so that he could lean his face in and kiss him on the lips. There were tears on Jimmy's cheeks. His eyes were wide and wild. "I'm sorry," Jimmy said. "I have to do it." And with that, Jimmy walked away. He slipped back out through the crack in the barn doors. He stepped once again into the dampness of the night air.

As soon as Jimmy approached the Askew house he saw the fire. Smoke streamed out of the side of the house, as if a chimney had been installed there. He could see the flicker and flash of orange and yellow flames behind that black smoke. Jimmy's rage was so intense that for a moment he felt as if he himself had willed the fire into existence. No one was outside. No one was stirring. He quickly deduced that the old man must still be in there, and that he must be burning up. Adrenaline rushed through his body. He was exhilarated. But then he remembered that it was Augustus who had the key—and he realized that fire or no, he had to get that key.

Without further deliberation, Jimmy dashed up the stairs of the house. He kicked open the front door. He stepped into the foyer. As soon as he stepped inside, he was confronted by the snarl of a menacing dog. And while the dog saw the knife gleaming in Jimmy's hand, it was not the fact of the knife to which the dog reacted, but to Jimmy's anger, which peeled off him in waves. Scout bared his teeth. He summoned up a ferocious growl with all the menace he could muster. The growl was foreboding—not so much a warning as a wind up for the attack Jimmy's hostility demanded.

Then, just as Scout's muscles tightened for a tremendous leap, the unmistakable sound of a human voice, crying for help, rose from out of the interior depths of the house. The dog stopped, arrested by his master's cry. Scout was forced by the sound to grapple with which was the greater menace, the fire or the man with the knife. Scout enacted his grappling by pacing in a circle, a space marking that Jimmy recognized as the same deliberating language he knew from Venus. The dog's movements, in fact, were so similar to those of Venus that Jimmy found himself picturing her in his mind's eye.

Scout, after his circular pacing, chose a gambit not entirely instinctive. He stopped moving. He looked at Jimmy not with menacing, but with pleading eyes. These were not the eyes of a creature merely intent on violent defense. These were the eyes of a creature desperate to save his master.

Jimmy looked squarely into the dog's eyes. He saw that the dog was acting instinctively, that by its growl it had meant to defend its master. But now he saw that this pleading look, this transition from predator to supplicant, this deliberate discarding of the violent defensive impulse was something new. And it occurred to him that this entreating look was the same kind of look that Venus might have summoned.

In the shining brown eyes of the strange dog, there was something recognizable. For a moment Jimmy thought, insanely, that Venus had taken over the very dog that stood before him. He could not make any sense of the recognition that filled him. But the force of that recognition hit him hard enough that he lowered his hand; he stumbled, as if he had been knocked back by the impact of a revelation, and he said the name "Venus" out loud with a small, hollow voice.

Upon hearing Jimmy speak, the dog cocked its head. It twitched an ear. Something passed between them.

Scout lifted his tail. Scout motioned with his snout. Scout understood the special demands of the moment. The master was in great danger. The danger was greater than Scout's ability to defy it. There was no choice but to collaborate with this ominous man. He transmitted, as clearly as he could via the wordless mechanism of eyes and gestures, an emphatic declaration of the right path.

Jimmy gestured toward the frantic dog with a nod of his head. Scout turned and led the way, leaping through the narrow wall of smoke that spread across the threshold of the study door. Jimmy followed.

Inside the room the heat and sound of the fire was intense. The fire had moved from the drapery, which covered a window to the left of the fireplace, in a straight line back toward the rear wall of the study. A bookshelf, which had sat along that wall, was a raging ball of flames at the heart of the inferno. Much of the back third of the room was burning furiously. The breeze, which flowed in at an angle from the open window where the drapery had been, seemed both to feed the fire and keep it pushed back against the wall.

In a matter of moments, Jimmy saw him. He was lying on the floor on his side in an unnatural position in front of the fireplace. His feet were dangerously close to the curtain of flame that fell across the back of the room. The man's free arm was stretched up. His arm slowly flailed, like a clock pendulum that had wound down to its last store of energy. As the dog approached, the old master rolled onto his back and exclaimed, "Scout!" with hope in his voice. But even as he spoke, the old man's eyes shifted from the face of his dog to that of the tall dark slave that stood above him, holding a knife.

Jimmy looked down upon the face of Augustus Askew. He had seen the man before, but never at such close proximity. Even now, in the flicker and shadow of the burning fire, the face was eerily familiar. He saw the recognizable juxtaposition of all that he loved and all that he reviled combined into a single face. There in the terrified eyes of the helpless slave owner was the blood source, the undeniable flesh from which

Cato had sprung. The face of the man he so loved was held in the ether of the face of the man he so hated. Jimmy placed the knife sideways in his mouth and held it between his teeth. He bent down toward Augustus, who recoiled instinctively.

Jimmy yanked on Augustus's body. He tried to pull him up, but the man resisted.

"Help," Augustus cried. He turned his head from side to side. He did not know what to think. He could not tell what was happening. He did not know what this rough Negro planned to do to him, but he could clearly see the knife that gleamed between the slave's teeth.

Scout barked. Augustus turned to Scout and in a weak, pitiable voice, he cried again, "Help."

"Shut up," Jimmy said.

Now Augustus unleashed the fullness of his terror. "Ahhhh-hhh!" He emitted a long, resonant scream, so shrill and high pitched that it did not sound like a man's voice. At the same time, in a helpless reflex he urinated on himself.

Jimmy saw the spreading stain of wet on the man's legs. Jimmy leaned down again, and once again, he yanked on Augustus's body—even harder this time. Augustus flailed against Jimmy's grip. He pounded weakly on Jimmy's arms with his fists. But Jimmy's arms tightened around him like a vise.

Scout paced frantically now. He too could not deduce what Jimmy meant to do. He barked again, and suddenly darted in to nip at Jimmy's legs.

"Hold still!" Jimmy shouted.

Cowed by the force of this command, the old man stopped his flailing. Slowly Jimmy rose Augustus's body up. Jimmy tried to stand him on his feet. When he saw that the old man was hurt, that he could not hold his own weight, Jimmy pulled him up hard and slung him, roughly, onto his shoulder. To keep from falling, Augustus slung his arms around Jimmy's neck. They both coughed at the same time. Smoke swirled around the upper half of the room. Jimmy had to crouch down in order to get his head low enough to breathe.

Augustus Askew, not knowing what else to do, whispered into Jimmy's ear, "Save me!"

# THE CROWS

*E*lla came to with a start. She was on Juba Jake's bed. Wally, Jake and Dorothy stood alongside the bed watching her.

Ella looked at the people around her. "What happened?"

Jake leaned over the bed. "You fell off the horse, honey."

"Fortunately," Dorothy added, "Walnut was kind enough to drop you in the bushes."

Wally touched Ella's forehead. "How d'you feel, baby?"

Ella stretched her body. She joined her hand to Wally's on her forehead. "I guess I'm OK," she said. "I feel all in one piece."

"You didn't break anything?" asked Jake.

Ella shook her head. "No." She wiggled her arms and legs. "Everything works." Then she looked at Wally and her expression changed. "We've got to go get Jimmy."

But Dorothy leaned in and touched Ella's arm. "You don't have to go get anybody. Wally told me what happened. Willis has gone to hitch Maple to the wagon. Willis and I will go get Jimmy," she said.

Ella sat up. "No! You've got to let me come with you," she said. Then she clambered off the bed and made a show of standing up straight. "I'm OK, see—and I have to go. Look here, he won't listen to you. I've got to go."

Dorothy pondered this.

"Don't worry. I'm OK," Ella said. She took Dorothy by the hand. "Come on now. I'm not hurt." She pulled on Dorothy's arm. "Let's go. We've got to hurry if we're going to catch him."

Without waiting for an answer, Ella went out into the yard. Dorothy and Wally went out after her. Willis was already there, sitting in the wagon. Maple was hitched and ready to go.

"Are you sure you're OK?" Dorothy asked.

"I'm sure," said Ella. She grabbed hold of the side of the wagon and climbed into it. "Come on."

"Ella baby," Wally said. "You ought to rest."

"You know I got to go get him, mama," Ella said. "Dorothy, come on."

Dorothy climbed into the wagon. "All right," she said. "Willis, take us up the road toward Hickory Grove."

Willis gave the reins a yank and they headed out onto Christmasville Road.

Back at Hickory Grove, Jimmy lurched out onto the front porch with Augustus slung around his shoulders. He took a deep breath and bounded down the stairs. At the bottom of the stairs, he slung Augustus onto the ground, then rolled him onto his back.

Jimmy leaned down and spoke directly into Augustus's face. "I need the key," he demanded. He removed the knife from his mouth and grasped it firmly by the handle.

Augustus stared at the knife. His leg was in pain. He heard what Jimmy said. But he didn't understand what was wanted. He looked at Jimmy with obvious confusion.

"I want the key to that chain you put on Cato," Jimmy

said. He waved the knife in front of Augustus's eyes. He forced his hand into Augustus's right trouser pocket. There was nothing there, but it was wet from urine.

Augustus cried for help yet again.

Scout barked. Then both Jimmy and Augustus heard a scream. Henry stumbled out the front door of the house. The shirt on his right arm was in flames. He ran down the stairs and threw himself onto the lawn. He rolled around in the grass until the flame was smothered.

Jimmy had to act quickly. He stuck his hand in Augustus's other trouser pocket—again he found nothing. "Where is it?" Jimmy yelled.

Augustus turned his head toward Henry. "Help! Help!"

Henry lay on the ground on his back about fifteen feet away. He was gasping with long, hard breaths. He seemed to be staring up at the sky. But then he turned to the side and saw Jimmy holding the knife above Augustus's neck. Instantly, he started to get up.

As soon as Jimmy saw Henry get up, he turned and brandished the knife in Henry's direction. "Keep back!" he shouted.

Augustus put his hands up to his collar—as if to clutch at something on his neck.

Jimmy glimpsed a thin strand of fine chain on Augustus's neck, just outside the right edge of his collar. Jimmy lowered the knife until his hand was above Augustus's shirt. Without loosening his grip on the knife, he looped one of his fingers under Augustus's collar. He took hold of the other side of the collar with his free hand. Then with both hands, he ripped apart the seams of the shirt. Buttons popped into the air as the shirt tore apart. Not a key, but a cross hung at the bottom of the chain around Augustus's neck. In disgust, Jimmy yanked on the necklace but it did not come off. Jimmy spit in Augustus's face.

Seeing this, Henry crouched down and held his hands toward Jimmy with his palms out. He took a step forward.

"Get back," Jimmy said. He pointed the knife in Henry's direction. Keeping his eyes on Henry, he felt around with his free hand, and slid it into Augustus's vest pocket. There he felt a solid iron key. He looked down to inspect it.

As soon as Jimmy was distracted, Henry took another step toward him. But Jimmy snatched the key out of Augustus's pocket, stood up and turned toward Henry. With the knife in his right hand pointed straight at him, Jimmy charged toward Henry. Henry backtracked quickly, until he almost tripped on a hydrangea bush.

When he saw Henry stumble, Jimmy stopped. "I'm going to go away now," he yelled. "If you follow me, I'll cut you. If you don't want the whole place to burn down, you better see to the fire." Jimmy lowered the knife, and began to back away.

Henry looked around at the burning house. It was true. He would have to rouse the others and get help to put out the fire. "I know who you are," he shouted at Jimmy. "They'll catch you!" Henry started to circle back toward Augustus.

"I didn't start that fire," Jimmy yelled, then he turned and ran straight toward the barn. When he reached the barn, he looked back. He saw Henry crouching over Augustus, trying to raise him into a sitting position.

Jimmy slipped quietly into the barn and went directly to Cato.

Cato had heard the shouting outside, but couldn't make sense of it. "What's going on?" he asked.

"I'll tell you later," Jimmy said. He put the key into the keyhole of the left manacle and tried to twist it, but it wouldn't turn. "Damn!" He pulled the key out and pushed it in front of Cato's face. "Is this the key?"

Cato squinted to try to see it better. "I can't tell," he said. "It looks like the right key. Try my other hand."

Jimmy tried the key on the other manacle. This time the key turned easily, and the cuff opened. Jimmy quickly put the key back into the left manacle.

"Don't force it," Cato said. "Be nimble."

"Nimble," Jimmy said. "Yeah, nimble." He fidgeted the key in the lock. After a moment, it turned. The manacle came off.

Freed from his position facing the wall, Cato turned around to face Jimmy.

"We've got to get out of here now," Jimmy said. "The house is on fire. They think I started it."

"What!"

"I don't know how it started," Jimmy said. "I went into the house and pulled your daddy out of there."

"You pulled him out of the fire?" There was doubt in Cato's voice.

"His leg got twisted up somehow," Jimmy said. "He couldn't walk. I carried him out."

"So you didn't hurt him?"

"No."

"Then how come they think you started it?" Cato asked.

"I don't know," Jimmy said. "But they're gonna blame it all on me. They saw me with the knife."

"Who else saw you?"

"Henry," said Jimmy. "Come on now. Can you walk?"

Cato took a few steps. "I think so."

"Let's go then. We've got to hurry."

When they got to the barn doors, Jimmy held them apart so that Cato could squeeze through. As soon as he got outside, Cato could see and smell the fire. Flames shot out of both sides of the house. A thick cloud of black smoke hung in the sky overhead. "Oh Jimmy," Cato cried. "The whole house will burn up!"

Jimmy slipped out of the barn doors after him. "Forget about the house," he said. "There's nothing you can do about it now. They're gonna come after us. We've got to make a run for it."

Overhead a circling crow cawed plaintively. Soon a dozen other crows flapped off nearby trees and formed a wide circle, flying in the dark sky above the house. Each crow cawed individually at first. But then, gradually they began to caw more and more loudly in unison. Since crows were rarely heard in the dark, the sound had the effect of an alarm, which roused the slaves who lived in the rows of cabins behind the burning house.

Jimmy and Cato began to work their way down the long driveway lined with hickory trees. Mr. Flint had taken away Cato's shirt before chaining him up. Now in the cool October night air, Cato shivered with chill. They tried to walk as quietly as possible. But they could not help stepping on the hickory nuts which lay everywhere on the ground around the trees. When Jimmy looked back toward the house, he saw dozens of field hands swarming around the perimeter of the house. The night air was filled with the sounds of men shouting, birds cawing, and the pop of hickory nuts being cracked underfoot.

Suddenly a new sound joined the others. The wagon carrying Willis, Dorothy and Ella rattled in a rush through the Hickory Grove gate. As soon as Jimmy saw who was in the oncoming wagon, he leapt out in front of it, and Willis pulled hard on the reins to try to stop Maple in her tracks. But the horse could not stop quickly enough, and Jimmy threw himself to the side of the lane to get out of the way. He landed on his side in the dirt.

When the wagon had stopped, Ella jumped out and ran

back to him where he was on the ground. Cato crouched over him. When Jimmy tried to stand up, he found that he could. But he walked with a limp toward the wagon. Cato and Ella walked on either side of him. Willis had gotten down from the driver's seat. He grabbed the side of the bit in Maple's bridle and led her in a tight circle, in order to turn the wagon around in the lane.

When the wagon was turned back toward the gates, Willis, Ella, Jimmy and Cato all climbed in—and once again, Willis drove the horse back onto Christmasville Road.

"Where's that damn knife?" Ella asked.

"I dropped it," Jimmy said. "When I jumped out of the way just now."

Ella and Dorothy had many questions. Why was the house on fire? Why had Jimmy taken the knife? How had Jimmy freed Cato from the chains? What had Jimmy done to Mr. Askew? How bad was Cato hurt by the whipping? How bad was Mr. Askew hurt by the fire? What had happened to Henry?

In the course of answering these questions, Jimmy made it clear that he had not started the fire, and that he had done nothing to Mr. Askew beyond rescuing him from certain death. But Henry had seen Jimmy wielding the knife and Mr. Askew had reacted throughout the ordeal as if Jimmy was going to kill him. Therefore, Jimmy concluded, once the authorities had come, once the fire had burned out, the local paddy rollers would be looking not only for Cato, who was now officially a runaway, but also for Jimmy, who was sure to be accused of attempted murder.

"Does Henry know where you live?" Dorothy asked.

"He knows me," Jimmy said, "because he's seen me with Cato, but I don't know if he knows where I'm from."

"Does he know your name?"

Cato answered this. "I don't think he does. Henry hardly

ever talks to me. I've never told him Jimmy's name, and he's never asked."

"I wonder if we should go back and get that knife," Dorothy said. "Was it a knife from our kitchen?"

"Yes." Jimmy answered.

"How would anyone know it was from your house?" Cato asked.

"Someone could recognize it," Dorothy said. "My mother has visitors over all the time."

"Stop the wagon," Ella said. "I'll go back and get it. Nobody will pay me any mind with that fire going on. But y'all need to keep going and get out of sight."

Willis brought the wagon to a halt. Jimmy looked at Ella. "I can go back for the knife," he said. "It was me who took it."

"Yes and it's you they'll be looking for," said Ella.

"We have to go into town," Dorothy said. "We have to go get the fire brigade. Ella, I think you're right—you should get out here. You should go get the knife, then walk back to the house. Willis and I will leave Jimmy and Cato at the house, and then we'll go on into town for help."

"How will you explain why you were out at Hickory Grove?" Cato asked.

"I'll just say we saw the fire from down at our house," Dorothy said. "It's practically true. We could see something was burning just after we got onto the road."

Ella got out of the wagon. "What about Cato?" she asked. "Where are we gonna hide him?"

"We'll have to hide him in your cabin," Dorothy said. "Just for tonight. I'll think of something better after tonight."

And so the wagon took off. Ella walked back toward Hickory Grove to look for the knife beneath the trees. Dorothy and Willis left Jimmy and Cato at the entrance to the Hollands' farm. Then they drove as fast as they could toward

Jackson to get the fire brigade—even though at this point they knew there was little hope of salvaging Augustus Askew's house.

At the Holland farm, Jimmy got some salve from Cora, which he rubbed onto Cato's back. Jimmy tucked Cato under a cover in his own straw bed, where he lay unabashedly beside him, holding his arms around him. Eventually, Cato fell asleep. Cato dreamed not of the whipping, but of the tinkling sounds of a piano, which Miss Bennet played for Mr. Darcy. Until in the midst of the dream, Cato saw that the pages of "Pride and Prejudice," along with all the other books in the Askew's library, were burning up in the flames.

## 33

## HENRIETTA'S INVITATION

*T*he next day all of Jackson was abuzz with talk of the fire. The brave old men of the fire brigade had saved all of the out buildings on the Askew plantation, but not, alas, the Askew home itself. Both Mr. Askew and his house servant Henry had been brought into town with great urgency to see Doctor Thorne. Dr. Thorne had determined that Mr. Askew had suffered a sprain in his right ankle, and that Henry had suffered second-degree burns on a portion of his right arm. The doctor wrapped up Mr. Askew's right ankle in a tight bandage to hold it fast. He wrapped up Henry's right arm in a loose bandage to let it breathe. He gave each of them a place to sleep in his home for the night.

What the citizens of Jackson did not know was that Ella had successfully retrieved a knife from a small ditch along the side of the entry lane at Hickory Grove. When the fire brigade came galloping into the plantation, she had ducked out of sight behind a hickory tree. Then she had walked back to the Hollands' farm without being noticed.

In the morning, Henrietta Holland heard the details of the

tragedy from Mrs. Greer. Henrietta decided that it would be appropriate for her, as Mr. Askew's nearest neighbor, to go to town to visit him and offer assistance. As she explained to Mrs. Greer, with the war and the general uncertainty in the world, she felt it was more crucial than ever that they should all stick together. Without discussing the matter with her husband or daughter, she had Willis drive her into town. Henrietta arrived at the entrance to Dr. Thorne's home, climbed the steps, and boldly rang the bell. Dr. Thorne's house servant answered, and said that yes, indeed, Mr. Askew was resting within.

"Pray inform Mr. Askew that his neighbor Henrietta Holland is calling to offer assistance," she said.

She waited while the servant delivered her message. When he returned, she followed him up the stairs to the small room where Mr. Askew sat propped in a bed, with his bandaged leg thrust out above the covers. He appeared to be still wearing the clothes that he had worn when the fire occurred. He did not have the appearance of having had any sleep.

"It is kind of you to come, Mrs. Holland," said Mr. Askew with words that were polite, but in a tone that was weary.

"Such a terrible tragedy, Mr. Askew," she said. "My husband, my daughter, and I—we are all shocked. These are unsettling times. It seems that anything can happen without warning."

Augustus looked at Henrietta and nodded, but his eyes were glazed over. He seemed, in fact, to look right through her. He attempted a cordial smile, but she saw that he seemed in a stupor.

"They tell me that your house has been lost, Mr. Askew" she continued. "But that all the other buildings were saved."

He nodded.

"Oh, what a tragedy! I suppose there's nothing to do but to

rebuild the house. Do you have any slaves who are skilled in carpentry?"

Augustus shrugged his shoulders. "I haven't had any time, Mrs. Holland, to consider what I will do, or what steps I should take," he said. Then he looked grimly down at his leg. "It seems for the moment that I shan't be able to take any steps at all."

Mrs. Holland nodded an acknowledgment in the direction of Mr. Askew's leg. "Oh yes, of course. Of course, Mr. Askew. There will be plenty of time to make arrangements for everything. But what about you? Do you have kin in the area? Do you have someone with whom you can stay? Someone to look after you?"

Augustus shook his head. "There is only my son, I'm afraid. And he, of course, is fighting in the war."

Without premeditation Henrietta said, "We have room in our home, Mr. Askew. Why don't you come and stay with us? It would be good for you to be near your property. We can look after you for a time—until you are back on your feet."

Now Augustus's eyes focused on Henrietta's face, and he visibly roused himself from his stupor. The kindness she intended was comforting. But it also made him realize the enormity of his predicament and the degree to which he would have to depend upon others for assistance. He did not relish being stuck in his neighbor's house, or being obliged to her because of her ministrations. Yet he had to admit it would be a convenient arrangement. He sighed. "Ah, you are too kind," he said. Then he looked around the room, as if he had suddenly lost something. "Oh dear!" he exclaimed. "What's happened to my dog? The dog helped save me, Mrs. Holland."

"Perhaps Dr. Thorne has your dog downstairs," she suggested.

"It's not like Scout to stay away," he said. "Mrs. Holland,

would you mind, could you ask Dr. Thorne to come up? I must find out what has happened to my dog."

Henrietta did as he requested, and Dr. Thorne came to the room. Dr. Thorne said that he was sorry but no dog had been brought to the house– no soul other than Henry and Mr. Askew had been handed into his care.

"But then what has happened to Scout?" Augustus cried. "I must find him. I promised my son that I would take care of him."

"Now, now, Askew, you don't need to worry about a dog just now," said Dr. Thorne.

"Oh but I must be sure that he is not hurt," said Augustus.

"Did you see the dog come out of the building?" inquired Dr. Thorne.

"Yes, yes, I'm certain he came out. Scout came out with me ... he came out with me and that ..." Augustus paused, not certain how to describe the man who had carried him out, "with me and that nigger that brought me outside."

"Who was it that brought you outside?" asked Dr. Thorne.

"I don't know," said Augustus. "It was a nigger I've never seen before. He came out of nowhere, and he was wielding a knife, though heaven knows why. He carried me out of the building. He stole a key from my pocket. And then he used it to unchain one of my slaves who was being punished. Then they both disappeared. It was the most extraordinary thing."

"When I get home," Henrietta offered. "I can have one of our servants go out to look for your dog. If the dog got out of the building, the poor creature is bound to be somewhere around the area."

"He must be so confused," said Augustus—feeling considerable empathy with that state. "Mrs. Holland, would it be possible for you to take me back home with you now? I must find out what has happened to my dog."

Before Henrietta could reply, Dr. Thorne said, "My dear fellow, you need to stay off your feet if you're going to get better."

"Yes, but I can't stay here," Augustus replied. "And if I'm to be moved to another location, they may as well move me today as move me tomorrow."

Dr. Thorne considered that there was some logic in this.

"Mrs. Holland has kindly offered to take me into her home as a guest for the time being," Augustus continued. "And it would be good for me to be close to Hickory Grove. Dr. Thorne, if you would be so kind as to make arrangements to send my servant Henry back to Hickory Grove, he has a sister who can take care of him in her cabin. And if you can also make arrangements to transport me to the Hollands' house, I would be happy to reimburse you for your trouble in both these matters."

"Oh, but I can take you," Henrietta said. "I came in our wagon with my driver. Dr. Thorne, if you have someone who could assist my driver, perhaps they could carry Mr. Askew to the wagon, and we could transport him back with us."

In consideration of these requests, Dr. Thorne agreed to have his servant help Willis carry Mr. Askew down to Mrs. Holland's wagon. He would then have his servant drive Henry back to Hickory Grove in his brougham.

And so it was that, acting on her own impulse, Mrs. Holland found at last what seemed to her to be a fitting retaliation for her husband's impulses in acquiring and then selling Sammy without her consent. She knew that under the circumstances, her husband could hardly refuse to take in Mr. Askew. It pleased her to think that George would have to bear with her decision, just as she had had to bear with his. But she was truly sincere in her desire to assist someone of Mr. Askew's caliber, not only because she had calculated that it would raise her social stature in the eyes of her friends, but also because she did, in fact, feel that it was morally the right thing to do.

So when Willis drove the wagon into the yard of the Hollands' farm with Mr. Augustus Askew lying in the back of it wrapped in a gray blanket, Wally, Sammy, Cora, and Ella came out to the yard to see him. Jimmy, who had caught a glimpse of Augustus from the door of the cabin, slipped back inside to warn Cato. Wally and Ella, no less aware of the danger of having Mr. Askew in such close proximity to Jimmy and Cato—listened intently as Mrs. Holland explained the situation.

After Henrietta had made it clear that Mr. Askew was to be taken in as a special houseguest, she said to Ella, "Now go and fetch Jimmy. He needs to help Willis carry Mr. Askew into the house. And then, Ella, you need to go look for Mr. Askew's dog. The dog has somehow become lost in all the commotion."

"Excuse me Missus Holland," said Ella, "but perhaps it would be better if Jimmy went to look for the dog. He's particular good with dogs. I can fetch Paymore to help carry Mr. Askew into the house."

"Very well then," said Mrs. Holland. "But hurry up and get someone. I'm sure Mr. Askew is none too comfortable lying here in the wagon."

"Yes'm."

Ella determined that she had best begin by getting someone to take Mr. Askew into the house. She went to Paymore's cabin, but found he wasn't there—so she asked Big Andrew and Little Andrew if they could assist Willis in transporting Mr. Askew into the big house. By the time Ella returned with help, Dorothy and her father had also come down to the yard.

"George, I've told Mr. Askew that he's welcome to stay with us until he can get back on his feet."

"Ah—yes, of course," George said quickly. "But where would you think it best for Mr. Askew to sleep, my dear?"

"Why in the back parlor of course," said Henrietta. "We can have a bed put in there. And George, one of Mr. Askew's house servants was hurt in the fire, and the other one, it seems, has run away. Under the circumstances, I think we should have our Sammy look after Mr. Askew for the time being, don't you agree?" This was Henrietta's coup de grace and it was not lost upon her husband.

"Ah yes, well … Sammy, or perhaps Ella, can look after him" said Mr. Holland with a note of doubt in his voice. "I'm sure we can make any necessary arrangements in due course."

"I can help carry him up," said Sammy, who had been leaning over the side of the wagon and staring at Mr. Askew in his blanket. "Did his mama die and he got sold to us too?"

"Hush up child," Wally quickly interjected, but not before Augustus let loose a strange, dry laugh.

"No, no, Sammy—Mr. Askew's house burned down," Mr. Holland explained. "That's how come he's going to live here for now."

"Oh," said Sammy, and he looked with great pity upon the man in the blanket.

"Now Ella," said Mrs. Holland, "you better run and get Jimmy. Have him go look for Mr. Askew's dog."

"I'll go right now," said Ella.

"I'd be much obliged, Mrs. Holland" said Mr. Askew, "if you could also send someone to bring round Mr. Flint, my overseer. I shall need to make arrangements with him for a great many things."

"Certainly, certainly," said Henrietta. "Ella, you take care of it."

Up until now, Dorothy had said nothing. Her mind was racing as she tried to calculate how she would be able to keep

Jimmy and Cato out of Mr. Askew's sight while he was a houseguest. The back parlor, she realized, was on the far side of the house from the yard. That meant there was little chance, at least, of Mr. Askew glancing out the window and seeing them. But it would require great care. Harboring a runaway would not only put her in legal jeopardy, it might also jeopardize her relationship with William. If only she and William were already married, Cato might even now be legally under her jurisdiction. Having heard what had happened during the fire from Jimmy, she didn't know whether or not Mr. Askew considered Jimmy his rescuer or his assailant. But she knew that he was aware that Jimmy had taken the key to free Cato and was therefore guilty of theft. So while Cato would have to be hidden from everyone, Jimmy would have to be hidden from Mr. Askew as well.

"Ella, I'll go with you," she said. "Mother, I can take Jimmy to look for the dog, and I would be happy to fetch Mr. Flint."

Augustus looked around at Dorothy, not having realized that she was among the many onlookers who surrounded him. "Ah, my dear," he said. "I would be most grateful."

While Big Andrew, Little Andrew, and Willis carried Mr. Askew into the house, Dorothy and Ella went to the cabin.

"What's he doing here?" Jimmy demanded to know.

"My mother wants him to live with us until his house is rebuilt."

"What! But if he sees Cato—or if he sees me …."

"We'll just have to make certain that he doesn't see either of you," Dorothy said. "In the meantime, mother wants someone to go look for Mr. Askew's lost dog. Ella suggested that you could do it, Jimmy."

"Me?" Jimmy turned to Ella with a look of disbelief.

"I had to say that," Ella said. "Missus Holland wanted me

to have you go out there and carry Mr. Askew into the house. I had to say that you'd be better at looking for the dog."

"I'll take you to Hickory Grove," Dorothy said. "You can look for this dog, and I can find the overseer, Mr. Flint. Does Mr. Flint know who you are?"

Jimmy grimaced. "I've seen Mr. Flint out in the field whipping the slaves," he said. "But he's never seen me."

"He knows me," said Cato.

Everyone turned to look at Cato, who had been sitting quietly on the bed. He was still in pain, and his voice was subdued.

"We're going to have to hide you," Dorothy said. She looked up at the ceiling, which consisted of a row of boards laid across the ceiling joists. "There is space up there, above the ceiling boards and below the roof. If we could get Willis to make a trap-door, you could get up there to hide if we put a chair on top of the table."

"How would he breathe up there?" Jimmy asked.

"Willis could find a space below the roof line to drill a few holes for ventilation."

"Miss Holland, you're taking too much risk on my account," said Cato. "I think I should go to him. I can tell him I just ran away for one night because of the fire."

"No," Jimmy said. "What's to stop him from chaining you up and whipping you again?"

"Right now he can't even walk," Cato said. "And his house burned down. All in all, he's got more to worry about than me knowing how to read."

"I think Cato may be right," Dorothy said to Jimmy. "At some point, when William and I get married, we can ask that his father give Cato to us as a gift. Then he'll be safe forever."

Jimmy glared at Dorothy. "No," he said. "I don't trust him.

Did you see what that man did?" He moved toward Cato. "Take off your shirt and show her."

But Dorothy held up her hand. "You don't need to do that," she said. She turned to Jimmy. She was surprised by how forcefully Jimmy had spoken to her. "I think we all need time to decide what's best. I'll ask Willis to make the trap door. That will give all of us time to think about what to do. For now, you and I need to go to Hickory Grove."

So Dorothy and Jimmy walked up Christmasville Road to Hickory Grove. Dorothy went in search of Mr. Flint, and Jimmy went in search of the dog. But Jimmy's mind was not on the dog. He was thinking that the time had come for him to run away. He would have to take Cato and escape to the North. It was impossible to stay in the same place where either of them could be recognized by that evil old man.

He was preoccupied with thoughts about various escape schemes as he wandered about in the woods looking for the dog. From time to time, he half-heartedly called out the dog's name. "Scout!" Cato had told him what the dog was called. "Come on you damn dog. Come and get me. You were ready enough to get me last night."

But the dog was nowhere to be seen. Jimmy searched the entire woods surrounding the perimeter of Hickory Grove. His trousers were covered with stickers. As the afternoon wore on, his musings grew more nostalgic. He remembered the day when Cato had pulled stickers out of Venus, and he had brushed Venus's ears. That day Cato had dared to touch his ear playfully. If only he had realized sooner what was possible. And now the situation compelled them to sleep together, with Jimmy literally hiding Cato in his arms beneath the covers. He tried to imagine a life in which they would be together all the time—maybe in the Union army—maybe in a shack some-where far from the rest of the world, somewhere out west.

Since he was tired, he sat down on a fallen log. Then after sitting for a while, he lay down on the log and closed his eyes. He imagined the crawl space in the roof of his cabin. He imagined lying in bed naked, looking up at Cato, looking back down at him through the trap door. In a matter of moments, he dozed into a nap.

When he awoke, the sun was noticeably lower in the sky. He sat up with a start. He couldn't afford to be caught without a pass after dark. He blinked his eyes. He thought he saw something move in the distance. When he stood up, whatever it was moved away. He walked toward the spot, which he had fixed in his mind as the juncture of two straight thin trees. When he got closer to the trees, he saw something move again. This time he was sure it was the dog. "Come on, Scout," he called out. "I'm not gonna hurt you, damn it." He took several steps closer. "Look," he said. "See. No knife." As he got closer, he saw the dog's tail as it moved behind a tree. "Come on, boy. You don't want to stay out here at night. Those paddy rollers will come and get you."

Jimmy crept as stealthily as he could toward the tree behind which the dog had hidden. When he got to the tree, he lunged around behind it—but the spot was empty. Then he felt something brush against the back of his leg. He looked around. Scout was standing right behind him, staring at Jimmy with his mouth open in a strange kind of smile. It was almost as if the dog were playing a game.

## 34

## SAMMY AND AUGUSTUS

*I*t may come as no surprise that in the dispute between Mr. and Mrs. Holland regarding which of the slaves would be temporarily assigned the role of servant for Mr. Askew, Mrs. Holland prevailed. It was agreed by all that young Sammy would be appointed to that position. Mrs. Holland negotiated the matter with Dorothy, who, it must be remembered, was Sammy's official guardian. Dorothy was receptive to the proposal because it was expedient. She knew that Ella had a poor opinion of Mr. Askew, and thus was not well disposed to being given the task. Whereas Sammy, who had ascertained that Mr. Askew shared with him the fate of having been cast into a relationship with the Hollands by cruel external forces, indicated that he would find it agreeable to undertake the job. Sammy's reasoning in this matter was not encumbered by any knowledge of Mr. Askew's biography. It was based rather upon a sense of collegiality which Sammy felt in response to seeing a fellow down on his luck, a fellow who might benefit from the tutelage of one who had already accumulated some experience in the hows and wherefores of fitting into a strange new household.

Insofar as Mr. Askew was confined to his bed, Sammy was obliged to forgo taking Mr. Askew upon an introductory expedition about the premises. In lieu of this, Sammy opted to impart his insights into the attractions of the Hollands' estate through narrative description. Since Mr. Askew did not grasp the fact that Sammy viewed him as having a shared predicament, he was unprepared for Sammy's sincere desire to orient him to his new surroundings.

"This room you're in," said Sammy, "this is what they call the back parlor. I don't know why they call it that, because it is nothing like the front parlor. They bring folks into the front parlor all the time. This back parlor is mostly where the women sit and sew, and they hardly ever bring the men back here at all."

"I see," said Augustus, who had already concluded that the boy was innocuous but mildly deranged.

"When I first got here," Sammy continued, "they took me around and showed me all the cabins, and the barn, and the garden, and the meat house. You'd be surprised how much there is to see when you first get here."

"No doubt," said Augustus, who nevertheless was sufficiently doubtful to make a point of surveying the view out the window as he spoke. He noted that it was beginning to get dark outside.

"When I got here they took me to the barn and showed me the horses Maple and Walnut," Sammy continued. "And the mules: Do, Re, Mi, Fa, Sol, La, and Ti. Only since I got here, Re and Fa died, so now there's only five mules. Also, Sol and La haven't been feeling too well lately. I reckon it's because they're old."

"Ah, old ... I see," said Augustus.

"Do you know how old you are?" asked Sammy. To Sammy's eyes, Mr. Askew appeared to be ancient. His hair and beard were grayer than Juba Jake's. Unlike Jake, Mr. Askew did, however, appear to retain some of his teeth. His skin, on the other hand, struck the boy as pasty and notably more wrinkled in appearance than Jake's skin. But while Mr. Askew seemed physically frail, no more than skin and bones, his demeanor gave him weight and importance that his body failed to supply.

"Yes, boy, of course I do."

"I'm not exactly sure how old I am. Jimmy says my birthday is in October because that's when Mr. Holland bought me—back in Memphis." Sammy rocked on his feet, with apparent pride in his lineage.

"Indeed."

"It's too bad you didn't get to meet Venus. Venus was our dog, but she died last year."

"Ah."

"She was my best friend. She was a good dog."

This mention of a dog reminded Augustus of his own companion. "I have a dog, too, you know."

"You do?" Sammy's eyes brightened noticeably.

"Yes, but he got lost after the fire. One of your brothers has gone out to look for him."

"That must be Jimmy," said Sammy. "Jimmy is good with dogs. I'm good with dogs, too."

"Are you now?"

"Oh yes. Venus minded me better than she minded anybody else. We taught Venus to warn me whenever Mrs. Holland was around. You see, I'm supposed to keep clear of Mrs. Holland on account of she's kind of upside down. She's mostly unhappy and I'm usually happy, so it's better if she doesn't have to lay eyes on me. So we taught Venus to go all around with me and keep a watch out for Mrs. Holland, then Venus would come and warn me with a special bark whenever she smelled Mrs. Holland nearby. Then I earn a penny for every day that Mrs. Holland doesn't lay eyes on me."

Augustus had been several times on the verge of calling Mrs. Holland and asking for new arrangements to be made regarding his temporary servant. But something held him back from this rational impulse. He was confined to his bed, and since neither Mr. Flint nor Scout had as yet been located, he was bored. Sammy's earnest banter intrigued him. "I don't understand that," he said. "Why would it bother Mrs. Holland to see you being happy?"

"Well," Sammy said, "that's a good question. I can't say I know why it bothers her. But Dorothy, Miss Holland, told me that Mrs. Holland is sad and it makes her sadder to have to see me being so happy all the time."

"How peculiar. So you're happy all the time?"

"Yes … that is … I was until Venus died. Since then I've been kind of sad like Mrs. Holland."

"Well then, I reckon there's no reason for you to keep clear of Mrs. Holland any more," Augustus observed.

Sammy smiled. "That's true. It probably wouldn't bother her too much to see me when I'm not so happy."

"You don't seem particularly sad today," said Augustus.

"No—I'm not! Ever since you got here I've been feeling happy again."

"Why is that?"

"Well I reckon it's because when you came it reminded me of when I first got here. I didn't have any friends. Then Venus came along. She was my friend. She helped me be happy. So now, I think it would be nice if I came along to be your friend. I can help you be happy too."

"I don't know," said Augustus with downcast eyes. "I don't

have much to be happy about right now. My house burned down."

"And you hurt your leg, too!"

"I did indeed."

Sammy made a point of bending over the bed to inspect Augustus's leg. "Does it hurt bad?" This was asked with fearful sincerity.

"Only if I move it the wrong way," said Augustus.

"But you're gonna get better, aren't you?"

"I suppose so."

"And then some men can rebuild your house, can't they?"

"I hope so."

"What did your house look like?"

"Oh it was a fine old house—even bigger than this one."

"Really?"

"Oh yes, much bigger, it had two parlors, a study, a library, a dining room. Why there was even a piano in the drawing room. And those were just the rooms on the first floor." Augustus spoke with pride about his house—but then, as he recalled that it was all lost, his voice darkened. "Oh, what's the use? It's all gone—all gone."

"But Jimmy's gonna find your dog," Sammy declared. "That will make you happy, won't it?"

"Yes, I hope he finds Scout."

"So that's his name," Sammy exclaimed, as if it were a momentous revelation. "Scout ...." Sammy said the name as though he were trying on a new hat.

"Yes."

"Does he do tricks?" Sammy asked.

"What kind of tricks do you mean, boy?"

"You know, like 'shake' or 'roll over' or 'play dead.'"

"Now what kind of a trick is 'play dead?'" Augustus asked, genuinely puzzled by the concept.

"That's when the dog pretends to be dead. He lies real still and doesn't move anything. Venus could do that ... and then we'd give her a bacon and she'd laugh."

"I've never heard of a dog laughing," said Augustus.

"Well it's more like a smile I reckon, but her tongue would laugh."

"I see."

"I could teach Scout to play dead, Mr. Askew, if you like," Sammy offered.

"You know how to teach dogs tricks?"

"Oh yes, and that one is easy. Dog's like to lie real still. I reckon it relaxes them."

Just at this point in the discussion, Dorothy knocked on the door, and Augustus invited her into the room. "I located Mr. Flint," she told him. "He said he would come to see you at seven o'clock tomorrow morning."

"Very good," said Augustus. "And the dog?"

"Jimmy has retrieved your dog. We have him in the front parlor. Shall I bring him to you?"

"Yes, by all means."

Dorothy went to get Scout. When she returned, Scout came in with his tail wagging. First, he went up to Augustus and nuzzled his arm. Then the dog turned to face Sammy.

"Scout!" Sammy cried. He was elated.

The dog barked in response to hearing his name expressed with such enthusiasm.

"Hi, Scout. I'm Sammy." Sammy kneeled down so that his face was at eye level with Scout's eyes. Scout moved up close to the boy. Sammy stroked his ears. Scout licked Sammy's chin, which made Sammy giggle.

"Has the dog been walked, Miss Holland?" Augustus inquired.

"Well, Mr. Askew, he appears to have been walking around

most of the night," Dorothy noted. "Jimmy found him in the woods."

"Ah, I see."

"Are you comfortable, sir? Is the boy bothering you?" Dorothy was alert to the fact Sammy's mannerisms might not be Mr. Askew's cup of tea.

"No, no. ... No bother" said Augustus. "He's promised me he's going to teach Scout new tricks. Apparently he thinks he can teach the dog to play dead."

"I don't doubt that he can, Mr. Askew," said Dorothy. "Sammy has a special fondness for dogs."

"So he told me," said Augustus.

"Well then," said Dorothy. "If everything is satisfactory, I'm going to attend to my mother. She's asked me to review the menu for today with her. Do you have any requests, Mr. Askew?"

"I'm particularly fond of pork," he replied.

"Very well," she said, and with that, she left the room.

Sammy had by now managed to entice Scout to lie down. Sammy was speaking softly to the dog, who though lying on his side, was not lying at all still. His tail thumped excitedly on the wooden floor, and he periodically raised his head so that he might better commune face to face with his instructor."

"No. Play dead," Sammy said, and he gently pushed the dog's head down and tried to settle the tail onto the floor. Subduing the tail, Sammy knew from experience, was the main challenge in teaching this trick. The dog was naturally quite excited about learning a trick. Excitement, inevitably, was conveyed in the tail. So to achieve the trick, the dog would have to master a most difficult task. He would have to suppress his enthusiasm. This is a feat commonly required of children by adults, but encouraged in dogs only by humans.

"Too bad I don't have some bacons to give him," Sammy

noted. "I reckon Scout would figure out what to do right quick if I had some bacon."

"Well then," suggested Augustus. "Why don't you go to the kitchen and get some. You may tell the cook that Mr. Askew has asked for some bacon for his dog."

"Really?"

"Oh yes, I'm quite serious," said Augustus, summoning up a quality of sternness in his voice that was amplified by the fact that he had much practice in being stern.

"OK then," said Sammy, and he rushed out the door, set upon his mission.

Augustus leaned back in his bed. This change of position caused him to move his right foot, which in turn sent a bolt of pain up his leg. He groaned. But then the pain subsided. He looked over at Scout, who was resting on the floor patiently waiting. Now that attention had been withdrawn from him, he was indeed lying as still as the dead. As Augustus looked at Scout, he thought about his situation. He had every reason in the world to be melancholy. His house was gone; his leg was hurt; and he was stuck in a stranger's home. But inexplicably, he was not melancholy. He was peaceful.

He thought about William. He knew he ought to write a letter to his son to tell him of the bad news. He hated to do that. William would want to come home immediately. But Augustus did not expect the army would allow a lieutenant to come home now under any circumstances. The Cause was first and foremost. Augustus agreed with that. Yet, he did think it was a shame that so much personal sacrifice was required. It was all the fault of the Yankees. His eyes grew dark. There was no need for any of this. The damned abolitionists! The damned Republicans! They were hell bent on turning the world upside down just because it wasn't convenient for them to have slaves. Augustus had no qualms about slavery. He was confident the

Negroes themselves would have no objection to the arrangement if they hadn't been insidiously encouraged by Republicans and gossip filtering down from the North. This
pickaninny Sammy was a perfect example. The boy's greatest
problem was that he was too happy, for God's sake. Ha! He
ought to write a letter to Abraham Lincoln and tell him just
that.

For some reason, his mind turned to Sophia, the young
Italian beauty he had met at a carnival when he was twenty.
She wasn't the sort of woman he could have married. He'd only
encountered her twice, and only once tête-à-tête. Yet
throughout his life, he thought of her from time to time. Just
after their last meeting was interrupted, he'd drawn rough
sketches of her, as best he could. And even though he'd drawn
those sketches so long ago, he still kept them in his study. Ah,
he thought, they are lost now! As he realized this, a tear gathered in the corner of his eye. He had come close to sexual
fulfillment with Sophia. He'd progressed so far with her that
day that she had removed much of her clothing—but then
they were caught by his father. Even now, forty-eight years
later, the memory of a few exquisite glimpses of her naked
body, as fleeting as they were, aroused him. He moved his hand
down his side for a moment.

But then Sammy was back with the bacon. "I got it," he
exclaimed, as he burst back into the room. Immediately,
Sammy saw the gather of moisture in Augustus's eyes. "Oh," he
said. "Does your leg hurt bad?"

Augustus looked down at his leg. "Yes, well … a little. But
I was just thinking of a young lady I knew long ago. I had
some drawings of her, and now I'm afraid they're lost forever
from the fire."

"Oh, you know, Mr. Askew I'm learning how to be an

artist," Sammy declared. "I reckon I could make you some new drawings."

"An artist?" This seemed most improbable to Augustus. "Does your master know about this?"

"Oh yes, sir. You see, I belong to Mr. Hicks now. Mr. Hicks is a painter. Mr. Hicks bought me from Master Holland last year after Master Holland didn't have enough money to pay for the painting he got from Mr. Hicks."

"Indeed."

"But you see, Mr. Hicks wants me to stay here with my family until I grow up. Then when I'm grown up, I'm going to go to Phil-delphia to help him with his painting."

"That sounds most irregular," said Augustus.

"Would you like me to do a painting of Scout? I already made a picture of my dog, Venus, on the wall of the barn. When your leg gets better, I can show it to you, if you like, Mr. Askew."

The details of Sammy's revelations knocked around in Augustus's mind. He saw that the boy was a veritable gold mine of private information. So George Holland had to sell a slave because he couldn't afford to pay the artist. Ha! It was just the sort of gossip that might be useful. Then there was the strange business about the wife being sad. He wondered what other interesting facts might be gleaned from his new charge.

"Tell me, boy, have you seen anyone new around here in the last few days? I mean any new slave?" Ever since Cato ran away, Augustus had wondered if someone nearby might be hiding him.

"Oh yes," Sammy said quickly. "Now my brother Jimmy has to share his bed with someone new." Then, in an afterthought he added, "Whoops, I'm not supposed to say anything about that."

"Why not?" asked Augustus, as he leaned forward on the bed.

Sammy's sense of right and wrong was viewed from a perspective that was different from the perspectives of most other people. Yet he understood well enough that the fact that Cato was living in their cabin was supposed to be a secret. He didn't know that it was especially supposed to be a secret from Mr. Askew. Yet he thought that he ought to be careful—not knowing how much he should or shouldn't say to his new friend. He quickly seized upon a strategy to obfuscate the situation. "Well, I reckon I shouldn't have told you, because in truth, Mr. Askew, they're not married—but they still have to share a bed." Sammy was prone to be scrupulously honest. This was his natural moral inclination. And he said what he said in a wording that he was satisfied was entirely truthful. Yet he was aware of what it implied.

"Ah, well …." Augustus's heart sank. For a moment, he'd hoped the talkative child might have information about Cato —but the boy was talking about his brother's sweetheart. It probably was a slave from Hickory Grove who ought not to be sneaking away at night. Ah well, at least it was something. "I suppose she's a slave from a nearby location," Augustus observed.

"Oh yes," Sammy said. "… a slave from somewhere around here. I hope you won't say anything, Mr. Askew … about them not being married. I know they don't mean any harm by it."

"So it's true love, is it?" Augustus asked.

"Well, I reckon so," said Sammy—though now he was veering into territory in which he was less certain of his veracity. "I know they like each other very much," he added to qualify his assertion.

Augustus sighed. He supposed he could track down which of his slaves was the culprit. But under the circumstances, it seemed rather a petty problem. True love was apt to cause unreasonable expectations in the niggers. It was best to lay down well-defined rules and limitations in all such matters. But he was feeling charitable. The brother in question had found Scout. He was grateful for that. And he supposed, since the Hollands lived so close by, that the girl's nocturnal assignations might not interfere with her work. He ought to find out who she was, though, so that he could instruct her in the terms she must abide by. But he decided to let the matter rest for the moment.

.

# "THAT'S WHAT I LIKE ABOUT
# WOODEN BOWLS"

*a*s the weeks went by, Augustus was unable to discover which of his slaves was the one being courted by Sammy's brother, Jimmy. Nor did he ever catch a glimpse of the elusive Jimmy. When after a few weeks Augustus was again able to walk about the house with the use of his cane, he did occasionally come upon Sammy's sister, Ella. Ella, however, seemed perpetually engrossed in a mundane task of one sort or another whenever Augustus encountered her.

In the meantime, Augustus saw a good deal of Sammy. Sammy was not only his servant, fetching with enthusiasm such articles as Augustus might require, but during the weeks of his confinement, Sammy was also the principal source of Augustus's entertainment. Sammy had no shortage of stories, facts, and trivial statistics to share. In addition, Augustus elevated Sammy into the role of principal warden of Scout. Sammy took the dog on numerous walks, taught him assorted tricks, and lavished upon him all such attentions as a dog might hope for. Sammy had Scout perform each new trick for Augustus. As evidence that Sammy took his job of entertaining

Augustus seriously, he brought in a deck of playing cards the better to pass the time. Sammy taught Augustus to play the sundry card games, which had been taught, to him by Juba Jake. Sammy took great care to allow his student to win as often as not, and was generally attentive to the old man's physical needs and comforts.

These arrangements suited Augustus quite well. It seemed to Augustus that having Sammy about was comparable to having a grandson of sorts. Augustus discovered that playing with a child was surprisingly pleasant. Play had for so long been absent from his life, that he had forgotten the pleasure of it. But now that he was removed from his ordinary life—no longer overseeing the daily affairs of Hickory Grove, the management of which had been turned over to Mr. Flint, he felt so unencumbered by responsibility that he saw no reason not to devote himself to achieving new triumphs in five card poker.

Despite his wishes, Augustus was forced to forgo rebuilding his house for the foreseeable future. Due to the war, it was impossible to get nails and other manufactured essentials. He told the Hollands that he could take an apartment in town, but the Hollands would not hear of it. Dorothy, in particular, was most solicitous. She wished to court his favor as her father-in-law to be—and toward that end, she was successful, for he had become fonder of her while living on the Hollands' farm. All parties instinctively avoided any talk of politics. And they were all, of course, united in their hopes for William's safety—and for a positive outcome from the war.

If there ever had been a moment when Cato might have reappeared and availed himself of Augustus's good graces, that moment had not arisen with sufficient clarity that Dorothy, Jimmy and Cato could agree upon it. In the mean time, Willis had constructed a rough trap door in the ceiling of the cabin.

And while Cato sneaked down from his hiding place to sleep with Jimmy at night, he spent most of his days sequestered in the cramped space between the roof and the ceiling. Willis chiseled out a discreet hole in the south side of the exterior wall, just above the joists. Under the right conditions, this aperture allowed just enough light so that Cato could read. Dorothy kept Cato supplied with reading material. Despite his unhappy circumstances, Cato was able to finish volumes two and three of "Pride and Prejudice," and many other novels. While his circumstances were physically uncomfortable, Cato savored the stories he read. Indeed, he could image no other circumstances in which he would have had nothing to do all day but read, and this, for him, was a bitter luxury.

The day after the fire, Augustus organized the hunt for Cato. He arranged for Mr. Flint to print and distribute wanted posters describing the runaway slave. He offered a substantial reward. At the same time, a search was undertaken for Cato's accomplice. Henry insisted that he could identify the slave who had wielded the knife; that he had seen this man before in Cato's company on numerous occasions, and that he was certain that the slave belonged to someone in the vicinity. Augustus instructed Mr. Flint to use Henry in his investigations. Mr. Flint took Henry around to all the nearby farms and plantations in order to perform a thorough search for the mysterious slave with the knife. Augustus was convinced that if they could find that slave, they might force him to lead them to Cato.

As a matter of courtesy to his hosts, Augustus had excluded the Hollands' farm from this search. But when the searches of all the other properties in the area yielded no results, Augustus determined that the Hollands' farm had better be searched as well. He called in Mr. Flint and Henry to give them instructions about how they might search his hosts' property in a tactful manner. While the three men sat in the back parlor, Mr. Askew rang for Sammy and asked the boy to bring them tea. Sammy went off to the kitchen. A quarter hour later Sammy returned with a tray on which Cora had prepared a teapot, two cups, and a bowl of sugar. As Sammy was placing these items on the small table at which the two white men sat, he heard them discussing their plans. Augustus and Mr. Flint determined that Mr. Flint would search the slave cabins, while Henry would visit the fields and inspect the field hands for the mystery man with the knife. Mr. Askew would speak to Mr. Holland to explain that these inspections were only being undertaken as a last resort.

Young Sammy knew that Cato was hiding above the ceiling in his cabin. But overhearing this discussion, he realized for the first time that his friend Mr. Askew might be, in fact, the individual from whom Cato was hiding. He could hardly believe it. But his ability to believe it was strengthened by the presence of Mr. Flint. Sammy instinctively distrusted Mr. Flint. The man had a loud and violent manner. He was coarse in his appearance. When Sammy realized that this rough man was about to commence a search of the cabins for Cato, he became nervous and alarmed—so much so that as he picked up the bowl of sugar from the tray to put it on the table, he dropped it onto the floor where it broke into pieces.

Mr. Flint called him a clumsy oaf. The house slave Henry, who had been sitting quietly in a corner of the room, audibly sneered at him. Mr. Askew told Sammy to clean up the mess, then go and get them some more sugar. Sammy did as he was told, but before he brought back the replacement sugar, he found Ella and told her what he had heard.

"Mr. Flint is going to search the cabins. Mr. Henry is going to the fields. Mr. Henry is looking for some man with a knife," Sammy told her.

"A man with a knife?!"

"I think that's what he said."

"Go back and do something to hold them up," Ella said. "I need time."

Ella knew that Cato was undoubtedly concealed in his hiding spot. Nevertheless, she dashed into the cabin to be sure. In a voice loud enough for Cato to hear from his perch above the ceiling, she described to Wally what was about to happen. Then she went out to the well, drew a bucket of water, and walked as fast as she could out to the fields. She brought the water directly to Jimmy, and whispered to him that Henry was about to come looking for him.

Just as Ella was explaining the situation to Jimmy, Sammy arrived in the field.

"What are you doing here?" Ella cried. "You're supposed to stay back at the house and keep them held up back there."

"Mr. Askew sent me to fetch Massa Holland," Sammy explained. "He told me to bring him back to the house so Mr. Askew can ask him a question."

Ella thought about this. "All right. All right. You go back to the house with him, then try to keep them busy a little longer."

Sammy delivered his message to Mr. Holland, who then accompanied Sammy back to the house.

"I think you better hide in the same spot with Cato," Ella said to Jimmy. "But you got to get back there before Henry comes out here."

"I can't leave the field," Jimmy said.

"Massa Holland's not here now. No one else will say anything. I'll tell the others to keep quiet."

Jimmy ran as fast as he could back to the cabin. There he found Wally pacing about the cabin, not looking at all calm. Jimmy put the chair on the table and climbed up onto it, and up through the trap door, then replaced the door. Wally took the chair off the table and, for the third time since Ella told her what was happening; she began to wipe the table with a rag.

Out in the field, Ella went around to each of the field hands. She asked them to say nothing about Jimmy no matter who might inquire in the next few hours.

Back at the house, after assuring Mr. Holland of his gratitude for his host's hospitality, Mr. Askew asked Mr. Holland if he might be permitted to instruct Mr. Flint to take a look around in the slave quarters while Henry inspected the field hands.

"I doubt that you'll find who you're looking for here," said Mr. Holland. "But, of course, it would be prudent to make certain. I should like to accompany Mr. Flint, if you don't mind."

"Of course, by all means," said Mr. Askew. "We shall all go together."

And so it was arranged that Mr. Flint and Mr. Holland and Mr. Askew would jointly inspect the cabins, while Henry went to the fields to survey the hands.

At this juncture Sammy arrived in the back parlor with Scout in tow. "Would you like to see a new trick?" he asked Mr. Askew.

"Not now, boy," said Mr. Askew.

"Don't bother us, Sammy," said Mr. Holland. "Go to the kitchen and see if Cora needs help back there. You ought to be able to help her with something."

"All right," Sammy said. "I'll go there. But this is a very nice trick that Scout can do."

Mr. Holland gave Sammy a stern look. Sammy still hesitated, wondering if there was anything more he could say that might delay them from leaving.

"What are you waiting for?" said Mr. Holland.

"Oh, I'm not waiting," said Sammy. "I'm going." And with

this, unable to think of any further excuse to delay, Sammy left for the kitchen.

Henry was dispatched to the fields while Mr. Flint, Mr. Askew and Mr. Holland went to the slave quarters. As it was the closest to the house, the men began their tour of inspection with the cabin where Wally, Ella, Jimmy, Sammy, and Jake resided. When the trio of white men arrived at the cabin, they found Wally inside, fastidiously wiping the table in the center of the room. Ella had by then returned from the fields. She sat by the door engrossed in the threading of a needle.

Mr. Askew spoke to Ella, "Is your brother Jimmy here? I should like to meet him."

"He's out in the field," Ella replied, not looking up from her task.

"Yes, that's true," said George Holland. "I just came from there. He's out with the rest of the hands. We've been working in the southeast field this morning. I can send for him if you like, Mr. Askew."

"No, that isn't necessary," said Augustus. "Henry has gone out to see them. There's no need to interrupt their work."

Ella was intent on keeping the eyes of the visitors from going up toward the ceiling. The trap door had been fashioned in such a way that two of the edges of the door were constructed from the sides of ceiling boards which had been attached together to form a solid plane. These edges were not noticeable. But the other two edges, where the wood had been sawed across the grain of the ceiling planks, formed visible breaks in the uninterrupted span of wood in those boards directly above the table. Ella was not sure how noticeable the outline of the opening was. But at that moment, to her the outline of the trap door looked quite prominent indeed.

"Oh, this thread! It just won't fit inside a needle," Ella said loudly. "Normally, I can thread a needle as quick as you like.

But ever since the war started, the threads we get nowadays are just too coarse. Look a there." And Ella held the thread up by way of example. She saw that Mr. Askew and Mr. Holland looked at the thread she was holding, but that Mr. Flint did not. Mr. Flint was looking around the room in a slow, methodical manner, though he had not as yet looked straight up, which he would have to do to see the spot above the table.

Like Ella, Wally was aware that Mr. Flint might look up. As a further diversion, she intentionally knocked one of her wooden bowls onto the floor.

"Oh my gracious," Wally said as she stooped over to pick it up. "But see there, wooden bowls just don't break. Ain't that something? That's what I like about wooden bowls." She thrust the bowl directly toward Mr. Flint, who looked at it and smirked.

"Who else lives here?" Mr. Flint asked her.

"My son Jimmy lives here," she said. "He's out in the field just now. This is my daughter Ella. She lives here too, of course. And Juba Jake lives here. But he's out in the barn with Willis I reckon. Then there's little Sammy. I believe he's back at the big house. Are you looking for someone in particular? Should I fetch Sammy, Massa Holland?"

Mr. Askew spoke. "No. We've just seen Sammy—and we'll visit the barn in due course."

And so the three men left the cabin to continue their inspection of the remaining cabins in the quarters.

In the meantime, Henry walked up and down the rows out in the southeast field. He looked carefully at each of the field hands.

"Is everyone here today," he asked Big Andrew.

Big Andrew looked around circumspectly at the slaves scattered about him. "Oh yes," he said. "Everyone's working."

"No one sick—is there?" asked Henry.

"No. No. We don't hardly get sick around here," Andrew explained.

Henry mumbled that he doubted that very much. Then he walked up and down the rows one more time, looking at each man meticulously. As he was doing this, Ella, who left the cabin the moment that the inspectors left it, came back out to the field and went straight to Henry.

"I saw Mr. Askew and Mr. Flint back at the cabins," she told him. "They asked me to come tell you that there are two men working in the barn, and that you should have a look at them." It was not true that anyone had asked Ella to deliver this message, but she gambled that such a message might not be questioned. "I can show you where the barn is," she said.

Ella led Henry back to the yard. She pointed to the barn. "There's the barn," she said. "Willis and Jake are working in there."

Henry went on to the barn to have a look at Willis and Jake.

As soon as he entered the barn, Ella went into the cabin, picked up a broom and poked the ceiling with its handle. "Hurry," she said. "Jimmy you got to get back to the field. I sent Henry over to the barn to have a look at Willis and Jake. He's in there now. If you go quick, you can get out before he sees you and get back out to the field afore Massa Holland knows you're gone."

Jimmy raised the trap door and peered down at her. "Put the chair up," he said.

Ella put the chair onto the table, and Jimmy climbed down. He slipped out the front door, then immediately veered around the side of the cabin to keep out of sight of the barn. He made his way back to the field in a roundabout fashion— keeping as far out of view of the barn as possible.

In due course, Mr. Askew, Mr. Flint, and Mr. Holland

completed their inspections. Henry reported that none of the field hands was the man they wanted. When Mr. Holland returned to the field, Jimmy was busy at work behind a plow.

And so over the course of the next several months, Mr. Askew, Henry and Mr. Flint had no success in their search for the fugitive. Eventually, Mr. Askew told Mr. Flint and Henry to put all their attention upon the work of the plantation. In his heart, Augustus had concluded that Cato and the furtive slave with the knife had run away to the North. At long last, Augustus wrote a letter to his son. He described not only the fire, but also how Cato had mysteriously run away in the midst of it.

Unbeknownst to Augustus, Dorothy had also written a letter to William. Dorothy's letter included details that Augustus's letter had omitted. She told William how his father had discovered that Cato could read; how he had chained Cato in the barn and whipped him severely. She confessed to William that she had, in a fashion, assisted Jimmy in helping Cato escape; that she could not bear to see Cato punished just because he wished to read Jane Austen; that even now she was harboring Cato in a hiding spot nearby. She asked William to tell her if he thought she was wrong to do so; she told him that if he asked her to, she would admit the truth to his father.

And so it was that William, whose regiment drilled and trained continuously, but still had not seen enemy action, was presented with two divergent points of view about the events at Hickory Grove. And once again, he felt that the contents of these letters were such that he could not discuss them with anyone. He wished that he could talk to Daniel Watson about what to do, but he felt that even his best friend could not be trusted with the information that Dorothy had shared with him. Under the circumstances in which William was living, with sharp awareness of the proximity of war, with a heightened sense of his own mortality, he could not reckon how the fact that Cato had learned to read was of any consequence. Yet he understood that his father must feel compelled to maintain the familiar order of the world that was now under assault. And harboring a fugitive slave was clearly against the law— even in the North.

In the abstract facts presented to him in Dorothy's letter, William reasoned that his father's reaction to discovering that Cato had learned to read had been intensified by many factors: his mother's death, the dangers facing William in the army, indeed the dangers facing all of them as the Yankees—who had won a decisive victory at Fort Donnellson, which sat a mere one hundred miles northeast of Jackson—pressed ever closer to his home. He could see it all around him—the way fear and apprehension led his men to snap at each other, the way the pointed nobility of their cause was gradually worn down by the harsh file of war. He had long since grown weary with regret about his commission. He had not yet resolved what he might or might not do when the time for battle came.

As the winter dragged by, his regiment began to move from place to place. Every time they moved there were rumors, talk among the men about the possibility of a looming battle. But it was not until April 6th, 1862, that the Sixth Regiment would engage in combat for the first time. Alas, the occasion of that combat was a battle fought near a church in Tennessee called Shiloh. It would be one of the most violent battles of America's most violent war.

# 36

## WILLIAM RAISES HIS RIFLE

*L*ieutenant William Askew marched near the front of the formation. Not too far behind him was his friend Daniel Watson. From time to time, William glanced around at Daniel, who smiled in return. Whether or not the smile was forced, William couldn't tell. But there was no doubt that each man's pulse was rapid—that each man had some muscle clenched, even as he marched. The drum sounded steadily, but it did not crowd out the sounds that wafted back from the distance. William tried to analyze those sounds. He could hear the complex sounds of gunfire, rapid staccato notes with long decays, combined with periodic big amorphous mortar booms blending into a sustained thundering monotone. And ... he could also hear other sounds—sounds from which his mind recoiled—sounds which he knew came from the throats of men, the choral cries of killing and the solo cries of being killed—as if these acts demanded vocal accompaniment.

As the sounds grew in a long slow crescendo, it was clear that danger was approaching. But there was no way to slow the progress of the marching unit—since no one man could slow the group's pace, though they all might wish it to be slower. Each man was compelled forward by the man behind him— and somewhere at the rear were men who were drawn forward by the men in front of them. Each individual might imagine jumping out of the machinery. Each man might pray for some miraculous cosmic time out. But though time was moving in slow motion, both time and the regiments were moving inexorably. William looked down at his feet. He wondered why they kept moving. Yet they did.

Most of the logistics of battle were already set in motion. The physical placement of the forces was determined; the timing of their movements was already commenced. There was little left for each individual soldier to do but to play his part as the machinery of the battle brought him to the fore. There was little mystery about what he was supposed to do. He would aim his weapon to shoot and kill the enemy. But there was great mystery about how it would feel. What exactly would happen? How would chance interact with the lifeblood of each participant? Most men's thoughts were strategic. How can I get him before he gets me? But some men put their minds onto the ideal—the great cause—and left the strategy to their reflexes, having learned that thinking is sometimes the adversary of prowess.

William's mind was perhaps the only one wrestling with a secret dilemma. Would he aim to kill? Now that the moment was at hand, now that he was out tramping in the field with his comrades, marching with those who looked to him for leadership, walking with those who would observe whatever he did— could he do aught but what was expected? He had often considered how impossible it would be for Dorothy to know anything of what actually happened in battle, except what he told her. Looked at from that point of view, it was silly to even contemplate a dilemma. Who has not embellished a story, altered a detail to achieve a more noble effect? And who—besides Dorothy and the Quaker—would even fault him for such a deception? He had nothing to reckon with, really, but his own conscience. What did he himself in his heart of hearts really believe was the right thing to do?

Before he had time to reach a conclusion, the moment was at hand. It came up fast, like an unexpected slap. All at once, he found himself at the front of the line. Now there was no one in front of him except the opposing forces facing him. He looked and saw the phalanx of blue uniforms mirroring the grays. He heard bullets whizzing by. The thought formed in his mind: "They are shooting at me," as if it were a surprise—as if it were the most improbable concept in the world. Aiming at him! He, who was a decent Christian man, a Southern gentleman, a man in love. He was filled with a sense of the rightness of himself, and with a kind of indignation that such as he should be the target of gunfire. His reflexes shot off conflicting signals—move left, move right—there was no safe way to move, and so he did not move. He raised up his rifle. He picked out a man at random. It was at random! He aimed the rifle at the center of the man's chest. He hesitated. From his right side he heard Daniel's voice shout, "I got him!" From the proximity of this shout, William could tell that Daniel stood right beside him—and the tenor of Daniel's voice was triumphant, as if what he had just accomplished was monumental. William looked at the Yankee whom Daniel had just got. The man crumpled, and fell flat on his face—he appeared to perish in an instant—in a quiet, yielding collapse.

William's finger was on the trigger. He was still aiming at the same random man—a man who stood three feet from the man Daniel had just killed. William sent commands to his finger. He told it to pull the trigger. His finger did not obey.

His finger gave no reason for this disobedience. It simply, mutely, would not abide by his order. It acted as if it had lost its strength, as if its little muscles were paralyzed. William could see that the man he was aiming at was aiming back—aiming right in his direction. It was unbelievable how slow time had become. There was all the time in the world to observe and ponder. William suddenly sucked in a hard breath —and a sound came out of the back of his throat, not a loud cry, but a gasping sound—like the sound someone might make who had held his breath too long. He raised the end of his rifle barrel half an inch. It was enough to change the bullet's destination to an airy space three feet above the Yankee's head. He fired. And just as he did, the Yankee fired back. There was an explosion to William's right. William turned his head just in time to see Daniel's blood and bones splattering out of his back like the eruption of a volcano. He saw Daniel's face. Daniel's eyes were looking at him. But there was no sound coming out of Daniel's mouth. There was only the stare that was coming out of Daniel's eyes to probe William's eyes. Without realizing it, William dropped his rifle. William's arms stretched out to catch Daniel's body. Daniel crumbled into his arms and the weight of Daniel's fall pulled both men downward. William let himself go down. He went down with Daniel, down, down, to the ground. And there he found himself down on a carpet of grass—dull, dark green flecked with blood—it was a separate world, a world in a lower echelon of the battle, which somehow magically seemed to be a fissure into which one might step away from reality. William watched Daniel's eyes all the way down, as they fell out of the reality of battle and into the fissure. He could not tell when it happened, but somewhere between the start and end of the fall, the eyes went lifeless.

William crouched over his friend's body. He was aware that

men all around him were moving forward. The swell of soldiers from behind him now moved over him like a wave. But he was anchored to the spot in the dark grass claimed by Daniel's body. He knew that the man whom he had chosen not to shoot at was the man who had killed his friend.

William knelt down and laid his own body on top of Daniel's—as if there were still a reason left to protect him. Then there was a period of no time. William did not know what happened next—or how many minutes elapsed—perhaps it was half an hour—perhaps it was an hour. The next thing William was aware of was that when he stood up, he could see that he was surrounded by a few remaining Confederate soldiers. All of his comrades had their hands in the air. He raised his hands also. His career as a soldier was complete.

## "WHAT ARE YOU DOING OUT HERE?"

It was not until Friday, April 25, 1862, eighteen days after it was over, that the Jackson, Tennessee, newspaper, the West Tennessee Whig, compiled the lists of dead, wounded, and captured soldiers from the Battle of Shiloh. In the two-day battle on Sunday, April 6th and Monday, April 7th, there were 1,723 Confederate soldiers killed, 8,012 Confederate soldiers wounded, and 959 Confederate soldiers captured or missing. Among the casualties were nearly five hundred men from the Sixth Regiment.

Dorothy was in town that Friday and was the first in her family to see the newspaper. In the alphabetical list of the dead, she soon came upon the names Daniel Allison, Adolphus Andrews, and Charles Baker. She stared at the sequence of Andrews and Baker, letting it become certain in her mind that there was no William Askew listed in the alphabetical spot between those names. She repeated the process of elimination on the list of the wounded. Again, there was no listing of William. Then, with her heart pounding, she turned to the list of missing and captured soldiers. There she found William's name printed in the harsh ink of the West Tennessee Whig: 'Lt. William Askew, captured April 7th, held at the Union prison at Camp Douglas in Chicago, Illinois.'

In a matter of seconds, Dorothy decided that she would go to him. It was one year to the day since they had made love in the barn. She'd seen him twice since then—once, on the day in May that he showed up at her house in uniform, when she renounced him, and the second time at their reconciliation in September, when he brought Cato back to Hickory Grove. For six months, she had been writing to him, urging him toward actions that she knew were treacherous. Now he was a prisoner in a Union camp. She could no longer abide sitting at home while the world and her future took shape beyond her influence. She had long considered that she might like to go to the North. Now he was a prisoner in the North, and she would go to him.

She would go to Chicago, find William at Camp Douglas —and marry him. Surely they would let a captured officer get married! And surely it was only fitting then, when they were married, that their personal servants would become their own property. Cato would be given to him. Ella would be given to her. So she reasoned—and so she conceived that she would bring both Ella and Cato with her to find him. Moreover, since Sammy—who belonged to Erastus Hicks—was in her charge, she would bring him, too.

The prospect of traveling to Chicago was daunting. She would be safer traveling with a man. Yet there was no white man she could imagine going with her. She considered that Augustus might be willing to go to his son—but she could not have both Augustus and Cato travel with her even if Augustus were willing to make the trip. In fact, if she wanted to ensure that Cato could go with her, she would have to be certain that Augustus did not think of going as well.

All this she considered before she returned home. When she arrived at the farm, she did not go directly either to her parents or to Augustus to tell them what she had learned. Instead, she found Ella. When no one was looking, she called Ella into the cabin. Ella's cabin was empty except for Cato, who was still hiding above the ceiling. She told Ella and Cato the news of William's capture. Then she explained her plans.

"How can we make a trip like that?" Ella asked. "A white woman alone with three slaves." Ella shook her head.

"I don't know," Dorothy admitted. "It would be better if we had a white man with us."

Cato peered down from the ceiling, where the trap door had been opened so that he could participate in the discussion. "Maybe I could pass for white," he said.

"I reckon part of you maybe could," said Ella, "but other parts—I don't think so."

"What parts?" Cato asked.

"Your hair—for instance," replied Ella.

"Why don't you climb down for a moment," Dorothy suggested. "So we can look at you."

Cato climbed down. He stood at attention while Dorothy walked around him to inspect the racial details of his appearance.

"You know your face does look a lot like William's," she said. "But Ella is right. Your hair doesn't fit."

"Too bad you can't put a wig on him," Ella said.

"Ha. ... Why not?" Dorothy's eyes lit up. "A wig. We can put him in a wig—and we can dab some powder on his face to lighten it up."

"Where you gonna get a wig from?" Ella asked.

"Well I suppose we could make one," Dorothy proposed. "Or I should say—maybe you could make one."

"Me!" Ella was astounded by this idea. "Where would I get hair to make a wig?"

"You can use my hair," Dorothy said. "My hair is long enough. If we cut off several inches of it, you can sew it all around the edges of a skullcap. Cato can wear a hat on top of that. Then we could make it so that just a little of the hair showed beneath the hat. That way it will look like his hair."

"You figure on telling your mama and papa that you're going away?" Ella asked.

"No. It's impossible. They'd never agree to my leaving."

"So you're just fixing to run away?"

"Well ... yes, I guess I am. It's the only way I can do this. I'll write them a letter. I can explain why I have to go. They still won't understand, but it's the best I can do. Besides, I have to be certain that Mr. Askew doesn't get the idea of going with me to find William."

"I don't think old Askew would go up North no matter what," Ella declared.

"If you did come with me...," Dorothy said, as she contemplated the consequences of her plan, "... both of you would be runaways. I'd understand it if you didn't want to take that risk."

Ella had never considered the prospect of leaving home. She and Dorothy had often talked of a future home together with William. But she had always imagined that home as being just down the road—not far from Wally and Jake and Jimmy. She had never considered being separated from them. "What about Jimmy?" she asked. "He's wanted to go north all his life. Maybe you should take him along."

"I don't know," Dorothy said. "If I took you and Sammy with me, my parents might understand that. But if I took Jimmy—they'd think I meant to undermine their livelihood here on the farm. I know how they think."

"I'd like to go to my brother," Cato said. "I'd like to help you make the journey. But Jimmy won't let me go away without him—and I won't leave him here."

Hearing how both Ella and Cato felt about the matter, Dorothy agreed that they would take Jimmy along. That night Cato told Jimmy of their plans. Jimmy was more than ready to escape to the North. But he did not like the idea of going to find William Askew.

"And then what?" he asked Cato. "Are we supposed to go up there and be slaves up in Chicago instead of down here?"

"I reckon we'd be free up North," Cato said.

"Then how come we need to go up there with them?"

"I want to help her find my brother," Cato said. "He's still my family."

This topic was a sore point between them. It was the one thing about which they disagreed. But it occurred to Jimmy that he ought to go along with the idea for the time being. Once they were in the North, they would have independent lives. They would be free men. And once they were there, he could get Cato away from William Askew and Dorothy Holland. It would be easier to do that when they were truly free. With this in mind, he agreed to the general plan.

That night, the news of William's capture reached the rest of the household at the Holland farm. When Augustus Askew was shown his son's name printed in the West Tennessee Whig —listed with those captured at Shiloh, he did not know whether to weep or be glad. He was glad that William was not hurt—but to be imprisoned by Yankees! It was horrifying to him to think what that experience might hold in store. Then, even as he was contemplating the dreadfulness of that, he also came upon the name of Daniel Watson printed in the first list —the list of those who had died.

Scout was at his feet when Augustus read Daniel's name.

He looked at the dog and shook his head. "Your master Daniel has died," he said out loud. "He was a brave man. My son has been captured. Now, I suppose, you will be mine alone." This was a bittersweet thought—for though Augustus undoubtedly was grieved at the death of his son's friend, he did not find it unpleasant to consider that Scout, as a consequence of that tragedy, must spend the remainder of his life with him.

Scout, in response to this, seemed almost as if he understood that something important had happened. When Augustus spoke, Scout got up from his spot. He came over to Augustus's chair. But just as Augustus was about to pet him, he turned and walked out of the room. Augustus called after him, but Scout did not obey his master. The house was quiet. The Hollands had all gone to bed. Augustus was obliged to get up to go after the dog. He found Scout standing near the window at the opposite end of the house. Scout looked out into the yard—as if he had spotted something. Augustus came up beside him to see what it was the dog had seen. There in the moonlit night Augustus saw the man, the slave who had both saved his life and attacked him with a knife, the slave who had set Cato free. This same slave was walking in the yard of the Holland farm! Augustus rapped hard on the window. The slave looked up, saw Augustus in the window, and instantly ran off into the shadows.

"It's him!" Augustus shouted. He rapped again on the window. But the slave was gone. Augustus went out the front door, onto the porch. He looked up and down the yard. There was not a soul to be seen.

Jimmy, when he realized that Augustus had seen him, ran down the yard, then back behind Paymore's cabin. From behind that cabin, he circled back around to the back side of his own cabin. He inched forward, creeping along the side of the cabin, until he was just at a point where he could see the big house. He saw Augustus standing on the porch, but he could tell that Augustus could not see him in the shadow of the cabin. He waited until Augustus went back into the house, then he ran to the front of his cabin and went in.

"He's seen me!" Jimmy shouted. Almost immediately, everyone inside knew what he meant. Jake was already in his bed. Wally and Ella sat at the table. Sammy played with something on the floor. Above them all, Cato pulled the trap door up from the ceiling and stuck his head into the opening.

"Askew saw me from the house," Jimmy continued. "He's in there now, telling everyone that he saw me. Soon they'll come out looking."

Cato spoke from above. "He still doesn't know who you are, does he?"

"No."

"He's gonna put two and two together," said Ella.

"Jimmy, you got to hide," said Wally.

"They think you robbed him with a knife," said Ella. "They could string you up."

"She's right," said Cato. "If they catch me, it's just for running away. But if they catch you …."

Suddenly everyone was quiet. All the faces around the room looked solemn—as if each person were coming to the same conclusion.

"I'm gonna run away then," said Jimmy. "I'm going North. I'm gonna go right now."

"Oh, baby!" Wally rushed over to him and threw her arms around him.

"I've got to do it, mama. There's no time to waste. I got to pack supplies." He looked around the room. And in an instant, he was rushing about pulling out articles to take with him, piling them onto his blanket.

"You're gonna need cash money," said Ella.

Everyone in the room went to their private spot. In a few moments, Wally laid a number of dollar bills onto the table. Ella laid two dollars and three quarters on the table. Jake laid down a ten-dollar bill and four ones. For his stash, Sammy went out of the cabin. Then almost as quickly, he was back with a handkerchief tied into the shape of a pouch, laden with pennies.

"Two hundred and forty two pennies," he announced. He set them on the table.

"You better keep those pennies little brother," Jimmy said. "That change makes too much noise. Anyway, you gotta keep that money for your art supply."

Sammy looked crestfallen.

"Look here," Jimmy said. He stuck his hand into the purse and pulled out a handful of pennies. "I'm gonna take ten pennies for good luck." He counted them out.

By now, Cato had swung his body down through the opening in the ceiling and dropped onto the table, and from there down to the floor. "You'll meet us in Chicago?" he asked.

Jimmy nodded his head.

"What!" Wally cried. She had not been told about the plan. "Who's going to Chicago?" She looked around at the faces of her children.

"There's no time to explain that right now, mama," said Ella.

Jimmy pulled the edges of his blanket up, forming it into a satchel filled with his supplies. "Run out there again and look, little brother," he said to Sammy. "See if they're coming yet."

Sammy went back outside.

Now Jimmy was hugging his mother. Then he hugged Ella, who could not hold back her tears.

Sammy came back in. "No one is out there—just Scout," he said. "Scout is standing out on the porch."

"You'd better watch him, Sammy" said Jimmy. "Don't let him follow me."

"What way will you go?" asked Ella.

"I'll go west, then north. I'll try to cross the river at Cairo —then up to Chicago."

"Hide in the woods in the daytime," said Wally.

"Better stay away from soldiers," said Ella. "Yankee or otherwise."

Jake had been pacing around the room. He came now to Jimmy's side. "I'm old," he said. "I may not see you again."

Upon hearing this, Jimmy could not stop his own tears from forming. "We'll all be together by and by," he said, though his voice cracked.

"Good luck, son," said Jake.

Now all that was left was for Jimmy to say goodbye to Cato and Sammy. He turned to Cato and threw his arms around him. The two men squeezed their bodies together.

"Make it three weeks in Chicago," Jimmy told him.

Cato nodded. "Three weeks."

Jimmy knelt down. Sammy came up to him. "You'll be careful, won't you?" Sammy asked.

"I'll be careful," said Jimmy. "You keep safe, too."

"I will."

"Look out there one more time," Jimmy told him.

Sammy went outside again, then stuck his head back in the door.

"Nobody's around," he said.

Jimmy stood up.

Wally stepped toward him, with her arms outstretched.

But Ella pulled her back. "Let him go, mama," she said.

And with that, Jimmy left. He ran behind the cabin, then straight back, back to the edge of the woods. He heard Scout bark. He heard voices coming now from the direction of the house. He ducked into the woods. He quickly circled back around to Christmasville Road. He crossed the road and ran into the woods on the other side. For five minutes, he ran as fast as he could through the brush. Then he slowed down. He realized he'd have to pace himself. He was traveling due west. He skirted across the southern end of the Greer plantation. Soon he came upon Dyer Creek. There was nothing to do but get his feet wet. He waded across. On the other side, the woods quickly gave way to cotton fields. Already he'd arrived at a farm he didn't know. He had to cut diagonally across the rows of cotton plants.

Abruptly, in the middle of the field, Jimmy stopped. He looked up at the sky. He realized how easy it would be to lose his direction. He searched the sky until he found the North Star. To go west, he would keep that star to his right. He looked around the field. The moon was low in the sky, but it shed enough light that he could see that no one was in sight. "Oh Jimmy," he said out loud. "What are you doing out here?"

WHEN AUGUSTUS CAME BACK in from the front porch, he climbed the stairs of the Hollands' house to the second floor. It was the first time he had ever ventured up to that part of the house, which he deemed to be the Hollands' private domain. He did not know which room belonged to whom. So he started banging on the first door, then on the next one. One of the doors opened and George Holland stepped out in his nightshirt.

"Good heavens, man," said Mr. Holland. "What's going on?"

"I saw him. I saw that slave I'm looking for. He was just outside in the yard!"

"Which slave?" asked George. "Your runaway slave, or the other one?"

"The other one," said Augustus. "He's out there right now. We must go out and catch him."

The other door opened, and Dorothy stepped out into the upstairs hall. She too was wearing her nightclothes. "What's wrong, Mr. Askew?" she asked.

"I saw that man with the knife," he said.

"Are you certain," she asked. "It's dark out there."

"Yes, yes! I'm sure of it," said Augustus. "You must go out and catch him."

"But Mr. Askew," said Dorothy. "None of us knows what this man looks like. If anyone is to catch him, you'll have to come along."

"Yes, of course," said Augustus. "But I need someone to drive my carriage. I'm sure he's running away already. But we might catch him if we use the horses."

In the throes of the moment, Dorothy could hardly think. If Jimmy knew that he had been spotted, she was not sure what he would do. "You say he's running away already. Did the man see you? Did he recognize you?" she asked.

"Yes, he saw me."

"Which way did he run?"

"He ran down the yard away from the house—then I'm not sure. He went somewhere behind one of those cabins down there."

"If he is on foot, Mr. Askew," said Dorothy, "I don't think it will do any good to chase him in a carriage. He's not likely to run down the middle of the road. Perhaps he's hiding in one of the cabins." Dorothy was following an instinct. She felt if she could take command of the search, she would be in a better position to control the outcome. "Why don't I fetch some lanterns, and we can go out to the cabins and look."

"Yes, yes," said Augustus. "But hurry."

"Certainly, let's hurry. Father, with which cabin do you think we should begin? The cabin closest to the house—or the one furthest away from the house?"

"I should think he'd hide in one further away," said George Holland.

"Perhaps you can round up some lanterns, father, while I get dressed."

"There's no time," said Augustus. "I'm going down right now."

"Oh but Mr. Askew," said Dorothy. "If the man is hiding in one of the cabins, he's apt to stay very still. So it will hardly matter if you wait for just a moment while we put on some proper clothes."

"But he might make a run for it," said Augustus.

"If he's making a run for it," said Dorothy, "I don't see how we can catch him—no matter how quickly we get dressed."

"The dog saw him," said Augustus. "Scout knows who he is. The dog can catch him!"

"Where is the dog now?" asked Dorothy.

"Scout is downstairs. He is probably out on the porch."

"Will he know what to do? I mean, will Scout know that you want him to find this man?"

"Yes. Scout knows him. He's the one who first saw him out in the yard. I'm sure he recognized him."

"Perhaps Scout has already gone off to chase him," Dorothy observed.

"Oh, Miss Holland!" said Augustus. He was now pacing in the upstairs hall. His voice was impatient. "All this talk is wasting time. We must hurry!"

"Yes, of course, Mr. Askew," said Dorothy. "Just wait one minute." Dorothy went into her room and closed the door. She ran to her bedroom window and looked out. Across the yard, she saw Sammy outside his cabin. He held something in his hand that looked like a pouch. The door to the cabin was open. Light shone from inside it. She caught the trace of someone walking about inside. Then Sammy went back into the cabin, and closed the door. Dorothy deduced that Jimmy must be in there. She looked down the row of cabins. The first cabin was the only one that had any visible commotion. She'd have to find a way to give Jimmy enough time to hide—or—to do whatever he meant to do. She went back to her bedroom door and cracked it open. "Are you still out there, Mr. Askew?"

"Yes."

"I was just thinking, maybe the man you saw was trying to find you," she said.

"No, no," said Augustus. "He ran off the minute he saw me. I rapped on the window, and when he saw me he was frightened."

"Was he still carrying that knife?" Dorothy had concluded that she'd have to keep up some kind of patter, while she changed her clothes—to make sure that Augustus stayed in the hall.

"No. I'm sure he's disposed of that by now," said Augustus.

"Has my father found any lanterns yet?"

"He's still getting dressed," said Augustus. "Please, Miss Holland. Time is of the essence."

"Yes, of course. I'm almost ready. I just need to get some shoes on."

"I really think I should go down myself and look for him," said Augustus.

"The slaves won't know what to think, Mr. Askew, if you start barging into their cabins. I'm sure they'll be most helpful if I come with you."

"I'm going back downstairs," said Augustus, "so I can see what's happening from the window."

"Wait just one second," said Dorothy. "I wonder if you could help me with my shoes. Ella usually helps me put them on. I'm all thumbs when it comes to doing it myself."

Augustus thought this was a strange request. Yet he hardly knew what other response to make than to oblige her. "Very well," he said. "Are you dressed?" he asked.

"Yes, you may come in," said Dorothy.

Augustus came into the room. Immediately he noticed the window on the far wall. He moved to go over to it—but Dorothy saw what he was thinking and picked up her shoes from the foot of the bed. She stuck them out toward Augustus to block his path. "Here you are," she said. "These are the best shoes for me to wear if I have to do some walking. We may have to walk about some tonight if we're to find this fellow."

Augustus took the shoes—then looked about him to see if there was somewhere he could sit so that he might shoe the woman as quickly as possible.

"Oh I suppose we'll need to get you a chair to sit on," Dorothy said. "Then I think perhaps if I sit on the bed here—then that will make it quite simple for you to assist me with these shoes. We can put the chair right next to the bed. I do so appreciate your help, Mr. Askew." Dorothy went toward a chair that sat against the wall. She made a visible effort to try to move it. "Can you help me with this?" she asked.

Augustus went over to help her with the chair. "Really, Miss Holland. This is all taking too much time."

"Well, let's hurry, then," said Dorothy.

They moved the chair next to the bed, and Dorothy sat down on the edge of the bed, raised her leg, and presented her foot.

"It generally takes quite a bit of doing for a woman to dress," said Dorothy. "Why this is taking no time at all! You should see how long it takes me when I have to put on a fancy dress. First, there's the corset, then the petticoats. It is quite an operation, I can tell you."

"I'm sure it is," said Augustus. He held out one of the shoes, and maneuvered to slip it onto her foot. The shoe went on easily enough, but then it was obvious that it would need to be laced.

"Would you be so kind as to lace it for me?" Dorothy asked sweetly.

At this point George Holland, who was now fully dressed, entered his daughter's bedroom. "Are you ready?" he asked.

"Almost, father. Nearly ready. Mr. Askew has only to help me with my shoes, and I'll be ready. Were you able to find the lanterns?"

"I haven't looked yet," said George Holland.

As they spoke, Augustus was furiously lacing up Dorothy's first shoe.

"I think there are two lanterns in the kitchen," said Dorothy. As she said this, Dorothy feigned to be too preoccupied with the conversation with her father to remember to present her other foot to Augustus, which she kept dangling below his reach. Seeing this, Augustus took hold of her foot and raised it up, in order to insert the remaining shoe onto it directly. Then, after he'd gotten the shoe onto her foot, he began to lace it. But Dorothy wiggled her leg in a kind of spasm that threw Augustus off the delicate process of threading the laces. As a result, he had to begin the lacing process over again.

"Oh sorry," she said. "I get tickled so easily."

"Perhaps I should help you with that," offered George Holland.

"No, no, man, I can do it," said Augustus. "Go and fetch the lanterns, if you would, sir. Really we're losing time, you know."

"I'll meet you downstairs presently," said Mr. Holland, and he left.

"How odd that this fellow should show up in our yard," said Dorothy. "I still can't help but think he came here on purpose. Perhaps he was trying to determine if you were still residing with us." Dorothy jiggled her leg again, but this time, Augustus didn't lose his place in the threading.

"The slave lives around here somewhere," said Augustus. "Henry told me he saw this same nigger with Cato long before the fire. I think someone is hiding him."

"Oh dear," said Dorothy. "I hope none of our slaves is complicit in this matter."

"They stick together, Miss Holland, and you can't trust any of them."

"Oh my," she said. "I've never thought of not trusting them. Why, I think they're just like our family."

"I'm afraid you are naïve, Miss Holland. When you've had as much experience as I have, you'll know better."

"Have you written to William about Cato's disappearance, Mr. Askew?"

"Yes, of course."

"Oh I hate to think of him up in that Yankee prison. He must be so lonely."

"His friend, Private Daniel Watson, was killed," said Augustus, temporarily forgetting his impatience in the flush of discussing his son's fate.

"Oh dear, no! I had not realized that."

"Yes, it was in the same paper today."

"Oh, poor William. He must be so sad."

"Scout belonged to Mr. Watson. I was going to look after the dog until the end of the war. But now I suppose I shall have to keep him."

"Yes, of course."

"There, that should do it." Augustus had at last completed the lacing of Dorothy's shoe.

"Thank you so much," said Dorothy. She stood up. "I suppose we may as well go downstairs now and see if father has found the lanterns."

When they got downstairs, they joined Mr. Holland and Scout on the porch. Scout barked a single bark.

"Have you seen anything?" Augustus asked Mr. Holland.

"No. All the cabins are dark, except the first one."

"I suppose if someone were hiding," said Dorothy, "they would hide in the dark, don't you think?"

"Yes," said her father.

"And they'd hide as far from the house as possible, wouldn't they?"

"Most likely," said George Holland.

"But if you think we should start with the first cabin, Mr. Askew ...," Dorothy said.

"We should start down there with the last cabin," said Augustus. "The man ran down that way. If he hasn't run off already, he's probably hiding back there."

The party proceeded methodically to investigate each of the cabins—starting with the last and working their way in due time back to Ella's cabin. By the time they arrived at Ella's cabin, it, too, was dark inside. As she had done at each of the other cabins, Dorothy knocked on the door, then entered. Inside, everyone was duly in bed and gave the appearance of having their eyes closed. The only thing that looked out of place to Dorothy's eyes was on the table. She saw Sammy's pouch of pennies on the table, but she could not from this deduce any further meaning.

"Pardon us," she said to the occupants of the cabin. "We're here with Mr. Askew looking for a man who was seen in our yard not long ago. Have any of you seen a stranger anywhere here tonight?"

"No ma'am," said Wally.

"I saw someone," said Ella.

Dorothy walked up to Ella's bed with her lantern, and peered into Ella's face, trying to decipher what signal she meant to give. "Who was it?" Dorothy asked.

"I don't know," said Ella. "It was some man I didn't recognize. He was out in the yard."

"That's him," said Augustus.

"Which way did he go?" Dorothy asked.

"Well he went down toward the other cabins," said Ella. "Looked to me like he was heading east."

"And you never saw him before, Ella?" asked Mr. Holland.

"No sir. Least I don't think so. I might have seen him somewhere around here a long time ago. He seemed kind of familiar, but not so's I could recognize him."

"Did you talk to him?" Dorothy asked.

"No ma'am. He looked like a no account kind of fellow. I didn't say anything to him."

"Did he see you?" asked Mr. Holland.

"Yes, sir. He saw me, and he said, 'Who you looking at?' all ornery like. Then he skipped off going east."

"East," said Dorothy. "That's over toward the Wadford estate."

"Yes ma'am," said Ella. "I reckon he's gone to hide over at the Wadford place. They got people over there of a doubtful nature. They never go to church, I can tell you that."

During all of this, Wally remained in her bed. Dorothy thought she could see signs that Wally had been crying—but she kept her lantern from shining in Wally's direction. Without moving her head, Dorothy glanced her eyes up at the ceiling. Nothing seemed out of place up there. Dorothy wondered if

Jimmy was hiding up there, or if he had, in fact, run away. If he'd gone anywhere, she presumed he hadn't gone east to the Wadford place.

"All right then," Dorothy said. "Mr. Askew, I suggest we pay a call on the Wadford estate and see what we can find."

The party left the cabin, and continued their search by visiting the neighboring Wadford estate. That investigation, however, proved fruitless. No one at the Wadford estate, of a dubious nature or not, had seen or heard of any stranger. After midnight, the members of the search party agreed that there was nothing more to be done, and so they went back home.

Out in the western portion of Madison County, Jimmy steadily made his way. As he walked, he imagined Venus walking by his side. He had always imagined that she would go with him when he journeyed to the North. Now it comforted him to imagine her so, walking along beside him, turning back to look up at him. "What do you think, girl?" Jimmy said. "Looks like we're gonna swim that river, after all!"

38

───────────

WIG AND HAT

he next morning Ella went to Dorothy's bedroom to whisper in her ear that Jimmy had run away. She explained that Cato and Jimmy had agreed to meet in Chicago in three weeks.

"Three weeks!" Dorothy called out, rather too loudly.

Ella held her finger to her mouth and made a "shhh" sound, then asked, "Will that be enough time?"

Dorothy lowered her voice. "I suppose it may be if we leave in the next few days. But we have so much to do! I must find a means of obtaining money. We need to pack clothes and food. You have to make Cato's wig. I want to write a letter to my parents."

"I told Sammy to go to the field this morning," said Ella. "I told him to tell your papa that Jimmy's too sick to work. That will do for a day or two, but by and by he's going to find out Jimmy is not here."

"You're right," said Dorothy. "I suppose we'll have to leave very soon, perhaps tomorrow—or the next day. We must be gone when my father discovers that Jimmy has run away. I don't know if my father will want to chase after Jimmy—or chase after us."

"If we're leaving soon, I better start on that wig," Ella said. "But what should I use for the cap?"

"I've thought about that," said Dorothy. "My father has a nightcap that ought to serve the purpose. I'll go next door and find it. Then I'll get a pair of scissors and meet you in your cabin."

And so the women set about their preparations. Under Ella's hand, George Holland's nightcap was altered. The long pointy end was cut off. The remainder was re-sewn and shaped into a snug covering sized to fit on Cato's head. Ella snipped several inches off the bottom of Dorothy's hair, then sewed the hair in strands around the edges of the cap.

Dorothy contrived a plan to get money. She told her mother that in honor of William she wanted to give a party to benefit the soldiers fighting in the war. She wished to throw a small charitable festivity at home. She would invite all her friends to come and dance and make donations. Dorothy declared that for this occasion she desired to buy a new dress. She told her mother she'd heard that Mr. Meacham, a merchant in town, had just received a shipment of dresses and other luxuries. She convinced her mother to provide her with a sum of money to purchase this new dress—then proposed that she might go to town the next day to buy it. She told her mother that she wanted to go to town alone—so that she might surprise her.

Having thus obtained a sum of money from her mother, Dorothy pursued a similar strategy with her father. She reminded her father that her mother's birthday on May 7th would be upon them in no time. She mentioned that insofar as she was going the next day to Mr. Meacham's she might well purchase a gift for her mother on her father's behalf—should he so desire it. Mr. Holland felt that it was most thoughtful of Dorothy to remember her mother in this way, and so he provided her with funds for that purpose.

But Dorothy did not wait until the next day to go to town. Without anyone's knowledge, she went that same day to Mr. Meacham's. She walked right past the dresses and other such ladies' attractions and, instead, selected diverse articles of clothing for a gentleman. She told Mr. Meacham that these were to be gifts for her fiancé. She promised Mr. Meacham she'd return the next day with payment. Mr. Meacham, who had known Dorothy since she was a young girl, believed her to be reliable. He accepted her promissory note.

In this way Dorothy obtained an assortment of new clothes for Cato, whose only remaining garments were the trousers he'd worn when he'd been shackled in the barn—and a shirt donated by Jimmy. After her shopping trip, Dorothy furnished him with a new set of trousers, a fine new shirt, an embroidered vest, and an excellent hat.

When Ella completed her efforts with the wig, she arranged the hat on Cato's head with the hairpiece beneath it. Once Cato was thus outfitted, Dorothy judiciously applied powder to his face both to lighten his color and to emphasize certain features and diminish others. In his new apparel, Cato became the very model of a gentleman. Indeed, he looked quite like his brother, except that, if anything, his features were even more symmetrical and handsome.

The time came for Dorothy and Ella to inform Wally about their plans. Wally vehemently opposed the idea of Dorothy taking Ella and Sammy away to the North. But after lengthy reassurances that she did not intend to break up the family, Dorothy was able to appease Wally with promises that she'd find a way to reunite everyone once things were settled down. It was decided that Dorothy, Ella, Cato and Sammy would start their journey the following morning, when Dorothy would announce that she was going to town to buy a new dress.

That night, Dorothy composed the following letter to her parents:

Dearest Mother and Father,

By the time you read this on Monday evening, I will be gone. I have taken Ella and Sammy with me to Chicago. We are going to the camp where William Askew is held prisoner. There it is my intention to marry him, and, if I am allowed, to provide him with such comforts and amenities as are permitted. I did not tell you about my plans, because I knew that you would not approve of what I am doing. Even so, I hope that I may help you understand why I am doing it.

You have heard me speak of my feelings for Mr. Askew. You have heard me speak of marrying him. But you have not heard me say how very much I love him. O mother and father, I do love him! William and I have pledged ourselves to each other. I have waited patiently for a year since the war began, but the war has only grown worse and worse. I can no longer stay at home waiting helplessly. I cannot stand by while he is in prison, without knowing if he has been wounded, or knowing anything of his present conditions.

I have presumed to take Ella with me because I have supposed that it is your intention that she would pass into my possession at the time of my marriage. I have taken Sammy with me also. Though he belongs to Mr. Hicks, he was left in my charge. I will contact Mr. Hicks and request that he meet me in Chicago. Should he agree to come to Chicago, I will transfer Sammy to his care. If he comes, I shall rely upon Mr. Hicks, since William is in prison, to provide me with such protections and guidance as he can while I am in the North.

It is my intention to marry William Askew, to see him safely through these present circumstances, and, when it is safe to do so, to return home with him to you. When we do, I hope that you and William's father will receive us as your own married children.

As you will discover, I have accepted money from each of you under false pretenses. What is more, I acquired various articles at Meacham's store in town, but I did not pay for them. I promised Mr. Meacham that he would be paid today—and I hope that you will do me the favor of honoring that debt.

If I have been successful, I will also by now have borrowed Mr. Askew's brougham under deceitful circumstances. I hope that Mr. Askew will find it in his heart to forgive me for taking his carriage for this journey. I pray that he will respect my good intentions toward his son.

I have learned that Jimmy has run away. Though I do not know where Jimmy is at present, I have reason to hope that I may find both Jimmy and William's servant Cato in the North—and that we may all be kept safe together

Finally, I pray that you will understand that I do not wish to cause you grief, even though I know that you will grieve over my actions. I love you both. I am doing what I am doing not because there is any diminishment in my love for you—but rather because my love for William compels me to act. I know my actions will not be judged proper for a woman—but they are the actions that my heart demands.

O mother, forgive me! Father, I ask that you do not endeavor to come after me, but rather, that you both pray for my well being, and that you endeavor to put your trust in my judgment. I promise that I will take every precaution

to remain out of harm's way while on my journey, and stay
safe until that day when we are reunited.

Your loving daughter,

Dorothy Holland

Monday, 28th April, 1862

During the night, Dorothy packed her clothes for the journey. These she put in a satchel, which she carried in secret to
Ella's cabin. In the morning, she spoke cheerily at breakfast
about her impending shopping trip to town. She asked Mr.
Askew if he would mind if she borrowed his brougham to go
into town—and asked him if there was anything she might
obtain for him while she was there. He told her that she was
welcome to borrow his carriage and that he would be most
grateful if she would visit the tobacconist to obtain a fresh
pouch of tobacco for his pipe. He gave her money for this
purpose. Then Dorothy mentioned to her mother that she may
as well buy spirits for the party and other provisions and
groceries while she was about it. For this purpose, her mother
gave her additional funds beyond those already supplied for the
dress.

Thereafter, things proceeded according to the plan that
Dorothy had worked out with Ella, Cato and Sammy the night
before. Dorothy drove the brougham up to Ella's cabin. When
no one was looking, Ella brought out Dorothy's satchel and her
own belongings and put them in the carriage. Dorothy and
Ella then headed toward town on Christmasville Road. But just
before they arrived at the bridge over Dyer Creek, they
stopped. Cato and Sammy, who had sneaked out of the cabin
before daybreak to hide in the woods, emerged from their
hiding spot and joined them in the brougham at the
prearranged spot just before the bridge.

Cato was fully dressed in his gentleman's clothes, wig and

hat. He wore his left arm in a sling. After much fretfulness on Dorothy's part about how Cato would avoid having to remove his hat in certain circumstances, Dorothy had hit upon the idea of using the ruse of a broken arm. They had agreed that Cato's left arm would be put out of commission in a sling, and that he would take the further precaution of always carrying Dorothy's satchel with his right arm—so that it would be apparent to all who encountered him that removing his hat would be unduly taxing for a gentleman thus disabled and burdened.

On the other hand, Dorothy did want Cato to have the use of his right hand, so that he might sign the register at any inn or hotel that gave them accommodation. Cato's ability to write was a skill that Dorothy wanted to be visibly displayed, as it would subtly work against any suspicion that he might not be white.

Dorothy and Cato had also discussed at length how they would identify themselves to strangers during the journey. Dorothy concluded that it would be safest if they traveled as husband and wife. Cato did not look sufficiently similar to Dorothy to be passed off as her brother without creating suspicions. Moreover, she wished to conserve money by taking only a single room at any lodging house—and this, too, required that they be married. When discussing what pseudonym they might use as a disguise, Cato had suggested that he should very much like to travel the world as Mr. Darcy, and couldn't Dorothy, therefore, be Mrs. Darcy. Dorothy, however, was of the opinion that this would be too risky, since for all she knew some innkeeper may have read "Pride and Prejudice" and might find the name peculiarly familiar. She suggested they use the name Dawson instead.

But Dorothy did like the idea that Cato should endeavor to comport himself in a fashion inspired by Mr. Darcy. She suggested that Cato ought to model his speech in public upon Mr. Darcy's manner of speaking. Toward that end, she had included a copy of "Pride and Prejudice" in her satchel. As they drove through Jackson, Cato rode in the brougham practicing playing the role of Mr. Fitzwilliam Dawson. He leafed through "Pride and Prejudice" as he rode, memorizing lines of dialogue that he might use on various occasions.

At the same time, Ella and Sammy were coached on strategies for audibly referring to Cato as Master Dawson. Inside the carriage Ella's tone, as she practiced addressing Master Dawson, was tinged with what Cato identified as sarcasm—accompanied by much rolling of the eyes. Sammy, however, thought it was great fun to play the game. He put all his skill into delivering a convincing performance as he humbled himself in the service of Master Dawson.

After heading southwest into town on Christmasville Road, Dorothy turned north back out of town on Picketville Road until she reached Ashport Road. She followed Ashport Road east until they rejoined Christmasville Road at a point just north of Hickory Grove. Thereafter they continued northeast on Christmasville Road until they reached the town of Christmasville itself. Dorothy's plan was to travel on the first day all the way to Bowling Green, Kentucky. She hoped to find Walter McNish, the man who had served as Erastus Hicks's postal agent by ferrying his letters from Bowling Green to Clarksville so that they might be put into the Confederate mail system.

It took them all day to travel from Christmasville, Tennessee, to Bowling Green, Kentucky, by way of Clarksville. They traveled across bridges over both the Tennessee River and the Cumberland River. Less than an hour north of Clarksville, they came to the Kentucky border. Dorothy feared they might encounter a border guard when they passed into Kentucky, which had not seceded from the Union. But by April, 1862, the Union Army had advanced south along the Tennessee River all the way to Pittsburgh Landing at the southern edge of Tennessee, which is where the Battle of Shiloh had been fought. Since the Union Army had won that battle and the Confederate Army had retreated south to Mississippi, the entire north central section of Tennessee was for all practical purposes under Union control. And so Mr. and Mrs. Fitzwilliam Dawson and their two slaves passed into Kentucky without encountering any troops.

The travelers found lodging at the Marshall House hotel in Bowling Green. Mr. Dawson entered that establishment with a satchel in his right hand and Mrs. Dawson and two Negroes at his side. He set down the satchel long enough to sign the register. When the hotel clerk, looking at Ella and Sammy, asked Mr. Dawson whether the two Negroes would also be staying in the room and whether, therefore, he ought to order two cots to be supplied for that purpose, Mr. Dawson replied, "I shall not say that you are mistaken."

Cato had come across that line of Mr. Darcy's in Chapter 8 of Volume II, which was a chapter that had particularly impressed itself upon him, insofar as he was reading it at the time Judge Samuels caught him in the woods. Since Cato thought it was a rather sophisticated way to say something in the affirmative, he had been eager to find an occasion to use it. Dorothy, however, immediately nudged her husband gently on his good arm, and added her own assent by saying to the clerk, "Yes, two cots will suffice for our servants."

Once they were alone in their room, Dorothy proposed that perhaps Cato should abandon the speech of Mr. Darcy in favor of that of a more recent literary model, such as David Copperfield. But Cato felt that now that he had satisfied his obsession by saying, "I shall not say that you are mistaken," he would be able to deploy future lines of Mr. Darcy with more conversational aptness. And since they did not have with them a copy of David Copperfield for Cato to study by way of reference, Dorothy decided to let the matter rest.

Insofar as they only had one bed and two cots in their room, it was determined that, with all due propriety, Dorothy and Ella should share the bed, while Cato and Sammy should man the cots. And on the off chance that someone might come to their hotel room door and rouse them in the middle of the night, it was decided that not only should Cato and Ella be prepared to change places quickly, but that Cato should keep his hat and wig at the ready as well. When Ella pointed out that it was unlikely that a gentleman would be wearing his hat while in his bed in the middle of the night, Dorothy replied that the oddity of a man being found wearing a hat in the middle of the night was a far safer offense than the sacrilege of a white woman being found in her bed with a Negro man. On this, they all agreed.

## 39

## "THE CURRENT GETS 'EM"

$\mathcal{H}$enrietta Holland was the first to read Dorothy's letter. Her reaction encompassed a gamut of emotions: rage, fear, remorse. But mainly she felt helpless. When she handed the letter to her husband, she sat on the sofa and she wept quietly.

When he read the letter, George Holland was dumbstruck. He did not know whether to go after Dorothy, or whether to go after Jimmy. Not knowing what to do, he did nothing. He sat in his chair.

When Augustus Askew came into the room, George Holland showed him the letter. When he had read it, he too sat in a chair. Like Mr. Holland, he said nothing. He was astonished that a girl could be so senseless. Yet he could not help but imagine the letter from the point of view of his son. When he looked at it from that vantage point, he was struck by the sincerity of the affection, which she said had 'compelled' her actions. His mind ruminated back and forth between his condemnation of her senselessness and his admiration of her fidelity.

The three of them sat for twenty minutes, the two men not speaking, the woman quietly sobbing—until, at last, Henrietta cleared her throat and said, "God help us, she's headstrong. I don't believe we could catch her, George. There is nothing we can do."

"I don't know which is greater, her imprudence or her devotion," said Mr. Askew.

"The world has gone mad," said Mrs. Holland. "The war … is a poison. Civilization disintegrates about us. I scarcely know what will become of anyone."

"Dorothy asked that we pray for her," said Mr. Holland. "I don't know what else we might do."

And so the cumulative effect of more than twelve months of war was that it quieted them all. They could not see where their lives were headed. They had become aware, as the war dragged on, of their age, and of an impression that the world was pulling away from them. A feeling of disorientation accumulated—and then Dorothy's letter shattered whatever remained of the hopeful defiance that had kept bewilderment at bay. The three parents saw uncertainty and vulnerability in each other—which amplified the atmosphere of impotence that descended on the Holland farm.

Augustus Askew did not attempt to replace his carriage. Instead, he began to walk back and forth from the Hollands' to Hickory Grove. Scout accompanied him. Augustus put his mind onto small things: Scout chasing a squirrel, the changeable spring weather, the cawing of crows, the emergence of worms when it rained. He grew preoccupied with smoking his pipe.

Henrietta Holland sought intimacy with Cora and Wally. Her loneliness for her daughter made her want the company of women. It comforted her to know that Wally missed Ella. She saw that Wally, like her, was adrift in the uncertainty of the world. Their familiarity—their certainty—to each other gained value.

George Holland prayed. All his life he had, as a matter of habit, attended the Methodist Church. But now he became truly attentive to the inner voice of his spirit. He grew earnest in prayers and meditations. The moments he stood in the church on Sunday morning singing hymns with his neighbors were, he realized, the only moments he felt comfort. And so he began to hum to himself, quietly, when he worked in the fields with his slaves. He hummed the melodies of his favorite hymns: 'Rock of Ages,' 'Blest Be the Tie That Binds,' 'Nearer My God to Thee.' The slaves left him to himself as he drifted in his own private space.

And so it was that no effort was made by any of them to seek after Dorothy, Ella, Sammy, Cato, or Jimmy.

\* \* \*

FOR JIMMY, day became night and night became day. The abrupt turning upside down of the natural clock left him in a bizarre state. He was giddy, but reality became like a dream. He crept through the woods at night. When dawn was nigh, he sought the depths of the forest, the innermost spot, where he searched for a large tree to screen his body from the view of those eyes which he presumed pursued him. It did not occur to him that he would not be chased—and so he ran from his own apprehension.

He was anxious about his course of travel. He had never seen a map. He knew only in a general way about Kentucky, Indiana and Illinois. He had an impression of where they were supposed to be. His only certainty was the North Star. He knew that if he went the right way, he would come to a river. The Ohio River, Jake had told him, was wide and deep. Dyer Creek was as nothing to it. Jimmy could not swim. Yet he could not imagine how else he might cross the river unseen. "Men drown," Jake told him. "The current grabs 'em." Jimmy panicked when he thought of the river. So he put the river out of his mind, and focused with much intensity on the present moments.

He worked himself into a wariness so pervasive that he could hardly go to sleep. Such sleep as he had was fitful. He frequently awoke when an animal walked nearby, or when the sun inched onto his face. Late one afternoon, just as he finally fell into a deep sleep, he was awakened by rain. He sat up and leaned against his tree, overwhelmed by a sudden loneliness. He was not sure why his face felt wet or why his eyes felt sore. He was not a man to cry easily, so he told himself it was the rain and not tears that wet his cheeks. He told himself that his eyes were sore only from lack of sleep. But his chest heaved and his body shuddered, just as it would from sobbing. And he wondered what force brought him into such a world, beset him so with trials, and left him so desperately alone. Why should it be so?

For most of his life, the North had meant one thing to him: freedom. But freedom was a word that he had understood only by its absence. Now the North also meant Cato. Now the North had a face he knew—a face he loved. Before Cato he'd only imagined freedom as an ambiguous state—the state of being away from the Hollands—out from under the Hollands —allowed to make his own choices. It was only after Cato that he could also understand what his own choices would be. There was no other thing that he was as certain of as his love for Cato. Yet it seemed so improbable to him that love for a man was what life had given him. For the world had conspired to say nothing of such a possibility—nothing, nothing, nothing. And yet—it had arisen as absolutely as the cloth of his trousers. It had unveiled a world of joy he had never imagined.

What else, Jimmy wondered, might rise up from the infinite? What other unimaginable thing might someday become more important to him than anything else? It was in this direction that his thoughts grew giddy and fantastic—for he had a sense of vast possibilities—of untold promise. He began to wonder if the whole of his life as a slave had been a ruse—if the white men had kept other wonders of the world hidden from him. Perhaps in the North men loved men as a matter of course. Perhaps the world was not what he thought it was. He waited for the rain to pass, because he could not see the North Star while the clouds blocked his view. And in the dark wet forest, he dreamed of a paradise. He dreamed that that paradise might be even better than he could imagine.

For three nights, Jimmy ate only stale bread. There had been half a loaf in the cabin the night he left. Wally had stuffed it in with his socks and shirts. He found water in the creeks and streams he passed along the way. But by the fourth night, the bread was gone. On the fourth night, he hid at dawn at the edge of a field. He hoped a gang of slaves might come alone to work. But when the sun was an hour up in the sky, he could see that no one was coming. He wanted to sleep, but he was more hungry than tired. He circled around the perimeter of the fields—staying in the woods—until at last he came upon two slave men with a plow and a mule, preparing a field for planting. He watched them long enough to be certain that no white man was with them.

When Jimmy ran out of the woods toward the slaves, their first reaction was fearful. They left the plow and mule and began to draw back. Jimmy called out, "Wait! Wait!"

One of the men, the shorter of the two, stopped. "Who are you?" he called.

"I'm escaped," Jimmy called back.

"Run away?" the man asked.

"Yes, run away," Jimmy said, "four nights ago." He was out of breath when he arrived at the man's side. "Where am I?" he asked.

"Beulah, Kentucky."

"Where's the river?" Jimmy asked.

"Which one?" the man replied. "You go west fifteen miles you'll see the Mississippi. You go north thirty miles, you'll see the Ohio."

"Where is the place that they come together?"

"About twenty-five miles that a way," the man said, and he pointed. "On the other side of the river is Illinois—Cairo."

"Cairo," Jimmy repeated. He looked in the direction that the man pointed and memorized the points on the horizon to mark his route. From his earliest memory, Jake had told him the name of the spot where the north began, where the rivers came together, where slavery stopped. He looked at the man who was pointing, suddenly curious how a slave could be so close to freedom and still stay put. "Have you been there?" he asked.

"Nope," the man said. "I ain't goin' nowhere to get chased by no dogs." He pulled up his pants leg and showed Jimmy a discolored scar. "Dog got me twelve years ago. I ain't run off since."

Jimmy looked around warily, as the idea of paddy roller dogs impressed itself upon his mind. "I'm hiding in the woods over there," Jimmy pointed. "Do you think you could bring me some food?" Jimmy pulled a bill out of his pocket. "I can pay you for it."

The man looked at the dollar bill in Jimmy's hand. Suddenly the guardedness in his eyes fell away. He pushed Jimmy's hand back. "You like cornmeal? Salt pork?" he asked.

"I like anything," Jimmy smiled. "Anything at all!"

"You'd better get on back there," the man said. "I'll bring you something at lunchtime."

Jimmy thanked the stranger, and went back to the woods. When he got to the edge of the forest, he turned and waved at the man, who waved back. Three hours later, at lunchtime, the man was as good as his word. He found Jimmy asleep twenty yards into the woods. He brought fried cornmeal with salt pork and three apples. Jimmy was so grateful he kissed the man on the forehead.

"Here now," the man blushed. "You best go further back in the woods to eat that." He looked back toward the field. "Somebody could see you if you stay here."

"When I get to the river," Jimmy asked, "What can I do? I can't swim."

The man scratched his chin. "If I was you I'd look for a boat," he said. "I hear tell of a man who found a rowboat tied up. He rowed across the river and tied it up on the other side. It was like as if someone'd left it there for him."

"Why would somebody leave a boat like that?" Jimmy asked.

"They say there's folks in the Underground Railroad that keep watch by the river. Maybe they put the rowboat out there."

"Underground Railroad," Jimmy said. "I heard about that. I thought maybe it was just a story."

"It may be a story," said the man. "But you're not the first fellow who's come sneaking up here. They all go somewhere. I never seen one come back." The man scratched his chin again.

"Course I also heard of men drowned in the river. The current gets 'em."

Jimmy was startled to hear the same words he'd heard from Jake. He held the food up in front of him. "Thank you for this food," he said. "I'm very hungry."

"God be with you," the man said.

Jimmy frowned at the mention of the word 'God'—but then he quickly covered it with a smile. He had no right, under the circumstances, to any ill feeling toward this stranger. He shook the man's hand, then retreated into the woods to eat.

When he had finished eating, Jimmy fell asleep—and it was the first good sleep he'd had since he left. He slept so long that when he woke it was deep in the night. He had no idea how much of the night was still left to him. He walked back to the field, back to the spot where he'd spoken to the slave with the dog bite. He looked for and found the points on the horizon that he'd memorized earlier. Then he looked up at the stars above those points and memorized the pattern of those stars. He walked as straight as he could in a fixed direction, keeping the guiding cluster of stars directly in front of him. Now the North Star was somewhat to the right, and he was walking in a north by northwest direction.

But after three hours, the first glimmer of sunrise appeared to his right in the sky. The man with the bite had told him it was twenty-five miles to Cairo—and he calculated that he'd walked no more than ten. And so he spent one more day hiding in the woods of Kentucky, one more day in the South, one more day in the land of slavery.

Near the end of that day, he awoke before sunset. He couldn't wait any longer. He began to move even before dusk completed its descent. After five hours of steady walking, he came upon the spot he'd been searching for. Even in the darkness, he could see it from a hundred feet inside the forest, the spot where the trees stopped. With his heart beating, he walked rapidly to the edge of the woods. There he stood on the bank of a wide dark river. The Ohio River—he could not believe how wide it was! And as he looked across it, he despaired. There would be no rowboat. There would be only drowning if he tried to swim. He climbed down to the edge of the water. He touched the water with his hand. The water was cold, foreboding. "I wish you were here, old girl," he said. "I know you could swim. You'd swim right across."

Jimmy walked back into the woods. He began to make his way due west, following the bank of the river. He stayed close enough to the river's edge so that if there were a boat of any kind, he would see it. He walked for more than an hour, until he came across a creek that emptied into the river. There at the spot where the creek met the river was a wooden pier. He went out toward the pier. He could not see anything in any direction that would provide a reason for a pier to be in this spot. He could see no road, no break in the woods. He walked slowly onto the pier. He heard a knocking sound. He saw the glint of a rope tied around one of the posts on the pier. He leaned over to see where the rope went. And lo, hidden under the pier, a rowboat was tied fast! And so for the first time he saw and believed with his own eyes the thing that had only been spoken of in whispered tones throughout his life. He whispered it now out loud: "the Underground Railroad!"

Suddenly he panicked. He ran back into the woods. It was too easy. It had to be a trap. He sat down and watched and waited. He watched and waited for thirty minutes. There he sat in the darkness watching it—the small wooden pier, about ten feet long, sticking out into the dark deep water. Under it, the boat was floating, was knocking against the wooden post of the pier, knocking in a rhythm that matched the sound of water lapping on the shoreline. Why did he hesitate? It was a moment he'd dreamed of—and yet, there was something ominous about the sound of the boat knocking on the pier.

He crept back to the edge of the water. He peered across the river. He could barely see the opposite shore in the darkness. The moon had set. There was only starlight. He took a deep breath. He decided to do it. He went out onto the dock, lay down on the planks, leaned over the side, and peered down under the pier to inspect the rowboat. He saw two oars in the boat. He saw a rope tied to the front of the boat, and a rope tied to the back. The boat was secured to the pier in two places. He untied the front rope. As he did so, the front of the boat swung away from the pier. In that orientation, he saw that it would be easy for him to climb down into the back of the boat. He threw his satchel into the boat. Then he lowered himself down into the boat, and steadied himself. He waited until he had his bearings. After a few moments, he untied the back rope. The boat drifted quickly out into the water.

Jimmy moved to the center of the boat—but as he did so, he felt how unsteady it was when he stood up. He sat down carefully in the center seat. He looked pensively at the oars. He sat for a long moment wondering what to do—for he had no idea how to row a boat. Then he realized that as he was sitting and wondering what to do, he was drifting out further and further into the river. And even as he observed this phenomenon, he saw that he was picking up speed, that even doing nothing he was being carried by the current down the river. He did not know how far it was to the point of the union, where the Mississippi joined the Ohio. But he realized that he might easily drift quickly into some public view, if he didn't act.

He swung the oars over the side of the boat. He tried to move them against the water. When he moved the oars, the boat did not react the way he expected. The boat went the opposite of the way he pushed! Then he pushed on one oar and pulled on the other. To his dismay, the boat began to spin around. Now the boat was both spinning and drifting—and he began to panic. He tried the opposite movements, pulling on one oar and pushing on the other. That stopped the spinning. Then he realized that he could use the spinning movement to point the boat in the direction that he wanted it to go. He gradually pushed and pulled on the opposite oars until the front of the boat was pointed toward the far shore. Then he rowed. But he had already forgotten the backward response of the movement of the boat, and he rowed the wrong way, back toward Kentucky.

He stuck the oars deep into the water, for he could tell intuitively that doing so would stop the boat's movement. Then he forced himself to row in the reverse way that made the boat go toward … the North! Once he had the knack of it, he rowed as hard and as fast as he could. He rowed and rowed steadily. The sound of the oars in the water made a rhythm like the rhythm of the boat knocking against the pier—until at last he came hard and fast upon the opposite bank of the river, upon the shore of Illinois. But on the Illinois side of the river, he found no pier. He tried to get the boat to stop, but it banged against the rocks of the shoreline and ricocheted back out into the river. Now the boat was spinning around again, and Jimmy could not calculate what to do with the oars to regain control. He jammed them in the water. He thought for a moment of abandoning the boat, of jumping into the water. Surely, he could swim a few feet to the shore. But Jake's words sounded in his ear, "the current gets 'em!"

He tried to row with one hand while he reached out toward the rocks on the shoreline with the other. But there was no rock tall enough for him to grab hold of, and rowing with one hand only made the boat spin more erratically. He tried to stand up, but he felt the boat instantly sway, and the swaying quickly tipped his balance, until he sat down again and clutched the seat to keep from falling out.

His head began to spin as the boat revolved. Suddenly he did not want to be in the boat any longer. The shore was so close. It was unbearable not to be able to get onto it. Earlier, he had dropped his satchel into the boat when he climbed into it from the pier. Now he grabbed the satchel and threw it as hard as he could toward the bank. It landed on the shore. And so the die was cast! He had to get out of the boat. Once again, the boat began to drift back out into the river. There was no time to lose. He stood up and yelped and half dived, half fell into the water. He'd hoped the water would be shallow, but he soon realized that he couldn't feel the bottom with his feet. He thrashed his arms. Despite his thrashing, his body sank down, heavy as a rock. In a moment, he was under the water, and he descended until his feet touched the riverbed. He tried to walk on the floor of the river toward the shore, but now he felt it— the current!

All at once, he realized that it was a matter of life and death. He pushed his feet hard against the bed of the river with all his strength. He bobbed back up above the surface, and gasped for air. Again, he thrashed his arms to try to pull himself toward the shore. This time he advanced a few feet before his body weight pulled him back down into the river. Now he was underwater again, but he had swallowed some water and he began to choke. One more time he pushed his feet as hard as he could against the riverbed, which catapulted his body back up. When his head broke the surface, he spat water out of his mouth. He gasped, sucking in air in a wild gulp, and again he thrashed and thrashed. He thrashed his way several more feet toward the shore, until again he sank! Now he was terribly frightened.

For a third time Jimmy propelled himself off the bottom of the river with his feet, springing up hard. The moment he resurfaced, he yelled out, "Help!" as loud as he could. But he knew there was no one to hear him, for his voice was surprisingly weak. He thought of Venus, of Cato. "Oh God!" And so in his terror he thought of God. But he was floundering. He slapped the surface of the water with his hands, desperate to make himself stay afloat. But these slapping, flailing movements only delayed his sinking for a moment. He felt himself sink again. He felt as if some great weight pulled him down. He descended—down, down, sucked back into the cold black depths of the river.

Now under the water he thought, "I'm drowning." He didn't know what to do. "I'm going to die!" He cast about wildly under the water, turning his head in all directions. Even submerged under the water his arms flailed in an unproductive way. Suddenly it occurred to him to try to use his arms—just as he had used the oars—to row his body toward the shore. He spread his arms out like oars and rowed with them. "Oh God, it works!" When he stroked with his arms he felt himself glide through the water in a direction opposite to the way he rowed. "This must be swimming," he thought. He stroked more forcefully—and this time he glided even more perceptibly. He changed the direction of his paddling movements until he felt himself impelled not only shoreward, but upward.

At long last, his head came up out of the water, and he could see that he was very close to the shore. Now instead of thrashing, he paddled with his arms—and this time, in a matter of moments, he hurtled up against a rock on the shoreline. He grabbed hold of the rock. He held fast to the rock while his legs dangled in the water. He caught his breath. Then in one last great effort, he heaved himself up and onto the shore.

He dragged his body away from the water. After he'd hauled himself six feet inland, he stopped. He lay face down on the ground, and for the third time in his life, just as he had done when Venus died, just as he had done when he saw Cato in chains, he cried.

# 40

# TRAVELS IN DENMARK AND SWEDEN

*L*ieutenant William Askew was one of 736 prisoners captured at the Battle of Shiloh and sent to the Union prison at Camp Douglas in Chicago. As an officer, he was entitled to special privileges at the camp, but he was too sullen to partake of those privileges. He stayed in bed. The Confederate doctor who attended him had seen other soldiers whose minds had been wounded in battle, but William would not speak, so the doctor could not glean any of the facts of his case. All he could do was determine that William had no physical injuries, and advise him to rest.

William was too ashamed to tell the doctor what had happened. He was certain he was responsible for the death of his friend Daniel Watson. In his mind, the Union soldier who actually shot and killed Daniel on the battlefield was only an unwitting participant in William's private moral drama. By rights, William told himself, he should have killed that soldier, but instead he purposefully shot his weapon into the air. He did so because he was reluctant to kill—and yet the consequence of his reluctance was that the one man who had befriended him was slain.

He hadn't meant for it to happen, and his mind kept returning to that point. But he would not exonerate himself. Although he hadn't meant for Daniel to be killed, he had meant to shoot into the air. He had broken a code of honor. He'd taken an oath to fight, but he had not done so. He'd taken a lofty but secret position against violence. He had not had the courage to defy war openly. His fellow soldiers marched beside him without knowing that he would not defend them. Why had he not considered that such a thing might happen? It had not occurred to him that he would witness such a direct consequence of his inaction. If only the Yankee had shot him instead of Daniel!

He lay in bed. He did not look at anyone. He could not bear to look his comrades in the eye. That his life should travel from its brightest joy to its darkest moments in just one year made the darkness more unbearable. He well remembered how happy he had been back in the Hollands' garden. He could conjure up a mental picture of himself pushing Dorothy on the swing. But the deadness of his present state of mind was like a dull knife that lacerated his remembered joy—until even that memory was bled of its pleasant feeling.

He resolved to put his thoughts onto something else— something to distract him. And so, when someone came around handing out books to the prisoners, he took the book that was handed to him. The book was called "Travels in Denmark and Sweden." As he lay in bed and skimmed the text of this book, it seemed truly foreign, as if it were written about a different species. His world had once been one in which such frivolities as cheese and mulled wine and the fairy tales of Hans Christian Andersen might seem, if not familiar, at least plausible. But now the cheerful Scandinavian world in the book seemed incredible. Only the harshness of the Swedish winter and the darkness of the long nights seemed credible to him. The book spoke of these phenomena as climatic curiosities, but William was in harmony only with their gloom. There was no coziness in fires, no sport in sleigh rides, no comfort in candlelit Christmas trees. No delectable descriptions of pastry could shake him from his dark state. He had acquired the mind of a skeptic, a pessimist, a misanthrope, a disparager of all things. He could feel the bitterness run through him, toxic, but as if it had always been there. He could no longer imagine the future. When he looked out past the next day, he saw nothing at all.

William slept fitfully at night. He ate mechanically when food was brought to him. Only when he trudged to the latrine did he feel anything like emotion. The filth and stench of that place made him feel nauseated. The nausea in turn put him on the brink of crying. He squatted in there, on the verge of actually expressing his grief, wishing he could break the façade of decorum that barred him from emotional release. Once, he vomited, but even then, he didn't cry. He trudged back to his bed, back to the pages of "Travels in Denmark and Sweden," back to the prison of his self-reproach, where he lay in solitary confinement.

One day the fellow in the bed next to him spoke to him. "Seems like you've been looking at the same page in that book for about three days," the man said.

William didn't reply.

"You were at Shiloh, weren't that so?"

Since he did not wish to speak, William merely nodded.

"Myself, I was at Fort Donnellson," the man said. "Saw things I can't shake out of my mind."

William nodded again.

"Did you lose someone? A pal of yours maybe?"

William's head moved again, in a barely perceptible nod.

"That's what I reckoned," the man said. "When you come face to face with a thing like that, it surprises you how bad it is."

William closed his eyes.

"I hope I get exchanged," the man said. "I hate the Yankees worse than before. This war's all their doing. They couldn't just leave us be."

William did not react at all to this.

"'Course I miss my wife pretty bad." He held up his hand, as if to marvel at his wedding ring. He had noticed that William had no ring on his hand. "I reckon you never married."

William shook his head.

"Don't know if it's better—or worse—to have someone back home while you're stuck up here in this rat hole."

There was no reaction.

"Maybe you got someone back home anyhow?"

A slight nod.

"Well, you're not the only secesh up here with a sweetheart back home. Where you from anyhow? I'm from St. Louis. Joined up with the Tennessee Third back in Memphis. Let's see, since you were at Shiloh, you must be from Tennessee or Mississippi."

William turned his head and opened his eyes. He really didn't want to talk to this man, but he could see that the man was not going to leave him be. "Tennessee Sixth Regiment," he said.

"Is that a fact? Where in Tennessee?"

"Near Jackson."

"I never got down that way. I think we marched north of your town when we went from Memphis to Fort Donnellson."

William nodded.

"So what's her name? Your sweetheart, I mean."

"Dorothy."

"I'm John Lewis. My wife is Emily. We have a daughter, Jane, and a son, Richard. Emily didn't like my joining up—but, hell, I wasn't going to stand by." Then he whispered. "Hooray for Jeff Davis! That's what I say."

This burst of patriotism caused William to turn back and stare at the ceiling.

The man continued. "I wish I knew how the war is going. I don't trust these Chicago papers they have in here. Yankee propaganda mostly. The fellow who was in that bed before you told me he was gonna sign an oath of loyalty to the Union. He said they promised to parole him right out of here if he signed it. But then if they ever captured him again in a Reb uniform, they'd shoot him straight out with no questions asked."

"Paroled to where?" William asked.

"Here in the North, I reckon. I don't suppose they'd let someone go back South if he took the oath. But anyway, like I was saying, it's all on account of the propaganda in those papers. That fellow believed what he read in the Tribune. He read that after Shiloh, the South was crushed. And he didn't want to rot up here in prison just waiting for it to all be over. He said he didn't care anymore about any of it. 'Let 'em put a nigger in the White House,' he said, 'for all I care.' He said he was going to sign the oath, get on a streetcar, and go straight up State Street to the nearest tavern and get drunk. I told him he'd be a traitor. He said, 'You can't betray something if it's already lost.' I told him, 'It ain't lost yet. That's just propaganda.' But then the next day they took him out of here—and brought you in."

The notion that he could sign a paper that would take him out of the war came as a surprise to William. He hadn't thought there was any way out of the nightmare, but there it was: sign a paper, go get drunk, and be done with it. "What oath did this man sign?" William asked.

"An oath of loyalty to the Union. The man renounced the South! It's shameful—truly, just shameful. But I think this fellow must've actually signed it, 'cause I ain't seen him since."

"Getting drunk sounds appealing," said William.

"Yeah," said the man. "I reckon it'd feel considerable good to get corned. But then you'd wake up in the morning, with nothing but a hangover, and ...."

"...the memory of your best friend getting a hole blown through his chest," William finished the thought.

This thought finally quieted the man. "Yeah," the man said. And then he rolled over and looked up at the ceiling and remained silent.

\* \* \*

WALTER MCNISH WAS A ROTUND MAN, sixty years of age, who showed few signs of his earthly tenure. His hair, though somewhat grizzled did not appear gray. His eyes shone bright and clear behind the spectacles perpetually perched at the end of his nose. He was lively in spirit and more energetic than many men of his age. This may have been due in some part to his Quaker piety, which abhorred idleness. But in a larger part, his liveliness sprang from his enthusiasm for the great system of Kentucky caves, of which Mammoth Cave was the chief attraction and Mr. McNish the foremost proponent.

When Walter McNish called at the Marshall House hotel for Mr. and Mrs. Fitzwilliam Dawson, he knew only that his wife had described them as a nice, but rather peculiar couple, who claimed that they were Shakers. Mr. McNish was given to understand that the couple wished to employ him as a tour guide to Mammoth Cave. He did not know that he had been especially sought out because of his connection to Erastus Hicks—or that 'Mrs. Dawson' was the woman for whom he had smuggled letters into the Confederate mail system more than a year before. Dorothy had determined, however, to enlighten Mr. McNish with at least a portion of the truth. She took Erastus Hicks's faith in Mr. McNish as evidence that he must be a trustworthy man. Even so, she thought it might be risqué to admit that the man traveling as her husband was, in fact, a slave—so she decided to leave that part of the story intact.

"Mr. McNish," said Dorothy, when they met face to face. "I must confess to you right away that we did not give our true names to your wife. In actuality, I am Dorothy Askew. Before I was married, I was Dorothy Holland. You may recall my name because last year our mutual friend Erastus Hicks asked you to forward two letters from him to me. This is my husband George, and these are our servants Ella and Sammy. We are traveling to the North because my husband's brother William, who is an officer in the Confederate Army, has been taken prisoner. He was sent to Camp Douglas in Chicago. We are going there to see if we can help William find his way out of this war, for you see, Mr. McNish, like Mr. Hicks, and perhaps like yourself, we are pacifists. I came here to contact you because I would like to inform Mr. Hicks of recent developments that I believe will be of interest to him, and I wonder if I might impose upon you to write a letter to Mr. Hicks on my behalf."

"My dear lady," said Mr. McNish. "I would, of course, be happy to oblige your request. But truly, there is no further impediment to your corresponding directly with Mr. Hicks. The Union lines are now at the Mississippi border. Even from Tennessee I think you might safely have posted a letter to Philadelphia, but here in Bowling Green anyone may do so."

"Then you mean to say … there are no censors who read the mail from here to Philadelphia?"

"No my dear, you are now quite definitely in Union territory. You can write in confidence to Mr. Hicks in your own hand and mail it at the post office near this hotel."

"Oh my," said Dorothy. "I feel foolish, then, to have troubled you. I did not realize that I could write to him myself."

"Well it's no trouble, my dear, truly. And since you are visiting here, perhaps you would enjoy seeing the cave after all. I would be honored to take you and your husband on an expedition to see it. It is my specialty. There would be no cost. Erastus Hicks is one of my dearest friends, and I should be happy to oblige any friends of his in whatever way I may."

"I thank you for your kind offer," Dorothy said. "But in truth, I must confess, we are eager to reach Chicago. I don't think we ought to take time for an expedition."

"Ah, but if you are traveling to Louisville," said Mr. McNish. "The cave will be on your route. And I would be pleased to accompany you as far as that. You must visit this wonder of nature, Mrs. Askew. But perhaps you would also like to discuss your mission in Chicago, for I daresay you are bound to find impediments if your brother-in-law is a prisoner."

"My brother was captured at the Battle of Shiloh," Cato said, feeling that at last he must say something.

"Ah yes, Mr. Askew, I believe I also forwarded a letter from Mr. Hicks to your brother. Lieutenant William Askew, is he not?"

"Yes," said Cato. "You are not mistaken."

"It would be kind of you, Mr. McNish," said Dorothy, "to travel with us. I would like to discuss our mission. I suppose we might talk at the cave as well as anywhere else. Is it very far?"

"It is about thirty miles to Cave City," said Mr. McNish.

"And then another ninety miles to Louisville. However, you may wish to journey only as far as Elizabethtown, which is but fifty miles north of the cave."

"Yes of course," said Dorothy. "Eighty miles is quite ample for one day's journey. Mr. McNish, would you be so kind as to meet us here in an hour. Before I go, I would like to write my letter to Mr. Hicks and mail it. Then we will be ready to visit the cave."

And so Mr. McNish departed. Dorothy wrote her letter to Erastus Hicks and mailed it. At the appointed hour, they reunited at the hotel, whereupon the party departed for Mammoth Cave—led by Mr. McNish on his horse. Within several hours, they had arrived at the historic entrance to Mammoth Cave. It was decided that they should all descend into the cave together, though Ella expressed reservations.

"It don't seem natural," she said, "to go down a dark hole in the ground on purpose."

"It is perfectly safe," said Mr. McNish. "The entrance leads into a large passageway, and I shall provide each of you with lanterns."

Mr. McNish, having prepared in advance, produced five lanterns from his saddlebags, which he distributed to each member of the party. Then down they went on rough formed steps and steep declines. When they arrived at the first sizable chamber, Mr. McNish halted the party so that he might speak at some length about the history and geology of the cave. His voice reverberated oddly, but he addressed them with much enthusiasm. He pointed out the odd cones and columns protruding from the ceiling and floor along the walls of the cave. "These formations are called stalagmites and stalactites," he declared.

"How did all this water get here?" asked Cato.

"Water, Mr. Askew, is the key to the formation of all the

intricacies you see about you—indeed, water formed the caves themselves. It seeps in from the surface above us, which is capped with sandstone, and travels underground until it drains at last in the rivers. It is the water that formed these corridors. And there are miles of passages. Beneath the capstone lies an unparalleled world. It is a labyrinth with mile upon mile of dark endless passageways!"

"I fear one might easily become lost down here," said Dorothy, "or go mad."

"Yes ... indeed one might," agreed Mr. McNish. "But do not alarm yourselves. I am quite familiar with these passages and know their markings."

Ella said to Sammy, "You hear that, boy, don't let go of my hand now. I ain't goin' chasing after you if you get lost. Did you ever see snakes down here Mr. McNish?"

"There are many small creatures adapted to life in the cave, Miss Ella, including harmless snakes, frogs, and lizards. There are even eyeless fish. But do not alarm yourself; the snakes and frogs will keep well away from us."

"Look," said Sammy, "there's a hole I can fit through." He pointed to an odd hole in the cave wall that was too small to admit any of the adults, but which was not too small for Sammy himself to climb into. It was evident that there was another chamber beyond the hole.

"Yes," said Mr. McNish, "There are many small or narrow passages that only a child could fit into. I've brought other children here. It would be safe for you to step into the other chamber for just a moment, Sammy—but you mustn't go past where we can see you—and you must come right back out."

Sammy pulled on Ella's hand. He clearly wanted to go in.

"You can go in there if you want," said Ella, "but you keep hold of my hand and don't go in further than I can hold onto it."

Holding Ella's hand, Sammy stepped through the hole and into the chamber on the other side. Both Sammy's arm and Ella's arm had to stretch to make this possible. With his other hand, Sammy raised his lantern to illuminate the antechamber.

"What do you see?" asked Dorothy.

"It's a big room," Sammy said. "And I can see more stalagites—and there is some kind of wind in here. It smells funny."

"Thermal air currents," said Mr. McNish, "are caused by temperature differences in different parts of the cave."

"There's a lot of colors on the wall," said Sammy. "It looks like somebody painted it orange and brown."

"Water seeping along cracks deposits mineral bands translucent enough to show colors from iron and other minerals," explained Mr. McNish.

"When we get to the North," Sammy continued, "I can paint a picture of this for Mr. Hicks."

"Come back out of there now," said Ella, "before my arm falls off."

Sammy climbed back through the hole to the main chamber. Cato, who had been standing near the hole to observe the proceedings, was curious to see the colors Sammy described. He leaned down into the aperture with his lantern to have a look. As he did so, the wind from the thermal air currents promptly blew the hat and wig off of his head. Dorothy and Ella gasped. The hat and wig blew several feet away, and Cato was obliged to stand up with only his own natural hair showing.

Dorothy blushed. Cato reddened. Ella clasped her hands together. And Mr. McNish, when he saw what was revealed, said, "Oh my!"

Sammy, however, perceived that the incident was amusing. He conveyed this by laughing out loud, "Ha. Ha. Ha."

Sammy's "ha-has', despite his young voice, echoed and reverberated around the walls of the cave.

As the echoes of Sammy's laugher died down, Dorothy retrieved the wayward wig and hat, then returned them to Cato's head. She carefully rearranged them so as to restore their credible appearance. As she did this, she explained, "Mr. McNish—as you can see, we have held back a portion of the truth from you. This is Cato—and although he is William's half-brother, he is not my husband. He is, in fact, William's servant who has run away. Since William's father owns Cato, we have taken the precaution of disguising him against the possibility that slave catchers might seek him. And we've taken the additional precaution of having him pose as my husband, both as a means of furthering his disguise, and as a means of avoiding the appearance that I am traveling unescorted. I apologize for misleading you."

"There is no need to apologize, my dear," said Mr. McNish. "I understand your motives, and—truly—I do not take offense. Honesty, though it is a high virtue, is not more important than safety."

"I think, under the circumstances, we should return to the surface so we can continue our journey to Elizabethtown," said Dorothy. "As we climb back up, perhaps we can discuss our mission in Chicago. You see, Mr. McNish, I hope to marry William in Chicago. And I would also like to find a way to secure his parole from the prison."

As they began their climb, Mr. McNish asked, "Did you write to Mr. Hicks about your intentions?"

"Yes I did," said Dorothy. "And there is a further matter I must explain, Mr. McNish. Some time ago, Mr. Hicks was visiting in our area. My parents commissioned him to paint a portrait for our family. When the painting was completed, we discovered that my parents were going to sell Sammy as a means of acquiring the money needed to pay Mr. Hicks's fee. When Mr. Hicks learned of this plan, he proposed to take ownership of Sammy in lieu of his fee. Then he further proposed to leave Sammy at our house in my care, which he did. Now I've written to Mr. Hicks to see if he would be willing to come to Chicago to take guardianship of Sammy. I also hope that he perhaps might be willing to speak to the local authorities at the prison camp on William's behalf."

Throughout this explanation Mr. McNish, as they climbed, kept looking back at Cato—as if he was trying to place someone he'd forgotten. He said to Cato, "Are you the lad Erastus used to model for Jesus?"

"Yes, sir, I am," said Cato.

"Ah now it fits," said Mr. McNish. "Erastus wrote to me about how very much he enjoyed painting you as Jesus without your master realizing it. Ha, Erastus is really quite seditious." Then turning to Dorothy, he said, "I daresay Mr. Hicks will want to see all of you, under the circumstances."

"That is my hope," said Dorothy.

When they reached the mouth of the cave, the party paused to take their leave of Mr. McNish.

"I commend your courage—each of you," said Mr. McNish, looking earnestly at each of his four companions. "Of course I do not approve of fighting. But I hope that when this business is over we shall be rid of slavery once and for all. Tell me, before you go, is there anything I can do to assist you? Do you have sufficient funds for your journey?"

"You've been so kind, Mr. McNish," said Dorothy. "I could not impose upon you further."

"Oh but you must permit me," said Mr. McNish. "Permit me to contribute twenty dollars to your cause. It is worth something if it helps bring three citizens out of slavery—or perhaps it may help rescue your future husband from prison.

Our principles must always be dynamic, Miss Holland. I believe there are times when bribery may be seen as a principled choice." He took a twenty-dollar gold coin from his vest coat pocket and handed it to her. "You may find that a guard at the prison will provide your fiancé with assistance in exchange for this."

"Mr. McNish," exclaimed Ella. "Is that real gold?"

"Oh yes, Miss Ella" said he. "Long before these troubles began I traded all my paper currencies for gold coins. I was not certain, you see, what value the paper might someday have if victory should go to the other side."

"I never saw a real gold coin before," said Ella.

"May I see it?" asked Cato. "I've never seen one either."

"Can I see it too?" asked Sammy.

Dorothy passed the coin around for all to see, then she said, "Now I think we must depart. Thank you for the tour and all your kindness," said Dorothy.

"If you see him," said Mr. McNish, "tell Hicks your impressions of Mammoth Cave. Tell him McNish says he must come make a grand painting of the cave so his Philadelphia friends will all want to come for a visit."

"I will tell him that," said Dorothy.

Dorothy, Cato, and Sammy climbed into the brougham. Ella climbed up to the coachman's seat and, as she drove the horses out onto the Dixie highway, Cato lifted his hat, and they all waved goodbye to Mr. Walter McNish.

# 41

# DARK HUED

*J*immy was face down on the ground by the Ohio River. Dawn had broken, but he was too tired to move. His ordeal in the water had sapped his strength. His right leg was in pain. He rolled onto his side to inspect his leg. He saw a bloody gash and a rip in his trousers below the knee. He supposed he must have cut his leg on the rocks, though he did not remember the moment when it happened.

He heard the meow of a cat behind him. He rolled onto his back, craned back his head, and rolled back his eyes so that he could see where the sound came from. It was a black cat—not very big, but older than a kitten. It sauntered in a circle around Jimmy's head, as though it were greatly inconvenienced to find a man lying on the ground blocking its path.

"Pardon me," Jimmy said. "I hope I'm not too much in your way."

The cat meowed and circled Jimmy's head with exaggerated steps.

"What do you want, cat?"

The cat stopped, and sat on its haunches. It looked Jimmy in the eye and meowed plaintively.

"Maybe you're hungry." Jimmy looked around. "You and me both. Do you see a big basket of food here?"

Now the cat stood back up and walked past Jimmy's head, brushing up against his face as it did so. It was customary for a cat to endear itself in this way to a human. But Jimmy had never before seen a cat so close. He'd never been nuzzled like that.

"Oh! So you like me? You want to be my friend?"

Jimmy sat up. He picked up the cat and sat it on his lap. The cat looked around warily, then peered up at Jimmy's face. After a moment, it sat down, tucking in all four legs until it was snugly nestled on Jimmy's lap. Jimmy stroked the fur on the cat's back. After a few moments of petting, it purred.

"You're soft," Jimmy said. "You're softer than Venus." Suddenly Jimmy caught a whiff of a sweet fragrance. The scent was flowery. It reminded him of Mrs. Holland's perfume. The smell came from a spot behind him. He turned and saw an old woman standing ten yards behind him. She was white. She wore a scarf tied about her head, and a lacy white shawl wrapped around her shoulders. She held a wooden cane, which she used now to point in Jimmy's direction.

"'Tis a fine morning," she said, "to be swimming in the river. I see you've made friends with Donahue. His name means 'dark hued.' Donahue thinks anyone dark skinned must be his kin. And who might Venus be?" She maneuvered her cane to propel herself several steps closer to Jimmy

Jimmy was startled. He looked around, but he saw that there was no one in sight other than the woman. He would have jumped up, but the cat in his lap made him hesitate. The woman was old. She had a frail appearance, but her step was lively. "Venus was my dog," he said.

"Was? Ah, she was your dog, eh? But she's gone now?"

"She died."

The woman nodded and took another step closer. "You like animals?"

Jimmy didn't answer.

"Well, lad, I see that Donahue likes you. And Donahue is quite fussy about whose lap he sits on, I can tell you."

Jimmy picked up the cat from his lap and set it on the ground. He tried to get up—but as he did so the pain in his right leg shot through him, and he fell back.

"Now, now, don't run off, young man. Look at me. Do I look like a paddy roller? You've hurt your leg."

Jimmy rubbed his leg and nodded.

"Did you swim all the way across?"

Jimmy looked back at the river, but the rowboat was gone. It had drifted out of sight. "I had a rowboat," he said. "But I had to swim the last part."

"Well, you're in Illinois now," she said. "'Tis the land of Lincoln, you know. God's blessing on the day."

Jimmy tried again to get up. This time he managed to stand.

"Can you walk?" the woman asked.

Jimmy hobbled a few steps. "Yes," he said. "I have to go on my way now."

"On your way? Oh yes, I suppose you will. You'll limp right on up to Canada in no time, you will. But before you go, perhaps you'd trouble yourself to have a bit of breakfast with me? My cabin's nearby, you know. And you could do with some bandaging on that leg."

Jimmy looked at her suspiciously. He thought it was not impossible that she might have bounty hunters waiting in her house. Perhaps she made a habit of luring slaves from the river to her trap. "Who do you live with?" he asked.

"'Tis but me and Donahue live in the cottage," she said. "I've shared breakfast with fellows like you before. Not just everyone, mind you. Plenty of ruffians come through these parts. But I trust Donahue's judgment. And you must do the same, lad. Look to your instincts. Be careful whom you trust. In the days to come you may well depend on strangers. You must watch out for the copperheads!"

"Copperheads?"

"Yes. Some of 'em wear a copper penny for a badge. But the bad ones don't. They'll catch you up. They'll put you in chains and try to collect a reward. There are bad men here in the North. Why they'd chain up Abraham Lincoln if they could."

Jimmy could not deny that he was hungry or that he wanted to rest. And what the woman said was true—he would have to trust strangers in the days to come. It went against his nature to trust anyone white. But this old woman seemed harmless. Her shawl was wrapped around her shoulders and tucked between her arms. The wisps of white hair that stuck out from under her scarf bespoke her age. Despite this, she wielded the cane with vigor. Though it was clear that someone like Jimmy could overpower her with little effort, her manner was fearless and forthright. She spoke to him with respect and kindness. "All right," he said. "How far is it to your house?"

"A few minutes' walk," she said. "It's not so much a house as a cabin—but it's home. Now come, Donahue. Come, my pet." She turned around and began to ply her way toward the woods.

Jimmy limped behind her. She was headed toward a path that led into the woods.

"I am Mrs. MacMurrough," she said, as they passed into the woods. "My husband, Mr. MacMurrough, has been dead these many years. Oh let's see, fourteen years ago it was. And what might your name be, lad?"

"Jimmy."

"Ah, Jimmy, that's a fine name! And do you have family back home, Jimmy? Or maybe up north?"

"I'm going to meet them in Chicago," he said.

"Ah, a wife or sweetheart, perhaps?"

Jimmy was not sure how to answer this. "A sweet … friend," he said. "And my brother and sister too."

"Oh a sweet friend, is it? Well now. You're a gentleman—that I can see. And your brother and sister, too. But you say you're going to meet them. Are they traveling as well?"

"My master's daughter is bringing them by carriage to Chicago. They're going by a different route. She hopes to visit the man she wants to marry. He's a soldier captured in the war, who was sent to a prison in Chicago."

"Your master's daughter, you say. Well, that's an uncommon trip for a lady to make, is it not? Does she mean to free your brother and sister and your sweet friend too?"

"We mean to be free," said Jimmy.

"Ah well," said Mrs. MacMurrough, "freedom you shall have then, by all means." She looked around to search for the cat, which had been following them, but now lagged behind. "Donahue, come!" she called. "You see how Jimmy here can barely walk? Yet see how much faster he is than you, you old cat." The cat scurried toward them, then ran ahead—only to look back at the humans and meow. "Oh you rascal," said Mrs. MacMurrough. "Yes, now you're fast—faster than an old lady on a cane, God bless you."

It was difficult for Jimmy to keep up. His leg hurt. The walking made it worse.

When the path climbed slightly uphill, Mrs. MacMur-

459

rough noticed that Jimmy slowed down. In response to this, she decided to stop. "I need to rest a moment," she said.

Jimmy looked around guardedly. He peered in all directions into the woods. The sun was well up in the sky. The daylight was bright.

"I suppose you've been traveling at night," said Mrs. MacMurrough.

Jimmy nodded.

"Well, don't worry, there's hardly a soul hereabouts—save Donahue and myself. The cabin is but a short walk up this hill and 'round the bend now, so there's no need to hurry. Nary a soul can see us here. No one comes out this way. I'm the crazy old woman who lives in the woods. The town folk take no notice of me. I keep to myself, you see. I don't like busybodies. Oh, and sometimes I play a bit daft. Then the town folk keep their distance. That's how I like it!"

After a few moments, they continued on. And just as Mrs. MacMurrough had promised, Jimmy saw a small cottage situated up the hill and around the bend. The cottage was no bigger than his cabin back home. This one had glass windows and a tall brick chimney. In front of the cottage was a garden planted with rows of pink and white tulips. The path led through a lath arbor laden with climbing roses not yet in bloom. A small cherry tree, just beyond the arbor, was lined with soft white flowers. Donahue trotted up the path, past the arbor, and went up to the door of the cabin. There he strutted back and forth in front of the entrance impatiently.

"Here we come, my pet," said Mrs. MacMurrough. When she arrived at the door, she opened it and the cat slipped inside. Mrs. MacMurrough followed him in. When Jimmy arrived, she nodded toward the center of the room. "Have a seat at the table there." She hung her cane on a hook by the door. "I have tea and biscuits and a bit of cold mutton. But how do you feel? Should I tend to your leg, or do you want to eat first?"

"I'm hungry," Jimmy said.

"Ah no doubt. Then we shall start with the food."

Mrs. MacMurrough took off her shawl, put on an apron, and set about preparing the meal.

Jimmy sat and surveyed the cabin. In the center of the room where he sat, the table was furnished with three chairs, two candles, and a vase that held six pink tulips. Against the wall stood a washstand, on top of which sat a wooden bucket. Next to that was a bookcase crammed with books of all sizes. A single small bed rested against the opposite wall near the fire-place. Above the fireplace hung an oval photograph of a man. Jimmy pointed at it. "Is that your husband?" he asked.

"Yes, that's Patrick himself." She stopped and wiped her hands on her apron. "An angel if ever there was one. The only bad thing he ever did in his life was that he up and died so many years before me. It's not good to live alone, Jimmy. That I can tell you. I have Donahue, of course. I talk to that cat all the time, you know. But bless him, all he ever says is meow. To tell you the truth, Jimmy—it's not so hard for me to play daft. Some days I play daft when I'm here by myself."

"You have friends who visit you here?" This was a matter of concern to Jimmy, who was still apprehensive of being discovered.

"I do have one friend who visits. Mr. Mack, he is. Mr. Mack and my husband worked together at the Illinois Central railroad. After Mr. MacMurrough died, Mr. Mack decided he would come out to see me once a week. He decided he ought to keep an eye on me! Hah! We play gin rummy and he always wins—that's why he comes. But if you want to get to Chicago, Jimmy, Mr. Mack's the man to help you. Trains leave Cairo for Chicago every day. Some trains leave with empty cars. That's the quickest way to go north. But here's the trick. You have to be sure to hide in a car that no one will look in. Mr. Mack has helped others, you know. He works in the rail yard."

"What happens if someone catches you?"

"That all depends. Some men will look the other way. Some men will turn you in. But you can get caught just as easily if you go on foot."

"Yes, but if I walk, I can travel at night and keep safe in the woods," said Jimmy.

"It's a long walk," said Mrs. MacMurrough. "And the woods are not thick everywhere you go. But let's not speak of it now. Now you must eat and rest." She put a plate of food in front of him, then poured him a cup of tea.

Jimmy ate in silence, while Mrs. MacMurrough fed some scraps of the mutton to Donahue. When Jimmy had finished, she cleared away his plate.

"And won't you go sit there on the bed now? I must tend to your wound."

Jimmy sat on the bed. He took off his shoes. He tried to roll up his trouser leg, but he could not roll the fabric high enough to expose the injury.

Mrs. MacMurrough arrived at his side with a bucket of water and a cloth. "Slip off those trousers, lad," she said. "Then I'll be disinfecting that wound and putting a nice bandage on it." As she spoke, she went to a bureau by the bed. From the top drawer she took out a bottle of whiskey.

Jimmy did not move. The prospect of taking off his pants in front of a woman seemed indecent.

"Come now. Don't be shy, Jimmy boy. As old as I am, you think I've never before seen a man in his unmentionables? You are wearing undergarments, are you not?"

Jimmy nodded.

"Well then? Good heavens man, be quick about it!" And Mrs. MacMurrough stood over him, brandishing her wet cloth.

Jimmy slid off his pants. He lay back on the bed fairly mortified. Mrs. MacMurrough with her cloth set about washing his leg with great diligence. When the leg was washed, the whiskey bottle came next. Mrs. MacMurrough poured an even dram straight onto the wound. Jimmy flinched. But Mrs. MacMurrough harrumphed and dabbed it gingerly with her cloth.

"There we are," she said. "Well, you cut yourself good on the rocks, I must say." She looked up and saw that Jimmy's arms were folded over his eyes. "Now, now, my brave lad," she said. "It's all right now." She patted his leg. "The worst is over."

Jimmy uncovered his eyes. He sat up. He propped himself up on the bed with his arms. "Thank you for your help, Mrs.," he said.

"Tosh, 'tis my pleasure to fix a man up." Now Mrs. MacMurrough began to rub the area around the wound briskly with her cloth. Jimmy was not used to having anyone touch him. No one, in fact, other than his mother and Cato had ever done so. But Mrs. MacMurrough was intent on cleaning every inch of his calf and knee. When she had finished, she went to another drawer in her bureau and took out a handkerchief. She ripped it in half. She wrapped each half around his leg to bind the gash. When she was done with the bandage, she picked up his trousers. "They've torn clean through where you cut yourself." She poked her finger through the tear to illustrate. "I'll have to mend them." Jimmy blinked his eyes. "I'll bet you're tuckered," she said. "Were you up all night?"

Jimmy nodded.

"Well then, you'd better get some sleep." She stood up. "You need to rest, lad, whatever you plan to do."

Jimmy did not reply. Instead, he fell back onto the bed and

laid his head on the pillow. His feet rested on a folded blanket at the foot of the bed. Mrs. MacMurrough lifted his feet, one foot at a time, and removed the blanket. She unfolded it and spread it over his body with a single deft throw. She tucked the end of the blanket under his feet. "Sleep as long as you like," she said. "I'll be out in the garden—and I'll be mending your trousers."

Jimmy fell asleep almost immediately. He dreamed he was at the bottom of the Ohio River. In his dream, he rowed with the oars under water. Donahue swam alongside him, meowing. When he got to the bank, Mrs. MacMurrough reached down and pulled them both up. Then she poured him a cup of tea. As he drank the tea, he lay in bed naked. Then Mrs. MacMurrough began to rub his leg, but when he looked up, he saw that it was Cato. Cato stood up and untied his belt. Cato's pants fell to his ankles. Cato, now naked, climbed on top of Jimmy and then …. Jimmy woke up. He thought he had been asleep only for a short while. But Mrs. MacMurrough was now sitting at the table reading a book and smoking what appeared to be a corncob pipe. He saw from the window that night had fallen. He sat up in the bed.

"Ah, you're awake now, are you?" said Mrs. MacMurrough.

"How long was I asleep?" Jimmy asked.

"Oh you've been snoring a good nine hours," she said. "You made such a racket that Donahue was frightened. He's not used to hearing a man snore." She stood, then went to the bureau, where she again took out the bottle of whiskey. "Here now," she said, "why don't we drink some of it this time? It's good Kentucky whiskey." Without waiting for an answer, she went to a cupboard and pulled out two small glasses, then filled them generously with the liquor.

Jimmy rubbed his eyes. The circumstances he was in struck him as most improbable. "Why are you helping me?" he asked.

Mrs. MacMurrough handed him his glass of whiskey. "Ah, why indeed! Have you never been helped before?"

"Not by a woman," he said. Then he realized that wasn't what he meant. "I mean, not by a … white woman."

Mrs. MacMurrough sat back down at the table, took a sip of her drink, then returned to puffing on her pipe. "Ah, Jimmy, perhaps the world is not so black and white as you think."

Jimmy sipped his drink and folded one of his arms behind his head. He stared at Mrs. MacMurrough. He did not know what to make of her. "You don't know anything about me," he said. "What if I was crazy? What if I was a mean, ornery, no-account runaway?"

"Lad, I told you. I trust my instincts. You must learn to do the same. For who will guide you through this world, if you can't guide yourself?"

Jimmy considered this. He did trust his instincts. It was his instinct that told him to be wary of anyone white. And his instinct also told him that an old white woman with a cat who fed him biscuits and whiskey was peculiar. "To me," he said aloud, "this world doesn't make any sense."

"Nor to me," said Mrs. MacMurrough. "But after many years of life, I think I've begun to understand why it is as it is."

Jimmy took a big swallow of whiskey. "Why is it as it is?" he asked.

"Because the world is just like we are," she said. "Look inside yourself, Jimmy. Something of everything you see in the world is inside you."

This seemed like arrant nonsense to Jimmy. Who in the world was like him? Certainly, nobody that he'd ever met was like him. "No!" he said, shaking his head. "I don't think there is anyone else in the world like me."

"Ah, indeed? And what is so special about you?"

"I'm a slave. I work in the field. A white man in Tennessee

owns me. There's nothing special about me. But it doesn't matter. I am not like anyone else. I don't believe in God. I don't believe in heaven. The only thing that I care about is my friend. And I don't know when I'll see him again." Even as he spoke, Jimmy was surprised by his own candor. The whiskey and something in Mrs. MacMurrough's manner made him feel that he could say anything.

"Ah," she said. "Do you speak of your sweet friend?"

Jimmy nodded.

"But you will see him in Chicago, won't you?"

"I don't know," said Jimmy. "I hope so.

"And there you will be free, won't you?"

"Yes," said Jimmy. He remembered his uncertainty about what freedom might be like. "But I don't know how it will feel," he said. "I don't know what freedom is like. Do you know? ... Are there men like me in the North? Are there men who ... love a man?"

Surprise registered on Mrs. MacMurrough's face. Jimmy's use of the word 'love,' and the manner in which he said it, implied more than she had previously thought he meant. Mrs. MacMurrough was silent. She was not certain how to answer him. Finally, she said, "Ah, lad, this is not a subject upon which I can speak with authority."

"Then it's true," said Jimmy. "You see ... there is no one in the world like me." There was satisfaction in Jimmy's voice, even though he understood that he had shocked his host.

For a long time, Mrs. MacMurrough did not reply. She took a swallow of whiskey, then absent-mindedly refilled her pipe from a pouch of tobacco that was tied with a string. When the pipe was filled, she tamped it on the table. She was not embarrassed to be silent and pondered at some length about how to reply. At last she said, "There must be others like you." Then she was silent again. She struck a match, lit her pipe and took several contemplative puffs. After a while, she spoke again. "If there's one thing I've learned, lad, it's that everything that exists in the world is inside each of us—and everything inside each of us, is also somewhere in the world."

This seemed completely wrong to Jimmy. He had seen evil in the world, but he did not believe any such evil existed inside him. "How can that be?" he asked. "I don't own slaves. There's no slave owner inside of me!" Had he been outside, he would have spit on the ground as he spoke.

"Is your owner not a man like you?" said Mrs. MacMurrough. "Is he so very different? Had you been born in his place, would you not be the same as he?"

"No," said Jimmy emphatically. "I would not! I would not treat any man as a slave."

"Ah well," said Mrs. MacMurrough. "That is a point of view that your situation has taught you. And if your owner was born in your place, would he not have been taught the same lesson? Would he not be the same as you?"

This question was harder for Jimmy to answer with certainty. But after a few moments he said, "I don't think there are other slaves like me. My mother ... my sister ... even my friend ... they all believe in God. They all believe in heaven. They all believe there's a big Master up in the sky, who made everything the way it is, and who must be obeyed."

"Well, perhaps if they saw the world through your eyes," said Mrs. MacMurrough. "They would believe as you do. What exactly do you believe in, Jimmy?"

"I believe in freedom."

"And what will you do with this freedom once you have it? Will you plant a garden? Will you sing a song? Will you eat rich food and grow fat? Will you accumulate money? What is it you seek in freedom?"

"I don't know yet, Mrs. I truly don't know yet who I may

be, just on my own. I know I am not like anyone else. But I've had to serve another man all my life. I need to be free to serve myself before I can know what I want."

"I see, then. You can't know what you want from freedom until you've been free to experience it—to see what it offers. Well I can tell you this; it's not too soon to start imagining what you might want—for you probably already know something of what there is to be had in this world. Is there nothing you can think of that you know you'd like to have?"

Jimmy took another big swallow of whiskey and smacked his lips. "I'd like to ride a horse," he said. "Yes, I'd like to have my own horse. And I'd like to have my own dog—and I want to raise my own chickens and pigs."

"Ah, lad, you do like animals."

"Yes. And I'd like to wear nice clothes. I'd like to have money to buy clothes for Cato—my friend—and for my sister Ella. I'd like to buy paints and things for my brother Sammy. I'd like to buy my sister Ella all the food she wants. She loves buttered corn. And Cato likes to read books. So I'd buy him all the books he wants. And my mother likes kitchen things, like bowls and pots and pans and knives. I'd buy her a right fine kitchen. And ..." Jimmy looked around the room. "I'd like to live in a house like yours. Your house is ... friendly."

"Ah, thank you."

"And I'd like to live in the house with Cato—and we would take care of each other—and tend our chickens and play with our dog. You know, I can farm anything. I know how to sow and plow and hoe and pick anything: corn, cotton, wheat. I did most of the work on the farm back home—more than anyone else. And I can harvest it and bag it and drive it to the mills. And Cato knows how to take care of a house. He can cook and clean and well ... neither of us can sew ... but my sister can sew and she can live with us ... and my brother. He paints pictures." Jimmy was breathless as he enumerated his unspoken dreams. The fact that he was allowing himself now, for the first time in his life, to voice these desires, which he had never before let himself contemplate, made him realize that this must be the first flush of his freedom. Exhilarating! It was more wonderful than he'd hoped for. He suddenly leapt out of the bed, heedless of the fact that he was dressed only in his under-garments, and went up to Mrs. MacMurrough. He knelt in front of her. His eyes shone. She had uncorked this outpouring of desires—and he was grateful for it. He looked at her more warmly than he had ever before looked at a white man or woman. "I can do whatever I want if I'm free, can't I?"

"Oh lad, yes, yes, of course you can. But before you begin all that, you'd better start by putting on your trousers." She pointed to the folded bundle on the chair next to her. "Give me your glass and put on your pants while I pour you another drink. Then I shall find you a gift you can give to your friend."

As Jimmy put on his pants, Mrs. MacMurrough refilled his glass. Then she got up and went to the bookshelves. She spent several minutes surveying the titles until she found the one she was looking for. "Ah, here it is," she said. She grasped a small volume, removed it from the shelf and brought it back to the table. "There now," she said. "There's a book you can give to your friend as a gift."

Jimmy picked up the book. He looked at it with curiosity. "I can't read," he said. "What is it?"

"These are the sonnets of William Shakespeare."

"Sonnets?" Jimmy did not know the word.

"Sonnets are poems. Does your friend like poems?"

Jimmy nodded.

"Good, well then some of these love poems were written by Mr. Shakespeare about his sweet friend." She picked up the book and began to leaf through it. "And if I'm not mistaken, judging from some of these poems, Mr. Shakespeare must have been a man who loved another man. So, lad, you may not be so special as you think." She scanned through the poems, as though she were looking for something in particular. "Well," she said at last. "Here's one that'll give you the idea of it. Shall I read it to you?"

"OK—but I don't know much about poems. Cato read poems to me, sometimes, but they just sounded peculiar to me."

"Well this will certainly sound peculiar, too. It was written long ago, and the language is old fashioned. Shakespeare was writing about how he must prepare himself for the time when even his sweet young friend would grow old and wrinkled." Mrs. MacMurrough winked. "In other words, just like me. Here's what he wrote:"

> *Against my love shall be as I am now,*
> *With Time's injurious hand crush'd and o'erworn;*
> *When hours have drain'd his blood, and fill'd*
>    *his brow*
> *With lines and wrinkles; when his youthful morn*
> *Hath travell'd on to age's steepy night;*
> *And all those beauties whereof now he's king*
> *Are vanishing or vanish'd out of sight,*
> *Stealing away the treasure of his spring;*
> *For such a time do I now fortify*
> *Against confounding age's cruel knife,*
> *That he shall never cut from memory*
> *My sweet love's beauty, though my lover's life.*
> *His beauty shall in these black lines be seen,*
> *And they shall live, and he in them still green.*

"So you see, Jimmy, even though his friend grew old, his

beauty still lives in this poem even today, hundreds of years later." She closed the book. "Tell me about your friend. You say his name is Cato."

"Yes."

"And is he as handsome as you?"

Jimmy reddened. "I don't think I'm so handsome, Mrs. But no man in the world is more handsome than Cato," said Jimmy. "His mother was a slave but his father is a white man. His skin, Mrs. MacMurrough, is golden! And he has eyes like a puppy."

"Oh my, well then Jimmy you must take pleasure in this beauty—and remember, do not take it for granted. Confounding age's cruel knife, you know…. Look at how it has worked upon me. You can't tell it now, but I too was a fair beauty in my day, lad."

Jimmy looked into Mrs. MacMurrough's eyes. "I believe it," he said. Then he added, "It is in you still."

471

# 42

# PRETTY AND CHARGER

*A*s they made their way north, Dorothy taught Cato, Ella and Sammy how to drive the brougham. The driver's seat accommodated two. The passenger box held four. Each of the slaves took turns sitting with Dorothy on the driver's bench, where she showed them how to control the speed and direction of the two horses. Insofar as the horses themselves required little more than an inkling of what was wanted by the driver, Dorothy advocated a restrained approach. This was particularly vital with Sammy, whose natural impulse was to incite the horses into a wild charge designed to assuage his impatience with the length of the journey.

Sammy was the most enthusiastic student—and the most willing to take over the task of driving whenever Dorothy was tired. Ella too found it agreeable to drive, since it lessened her boredom. Cato, however, was more interested in reading his novel and practicing nuances of aristocratic speech than in driving—though he did enjoy driving in the morning when the air was fresh and the sunshine moderate. On such occasions, he pronounced it 'a capital time to drive.'

The travelers made stops in Elizabethtown and Louisville in Kentucky, then went on to Indianapolis. There they stayed in a hotel in which the lobby featured a display of cages of exotic birds, including a toucan and a parrot. The toucan, with its long, brightly-colored beak, was a source of particular fascination to Sammy and Ella, while the parrot's ability to talk provided Cato with sundry opportunities to try out new dialects discreetly. Although he did not succeed in teaching the parrot to say, "You are not mistaken," the parrot did teach Cato to say, "God bless America."

As they continued their journey, it was decided that it would be more credible, for the sake of appearance, if Ella and Sammy sat together on the driver's bench, while Cato and Dorothy played the married couple inside the passenger compartment. This was the configuration they adopted whenever they traveled through a populated area. Although Sammy and Ella spent little time talking, Dorothy and Cato began to spend much of their time together conversing about matters of importance to each of them. The circumstances of their journey favored a deeper intimacy.

They both expressed the hope of meeting new people in the North whose views of the world would be in keeping with their own. They both spoke of Erastus Hicks as exemplary of the kind of person they hoped to encounter. Dorothy imagined ladies and gentlemen who would share her interest in the world of ideas. Cato imagined gentle, well-spoken citizens with delicate manners and a love of Chopin, who would be indifferent to his racial composition.

Cato wondered if, now that they were in the North, he would be free to pursue his own desires. Might he and Jimmy, for example, go to Philadelphia, the city of brotherly love?

Dorothy allowed that they might, although she confessed that she did not know how the world might regard former slaves once the war was over. She cautioned Cato against taking risks. She assured him that he and Jimmy would always be welcome to reside wherever she called home and enjoy whatever protection that might offer.

"But no doubt both of you will eventually want to find wives and have children," she said. "Would you rather do that in the North or back home? Perhaps your father will regard you with more affection when you are married—especially if you have children. After all, when William and I have children, they will be related to your children—and Augustus will be the grandfather of all of them."

One result of having worn a disguise throughout their journey was that Cato understood that if he chose to do so, he could pass as white. When he added to this the prospect of marrying and having children, he could imagine a life with numerous agreeable qualities. Why not be like Darcy and find an Elizabeth? Why not choose a life upon which the world would smile? For him there would be no more pretense in being white than there would be in marrying. The latter would require a greater leap on his part than the former, yet he could imagine carrying it off—especially if he ever were to find a woman as sympathetic as Dorothy. And he had to admit that the idea of having children was attractive, insofar as he longed for the kind of family he had never had. Yet he realized that if he had a family, he, like his father, would spend his life protecting a secret. Though in his mind his secret was of a different order than Augustus's secret—when he considered the complications of how to arrange things with Jimmy within the circumstances of a conventional family, it was the first time he thought of his father with sympathy.

Cato's natural preference was to spend his life with Jimmy

alone, even though it was an unprecedented idea. The shape and arc of such a life was unimaginable to him. Yet the world was on the brink of unparalleled change. A whole race of slaves might be freed. Thus, the course of all their future lives was unknowable. The radicalism of the moment was both an invitation and a caution. The upheaval of the war seemed to beckon still more drastic changes even as it sharpened the appetite for the comfort of the conventional. The dual impulses of singularity and conformity wrestled within Cato. But Cato was the embodiment of compromise, for he was both Negro and white.

"I should like to have a family," he replied at last. "I should like to have children. But I do not think I will find a wife." This was as much as he dared say on the topic. He hoped that even from this gentle renunciation of her expectations, Dorothy would surmise the deeper currents of his nonconformity.

But Dorothy mistook his reticence for modesty. "Oh but you could easily find a wife," she said. "Do you not know how handsome you are? Do you not realize how a woman would appreciate your superior sensibility? You have more than a few qualities, I can tell you, which are attractive."

"I should have said," Cato ventured, "that I do not think I will seek a wife. I am fonder of friendship than of marriage."

Dorothy saw something in Cato's eyes as he said this that hinted at the seriousness behind the ease of his words. But she mistook in what he said a desire like her own for a relationship which prized independence as much as intimacy. "I'm sure there are women like me," she said, "who would value autonomy in a spouse above all else. Marriage need not preclude friendship."

"No, it need not," Cato agreed. "But friendship can preclude marriage … if the friendship is with a man."

Dorothy still did not grasp what Cato meant. She saw no obstacle to marriage in friendship with a man. "Why should friendship be an impediment to marriage," she asked. "I will have friends when I am married. I expect that William will have friends. I hope that Ella will always be my friend."

Cato stared out the window of the brougham at the passing trees. His urge to divest himself of the secret was as potent as his fear. It needed but a prod, a moment of impulsiveness. He turned to her abruptly. "I want to live with Jimmy," he said. "I would rather live with him than with a wife."

Dorothy stared at Cato as if her eyes might penetrate what her mind could not follow. "You are friends. But why would you want to live with him?"

"For the same reason you want to marry my brother," Cato said, as he sucked in his breath. "Because I love him—just as you love William."

Dorothy's eyes continued to dart back and forth, as she stared at him. She did not speak. She felt a tremendous desire to comprehend what Cato meant. Then a door opened in her mind that she had not realized was there. "Oh you …." She stepped through the door. She felt her face flush. The deviant truth of it filled her with adrenaline. It was only the kindness of her nature that restrained her from expressing the first gush of what she felt. She averted her head to avoid revealing her shock.

Cato saw that she understood. Tears welled in his eyes. "I have not been able to tell anyone," he said.

She could hear the tears in his voice before she turned back to see them. She reached out to take his hand. "Oh yes," she said. "I did not know. But I understand you now."

They sat in silence for a long time. Each stared out the window, yet neither saw any of the passing scene. So inward was the focus of their thoughts that had they passed a battalion of marching soldiers, they would not have noticed. In time, Cato felt compelled to elaborate. "I should say that we love each other. I don't think either of us expected it—but from the day I first saw him, I ...."

Dorothy continued to hold his hand even as she persisted in staring out the window. "Forgive me," she said. "I have to accustom myself to this subject. Pray, be patient."

Cato waited in silence as he watched Dorothy ponder what he had told her. After a while, he did begin to notice the trees and the tall grasses in the fields as they drove by. At last, he asked, "Do you think it is a sin?" Then he added. "I have prayed about it."

"If it is," said Dorothy, "It is nothing compared to slavery—to how your father has treated you." She looked at him directly now. "You are a good and gentle man, Cato. It's not for me to judge how your heart should speak to you. I am disoriented by what you say. But perhaps you are no more out of step with the world than I am. I can imagine a world that is so different from the one we live in—yet I cannot yet see the fine details of it."

"Erastus says we are like seeds," Cato said.

"So Mr. Hicks knows of this?"

"I cannot say for certain," Cato said. "But I think he does."

"It would not surprise me," said Dorothy, withdrawing her hand from Cato's hand. "He is like a soothsayer. He seems to understand everything. He may be the only man who has really understood what matters to me. He understands my friendship with Ella."

"You mean your friendship with Ella is like mine with Jimmy?"

"No—not like that. But it hardly matters. The fact that Ella and I are truly friends seems at once both so natural and so contrary to the order of things. I might just as easily have been born her slave and it would not have mattered a whit to me. I don't know how to express the connection I feel. It isn't sexual. But it is more than friendship."

"I would like to be your friend," said Cato.

"Oh well, you'll be more than that," said Dorothy. "When William and I are married, you will be my brother, will you not?"

"Yes, I suppose I will. I've always wished for a sister."

Upon this prospect, both of them smiled. Then they remained silent for many hours.

After Dorothy and Cato had grown silent, Ella and Sammy began to converse.

"You want to hold the reins?" asked Ella. Without waiting for an answer, she handed them to Sammy.

"Can the horses tell who's driving?" Sammy asked.

"I reckon they can tell when it's you," said Ella. "On account of how you yank it. It's a good thing those horses have a lot of horse sense. They know when to mind and when not to mind."

"They mind me," insisted Sammy. "Watch!" And he jerked the rein up and down to urge the horses faster. But the horses increased their speed only a little.

The horses, like the brougham, had belonged to Augustus Askew before Dorothy borrowed them. Not knowing their names, Ella and Sammy had named them Charger and Pretty.

"Oh they mind you." Ella chuckled. "But Charger makes up his own mind about how fast to go, and Pretty does whatever Charger does."

"I wonder what they think about all the time," said Sammy.

"Oh they think about what they're doing, I reckon," said Ella. "They got to watch out for holes, and look out for how the road curves. They got to swat flies with their tails. They got to make sure they don't step on each other's feet."

"It's too bad they can't talk to each other," observed Sammy. "Then maybe they would have more fun."

"Child, who ever heard of two horses talking to each other? What d'you think they'd say anyway?"

"I bet Charger would say, 'Hurry up, Pretty, you're always going too slow.'"

"No. No." Ella shook her head. "That's where you're wrong. Charger would say, 'Don't be going too fast now Pretty, you got to follow my lead.'"

"Pretty never goes fast," said Sammy. "She's so slow if it weren't for Charger, we'd still be in Kentucky."

"If Pretty let Charger run as fast as he wants to, why they'd get all tired out in no time. Then we'd still be in Kentucky for sure," said Ella.

"I guess they work good together," said Sammy. "But if I was a horse, I'd be like Charger."

"Well I'd be like Pretty," said Ella. "She's got more sense."

"How come you don't like to go fast?" asked Sammy.

"There's no rush," said Ella. "Chicago ain't goin' no place. Besides, I don't know what we're gonna run into when we get there. I'm in no hurry to find out, neither. If you ask me, Miss Dorothy's gonna have a hard time getting into that prison to see Lieutenant Askew, let alone getting married to him. I don't know what those Yankees are like, but I don't like how they look at me."

"Who looked at you?"

"Some Yankee back at that hotel in Indianapolis. He looked at me like I was one of those birds in the cage. Like he never before saw someone so peculiar as me. Ain't nothing strange about me! I'm just ordinary."

"Maybe that man doesn't have any slaves," Sammy speculated. "Maybe he never saw a slave before."

"Well I don't care," said Ella. "If he was a gentleman he oughtn't to have stared like that."

"Maybe he stared at you on account of he was sweet on you," said Sammy.

"What? Hush your tongue child. Ain't no white man sweet on me! He looked more like he was fixing to spit on me. Even old Mr. Askew never looked at me like that."

"I hope Mr. Askew ain't too lonely," said Sammy. "I reckon nobody'll play cards with him now."

Ella shook her head. "Child, that's bunkum. I don't know why you give a hoot about that old cracker."

"Scout likes him," said Sammy.

"Yeah, well Scout's just a dumb dog. You've got more sense than a dog."

"Scout ain't dumb," Sammy protested. "He knows all kinds of tricks. He knows more tricks than Venus did even. And besides, Scout don't have any friends 'cept for Mr. Askew and me. Who's he supposed to like, if he don't like us?"

"Well, he don't have to like anyone."

"So you just expect Scout to go around being sad all the time—just 'cause he don't have any friends? That would be dumb."

Ella had to concede that Sammy had a point. The dog had little choice about his companions. "We should've brought that dog with us," she said. "Scout would be better off with you than old Askew."

"If we did that, then Massa Askew'd be lonely for sure," said Sammy. "Scout's the only friend he has left. He told me his wife died. And then his house burned down. And now his son got caught prisoner." Sammy shook his head at the obvious pity of it all.

"That man deserves to be lonely," said Ella. "He's a bad man, Sammy. You're just too young to know any better. He's done terrible bad things to folks."

"He's nice to Scout. He was nice to me."

"Confound it boy, just because an old cracker plays cards with you, it don't make him a nice man. Do you know he whipped Cato in there? His own son, too. He whipped him real bad—and he left that poor man chained up till Jimmy came and rescued him."

"Master Askew is Cato's father?" Sammy had not realized this. "How did that happen?"

"Never mind about how that happened," said Ella. "But that's just one more reason he's a bad man. And another thing: he sold away Sara's two little children—all on account of they were hungry and she took some food. You remember when you got sold away?"

Sammy nodded.

"Well that's what kind of man he is. It's all right you playing cards with him and all—but don't pity him. He'd just as soon sell you away as whip his own son."

Sammy was chagrined to hear these facts about Mr. Askew. He trusted Ella's judgment too much to doubt what she said. But he could not reconcile this new image of Mr. Askew with the one he had already formed. "Why is he so mean?"

"Some people are just plain mean," said Ella. "That's how they are."

"Well maybe if someone is nice to them they won't be so mean," said Sammy.

"You're just crazy, boy," said Ella. "You can be nice to white folks from now until Christmas, and that won't make them any less mean."

"Do you think he's mean to Scout?"

"Probably. Mean people are mean by nature."

"Then I'm going to have to go back home and get Scout," Sammy declared.

"How're you gonna do that?"

"When I get bigger, I'll go back and get him."

"Look out, someone is coming at us," Ella said. There was another carriage approaching from the top of a crest in the road. "You'd better give me the reins."

Sammy handed the reins to Ella, and sighed. "I never get to drive when someone is coming."

"When you get bigger," said Ella. "You can drive whenever you want."

Ella slowed the horses, while the carriage passed by. Then she gave Charger a restrained 'giddy up.'

"What about Abraham Lincoln?" Sammy said, once they were going again.

"What about him?"

"Miss Dorothy showed me a picture of him. He looks kind of like Mr. Hicks. He's a white man, and he's not mean, is he?"

"He's the president. He has to be nice so as folks will vote for him," Ella explained.

"I wonder if he knows how to play cards," said Sammy, yawning—and inasmuch as Ella was now driving, he leaned back and took a nap.

## 43

"A GOOD PIOUS OUTFIT"

*W*hen Jimmy awoke, it was well past dawn. He saw a tall, slender man with long white whiskers, a ruddy face, and pale gray eyes standing over him. The man held a saucer in one hand and a teacup in the other. Jimmy had removed his shirt and trousers before going to sleep. He lay on the floor wrapped in a blanket. When he saw the strange man, he shot out of the blanket and—despite not being dressed—bolted toward the door. But Mrs. MacMurrough, who was nearer the door than Jimmy, saw where he was headed. She stood and kicked the door shut before Jimmy could reach it.

"Here now, Jimmy," she said. "Don't be jumpin' out of your skin! This gentleman's none other than Mr. Mack, the very same man I told you about from the Illinois Central."

Mr. Mack, without spilling a drop of his tea, swiveled on his feet to observe Jimmy's course toward the door. "Oh he's a sharp one, he is," said Mr. Mack. "Sharp reflexes! That's just the thing to have in a situation like this. You can't be too careful. But I did not mean to startle you, friend."

When Jimmy saw that the door was blocked, he turned instead to retrieve his clothes, which sat on the washstand across the room. Donahue was curled in a ball on top of Jimmy's clothes. He raised his head when he heard the commotion, and blinked when he saw Jimmy coming.

"We thought you were asleep, lad," said Mrs. MacMurrough. "Mr. Mack meant no harm. He only meant to take the measure of your size with his eyes. He may be able to fit you up with some new clothes."

Jimmy picked up the cat with one hand and slid his pants and shirt off the washstand with the other. Donahue meowed loudly, and Jimmy set the cat back on the washstand. He hastily began to put on his trousers. "What do I need new clothes for?" he asked.

"It's so you can get yourself a job, lad, in Chicago," said Mrs. MacMurrough.

"We're supposing you may not have a sack of money with you," said Mr. Mack. "We're supposing you'll be wanting to earn some money when you get to Chicago. I know a firm there, you see. It's on Clark Street facing Courthouse Square. It is a catering firm, you see, called Ambrose & Jackson. The firm is owned by colored gentlemen, not a common thing I can tell you that! Mr. Ambrose and Mr. Jackson may be able to give you a job—but you must present yourself to them as a free man. They won't hire a runaway slave. They dare not, you see, or they'd soon be in trouble with the authorities. So you'll need to tell them you're a free man. And you'll need to look good and proper, with proper clothes."

When he'd put on his shirt, Jimmy sat on a chair at the table to put on his shoes. "What kind of work do they need?" he asked.

"Well, it is a catering firm," said Mr. Mack. "I can't say for certain that they'll need anyone just now. But I suppose it may be possible that they'll need a well-dressed man to deliver the food and serve it—unless you know how to cook."

"I don't," Jimmy said. "I served table only on special occasions. My friend, the man I'm going to meet, is better at that than I am. He was a house servant. I worked in the field."

"Yes, I see you're strong," said Mr. Mack. "Perhaps they'll need a strong fellow to carry supplies about—and another one to serve. But, whether you serve or not, you must be dressed to look the part of a free man. I can bring you proper clothes if I know your size."

While they were talking, Mrs. MacMurrough rummaged through a drawer in her bureau. "Ah, here it is," she said. She held up a long narrow strip of cloth on which markings at regular intervals could be seen. "Here's the tape I used whenever I needed to measure Mr. MacMurrough," she said. "Now stand up tall, lad and I'll take your size."

Jimmy stood—and Mrs. MacMurrough appraised him with her tape. Mr. Mack wrote down the measurements as Mrs. MacMurrough called them out. She ran the strip around Jimmy's chest. "One yard, six inches," she called. Then she stretched the strip down his arm. "Two feet, eight inches," she reported. Then she measured down his leg from his crotch to his ankle. "One yard."

In this manner, Jimmy was fitted for new clothes. Mr. Mack, once he had the measurements, finished his tea, and took his leave.

"I'll be back before nightfall," he said.

True to his word, he returned after dinner. He brought with him a black frock coat, a white vest, and a pair of black pantaloons. To these Mrs. MacMurrough added a black silk tie, which had belonged to her husband.

"'Tis a good, pious outfit," said Mrs. MacMurrough. "And how did you get all of this tailored so quickly?"

"I have ready-mades set aside for this purpose," said Mr. Mack. He held the clothes up in front of Jimmy. "He'll look very much like a Quaker," said Mr. Mack. "All he has to do is carry a Bible and wear a top hat."

"No Bible," said Jimmy. "And no top hat. I will dress like a free man, but I won't act like someone I'm not."

"Jimmy does not believe in God, Mr. Mack," said Mrs. MacMurrough. "He has no use for a master of any kind, whether human or heavenly."

"Ah, I see," said Mr. Mack.

"If I'm to be free," said Jimmy, "I should be free to believe whatever I want."

"Indeed," said Mr. Mack. "You may believe as you like. But I would advise you to keep such talk to yourself. You'll have to make your way in the world now, Jimmy. You'll want to have the air of a respectable man. Be courteous and humble. You can say what you like to us. But when you're on your own, you'd best make yourself as agreeable as possible—especially with whites."

"Don't forget," said Mrs. MacMurrough. "There are copperheads about. You can never tell what might happen if you cross a white man. So be very polite to everyone."

"I plan to keep to myself," said Jimmy. "As much as I can."

"Come, Mr. Mack," said Mrs. MacMurrough. "Let us take a walk down to the river, shall we, while Jimmy tries on these clothes."

When Mrs. MacMurrough and Mr. Mack had gone, Jimmy hurriedly put on the new clothes. He looked at himself in the glass. The clothes did make him look respectable. Though he was grateful for the kindness and good intentions of Mrs. MacMurrough and Mr. Mack, he was not comfortable with their idea of who he should be. He was eager to be on his way—to be on his own once again. He wondered what it might be like to work for two colored gentlemen. Serving food to white people was hardly the work he dreamed of doing. Yet he would need to find some temporary work, and find it soon. He could not depend on kindly old ladies to feed him mutton wherever he went.

The next morning Mr. Mack arrived to take Jimmy to the rail yard in Cairo. When they were ready to leave, Jimmy bade farewell to Mrs. MacMurrough. "I will not forget your kindness, ma'am," he said. He picked up the cat and kissed it on the nose. "And you brought me luck, Donahue." He petted the cat, and shook hands with Mrs. MacMurrough.

"You know where to find us," she said, "if you ever come back this way."

Mr. Mack had come in a buggy. In the buggy, he and Jimmy drove to Cairo. Jimmy was wearing his new clothes. His old clothes were stowed with the rest of his possessions in his satchel, which had grown larger and even more conspicuous with the added cargo.

"When you visit Ambrose & Jackson," said Mr. Mack, "leave your bundle hidden somewhere. You don't want to look like a drifter, you see. Give them an address where you live. Tell them you live with your family in a boarding house."

"How will I find their office?" asked Jimmy. "I can't read. I'll have to ask someone where it is."

"When you get off the train, you must first find the courthouse. The courthouse is in the middle of Courthouse Square, you see. The street east of the square is Clark Street. When you get there, ask someone which office belongs to Ambrose & Jackson. Ask a policeman, if you can. I'm going to put you in an empty boxcar. They won't load that car up until it gets to Chicago."

"How will I know when I get to Chicago?"

"Chicago is the last stop. The rail yard there has many

tracks, more tracks than any of the stations along the way. If
the train stops for more than an hour, and if you see a lot of
tracks in the yard about you, and if you see large buildings all
around you—then you'll know you're in Chicago. Now be sure
no one sees you when you get off the train. Slip off quietly,
then walk away from the train. Don't run or do anything to
call attention to yourself. If anyone sees you, just tip your hand
to them and say, 'Good day.' If you don't act suspiciously, no
one will suspect you."

Mr. Mack drove the buggy directly into the Illinois Central
rail yard. He drove up to a shed, which stood by itself apart
from the main cluster of warehouse buildings. There he got out
and hitched the horses to a post.

"Let me carry your satchel," said Mr. Mack. "Then you
should walk beside me, and as we're walking gesture with your
hands like we're talking about something to do with freight."

They walked down a line of boxcars until they came to one
that was four from the end. Mr. Mack slid the door of that car
two feet open.

"Now don't climb up there until I tell you. When it's time,
I'll hold my hands together down low to make a step—and I'll
boost you up. But first I'm going to put your satchel inside the
car."

In a casual manner, Mr. Mack leaned against the wall of
the boxcar, and slowly—as if he weren't even conscious of
doing so—he placed the satchel onto the floor of the empty car
with one hand, while gesturing with his other hand away from
the car, smiling and talking with great animation.

"Once you're inside, change back to your old clothes, then
fold the new clothes so they won't get wrinkled. When you get
to Chicago, change back into the new clothes before you get
out of the car."

Mr. Mack had another small parcel, which he handed now

to Jimmy. "There's some food in here," he said. "It should be enough for today at least." As he spoke, he looked up and down the yard. "Well sir, I think it's time. Step on my hands and up you go, smooth and slow."

Mr. Mack formed his hands into a step. Jimmy set the parcel of food on the floor of the car, stepped onto Mr. Mack's hands, and was hoisted up and into the car. From the inside, he turned to shake Mr. Mack's hand.

"No time to shake hands," said Mr. Mack. "Just close the door from the inside. I'm going to walk away now."

"Thank you," said Jimmy. But even as he spoke, Mr. Mack was walking away and did not look back.

Jimmy closed the door of the boxcar. It was dank and dark inside. He made his way to the corner of the car farthest from the door. He took off his new clothes, folded them carefully on the floor, took his old clothes out of the satchel, put them on, and then sat down to wait. After about an hour, he heard the train whistle, followed by the sound of metal lurching into motion. Then the train began to move. As the train started, Jimmy heard the sound of men whose voices he did not recognize talking outside. Then, without warning, the door slid open several inches. Jimmy huddled into the corner. His heart pounded. He stayed as low to the floor as he could. Bright light streamed in through the opened door in stark contrasted with the darkness in the rest of the car. Jimmy could not tell if the door had been purposely opened, or if it had simply slid a few inches when the train began to move. Two men were talking outside. One of the men shouted something that sounded like "Oh, Paddy." Jimmy saw a hand reach in—bright and white in the glowing light from outside. In an impulsive reflex, Jimmy stood up fast. He pushed his body back hard into the corner of the car. He thought about making a run for it. "If there are only two of them," he thought, "I can take them." He started to step forward, then stopped. "But what if they have guns or sticks or dogs?" He stepped back into the corner. "I could jump out the door as far as I can, then run before they catch me." The train was still moving slowly. Whoever belonged to the hand was walking at the same speed as the train. Jimmy moved along the wall of the car until he was at the edge of the darkness. One more step and he'd be in the light. He sucked in his breath. He would run and make a tremendous leap. Just then he heard a man yell, "Clear." This time it sounded like Mr. Mack's voice. Then the hand grabbed onto the door and slid it closed. The door closed with a bang, and Jimmy was again in darkness.

Very soon, the train picked up speed, until it was moving as fast as a horse and carriage. Then the train went faster still. Soon Jimmy realized that he was moving faster than he'd ever moved in his life. The train accelerated—and now it was going faster than a galloping horse. Jimmy wondered if something was wrong. Was it meant to go so fast? He could hardly imagine that it was normal for a machine to travel at such a speed. He sat down in the corner—fearing that the car might soon go flying off the track. But then the train stopped accelerating, and the speed remained constant. After twenty minutes of steady speed, Jimmy concluded that the train was riding smoothly on its track, and there was a steady rhythm of clicking and clacking that reassured him.

At first, Jimmy did not think he could easily sleep while the train was traveling at such a high speed. But after another hour, the darkness inside the car and the sound of the clanking rails began to work their effect upon him. He slumped down lower and lower against the wall of the car. Soon his head was lying on the soft cushion of his satchel. He thought of Cato. He pictured the two of them in fancy clothes, serving platters of food. Cato bowed and winked at him. Slowly his eyes fluttered closed—and he was asleep.

Sometime later, he awoke. He was not sure how long he had slept. Mr. Mack had told him that the entire trip, with stops, would take about eight hours. He was certain the train must have stopped at least once while he was asleep. He remembered sensing a quiet period, when he must have slipped deeper into his dream. Then there was a lurch when the car began to move again, and it woke him for just a moment till he fell back into his dream.

But had that happened only once? Jimmy couldn't remember. He crawled over to the door of the car, and pulled it open a crack. From the angle of the sun, he gauged it to be about mid-afternoon. The train had left two hours after sunrise. He calculated that he'd been traveling six or seven hours. He sat by the door and stared out the crack, watching the scenery go by. The land was flat. It stretched out for miles, receding into the distance with no sign of any hills at all. He saw clumps of trees here and there, but mostly there were fields of tall grass, interrupted occasionally by stretches of cultivated land. He saw no cotton. There were some fields of corn—and some fields with a crop he took to be wheat.

After a while, several buildings came into view. Not long after that, the train came slowly to a stop. Jimmy reasoned that he was not yet in Chicago. He saw no extra tracks. He could only see a few buildings nearby. And after ten minutes, the train began to move again.

Jimmy went back to the corner of the car. He realized he was hungry. He dug into the parcel Mr. Mack had given him. He found some crackers and a slice of ham. He ate the crackers and ham, consuming all of it even though he knew he should save some. Then he was thirsty, but there was nothing for him to drink. Despite his thirst, he also had an urge to urinate, which he could no longer ignore. He stood and went to the door. He opened it wide enough to stick his head out. About half a mile away, he saw a road. On the road, a figure was riding a horse in the opposite direction from the train. He waited until the figure receded. Soon there was no one else in sight. Jimmy relieved himself, pissing out the door of the boxcar in a hard, steady stream—peering into the distance as he did so, to see if anyone else might be about to come into view. Soon he saw another figure on horseback on the road, far in the distance, but coming closer. Jimmy could not stop—did not want to stop—peeing. He was so unused to the speed of the train that it was hard to gauge how soon the rider would come close enough to see him. He stepped back discreetly—as far as he could while still keeping the stream flowing out the door. Suddenly there was a crescendo of sound, then a thunderous whoosh, as another train—going in the opposite direction on the adjacent track—rushed past. The force of the air from the passing train blasted the arching stream back at Jimmy, and he was instantly sprayed with his own urine.

"Damn!" He stopped peeing and yelped with annoyance. But after a moment, he laughed. "I pissed on myself!" he said out loud. He imagined telling Cato the story. He waited until the other train passed, and then, at last, completed his task. "That was the longest damn piss I ever took," he said to himself. Then Jimmy realized, that if he was going to impress Mssrs. Ambrose & Jackson, he'd have to find some place to wash up as soon as he arrived in Chicago.

## 44

A PLAIN WHITE RIBBON

*J*immy's financial woes were dire. When he fell into the Ohio River, he had lost most of the money that he had received from his family. Only nine of Sammy's ten pennies had stayed lodged in his pocket when he dragged himself onto the bank. He wished his pocket had managed to hold onto more. When he got to Chicago, he was already hungry, and he knew nothing about the cost of food in Chicago—or even where he might buy some.

Jimmy had no doubt that he had arrived in Chicago. He saw both a large number of buildings and a large number of tracks. When the train had been stopped for about twenty minutes he decided that he'd better get out. Contrary to what Mr. Mack had advised, Jimmy chose not to put on his new clothes. He wanted to wash himself first. He climbed out of the boxcar, walked across the tracks, looking every which way as he went, until at last he stepped onto the streets of Chicago in his field clothes. He nodded at the first person he encountered and—with exaggerated politeness—wished him a good day. The stranger returned this greeting with a suspicious look, but kept walking.

Jimmy soon came to a busy street, where he was surrounded by carriages, streetcars, and people walking. He saw that he was conspicuous in his farm clothes. There was no convenient place for him to wash up or change his clothes. The street was lined with tall public buildings. How would he ever find Cato, Dorothy, and Ella in such an enormous place? They had not agreed on a meeting spot.

Jimmy passed a building with plate glass windows, inside which he saw dozens of white people, seated at tables in pairs, or in groups of four or six, eating lunch. Jimmy had never before seen a restaurant, but he quickly understood the appeal of such a place. Inside the restaurant, he saw two Negro men in uniform waiting on the diners. One of these men saw Jimmy, and gave him a look that seemed to say, "Watch out!" Jimmy, who had been peering unselfconsciously into the window, instantly backed away from it.

Jimmy knew it was out of the question for him to walk into this eating establishment. But it occurred to him that there might be a back door, and that by approaching the building from behind, he might find a way to talk to one of the uniformed servants. He walked to the side of the building. He found himself on an alleyway much narrower than the main street. This alleyway had no sidewalk. It receded back toward another small lane, which ran along the rear of the building.

Jimmy walked into the alley. As he did so, he sensed that he was moving out of the public space. The light in the alley was darker than the light in the street. The alley smelled different from the street. The odor of urine reinforced the feeling that he had stepped into a private world—a space more suitable to the clandestine needs of a runaway slave. He walked to the back of the building. There he saw a door. Next to the door was a bulky wooden bin filled with refuse.

He approached the bin cautiously. He smelled food—rotting food—but food, nonetheless. Jimmy wondered if it was too decayed to eat. He peered down into the bin to determine what was inside. Just as he did so, the door at the back of the building opened. One of the Negro men, the same one he had seen earlier, stepped out. The man held a small can filled with kitchen waste. It was evident he meant to dump the waste into the large bin into which Jimmy was peering.

Jimmy stepped back from the bin. The man hesitated for a moment, then chucked his load of scraps into the bin. He glared at Jimmy. "What are you looking for?" he asked.

Jimmy took another step back. "Just food," Jimmy replied. "And a place to wash and change clothes." He dug into his pocket and help up a penny. "I have some money."

"You can't skulk around here," the man said. "Go on back to Shanty town." With that, the man went back into the building and closed the door.

Jimmy felt his blood rise. Although the man had skin as dark as Jimmy's, he had spoken with a superior air. "Hello to you, too," Jimmy said out loud.

Jimmy reasoned that the man would not come out again—at least for several minutes. He returned to the bin and dug inside it until he uncovered the remains of a sandwich. He also found a leftover piece of meat. Having satisfied himself with this bounty, he walked further down the alley. At length he came upon a recess in the building wall—an alcove that appeared to have held a door at one time. The doorway was boarded up. The alcove smelled strongly of urine, but it was sufficiently recessed to be private. Jimmy sat down in the recess to eat the food that he had found.

When he was finished eating he told himself that he might

as well change his clothes. He reasoned that he was not likely to find a place to wash—nor was he apt to find anywhere as private as the alcove to change. He rapidly undressed, then began to put on the clothes Mr. Mack had given him. He had just put one of his legs into his trousers when a young white boy came walking down the alley and saw him. The boy stopped—looked at him with wide eyes, then dashed off, running down the alley with an alarmed look. The boy disappeared around a corner.

Jimmy shook his head. He'd begun to feel serious misgivings about the North. He'd spent his life imagining this escape to freedom—but now that he was really here, he was astounded by the unfriendliness of the people. He had felt safer on Christmasville Road at night—paddy rollers or no.

Just as he was thinking these thoughts, the youth, who had run from him moments ago, returned—accompanied by two grown men. From the other direction, a third man appeared, a large man, more ominous than the other two. This third man smoked a cigar.

"What have we here?" the cigar smoking man said.

"Nigger with his clothes off," said one of the others, who had a stubbly beard. At this point, the youth, whose principal role appeared to be that of a lookout, ran off again around the corner.

"This isn't a public changing room boy," said the cigar man.

Jimmy said nothing. He continued to put on his clothes.

"Show us your papers," the cigar man demanded.

As the man spoke, light glinted on a shiny copper penny in the lapel of his coat. Jimmy said nothing. He reasoned that if he remained calm and deliberate while he finished putting on his clothes, it might discourage the men from making any sudden moves.

"Answer me boy," said the cigar man, who stepped forward. "Where are your papers?"

With his clothes on, Jimmy stood and looked the man directly in the eyes, but he said nothing.

"Nigger's got to be a runaway," said the stubbly man. "If he had papers he'd show 'em."

"Is that it?" said the cigar man. "Did you run off? Does your master know where you are?"

"Looks like a field nigger," said the stubbly man, "who's trying to put on airs."

"That's a mighty fine coat you've got there, boy," said the cigar man.

Without taking his eyes off the cigar man, Jimmy bent down to pick up the clothes he had just removed. He calculated whether or not he could make a run for it. He speculated that if he darted in one direction—but then changed course at just the right moment—he might slip by them.

"I reckon he stole that coat," said the stubbly man.

Jimmy leapt in the direction of the stubbly man. He leapt so violently that the stubbly man instinctively stepped back.

"Grab him," said the cigar man.

Jimmy pounced two steps to the right. When he was certain that all three men had begun to move to grab him, he abruptly bounded back to the left, and then, just as abruptly, switched directions again and lurched forward. Jimmy's feint confounded his assailants. They were unable to grab him. When he got two yards ahead of them, he ran. He hoped that once he got back onto the public street, they'd give up the chase.

Jimmy ran fast enough so that when he reached the end of the alley he had increased his lead by several yards. There he turned right onto the main street, which put him in the path of several people on the street who were walking toward him. He kept running—heedless of the stares of strangers. Soon Jimmy's attackers emerged from the alley behind him, and to his dismay, they continued the chase.

"Stop him," the stubbly man yelled. "He stole a coat!"

Several people on the street reacted to the stubbly man's shout. Three of them stepped aside—giving Jimmy wide berth. But two men paused and positioned themselves to try to catch him as he passed. Farther away, at the end of the block, a policeman was directing traffic. Jimmy quickly concluded that the policeman would take the side of his pursuers. Since he had no papers—and was, in fact, a runaway—he could imagine no other possibility. He made a sharp left turn and ran out into the street itself—hoping to get to the other side—dodging oncoming carriages as he did so.

There was too much traffic on the street for Jimmy to go straight across it. He ran down the center of the roadway, dodging horses and buggies. When he saw an opening, he darted to the sidewalk. He was now on the opposite side of the street from the policeman, who started down the street toward the men who were chasing him. Jimmy looked back. The men chasing him abruptly slowed down, as if they too wished to avoid the policeman. They stepped into the street—then tried to cross it in the same manner that Jimmy had just completed.

The policeman blew his whistle. He pointed his baton toward the three men who were crossing the street. Even though Jimmy was still running, the policeman did not—as yet —show any sign of having seen him. Jimmy arrived at another alley in the middle of the block. He hoped to get out of view before the policeman saw him. He turned hard into the alley, which he saw was one block long. Although he was already breathless, Jimmy ran harder and faster than he had run previously. He wanted to get to the end of the alley before his pursuers could see which way he turned at the far end.

When he got to the far end, he turned to the left. Then, after he was all the way around the corner, he stopped. He turned completely around, then walked slowly and deliberately back across the alley, looking straight ahead, as if he had all the time in the world. He continued to walk unhurriedly when he got across the alley. He saw people walking toward him, but now no one paid him any particular notice. Three doors down from the intersection of the alley, Jimmy turned into the door of a shop. He opened it and found that it led up a flight of stairs. He walked up the stairs—forcing himself to climb the stairs as slowly as a man in a hurry could manage.

When he arrived at the top of the stairs, he stopped. He was in a hat shop filled with tables and stands, which held artfully, displayed ladies' hats. A counter stood at the side of the room. The counter was commanded by a shop clerk, a young man dressed in dapper finery, who stood when Jimmy arrived. The clerk's face flickered with alarm. But this expression was quickly replaced with a cautious smile.

The young man spoke with cool cordiality. "May I help you?"

Jimmy was still panting from the exertion of the chase. He knew that his breathlessness must seem odd to the young clerk. "I'm winded," Jimmy explained. "I've been climbing stairs. I've been climbing stairs all day. I'm looking for a hat store. I'm supposed to pick up a hat for Miss Holland.

"Miss Holland?" The young man wrinkled his forehead to indicate that he did not recognize the name.

"Yes, Miss Dorothy Holland."

"Which hat shop were you looking for?"

"That's the trouble," said Jimmy. "I can't recollect the name of the shop. Miss Holland told me the name."

"This is D. B. Fisk Millinery," said the young man, with an affectation of pride.

"D. B. Fisk," Jimmy repeated the shop name as though he were pondering whether that name might be the name he'd forgotten. But he was actually pondering how he might keep up a patter with this man long enough so that the men in the street would continue to move farther away. "I don't rightly know," he said at last. "That might be the name."

"Well," said the young man, "I'm very much afraid that we don't have an order for Miss Holland here."

Jimmy nodded. "Do you mind, sir, if I stop here for a moment to catch my breath?"

"No, that's quite all right," said the young man, who was staring at Jimmy with unabashed curiosity. "I am Mr. Ames. I am the shop clerk for D. B. Fisk."

"Thank you kindly, Mr. Ames."

"Perhaps I can help you locate the shop you want," said Mr. Ames, and he stepped out from behind the counter. "I know all the millinery shops in this area."

Jimmy looked around at the elaborate hats on display. "Miss Holland is partial to simple kinds of hats," he said. "Miss Holland is a Quaker. She likes plain things." Jimmy surprised himself with his own lie. "She told me the hat she ordered has a plain white ribbon."

"A white ribbon?" Mr. Ames arched his eyebrow as he said this, as though it were an important clue. He moved closer to Jimmy.

"Yes, sir, a white ribbon."

Jimmy heard voices coming from the street below. Instinctively, he stepped farther away from the stairs. He surveyed the hats in the room—hoping to see something like the one he had just described, so that he might walk in the direction of it. But there was no such white-ribboned hat to be found, simple or otherwise.

"Ribbons … ribbons," the shop clerk repeated. As he

spoke, he stepped closer still to Jimmy. When he did so, Jimmy smelled a waft of spicy fragrance, like a perfume, emanating from Mr. Ames's environs. "I know of a shop that carries hats with ribbons," said Mr. Ames, taking another step closer. "There is a shop on Clark Street."

"Yes, Clark Street." Jimmy repeated the name. This was the street name that Mr. Mack had made him memorize—the street where the caterers shop would be found. "Is it near Ambrose & Jackson's?"

"Ambrose & Jackson?" Mr. Ames shook his head. He had stepped as close as he dared for the moment. He looked at Jimmy with an open gaze. "I'm sorry," he said. "I am not familiar with that establishment. The shop I have in mind is on Clark Street between Lake Street and Couch Place. The shop I refer to is called Shaw's. They sell millinery goods, cloaks and mantillas."

"Shaw's," said Jimmy. "Yes, I think that's the place Miss Holland told me. How do I get to Clark Street?"

Even though he was standing close already, the young clerk, in a deft movement, stepped closer still. "When you leave here, you'll be on Lake Street. Turn left." The young man indicated the way with his left hand, sweeping it almost to the point of touching Jimmy's arm. "Go three blocks. The first street you'll come to is State Street. Then the next street you'll come to will be Dearborn Street. And then the third street you'll come to will be Clark Street. There you will turn left again." Once again, the clerk indicated the direction with his hand in an arcing gesture, which at its culmination grazed past Jimmy's waist. "Shaw's establishment is four doors from the corner."

Jimmy sensed some unspoken feeling was being conveyed to him by the young man, who continued to stare at him with wide eyes. It was not the sort of look he was used to seeing in a white man. "Thank you, Mr. Ames," said Jimmy. "I surely do hope I can find that hat shop. I'm sorry to trouble you." As he said this, he gave the clerk a broad smile.

"No trouble at all," said Mr. Ames, who tossed his head back. He smiled at Jimmy—and at the same time, he blushed.

Jimmy turned to go down the stairs. As quickly as he had climbed the stairs, he was now set upon going down them as slowly as possible. He made a show of mumbling the name of the millinery shop "Shaw's"—as if he were trying to memorize that name, and as if doing so required him to halt each time he said it. In this way he made his way down, pausing and exclaiming "Shaw's" every few steps, thus drawing out his passage on the stairs for several minutes. Throughout this process, Mr. Ames stood at the top of the stairs, watching Jimmy's descent with candid interest.

When Jimmy arrived at the street, he proceeded even more slowly. He opened the door, then backed out of it—waving his hand—as though he were saying goodbye to the young man at the top of the stairs. Mr. Ames waved back, smiled and tossed his head again. Mr. Ames even went so far as to take a tentative step down the stairs in Jimmy's direction. But then Jimmy closed the door and turned quickly toward State Street. He walked with deliberate but hurried steps. He saw none of his assailants in front of him. The people approaching him exhibited an indifference that suggested that there was nothing awry behind him. Based on the reaction of those coming toward him, he was sufficiently reassured that he chose not to turn 'round to look behind him.

## 45

## A STREETCAR ON STATE STREET

*N*ot long after receiving Dorothy's letter, Erastus Hicks left Philadelphia to travel to Chicago. He did not know whether he could do anything for William Askew. He was not sure if he could help Dorothy obtain her beloved's release from prison. But he was willing to try. Moreover, he was eager to see Cato—to see him walking free in the North, free to choose a new path in life, free, Erastus hoped, to renew his apprenticeship with an appreciative mentor. Erastus also considered that seeing Cato would revive his spirits. He was more than a little depressed by the war. Working as a nurse, he had seen horrific sights. Those horrors had seemed like poison. He wanted the balm of Cato's beauty to refresh him, to cleanse away the dreadful images. Though Erastus had stored many visual memories of Cato in his mind, he was eager now to revisit Cato's beauty in the flesh. The very thought of it lured him forward. He rode quickly on his horse.

Cato knew that Dorothy had written Erastus, and that she had asked him to meet them in Chicago. As he sat riding quietly in the brougham, Cato, too, thought that such a meeting would be pleasant. He missed his friend and teacher. He imagined that seeing Erastus would be an antidote to the uncertainties of his situation. Erastus was a familiar rock, a source of sound advice. He could count on Erastus to help him begin a new life with Jimmy. He was certain that Erastus could advise them about where and how to live—perhaps in Philadelphia.

Cato was also curious to see how Erastus would regard his posing as the white husband of Dorothy. Would Erastus not think him fetching in the clothes he now wore? He was certain that Jimmy would not. In fact, he had already concluded that it would be best if he abandoned his disguise before Jimmy ever saw it. But it would not disappoint Cato if he had a chance to show himself to Erastus while dressed in his wig and hat and expensive coat.

As she sat beside Cato, Dorothy likewise mused about Erastus. She, too, was eager to apply the painter's wisdom to her uncertain situation. She hoped that if Erastus, as a Yankee, put in a good word for William, the Union captors would … what? She hardly knew what to hope. At the very least, she hoped they would allow their marriage to be performed.

Dorothy also hoped that Erastus would be prepared to take custody of Sammy. She was not eager to part with the boy, but she was anxious about the cost of caring for so many with the money she had remaining. Even if Erastus were to take care of Sammy's needs, she and William and Ella and Cato—and, of course Jimmy, once he rejoined them—would all have to live on her funds. In addition to the money she'd obtained at home, she had the twenty-dollar gold coin that Mr. McNish had given her. He had hinted that she might want to use the coin to bribe a guard at the prison. If such a bribe were successful, if William could be freed—they could go home directly. She would not need the money to last so long. But if the bribe failed—she might lose the coin and have that much less to live on. So she fretted about the safest course of action—and whether she even ought to attempt something as unsavory as a bribe.

Ella, for her part, thought of her brother. How would he travel? How would he eat? If he got to Chicago, how would they find him? The more she thought about the plan to meet him in Chicago, the more she felt that it had been thoughtless and impulsive. Jimmy should have hidden in the woods until such time as they could think through a more precise plan. But it was too late for that. She tried to put her mind inside Jimmy's. She tried to think as he might think. She thought that it might occur to him to choose a public place to meet them: some easily found location such as the train station, or the post office. Or he might think to meet them somewhere near the prison camp. But then she wondered if the camp might be located somewhere outside the city. How would he get there? How would any of them know when and where to meet?

Ella was also worried about Dorothy's plans to marry William. Ella knew that Dorothy had not written to William. Dorothy feared that if William knew her plans he'd be bound to insist that she should not come to Chicago. Yet Ella could not help but think that it would be better if Dorothy knew for certain that William was prepared to marry her from his prison camp. There had been no communication from William since his capture. All they knew had been gleaned from the news-paper reports. What if there was a mistake? What if William was not even in Chicago? But Ella dared not raise these ques-tions to Dorothy. She saw that Dorothy was fixed upon her purpose, and would not be receptive to hearing Ella's misgivings.

While the travelers contemplated these matters, William Askew pondered whether or not he ought to take the loyalty oath which John Lewis had told him about. Since the day he heard about it, William had been alert to conversations about the oath. None of his fellow Confederate soldiers spoke openly of signing it. Yet there were those, like him, who did not vehemently repudiate it. William had an advantage in the matter. He had been morose for so long, his despondency was a distraction, which diverted attention from his neutral response to the oath. Whenever it was mentioned, he shook his head. He let his eyes glaze with pain. But he did not renounce it. He did not swear that he would sooner die than sign it, nor did he spit and curse at the very mention of it, as did many of his comrades.

The existence of the oath had been revealed to William at his darkest hour. The prospect of parole had been the first flicker of hope in that darkness. He needed only to sign a paper, and then … he'd be free, free to leave, free to go get drunk, free of the nightmare of war. And what was that paper but a collection of words about loyalty to the Union? His comrades spoke of the treachery of it, of the dishonor of even contemplating such a thing. But what did he care for honor? He had forever lost his honor at Shiloh. For dishonor to be felt there must first be a morsel of pride. William no longer had any pride. Unlike his fellow soldiers, he had nothing to swallow.

Yet William was alive to the fact that he could give no hint to anyone of the thoughts that played in his mind. It was clear to him that if his fellow prisoners knew that he had any thought of signing the oath they would revile him; they might even wish to attack him. John Lewis, the man who had first told him about the oath, had sworn as much. He grumbled at length about the secesh who after reading about the oath in the Chicago papers had declared the Southern cause to be lost, and who had then mysteriously disappeared from the prison camp.

It was taken as a fact that this traitor had signed the wretched pledge. And now John Lewis and his fellow Confederates cursed the man. They swore vengeance. They declared that some day they would find the rat and that his treason would be remembered long after the South had triumphed.

But these were empty threats. The man in question had long since been free to drink his fill at a jolly tavern on State Street, while his comrades languished in the harsh incommodity of Camp Douglas. There was a streetcar that ran on State Street all the way from Camp Douglas to the city center. William concentrated his daydreams on that streetcar. He imagined signing the oath and being paroled. He would picture himself alighting on the streetcar. He would imagine himself in civilian clothes, stepping onto the car, sitting down in a carriage filled with strangers. He was beguiled in his musings by the feeling of anonymity that this reverie conveyed. He was no longer a soldier, no longer a Southerner, no longer a man who'd once shot bullets into the air while his friend was blasted into bits at his side. He was no longer a defeated enemy, nor a despondent casualty of war. He was transformed in his dream into an ordinary man, riding the streetcar, marveling at the commonplace, reveling in the mundane. He would ride the streetcar to the city center, where he would become lost, absorbed into the crowd, a man without a past or a future.

William did not follow his daydream beyond the streetcar. It was the streetcar, with its forward motion, its rumbling progress, its moving away while moving toward, that comforted him. He could not discern what might lie beyond it. He could only reason that physical movement would help him, that being bodily transported would shift him out of his senselessness. The horses pulling the streetcar forward would be the engine of his transformation. The rails upon which the streetcar rode would guide him to a new place. When he stepped off the streetcar, he would nestle into the bosom of the anonymous crowds. So went his thoughts. But of these thoughts, he said nothing. He watched and waited for an opportunity to speak to a Union officer in private.

After a while, the doctor attending William concluded that there was no longer any reason why William could not get out of bed and participate in the ordinary routines of prison life at the camp. The secret thoughts of parole that played in William's mind had animated him. He was no longer seen to be in a dark cloud of despair. So it was decided that William would join the daily roll call in the yard at which the prisoners were counted. At the conclusion of the roll call the prisoners were allowed to fall out, after which they broke their ranks and milled about the yard. Some of the prisoners went to a spot in the perimeter of the camp where a small rectangular hole in the fence had been fashioned by an enter-prising Chicago woman. At convenient times, this woman stood outside the wall of the camp and sold food and bever-ages to the prisoners through the service window she had devised. For a short time, the Union officials tolerated this practice, though not without keeping a close watch on the transactions to ensure that nothing but edible fare was thus obtained.

One day William joined the others who waited in line to buy food from the vendor. He purposefully dawdled so that he was the last one in line. Then, after he had purchased his food, he stood close by the fence while his comrades wandered back to their barracks. The Union guard who had been monitoring the vendor's operation watched him while he stood munching on his food. William waited until he was alone with the guard. When he was certain that all of his comrades were out of sight, he spoke to the man.

"Can you tell me whom I should see about the oath?" he asked the guard.

"What oath?" was the reply of the guard, who, being uncertain of what William was about, raised his weapon in such a way as to indicate that he would tolerate no chicanery.

"The loyalty oath," said William. "I'm told a prisoner can get a parole if he swears an oath of loyalty to the Union."

"I don't know anything about that," said the guard.

"I've been told that there is an oath," said William, who was conscious of the fact that while he was a Confederate officer, the guard to whom he spoke was merely an enlisted man. "Would you tell your commanding officer that Lieutenant Askew inquired about the oath? My safety depends upon your discretion," he added.

"Go back to your barracks," said the guard, who regarded William with suspicion, and was unwilling to promise any favors in matters about which he knew nothing.

William left. Nothing more was said, nor did there seem to be any consequence from his query in the days that followed. For a week, William returned each day to the food vendor's service window. But each day a different guard was on duty. When at last the guard to whom he had spoken reappeared, the man avoided making eye contact. William could not tell if this was merely the discretion that William had requested, or willful disregard.

Then one morning, before the daily drills began, a group of three guards entered the barracks. They told William that he had been assigned to new quarters and that they would escort him to his new location immediately. He was told to pack his belongings. Several prisoners, including John Lewis, were nearby when this announcement was made. John Lewis looked at William with immediate suspicion. William, for his part, gave the appearance of being surprised. He feigned outrage that such an unprovoked demand should be made of him. He went so far as to shake hands with John Lewis, promising that he'd see him as soon as he straightened the matter out.

William was, in fact, surprised at what was happening. He had presumed that the guard to whom he had spoken had not acted upon his inquiry. Even now there was nothing in the circumstances of his being moved to a new location that assured him that his message had been delivered.

William was not escorted to new quarters. Instead, he was escorted to the office of the commanding officer of the camp, Colonel Joseph Tucker.

The lead soldier saluted the colonel, and announced the arrival of the prisoner. "Lieutenant William Askew," he said

"At ease, gentlemen," said the colonel. Colonel Tucker was a thin man with brown eyes, and a Van Dyke style beard: a pronounced moustache with a tuft of hair on his chin. He sat at a wooden desk upon which several architectural drawings had been unscrolled. "You may leave the prisoner here and wait outside," he instructed the guards. When they were alone, the Colonel spoke. "Lieutenant Askew, I am told that you inquired about the oath of allegiance to the United States. Is that correct?"

"Yes, sir."

"Lieutenant, are you aware that the oath of allegiance and the terms of parole are generally authorized only for enlisted men?"

"No, sir." William blushed as he realized his blunder. Officers were not enlisted men.

Colonel Tucker saw William's face color, but he continued. "Sir, it has not been considered likely by the government of the United States that a Confederate officer would consent to renounce his office, nor forswear allegiance to the Confederacy.

Are you not an officer in the Confederate Army with the rank of Lieutenant?"

"Yes, sir," said William. "I am a second Lieutenant in the Tennessee Sixth Regiment."

"And yet, despite your office, despite the faith placed in you both by the men who serve you and those who command you, you would renounce your commission, betray your government, and undertake to swear an oath to the United States?" The colonel described the matter using harsh words, the better to convey his skepticism that a Confederate officer would defect.

"Sir, taking the oath means nothing to me. I have already betrayed my men far more gravely."

"Lieutenant, what do you mean?"

And then William told his story. He told how he had taken his commission in the army on impulse, without consulting his betrothed, Miss Holland. He told how Miss Holland had been opposed to the war, had then renounced him, and would not forgive him until he had promised her that he would not commit violence. He told how she had been persuaded by her Quaker friend that it was wrong to kill, that this friend had also written to him and urged him to forgo bloodshed, proposing that he might give the appearance of fighting without actually shooting with deadly intent. He told how he had wrestled for months with the quandary into which his promise had put him, how he had pondered his dilemma from every point of view, and how he had not been certain even upon the brink of battle what his actions would be. Then he told the story of the battle itself. He told of his friend Daniel Watson who marched at his side. He told how Daniel Watson had been his friend back in Tennessee, and was a loyal enlisted soldier who depended upon him as a commanding officer and a comrade. Then he told Colonel Tucker in stark detail how they had reached the front lines. He told how there he had aimed his rifle to shoot above the head of the Union soldier opposite him. He told how that soldier had then promptly killed his friend, and that his friend had died in his arms, looking up into his face.

Upon telling this last detail, William's voice grew choked and faint, such that it was barely audible. Colonel Tucker, who had been watching William closely during the telling of the tale, looked away when William revealed the last crucial detail. The colonel averted his eyes because he did not wish to look directly at William while he weighed his reaction. He was both repulsed and moved by the story. He himself had never entertained any compunction about the necessary evils of war. He had little sympathy for pacifists, whom he regarded as spineless hypocrites whose cowardice was wrapped in religious pretexts. And yet he was sensitive to the element in William's story that was born of romantic feelings. It was not lost upon him that the young man had undertaken a promise of nonviolence to satisfy his lover's wish. Women were, he felt, inclined to be foolish and sentimental about war. He saw that the young man had suffered for his actions. Moreover, it was awkward for Colonel Tucker to place his own sympathies in the matter, since the lieutenant had spared the life of a Union soldier and thus forfeited the life of his Confederate friend. But the act was, in the colonel's mind, an unconscionable action for an officer. What form of repudiation was warranted for such a man?

It was incumbent upon Colonel Tucker to ferret out the true inner feelings of anyone who proposed to take the oath. He had to discern the sincerity of the applicant. In this case, the colonel was convinced that William sincerely desired to remove himself from the company of his fellow soldiers. It was a wonder to the colonel, in fact, that William could look his fellow soldiers in the eye at all.

At the time of William's interview, negotiations were under way between the North and the South to exchange prisoners. Colonel Tucker had received orders instructing him to allow prisoners to decline the pending exchange by which Confederate prisoners would be returned to the Confederate army in exchange for Union prisoners who were likewise exchanged. To decline the exchange, Confederate prisoners had to take an oath of allegiance to the United States and promise to remain north of the Ohio River. The colonel was convinced that the pitiful young man before him was unlikely ever to bear arms against the Union —or ever again even pretend to do so. It would be expedient to be rid of him. "If you choose to take the oath of allegiance, Lieutenant Askew, I will tell you that the Army of the United States would never accept a man such as you in its ranks. Therefore I hope you will give no thought to joining the army of the North."

These words fell hard upon William's ears. He had confessed the secret that burdened his heart only to see his shame confirmed in the scorn of this Union officer. Though his actions had benefited the enemy, even his enemy, it seemed, was appalled by his actions. But what did it signify? He was already so mortified that this further reproach did not much matter.

"If you take the oath of allegiance," the colonel continued, "you must swear to remain north of the Ohio River."

William nodded his head. He would like nothing better than to return home. But how could he face anyone in the South? Even if no one there knew what he had done at Shiloh, they would certainly discover that he had been paroled from prison by renouncing the South, by taking an oath of allegiance to the United States. He could not face his father.

And as he thought of his father, he felt an impulse to cry, which he could not entirely suppress. He knew that Hickory Grove had burned, and that while his father had lost his home, he still had pride in his son. When William pictured meeting his father and imagined his father's burgeoning shame, he realized that he could not go back home. It was simply out of the question. But if he stayed in the North, what would become of him? He would be cut off from Dorothy, from Cato, from his father, and from everyone about whom he cared. It was a dismal prospect. But, as he pondered the choices, he realized it was really the only choice he could make.

"Colonel, I desire to swear an oath of allegiance to the United States and be paroled in the North."

The die was cast. The oath was taken. In a matter of hours, William was dressed in civilian clothes and escorted out the gate. He walked around the perimeter of the camp until he came to State Street. There he waited for the streetcar. He had little money, just enough for the fare and then perhaps for a meal or a drink. When he finally stepped onto the streetcar, he found it surprisingly empty. Although he was now just an anonymous traveler, he did not feel anything of the transformation for which he had hoped. He sat alone in a seat near the back of the car with his eyes lowered—and wondered what he had done with his life.

# 46

## CHOCOLATE ICE CREAM

$\mathscr{A}$lthough William had thought that he would get off the streetcar and go directly to a saloon for a drink, when the time came he did not do so. He got off the streetcar at State and Madison, at the very heart of the city. At first, he walked aimlessly, absorbing the impact of the transition from the somber world of the prison camp to that of the bustling city. He was, as he had expected, comforted by the anonymity. He hoped that he looked like any other Northerner. He found himself studying them—the Northerners walking the streets— to see if there was any physical quality, anything in their manner or appearance that was different. He saw a certain air of disinterestedness in the passers by—as though they were minding their own business. They appeared impartial, or at least, unconcerned about interacting with their fellow citizens. It was noticeably different from the manners of Southerners, but it suited his purposes, since he did not wish anyone to be curious about him.

As he was walking, he came upon an ice cream saloon. He thought of the first time he'd tasted ice cream. There was none sold in Jackson. In his childhood, ice cream had always been a special treat that he associated with travel. His father and mother had taken him to Memphis. He remembered being a young boy and watching his father eating strawberry ice cream in Memphis. It was one of the few memories he had of his father showing unabashed pleasure. He remembered his father's excitement in describing how the marvelous cold confection was produced and made available even in the heat of summer. During the winter, huge blocks of ice were cut from the Mississippi River, then stored in deep holes in the ground where they were protected by straw and sawdust. Then throughout the warm months, chunks of ice were brought up and transformed with salt and cream and eggs and fruit into the velvety extravagance that made him smile.

William remembered his mother's soft, wistful smile. She, like him, was as pleased by Augustus's unusual display of happiness as by the ice cream itself. On impulse, William turned into the ice cream saloon at State and Washington. He did not have much money—but he thought to himself, 'eating ice cream will be better than getting drunk.' He went to the counter. He surveyed the choices—far more choices than he remembered having as a boy in Memphis. But he settled on chocolate—the same flavor he had always chosen as a boy. He was seeking the comfort of nostalgia, and he knew that chocolate ice cream would be a palliative for all his remorse. He sat down at a table by the window. He looked out the window briefly, then took his first bite. He smiled. And as he smiled, he realized how much he was like his father. For it had been many months—maybe more than a year—since William had shown any outer sign of happiness.

As he was thinking this—and perhaps because he was thinking it—his eye settled on a man making his way down the street. It was an old man—a stranger to Chicago who was walking down the street in an uncertain way, looking about him as if not sure where he was going. The man looked rather like his father—, which added to the surge of homesickness that William began to feel. He had thought only briefly—for the thought was too painful—about the exile to which his parole and oath had condemned him. But now the sorrow of his banishment issued forth. It stabbed his heart like a knife. He watched the strange old man as he slowly made his way down the street. Then, as if by a force of his own mental exertion, William willed the man to stop in front of the ice cream shop.

At that point, William was struck by how much this strange old man looked like his father. The resemblance was striking. He felt an impulse to rush out into the street, to greet the man—to offer the poor fellow some gesture of Southern hospitality—to show him a kindness in a city that was so egalitarian in its indifference.

William waved—and as he did so he saw the old man's eyes focus upon him. The old man looked at first at the window where he doubtless saw the reflection of the street. But then, drawn in by the waving of William's hand, the old man's eyes concentrated on the shape of the stranger inside the ice cream saloon. Suddenly the man staggered. He appeared flabbergasted. He put his hand up to his heart. Then he came to the door of the shop, opened it and stood in the doorway.

"Son!" the old man shouted.

William laughed. He could not believe that the bizarre thoughts he had harbored in his imagination had somehow conveyed themselves to this stranger such that even the stranger had taken up the idea. But then he, too, suddenly looked again—unimpeded now by the layer of glass or the filter of his expectations. He saw that it was his father. It was Augustus Askew.

William leapt up from the table. Augustus lurched toward him. They embraced. Each was so stunned by the circumstances that they did not speak, but held each other in a wobbling, deeply-felt hug for many moments. When they stepped back, both men had tears in their eyes, which were quickly wiped away.

After the long silent hug, there came a hundred questions. Each man spoke rapidly. Augustus explained that he had just arrived by train, that he had been walking down the street searching for a hotel—that after several days of feeling helpless he had suddenly decided that if Dorothy Holland could do a thing, he could do it, too. Then he had to explain what Dorothy had done—that she had deceived her own parents, had stolen—for all practical purposes—his own brougham— and had set out to come to Chicago to see William—and that even now she must be close by if she were not in Chicago already. He told how Dorothy had taken with her two of the Holland slaves—and that another Holland slave had disappeared.

"But why is she coming?" William asked.

"She means to marry you—and to rescue you I suppose. But what are you doing out of prison?"

Then William had to explain. There was not enough time for him to invent a lie. If he had had days or weeks or months to invent some prevarication he would undoubtedly have done so. But the suddenness of seeing his father, and the emotional relief it brought him left him in a state of childlike candor. In the course of five minutes, he told the whole story. He revealed not only the disgrace of the oath and parole—but also the greater shame that occurred at Shiloh.

Augustus listened to his son in silence. There was perhaps still some part of him wherein a faint upwelling of anger and shame flickered. But much had happened to change Augustus

Askew since he had last seen his son. The burning down of his house, his brush with death, the onslaught of the war, the months of living in the Hollands' back parlor, the overwhelming feeling that he'd lost his wife and his son and that everything in the world that he'd known had fallen away—all had combined to temper the soul of Augustus Askew. His certainty about the way things were had diminished. He was no longer as sure as he had once been about what was right and what was wrong. Moreover, his joy at seeing William alive, at the undeniable miracle of sitting with him in an ice cream saloon, at watching his son eat chocolate ice cream just as he had done when he was a boy, was too wonderful to squander in anger. And so without premeditation, he forgave his son. It happened so quickly that he did not have time to reconsider it. Just as he had done when William was a boy, he took a bite of the ice cream from William's bowl—and smiled.

Now William cried without restraint—for he had told his deepest shame to the man whose judgment he most feared—and the man had only smiled. William's tears did cause Augustus to be embarrassed. He looked around. No one seemed to notice. The Northerners continued going about their business. Augustus took out his handkerchief and handed it to his son. William wiped his eyes.

"Finish your ice cream," Augustus said. "I'm going to have some, too."

And with that, Augustus went to the counter where he ordered a scoop of strawberry ice cream, just as he had always done in Memphis. Then father and son spent thirty happy minutes sitting in the window of an ice cream saloon in Chicago saying very little, but feeling a great deal.

47

## "YOU LEFT YOUR HAT"

On Saturday, May 17th, 1862, Erastus Hicks arrived at the six-story Sherman House hotel, reputed to be the finest building in the city. The Sherman House boasted amenities such as steam heat, gas lighting, and a restaurant with a French chef. It was situated on Randolph Street between Clark and LaSalle Streets, across from the northern edge of Courthouse Square. On the same block were two establishments that caught Erastus's attention. The first was the office of Otto Steitz, sign and banner painter, and the second was the shop of G. F. Frazza, wig maker, hair cutter and perfumer.

Erastus considered that he might have something in common with each of these gentlemen, though not the same thing in each case. With the sign painter, he presumed to share a common trade interest, since during his travels Erastus had painted signs and banners as often as he had painted portraits. With the Italian hair cutter, Giovanni Frazza, Erastus hypothesized a less obvious mutuality, one that might only be hinted at, but which arose out of the affinity of tastes indirectly suggested by wigs, hair cutting and perfume. There was in fact another wig and perfume purveyor on the same block, a Mr. F. Hudson, Jr. But Erastus felt that Mr. Frazza, since he had added hair cutting to his repertoire, seemed the more promising.

Upon his father's death, Erastus had come into possession of considerable wealth. He thought seldom of the luxuries that money afforded, but there were one or two indulgences that roused his interest. He was fond of a good cigar, when one could be found, and so he noted that around the corner from Mr. Hudson's wiggery was the shop of William Daniels, whose sign proclaimed "tobacco and segars." Between the sign painter, the hair cutter and the tobacconist, Erastus felt he had much to explore.

Once he had checked into his fifth floor hotel room, Erastus began by taking a bath to clean away the dust of his travels. After his bath, he dressed, and then walked down to the lobby, whereupon he immediately had to walk back up to the fifth floor because he'd forgotten his hat. Once he had retrieved his hat and descended again to the lobby, he ventured down the street to pay a call on Mr. Steitz, the sign painter.

Mr. Steitz, as his name suggested, was German. He was of a certain age—some years older than Erastus was—an old world artisan, whose exemplary signs included both cursive script and fine serifs. When Mr. Steitz heard the jingle of the bell on his front door, he was working in his studio on a sign for a coffee merchant. Once he ascertained that Mr. Hicks was a colleague rather than a prospective customer, he invited Erastus back to the studio so that he might continue his work while the two men conversed.

Erastus asked him about the local painting business, about life in Chicago, about life in the old country, about the impact of the war on the local citizens. Erastus told Mr. Steitz something of his own story: of his life in Philadelphia, of traveling through the South before the war, and of his interest in portraiture. They discussed the intricacies of sign painting. They found they had a common interest in Goethe, the German poet and philosopher. Together they agreed that passions must be deeply felt. At last Erastus came around to a question of gossip. What was Mr. Steitz's opinion of his Italian neighbor, Mr. Frazza?

"Ah, the perfume gentleman. Well... he's a pompous peacock, always smelling of toilet water and soap, too precious if you ask me. Bah! But he does a good business ... has ladies galore in his shop ... none quite as pretty as he is, though," and with this Mr. Steitz rolled his eyes. "If you know what I mean."

Erastus allowed that he did know what Mr. Steitz meant, but suggested that as he was seeking to buy a bottle of perfume for a gift, he wondered if Mr. Frazza might not be the best man to call on.

"I'd go to Hudson around the corner if I was you," said Mr. Steitz. "I'm afraid Hudson's as much of a dandy as Frazza, but at least he doesn't smell of perfume."

"And what about the tobacconist? I'd like to find a good cigar."

"Don't smoke them myself," said Mr. Steitz. "I tried one once, and the ashes fell on my work—very messy. But I've heard no complaints about Daniels. He's a regular enough fellow."

So Erastus gleaned what he could from Mr. Steitz. He was intrigued by Mr. Steitz's comment about Mr. Frazza's prettiness. Although Mr. Steitz meant it as a derogatory remark, Erastus took it as complimentary—although Erastus did conjecture that Mr. Steitz's conception of prettiness might not be in agreement with his own.

Having collected such insights as he could from Mr. Steitz, Erastus walked two doors down Randolph Street to the wig, haircutting and perfume emporium of Giovanni Frazza. He found Mr. Frazza sitting on a dais at the rear of his shop adjusting the contours of a wig, which sat on a smoothly sculpted wooden bust that approximated a woman's head. The raised platform on which he worked also held an adjustable swiveling chair, intended, apparently, for haircutting customers. Erastus was glad to see that no customer occupied that chair. For the moment, Erastus was the only patron in Mr. Frazza's establishment.

When Erastus entered, Mr. Frazza interrupted his work and stood on the dais with one hand on his waist and the other at his side. He was, as Mr. Steitz had indicated, a striking figure. His attire was splendid. His posture was impeccable. His hair was immaculately arranged. The delicacy of his features was accentuated by his comportment. At first, he reacted to Erastus's arrival with a degree of wariness. But this hesitation passed like a cloud across the sun. He quickly surmised that he was in the presence of a sympathetic soul. Soon his eyes sparkled. He unloosed a limber animation. He stepped off the dais and came to shake Erastus's hand.

"How nice to meet a gentleman from Philadelphia," he said. "Life is not so refined here in the west. But we strive, we strive."

Mr. Frazza appeared to be about thirty years old. He was young enough to have fair features, thick wavy hair and a glowing complexion, but not so young as to be boyish in his manner. To Erastus he seemed ripe, elegant and sensitive, marred only by an excessive emanation of fragrance. Unlike Mr. Steitz, Erastus was inclined to overlook this defect in favor of Mr. Frazza's more comely qualities.

"In any event," said Erastus, removing his hat and setting it on a counter. "I see that you have succeeded in creating a haven of refinement here." He looked around the shop at the bottles of perfume. "And I'm told by your neighbor that your business is thriving."

"By my neighbor?"

"Yes, by Mr. Steitz, the sign painter. I visited him before coming here. I dabble in sign painting myself when the situation calls for it—though my greatest passion is for portraiture. Steitz and I had a long chat."

"Ah, Mr. Steitz! Well to be sure, he is a fine craftsman," said Mr. Frazza. "But his manner is so gruff."

"He is not an aficionado of perfume, I fear."

"So many men are coarse by nature."

"I suppose most of your customers are women."

"Oh yes—though I do sometimes see men who wish to buy a gift—not an unreasonable thing to do as far as I'm concerned—yet they cower in shame when they come in here lest someone should see them."

"Then you won't be surprised to learn that I too wish to buy a gift, and I hope I may do so brazenly."

"A gift ...." Mr. Frazza let his eyes linger for a moment in contact with Erastus's eyes. "For your wife?"

"No, no," Erastus raised his eyebrow. "I am not married. But I have come to Chicago at the behest of a friend. She herself is traveling here from Tennessee to rescue her lover, who is now a prisoner at Camp Douglas."

"A Confederate!"

"Indeed, a handsome young Lieutenant to whom she is betrothed. He was captured at the battle of Shiloh."

"So he's in the prison here?"

"Yes, she hopes to secure her lover's release, and then to marry him. She hopes that I may intercede in some way with the Union commanders at Camp Douglas. I have friends in Congress, you see, though really I don't know what influence I might have. I am here in the main, you could say, for moral support."

"I see."

"But I'm also here to see her servant. He is the brother of the Lieutenant who's in prison. I am quite fond of this brother. I painted his picture last year, a very handsome boy."

Mr. Frazza's eyes sparkled with curiosity. "You say this fellow is your lady friend's servant—yet it is his brother that the lady hopes to marry?"

"Yes. You see, the brothers have different mothers," explained Erastus. "The Lieutenant's mother was his father's wife. My friend's mother was his father's slave."

"Oh dear."

"Well I suppose it was an unfortunate origin. Yet I will tell you that this genesis produced the best-looking man I have ever known."

"Ah." Mr. Frazza clutched himself. "I see. I see." Then he cocked his head. "So who is it you wish to buy the gift for?"

"Ah, for the lady of course. Though I suppose the young man is fond of perfume as well. I had occasion to wash his feet once. It was a ceremony connected with the portrait. We used perfume as an anointment. He seemed quite excited by it."

Mr. Frazza nodded and took a step closer to Erastus. "So your friend is traveling here with the lady?"

"Yes. She's transporting an entourage of servants. She's bringing my friend, and another young slave, who actually belongs to me, and his sister."

"You mean to say you own a slave as well."

"Yes, I'm afraid I do. I bought the boy with the intention of setting him free. But it was agreed that he should remain in the South with his family while growing up. Now she's bringing him here—so I suppose I will have to look after him."

"How long will you be in Chicago?"

"I can't say. There are several dilemmas that must be resolved before I can leave. I'm staying at the Sherman House."

"Ah yes—the Sherman House—very nice. I was in there some years ago. Lovely rooms." Mr. Frazza paused for a moment. "Another gentleman showed me his room once."

Erastus raised his eyebrow. "Did he?"

"Yes."

"How unusual."

"He was an unusual gentleman." Mr. Frazza spoke with a mischievous smile.

Erastus felt the force of the innuendo growing between them. "It sounds as if this gentleman was friendly, at any rate."

"Oh yes—quite friendly."

"Was that the only time you were at the Sherman House?"

"I'm afraid so."

"Ah."

Mr. Frazza hesitated, then said, "I wonder if the rooms have changed." He hesitated again, then bit his lower lip. "Perhaps you'd show me your room."

Erastus smiled. Here once more was a window he might open. But as appealing as Mr. Frazza might be, Erastus did not wish to be distracted from his main objectives in Chicago. "I'm afraid I shan't have the time, dear fellow—though I'm sure it would be most pleasant."

It was evident from Mr. Frazza's eyes that he was crestfallen. But he tried to shrug it off. "Too bad. I so seldom meet a man who appreciates the same things I do."

Erastus looked at him with what he hoped was an affectionate paternal smile. "No doubt there are younger men than I who share your appreciation."

"Younger perhaps, but certainly not more agreeable."

"You're too kind!"

Mr. Frazza stared into the air for a moment, then turned

back to survey the collection of bottles on his counter. "So what kind of perfume do you think your lady friend would like?" he said. "Something floral, something spicy?"

"She's Southern," said Erastus. "So I think of honeysuckle."

"I have just the thing."

And so Mr. Frazza sold Erastus a bottle of perfume. On the whole, the visit did not disappoint Erastus. For when he traveled, he liked to locate kindred souls. Though he never acted upon these alliances, he found it reassuring to discover them. And then he felt that perhaps someday he might come back to such a friendship with an eye to advancing it. Having a collection of such possibilities was a source of contentment for him.

Erastus concluded his expedition by stopping in William Daniels' cigar store. There he found a decent cigar—though not, perhaps, of the caliber he might find in New York or Boston. Then just as Erastus was completing his purchase, the clang of a great bell in the tower of the courthouse across the street informed everyone in its range that it was time to eat dinner.

Erastus returned to the hotel in order to sample the work of the French chef, whose condescension to cook in Chicago was loudly extolled via signs in the hotel lobby—signs painted, perhaps, by Mr. Steitz. Erastus ate an excellent dinner, worthy of the pride of the French nation—then had a glass of brandy with his cigar in the smoking parlor, which was provided next to the dining room. In her letter, Dorothy had suggested that after arriving in Chicago, Erastus should leave a note with instructions about where to meet him, addressed to her in care of general delivery at the Chicago post office. While Erastus smoked his cigar and drank his brandy, he wrote Dorothy a note instructing her to call on him in his room at the Sherman House, and dispatched the note via a hotel messenger. In the meantime, he would pay a visit to Camp Douglas, to see what prospects there might be for providing assistance to Lieutenant Askew.

With these intentions settled, Erastus retired to his hotel room. He was just on the point of undressing for bed when there was a knock on the door. When he opened the door, he was startled to see Giovanni Frazza.

"I'm sorry to disturb you," said Mr. Frazza. "But you see, you left your hat." And indeed Mr. Frazza held forth Erastus's hat, which he had been holding behind his back.

Erastus did not doubt that he had left his hat at Mr. Frazza's store. He could not remember doing so. Certainly, he did not do so intentionally. Yet he could see in Mr. Frazza's eyes that a good deal of hope had been acquired in consequence of the forgotten hat.

"Thank you," said Erastus. "Please do come in."

Mr. Frazza stepped into the room.

"And so it seems you shall see if the rooms at the Sherman House Hotel have changed, after all," said Erastus.

"Yes," said Mr. Frazza, "it seems I shall!" And he smiled in a most agreeable manner.

48

## AN I BECOMES A J

$\mathcal{B}$y the time Dorothy, Ella, Cato, and Sammy had
arrived in Chicago, they were weary of travel.
Throughout the early days of their passage, Dorothy had imagined that upon arriving in Chicago she would go straight to
Camp Douglas. But now that they were at last in close proximity to the Camp, her desire to recuperate from the journey
was greater than her eagerness to fulfill her mission. She
thought at once of finding a hotel. But then she considered
that she ought to check for a message from Erastus Hicks. If he
were already in Chicago, it would be better to see him first, and
find out what he thought she should do.

After inquiring for directions, Dorothy pulled up to the
Chicago Post Office and Custom House, an imposing three-
story building at Dearborn and Monroe streets. As they
stepped out of the brougham, Sammy, Ella, Cato and Dorothy
were each awed by the tumult of the city. Accustomed as they
were to rural life, the hubbub in which they found themselves
seemed tremendous. There was a congestion of buggies, horses,

and people, each flying this way and that. Every citizen, it seemed, zealously pursued his or her private objective.

"There must be a fire someplace, seeing how everyone is dashing around," said Ella.

"I think this is how folks live up here," ventured Dorothy.

"It makes me dizzy just to watch them," Ella said.

And indeed all four of them stood looking about at the streets and buildings and the crowds of people with wonder. At last, Dorothy went into the post office and returned holding an open letter.

"Is it from Erastus?" asked Cato.

"Yes, he is already here. He's at a hotel called the Sherman House."

"Sherman House," said Ella. "Ain't that a bigwig Yankee general?"

"Ella, I doubt that the hotel is named after General Sherman," said Dorothy.

"Will the Yankees want to shoot us?" asked Sammy.

"We don't look like Rebels," said Cato. "As far as anyone can tell, we just arrived from Philadelphia."

"I don't know," said Ella. "They talk mighty funny up here. I think if they heard us say a word, the jig would be up."

"I can talk Yankee talk," said Cato. "You've got to speak fast and short."

"Maybe you'd like to try it out, then," said Dorothy, "by asking someone how to get to the Sherman House."

Cato did try it out. He picked an older man with a big moustache who appeared to be walking more slowly than anyone else. "Excuse me, sir, can you direct me to the Sherman House hotel."

At first, the man continued walking, as if he would not stop to answer the question. But then, surveying the hapless foursome, at last he did stop. "Sherman House?"

"Yes, sir."

"It is on Courthouse Square."

"Ah yes," said Cato, trying to be brusque in his enunciation. "And where is Courthouse Square?"

The man pointed north on Dearborn Street. "Go north to Randolph, then west to La Salle. You'll see it."

"Thank you, sir."

And so, at about 1:00 p.m. on Monday, May 19th, Dorothy drove the brougham to the Sherman House hotel on Courthouse Square. After learning that Mr. Hicks had been established in room 503 on the fifth floor, the four visitors climbed the stairs to call upon their friend. By the time the party arrived on the fifth floor landing, each of them was breathing rapidly.

"That's the most stairs I ever climbed up in my whole life," said Sammy, who put into words what they all felt.

The party waited for several moments in front of the door to room 503, and then at last Dorothy knocked.

When the door was opened, Dorothy, Ella, Cato and Sammy found themselves inside a room occupied by two gentlemen. There was an awkward moment before anything was said. Erastus was so surprised to see Cato in his wig and powder and fancy coat, comporting himself more like a gentleman than a servant, that he had to stop to calculate how he should word the introductions.

"This is Mr. Frazza," he began—and all eyes turned to look upon the gentleman who was in the process of putting on his coat. "Mr. Frazza has been kind enough to personally deliver an item of merchandise that I purchased from his shop." Erastus paused—as though he were weighing what to say next. "I asked him to have a cup of tea with me. As you will have seen, it is quite a climb to the fifth floor, and I thought it my duty to repay his kindness with an opportunity to rest."

Erastus turned to his guest. "Mr. Frazza, these are my friends from Tennessee, whom I mentioned to you." Mr. Frazza nodded in the general direction of the visitors. "Mr. Frazza and I have just been talking, and I mentioned to him that I hoped that you would receive my message—and so it seems you have!"

Again, there was much nodding all around. Then Dorothy spoke, "I am pleased to meet you. I am Miss Holland." Then gesturing toward each of her friends, she said, "This is Ella. This is Sammy. And this is Mr. Askew."

"Ah yes," said Mr. Frazza and he looked at each of the visitors in turn, looking with particular scrutiny at Mr. Askew. "Well, I suppose I'd better take my leave. Thank you, Mr. Hicks, for the tea. I hope that you will enjoy your visit to Chicago."

When Mr. Frazza had left, Erastus shook hands with each of his visitors and asked them to sit. "It is good to see you all," he said.

"No doubt you are wondering about Cato's appearance," said Dorothy. "We decided that he should travel in disguise. As I mentioned in my letter, he was compelled to run away following an incident at Hickory Grove. And we thought it would be safest if I were seen to be traveling with my husband."

"With your husband!"

"Don't you think I make a good husband?" asked Cato. "I've learned to speak just like Mr. Darcy from 'Pride and Prejudice.' And everyone thinks that we are man and wife."

"It is merely a charade, of course," said Dorothy. "But as far as I can tell, no one has suspected it."

"Humph," said Ella. "No one has paid us much mind one way or the other. Folks up here don't seem too friendly."

Erastus looked at Cato. "Is that a wig you're wearing?"

"I made it," said Ella. "Out of Dorothy's hair and a skull cap."

Cato stood up, and began to promenade about the room. "How do you like it?" he asked.

"I don't know if I would have recognized you," said Erastus. "You are ... transformed."

"He looks white," said Sammy—feeling somewhat ignored by the adults.

"Indeed," said Erastus. "And how have you been, young fellow?"

"I learned how to paint."

"Miss Holland wrote me that you painted on a very big canvas."

"Um ... I painted on the barn. I painted Venus. But then she died after that."

"Ah, gracious. Well it's good that you painted her. Now you will remember her."

Sammy nodded.

"And now you've come all this way."

"It's really been quite an adventure," said Dorothy. "We've used counterfeit names. I took money from my parents under false pretenses. I even borrowed Mr. Askew's brougham without telling him."

"Oh dear. Your parents must be quite alarmed by all this. Do they know where you are?"

"I left a letter explaining my intentions."

"And I suppose there is a reward for Cato's capture."

"Yes," said Cato. "And probably one for Jimmy's too."

"For Jimmy?"

"Yes, he had to run away even before we did. My father saw him in the yard and recognized him. Jimmy saved my father from the fire when his house burnt down, but somehow my father thinks that Jimmy tried to kill him."

"So where is Jimmy?"

"We plan to meet him here in Chicago," said Dorothy. "He left in such a hurry though; we did not make arrangements as we did with you." And then she added, "Of course, he's traveling on foot."

"So you don't know where he is?"

"No."

"Well if he walks all the way to Chicago from Tennessee, I should think it would take him several weeks."

"Yes," said Dorothy. "I don't imagine he will get here for yet another week or two."

"Under the circumstances, I think we'd better take a room for you here at this hotel," said Erastus. "Dorothy, for your future husband's sake, I think you ought to abandon the pretense that you're married. I can reserve a room for you and Ella and Sammy. The hotel can add a bed to my room for Cato."

"I have money to pay for our room," said Dorothy.

"Yes, but you ought to conserve your money," said Erastus. "And truly, since my father died, I have more money than I know what to do with. You must allow me to pay for your lodging. Some day after you're married, you can repay me with room and board in your house when I come to visit."

"But you've done so much for us already in coming here."

"I insist."

"Very well."

And so at Mr. Hicks's behest, Dorothy, Ella and Sammy were put into room 207 at the Sherman House hotel. They were relieved that their accommodation involved traversing far fewer stairs than room 503.

Notwithstanding the stairs, Cato was happy to lodge with Erastus. He was eager to talk to his friend about his relationship with Jimmy, and to see if, as he had speculated, Erastus had guessed the truth of it.

Erastus, for his part, was elated that Cato would now sleep in his room, with the possibility that further intimacy might ensue. From the moment he had seen Cato in gentleman's raiment, with his fine silk trousers, his embroidered vest, his felt hat and polished boots, Erastus's ardor had risen like adrenaline. The sight of Cato's delicately chiseled features powdered to a lighter hue and his seductive dark eyes framed with Caucasian locks, left Erastus weak-kneed and light-headed. For all his charm, Mr. Frazza did not arouse in Erastus a feeling that left him half as giddy as did Cato's smile. There was great allure in that which appeared unobtainable but which was now not so far out of reach.

Erastus was mindful of the fact that Cato had written to him a line of verse, 'I travel a road which no one beholds except my friend and lover,' which Erastus had concluded must refer to his friend Jimmy. For the moment, Jimmy was far away, and Erastus wondered what depth of feeling Cato had for his friend. Perhaps their affair was superficial, a product of proximity and isolation. Surely, Jimmy could not rival Erastus when it came to worldly matters. Erastus knew that Cato craved cultural tutoring, that he desired gentlemen's conversation and a gentleman's clothes, and that he would gain few insights about poetry, philosophy, art or literature from his field hand friend.

And yet Erastus was also mindful of the fact that he was much older than Cato, that Cato regarded him as a mentor and as a friend, and that while it may be pleasant to have common interests, attraction is fueled in no small measure by differences, by otherness, by complementation, and—not least —by brute physical appearance. Erastus did not have much faith in his own good looks, whereas he knew that Jimmy was a strapping, handsome he-man. In fact, Erastus himself had not been immune to Jimmy's sheer physical appeal.

Cato had articulated something of the complex feelings that arose from his racial mixing. While the white world regarded him as a slave, his fellow slaves felt him to be in a category set apart. Erastus guessed that Cato enjoyed a degree of kindred acceptance from Jimmy that he could not get from the other slaves, or, indeed, from Erastus. And so he feared that the racial expectations of whites and Negroes worked against him. He worried that Cato regarded him as carrying an air of superiority. Therefore, he was resolved to divest himself, as best he could, of any hint of aloofness—to treat Cato entirely as a peer.

"You are a gentleman through and through, I see," said Erastus as they sat in room 503 with two hours to fill before dinner.

"It amazes me," said Cato, "how differently I am regarded in this disguise."

"Well, perhaps it is not so much a disguise as you think. Perhaps it is the revelation of your natural state."

"It's odd that you should say that. Lately I have been pretending to be like Mr. Darcy."

"Ah, yes, Jane Austen."

"I spent many weeks hiding in the crawl space above Jimmy and Ella's cabin. While I was confined there, I finished reading 'Pride and Prejudice.' I don't think I could have endured the circumstances without it. But the only reason I got caught reading in the first place was that I was so engrossed in the novel that I didn't notice Judge Samuels approaching when I was out in the woods. Jane Austen was my downfall and my salvation."

"Well, perhaps it would be fairer to credit Jane Austen with your salvation and Judge Samuels with your downfall."

Cato smiled. "Don't worry. I love to read. I wish everyone knew how to read. I am so grateful that you taught me."

"Ah, my friend, such a gift is a blessing to the giver. Perhaps you will do the same. You can, you know."

"You mean I could teach someone to read."

"Yes, why not?"

"I tried to get Jimmy interested in learning. But he doesn't see any point in it."

"Well … no doubt he does not know what he's missing. Have you made an effort with anyone else?"

"No."

"You should take it up with Sammy. Children take to it easily."

"Sammy has certainly warmed to the idea of painting."

"I wish I could see his handiwork on the barn," Erastus said. "What do you think of it?"

Cato smiled. "It is ambitious."

"Oh that is tactfully put."

"Well—you see, that's what I like about Mr. Darcy. I admire tact."

"Certainly he was most tactful on the whole. But he began by being rude. It is a requirement in novels that characters must grow and change, just as they do in real life."

"Do they? There are some people in my life that I can't imagine changing. My father, for one."

"Ah yes, I heard what he did to you."

"All because I was reading."

"If he were to accept you for the gentleman you really are, he would never forgive himself for having raised you as a slave. He punished you because you dared to show yourself as an equal."

"He whipped me."

"Ah, my dear … was it quite painful?"

"Yes."

"Did he whip your back—or elsewhere?"

"Just on my back. He got himself worked up into a terrible frenzy. I passed out."

"Damn him!" Erastus stood. "Forgive me, Cato, but I must curse the man. Some men are not worthy of their own blood."

"Oh, you should have seen Jimmy. He was in as much of a frenzy as my father had been."

"Yes …. Yes, I understand the impulse for revenge. Violence begets violence."

"You know, the truth is, I believe Jimmy did intend to kill my father after he whipped me. But something changed his mind. He saved him from the fire instead."

Here was a point upon which Erastus could not begrudge Jimmy his due. "Thank God that he did so. I admire him for that. And I do believe that rescue is a more fundamental human impulse than murder."

"You believe in the goodness of mankind? Even with this war?"

Erastus sat down again. "The war has tested my faith, Cato."

Cato blinked his eyes. He had never before known Erastus to admit of any doubt. Nor had he ever heard Erastus curse, as he had just cursed Augustus.

"But men are like children," Erastus continued. "They want experience. Life supplies it. It is wearisome to pursue evil for a lifetime. Even the worst fellow must learn, eventually, that the greatest pleasures come from good."

"For me the greatest pleasures have come from love," said Cato. He hesitated a moment. "Once, when we first met, you foresaw that I would find love … and you were right …. I have."

Erastus colored. He did not want the conversation to turn

to this subject as yet. "Yes, of course. You are loved. Certainly by me."

"Oh Erastus, I ... have the greatest regard for you."

"But we need not speak of that." Then, to change the subject more forcefully, he said, "As terrible as it was, perhaps it has been good for your father to experience the loss from the fire. Tragedy begets growth."

"It was my home, too, that burned."

"Ah yes, of course. But you were not meant for life as a servant in such a home as that. I hope that does not sound callous. By rights, you should share a home with someone who respects and appreciates you ... as I do. Someone who will regard you as an equal."

Cato was not sure whether Erastus was offering to share his home with him ... and yet it did seem that he was saying as much. He had come to understand that Erastus was fond of him. After all, ... the man had gone so far as to kiss him goodbye when they last parted. Yet, he did not fully fathom the extent of Erastus's fondness. Certainly, it would be exhilarating to live with Erastus, to have his guidance. And there would be so much to talk about, so much to share. Yet he had never considered sharing the most intimate activities—that which he had shared, which he wished to go on sharing—with Jimmy. But for a moment, he did think of it. And he could see that Erastus was thinking of it too. "Are there novels, Erastus, in which a man loves two different people?"

Erastus laughed. "A ménage à trois? Yes, there are such stories. But I'm not aware of any happy ones. As a general rule, the men in such stories must eventually choose."

"I do not like making choices. I feel as if all my life I've had to choose between things that are not separate inside me."

"That which is blended in you is beautiful indeed," said Erastus, who was staring at Cato with unabashed desire.

"Would you like to draw me?"

Erastus blinked. He was startled. But slowly, he nodded.

"Do you have your charcoals?"

"Yes … but … do you mean draw you now, this very afternoon?"

"Why not? I would like you to draw me."

Erastus sucked in his breath. This was a turn he had not expected. He was not sure where Cato meant to lead him. "All right." Erastus went to the window and opened the drapery wider. They were up on the fifth floor, above the roof of the courthouse building across the street. The light was perfect, soft, cloudy, bright. "How do you want to pose?"

"In a classical manner," said Cato.

"Classical?"

"Yes … why not?"

"Well you should stand by the window. Let the light fall on half of you, while the rest is in shadow. It adds dimensionality to your figure."

Erastus went to his trunk and opened it. He had a sheaf of drawing paper pressed between two boards. He gingerly slid out a single sheet, and removed the top board to use as an easel. He took up a bundle of charcoal sticks of different dimensions. He went to a chair that was next to a small table, and turned it to face the window. In this chair, he sat, and onto the table, he laid his sticks.

Cato stood at the window. He was wearing his silk trousers, his embroidered vest, and a muslin shirt. He had already removed his felt hat and the wig. Now he unbuttoned his vest, removed it and tossed it aside.

Erastus sat with the board and paper in his lap. He picked up a stick of the charcoal. He was not sure what Cato intended to do—was not certain what Cato had meant by a 'classical manner.' He was breathing hard and his hand, when he looked at it, did not look steady.

Cato unbuttoned the top buttons of his shirt. Erastus had glimpsed this part of him before. He had seen the hairless chest peeking through his opened shirt—sometimes beaded with sweat. But now Cato's chest was dry and smooth, and the bright soft light made his skin glow.

Cato looked at Erastus and smiled. He saw that Erastus's eyes were wide. He unbuttoned the remaining buttons on his shirt, and took it off. He tossed this aside as well.

Now Erastus gulped. He had never seen Cato without a shirt. His hand began to move involuntarily. He wanted to draw him quickly. He wanted to get it done, to get it fixed on paper before Cato had a chance to change his mind. Cato's impulse had come with such haste, Erastus was not sure it would last.

Cato turned to a three-quarters profile. He saw that Erastus had begun to draw. "Wait!" he commanded.

Erastus stopped drawing. He lowered his hand to his side. He cocked his head. Cato nodded. Then he took hold of the cord that cinched his trousers at his waist. He began to untie it. All the while, he watched Erastus with keen interest. Erastus sighed audibly. Cato let the trousers fall to his feet. Now he was wearing nothing but his cotton underwear, his unmentionables.

Erastus shifted on his seat. He did not know what to think. He could see straightaway the clear outline of Cato's genitals in his undergarment. He had not expected this to come so suddenly. He felt that he ought to do something, to say something. Yet all he could do was stare. It was obvious that Cato had deliberately stripped in a provocative manner.

Erastus exhaled and raised his arm. He commenced, once

again, to draw. But Cato held up his hand. And again, Erastus paused.

Now Cato put his fingers into the top seam of his undergarment. Then, he looked up at Erastus, and when he was certain that he had Erastus's undivided attention, he slowly began to slide the garment down his legs. When he arrived at the crucial moment of unveiling, he saw in Erastus's eyes a reflection of the very instant when his penis came unsheathed from the garment. He pulled the cloth past his genitals and paused. As there was no more tension in the cloth to hold them up, he raised his hands and let the unmentionables fall gracefully to the floor. Then he bent down, picked them up, and tossed them aside. He stood then, with unabashed poise, absolutely naked, bathed in the soft, bright light of the window —aware that in this three quarter profile, his penis formed a gentle downward arch, while the nipples on his chest had stiffened in response to the coolness of the air.

And so, the moment had come at last. Erastus had imagined Cato's body. He had imagined it most vigorously on countless occasions. And he would almost have been relieved, if in this moment of which he had dreamed, he could see some imperfection, if he could feel some modicum of disappointment that might slow the beating of his heart. But Cato was twenty years old. Every inch and contour of his flesh was ripe and firm. And thus, there was no relief for Erastus's rapid pulse or his shallow breaths. He could no longer remain silent. "Ah, my boy," he cried out. "You are so beautiful, so beautiful." Instantly tears formed in his eyes. He suddenly did not want to go on. A feeling of shame and unworthiness washed over him. Why had God brought him this gift? He had not the skill. He had not the talent to draw such beauty. He felt absolutely impotent. It was too much for him. How had any of his forebears managed such a thing? How had Michelangelo done it?

Surely there had been some such boy, surely there had been a flesh and blood prototype for David, surely there was a moment just like this when Mr. Buonarroti had stood before some naked young model of extraordinary beauty, and wondered if he could accomplish the great thing that cried out to be done. How had Michelangelo wrested his erotic longing into aesthetic service? Erastus could barely hold the board flat on his lap. His own erection was so forceful that it pushed up against it.

Cato remained standing calmly, almost humbly, with a half-smile—watching Erastus struggle. He was acting entirely on impulse. And yet he felt that he had to do what he was doing. It was a very different thing from what he sought to do with Jimmy. He wanted to do this for Erastus's sake—as a kind of gift, a repayment for what Erastus had given him. Yet he also was aware that something in him was stimulated by Erastus's adoration. It was a stimulation that bordered on the erotic. He was aware that if he let his mind move a few degrees in that direction, it would be reflected in his own tumescence. But that was not the thing he wanted to do with Erastus. If he had not loved Jimmy, he might have let himself feel the force of arousal that Erastus's desire engendered in him. He might have allowed himself to begin to get hard. But he did love Jimmy— and he felt such a strong fidelity to Jimmy that he sincerely wished to remain chaste. Therefore, he turned his mind away from the thoughts where his exhibited nakedness would other- wise have led him. Even so, the very sensation of Erastus's eyes burning into his body was exciting. He could see, by the slant of Erastus's drawing board in his lap, that Erastus was fully aroused. And then, despite himself, he felt an ever-so-subtle pneumatic movement stir below his waist.

Erastus, of course, saw this too. He saw Cato's penis stretch half an inch—not nearly as much as it was capable of doing.

The stretching was almost entirely at the tip of Cato's penis, in the area of the foreskin. The effect was to make a J out of an I, but not enough to elevate the organ to a more perpendicular state. Yet it was something; it was an acknowledgment of reciprocated sexual feeling. There was simply no other explanation for such stirrings. Erastus was certain that Cato knew full well what was happening. He had seen the way in which Cato had glanced at his own lap. And Erastus had all he could do to keep from throwing down his board and rushing up to kneel before his beloved. But he didn't. He could not. He felt constrained by honor. He did not regard such preliminary stirring as had occurred in Cato as sufficient invitation to act. And he was, after all, a gentleman. He had been asked to draw Cato in a classical manner. He himself wanted to draw the boy. Drawing was at the very core of his soul. And so, he waited. He watched the pendulous organ with voracious scrutiny. Once he saw that the elongation had paused, and that no further distending was occurring, and when after several moments it was clear that this was the boundary which Cato had marked in his feelings or achieved—at least—through his own volition, Erastus raised the charcoal up above the paper—and through the most profound force of will, he began, once again, to draw.

In time that which began with a carnal charge, was transformed by degrees into the concentration that craft demanded. Erastus put all of his skill into the drawing. Cato stood still. The erotic stirrings abated. All in all, it took Erastus about ninety minutes to complete his portrait. And when it was done, he said simply, "I'm finished."

Cato turned around. And then for the first time Erastus saw the scars on Cato's back. The skin had healed from the whipping, but it was no longer smooth and lustrous as it was on the rest of his body, but defaced with rough, ragged violent stripes. The mutilation was all the more heartrending because of its contrast with the rest of Cato's body. Erastus stood instantly, and walked up to Cato. He hugged him. He touched the skin on his back with his fingers, and caressed it tenderly. "You are altogether beautiful," he said.

"Thank you." Cato knew what Erastus had just seen, and what this last compliment had meant.

And then, since there was nothing more to be said, Cato put his clothes back on, and the two men prepared to go down to dinner.

# 49

# JIMMY POURS THE PUNCH

*M*r. Ambrose and Mr. Jackson were the owners of the catering firm located on Clark Street near Courthouse Square that Mr. Mack recommended to Jimmy as a likely employer. Jimmy went directly to Clark Street where a stranger pointed out to him the office bearing the sign for Ambrose & Jackson. In the office, Jimmy was directed to speak to Mr. Jackson, a well-dressed colored gentleman, whose rotundity served as a visible affirmation of the success that his business enjoyed. Jimmy told Mr. Jackson that he was ready and willing to work, that he had just come from D. B. Fisk Millinery—for whatever that was worth—and that he lived on the south side with his uncle George.

All this Mr. Jackson listened to, though he was frequently interrupted by staff members who had messages of one kind or another pertaining to the day's catering concerns. To Jimmy it appeared that the firm was staffed entirely by Negroes and that none of them was so very different in speech or bearing than Jimmy himself. Jimmy emphasized to Mr. Jackson that he had experience serving table, that he had done so on the south side, though he did not mention how far south this had actually been, and that he was quite familiar with the deferential manner which Mr. Jackson had indicated was wanted by wealthy diners.

"Nay, not just deferential, but invisible," said Mr. Jackson. "They must hardly realize that you are there."

"Yes, sir. I'm nimble and about near invisible."

After looking him up and down and tapping his hand on the table one or two times, Mr. Jackson told Jimmy that he could work on a trial basis. He must prove his fitness to handle the job for two weeks before Mr. Jackson would consider making him a full time employee.

Jimmy was immediately put under the tutelage of Mr. Nat Johnson, the experienced and educated headwaiter who had been with the firm for several years. Nat Johnson took Jimmy to the linens and uniform storeroom, measured him with a tape, and then selected for him an official uniform similar to that worn by all Ambrose & Jackson employees. Mr. Johnson remarked that it was fortunate that Jimmy had happened to have his interview with Mr. Jackson. Mr. Jackson was the nice fellow that everyone liked. Mr. Ambrose, on the other hand ... well, he was not anyone's favorite—except perhaps for Mrs. Ambrose, who worked in the kitchen and supervised all the cooking. Mr. Ambrose ran the financial end of the business, while Mr. Jackson supervised the day-to-day operations.

"What you got to remember," said Nat Johnson. "Is that no matter how hungry you are, don't ever eat any of that food before it goes out to the customers. If Mr. Ambrose heard about you doing anything like that, he'd kick you out right quick."

Jimmy vowed that he would not even think about the food in that way, although he had to swallow when he said this, since, considering how terribly hungry he was, it was hardly true that he could control such thoughts entirely. Nat Johnson, however, seemed satisfied that Jimmy gave a proper answer to each question put to him—and immediately assigned Jimmy to a job. Jimmy would begin work at a reception at Buters & Company, which was an auction house on Dearborn Street. Hors-d'oeuvres would be served at 3 p.m.—accompanied by tea and punch. Jimmy's job would be to work with Nat serving the punch. Each of them would serve from punch bowls at opposite ends of a long table. The tea service was to be in the center of the table, and the hors-d'oeuvres were to be set in between the tea and the punch bowls. Three other workers would handle the tea and hors-d'oeuvres service. Thus, there would be a total of five uniformed Ambrose & Jackson waiters serving at the reception.

Jimmy soon discovered that this 3 pm reception was a regular affair, which was catered, by Ambrose & Jackson once each week immediately preceding Buters & Company's Friday 4 pm auction. From the worker who handled the tea service, Jimmy ascertained that he could expect to receive greater patronage at his punch bowl than his comrade would receive at the teapot. The punch, he was told, was a very nice rum-punch, which Buters & Company had found to be a more elevating libation than tea, elevating, that is, with respect to the auction prices. Jimmy learned further that his immediate predecessor at Ambrose & Jackson, who had also operated the punch bowl, had been discharged the week before when he had been observed to be drunker than were the patrons at the auction. How his predecessor had achieved that state was a mystery, since no one had actually seen him sample any of the punch.

After the catering crew arrived at Buters and Company and all the food had been neatly arranged on the table, Nat

Johnson demonstrated to Jimmy the proper method for filling a cup with punch.

"You must always have several cups filled with punch already sitting in front of the bowl for folks to take up. Those folks who've already had a cup and have come back for seconds, will walk up to you with their empty cup in hand. You dip the ladle like this. See how just one dip of the ladle will fill the cup. Be sure you hold the ladle over the bowl so that if anything spills it won't spill on the tablecloth."

"What if somebody holds out their cup for punch, but they don't hold it right over the punch bowl?" Jimmy asked.

"Ah, yes," said Mr. Johnson. "In that case you say, 'allow me' and you take the cup from out of the gentleman's hand, you hold it over the bowl and fill it, then you hand it back to him. Be sure to keep your eyes on the ladle and the cup and not on the gentleman you're serving."

"How many cups are they allowed to drink?" asked Jimmy.

"They can drink as much as they want. However, if you get the same fellow coming back quite a few times, and if that fellow looks like he's getting wobbly on his feet, you'd better start pouring less than a full cup. But if you do that you've got to do it so that the man doesn't notice."

When the doors to the reception opened at three o'clock, there was already a substantial group of customers waiting to enter. It was evident from their attire that the clientele of Buters & Company were quite well to do. They were also quite hungry, it seemed, since they all came straightaway to the reception table and began to collect refreshments.

For the first thirty minutes Jimmy had a great deal of cup filling to do—and it seemed that no matter how many new or returning cups he filled, there were still more cups waiting to be replenished. At forty past the hour there was a lull. Several patrons were still standing in the vicinity of the food table, but, for the moment, no one's cup wanted filling. Jimmy was able to ask the nearest hors-d'oeuvres server what exactly it was that was being sold in the auction.

"They auction all sorts of things: rugs, pictures, silverware, jugs, candleholders, plates, jewelry."

"Where's it all come from?"

"They bring it out from the back of the house."

That wasn't what Jimmy meant, but he nodded anyway. Just then he saw that a young woman who had already come to him for refills twice before, was back again. She smiled with a brightness that appeared to have been enlivened by the punch.

As she held out her cup she said, "I'm an abolitionist you know."

Jimmy nodded, but he did not look up from his operations with the ladle. Nevertheless, he could tell, from the sound of her dress brushing against the serving table, that she was wearing a fancy hoop dress.

"I think slavery is an abomin ..." She paused. "... I think it's just awful." The woman was holding her cup over the punch bowl, but her hand was noticeably unsteady. Jimmy had to follow her cup about with his ladle as the cup wobbled around. In response to her unsteadiness, he was forced to pour the punch very slowly. He decided that it would be best if he did not fill this particular cup entirely.

"I hope that Abe Lincoln frees all the ... oh, oh." As she spoke, she stepped back and tipped her cup, and in doing so, spilled punch onto her dress.

Jimmy picked up a napkin and reached out to blot the spill. But he quickly thought better of it and handed the napkin directly to the young woman.

"Oh dear, papa will not like this." She dabbed at the spill but her efforts had little effect. She looked up at Jimmy. "Do you have some water?"

Jimmy was not sure if he had some water or not. "One moment, Miss," he said, and he ran to the other end of the table to ask Nat Johnson what to do.

"Go look down below by the tea. There's a jug of water under the table there," said Nat. "Take a napkin and dip it in the water for her to use."

Jimmy took a napkin, and at the middle of the table he bent down and dipped it into the jug, which was hidden from the view of the diners by the tablecloth which covered the serving table. He then brought the wetted cloth back to his guest and handed it to her. Now again she dabbed on the stain and it was transformed into a large wet area on her dress, but its color was not greatly diminished.

"Now what have you done?" An older man who had come up to the young woman with a scowl on his face spoke this.

"Oh papa, I didn't do anything."

"Then what has happened to your dress, Lily?"

"It was an accident."

"Have I not just purchased that dress for you? Do you think so little of money that you cannot take care of your own clothing?"

"But papa, I couldn't help it. The waiter spilled punch on me—that's all."

Now the older man turned his gaze upon Jimmy and his expression was very black. Jimmy, for his part, upon hearing himself thus accused, was barely able to conceal his outrage.

"I did not do that," said Jimmy.

"Boy, do you contradict my daughter?"

"Sir, an accident occurred, but I did not cause it."

Having noticed the commotion, Nat Johnson came around from the other end of the table, the better to mediate the situation. "Is everything all right, sir?" he asked the older gentleman.

"Are you the headwaiter, then?" asked the older man.

"I am."

"Then no, by George, everything is not all right. One of your staff has spilled punch on my daughter's very expensive dress, and now he has the impudence to deny it."

Jimmy could not restrain himself. "I didn't spill any punch! Mr. Johnson, what happened was, this lady spilled it on herself."

Now the father whirled around from Nat Johnson to Jimmy. "What! Is this how guests are to be treated at Buters and Company? Will you accuse my daughter to cover up your own clumsiness?"

"I poured a little bit of punch straight into her cup. She stepped back from the table and then she spilled it on her dress," said Jimmy, keeping his voice as calm as he could.

The young woman, who had been watching this exchange with a dazed look on her face, now found everyone looking at her. "I did not spill it, papa" she said. "You know I am very careful with new clothes."

"However the spill occurred," said Nat Johnson. "I can assure you, sir, it was undoubtedly an accident. I suppose the stain can be easily cleaned."

"We shall see about that," said the old man to Nat Johnson. "I shall expect your employer to pay for the cleaning bill for this dress when I submit it." Then he turned again to look at Jimmy. "And this inept boy should not be allowed to serve drinks!"

Now Jimmy, though he well understood that it would be better for him if he should say or do as little as possible, could not countenance such injustice with meek subservience. He dropped the ladle loudly into the punch bowl—which caused some of the punch to splash over onto the tablecloth. "I am not clumsy. I ... I am nimble. I poured eighty three cups of punch without spilling a drop!"

The young woman shook her head violently at this point. "I was very polite to him," she said with a sneer. As she spoke, she took several steps backwards—looking for a moment almost as if she might trip.

"Look at her," cried Jimmy. "She's had too much to drink. That's why she spilled her cup. She's drunk!"

"I'm not the least bit drunk," protested the girl, who in response to this accusation abandoned any pretense of politeness. "I haven't had two cups of punch." She lurched forward. "Papa, I think he did it on purpose so he could try to touch me with that napkin."

Now the father was livid to the point of raising his fist in the air. "Oh, dear God. Did he touch you, Lily?"

"I didn't let him," she said.

Now Nat Johnson, who was by no means convinced that Jimmy had done anything wrong, was nonetheless sufficiently experienced in the ways of the world to realize that no good could come of these events. If he were to ask any of the others whether or not anyone had witnessed the unfortunate accident, he would, he was certain, enrage the father even further— simply by questioning the daughter's word. The acrimony had escalated to such a degree that now there were accusations of improprieties, which were nearly criminal in their implications. He quickly concluded that the most expedient way to defuse the situation would be to offer the aggrieved parties retribution. "I assure you, sir," he said to the old man. "That Buters & Company does not abide any inconvenience to its patrons to be caused by our staff. If this waiter has spilled punch, I am certain that it was due to an accident and not as the result of any improper intention. However, we will be happy to accept the cleaning bill for your daughter's dress, and

I can guarantee you, sir, that this waiter ..." and here he pointed to Jimmy, "... will be discharged."

Upon hearing these words, Jimmy raised the ladle, which was full of the dregs of the punch. He felt a tremendous impulse to toss it in the faces of all three of his accusers. But instead, he raised it to his lips and, glaring defiantly at Nat Johnson, slurped the liquid loudly into his throat. Then, without taking his eyes off Nat Johnson, he reached over and grabbed a handful of the hors-d'oeuvres, and proceeded to eat them. Upon seeing this, the young woman shrieked with disgust.

"You are discharged," said Nat Johnson. "Go back to the office immediately and turn in your uniform."

By now, the rest of the staff had gathered near Jimmy's end of the counter, and several other guests had drifted back to the refreshment table to see what was going on. Having inferred that under the circumstances he certainly would not be paid any wages for his work, Jimmy picked up a napkin and filled it with bits of food from the table. Then he raised the napkin up high—and, with a triumphant smile on his face, marched out of the room carrying the napkin above his head past murmurs in the crowd, as though he held a trophy prize from a great adventure.

When he got out to Dearborn Street, Jimmy stopped long enough to eat all the food he had gathered. Then he took the napkin and carried it to the offices of Ambrose & Jackson. There he took off his uniform, and put back on the clothes given to him by Mr. Mack. Then, without saying a word to Mr. Jackson or to Mr. Ambrose, Jimmy left the office. His career as a caterer was ended.

All this had transpired on the same day that Jimmy had arrived in Chicago. And though he still had no money, he had at least eaten something—first he'd eaten the sandwich he found in the refuse bin behind the restaurant, and then he had eaten the snacks pilfered from the reception. His adventures in the city thus far had not left him with a favorable impression of the North. And now as the sun was setting, and he found himself so poorly circumstanced as to be walking about the city streets wondering where he might sleep, he began to wonder for the first time if he should ever have run away at all. Might it not have been better to endure a whipping at the hands of old Askew than to be penniless and homeless in such a place, where copperheads might chase him for no apparent reason, and drunken white girls accused him of spilling punch? If it were not for the fact that Cato was already on his way to meet him, he would be more than a little inclined to go back to the Illinois Central and go straight south to home.

But then as he thought of Cato his mood changed. His anger gave way to longing. He was in great need of seeing a friendly face. And as he reflected upon rejoining Cato, his thoughts turned further out to the future. He wondered, what would they do, the two of them, in this foreign, unfriendly place? How would they live? He supposed Cato would have managed the whole episode with the punch in a different way. Cato would perhaps have been deferential, apologetic, doing what he could to smooth things over. And the white girl, he imagined, would not have been so quick to accuse his more eloquent friend. So his thoughts alternated between indignation and longing, between pride at saving his dignity and regret about losing his one great chance for a job.

When night had fallen, he made his way to an alcove in an alley where he found and ate the remains of a discarded sandwich. There in the darkness, he lay down, and, despite the acrid smell of urine, he slept.

## "I REALLY LOVE HIM"

When Dorothy Holland and Erastus Hicks arrived at Camp Douglas, they were told at the gate that no visitors were allowed. Dorothy was permitted to write a note, which the gate sentry assured her he would have delivered to the prisoner in question. She asked if she could call the next day for a reply and was told that she could. In her note, Dorothy wrote that she had arrived in Chicago, that she was with Mr. Hicks, and that they were going to attempt to intercede on William's behalf. She asked William to reply with a note of acknowledgment and to report the status of his health and well-being. But when they returned the next day Dorothy's note had been sent back to her unopened.

"We do not have a Lieutenant Askew in this prison, ma'am," the guard said.

"There must be some mistake."

"Perhaps you'd better write a note to the commanding officer, Colonel Tucker," the guard suggested.

Dorothy wrote a note to Colonel Tucker, and she and Erastus were told to wait for a reply. For his reply, the Colonel sent back word that Miss Holland and Mr. Hicks should be brought to his office.

Dorothy could only imagine one kind of news that would be considered so delicate that it must be delivered in person. But Colonel Tucker simply wanted to assure himself of the identities and the intentions of those who had inquired about the man he had recently paroled, since that information must be treated as confidential. When he discovered that the visitors were the parolee's betrothed and a Northern gentleman, he was reassured about their intentions. Yet he still was cautious.

"It is most unusual for a prisoner's fiancée to travel hundreds of miles to visit him in the enemy's prison," said Colonel Tucker. "I would have thought your allegiance to the Southern cause would keep you from traveling in the North and consorting with Northerners?"

"I have no allegiance to the Southern cause," said Dorothy. "Indeed, I have opposed this war and Lieutenant Askew's participation in it from the beginning."

Upon hearing this Colonel Tucker recalled the story told to him by Lieutenant Askew of the affianced lover who had renounced the war and had extracted a promise from him that he would commit no violence. And as he remembered the behavior that this promise had led to, his manner grew cold. He spoke officiously. "Lieutenant Askew took an oath of loyalty to the Union," he said. "He has sworn to remain north of the Ohio River. He was paroled last Saturday and left the camp. That is all that I can tell you. He is no longer here. And now I must bid you good day."

And so Erastus and Dorothy were dismissed and left the camp.

Dorothy was astonished by what they had heard. "He swore to remain north of the Ohio River," she exclaimed. "That means he cannot go back home."

"Not unless he breaks his oath," said Erastus.

"But where can he be?"

"I suppose he could have gone into the city in order to write you a letter."

"Then we must find him."

"Yes, but now we have two men to find," said Erastus. "We must find William, if he is still here, and we must find Jimmy, as soon as he arrives here."

"Yes, of course, but how can we find them?"

"I don't suppose either of them has much money."

"William may have had money with him," said Dorothy. "I just don't know. I never imagined something like this could happen. Jimmy had some money from his family, thought not a great deal."

"We should check the local hotels," said Erastus. "That is the logical place to begin. As a starting point, I think we should check with the Sherman House. For all we know William may have taken a room there."

And so they resolved to return to the Sherman House. Once they determined that there was no William Askew staying at the Sherman House, they decided to divide the task of checking the remaining hotels. Dorothy would go with Ella and Sammy to check the Briggs House and the Adams House, while Erastus and Cato would check the Tremont House and the Matteson House.

Now it happened that William had found his way with his father Augustus to the Tremont House on Lake Street, and it was there that they took lodging. Since Augustus had speculated that Dorothy and two of the Holland slaves would by now already have arrived in Chicago, Augustus and William had likewise concluded they should embark upon a search of the other hotels. They decided to go out together to look for Dorothy, since it was understood that given the circumstances it would be most awkward for Augustus to encounter Dorothy alone.

Finally, Jimmy, who had similarly concluded that Dorothy, Ella, Sammy and Cato should by now have arrived in Chicago —had also determined to look for them at a hotel. But whereas Dorothy and Erastus had simply asked for and received a list of the names and addresses of other Chicago hotels from the Sherman House, and William and Augustus had done the same at the Tremont House, Jimmy had no one to ask for such a list, nor any way to read such a list had he been able to obtain one. Furthermore, he was aware that he would not even be allowed to enter a hotel by himself unless he was seen to be accompanying a white guest to whom he might be understood to be a servant with legitimate duties in the hotel. Therefore Jimmy was obliged simply to wander about the streets of downtown Chicago looking for a likely hotel. He had an idea that if he lingered somewhere in the vicinity of the entrance to a hotel, he might, with luck, spot his friends coming or going.

After walking up and down the streets for more than an hour, Jimmy at last came upon a building that he judged might be a hotel. It was a large brick building into which many people were going and from which many others were coming. He positioned himself across the street. At first, he stood in a doorway. Then he paced up and down the block. It seemed necessary to keep moving in order to avoid calling attention to his loitering. After a while, he began to wonder whether or not the building in question was really a hotel. And so, when he saw a passer-by whose face looked friendly, he gathered up his courage and spoke.

"Excuse me, sir," he said. "I am a stranger here; is that a hotel across the street?"

Surprised, the man looked up, and then looked at the

building across the street to which Jimmy had pointed. "Why yes, that is the Tremont House, which is indeed a hotel."

"What street is this?"

"We are on Lake Street."

"Thank you, sir."

Now that he was certain that he was watching a hotel, Jimmy settled in to his job as a lookout. At first, he was patient. But with time, he thought more and more about how hungry he was feeling. As the hours ticked by there were moments when he reasoned that he might go back to the alley behind the restaurant, where he could again search for leftover food. But then he argued to himself that it was far more important that he find Dorothy and Cato. Once he found them, he told himself, he would have no further worries about food or sleep—and he would at last be reunited with Ella and Sammy and, most agreeably of all, with Cato. And so he stifled his hunger as best he could, and kept close watch on each person who came and went from the Tremont House.

Jimmy had taken up his post watching the hotel early in the morning. By the time the noon lunch hour had arrived, the hunger gnawing at his stomach grew harder and harder to stifle. He had eaten nothing since he'd consumed the hors-d'oeuvres he'd snatched from the auction, followed by a half-eaten discarded sandwich the day before. He found himself wondering if it might not be safe to take a break from his watch to find some food. It was lunchtime, after all. Dorothy and the others, he imagined, were likely to be sitting down to a nice meal, and thus not at all apt to be coming or going from the hotel during this hour. As he stood weighing the reasons to go against the grounds to stay, he realized that there were two men coming out of the Tremont hotel whose likenesses were more familiar to him than those of anyone he had seen in weeks. He saw Augustus and William Askew! Jimmy stepped back quickly into the shadow of a doorway. He could hardly believe his eyes. William, by rights, should be in prison. Augustus, just as rightfully, should be back in Tennessee. Yet here they were as plain as day, walking out of the Tremont hotel in Chicago. The two men stopped for a moment out on the sidewalk. Then William held up a piece of paper upon which something was written, and pointed, as though indicating a direction. After that, they walked off, rounded the corner and disappeared.

Jimmy was dumbfounded. He could not imagine any explanation for what he had seen. Yet he could not deny having seen it. As he contemplated the implications of what had passed before his eyes, it occurred to him that if Augustus and William were in the hotel, Dorothy and the others might be there as well. But then he remembered that Cato had run away from Augustus, and so he concluded that it was not possible that Cato could also be in the hotel. When he came to this conclusion, he reasoned that Dorothy, Cato, Ella and Sammy must have taken lodging at some other hotel.

He made up his mind to leave, to go back to the alley behind the restaurant in search of food. There was no longer a reason to stay at the Tremont. In fact, there was good reason to get further out of sight. After all, it was because Augustus Askew had spotted him back home that he had had to run away in the first place. But just then, he saw two more men come around the corner across the street. Jimmy stopped. Once again, he stepped back into the shadows.

Jimmy had no doubt that one of the two men was Erastus Hicks, the painter, who in Jimmy's mind had no more business being in Chicago than Augustus Askew. The painter ought to be back in Philadelphia. Jimmy was certain the man had returned there many months ago. But the other man! The familiarity of the other man shocked him. He looked very much like Cato. Yet the man walking with Erastus Hicks was white. This man was wearing a fine felt hat from which locks of straight brown hair extended. He wore silk trousers, an embroidered vest, polished boots. It was not possible that such clothes could belong to Cato. And yet! The gentleman's walk, his bearing, and most of all, his face, were unmistakable. Jimmy could not deny that he was looking at his very own friend, his fellow slave, and his lover. But why was Cato with Erastus Hicks instead of Dorothy? Why was he wearing such clothes? Why did he have false hair? And where, then, were Dorothy, Ella and Sammy?

Jimmy wanted to shout these questions out across the street. But something held him back. Something told him he should wait a moment, that he should watch a bit longer to better ascertain what was happening. Erastus and Cato seemed to be headed for the Tremont hotel. But then they stopped in front of a shop window. Since Jimmy could not read, he could not tell what the sign above the shop said. But he could see quite plainly that books were displayed in rows in the window, and so he presumed that the shop was a bookshop.

Erastus and Cato stopped in front of the window with their backs turned to Jimmy, who was across the street. Erastus said something and lifted his left hand to point at a book in the window. At the same moment he silently raised his right arm and swung it behind Cato's back and let it come to rest on Cato's shoulder. Then—with barely a second of hesitation— Cato, likewise, raised his left arm and let it rest on the shoulder of Erastus Hicks. There was in this gesture an easy and intimate familiarity. The two men stood there for just a moment—like comrades in arms—with their hands squeezed around each other's shoulders. Then they turned, and a certain look passed between them. Jimmy saw Cato's face clearly. Cato was beaming—smiling and laughing—and he said something that caused Erastus Hicks to laugh also. Then the two men continued walking, and they walked directly into the Tremont hotel.

Jimmy, seeing them turn into the hotel, called out Cato's name. He bolted out of the shadow, then, with sudden impulse, ran across the street, shouting Cato's name. He got quickly up to the entrance to the hotel. He began to open the door. But as he did so, a tall man in a uniform grabbed hold of the door and stopped him.

"What is your business boy?"

"My friend is ... I ...."

"Your friend?" The doorman looked down at Jimmy with professional disdain.

"I need to speak to a friend of mine. He went in the hotel."

"This hotel is for guests only. Walk away and go about your business, and there will be no trouble."

Jimmy looked into the man's eyes. He could see that there was no hope of reasoning with such a man. He called out Cato's name one last time—but his voice was blocked by the panel of the door, which had been closed in his face. He turned and walked back across the street.

Jimmy stood again in the vicinity of a doorway. His first thought was that he could wait until Cato came out of the hotel again. But time had slowed down. From the moment Jimmy had witnessed that affectionate embrace between Cato and Erastus Hicks, he felt as if he had stepped outside of normal time, and was now watching a mental review of what had happened. He watched himself run across the street. He watched himself shouting Cato's name. He watched himself being rebuffed by the doorman. But as he was watching these actions, he was also aware of an alternative sensation. A tremendous aching pain had detonated inside him. And the pain was so distracting that he could hardly focus his thoughts.

563

He tried to concentrate. He tried to construct painless reasons and explanations for what he had seen. But these efforts were like the efforts of a man in a nightmare who cannot make his legs move. He was helpless against the onslaught of thoughts, which told him that what he had seen was evidence of the very thing he had feared back when Cato first confessed that Erastus Hicks had kissed him. He saw. He felt. He intuitively understood—that something had changed, that there was now some new kind of intimacy between Cato and the older man.

But it was not the affection between Cato and Erastus Hicks by itself that had caused Jimmy's pain. It was also the vision of Cato in the guise of a white gentleman, the vision of Cato in his fine clothes, the vision of Cato engrossed in animated conversation discussing books with his learned friend, the vision of the half-white mulatto who now appeared to have entirely shed that half of himself which the world had judged to be chattel but which had been his bond with Jimmy; it was that vision that burned a hole in Jimmy's heart.

"Oh Cato, Cato!" Jimmy heard his own voice speak out with a weak, muffled sound that no one else could hear. Cato had told him again and again, "I'm not white." But this was the very thing Jimmy had always feared—the thing that had actually come to him as his first impression of Cato. "You seem almost white," he had said. And now, as if to prove that this very fear had actually been a premonition, Cato had made himself white. The deception, the opportunism, the betrayal were as wormwood to Jimmy.

And yet … Jimmy could not deny the happy look he had just seen on his friend's face. He wanted such happiness for him. He truly did. Nor could Jimmy say what he himself would choose to do if he too could don fancy clothes, wear impostor hair, or powder his face, knowing he might thus free himself of subjugation. Would he not also be tempted? He certainly knew as well as anyone how much there was to gain —and how much wretchedness and difficulty might thus be avoided.

Jimmy was also aware that he did not fully know Cato's heart. How could he? He had never experienced being mistaken for white. He had never been an outcast among his own people. He had never looked at a man like Augustus Askew and wrestled with the feelings a son must own for his father. Instead, Jimmy had assured him, "You can't help who your father is." Jimmy had been the first to exonerate Cato of his blood. He had teased him and lovingly guided him to rebuke his uppity ways. Jimmy had affectionately subverted the righteousness Cato might have felt about his station. And Cato had responded to this with something like relief, as though he had needed only the slightest encouragement to slip fully and joyfully into his Negro skin.

Then there was the special bond between them—the one thing that they could never share with anyone else. Had Cato not said, "I love you." Had he not yielded his most private part to Jimmy? Had he not taken Jimmy and all that Jimmy stood for deep inside him?

But now again there was the painter—the painter who had ever worked and schemed to acquire the prize—as though to reassert the power of the white race to take possession with impunity, disregarding all other claims. Jimmy despised him. What did Jimmy have to offer compared to this rich white man? Jimmy who could not read, Jimmy who could not paint, Jimmy who knew nothing of poetry or novels or philosophy, Jimmy who had no money or power, Jimmy who had naught but the muscles in his arms and legs to call his own, Jimmy was keenly alive to the contrast between himself and Erastus Hicks.

But Jimmy was certain he had one thing that the painter

did not have. He was certain that he loved Cato more than anyone else ever could. And Jimmy further believed that his love was not merely that which is born of desire. Yes, he saw how attractive Cato was. Who would not respond to such loveliness? But this attraction had always been secondary. Cato's physical beauty was only the wrapping on a gift whose contents were the real treasure. It was the heart and soul of Cato that he loved. It was Cato's gentleness that he loved. He loved the playful goodness of Cato, and he knew that Venus had also loved this. He loved Cato's poise and composure, his generous spirit, his kind regard for everyone no matter the race. Jimmy even loved the scared rabbit in Cato, which he had shown in that awful moment when Jimmy was angry with him.

But what Jimmy judged to be in the eyes of Erastus Hicks was base lust, the perverse unseemly lust of an old man who ought to have kept his eyes off a boy who was set so far apart from him in age and station. Erastus Hicks could never see into the heart of Cato's life, see the day-to-day reality of it, or know what it was like to be a slave. Erastus Hicks was a man who simply bought what he wanted, as he had bought Jimmy's brother. He was a man who had used his wiles to seduce Cato, with reading and painting and exotic talk.

Jimmy could not deny that these things were good for Cato. He could not deny that he had seen how Cato's mind had blossomed under the painter's influence. Though he would never admit it to anyone, he had been proud of how quickly Cato had learned to read. Though it was mysterious to him, he had been no less proud of Cato's intellect, of his easy mastery of the worlds of poetry and novels, and of his subsequent desire to share these worlds with his field hand friend.

And now ... now that he had seen Cato with Hicks in an uninhibited moment—unaware that they were being watched —he could not deny the credibility of the happiness he saw.

And Jimmy allowed himself to indulge in a noble thought. "I should give him up to the painter," he thought. This thought came quietly, with no fanfare. It had no hidden motive behind it. It was not a thought behind which lay any spite. He did not taint this thought with a bitter reflection on how someday Cato might realize that no one had ever loved him as he did. Indeed, he told himself it was precisely because he loved Cato so much that such a thought could exist.

Why should Cato not have the things he longed for? Jimmy knew that Cato wanted to have someone to talk to about books and poetry and painting and music. Jimmy knew that Cato wanted to have fine clothes, wanted to have a library, wanted to walk with ease in the world. He knew that Erastus Hicks could give him these things. Moreover, Jimmy knew that he could only give Cato the opposite: hardship, uncertainty, and all the struggles that would attend two slaves who tried to make their way in a hostile world. What did it matter that Jimmy loved the heart and soul of Cato if he was so selfish as to deny him the opportunity to fulfill a greater destiny? For Jimmy imagined that if Cato had half a chance, if Cato were truly able to go into the world unencumbered by slavery, that he would undoubtedly become a great man. He would be a man of consequence—a man whose unique heart and intellect could affect the souls of other men. Jimmy did not know why he believed so strongly in Cato's potential for greatness. It was not something he had ever felt about anyone else—and yet there it was, a feeling as clear and undeniable as any he had known.

He let his imagination play with this belief. He could imagine that Cato might move to Philadelphia. There Cato could become a student—not just of Erastus Hicks, but a real student, sent to the university. And no doubt, Cato would enjoy the privileges of wealth: an expensive home, a private carriage, a library of books. Then someday Cato might in turn become a teacher. Perhaps he would even teach the slaves. He would do so with the benefit of having once been a slave. He would be a model of how a slave could rise up in the world, how a slave could learn to read, how a slave could become a gentleman. He would be a source of inspiration. Erastus Hicks could make all this possible.

The only prerequisite that was necessary for this greatness to emerge was for Jimmy to remove himself from the picture. He tried on the feeling of doing just that. He imagined the future of his life—alone, without Cato. It was an anguishing vision. And yet—it was not so different from what he had always imagined his life would be. As a boy, he had never dreamed of having a relationship with anyone—certainly not with someone like Cato. It had come to him as an unexpected gift—indeed, it was the only gift in his life for which he was truly grateful. And though fate had dealt him a life with circumstances he thoroughly despised, this one gift had seemed to redeem all the rest of it.

"I really love him," he said to himself. For this was the only excuse he could fall back on to explain why he would even consider parting with the great gift of his life. Such nobility, such moral purpose, was not familiar to Jimmy. He had not cultivated an image of himself as one who might make such an extravagant gesture of self-abnegation purely out of love. Quite the opposite, he had always portrayed himself as the bad fellow, unwilling to submit to God the master, a loather of church-going, a rejecter of turning the other cheek, an advocate of resistance, a disciple of passive subversion, a despiser of the white race. Such nobility as he had was poured into a rebellious spirit, an unwillingness to accept injustice. Justice and injustice had always been so clear to him. But here—in the case of Cato, in the case of Erastus Hicks, despite Jimmy's inherently unfair disadvantage, despite his inability to offer what the rich white man could offer, however innocent he was of this inability— something had upset his clear commitment to seeing justice— and only justice—prevail. Now he envisioned doing something that would accommodate the unfair advantage of privilege rather than resisting it. And the only reason for this was that he loved Cato to the point of feeling that Cato's destiny, Cato's happiness, Cato's potential was more important than his own —or rather, Cato's happiness was his own.

Jimmy knew that he was capable of great love. Venus had taught him that. He understood that he would have done anything—he would have made any sacrifice—forgone any personal need to enrich the dog's life. But he had always thought that the special feeling he had for Venus was an exception—and now he realized, in a moment of bittersweet insight, that such an impulse might actually be a part of his character.

And so this thought took shape and it quickly grew, until it became a resolution. Jimmy's deliberation had taken place in the course of twenty minutes while he still stood across the street from the Tremont hotel watching people come and go. And as he was thinking, he saw Erastus and Cato reemerge from the hotel. Jimmy stepped back into the shadow of the doorway. He had reached a decision. He would not call out to Cato after all. He would not place the dilemma of choosing on Cato's shoulders, would not tempt him to forgo his destiny out of sentiment and fondness for what had passed between them. Instead, he would follow Cato in secret, for he supposed that Cato and Erastus Hicks would eventually lead him to Dorothy and Ella and Sammy. It was to his sister that Jimmy now wanted to go. It was with Ella's assistance, he had decided, that he would carry out his new resolution.

## JIMMY DEPARTS

*W*hen Erastus and Cato left the Tremont hotel, they went directly back to the Sherman House. Having been informed by the clerk that William Askew was indeed staying at one of the hotels on their list, they were the first to discover his whereabouts, which made them feel as if they'd won a competition. They were eager to return to Dorothy to tell her the good news. But the good news came with an unexpected addendum: the hotel clerk had informed them that William was staying at the hotel with his father, Augustus.

"Oh dear," Dorothy exclaimed when she heard this. "I wonder how he managed to get here so quickly!" As she reflected on the prospect of meeting him again, she said, "I don't know if I can face him. I literally stole his brougham."

"I can hardly face him any better," said Cato. "The last time I saw him he was whipping me—and then, I ran away."

"I think it would be best," said Erastus, who had already formulated a strategy, "if Dorothy were to take Ella to see William and his father, while Cato, Sammy and I remain here."

But Ella shook her head. "I don't know, Mr. Erast. If it was up to me, I'd take Sammy with us. Mr. Askew got to be fond of Sammy while he was staying at our house. And, if you'll excuse me for saying so, Sammy's the only one of us who more or less likes him."

So it was decided that Dorothy, Ella and Sammy would go to the Tremont House hotel to find William and Augustus. Erastus also proposed that Dorothy should look for an opportunity to mention Cato's name to Augustus to see if she could gauge his present state of mind regarding his runaway slave. She ought to mention his name, Erastus added, without actually revealing that Cato was present in Chicago.

After leaving the Sherman House, Dorothy, Ella and Sammy walked north toward the Tremont. But the trio had only walked a single block when someone came up from behind them and swooped Sammy up into his arms, pressing the boy in an embrace. "Hey little brother," said Jimmy.

"Jimmy!" Ella shouted. Before Jimmy could set Sammy down, Ella threw her arms around her brothers, and squeezed them both. Then, holding them tight, she flung back her head and whispered, "Oh thank you, Lord. Thank you!"

"I was afraid we'd never find you," said Dorothy, shaking Jimmy's hand when Ella had released him.

"Well I believe I found you," said Jimmy. "I am thankful I did. I've had many adventures, and some of them were terrible."

They stood on the street for half an hour while Jimmy told them his story. He told them how he'd come upon a hidden boat in which he rowed across the Ohio River. He told them how he had to jump into the water just before he reached the far bank. He told them that he'd lost all his money and that he'd almost drowned. Then he told them about the black cat that found him lying on the Illinois shore—and how Mrs.

MacMurrough, the cat's owner, took him in—and how she'd introduced him to Mr. Mack, who was part of the underground railroad. He described how Mr. Mack brought him to the Illinois Central rail yard in Cairo and stowed him onto a freight car—and how he'd traveled all the way from Cairo to Chicago in just eight hours.

Then he told the story of being chased by copperheads his first day in Chicago. He told how he'd eluded his would-be captors by pretending to search for a hat in a millinery shop. Finally, he told how he had been hired by a colored catering firm to serve punch—only to lose his job on the first day without ever having been paid.

"I've had my fill of the North," Jimmy said in conclusion.

"We are on our way to find William and his father," said Dorothy. "He was paroled from prison—but in exchange he had to take an oath to stay north of the Ohio River. So I'm afraid we'll have to stay in the North for some time."

"I saw them coming out of a hotel this morning," said Jimmy. "I was looking for you."

"Did they see you?"

"No, they didn't see me," said Jimmy. And to be quite clear about it, he added, "I reckon it would be best all around if Mr. Askew didn't see me."

"Of course," said Dorothy. "You're quite right. Perhaps you and Ella should go back to our hotel. We have rooms at the Sherman House, along with Cato and Erastus Hicks."

Jimmy nodded.

Dorothy turned to Sammy. "I suppose it will just be the two of us who will go to visit Lieutenant Askew and Mr. Askew. Is that all right with you?"

Sammy nodded.

As everyone was in agreement with this strategy, the party split into two. Ella led Jimmy back toward the Sherman House hotel, while Dorothy and Sammy continued north toward the Tremont House.

"How did you find us?" Ella asked Jimmy. "This place is so big; we didn't know where to begin to look for you."

"I followed Cato to the hotel. Then I waited until you came out."

Ella found this very strange. It was so strange that she stopped walking. "You followed Cato to the hotel! How come you followed him?" she asked. "How come you didn't go up to him and say hello?"

"Because I've changed my mind about staying up here in the North."

"What?"

"I've decided I want to go back home. These Yankee whites are worse than the ones back in Tennessee."

"I don't understand. What does that have to do with Cato? Why didn't you talk to him?"

"I don't want to see him."

"That makes no sense. Why not?"

"If he sees me, he'll want me to stay here in the North. But I know it will be better for him if he stays here and I go."

Ella clasped her hands together. Her eyes were wide and fixed. "Jimmy, are you serious?"

"Yes, I am. I want you to give Cato a message from me. Tell him I've gone back home to Tennessee. Tell him that I think the painter should buy him from the Askews and take him to live in Philadelphia. Tell him I think he'll be happier living in the North with someone who can help him with his books and his clothes—and someone he can talk to about those things."

Ella's mind stuck on the words, 'Tell him I've gone back home to Tennessee.' "You talk like you're fixing to go back home right this minute."

Jimmy nodded. "I am. I'm not going to the hotel with you."

"What! But Jimmy, you can't do that. We just found you. How can you run off again? I don't understand."

"I don't know how else to explain it," said Jimmy. "I'm leaving because of Cato. I think life will be better for him if I don't see him."

"But why can't you tell it to him yourself?"

"Because if he saw me ... I know him ... he'd try to get me to stay here. He wouldn't think about what's best for him. But it will be better for him," Jimmy repeated, "if I go."

Ella shook her head. "You're saying he doesn't know what's best for him, but you do."

"Yes, I do. I want to do this for his sake, Ella. Don't you see, Cato can be somebody in the world. He can't be nobody if he sticks with me."

Jimmy's proposition had taken Ella by surprise. At first, she could find no sense in what he was saying. Gradually, she came to the point of weighing the logic of his argument. On the face of it, she agreed that Cato would be likely to rise higher in the world if he were bound to Mr. Hicks. But this didn't explain the connection between Cato's future with the painter and Jimmy's plan to disappear without seeing his friend. Ella knew their friendship was special. But she did not see why Jimmy and Cato's friendship should have any bearing on Cato's connection with Mr. Hicks. She had a vague sense that there was jealousy between Jimmy and the painter regarding Cato— and she knew that Cato was fond of them both. But the notion that Cato must be made to choose between them puzzled her. "So how do you plan to get back home?" she asked, speaking not in a whisper, but saying words that were clearly hard for her to articulate.

"I'll go home the same way I came. I'll hop in a freight car and ride back down to Cairo. I reckon Mrs. MacMurrough or Mr. Mack will help me get back across the river."

"Are you really fixing to do this?"

"Yes, I am. I'm sorry. I'm going to miss you."

"But Jimmy, I don't know what will happen to me here. I don't know what Dorothy and William will do. William had to take an oath, and now he's got to stay in the North. That means we can't come home."

"They'll come home when the war is over."

Ella had been speaking as calmly as she could, but now she could bear it no longer. She burst into tears. "Oh Jimmy! Please don't do this. Don't run off again. I don't want to be up here in the North without you. Can't you fix it with Cato some other way?"

Jimmy lowered his head. The force of his sister's entreaty was almost more than he could refuse. He had been so preoccupied with the accomplishment of his purpose that he hadn't considered the impact of his scheme on Ella. Now he realized that she had counted on him to be with her while they were all away from home. He felt that it would be selfish of him to abandon her altogether. He hung his head and thought for several moments. "I suppose," he said, "that after Cato leaves for Philadelphia, I could come back up here and stay with you. Once Cato has gone, Dorothy could write a letter to her parents to let me know."

"And then you'll come back?"

"Yes, I promise," he said solemnly. "I'll come back as soon as Cato has gone."

"But what if Cato and Mr. Erast don't leave?"

"If they don't leave here after three months, I'll come back no matter what happens."

Ella nodded. But then she said, "I still don't understand. I don't understand why you won't just talk to him."

Jimmy tried to think of a way to explain it. "You love Sammy, right?"

"Yes …. So?"

"Well, you know how the painter's fixing to take Sammy off to Philadelphia, right?"

"I reckon he will—on account of he bought him."

"And you'll miss Sammy when he goes, right?'

"You know I will."

"But just the same I know you believe that Sammy will be all right. He's gonna start a new life. He'll have a chance to do things he could never do before. Maybe he'll become an artist like he's always talked about. I feel the same way about Cato. He'll have prospects with the painter. He'll be able to make something of himself. I know he will. That's the only way I can explain it. It's not something I want for myself. It's something I want for him. But Cato is fond of me—so fond that he'd give up all those prospects."

"And before he can give up his future to be with you, you're fixing to give up your friendship with him?"

Jimmy nodded.

"How will I ever explain this to anyone?"

"Now, Ella, please, you can't tell Cato the reason I'm going. You can't tell him I'm doing this for his sake. I want you to tell him I decided I hated the North and I couldn't wait to get back home. And don't tell him anything about which way I'm going. I don't want him to come chasing after me."

Ella nodded. But in her mind, she could not see how she was going to explain Jimmy's scheme to anyone.

It occurred to Jimmy then that if he lingered much longer, either he would lose his resolve or Ella would decide not to help him. So he stepped forward, flung his arms around his sister and hugged her. "Don't worry," he said. "Take care of yourself. I'll come back to you again in three months. Goodbye." And with that, he turned and walked away. He did not know if she would run after him. And since he did not want her to have an excuse to call him back, he did not glance around, but kept walking with his eyes fixed forward.

Ella watched him walk away. She waited for him to look back, and when he didn't she continued to watch him. She watched him until he disappeared around a distant corner. Then she felt a surge of dread. She had not minded leaving home to travel to a strange city as long as she was with Sammy and as long as she expected to be reunited with Jimmy. Now, however, she had to face living in an unfamiliar world for several months with no family or friend except Dorothy. It would be just three months if Jimmy kept his promise. But Jimmy had acted so unreasonably that Ella felt she had cause to wonder whether he could be relied upon to keep his word.

For the first time she had to face a fear she'd kept at bay. She was afraid that her relationship with Dorothy would change after Dorothy married William. She was afraid that the delicate balance she had shared with Dorothy between friendship and slavery would tip severely toward the more conventional relationship, which was mistress and slave. She had been able to disregard this fear as long as she thought Jimmy would be with her. Jimmy, she knew, would be her ally—and could be counted upon to help her should she ever wish to free herself from the bond to Dorothy. But now it was clear that for the time being she would have no choice but to submit to William and Dorothy's whims—wherever they may choose to go and however they may choose to live. It was already ordained that they could not go back home. William had taken an oath to stay in the North as a condition of parole. This action made Ella uneasy because it showed that his behavior was unpredictable.

With Jimmy's departure, she felt vulnerable. She felt how

little control she had over her destiny. She wanted to honor his wishes. Jimmy had asked her to keep his true reason for going away from Cato. But she found herself contemplating two alternatives that might bring Jimmy back right away. If she were able to induce Cato and the painter to leave immediately, she might quickly go and find Jimmy at the train yard and convince him to stay. On the other hand, if she were to tell Cato the truth, she believed that Cato would seek out Jimmy himself and convince him to stay.

She resolved to begin with the first alternative, to honor Jimmy's wish, to do what she could to encourage Cato and Mr. Hicks to leave right away. But she was also resolved to fall upon the second alternative in defiance of Jimmy's wish, should the first strategy fail. As she walked back to the Sherman House, she considered what seemed like an obvious reason for Cato and the painter to leave. Dorothy and William might show up at any moment with Cato's master, old Mr. Askew. Cato could be captured and brought home to be whipped. It would be foolish for him to sit around the hotel waiting for this to happen. He ought to go at once and get as far from Chicago as he could.

As she formulated this line of reasoning, she felt the urgency of her situation. If she was to have any hope of catching Jimmy before he left, she must set things in motion as quickly as possible. She stopped walking toward the Sherman House and began to run. When she reached the hotel, she climbed the stairs to the painter's room on the fifth floor as quickly as she could. Breathless and nearly frantic, she knocked on the door. The door was opened and she stepped into the room holding her hands to her breast.

"I've come back because we found Jimmy."

Cato jumped to his feet. "Where is he?"

"He's on his way back home," she said—raising her hand to

bar Cato from leaving the room. "He had all kinds of terrible trouble up here in the North. He said to tell you he's going back home and you should leave him be. He thinks you and Mr. Erast ought to leave right away for Philadelphia. He said Mr. Erast might someday send money back to Mr. Askew to buy you free, but for right now you'd better skedaddle before old Mr. Askew comes looking for you."

"What?" Cato's face showed terror, but it was not from fear of his father. "Where did you see him? Where did he go?"

"He's gone."

"How can he be gone? He must have told you where he's going."

"He's gone back home," said Ella. "So y'all may as well pack up and go right quick before Dorothy and them get back here."

Cato walked up to Ella and took hold of her. "Ella, you've got to tell me where he is. Please!"

Ella saw the panic in Cato's eyes. "Don't you think you ought to get away before your daddy comes looking for you?"

Cato began to shake Ella bodily. "Where is he? You must tell me!"

"Please don't ask me. Please go on and leave before they get here. That's the best thing. That's what Jimmy wants."

"I'm not leaving without Jimmy," said Cato.

"It's too late," said Ella.

"Where is he?"

"Oh, I can't!" Ella now clutched Cato as hard as he was holding her. "He told me not to tell you."

"But why? Why would he do that?"

"He doesn't want to see you. He wants you to go away right quick."

"That's a lie!"

"No, I'm telling you the truth. He wants you to go with Mr. Erast."

Cato face became wrenched with anguish. He let go of Ella and fell down to his knees. "Please!" he cried. "For God's sake, Ella. Tell me. Where is he? Where is he?"

Ella could hardly stand it now. "He said you'll be better off with Mr. Erast. That's the reason. He wants you to find a better life."

Cato leapt back to his feet. He was in a frantic state. "I'm going to find him," he shouted to Erastus. "If she won't tell me, I'll go out and find him myself." He pushed past Ella and went directly to the door.

"Wait," said Erastus. "I'll help you look."

"Oh!" cried Ella. "Why won't you just go? It's not what he wants!"

"Come on," said Cato. "There's no time to waste."

"Give me a moment," said Erastus. "I need to get something." Erastus went to the bureau and took a leather satchel out of the drawer. "All right," he said, "let's go."

Before Ella could speak, the two men had left the hotel room and had begun to walk quickly down the stairs. Ella was in a daze. She could no longer resist the force of Cato's determination. It was clear to her that the first alternative was not going to work. Cato was decidedly not going to leave without Jimmy. She had tried valiantly to honor Jimmy's wish, but what choice did she have now? She ran to the top of the stairs and leaned over the banister."

"He's gone to stow away on the train," she shouted. "Go to the train yard. He's going in a freight car on the Illinois Central Railroad to Cairo."

## "YOU HAVE TO DECIDE!"

*W*hen they arrived at the Illinois Central rail yard, Erastus and Cato counted thirty freight cars. After a brief discussion, they decided to divide the task of checking the cars. Cato would start with the front car, while Erastus walked halfway down the train to begin his search. After twenty minutes, they had each checked ten cars. It was in the eleventh car, not far from the end of the train, that Erastus saw a man curled in the corner of the car. He climbed into the car and crept up close to the unmoving form. The sound of muffled snoring told him that the man was asleep. A waistcoat lay on the floor of the car two feet in front of the sleeping figure. Erastus picked up the coat and scrutinized the body of the sleeping man. Even in the darkness, he knew that muscular shape. It was Jimmy.

Erastus stood for a moment looking wistfully at the sleeping form of his rival. He sighed, blinked his eyes, then withdrew from his pocket the leather satchel he had brought from the hotel. He looked around to be sure that no one was watching. He stuffed the satchel into the pocket of the coat he'd picked up. Then he returned the coat to the floor of the car, arranged it next to Jimmy just as he'd found it, and noise-lessly climbed out of the freight car and back onto the ground of the rail yard. A few minutes later, he brought Cato down to the car where Jimmy lay sleeping.

"He's in there," said Erastus. "Go and wake him. I'll wait out here."

Cato climbed up into the car. He found himself trembling, as if his body were made of springs. From the moment Ella had delivered Jimmy's baffling farewell, Cato had been beside himself with worry. But now his anxiety gave way to exhilara-tion. He rushed to the corner of the car—then stopped. Like Erastus, he stood for a moment looking at the sleeping man before him. Even in the dim, strange environment of the freight car, Cato felt the erotic thrill of his desire for Jimmy. He wanted to throw himself onto his lover and wake him with a kiss. They had not seen each other for nearly a month. He knelt down and placed his hand gently on Jimmy's shoulder and shook it. In a moment, Jimmy opened his eyes.

"Cato!" he cried. He bolted to a sitting up position.

"I've found you," said Cato.

Jimmy put his hands up to his eyes and rubbed them. "I was asleep," he said. As his eyes focused, he saw that Cato still wore his expensive clothes, but had removed his wig and hat. Although he was angry at having been found, the sight of Cato's fuzzy natural hair disarmed him. Impulsively he reached up and stroked Cato's head.

"Yes," said Cato. "That's why I woke you."

"How did you find me? Did Ella tell you?"

"Yes."

"Damn it. Why'd she do that?" Jimmy scowled to show his displeasure

"I begged her to tell me. Don't blame her. She only spoke

after I was already out the door and on my way to search the entire city."

"You were supposed to go to Philadelphia," Jimmy asserted.

"Philadelphia? Why would I go there without you?"

"But ... you ...."

"You thought I'd go somewhere without you?" Cato rolled his eyes. "How could you think that?"

"I thought you should go with him. You'd be better off without me."

Cato put his hand on Jimmy's mouth. "Don't say that. Don't you know there's nothing for me without you?"

"But you could be somebody. You could read books. You could go to school. You could have all his money."

"His money!" Cato eyes flashed, with more than a hint of anger. "What do I care for money? You think I care about money more than I care about you?"

"But I can't read."

The tone of Jimmy's lament made Cato soften his voice. "What difference does that make?" He rubbed his hands on his cheeks trying to think of how to respond. "I can't farm," he said. "I can't do much of anything except be a servant."

"But you could go to school."

Cato nodded. "Yes, I could." Now his nose wrinkled in exasperation. "And what's to stop me from going to school? You and I, we can make whatever life we want!"

"What kind of life can we make?" Jimmy said, with plaintive sincerity. "Two runaway slaves."

"We won't know unless we try."

"But ...."

"I know it won't be easy. I've never expected life to be easy." Cato understood why Jimmy was afraid. He himself was worried about how they would live, about what work they would find. But his recent experiences had given him an unexpected taste of his own power. "Acting white has shown me something," he said. "Folks treat you the way you expect to be treated."

"Are you gonna be white now?"

"No. Jimmy—no more. I just did that for Dorothy's sake. She wanted me to pretend to be her husband as protection while we were traveling."

Jimmy's head nodded involuntarily as he processed this information. Then he spoke in a low, even tone, with his eyes fixed on Cato. "But when I saw you, you were in that wig and you weren't with her, you were with him."

"You saw me?"

"You were walking down the street with him. Then the two of you went into a hotel. I called to you but you didn't hear me. Then I tried to go in the hotel after you, but they wouldn't let me in." Jimmy's face screwed up into a bitter expression. "I guess since I forgot my wig."

Cato was stung by the acrimony in Jimmy's voice. Yet he now understood—really, for the first time—why Jimmy had acted the way he had. He had never intended to let Jimmy see him in the wig. "Oh Jimmy." He reached out and grabbed his friend's hand. He squeezed it hard. "I'm sorry." His voice was racked with guilt. He lowered his head, then lifted it sheepishly. "I didn't know you were there. I only wore the wig because Erastus and I had to go in and out of hotels looking for William. I thought it would be easier if I were dressed that way."

"You had your arms around each other's shoulders. And you acted different with each other. You looked like you belonged together. You were talking about some books in a shop window. And all I could think about was how you and I can't talk about books like that."

"You could learn to read if you wanted to." Cato said this

gently and without reproach. "Remember when you showed me how to pick cotton? It's no different. We can teach each other everything we know."

"I don't know …." Jimmy remembered the moment to which Cato alluded—that blissful day in the field when he'd plucked a hair off Cato's chest.

"Nimble fingers," said Cato, "take a nimble mind. You can learn whatever you put your mind on. I know you can."

"I don't know," Jimmy repeated. He shrugged his shoulders. "I'm always too tired after working in the field to do anything else."

"But what about now? Now we're free. Now you can do whatever you want. Isn't that what you've always dreamed about? How could you even think about going back to the Hollands?"

"Because the North is no good. It's no different here than back home. In fact, it's worse. Here you got nowhere to go and no one to protect you."

"We can protect each other," said Cato.

"Where we gonna live? How're we gonna eat?"

"We'll get jobs."

"I tried that. I didn't even get paid. And you know why I lost that job? Because some dumb white girl spilled punch on her dress and she blamed it on me rather than admit it herself." Jimmy smirked. "You think we can survive in this world?"

"Maybe not alone."

"That's just it. I'm no help to you. But it could be so easy for you. At least one of us should have it easy. If you went with him, you could forget about all the shit. You could be somebody in the world. You could be somebody great. You could change the world."

Cato was moved by this speech. He had never before heard Jimmy speak like that. Nor had he understood that Jimmy's wanting him to go with Erastus arose from something other than jealousy. He let the substance of Jimmy's vision sink in. It was true. He felt capable of a life that might be extraordinary. Reading had stimulated a free, unbounded imagination in him. Yet in all his flights of fancy he had never imagined that his accomplishment might be something facilitated by Erastus. If only Jimmy could understand that it was Jimmy and not the painter who was his true complement. It was Jimmy who fleshed Cato out. Erastus merely reflected.

"But don't you see, Jimmy," he said at last. "I can't change the world with Erastus. I can only do that with you. With him —with me acting white—the world wouldn't be changed. It would be the same as it has always been. The only way I can change the world and be somebody in the world is if I stay with you. That's the somebody I want to be."

"But ...."

"Please ... don't say more. There's nothing you can say to get rid of me, really, there isn't—there is nothing you can say."

For a moment, the two men looked at each other as if to take a measure of their feelings. The longer they looked into each other's eyes, the more immense that feeling became. They had been speaking calmly for a quarter of an hour. Throughout that time, they'd held back any trace of their ardor. But now as they stared deeply into each other's eyes, each of them felt like he might burst. At last, Cato threw himself onto the floor and hung his arms around Jimmy's neck. "Oh Jimmy! Please stay with me!" he cried.

Jimmy could do no more. He had tried as best he could to do what he thought was right. He had hoped Cato's friendship with the painter would be enough to let him choose an easier path. But Cato's loyalty was unwavering. As he thought of Cato's fondness and fidelity—as he let himself reckon how it felt to be so loved, a wet drop fell from his eye and rolled down his cheek. He thrust his arms around Cato's neck and pulled his lover's face close to his. "Oh Cato," he said. "You know I love you." He kissed him deep—and their tongues were quickly loosed inside each other's mouth.

"I'll never leave you," said Cato. "I'm yours."

"You're mine!" said Jimmy.

Cato laughed. "I am! I am your own—I am your very own."

The air quickly filled with a sexual aroma as each man's sweat glands leaked amorous odors that recalled them to their great desire. Soon each man's hands compulsively tried to comprehend the contours which lay in the other's flesh, as if feeling and sensation alone could solve the riddle of their mutual desire.

"You are mine," Jimmy whispered. "And I will hold you to me now and for always, come what may. I will always do for you. I will!"

"Do me now," cried Cato. "Oh Jimmy I want it." As Cato said this, he grasped at the bulge in the crotch of Jimmy's black trousers, which stiffened forcefully in response to his touch.

"Damn!" Jimmy cried out. "You gonna get it now! You gonna get it good and hard now." He pulled his trousers down to reveal the same unmentionables that Mrs. MacMurrough had once seen, but which now looked like a tent supported by a single arching pole. Jimmy struggled to quickly take off his shoes and then to remove his trousers.

Cato did not answer, but pushed Jimmy down onto his back. He positioned himself over Jimmy's body and slipped his fingers into the waistband of the unmentionables. "Looks like you're gonna bust out of these if I don't get them off you," he said. He pulled Jimmy's undergarment down until it snagged on its obtruding contents, then with a final tug, he cleared the hurdle and Jimmy's penis leapt up like an uncoiled spring.

In an instant, Cato had slid both his pants and his underwear down to the tops of his boots. Now the tables were
turned. While Cato labored to remove his boots, Jimmy stared
at Cato's penis as it waved about. He gingerly plucked at it as if
it were a small animal darting about to evade him. "Come here
you frisky thing," Jimmy teased, and Cato giggled while
Jimmy's fingers picked and pulled at the bobbing organ. When
Cato had finished stripping, Jimmy clasped his hand firmly
around its prey. "Gotcha!" he said gleefully.

When his boots were off, Cato threw his body down hard
onto Jimmy's. "Let me rub you up."

With a sudden energy, the two men slid around on each
other, perceiving in distinct successive sensations the feel of
each other's chest, nipples, stomach, groin, knees, and feet.
Their bodies explored, rubbed, and massaged together, simultaneously giving and receiving impressions.

Jimmy stroked clumps of Cato's hair with curious fingers,
while Cato's tongue dipped in and out of Jimmy's ear, smelling
the sweat on the back of his neck. When his nostrils were filled
with the acrid smell, Cato withdrew his tongue and whispered
into the cup of Jimmy's ear in a soft tender voice, "I love you."

Jimmy quickly reached down to find Cato's buttocks as if
to remind himself how badly he craved them. Then in an
instant, he grabbed Cato's body and he pulled him over and
onto his back, where with a single commanding maneuver he
parted Cato's legs and lifted them up and onto his shoulders.
"I'm gonna do it now," he said.

Cato nodded, smiling. His eyes shone like a child who's
been promised a wondrous gift. He had enough experience by
now to know that to accommodate Jimmy's size he had to
simultaneously relax and open. It was a state he could achieve
only by letting his lust well up until his brain understood how

badly he wanted it, so that desire could work the secret mechanisms that unlocked the passage.

Jimmy likewise knew that he had to enter slowly, pressing with firm intentionality, but mindful of any resistance. Once he was lodged inside to the full reach of his penetration, Jimmy knew the path would be open for more rapid thrusts. His physical impulse was to begin fucking Cato violently, but his heart was filled with an emotion that held him fast and still.

Jimmy was fully extended inside Cato. The image of this bond rose in each of their minds now like a sacred symbol. Were they not like the coupled rail cars, locked together at last in their journey in life? There would be no more separations, no more impediments, nothing more to derail their passage to freedom. They would be free from slavery and from their own self-doubt, for the unspeakable love was now manifestly enduring. It had passed a trial and been found to be unwavering, persistent, safe to trust with a lifetime. And so they each restrained the physical urge to move. They lay in a long still interlude, marveling at the joy they felt to be so joined, looking deeply into each other's eyes as if the entirety of the heavens could be seen in them.

The passage of time was suspended. They lay in the corner of the Illinois Central freight car holding each other in this embrace for a longer time than either of them realized, until simultaneously they both began to quiver. As if by mutual agreement, Jimmy began to thrust fervently, propelling himself in and out of Cato with an urgent intensity that quickly built upon the high plateau of their accumulated desire to a peak. They could each feel the sexual chemistry form quickly into a pending explosion, matched by the rising pitch of their voices. In rapid succession, they each ejaculated violently, first Jimmy, then Cato.

"Oh damn. Oh damn." Jimmy's guttural sounds coalesced into words.

"Oh damn is right!" Cato cried and then he began to laugh, in shock from the unprecedented intensity of his orgasm.

And they both looked down at their bodies, wet with sweat and fluids, awed by the evidence of Cato's prodigious output.

Jimmy spoke first. "Damn, boy, you must have been saving that up for a month. I never saw so much stuff come out of you."

"You know exactly how long I've been saving that up," said Cato. "I hope I never have to save it up that long again!"

"After this, you'll be lucky if you can save it up for more than a day." Jimmy winked. "Cause I ain't gonna give you much rest from now on."

Once again, they fell into a bodily embrace, lying now side-by-side, quietly absorbing the bliss of their reconciliation. When at last they reached a sense of ampleness in this meditation, they sat up and put their clothes on. They knew that they had to discuss what to do next.

"Come with me back to the hotel," said Cato. "We need to talk about what to do. But it's dangerous to stay here. Let me tell Erastus."

"What? Where is he?" Jimmy hadn't expected this.

"He's waiting outside."

"Outside?" Jimmy stood up. His mood darkened. "He's here?"

"Yes—of course. He helped me find you."

Jimmy looked warily at the door of the freight car. "I don't want to see him," he said.

"But he's been so thoughtful … and patient." Cato stood up now, too. He walked to the door of the freight car. "Wait a moment. I'll go and get him." Cato hung his head out the door of the car. But when he looked outside, he saw that Erastus was not there. He held on to the side of the car so that he could lean even farther out—and he looked up and down the rail yard. There was no one in sight. Cato turned back into the car. "He's gone!"

"Gone?"

"I don't see him anywhere."

"Maybe he went for a walk."

"No I looked up and down the whole length of the train. He's not anywhere."

"Maybe he thought you'd meet him somewhere else."

"No." Cato shook his head. "He was the one who found the car you were in. Then he brought me down here and told me, 'You go in and wake him. I'll wait out here.'"

"I guess he got tired of waiting."

"Let's go. We have to go look for him."

Jimmy picked up his coat and put it on. But as he did so, he felt a weight pulling inside it. He reached into his pocket, extracted an unfamiliar article and held it up.

"What's this?" he asked.

Cato looked at the mysterious object. "I don't know," he said. "Where did you get it?"

"It was in the pocket of my waistcoat."

"It looks like a leather purse," said Cato.

Jimmy opened the satchel and saw that it was filled with coins. He knelt down and poured the contents onto the floor of the rail car.

The clanking sound of the trove of coins was so loud that Cato was startled. He stared at the money with wide eyes. "It looks like at least a hundred gold coins," he said.

"Where did this come from?" asked Jimmy.

"Erastus must have put it in your coat. I don't know what else it could be. He had to have put it there."

591

"But why?"

Cato thought for a moment. He could think of no explanation except the most obvious. "He must mean to give it to you as a gift."

"To me?"

"Yes. He put it in your pocket." Cato looked at the shiny coins and calculated their worth. "If there are a hundred gold coins ... and each coin is worth twenty dollars—that would be two thousand dollars."

"Two thousand dollars!" Jimmy looked at Cato then back at the coins. "Damn!" He had never seen that much money in his life. "You think he means to give us all that money?"

"Yes," said Cato—letting the magnitude of the gift sink in. "I'm sure that he does."

Jimmy was speechless. He felt an impulse to be suspicious of such an unreasonable act, even though he himself had recently endeavored to act in an unreasonable but selfless way. The evidence of the painter's generosity sparkled on the floor in front of him. He could not deny it. "Fuck him," he said out loud. And as he spoke he began to pace about the rail car. He felt as if he wanted to spit. All of his instincts told him to reject such a gift. He could not be bought! But then he tried to focus his mind on what exactly the painter hoped to buy, what was it he wanted? It was clear that he had not only left the money but had removed himself, as if he meant to take himself sharply out of the picture at the precise moment that Jimmy returned to it. Try as he might, Jimmy could not impute a selfish motive to the gesture.

For the first time, he let himself wonder if he had been wrong about the painter. So much of what he had always believed about the world had been proved wrong. The North was not paradise. Freedom was not a magic potion. And now this gift. He'd had some idea that the painter was wealthy, but he had never imagined such a gift was possible even from someone who might afford it. And that it should be put into his pocket instead of Cato's! He could not help but appreciate the meaning of that gesture. He had borne nothing but ill will toward the painter. He had been sore with jealousy and resentment. Now he was suddenly humbled by the contrast of his own insecurities against the painter's generosity. Had he always been so self-doubting? Had the painter always been so charitable?

He searched his memory for clues that might have predicted this turn of events. He had to admit that he did not really know Erastus Hicks. He had never allowed the man to be more than a symbol. He had intuited almost from the beginning that the painter was in love with Cato, and that he had advantages Jimmy could never match. He was white. He was educated. He had money. Jimmy had convinced himself that Cato would be better off with this man. He had feared that he himself was not good enough. As he thought of this, he looked at Cato who was hunched down beside the coins. Cato wore the same scared rabbit look Jimmy had seen back in the barn the day they argued. His appearance said that he was passively but anxiously awaiting Jimmy's assimilation of the meaning of the unexpected gift. His posture made it clear that for the moment he would not presume to speak about it. And just as it had before, Cato's expression of passive vulnerability defused Jimmy's anger. Jimmy had said "Fuck him!" before he knew what he was saying. He had been angry because the gift did not mitigate his feeling of financial impotence, but had seemed to underscore it.

But none of that mattered, Jimmy told himself now, because Cato really did love him—him!—more than anyone else. And in the confidence of that certain love, Jimmy could afford to be more generous. With a palpable shudder, he released the desire to resist the gift. He did not need to make it wrong. He stopped pacing. He gazed at the pile of twenty-dollar gold pieces on the floor of the rail car. "He must care for you more than I thought," he said.

"We have to find him," said Cato. "We have to thank him."

"Do you think he went back to the hotel?"

"He must have," said Cato. "Will you go there with me?"

Jimmy nodded.

Cato's look of apprehension melted. He stood and moved close to Jimmy. He kissed him. "Thank you," he said.

But when they arrived at the hotel, they were faced with a quandary. Without saying anything, they both understood that there would be a problem getting inside the hotel. In the absence of a white escort, they could not simply walk in the front door.

"What should we do?" Cato asked. He had an idea of what to do, but he didn't want to be the one to suggest it.

"Do you think they will recognize you," said Jimmy, "if you put that ugly cracker hair back on your head?"

Not knowing what else to do with the hat and wig, Cato had been carrying them in his hand since they'd left the railcar. "The doorman should know me," he said. "I've been in and out of here a dozen times with the wig on."

"All right, then. Put it on."

"You'll have to walk close by me, so it's clear we're together."

"I could stick my dick in your butt and we could walk in that way."

"Ha. Ha." Cato laughed nervously, but he put the disguise back on.

With Cato in the lead, they got past the doorman without incident, but when they arrived at room 503, no one answered the door. They descended to room 207, where they found Ella alone. When she saw Jimmy, Ella threw her arms around him, just as she had done earlier in the day. She repeated her thanks to the Lord—but now also to Cato.

"Do you know where Erastus is?" Cato asked.

"He left here twenty minutes ago," said Ella. "And guess what? That Mr. Frazza was with him. He said Mr. Frazza has a perfume shop just down the street. And Mr. Erast bought a great big bottle of stink good for me, and one for Dorothy. Look here." Ella held up two bottles of perfume.

"Who is Mr. Frazza?" said Jimmy, thoroughly perplexed.

"He's a friend of Mr. Erast," said Ella. "Mr. Erast said they was going over to the hotel where Dorothy went to fetch Sammy. He said he and Mr. Frazza are fixing to pick up Sammy and then head out to Philadelphia to see about opening a perfume shop there. He said once they get situated we ought to come out there and visit Sammy any time we want."

It only took a moment for Cato to grasp what this meant. He had suspected something unspoken was afoot after they'd found Erastus alone with Mr. Frazza in the hotel room when they first arrived. But Erastus had never confided anything to him about Mr. Frazza. This hardly seemed fair to Cato, since he had spoken to Erastus candidly about his feelings for Jimmy. He understood that Erastus was habitually discreet and circumspect. Yet it seemed as if a great deal of conspiring had gone on without his knowledge. First, there was the purse full of coins that Erastus took with him when they went to look for Jimmy. And now it seemed that an entirely new life had been planned with Mr. Frazza, to whom Cato had been barely introduced. Despite his mild irritation at not being taken into Erastus's confidence, Cato was delighted to realize that Erastus not only seemed to be not pining over him, but appeared to have found someone closer in age and station. Mr. Frazza was clearly a man of aesthetic refinement. And underneath his fussy attire, Mr. Frazza had also struck Cato as a fine looking man. From Jimmy's bewildered look, he saw that Jimmy had no clue as to the real meaning of Ella's information. He whispered something in Jimmy's ear. Jimmy's eyes went wide, and he whispered something back.

"What's all this whispering about?" Ella asked.

"I was just explaining to Jimmy who Mr. Frazza is," Cato said.

"Humph." Ella did not see why this should be a private topic. "Well I don't think you're going to get to meet him, Jimmy," she said.

"Why not?" Cato asked. "They'll come back here before they leave, won't they? To say goodbye?"

"I don't think so." Ella shook her head. "He said to tell you goodbye. He said he hoped you'd understand." Then seeing how crestfallen Cato looked, Ella added, "I'm sorry. Seems like everybody wants to run off from you before you get a chance to change anybody's mind."

Now Jimmy whispered something into Cato's ear. Cato thought for a moment and then he whispered something back. Jimmy whispered yet again, and to this, Cato finally said out loud, "Yes. I think we should."

"Should what?" Ella asked. "Why d'you two keep whispering to each other?"

"We were just talking about whether or not you'd want to come live with us," said Jimmy.

"Come live with you?"

"Yes," Jimmy said. Then he held up the leather satchel full of coins. "Mr. Hicks has given us two thousand dollars."

"What!" Ella rushed to Jimmy's side. Jimmy held open the purse so that she could see the evidence inside it. "Lord, the man's gone crazy. Why'd he give you all that money?"

"He knows we can't wait here for Dorothy and William to come back with my father," Cato explained. "If we want to be free, we have to do something about it now. Erastus gave us this money so we could start our own lives."

"Oh my gracious!" Ella was as speechless as Jimmy had been.

"So you have to decide," Jimmy said. "If you want to come live with us, or if you want to stay here and live with the white folks."

Ella found herself shaking as she grasped the implications of what was being put to her and the suddenness with which she was being asked to respond to it. "You mean you're fixing to just run off right now and never see them again?" she asked.

"We have to," Jimmy said. "We mean to be free."

"But where will you go?"

"We haven't decided," Cato said. "We've hardly had any time to talk about it."

Ella shook her head. "I can't decide something like that so fast," she said. "And I can't just leave without telling Dorothy what I'm doing."

Jimmy nodded. He understood Ella's reluctance.

"Before we go," Cato said, "I can write Dorothy a note and explain it all to her. It doesn't mean you'll never see her again."

"I don't know," Ella continued shaking her head. "I haven't had any time to think about it. It's all happening too fast."

"We have to go soon," Jimmy said. "If they come back here, there's no telling what might happen to Cato and me."

Ella's face was contorted by her indecision. She looked at Jimmy with pleading eyes. "What should I do?"

"Come with us," he said simply.

## "DO YOU LOVE HIM?"

$\mathcal{A}$ ugustus Askew returned to the Tremont House hotel by himself. He had grown tired from walking, but William had been determined to keep looking for Dorothy, and so they had parted company at mid-afternoon. When Augustus arrived at the hotel, the desk clerk handed him a note addressed to him and to his son. The note was from the painter Erastus Hicks. It explained that Mr. Hicks had been informed by the clerk that both Mr. Askews were registered at the hotel. It noted that Mr. Hicks had then determined that both gentlemen were out. It told how Mr. Hicks and Miss Dorothy Holland had been searching for William, and that they were staying at the Sherman House hotel. It suggested that after reading the note both of the Mr. Askews should remain at their hotel, since Mr. Hicks would arrange for Miss Holland to come there to find them as soon as possible.

Having read this note, Augustus was not surprised when Dorothy, accompanied by Sammy, knocked on his door an hour after he returned to his hotel. Augustus and Dorothy greeted each other awkwardly. Dorothy was embarrassed because she had both deceived Augustus and her family and had taken his carriage. Augustus felt awkward because he knew that his arrival in Chicago was an unwanted intervention. The awkwardness of both parties was not helped by the fact that William had not yet returned. As a result, Dorothy and Sammy were obliged to pass the time alone with Augustus as they waited in his room.

Sammy felt an impulse to counter the uneasiness between the adults, and so he began an explanation to Mr. Askew of his forthcoming itinerary.

"I'm going to go to Pennsylvania with Mr. Hicks," he explained. "I want to learn how to paint from Mr. Hicks. Did you ever see his paintings Massa Askew? He paints so good that everything looks just like real."

"Yes," Augustus told the boy. "Mr. Hicks painted my late wife and he also painted a story from the Bible about when Mary washed the feet of our Lord."

"Was Mary the Lord's slave?" asked Sammy.

"No, no, my boy, she was a white woman."

Sammy nodded but was clearly perplexed. "Was she the Lord's wife?"

"No, boy, she was washing his feet, you see, to honor the Lord because he had raised her brother Lazarus from the dead."

Sammy's eyes went wide. "You mean someone could come back to life after they died?"

"The Lord had that power, my boy. He was the son of God after all."

"Could the Lord bring Venus back? She was a very good dog."

"The Lord went up to heaven a long time ago, my boy. So now he doesn't do that anymore," said Augustus. He took the boy's hand. "You're fond of dogs, aren't you?"

"Yes," said Sammy. Then remembering that he and

Augustus had shared a fondness for one dog in particular, he asked, "Did Scout come to Chicago with you?"

"No, Scout is still back home with Miss Holland's parents."

"Oh."

"Perhaps when you get to Philadelphia you'll find that Mr. Hicks has a dog."

Sammy's face brightened at this suggestion. "I never asked him," he admitted. "I reckon he does have a dog. He's very rich. I think he can buy anything he wants. He bought me a long time ago when I was little."

Dorothy spoke up now. "It was in order to bring Sammy to Mr. Hicks that I brought the boy with me, Mr. Askew. Mr. Hicks had agreed to come to Chicago in order to intercede on William's behalf at the prison camp. But when we got to the camp, William had already been discharged."

Augustus sighed. "Yes, he signed an oath. They paroled him on the condition that he must stay in the North. Miss Holland, I don't know what you mean to do. But I hope you will encourage him to come home as soon as he can."

"The most important thing is that he's safe and out of prison," said Dorothy. "Once the war is over I don't doubt that we'll be able to come home. How were my parents when you left them?"

"Well of course they're worried about you. Have you written to them since you arrived here?"

"Yes, I wrote to them yesterday. I told them about the parole and the stipulation that we must remain in the North."

"He came out of the prison with no money," said Augustus. "But I have made financial provisions for you both." He smiled earnestly as he said this, but then quickly his smile melted and he began to pace. "I'm afraid he's not himself, Miss Holland. This war has got the best of him."

"You mean he's ill?"

"No I don't mean physically ill. It's his mental state. He blames himself for the death of his friend Daniel Watson."

As he paced, Augustus told Dorothy what he knew of the events that occurred at Shiloh and how they had affected William. As she listened she began to pace along with him in the opposite direction. She asked several questions, then sat down. Augustus at last sat down as well, and after that, both the father and the fiancée sat in silence. They remained so until at last there was a knock on the door. Augustus rose to answer it. When he opened the door, his son stood before him.

"I couldn't find her," said William.

Without saying anything in reply, Augustus stepped aside so that William could see Dorothy standing in the room behind him. William stared for a moment. He looked from Dorothy back to his father then back to Dorothy. Then all at once, he rushed to her and clutched her to him tightly.

"Son, why don't you take Miss Holland next door to your room so you can talk? If you leave the door open, I'm sure it will be all right," said Augustus. "Sammy and I will stay here. Perhaps we'll play cards."

The couple walked next door to William's room. To honor Augustus's request, they left the door ajar by some inches, but this did not prevent them, once they had reached the interior of the room, from kissing each other deeply.

Then William gently pushed her away and held her by the shoulders. He had resolved to make a clean breast of his story right away, to get it all out in the open, for it was the only way she would be able to understand his state of mind. He told her, "I tried to do what you wanted. When I went into that battle, I aimed my rifle high so as not to harm anyone. But because I did that, my friend Daniel, who stood right next to me, was killed by the very Yankee over whose head I had fired my shot. Ever since that moment I have felt so guilty that I feel like I may as well have died myself. What I did was inexcusable. Even the Union general at the prison camp was appalled when he learned of what I had done."

Dorothy looked into his eyes in silence for a few moments. Then she took his arms in her hands, lowered her hands to his forearms, and held him gently by the wrists. "It is not appalling, my darling. Indeed, to me you are innocent." She said this as soothingly as she could. "Daniel Watson did not die because of what you did. He died because that Yankee killed him. You cannot blame yourself. You have killed no one. You were the only one in that battle who was innocent."

"Oh, Dorothy. Daniel saw what happened. I could see it in his eyes, just before he died. He could see what I had done.

"If Daniel is in heaven then he will surely know that what you did was virtuous in God's eyes," said Dorothy. "Christ instructed that we must love our enemies. Mr. Hicks has shown me these teachings, which are in the Bible itself. In the gospel of Matthew, the fifth chapter, Christ said …." She changed the tone of her voice as she recited the scripture, which she had committed to memory, speaking with what she intended to be a tone of authority: "'Ye have heard that it has been said, thou shall love thy neighbor, and hate thine enemy. But I say unto you, love your enemies, bless them that curse you, do good to them that hate you, and pray for them that despitefully use you.' Don't you see William? That is the reason the Quakers don't fight in this war. It is not because of cowardice. It is Christ's teaching that they obey."

"Why did God spare me and take Daniel?" William asked. His eyes were wide and earnest.

"It was the Yankee's decision to take Daniel, not God's," said Dorothy. "It was the Yankee who acted. He acted in the free will which God has given to us all, and through which we are able to choose any action—even to choose to do evil to one another. But evil, however deadly, does not validate more evil, William. Oh darling, you must not blame yourself for any of the consequences of this horrible war."

"But I was the leader of my men. I took them into battle. They trusted me." William's voice choked on these last words, for it was that betrayal of which he was most ashamed.

"You could not help that," said Dorothy. "You took your commission before you knew what I felt about it. And after you agreed to my wishes, you could not get out of the army. You told me yourself that the army kills deserters. You were trapped by the rules. You were trapped by the conventions of those whose tactic it is to wage war and kill ... and for what reason? To keep the Negroes in slavery! Do you really think that God supports such actions?"

"I could have saved him," William said. "Regardless of how I got there, I was there. I had the power to save him, but I didn't."

"You could not stop the Yankee from killing. You could only stop yourself from killing."

William looked at Dorothy, his eyes full of anguish. "I wish that I could see it as you do, but I can't."

"It's all right," she said. "You must give yourself time. You've been in the company of those who revere war and belittle the peace beloved by God. Now you are back with someone who honors what you did, who understands your valor, who adores you for having the courage to do what was right under awful circumstances. You know that I love you all the more for it." As she said this, she took his hands and looked deep into his eyes. "Can you not find peace in my love?"

"I want to," he said. "Oh Dorothy, I have not forgotten how beautiful you are."

"Am I?"

He released her hand and reached up to touch her neck,

which was warm and soft. She took hold of his arm and slid his hand down to her breast. He was able to discern the pliant contour of it even through the fabric of her bodice. His breath quickened. He looked around at the door. "My father is in the next room," he said. "We dare not do anything now."

"Let us get married right away," she said. "Once we're married we can do whatever we want."

"Shall we get married? Just like that?"

"Why not? What does it matter now? You've taken an oath and we can't go back home. At least your father is here. He can be with us when we marry."

William still had his hand on Dorothy's breast. It had been a long time since he'd found himself so aroused. It allayed the numbness, which had lain upon him like a shroud. As he felt the warmth of Dorothy's body, he wondered if he might find a way out of the deadness he had felt since Shiloh. Might he not be raised from the dead by the balm of Dorothy's touch?

As if she could read his mind, she clasped her hand around his groin. She gasped audibly to discover that he became hard so quickly. "You seem quite ripe for marriage, Lieutenant Askew," she said.

"I am."

"Then let us go now. Let us get married right away, today."

"We'll have to talk to father. I don't know what he will say."

"He'll be happy to have it settled. He told me he's made provision for both of us. I think he'll be glad to know that I will look after you. And there is hardly any point, under the circumstances, in planning a ceremony. Surely he'll want to see us get married while he's here."

"I suppose so."

"Your brother is here, too."

"What?" This information seemed to William to come without warning. You mean Cato is here?"

"Yes, Cato came with me to Chicago. He came to escort me on the journey. We dressed him up in a wig. We put a sling on his arm. You should have seen him. He looks rather like you when he's made up to look white."

"But Cato ran away. Father wrote me that he ran away after the fire."

"Yes, he ran away because your father whipped him severely after he was caught reading a book. 'Pride and Prejudice' of all things! But then Cato hid in the roof of one of the cabins on our farm," said Dorothy. "Jimmy and Ella took care of him. Ella told me where he was. Ella and Jimmy are here too. We all came to get you."

"You traveled with my brother?"

"Yes. He was a perfect gentleman."

"Where is he?"

"He's waiting back at the other hotel with Mr. Hicks. He was reluctant to come here because he doesn't know what your father might do to him. You must speak to your father about it, William. It hardly makes sense to punish Cato now. I would not have felt safe traveling here without him. Your father seems to have forgiven me. I deceived him quite shamefully in order to get here. Perhaps he can forgive Cato also."

"Yes, my father told me that you ran away with his carriage." William smiled as he said this, just as he had smiled when his father told him about it. Dorothy's pluck both astonished him and endeared her to him.

"Yes, I took his old brougham."

"And all that just to come and see me?"

"Of course. I had to come. I couldn't sit at home mending socks while you were in prison."

"Oh Dorothy." He hugged her and they kissed again. The force of the erotic desire provoked by each other's touch was almost more than either of them could resist. But they were

605

both determined to act honorably. "Let's go and talk to my father," he said. "I'll speak to him about Cato, too."

They returned to Augustus's room, where William launched immediately into the topic at hand.

"Father, Miss Holland and I would like to be married. We plan to do so right away. We'd be honored to have you present. But you must understand that any ceremony, under the circumstances, would be quite modest."

Augustus looked first at William and then at Dorothy. He had expected that they would marry soon. He knew that they could not return home. As he considered the circumstances, he concluded that there was no reason to object. "Very well," he said. "I congratulate you both."

"Thank you," said Dorothy.

"Father, there is another matter that I must speak to you about. Dorothy traveled here under the protection of another member of our family. She was escorted by my brother."

"What!" Augustus's face was transformed. He had never before heard his son refer to the other boy as 'my brother.' That he should do so now shocked him.

"Cato was hiding near the Hollands' farm," William continued. "Miss Holland's servant Ella knew where he was, and when Dorothy decided to come here, they concluded that it would be safer to do so in the company of a gentleman."

"A gentleman!"

"He was dressed as one at any rate," said William. "And I'm told he looks very much like an Askew when given the right attire. Father, Miss Holland and I would prefer it if you and my brother were reconciled. I know he disobeyed you. But surely now, here in this distant place, the bond of blood, the familial tie is all that matters."

"You are his father and I am certain that Cato loves you," Dorothy said. "He has no other family."

"But he broke the law. He learned to read in secret!" Augustus felt that this all was too much to ask. "Then on top of that he ran away—on the very night the house burned down. What family member does that?"

"As I understand it, father," said William, "you whipped him that same night as well. You can hardly blame him for wanting to run away."

"Yes, he was punished. He had disobeyed. I wasn't going to go on punishing him forever. He had no right to leave me at that time."

The tone in Augustus's voice made it clear that he felt abandoned by Cato. But Dorothy heard in it an indication of some deeper feeling.

"Do you love him?" she asked.

Augustus was startled by the question. He had never become used to the directness with which Miss Holland spoke about such things. And no one had ever considered putting such a question to him before. On the face of it, the question was absurd. The boy was a slave. That he was also a son was a regrettable accident. Augustus had regarded Cato as a responsibility, just as he had regarded all of his slaves. He had raised him, taken care of him, taught him right from wrong. It was true that sometimes when he looked into the boy's face he saw himself, a young, earnest version of himself. At times, it seemed as if Josline's blood had had almost no portion in the child, for his physical features favored the father. Yet Augustus had done what any other slaveholder would have done—more perhaps. He'd heard of cases where some heartless owners had sold their little mistakes away right after birth, just to be rid of the reminder. But he had always done right by the boy in his mind, according to his thinking. And he was not immune to the attachments that form among people—especially with such a one as carried his own blood.

Until the day he learned that Cato had secretly learned to read, he would have boasted of Cato as having led an impeccable life. After reflecting upon all this, Augustus said simply, "Of course, I love him."

"If you could only tell him that," said Dorothy. "Tell him that you care for him. I don't think he knows that, and it would mean so much to him to hear you say so. Cato's a good man, Mr. Askew—a credit to your family. He looked after me during our journey. He was as chivalrous as any Southern woman could hope for."

"Cato is your brother, isn't he?" This question was directed at William and came from Sammy, who had been quietly listening to the adults' conversation with great curiosity.

"Yes, in a way, Sammy," Dorothy said quickly.

"Cato is my half-brother," William explained.

"I reckon Jimmy is my half brother too," Sammy speculated. "I got born from a different mother and father than Jimmy, but it don't matter. We're still brothers. He told me so."

These observations were met with a general silence in the room, which was eventually broken by the sound of another knock on the door. This time when Augustus opened the door, he found Erastus Hicks standing outside with another gentleman.

"Mr. Askew, I've come to fetch Sammy," said Erastus, feeling it best to be direct and to the point. "Mr. Augustus Askew and Mr. William Askew, may I introduce Mr. Giovanni Frazza. Miss Holland, I believe you will remember Mr. Frazza from our previous meeting. Mr. Frazza will be traveling to Philadelphia with me on business."

"I'm pleased to meet you," said Mr. Frazza. "And Miss Holland, it is an honor to see you again."

"Mr. Hicks, we have just been talking about marriage. William and I are going to be married," said Dorothy. "Surely you will stay long enough to join us. We want to get married very soon, perhaps tomorrow."

"Tomorrow!" Erastus smiled. "Ah that is soon indeed."

"Yes. I was just speaking to William's father about whether we might not have Cato join us at the wedding," Dorothy added.

"Ah. Well, I would like nothing better than to attend your wedding," said Erastus. "But Mr. Frazza and I have already hired transportation. We've made arrangements to leave this afternoon. I'm sorry. Perhaps you and William would do me the honor of coming to Philadelphia for your honeymoon? I should be happy to have you as my guests. That would allow me to pay tribute to your marriage even though I am unable to attend the wedding."

"That's very kind of you Mr. Hicks," said William. "We haven't had any time to discuss our plans—but we will give your invitation every consideration."

"It seems that fate has brought us all to Chicago," said Erastus, "and I do believe that all of us came with a desire, whether conscious or not, to fulfill a destiny. It is, I am disposed to believe, the result of our compliance with inclinations, which God, in His wisdom, has favored within us. Providence smiles when we follow the deepest yearnings of our souls. Therefore, I have no doubt that your marriage will be a union blessed by good fortune and by the love you bear each other. May you have many years of happiness. And may we all achieve the highest good to which our souls aspire."

"Mr. Hicks, your words are so felicitous and so wise, that I wish we could honor your blessing with a toast of champagne," said Dorothy.

"Hear, hear," said William. "Perhaps we should toast with imaginary glasses."

They all raised their hands in response to this sentiment, as if to pretend to clink their glasses—and in doing so there was a feeling among them that the hand of fate was joined with theirs in honoring all the events which had led them to such a momentous reconciliation.

While these civilities were being exchanged, Sammy gathered up his small parcel of belongings, which included a bundle of brushes that had been left for him by the painter, and which he had carried with him throughout his journey. These brushes were in fact the only material possession he had in the world, and he wrapped them as carefully as he might have wrapped a jewel. Then he walked over to stand by Erastus to indicate his readiness to begin his new life. "Do you have a dog, Mr. Erast?" he asked.

"No Sammy. I haven't a dog. I've been traveling around the country too much to look after a dog."

"Oh," Sammy shrugged. His expression was dejected.

"But you know I might very well get a dog," said Erastus. "You see, Mr. Frazza and I have been discussing opening a business. And now that you are coming to live with me, my boy, I reckon I'll settle down. Would you like to have a dog?"

"Oh yes!"

"Then I see no reason why we cannot do so."

"Why don't we all go back to the Sherman House?" said Dorothy.

"I'm afraid we must leave directly," said Erastus. "Sammy, you'd better say goodbye to everyone."

Sammy walked up to Dorothy and William. "Goodbye Miss Holland. Goodbye Mr. Askew." Then he turned to Augustus. "Goodbye Massa Askew, please say goodbye to Scout for me when you get back home."

"I will," said Augustus, who was genuinely sad to see the boy leave. He reached into his pocket and took out a coin.

"Here," he said, handing the coin to Sammy. "I think I owe you at least this much—since you won the last two hands."

"Thank you, sir."

When Sammy, Mr. Hicks and Mr. Frazza had left, William returned to the discussion of his brother.

"What about Cato, father?" he asked.

Augustus sat down in a chair. He had been worn down by what seemed to him like overwhelming forces. First his wife's death, then the coming of the war and the loss of his house in a fire, after which he had been obliged to live for many months with the Hollands. With William gone for so long, he had felt alone and helpless. One day he realized that no one who loved him had remained in his life. He had been so angry with Cato for learning to read and for running away—but he had not thought much about whether Cato loved him. 'I am certain that Cato loves you.' Dorothy had said. And as Augustus recalled these words, he wondered if it was possible that Cato did indeed love him.

"Yes," Augustus said at last. "I suppose I may as well go and see Cato."

"Oh yes!" said Dorothy.

"Thank you, father," said William.

And so the three of them set out to go to the Sherman House hotel.

* * *

AT THAT HOTEL, Jimmy waited for Ella's reply.

"Come with us," he said.

And Ella felt as if she were standing on the edge of a precipice. Her mind dashed about in a panic; for there seemed to be nowhere she could set it that would be a safe perch from which to consider the alternatives put before her. On the one side lay the prospect of familiar drudgery, from which a chance might never again open up for escape. On the other, there was a dizzying uncertainty, in which freedom loomed as a permanent loss of security. She had worried about how her relationship with Dorothy might change upon Dorothy's marriage to William. She had worried even more about the unpredictability of William's actions. But upon that path, her anxieties were confined to the boundaries of a servant's interactions with a master, which was a terrain that was so familiar to her as to be reassuring. She did not doubt that she would be clothed and fed and housed in a manner at least as palatable as that to which she had become accustomed.

But the prospect of living with Jimmy and Cato—all of them runaway slaves—none of them having experience with the responsibilities of paying bills or securing lodging or finding employment, was one in which the terrors were heightened by their abnormality. She could not easily conjure an image of what her role might be in relationship to her brother and his friend. The bond between the two men was mysterious to her. She sensed that it was unique in some way that was not disclosed. She had an instinctive feeling that her part in such a household would be out of balance—more aligned with Jimmy than with Cato, but not, somehow, on the same footing as that relationship, which seemed volatile and full of riddles.

As she tried to form an image of her life with them, she only experienced a rapid succession of disjointed images, something like a dream that might teeter into a nightmare if it all did not unfold just so.

She was overwhelmed by a sense of consequentiality in this decision. It pushed her into a place where she felt thrown upon the primacy of her own soul to guide her. At first, this made her feel tremendously alone, alone in an even more profound way than the solitude created by her own flesh. She knew that no soul but hers could make this choice. But as she winced at the loneliness of making such a choice, she suddenly sensed something of her deepest self that was greater than she had ever sensed before. The more deeply she went into the reserves of her spirit, the more cavernous those reserves seemed. She felt then that in the cavern of her soul she could sense a larger self, a grander pattern from which she was being spun. The impetus of this sensation was soothing—and it seemed to tell her not to fear the loss of the opportunity offered by Jimmy and Cato.

When Dorothy, William and Augustus arrived at the Tremont Hotel, they found Ella there, alone in Dorothy's room.

"Cato and Jimmy have just gone," said Ella. "They said they's fixing to stay free now that they're up North." She handed Dorothy the note that Cato had written.

Having resolved to reconcile with Cato, Augustus was disappointed to find that he had run away once again. "Who's Jimmy?" he asked.

"Jimmy's the one that pulled you out of that fire, Mr. Askew," said Ella. "He and Cato are good friends."

"So it was him!" said Augustus. "The one that tried to kill me."

"He never tried to kill you, Mr. Askew. Jimmy only ran into that burning house to pull you out of it. He had a knife with him 'cause he was fixing to cut Cato loose from those chains, that's all. He's powerful fond of Cato, Mr. Askew. He couldn't stand to see Cato chained up, is all."

Augustus had been surprised to find the painter Erastus Hicks in Chicago, but now he was even more astonished to learn that Cato and his accomplice had also rendezvoused within the same city. Cato had accompanied Dorothy both as an escort and to see his brother. This Jimmy, it seemed, had come both to elude Augustus and to be with Cato. But now

Augustus thought that in this grand convergence the hand of destiny was truly astounding.

"I'm afraid they've gone," Dorothy said. "And he doesn't say where to." She handed the note to Augustus.

After Augustus had read it, he turned to Dorothy, "He writes well, doesn't he?"

"Yes," said Dorothy, "he does."

\* \* \*

The End

# AUTHOR'S NOTE

I first began writing *Unmentionables* as a result of an unexpected experience. I attended a "past life regression" study run by a writer named Dr. Helen Wambach, who was compiling statistics about past life memories for a book she eventually published called *Life Before Life*. I went with two friends of mine as a lark. We were skeptical but curious.

When we arrived, we were instructed to lie on the floor of the vast meeting room at the Holiday Inn in Elmhurst, Illinois, along with about fifty other subjects. Dr. Wambach intoned hypnotically, as she guided us to find memories of our past lives. At the end of the session, we were awakened, at which point one of my friends said to me, "What a crock!" He had been lying on the floor for an hour wide-awake. He had no past life recollections whatsoever.

My other friend recalled himself to be a Buddhist monk in the 4$^{th}$ century. I too experienced a trance, which felt like a dream. It was in that hypnotic state that I imagined a past life as Ella, an enslaved woman on a small family farm in Madison County, Tennessee. I filled out Dr. Wambach's questionnaire. My answers there about who I was, who my family members were, and where I lived, were the genesis of this novel.

Of course, I cannot know for certain whether or not I may have had a past life as an enslaved woman. But I am certain that these characters became a vivid part of David Greene's life for eighteen years while I researched and wrote this book.

\* \* \*

Prior to the publication of *Unmentionables* in 2010, I was unable to find any written account of the lives of enslaved gay men in history books or published primary documents. Nor was I able to find any instance in which the story of enslaved gay men had been told in fiction. The publication of *Unmentionables* marked the first time that these characters, who had previously been expunged from history, were the subject of an historical fiction novel.

The logo reflects the love between enslaved men that society refused to acknowledge. These enslaved men were people who had been deemed "unmentionable" by historians and writers.

To learn more about all my books and to join my mailing list
go to
www.davidgreenebooks.com

ALSO BY DAVID GREENE

*All to Pieces*

In this second installment the *Unmentionables* series, slave catchers kidnap Jimmy and resell him into slavery. Cato risks his own re-enslavement to travel deep into Confederate territory in an all-out search to find his lover.

"All to Pieces" is a 19th-century phrase that means "completely, absolutely."

*The Winkler Case*

When insurance salesman Elliot Blake makes a house call at the home of fight promoter Walt Winkler, it's handsome boxer Vito Vellucci who comes to the door. In this gay re-imagining of the classic noir novel *Double Indemnity*, obsessive desire unfolds in an unexpected direction.

*Detonate*

Ride from Niagara Falls to New York City on a speeding train with biracial, bisexual private eye, Tyrone King, and fellow passenger, Sarah, as they race to stop terrorists from blowing up the Statue of Liberty.